I have heeded your warning ... is it true? Is she now amongst us, on the Earth plane? the Elder questioned.

Yes. The seventh incarnation has taken place. The prophecy will be fulfilled. Now the Cat plays with the Snake, teases him, tempts him, but soon she will command him. Father's thoughts were crystal clear, the communication penetrating, imprinting the Elder's mind-source.

Then it is time? The Elder echoed a sense of reluctance from deep within his Earth nature.

Have you trained him, prepared him? The question was quick, to the point.

We have, Father, we have, the Elder confirmed, once again in perfect tune with his host.

And you did not violate our trust? Father's aura vibrated less brilliantly as the six held close to him, their energies fuelling the last moments of their contact.

He knows nothing of his origins, the Elder responded.

Good. Then you will know what to do when his moment comes ...

A book that captures both the spirit and the violence of the Martial Arts. Fiction it may be, but the fights are for real. The most vivid descriptions of mortal combat I have ever read'
Terry O'Neill, Fighting Arts International

TEGNÉ
WARLORD OF ZENDOW

Richard La Plante

SPHERE BOOKS LIMITED

SPHERE BOOKS LTD

Published by the Penguin Group
27 Wrights Lane, London w8 5TZ, England
Viking Penguin Inc., 40 West 23rd Street, New York, New York 10010, USA
Penguin Books Australia Ltd, Ringwood, Victoria, Australia
Penguin Books Canada Ltd, 2801 John Street, Markham, Ontario, Canada L3R 1B4
Penguin Books (NZ) Ltd, 182–190 Wairau Road, Auckland 10, New Zealand

Penguin Books Ltd, Registered Offices: Harmondsworth, Middlesex, England

First published in Great Britain by Sphere Books Ltd 1988
This edition 1989
1 3 5 7 9 10 8 6 4 2

Printed and bound in Great Britain by
Richard Clay Ltd, Bungay, Suffolk

For Richard Girling Sears, my grandfather

AUTHOR'S PREFACE

Although *Tegné* is a work of fantasy and fiction, I have grounded my text on actual personal experience. Most events and conditions which are described, both physical and psychological, are based upon similar occurrences which I have participated in, witnessed, or have seen documented. Having had a long and avid interest in Eastern philosophy, including the internal, spiritual practices of meditation as well as the more external forms of Japanese armed and unarmed combat, I have used both Indian and Japanese terms throughout the book.

However, as I have stated, the book is fantasy and fiction, and no historical foundation or factual chronology exists within its chapters. Yet I do hope there is a certain truth in *Tegné*, for truth, by nature, transcends the confines of time and space.

ACKNOWLEDGEMENTS

I wish to acknowledge and thank the Gower Publishing Group for their kind permission to use selected pieces of the *Tao Te Ching*, written by Lao Tsu in the sixth century BC and translated into English by Gia-Fu-Feng and Jane English.

I would also like to thank my friend Professor Roger T. Ames for his kind permission to use selected pieces of Lao Tsu, *Tao Te Ching* as adapted and translated by himself and Rhett Y. W. Young and published by the Chinese Material Centre.

Special thanks are also due to Senseis Terry O'Neill and Dave Hazard for their friendship, encouragement, and ability to provide accurate technical advice on the many forms of combat relevant to Tegné.

To my agent Ed Victor, my editor Mary Loring, and my secretary, Elaine Causon.

Lao Tsu

Lao Tsu, an older contemporary of Confucius, was keeper of the royal archives at Loyang in the province of Honan in the sixth century BC. According to ancient legend, as he was riding off into the desert to die – sick at heart at the ways of men – he was persuaded by a Chinese gatekeeper to write down his spiritual teachings in order to preserve them for posterity.

CONTENTS

I

THE VISION

Under Heaven
All can see beauty as beauty
Only because there is ugliness
All can know good as good
Only because there is evil

(Lao Tsu, Honan Province,
sixth Century BC)

The Elder entered the nine-foot-square stone meditation chamber. He placed his hand against the heavy iron shutters of the single window and pushed outwards. The rusted metal, grown thick and porous during the ninety days of the monsoon, held firm against the small, almost effeminate, hand. Yet there was an uncanny strength to this diminutive man, a strength that had little to do with sinew and bone, and gradually the shutters gave way, allowing the first cascading rays of the rising sun to penetrate the grey cell.

The Elder squared his shoulders, inhaling the chill air. Daylight played upon the braided strands of silver hair which began in a knot on the crown of his otherwise smoothly shaven head and fell down the back of his silken robes. From the open window he could just make out the hazy outline of the high mountain peaks which formed the eastern perimeter of Lunan province. His views to the north and south were blocked by the jutting Tiyuku face, for the Temple of the Moon was built into this enormous mountain and its inner recesses, including the fifty meditation chambers, were carved from the rock itself.

He stood perfectly still, and, for a moment, reflected upon the sheer strength of purpose which had enabled his predecessors to create this impenetrable place of peace. Then he knelt upon the small Mandarin rug, sitting back to rest his hips upon the heels of his feet in the traditional sei-za position. His slow exhalations formed a fine, white mist in the morning air, and the faded gold threads of the carpet merged with the yellowed silk of his heavy robes. He inhaled deeply, filling his lower abdomen, retaining the breath for an interval of sixty heartbeats, then exhaled to the same count. He remained focused directly ahead, concentrating on the small copper disc which was attached to the grey stone wall in front of him. Mounted upon the disc was the insignia of his Brotherhood, a polished golden quarter moon with a single silver star positioned below its southern tip. At first the moon

3

and star simply reflected in the Elder's close-set brown eyes. Then, as the meditation deepened, his eyelids closed and the reflected sign internalized, penetrating his surrendered consciousness. Finally, the Elder increased his breathing rate, creating a rapid, chugging respiration. His body temperature soared in response, taking him into the Dragon Zone.

The kundalini energy was awakening, uncoiling with tingling, electric pulses in the base of his spine, climbing up the central nerve, entering, opening, energizing each of the seven chakras en route to its final destination.

The Elder had been 'open' for six yeons, yet still hovering on the surface of his consciousness was the memory of the original procedure. The excruciating pain which had accompanied the slow twisting of the diamond drill. The concentration required to bore into the frontal bone, an exact finger's breadth above his nasal bridge, dead centre between his eyes. The memory of the infinite strength which held both his arms and legs, allowing not the slightest movement, while the Exalted Priest performed the operation. Twenty minutes which became eternity. The high-pitched, metallic whine, the perspiration and blood dripping down his cheeks, the superhuman effort to control his breathing, to maintain silence, not to scream out. And finally, the searing blue light, brighter than any light on earth, exploding in his brain.

And now, as then, the Elder was in Vakos, the State of Inner Vision. Viewing through ajna, the third eye. There were shadows moving in the void, silhouettes; then his cerekinetic focus, activated by his controlled respiration, began to make the 'vision' crystallize. His last, fading threads of consciousness beheld a vast desert landscape.

Desolate, barren, burnt chalk-white by the four suns which rose in the north, south, east and west, converging at centre-point to form one, enormous, burning white nebula.

There was no wind, no life amidst the jagged rock formations and wide, uneven craters, only the thick, vaporous heat rising from the sun-bleached earth.

In the distance, a thin humming began — like the beating of fine, silken wings. Gradually, the sound took a physical form, rising through the vapour. The form moved closer, closer, finally materializing into a horse and rider.

The rider wore billowing, flowing robes, his hair shimmered gold, yellow and blue. An aura was formed by the colours, encircling his ivory-white face; his deep, wide turquoise eyes were fixed firmly ahead. The horse was gleaming silver, its hooves flying across the earth, but not touching. No sound accompanied the horse and rider. They were perfect beauty; the swirling colours so exquisite that they totally captivated the Elder. There was such joy, such great vitality to the rhythm of the movement . . .

All pain was past, a state of harmony realized, a supreme euphoria; an understanding that this was the way it was supposed to be, always . . .

Then, from the vapour, rose the black, shadowy shape. The shape became firm, forming into a long, sinewy, cat-like body. The eyes burned red and the snarling mouth was pulled back to reveal long, white fangs. The fore-claws were extended, fully unsheathed, as the Cat leapt, tearing the rider from his silver mount.

Rider and Cat fell to the ground; forming a grotesque union. The man did not struggle as the frenzied animal ripped the limbs from his body, finally biting through the fine, ivory neck, severing the head.

Only now did the Cat look up, only now did she see Him. He was the Father Protector, tall, exceedingly broad-shouldered. His long, golden hair hung mid-way down the back of his fine, white, silken robes. His skin was the same ivory as the skin of the rider. The Cat knew him; she snarled as she backed away. He raised his right hand, the long, graceful fingers extended. From the fingers a blue stream of light emanated, forming an arc between the hand and the savaged rider. The Cat backed further away, her image growing faint, as the blue light encircled the fallen man, wrapping round him, strand by luminous strand, finally encasing him completely.

The Cat disappeared within the vapour as the Father Protector turned and faced the Elder. His face was beautiful in a way which exceeded the confines of male or female. The cheekbones high and defined, the ivory skin flawless, the lips pale, the huge, turquoise eyes watery pools of prana, Earth energy, forever vibrating, forever in flux. The face was close now. Nothing else was important. A single tear formed in the right eye; the tear built and fell, rolled down the cheek, rolled forward, forward, until there was only this single tear, rolling through time and space. Closer, closer, until the tear became defined . . . the tear became the Golden Foetus, flying forward from infinity. The embryo was nearly formed; the Elder could almost see

*the Earth body. From some primordial recess of his soul, the meaning
of this vision began to surface:*

IT WAS THE TIME OF THE BEAST. IT WAS ALSO THE HOUR
OF CONCEPTION. THE GOLDEN SON WOULD RISE. THE
EARTH WARRIOR WAS COMING.

The energy was so intense, near the break-point . . . the cry of
birth shattered the vision.

Tabata stood above the Elder. 'Are you not well, Elder, I
heard your scream?' Tabata spoke as he looked lovingly down
upon the senior, exalted Brother of his Order.

The Elder pulled himself up from the prayer rug. He cupped
his head in both hands. The point between his eyes throbbed.
Looking up, the Elder searched Tabata's eyes.

'We can wait no longer. I have spoken to you of a mission . . .
far from here, beyond the Valley, deep into Vokane.'

There could be no weakness, no hesitation, no questions.
Tabata, Shihan of the Temple, Grand Master of Empty Hand,
had been chosen. The Elder had chosen him nearly two yeons ago.
He must be prepared to leave, to turn his back upon the Order,
to walk forth from the cloisters of the Brothers of the Moon. A
mission from which he would never return. Tabata was completely still, he did not allow his heart to increase its beat. He
entered zanshin, the state of calm, complete awareness.

'I am ready, Elder.'

Tears welled in the older man's eyes, tears that came from the
depths of him. How he loved this great, bearded bear of a man.
He extended his arms towards Tabata in a final embrace.

2

THE BIRTH

Evil is born from good
Good from Evil
The two spring from the same source
But differ in name
Light from darkness
Day from night

(Lao Tsu)

Midday in Lunan; daybreak in Vokane. Three thousand vul, a time difference of six hours and a desert as wide as the Great Sea itself separated the Temple of the Moon from the mighty Zendow, which stood like some dark, conquering giant in the far corner of the eastern province.

This fortress-like city stretched an even nine vul from east to west, and was nearly five leagues from north to south. Throughout the seven hundred yeons of its existence it had been the home of two religious orders and three powerful, warring clans.

It was a religious sect, the Kundani, who constructed the city; the building taking the better part of two hundred yeons. And although most of their records were destroyed in the Great Fire of 400, remnants showed that the Kundani were a sect of sun-worshippers. Peaceful and productive, they occupied the city for most of its original three hundred yeons.

Then came the Manons, a fierce, nomadic tribe from the great northern steppe region. They descended with their steel-tipped arrows and heavy wooden clubs, thousands of them, travelling from the arid, treeless steppes and through the lush Forest of Shuree.

The Kundanis' sole means of defence was a mass prayer to D'Oro, their sun god. Consequently, they were slaughtered to a man, and their city taken.

However, it was legend that D'Oro finally did respond to the Kundani prayer. For, one hundred yeons later, a solar explosion caused the Great Fire, destroying the Manons in a single spontaneous combustion, leaving the walled city vacant and cindered with the exception of the huge, circular configuration of slab-like stones, some ninety feet in height, which formed the Kundanis' timeless tribute to the god they had worshipped. The walled city stood, burnt and empty, for nearly two hundred yeons.

It was in Yeon 700 that a small cluster of travelling monks rediscovered it. There were no more than three or four hundred of them. They had survived the arduous eastern journey from the upper Lunan Province, travelling across the Valley of Sand, and making their way deep into Shuree. They hailed the walled city as their promised land, named it Lunalle, and began the enormous task of renovation.

Twenty-five yeons they laboured, day and night, rebuilding the northern wall and carrying fresh timber from the surrounding forest to replace the charred floors and fallen beams. No sooner had they completed the bulk of their restoration than the wandering Yusun Clan invaded from the west. The Yusuns scaled the high walls and drove the monks from their holy grounds; not without resistance, for these Brothers were from the Temple of the Moon, a martial order, and many Yusun were amazed at the instant ferocity and practised skill with which these empty-handed monks fought. Sheer numbers decided the outcome and the surviving Brothers fled, driven back through the forest and into the Valley, where the burning sun scorched their unprotected skin, finishing the slaughter that the Yusuns had started. Thus the Valley of Sand became known as the Valley of Death.

The Yusun rule was brief; they were a cattle- and horse-breeding clan and were unable to settle properly within the confines of the city. Irrespective of its size, they needed the prairie and the grazing land at the base of the Western Mountains. Most of the clan had, in fact, moved on by the time the first party of Zendai descended upon them.

The initial Zendai war party was barely one thousand strong, yet their impenetrable, shining black body-armour, distinguished by the Sign of the Claw, and their precise discipline in the military arts made them invulnerable. It was the first time any Yusun had gazed upon the fine, single-edged, curved blade of the katana. A perfect killing weapon, and wielded with such skill and grace that more than once its victim was so mesmerized by the flashing steel that his limbs were severed before he thought of defence.

The Yusun Clan either fled or surrendered in the face of these huge-boned, bronzed, god-like Warmen. For the Zendai were a pure race, finely bred, and would tolerate no less than perfection in their offspring. Zendai bred with Zendai; it was more than law, it was religion.

They had come from the deep sun of the south, beyond Miramar, and beyond the High-Peaked Mountains, from a land bordered by the Great Sea. Yet this master race had grown, multiplied beyond that dry land's ability to support them. And, like the Manons, the Zendai travelled away from the sun and towards the moist, fertile soil of Shuree.

It was the Zendai who named the province Vokane, which in their ancient tongue meant 'Mother of Life', and the Zendai who called the walled city after their own clan, the City of Zendow. It was this conquering clan who were first led by the great Warlord, Volkar, the invincible giant, the purest of pure. Volkar, of whom each succeeding warlord for six generations was of direct descent. Volkar, the forefather of Renagi . . .

The sun was just beginning its climb above the sky-scraping, spiked ramparts, casting long, dancing shadows onto the paved streets below. The morning was tranquil, its quiet, still energy like a newly born babe waiting to be slapped into life. Voices, small yet distinct against the high stone walls, echoed in the inter-connecting courtyards surrounding the palace. Slowly, Zendow was awakening . . .

A single knock on the thick carved oak door and Zena entered Renagi's chamber, carrying the large wooden bowl, steam rising from the water. Close behind, Hiro shuffled, two clean, thick, white cotton towels folded over his right arm.

'Good morning, Master,' Zena said, and the two servants bowed.

The sunlight streamed through the arched stone window as the Warlord slid from beneath the deep blue, embroidered blanket. Still partially erect from a night of dreams and a bladder full of red wine, he strode, uninhibited, in front of his attending servants.

At thirty-five, he was nearing his peak; that time when mind and body become one, the mind sharp, seasoned by experience, the body supple, strong and quick. Watching him move to the bath-chamber, Zena marvelled at how the lean, muscular frame seemed rooted to the floor, the Warlord's feet able to grasp the bare wooden boards as assuredly as his hands were able to grasp the katana.

Renagi watched the deep yellow stream arc towards the porcelain bowl.

'Today is the first day of Celebre – the show of strength, the ride through the Province,' he spoke aloud to himself, 'Once a yeon they must see me, see their Warlord ... they must bow down to the Red and Black ... yes, I will ride Kano.'

His voice trailed off as he shook the last drops from his now flacid penis. Still thinking of the day ahead, Renagi turned and gracefully took the step down from the bath chamber.

This Celebre I must put the fear of God into them. Six Celebres since I've been there, and each yeon their grain production has diminished. Most certainly time for a visit ...

Zena and Hiro waited, motionless, the water still steaming in the bowl. Renagi moved to the centre of the floor and stood, feet together, facing the sun-filled window. Arms to his sides, he bowed to Sol-Ra, God of Light. Eyes concentrated, Renagi eased his clenched right fist to the point slightly above his chin, a hand's breadth away. His open left hand, equally slowly, came up to cup over his right clenched fist. He inhaled deeply, the breath filling his lower abdomen, then, eyes never wavering, he began the Morning Form.

His clenched right fist shot upwards towards the left ear, then sharply down in the defensive gedan position. His open left hand now clenched hard into a fist as he stepped back on the right leg. Pivoting, he executed the palm-heel defence, followed by a lunging spear-hand. Now, sinking low into the straddle-legged horseback stance, he performed a left leg sweeping block followed by a sharp side-thrusting kick. Never did his eyes waver, never did his breathing become irregular. The Morning Form was three hundred yeons old, passed from Warlord to son – forbidden to be taught outside the lineage.

Renagi had performed the Form every morning for twenty-five yeons, and now as he neared 'The Peak', its powers were opening to him. With each lower breath he was able to take energy from Sol-Ra and, with each exhalation, transfer that energy to his fist, or his knife-foot.

The Form took twenty minutes, not a second more, not a second less. By the last thrust his energy force had built to explosion; and with the final expulsion of breath from his diaphragm, the ki-ai cut the morning air, echoing in the lower courtyard.

Assuming the first position, Renagi bowed again to Sol-Ra, crossed his arms in front of his body and returned to normal stance. Only now did the Warlord acknowledge Zena and Hiro. He turned, and ever so slightly nodded towards them. In unison, the wizened, white-haired Zena and the younger, dark Hiro, bowed to their master. The water was now the proper temperature, the thick, white cotton towels ready. They were honoured to bathe Renagi – particularly on this first day of Celebre.

YEON 966
SLAVE STATE OF ASHKELAN
VOKANE PROVINCE

One hundred vul to the west of Zendow, Asha-1 baked beneath the sun. It was the first of six such village communities which lay within the Green Triangle, a particularly fertile zone which ran five hundred vul from north to south. The entire area was designated Ashkelan, the 'state of slaves'.

The practice of 'culling' this group of people, of specifically disposing of their strongest, most dominant, males, thus interbreeding only their weaker genes, had begun two hundred yeons previously, with the Yusun Clan. The practice was instigated by a need for a controllable labour force to produce the grain required within the walled city. The procedure had resulted in a working tribe of albinos. A cruel tradition which the Zendai had carried on. 'A tradition born of necessity.'

*

The sun was just reaching danger level as Maliseet looked up to the clear, azure sky. She placed the last of the carotene into the round straw basket. *Mother will be pleased*, she thought, *there is enough carotene to last until High Solstice. Strange that without this long, pointed, orange vegetable we could tolerate no sunlight at all. How awful it would be, never to feel the warmth.*

Maliseet looked at her forearm. The white Ashkelite skin was nearly translucent, and a circuitry of delicate blue veins ran beneath the fine epidermis. She had no natural pigmentation, like the rest of her people, only the temporary protection which the regular ingestion of carotene provided. She glanced again at the brimming basket. Yes, Mother would be very pleased.

A single bead of moisture formed on her brow – a warning. Maliseet reached into her apron, found the blankers; thick, black-lensed spectacles which protected the retinas of her eyes from the ultra rays. She fixed the blankers in place, bent down, took hold of the leather strap and hoisted the basket to her shoulder.

Raine's eyes searched the horizon. Behind her, the tiny, windowless, thatched cottages of Asha-1 formed uniform rows on each side of the dirt road. Maliseet had been gone since daybreak; why was she always the last home? Every other family would be indoors by now, asleep or spending the heat of the day huddled, conserving energy, around the underground ventilation shaft. But no, not Maliseet, she loved the sun, even though it could kill her.

This time I will teach her, thought Raine, *this time she will stay indoors for three days . . . this time.*

Raine's plans for punishment melted as she saw Maliseet round the bend. Her daughter was exquisite; tall for an Ashkelite, nearly five feet, six fingers, and remarkably full-bosomed. The fine, silken white hair hung well below her slim, strong hips. And the legs – they were the best feature of her body – long, long legs, feminine yet muscular, and sure. The face was her father's; proud, high cheekbones, full sensuous lips, large eyes set wide apart. Warm, glowing eyes, nearly amber in colour, unusual in comparison to the vapid pink eyes of the other Ashkelites.

Maliseet's father had indeed been a fine-looking man, until the Clan singled him out – made him responsible for the entire grain production of Asha-1. They demanded quotas that were impossible to fill – impossible, unless he worked the danger levels. They threatened his family with death. Every day, Akid worked from sunrise to sunset, and into the night, for one full harvest he worked. One full harvest and his single, thin layer of skin was burnt to the bone.

'Mother!' Maliseet called, holding out the full basket of carotene. Raine ran to her daughter and took the heavy wicker basket from her.

'Come, come, girl, we must get inside,' she said, putting one arm around Maliseet and urging her towards the village and the shelter of their hut.

*

Five days into the ride. Two more to travel, Renagi noted as Kano surged forward. This stallion had a rhythm unlike any other horse

14

he had ever ridden. A full eighteen hands of white, throbbing muscle and a wild spirit which merged with Renagi's own. Only the Warlord could mount Kano; it had been that way since the Yusun breeders had presented the stallion as an offering of peace. Renagi and Kano, the perfect wakan, that mysterious merging of souls.

Today was no different. Renagi, mounted on the white giant, was invincible. Kano bucked and pranced, aware of the power he surrendered to his master.

The Procession of Celebre wound its way through town and village. Renagi's jet-black hair was oiled, pulled tightly back and plaited, his brown, slant Mongol eyes alive with fire, his broad shoulders made even broader by the black Zendai war armour; its blood-red 'Sign of the Claw' cut deep into the shining leather and alloy. Renagi held his back straight – perfect posture, his square jaw set; he spurred Kano onwards.

Behind him, riding in exact formation, was the Procession. They were the Twelve Chosen Warmen. From village to village they galloped, and in each village Renagi's minions kissed the earth as he passed. Failure to pay homage resulted in death. The speed of the katana, the Zendai long sword, was well known, and once drawn, the katana must take life – that was the law.

Sunset, the Procession galloped on. Tomorrow would bring the homeward journey, and the midnight feast of Celebre. But, for now, there was one more village, and that village was Asha-1.

The ultra rays were at safety level. The blankers could be removed, the field-work continued. One by one, the doors of the small cottages opened. Small groups of Ashkelites walked out into the dirt road. There was the usual conversation, a minimum of anxiety – each knew it was the time of Celebre, yet the general feeling was that the Procession would not enter Asha-1. The Zendai had not bothered with the village for six harvests. What interest could Renagi have in the Ashkelites? As long as they produced, kept their place, Renagi did not need to view his slaves.

Maliseet joined a work party, two boys her own age, and a woman slightly older than she, perhaps twenty. The four walked slowly towards the Easterly Fields. They were just nearing the point where the road narrowed to a small path when the ground began to tremble, as if the earth had come alive with thunder. Maliseet looked in the direction of the sound, straining her eyes against the sun. In the distance, she could see the dust billowing from under Kano's hooves; she could distinguish a black-suited figure in the horse's saddle. The Procession galloped towards them.

Those Ashkelites already in the fields were, by now, running back towards the village. Maliseet fell into step as they ran for home. Raine stood waiting nervously at the door of their cottage.

'Do not be frightened,' Raine spoke as much to herself as to her daughter, 'No harm will come – show them respect. Remember, show respect.'

On each side of the road, the Ashkelites formed straight lines. The women who had been in the fields were brushing the dust and earth from their heavy cotton dresses, the men straightening their tunics and trousers. The Procession entered Asha-1 through the east gate. The Warmen broke gallop, tightened ranks, as the panting, snorting horses moved slowly forwards, between the two lines of Ashkelites.

Maliseet had been twelve yeons when the Procession last came. The fear had been contagious, yet she also remembered the fascination. This time was no different. Now, she could see the giant white stallion, the silver and turquoise amulets hanging from the great leather saddle. She could distinguish the in-destructible, black shining armour, the red claw. She could clearly see him, the Warlord. In spite of her fear, she found it impossible not to stare . . .

'Get down, child!'

Raine's desperate voice cut through Maliseet's thoughts. In-stantly, she knelt, joining the others, kissing the earth, paying homage to the Warlord.

The Procession stopped. Renagi and his twelve Warmen sat still. The Ashkelites remained prostrate, the black cloud of death hanging heavily above them, and for a long, tortured moment every rustle of clothing, every uneven breath, even the beating of a single heart, foretold doom.

The body-hugging chest protectors and the wide, tubular arm-guards gave each of the Warmen a pronounced muscularity, a malevolent power. They remained poised, their blackness in contrast to the tranquil blue of the sky, as if together they formed the barrier which prohibited access to all that was sure and certain.

'All of you. Up. Stand up,' Renagi's voice rang out, clear, deep, resonant.

Some visibly trembling, others controlling themselves, the Ashkelites stood at attention. The Warmen studied the faces, searched the eyes. If even a flicker of defiance shone, the katana would be drawn.

Stillness, deathly quiet, that time when each Ashkelite fought to control the nervous energy. No sudden cries, no whimpering, no rapid movement . . . nothing . . .

The deep, controlled voice; 'It has been brought to my attention . . .' Renagi scanned the faces, as if he spoke to each of them separately, 'that the quotas for Asha-1 are below any other village in Ashkelan . . .'

Silence. A long pause . . . 'That grain production has fallen by half . . .' looking, questioning . . . 'Did you not think that I would know this?'

The pitch of his voice began to build; 'Did you not think I would care?' Renagi's voice was louder, deeper, 'Did you not expect me to come here?'

The voice was a weapon, filling the air, inescapable.

'Did you not think that you would answer to me,' now a deafening, punishing roar, 'Answer to ME!'

The black silence again fell upon the village. The Warmen, eyes darting from face to face, itchily fingered the hilts of their katanas. Finally, Nakos, the production leader, stepped from line, prostrated himself, kissing the earth. Renagi, with a gesture of his gloved hand, signalled the frail man to rise.

'Master, Warlord, I beg your forgiveness.' The voice was thin and reed-like, yet bore a certain resigned strength.

Renagi nodded, indicating that Nakos should continue.

'Within the last six solstices our male population has decreased by four score. Our work-teams are primarily composed of women and children.'

The voice droned on with excuses: the lack of rain, the rampant carcina amongst the male population, the shortage of carotene, the increase in ultra rays.

Renagi was now only half-listening. His attention had shifted. She stood half a head taller than any of the women around her.

Even in the heavy cotton work-dress the breasts seemed swollen, ripe. The parts of the legs that were visible, the calves and the bare feet, were unusually muscular for an Ashkelite. And the face, not the usual thin lips and sunken eyes, the face was superb.

'We have now trained our younger, mixed work teams to an efficiency level comparable to the level achieved by the male teams of the Fifth Solstice . . .' Nakos felt he was getting through, convincing the Warlord.

Renagi held up his huge, black-gloved right hand, stopping Nakos in mid-sentence.

'What is your name?'

'I am Nakos.'

'Nakos, I have heard enough. I do not want excuses, I want grain. Nakos − from this Celebre you are solely responsible for the grain production of Asha-1. That production will equal the production of the Sixth Solstice. If it does not, I will be able to find no reason for the existence of Asha-1 − do you understand?'

Nakos knelt, kissed the earth, and accepted the certain sentence of death. The matter closed, Renagi turned his full attention towards Maliseet.

She knew he had been watching her. She could feel the sharp, burning energy from the snake-lidded eyes. She was frightened, yet the fear was counterbalanced by sheer fascination.

Renagi felt no need for discretion. He turned in his saddle, facing her completely.

'What do they call you?'

The voice had regained its velvety richness, no longer threatening, but still commanding.

'I am speaking to you.'

He now gazed upon her fully. There could be no question, no doubt as to the object of Renagi's attention. As she stepped forward, she felt Raine's hand grip her left shoulder, then fall away. She felt naked, alone and, finally, fully frightened.

She knelt and kissed the earth.

'Maliseet. Maliseet is my name.'

The high, quavering voice hung momentarily on the still air, then silence . . .

'Maliseet . . .' His pronunciation, the emphasis on the last syllable, the slowness in the delivery, all gave the name a gravity, a fated quality.

The Warmen sat alert; they waited. Any resistance would be instantly stopped. They waited . . . waited. Renagi's hand rested dangerously on the hilt of his katana.

Menra sensed the process of decision. Why was Renagi not drawing his sword? Why was he not now holding up the head of this Ashkelite bitch? Surely, he had singled her out for slaughter; and now the Warlord would demonstrate how little one Ashkelite life meant . . . He would gain great face with the Warmen. He would remind these slaves of his omnipotence . . .

'Maliseet . . . a fine name.'

Renagi smiled generously, straightened in his saddle, turned, heeled Kano, and galloped up the dirt road towards the east gate.

The dangerous moment past, the relief was clearly audible. The Ashkelites fell to their knees. The Kiss of Earth never held such meaning, never were they in greater awe of their Warlord.

God of the Sun, he is a master . . . The thought flashed through Menra's mind as he waved the Procession on, following Renagi to the east gate and out of Asha-1.

To let those poor idiots feel his power of life and death, and then to give life, what a stroke!

The Procession, now in perfect formation, galloped as one, Menra in the lead position, a perfect twelve paces behind Renagi. Twelve paces, a long enough distance to show respect, a short enough space to close quickly if trouble threatened.

Suddenly, Renagi pulled heavily on Kano's reins. The giant stallion came to a snorting halt. As quickly, the Procession halted behind. They were barely two miles east of Asha-1.

Renagi turned, 'Menra, come here. I want a private word.'

The Warmen sat, stony-faced. Menra edged forward, towards Renagi. What could be the meaning of this, had something been overlooked, had something displeased him . . .?

Menra's mount was now side by side with Kano, ahead of the halted Procession. Still, Renagi's voice was hushed.

'The girl, the one called Maliseet. Go back, bring her to me. I am trusting you. Not one Warman must be aware of what you do . . . no one must see her enter the castle.'

Menra's mind whirled. What reason? To bring an untouchable, a slave, into Zendow . . .

'Do you understand?' Renagi's voice jogged Menra's attention.

'Oss, Master, I understand.'

'Go then, and remember, no one must see the girl.'

*

Perhaps it was premonition, perhaps mother's instinct. Raine felt a foreboding . . . she had refused to allow Maliseet to join the evening work-teams. The others had turned on her – how could she refuse? She, of all Ashkelites, should know the impossible demand placed on Nakos, how could she withhold her full efforts? Surely, she must remember her own husband, staying in the fields alone, long after the others had taken shelter. Still Raine held firm – no, the girl would return to full labour at dawn. Tonight she would remain indoors. At one point Maliseet had turned to ask Raine why, what could be wrong with going to the fields tonight? Raine's eyes had halted her; the capillaries had expanded – from fear? From anger? The usual pink quality was now near crimson. Raine's full protective energies had activated. Maliseet would not go to the fields this eve.

Once inside their tiny hut, Raine ordered Maliseet into the far bedchamber. Why was her mother acting this way? It wasn't at all like Raine, yet there was no arguing with her, her command was final, giving no room for disagreement.

Maliseet drew the curtain to the bedchamber. A cot and a small oak chair filled most of the space. Maliseet lay on the cot, closed her eyes, drifted. *Maliseet* . . . His soft, rich, velvety voice said her name over and over again . . .

Raine sat on the bench next to the central ventilation shaft. She stared at the door . . . what was it? The feeling was so strong. Was it the memory of Akid, her husband? Yes, that was it; the Procession had triggered the association with death. They had killed her husband, just as they would kill Nakos.

It had begun the same way. Everyone had joined in, worked to their limits to help Akid maintain production. Worked into the danger levels. Then . . . with the first symptoms of carcina, with the first tiny, white water blisters on their backs, the panic took hold. Soon, it was Akid who laboured alone, just as it would be Nakos. Give them three moons, at most six. God, they were a weak race, a pathetic race. Yes, that was it; that was the reason for this irrational fear.

It will be over by morning, the Procession long gone. Yes, it will be over by morning.

*

At first it sounded like someone running, far in the distance. Then, as the sound drew closer, it became more distinct. The steady rhythm of a single horse.

Raine sat bolt upright, every ounce of her attention directed to the clatter of the hooves. No one in Asha-1 had a horse, they were forbidden. Could it be a messenger, someone lost?

The horse was close now, slowed to a walk. Directly outside the door . . . now moving past . . . silence. Raine tried to control her short, gasping breaths. She must not panic.

The knock was hard and sharp. Raine stood, stared at the door. Three more knocks, more insistent, the old door shaking in its frame. Raine inhaled deeply, held the breath, then slowly exhaled. Steeling herself, she walked to the door.

'I have been told by those in the field that I will find the girl called Maliseet here?' asked Menra.

Raine remembered this one. He was the closest to the Warlord, the senior rider in the Procession. Now, alone, his huge body filled the entire space of the door. His deep brown eyes searched the room behind Raine, his bearded face concealing any intent or emotion.

'I am her mother.' Raine's voice betrayed her; it was a frightened, pleading voice.

'Then you will be honoured to know that the great Warlord Renagi requests your daughter brought to him.'

'Why? For what purpose? What need does he have of my daughter?'

Quickly, with complete economy of movement, Menra was inside the hut.

'Where is the girl?'

Maliseet stepped from behind the curtain, walked from the bedchamber. Menra's eyes focused on her. She was inexplicably calm. A feeling exuded from her, an aura. Perhaps she would not be hurt. The feeling extended, took hold of Raine, wrapped her in its safeness, calmed her.

'I am Maliseet.'

Raine stood transfixed. Menra walked to the girl, gently extended his hand. Maliseet took the hand, allowed the enormous man to lead her from the door.

It was as in a dream, Raine watched, unable to speak, to protest, to fight. As if it had all happened before – she was merely watching for the second time . . .

Menra mounted the rippling black stallion. Once securely in the carved leather saddle, he bent down and, with a single effortless motion, lifted Maliseet into the saddle behind him.

He looked once at Raine, a deep, searching look, a look that was almost an apology. Raine stared, drained of emotion, captive in the vacuum of what was taking place. How delicate Maliseet seemed, her pure, nearly translucent, white skin, the fine, long, white hair, the rough, white, cotton dress; all so vulnerable in comparison with the blackness of the Warman.

Finally she made contact, held Maliseet's eyes. And in that moment, the mysterious calm which prevented the pleading tears and screams held Raine's instincts at bay. One long moment of contact and the Warman's heels dug lightly into the black, muscular flanks. They were gone.

Raine watched them ride through the east gate, watched as the horse became a tiny speck in the distance, finally disappearing. Still, she looked after them, as the hollow inside her began to fill. Now it was coming, the aching, the throbbing, growing with every breath. Slowly, she turned to face the desolate, empty room.

One step, two steps, and the feelings began to rise up from the depths of her; deep, primordial feelings, engulfing her, overcoming her. It seemed her life energy had been, in one instant, sucked from her loins. Raine collapsed, tasting the earthen floor; finally, crawling on her hands and knees, she began to sob. A sob that became a howl, a howl that became a shrieking, desperate scream; a scream that became blackness.

*

'Yip!' The ki-ai was short, sharp. A quick expulsion of breath from the diaphragm. The squat, barrel-chested, bare-footed Warman back-shifted slightly. The lunging mae-geri fell short of its target, the solar plexus.

No hips, you cannot make distance with a kick without pushing from the hips.

The observation passed quickly through Renagi's mind as he studied the two Warmen. This was Renagi's favourite physical event, the freestyle kumite. Any man from any province could participate. All techniques were permitted, including joint breaks and strangulation. A contest was decided on submission only, one contestant either unable to continue, or unwilling. No one was ever unwilling, the loss of face would be too great. Better to die, much better.

The taller man readjusted his stance. In spite of his long legs he had been unable to connect with this little bull of a man.

The bull studied the taller man's intake of breath. Just starting to break up, lose its regularity. That was good, the tall man was just starting to become anxious.

The bull shifted forward, then back, in a steady, mesmerizing rhythm. No need to commit, unsettle him first, make him anxious. It was obvious that the taller man did not want to enter punching distance, and certainly not grappling range. No, his opponent was much too well-rooted to risk close-in fighting. The two stood face on, both loosely in sochin stance. They were nearly still, motionless. They studied each other, waiting for the break in breath.

Renagi sat in the Velchar, a carved stone seat, lined in black and red velvet cloth, three body-lengths above the fighting square. Zena and Hiro knelt in sei-za position on each side of their master. On the next level, one pace below, the select Warmen of the Procession sat, their silver goblets brimming with heavy red wine.

In each of the four corners of the Great Hall, a member of the Council of Zendai occupied a carved stone seat. One hundred more Warmen took kneeling positions at ground level, surrounding the square. No civilians entered the Great Hall while the kumite took place, and certainly no women. Today there had been eighteen combatants; there had been six deaths, four men crippled permanently from joint displacement, one blinded, three dehydration blackouts, and two concussed. Two combatants remained in competition; the finalists.

Renagi scrutinized the two in the square. The taller man had the physical advantage, yet the short one was distinctly more centred. Even from this distance Renagi could feel the dark, deep-set eyes bore into the tall man. There was nothing more intimidating than stillness, and the little bull had certainly mastered the slow, deep, lower breathing that enabled a warrior to be calm in the midst of battle. Renagi watched the short but thick feet as the toes curled, pulling the floor, allowing the energy to flow upwards.

Renagi saw the movement before it began. The low, lunging

slide from sochin to an extended zenkutzu stance, the right hand drawn back in nihon-nukite, the two-fingered spear. This would be it, the little man flying towards the tall man, the spear-hand shooting towards the eyes, the force great enough to penetrate the soft tissue and go up – up into the brain.

'Hissss' . . . the ki-ai sizzled through the Great Hall. And then, the unexpected, the waza. As the fully committed nukite attack crossed the half-way mark of the square, the tall man spun and performed a fine back-thrusting kick pulled round at impact. The full force of the small man's charge was met with this perfectly balanced technique.

The snap of the seventh cervical vertebra was marginally louder than the 'yip' ki-ai. For a moment, the small man froze, his head bent back, paralysed, gazing in agony . . . the tall man used the moment to spin forward, the kicking leg now a pivot as he drove his elbow up into the tip of his opponent's mandible. The smaller man's head was now held only by skin, the vertebrae and spinal cord severed as he fell dead to the stone floor.

Everything – the breathing, the anxious eye contact, the short mae-geri – had been a ploy, a feint, a method of making the small man confident, of making him commit.

The tall man turned, and amidst the loud, staccato hand-claps which constituted the Zendai sign of acceptance, he bowed deeply to the Warlord.

Renagi stood, turned slightly to his left. Zena was there, the fine, shining katana held forward, its etched silver hilt glowing through the silk braiding. Renagi took the katana, cradled it, and slowly walked down towards the square. By the time he arrived the combat zone had been cleansed of blood, the dead man removed, and the tall man bowed in rei position before his master.

The katana was two hundred yeons old, the fine steel of the blade had been pounded flat, folded over, pounded again, folded and tempered one hundred times. Never used in battle, never held as a possession, never given life, never given soul, the katana was clean, new. A katana could belong to one man only, carried always by his side, and finally buried with its master.

Tanak wept openly as Renagi bade him to rise and accept the fine, long sword, thus welcoming him to the honoured and select Clan of Warmen.

*

The ride had been comparatively easy; the beautiful, white-skinned child seemed weightless behind him. Menra had, on two occasions, been conscious of the warm, round breasts pressing against his back. Yet only once, when they had stopped to rest and she lay quiet, asleep beside him, did he contemplate the heat of her body, the sweetness of her loins. And even then he had controlled his thoughts, halting them. After all, it was an act punishable by death to fornicate with an untouchable, an Ashkelite. So the journey had continued and now they were entering the outskirts of Zendow. Menra remembered the Warlord's command, 'No one must see the girl'. He would use the secret tunnel, enter the castle by its bowels, then take her to a holding cell before he summoned his master.

As Menra left the fifteen-foot-square cell, lit by a single torch, he could not help but again notice her eyes. If she was frightened it was not evident, not in those wide, amber, open eyes. Menra would have known – after all, he was the senior Warman, trusted above all others. His life, his death, rested on his ability to read men, to read what was written in their eyes. This Maliseet was indeed a strange one; he looked once more at her, sitting alone on the solitary wooden bench. She was definitely not frightened.

*

By the time Menra entered the Great Hall, the Feast of Celebre had begun. The same vast space that hours before had hosted the freestyle kumite, the same vast space that had seen seven deaths, and one great, honourable victory, the same Great Hall that had, for twenty yeons, hosted this event, was now a place of laughter, of boisterous camaraderie, of warm red wine, of drummers, acrobats, women and children. In the hall's centre was the Warlord's table, the Twelve Warmen of the Procession seated in lines to either side of Renagi. Beyond them sat the Military Council the chief advisers, and one hundred of the most honoured Warmen.

As Menra walked towards the table, he was quick to notice the glowing young face of the newcomer. He sat at the end of the table facing Renagi. Tanak looked up, caught Menra's eyes and bowed his head, humbly acknowledging the older man's entrance. Menra bowed quickly to Renagi, and took his place in a heavily carved oak chair, on the right-hand side of his Warlord.

'And it was a successful trip?' Renagi lifted the silver goblet, knowing full well that Menra would not have returned otherwise.

The serving-girl had just finished filling the large goblet when Menra grasped it and lifted it in a toast. He wanted to say, 'A prize worth waiting for', but thought better at the last; perhaps it would show impertinence, or a pre-supposition of his master's purpose.

'A successful trip,' was all Menra said.

Renagi smiled broadly, the great white teeth brightening the face, as the slant, hooded eyes became tightly closed slits in the wide, olive-skinned brow.

'Then drink, drink!' Renagi bent closer, hushed, conspiratorial in tone, 'Madame Wang has two new ones for you tonight – a gift from me ... virgins, true virgins, not Wang's usual re-stitched impersonators.'

Renagi bellowed with laughter at his own comical description. Yes, Wang was known to use the needle and thread. But then, a continual supply of clean, fresh girls below the age of twenty was not always easy to produce, even with the standard fifty golden kons paid to the parents.

Menra relaxed, the heavy red wine soothed him, taking hold and giving him a warm confidence. The toasting began, the traditional raising of glasses. First to each of the Warmen, then to the members of the Military Council. Now the goblets had been re-filled at least one dozen times, for it was the custom to gulp, not sip, the wine. Drunkenness was desired on this night of Celebre. All actions were condoned, even verbal insult to the Warlord – as long as it remained in jest – no one was accountable. The drunken Zendai was clearly a different man to the same Zendai in a sober state. All was forgiven.

The new Warman, Tanak, stood for his toast. Barely stood, as he raised his glass and fell backwards to the cheers and applause of the now roaring Zendai and Warmen. Tanak picked himself up, knowing that even through the haze of his drunkenness he must maintain face this evening. He hoisted his body back to the impossibly long table. All eyes were upon him, the table had quieted, he could feel them urge him, will him.

Taking control, Tanak stood, lifted the once-again brimming goblet.

'To my Warlord, whom I am, from this night onwards, honoured to serve.'

The Great Hall shook with the shouts of 'Hei! Hei!' as clenched right fists punched into the air. Finally, Renagi stood, firm, secure.

'I declare the Feast of Celebre.'

On cue, the bare-chested drummers began the beat. Deliberate, then slowly building, building, as the finest serving-girls carried in the gigantic boar, sitting atop a silver tray, an apple in its huge, tusked mouth.

Four hours later, the table began to quieten as one man, sometimes two at a time, stood, bowed to Renagi, and wound his way to the Willow World. Wang would have a good night, the Feast of Celebre could see her to a fortune in golden kons. Each girl fetched five kons for an hour, and in this state many of the men required a fraction of that time before they gave up, their precious sceptres refusing to rise. Some merely entered the pleasure chambers and collapsed from the wine.

Menra had conserved himself, had drunk just enough to fuel his fire, to promise a long, hard ride to the heavenly plane. His thoughts travelled more and more to Renagi's 'gift' . . . virgins? Yes, it was time to make the move. He stood.

Renagi's hand shot out, caught him by the sleeve of his red battle tunic. Menra looked down, into the hard, dark eyes. He knew the question.

'She is in the holding cell, beneath the escape tunnel,' he said.

'Did anyone see you enter?' Renagi's voice was insistent.

'No one.'

The hand released its iron grip. Renagi grinned his white-toothed grin. Menra walked towards the door.

*

'Maliseet.'

The voice was the same rich velvet, but the timbre was somehow changed, there was a gravelly, slurred quality. The girl looked up; she had been sitting as Menra had left her, on the wooden bench. She had been expecting the Warlord; ever since she had seen him that afternoon it had been impossible for her to think of anything else. Somehow, this handsome, fierce man had captivated her thoughts. Now, here in front of her, he stood. For a moment she panicked . . . what was the correct response, what should she do . . .?

Quickly, she knelt before him and kissed the hard, cold stone floor.

The hand was warm against her neck.

'No, no, no, get up. Let me look at you.'

Maliseet raised her head, her gaze riveted on the reddish-blue, claw-like mark which extended from the right wrist to the mid-point on the top of the wide, muscular, veined hand. He noticed her gaze.

'The Royal birthmark,' he said proudly.

She was standing now, close to him. The smell of wine from his mouth was not unpleasant, but there was a wildness to the man that made her uneasy.

'Like my eyes, it is a sign of purity. Like my eyes,' he repeated the words slowly as if they were a command.

Maliseet looked into the slanted, deep brown eyes. She was, at once, lost. For the first time since the Warman had come for her, she felt the protective shell of her fantasy broken. A quiver began deep within her as she stared into the Warlord's face; she felt his uncompromising dominance. Her body began to tremble.

'You are cold?' Again the warm hand touched her, 'Come with me, this is no place for a . . .' he hesitated, then, bordering on sarcasm, '. . . princess. An Ashkelite princess.'

*

Menra had been twice to the heavenly plane with the first offering. Twice before the screams of pleasure had given way to screams of pain; she had, indeed, been a virgin, yet schooled brilliantly in the art of arousal and inner contraction; probably by Wang herself. Now Menra relaxed, drew slowly on the long-stemmed pipe, filling his lungs with the smoke of the elixir. Somehow the smell always reminded him of violets. As to whether the elixir actually prolonged life Menra was uncertain, but surely the state of total ease which the drug induced was reward in itself. Forty minutes longer and he would be ready for the second 'gift'.

His thoughts drifted with the white smoke as the small, tight rings floated lazily towards the top of the canopied bed. What was his Warlord doing right now? Was he questioning the young girl – but about what? Surely, Renagi could not find the Ashkelite attractive?

Menra's flaccid serpent answered the last question, filling out at the memory of the full, warm breasts pressing aginst his back during the ride to Zendow. What would those breasts look like?

With such a delicate skin, the nipples would have to be pale and pink. Would the aureolas be large, would they cover the entire curve of the breast? And the sacred triangle; the hair must be fine, silky and white. He had never seen a woman with a pure white mound.

Menra was now fully erect; he reached to the top of the round, ebony bedside table, picked up the tiny brass bell, and summoned Madame Wang.

*

Maliseet allowed Renagi to guide her through the dank, narrow stone passages, the torches providing a flickering light. They were completely alone, and their footsteps echoed in the high ceilinged corridors. Finally they came to a solid, high stone wall. Renagi had kept his hand upon her shoulder as they walked, and now, turning to him, she felt the hot hardness beneath his robes. She stepped backwards, away from him, and into the cold stone.

'Be still, I will show you something,' he said brusquely, his face half-covered in shadow. Then, turning, he shoved the heel of his palm firmly into the wall, to the right of her head. Involuntarily, she jumped forward as the concrete moved behind her. Renagi caught her, laughing.

'Go ahead, go up,' he said, indicating the narrow, winding, stone steps behind her. Maliseet was terrified, yet powerless to do anything other than what he asked.

Up, up she walked, feeling his hot breath on her neck as he followed. Her upper thigh muscles were strong, well-developed from the continual squatting and standing motions of the harvest, yet the winding stairs tired her; they seemed to have no end. She moved on and on through the blackness . . . Thump! Straight into another solid wall. Maliseet fell backwards, momentarily stunned.

'Yes, we have arrived. Yes,' Renagi's voice was teasing, almost playful, as he broke her fall.

Another thrusting palm-heel. The concrete rose, revealing a high, domed room – the shape of the quarter moon and a myriad of six-pointed stars cut through the ceiling, allowing the full natural moon to illuminate the canopied bed and thick red gold Miramese carpet.

'Come into my temple,' Renagi urged, as he nudged the stunned girl across the threshold, and the concrete slab creaked

29

back into position behind them. 'Would you care for wine?' he asked, a mocking tone in his voice as he picked up the cut crystal decanter from the ebony table and poured the thick red wine into a huge silver goblet. 'There are ten of these chambers, used by the former occupants as meditation rooms. We have a more worldly purpose for them ... This one is my private, ah, entertaining room.'

Renagi's voice was hardening, becoming more insistent. He began unfastening the sash, loosening his red-and-black embroidered robes.

'Maliseet, shall I entertain you?'

He let the robe fall. In one dramatic moment, Renagi stood naked in front of her, his throbbing, erect penis jutting out, appearing enormous in comparison to his tight, sinewy body. She stood, frozen in fear, unable to stop staring at this man whom she had fantasized as some fine prince or king. He walked forward, gripped her.

Her body recoiled. 'No! No! Leave me ... Leave me! You cannot do this! Leave me!'

With a single sweep of his arm he ripped the thick cotton dress from her; she wore nothing underneath. Her breasts were larger than he had imagined, beautiful pink pendulums, the aureolas huge, covering the entire front of each orb, the nipples delicate but thick.

Maliseet broke his grasp for an instant. There was no escape, but still she ran. She got as far as the bed before he was upon her.

She screamed, 'Please, please, dear God, don't do this to me. Please, my lord ... Please.'

By now Renagi had her pressed backwards on to the heavy silk bedcover, holding her down, his hands against her shoulders while he spread her legs with his powerful thighs. He lowered his head to her, licking her skin, working downwards, below the navel. His tongue felt the fine, silken hairs growing in a thin line, leading him towards the place of magic.

'Please, stop, please, please!' Maliseet screamed.

Her screams echoed over and over, shattering her consciousness, becoming meaningless, animal noises. Then she felt the iron grip upon her hair, pulling her head back as his mouth lowered upon hers, cutting off her voice, the hot, thick tongue pushing inside her mouth, nearly choking her.

She was vaguely aware of his other hand upon her vagina, the fingers roughly prying, opening the contracted lips. Then he released her, raised up and away from her, and quickly brought his clenched fist round in a vicious swipe to the side of her head.

'Be still!' he commanded, as she sank back on to the bed in semi-consciousness. It was then that he entered her, using the spittle from his own mouth as lubrication. The pain was somehow detached, dull, yet ripping.

*

Three days later a work party, harvesting far on the outskirts of the Easterly Fields, found Maliseet wandering towards Asha-1, her white cotton dress in shreds, her body red and swollen from over-exposure to the ultra rays, her face, legs and arms blue with bruises. The amber eyes were vacant, staring; she seemed incapable of speech.

Carefully, touching her only enough to guide her, they led her to the village.

Raine heard the knock on her door. She didn't move; some had been more persistent than others, but eventually they had all gone, leaving her to her anguish. This one would not stop. Knock! Knock! It continued. Finally she stood, rubbed her tired, sunken eyes, ran a hand through the hair she had twisted into knots, and walked to the door. Knock! Knock!

She pulled it open, and was at once blinded by the sun. Slowly, as her eyes focused, she thought she was dreaming. In the centre of the two men and one woman stood her beloved Maliseet.

'We found her in the fields.'

The woman's words were empty, unnecessary to the mother whose deepest prayers had been answered. Her eyes full of tears, Raine looked from face to face in grateful reply, then gently took her daughter by the shoulder and led her to the small, narrow cot in the back sleeping chamber.

*

Day and night she attended Maliseet, laying cool, vinegar-lemon compresses on the swollen forehead, encouraging her to sip the warm broth of carotene and crushed almonds which would, she prayed, restore a balance to the severely damaged skin. And all the time she prayed, prayed for her daughter's soul.

On the seventh day, Raine noticed a subtle change in Maliseet's expression, a new light in the child's eyes.

'Are you feeling a little better?' she asked hopefully, as she held Maliseet's head and guided the cup of carotene to her mouth.

'Yes, stronger, much stronger,' Maliseet replied, the first words she had uttered in more than a week.

Odd, Raine thought, *she seems so void of emotion, empty of gladness. She must know she is safe, she is home.*

The next morning, Raine found her standing naked by the side of the cot, examining her body with her hands, rubbing hard over her abdomen, squeezing her breasts. It was a personal, intimate moment, and Raine turned quickly to leave, hoping the girl had not seen her.

Maliseet looked up, and Raine halted.

'Do you think I can return to the fields soon?' Maliseet asked. The words were more statement than question. The bruising was much fainter, the redness less raw, the compresses and carotene were working. Raine moved towards the girl, to help her back to the cot.

'You still need rest, the skin is not completely healed,' Raine said.

Maliseet stepped back. A look crossed her face, a look Raine had never seen before, a hard look. 'I am fine, Mother. Please, don't touch me,' she said.

Raine backed away, wounded. She told herself that all this would pass, as soon as she could talk to her child, find out what had happened, comfort her.

But it did not pass; not for days, then weeks, finally one month. Any attempt to rekindle Maliseet's memory of the five missing days was met with the hard, stone stare. She was now fully recovered, physically, and she had resumed full work shifts, yet there could be no real contact with her. Raine's feelings of sympathy for the girl, and of her own inadequacy in the face of Maliseet's ordeal, were now giving way to anger. Anger at her daughter for shutting her off; the one person in the world that Raine would die for, and Maliseet was refusing to share her feelings, her thoughts, her warmth.

Five months had passed. The interaction within the close walls of their tiny cottage had been cold, basic. Raine had cooked, cleaned, washed, worked the early harvest shift; Maliseet had worked with the dawn, dusk and alternate night teams. The pattern was always the same; the girl would return from the field, sit briefly while her mother served food, answer only with 'yes' or 'no', refuse conversation. Then she would go to her chamber, pull the curtain, and not re-emerge until it was time for her next work-team.

Five months of living with a total stranger, thought Raine, as she watched Maliseet enter the bedchamber and pull the curtain across the door behind her.

Raine sat on the wooden bench, looking at the heavy, drawn curtain. Five months with no human warmth, hardly any contact. Her anger was sharp and focused. Five months was too long; her daughter's behaviour was inexcusable. Raine stood and walked purposefully towards the drawn curtain.

In eighteen summers, she had never laid a punishing hand on Maliseet, but if now that was what was needed, then so be it. Raine drew in a breath, felt the bottled anger ready to explode, and tore back the curtain.

Maliseet stood naked, her eyes bulging with fear and shame, her hands cupped over her swollen stomach.

'I am carrying his child.' The words gushed forth as if some great, dark, emotional block had finally given way. 'I am carrying the Warlord's child.'

In one gasping intake of breath, mother and daughter were reunited, drawn close by this deep, horrible truth.

By the seventh month the outward signs of the pregnancy were impossible to hide. The morning sickness had continued and, in fact, grown more severe with the passage of time. Finally, Raine had forbidden Maliseet to work in the fields. The last four weeks had been an exhausting and silent exercise in the repression of fear, fear for what was to come.

The contractions began on the eve of the last day of summer; the child came with the rising sun, the head first, and as Raine pulled the bloody infant outwards from the spreading pelvis she was astounded at the thick golden hair which adorned the emerging head.

Not the white hair of an Ashkelite, she thought as she tugged in synchronous rhythm to Maliseet's strained efforts to force the child from her body.

Maliseet did not cry out. Not once. Instead, her face was set in a grim, determined mask of stone, emotionless, intent only on ridding herself of this curse. Now the infant was nearly clear of the stretched and weeping vagina.

'A boy! It is a boy!' Raine shouted aloud, overcome with the miracle of birth and forgetting, for an instant, the circumstance.

'Shut your mouth!' Maliseet spat the words as she completed the delivery.

Raine stepped back, stung, holding the quietly breathing baby in her arms. Then she took the heavy shears from the table and cut the umbilical cord, separating the baby from its mother.

The cord! The cord is like spun silver, she noted, shocked, then turned quickly as the baby screamed in her arms. *And the eyes! The eyes are blue!*

3
THE MISSION

Know the strength of man
But keep a woman's core

(Lao Tsu)

Tabata sat cross-legged on the outer edge of the clearing. Concealed by the late spring leaves of the tall oak tree, he sat in the shadow of Zendow. The stronghold was breathtaking – thick, bonded stone walls standing half an octavoll in height, an intricate complex of sentry-boxes, open guard-posts and iron spikes designed to discourage even the most ambitious of climbers. And, hanging from every rampart, the great billowing banners of the Clan, the red claw painted boldly on to the black silk cloth.

How many Earth lives have led me to this moment, mused Tabata, as he rubbed more dirt into his already filthy begging robes. *How much training, how many months of fasting? How many days of solitude?*

He recalled the last nine months; the long trip west from the Temple, the thirty solitary days in the burning, desolate Valley which separated Lunan Province from Vokane. He remembered the dreams which began in the Valley. Strange, recurring dreams of ivory-skinned men with infinite, turquoise eyes. Men of the spirit, who would guide him, protect him. Men he could nearly recognize, as if he had known them but forgotten or, perhaps, was about to know them.

These spirit-men often remained in his conscious mind as he began his daily meditation. Their image helped him to achieve the transcendental state. A state so free, so void of constraint, that on many occasions he had felt vast sorrow in returning to conscious function. Yes, the last nine months had opened new doors, given him new self-awareness.

Yet, many nights he had lain looking at the stars, listening to the sounds of the forest, and imagining himself once again in the warmth of the Brotherhood, at the Temple. In the early mornings he would find himself listening for the clatter of donkey-drawn carts across the cobbled courtyard, or the laughter of the apprentice brothers as they assembled for morning kata. He had learned that in these ways he was still a man of sentiment, a man who yearned for human companionship, for deep spiritual conversation. At first, he had thought of this as weakness; now, in the last months, he had come to accept the longings, to recognize them as no more or less than a facet of his earth nature, the outer layer of his Earth soul. He recognized in them the very basis of what he was: an artist, whose form of self-expression was his own body. The forest had taught him, expanded him. He had studied the ways of its life, the insects, the animals, the birds. He spent countless hours observing their survival, the techniques with which they hunted, defended their territory, raised their young.

Tabata continued his daily practice of the classical Temple Forms of Empty Hand. He held the fine linear movements of the Jion-ji katas in deepest respect. Yet now he had begun to expand them, incorporate into them the stances and motions of the forest life he studied; the upright, darting strike of the praying mantis, the low, slinking stalk of the margay, the patience and quick ferocity of the coyote, and the visual concentration of the predatory hawk. Taking the classical form Jiin as his foundation, Tabata elaborated upon the kata by adding the 'forest' movements. He practised the new kata each evening at sunset and, through its practice, he grew in tune with his surroundings. The forest became his teacher.

His body had also changed. Gone was the superfluous weight he had carried at the Temple. He had carefully followed the Elder's instruction regarding his intake of food. He had learned to prepare the young leaves of the oak and beech trees, to boil their bark, creating a broth which both nourished and cleansed his system. He had cut back on the traditional Temple diet of rice and grain, thus limiting the soft yin thoughts and righteous attitudes that the diet produced and increasing his harder, more aggressive yang self.

'You must become aware of the ambitions and desires of the men outside this Temple,' were the Elder's exact words as he explained the new regime. Tabata had adhered to every detail, and now, finally, on this thirtieth day of the lunar month, Mayo, he was in Zendow, as instructed, dressed in the guise of a beggar.

The birth had been visible in the astrological charts for many yeons; the Senior Astrologers had been able to pin-point the precise time and date. With the signs imminent, a select unit of beggar-monks were despatched from the Temple, trained to be unobtrusive yet totally observant. Renagi's secret liaison was discovered, the subsequent pregnancy monitored. The Elder's vision of 'The Birth' was the last sign, the final link in the complex pattern of events which led Tabata here, now, as he watched and waited for fate to unfold.

Hours passed, the sun burnt to an ember, night fell. Tabata maintained his cross-legged vigil, allowing himself only periodic phases of light sleep. He had fasted for three days in preparation – not enough time for his body to grow weak, but time enough to clear his physical system and ensure the sharp function of his mind.

He breathed in deeply; the smell of morning was on the light, southerly breeze. His eyes were gently closed, resting. He could feel the faint footsteps, perhaps one hundred paces to his right. In spite of his immense self-control, Tabata was aware of his own excitement, the increase in his heartbeat. He opened his eyes.

She was just entering his field of vision. A young woman, perhaps sixteen or seventeen yeons, with the long white hair and distinctive pale skin of an Ashkelite. The young woman carried the bundle close to her chest, carried it carefully, as if it were alive. Yes, this was *it*, it was actually going to happen.

Tabata performed slow breath retention as he brought his quickly increasing heartbeat back to calm-focus level. The woman walked ahead, proud, her face set firm, the eyes aimed forward. Her gait was nearly a march as she entered beneath the first sentry position.

The voice came from a mechanical voice enhancer, the words echoed.

'Halt! Do not step beyond the designated threshold. Halt.'

The woman ignored the command, as she continued forward.

'Halt,' again the word echoed.

Tabata watched intently as two fully armoured guards moved smoothly from the main gate, barring her way. There was a brief exchange of words, one guard looking to the other, then back at the young woman. She extended the bundle; Tabata could now make out the outline of the infant.

One guard bent down, looked closely, backed away in what appeared to be amazement. He said something to the other guard, then turned and ran towards the main building. Once, the young woman attempted to push past the guard who stood with her. She was easily repelled and held in check.

Perhaps fifteen minutes had passed since her arrival at the gate. She stood sullen, silent, looking down at the infant. Finally he came. Tabata instantly recognized the shining, oiled black hair, the slant-hooded eyes. How often had this fierce Warlord been described to him?

Accompanying the Warlord was an older man, of perhaps fifty yeons. Tabata backed further into the shadow of the huge, gnarled tree.

Renagi bent close, looked at the infant. He seemed relaxed as he turned to the older man, his attendant, and spoke. The young woman reacted to his words, pulled away, her body movements conveying anger.

Sharp and fast, Renagi's attendant snatched the infant from her grasp. She flung herself upon him, was lifted off and held in the air by one of the armoured guards. Renagi was agitated; he snapped an order to his attendant. The man looked at him once, a long, questioning look; Renagi repeated his order.

Carrying the infant, the attendant turned and moved quickly away, taking a dirt path which branched off from the main road.

Tabata could just hear the young woman's screams as the armoured guard carried her into a dark recess below the main wall, out of view of the sentries. Renagi and the second guard followed.

Tabata stood up, straining to see. His eyes just caught the gleaming, long steel blade as it flashed through the air, severing the young woman's head – continuing on its path, cutting through the neck of the armoured guard; woman and Warman fell as one, their blood mixing and soaking the earth.

The second guard stood in horror, his eyes wide, his mouth half-open in question. Renagi spun, and with an overhead motion, the blade arcing high, pulled from the hip – brought the katana downwards, splitting the man's skull into perfect halves, cutting down through the neck and into the torso. At first there was no blood. The man stood, frozen. Renagi pulled the blade from the man's sternum, re-sheathed it as quickly as it was drawn, and took one step back. The man began a twitching, spasmodic dance, the blood shooting, gushing from the long incision.

Renagi turned, and started for the main gate as the Warman fell heavily to earth. The young woman and the two guards lay dead.

Tabata closed his eyes; he could feel Maliseet's sad young spirit travel through him, then up, up, and into the void. He bent his head forward, touched the thumb of his right hand to his right temple, the middle finger to the left.

'May your transition from earth body to spirit be gentle. May your next birth be at one with the light.' He whispered the ritualized words from the Temple's Book of Passage. Then Tabata turned and followed the trail of the attendant and the infant.

Tabata used hengetsu, the swift, silent, half-moon sweeping run, as he moved through the brush. The attendant was in his eye-line, only a hundred paces ahead. It was essential that Tabata be neither seen nor heard.

The river was a quarter-voll away when the attendant broke into a run, carrying the infant towards the water's edge. Tabata noted the man to be in excellent physical condition, his strides long and even.

Tabata was close now, close enough to hear the broken, anxious breathing. Clearly, the attendant did not like his assigned task . . .

Menra veered to his left, ran up on to the grassy knoll overlooking the fast-moving, blue-white water. He stood completely still, calming himself. He had served Renagi for thirty-five yeons; had been assigned as his personal attendant from the day of the Royal birth. How honoured he had been to be selected as guardian to the Royal heir. He had watched Renagi grow, mature, assume the position of Warlord. He had loved and obeyed his master, never doubted him, never questioned his commands – until now, at this moment.

He looked at the strange infant cradled in his arms. The baby no longer cried; in fact, it seemed perfectly content. Could it be so? Menra knew he must never ask. Yet she was the same young woman he had brought to Zendow just under a yeon ago. Yes, it was Maliseet who had brought this child to Zendow, who claimed him to be the Warlord's son. It was Maliseet who had the courage to confront Renagi.

The infant had light hair, similar to that of the Ashkelites, and the skin was pale, but the eyes? They were not pink, they were blue. No Ashkelite had blue eyes. God, could it be true? Could his Warlord have broken the most sacred of laws, could he have mixed his Royal blood with an untouchable? The infant was bundled, led, the body hidden by the old woollen blankets. Should he dare to look? With his right hand, Menra pulled the blanket aside, reaching into the cotton-cloth, grasping the infant's right arm, freeing it from the wraps.

'A male child, a boy!' he gasped. And there in front of him, on the infant's right wrist, was the Sign of the Claw, the royal birthmark. Menra stared, on the edge of shock.

'God of Light, I pray that I am forgiven for what I have done. May I be forgiven for the knowledge I must bear, for what I must do,' he intoned.

Then, near sobbing, Menra re-wrapped the infant, steeled himself and threw the bundle into the swift currents of the river below. The small body hit the water with a dull thud, landing on its back, the face placid, the eyes open. The woollen blanket and cotton padding broke most of the six-foot drop.

Quickly, the water engulfed the small bundle, taking it under. Menra watched, transfixed. Up it bobbed, moving quickly downstream. Under again, then resurfacing.

Is the baby dead? Surely he has drowned. What should I do? Menra's mind raced, *I must make sure he does not live.*

Ahead was the waterfall, certainly he would not survive the fall. *But I must be sure . . .* Menra pushed back his human feelings, buried his heart. *Now, of all times, I must not fail my master.*

He was about to start after the boy when he heard the growl. A low, deep, guttural growl. A sound so menacing that the hairs on his neck stood rigid. Menra looked up.

There, standing on the opposite shore, was the Cat. Menra stared, blinked, then stared again. Surely he was dreaming. No panther could be this large, nearly the size of a stallion; shining black, eyes burning with a red glow, the glistening white fangs extended.

'A sign of the Devil,' Menra uttered as he turned, sprinting full-out, back up the dirt path towards Zendow. Behind him, the howling came.

Tabata listened, heard the howl, recognized this final omen, and dived headlong into the swirling water. The pounding river beneath the waterfall dragged him under. He allowed himself to be taken, to sink down into the dark, churning froth. Finally he touched bottom, his bare feet could feel the cold, large stones beneath the mud. He pushed hard against them, using all the strength in his hips, thighs and lower legs to drive upwards.

His thrust coincided with the baby's fall down the rushing chute of water. As Tabata broke the surface, arms extended, the infant crashed roughly into his chest. Tabata folded himself around the screaming baby boy and kicked hard for shore . . .

4

THE FIRST TEACHING

What others teach, I also teach; that is:
'A violent man will die a violent death!'
That will be the essence of my teaching.

(Lao Tsu)

The clearing was man-made, the ground free of stones and shrubs and the entire area slightly more than twenty paces in diameter.

Yesterday's wood now burned as embers in the deep, square fire-pit which was positioned in the far corner on the perimeter. A simple earthenware pot hung suspended by a single chain above the pit; a thick stew of herbs and forest vegetables simmered slowly.

Several feet to the side and behind the fire stood a sturdily constructed thatched hut. The hut was easily large enough for two men, its reed and grass thatch pinned tight against the latticework of the timber frame.

The forest surrounding the clearing was dominated by the silver-grey bark of the ash, the jagged foliage of the oak and the sheathed clusters of needle-sharp leaves on the high evergreens. The trees provided a natural tent of protection above this forest home of Shihan Tabata and his student, Tegné. Only during the most severe winters were the master and his pupil forced to temporarily vacate these premises and take up short-term residence in the caves to the west, near the lip of the Valley.

Three hundred vul to the east, further than Tegné had ever travelled, was the southern tip of Ashkelan, and, beyond that, lay Zendow.

'Ich.' The strong, full voice rang out, cutting the chill of the early November morning.

Tegné's fist shot towards the flame of the thick, lighted meditation candle. Tabata scrutinized the hip movement, the rotation on the central axis as the fist stopped half-a-hand before the flame.

'No kime. Without kime there is no technique. Again, focus your energy,' Tabata demanded.

'Ni.' Again the punch. The flame quivered slightly. 'San, chi. Ich, ni, san, chi'; over and over Tabata shouted the command to strike. Over and over Tegné responded, the sweat building on his brow, frustration causing his forehead to furrow.

'Ich!' Tabata yelled. Tegné was angry; angry at himself for his failure to succeed at this lesson, angry with Tabata-Sensei for pushing him onward. He readjusted his loose, low, sochin-dachi stance, brought his right fist back, close to the fully twisted hip. 'Yeii!' Tegné ki-aied as his hip snapped forward, throwing the fist towards the flame. The flame blew backwards, almost extinguishing. Tegné willed it out. On the verge of his wishes the flame flickered, then burst back into full life.

Tegné stared at the flame, looked once at his teacher, then turned away in disgust.

The Sensei studied the boy, the face, the posture. For sixteen summers he had nurtured him, taught him, trained him, loved him as a father. Tegné had been a spirited infant, waking at all hours with fits of violent screaming. More than once, Tabata felt cursed with this 'mission'. Never had he dreamed, as he swore the sacred vows of his Order, that his greatest contribution would be the parenting of an outcast son.

Tegné stood before him, the sweat causing his pale skin to glisten as the young blood surged through his veins, defining the newly muscled upper torso. Tabata looked into the deep-set blue eyes. *Tegné – born of the angry water,* he reflected, as he raised his hand, preventing the next punch. His voice was gentle, 'I believe you are missing the meaning of this lesson.'

Tegné avoided his Sensei's gaze.

Tabata continued, insistent. 'The flame will extinguish only if the punch is perfect. Perfect kime, perfect timing, and perfect attitude. To be perfect you must relax, be natural.'

'Perfect?' Tegné repeated the word as he raised his head. There was the slightest hint of a challenge in the breaking adolescent voice.

'Yes.' The strong tone of Tabata's answer quickly restored his student's manner to one of respect. Tabata used the moment, contorting his face, imitating the frustrated, angry boy; he flexed his biceps and performed a stiff, comical punch in the air.

'Perfect,' Tabata said, flatly.

Tegné exhaled; his tense, tight shoulders relaxed, and his lips parted in an easy, engaging grin as he saw the flicker in his Sensei's twinkling brown eyes.

'Now, come with me,' Tabata continued, placing the lighted candle on the ground. Bending, he picked up the soft cotton top of Tegné's training gi and placed it around the boy's shoulders. Then he guided him to a spot on the outer perimeter of the clearing.

'Sit down,' Tabata said. 'Perhaps it is time for a new Sensei,' he added, as he urged the boy into a comfortable half-lotus position. 'Keep your eyes straight ahead, regulate your breathing,' he instructed as he moved behind the boy towards the underground food stores.

Tegné stared into the dry, dense underbrush. The thick evergreen trees overhead blocked the sunlight.

What is he doing? Tegné wondered. He turned towards the hurried sounds behind him.

'Do not look at me. Look straight ahead. Raise your ki from your seika-tanden. Focus through your eyes. Become aware,' Tabata snapped.

Tegné turned back abruptly, concentrating on the forest in front of him. Tabata soon appeared at his side, their evening meal in hand. The filleted trout was attached to a ball of cotton twine, secured on the carved wooden fishing hook.

'Straight ahead,' Tabata reaffirmed his last command. He moved quickly, quietly into the underbrush. He looked towards the east, towards the west, then turned his eyes north. Satisfied, he pivoted and stared enigmatically at Tegné. The boy's curiosity was consuming his discipline. Tabata anticipated the question and put a finger to his lips. Tegné remained silent, but watched, intrigued, as Tabata carefully placed the trout underneath a pile of crisp, golden leaves. Then the Sensei stepped backwards towards the clearing, unravelling the twine as he moved.

'Watch the bait carefully,' said Tabata, as he laid the remainder of the ball of twine on the ground. Then he began to howl, 'Whoo-oop! Whoo-oop! Whoo-oo-oo-oop!'

Tegné turned and looked up at his Sensei. Tegné had removed the jacket-like top of his gi. Bare-chested and moving his arms in a counter-rhythm to his legs, Tabata was alternately bringing each knee up tight to his chest and stamping his bare-soled foot solidly against the hard ground. His fingers were extended and bent claw-like, causing the total effect to be that of a stationary running movement with the legs while the hands and arms seemed to assist by pulling at the air in front of him. The entire sequence was performed in unison with the howl. Tegné stared, genuinely moved by the sheer physical grace of the strange movement and constant beat.

Is this a kata, some form I have never before seen? he wondered, in constant awe of his Sensei's ability to inject such controlled spontaneity to virtually any physical act.

It was then that the light breeze caught the leaves above them and eclipsed Tabata's body in a fluttering half-shadow. Perhaps it was the sudden movement against his Sensei's bare flesh, perhaps even the deepening twilight, but for a moment Tegné was certain that he saw a four-legged animal before him, running against the wind, its eyes caught fierce and bright, staring from the shadows.

'Not at me . . . concentrate on the bait.' Tabata's words broke the illusion as the Sensei halted his movement and stood still before him.

'I have not done this for a long time,' Tabata said, smiling himself now and looking truly puzzled. 'Ah, yes . . . yes . . .' he motioned again for Tegné to turn towards the forest, '. . . different rhythm, that's it, a different rhythm.'

'Whoop. Whoop, Whoo-oo-oo. Whoop!' Tabata howled, with renewed vigour.

Tegné studied the clearing, He focused his eyes on the pile of leaves, straightened his back and centred his breathing. His ki began its flow from the seika-tanden point below his navel up, up towards the optic nerve. The steady, low, 'Whoop. Whoop. Whoo-oo-oo. Whoop!' became mesmeric. The initial curiosity passed, and Tabata's rhythmic dance produced an overwhelming, calming effect within Tegné as he began to feel warm, secure. The feeling crept from his spine, spreading outwards through his limbs. His very heart seemed in perfect synchronization with the 'dance'.

It was dusk when he awakened. He could feel Tabata's presence to his right side. He dared not turn and look, realizing he had dozed off, perhaps missing his Sensei's lesson. He focused his gaze on the forest directly ahead. Thirty paces away, the glowing, black eyes stared back at him. The prairie wolf sat motionless.

'Pay attention to your teacher,' Tabata whispered as he pulled the twine, moving the mound of leaves forward. The wolf did not budge; wonderfully alert, alive, yet completely still. Again, Tabata tugged on the twine; no response. Tegné was fascinated by the creature, the completeness of it, the total awareness.

'Concentrate your eyes, release your mind,' Tabata whispered. Tegné allowed his mind to drift, focusing his eyes on the animal. He brought his breathing to a slow, steady rate, practising a slight retention before exhalation.

The wolf was clearly silhouetted in the moonlight. Tegné studied the expansion and contraction of the chest, becoming gradually aware that the rhythm of the wolf's breathing was exactly in time with his own.

Tabata tugged again at the twine. The hungry animal eyes followed the movement of the bait. Again, Tabata pulled, and this time Tegné felt the tug deep within his own solar plexus, as if Tabata's action had actually touched a point in his own abdomen. His eyes moved involuntarily; he watched the bait jerking through the underbrush. Now he could feel the hunger, the control, the earth beneath him.

Snap! The movement was lightning quick. Tegné jerked forward, his stomach in mild spasm. As he recovered, regaining his seated position, he glimpsed the wolf, the trout in its mouth, springing through the underbrush, disappearing into the moonlight. The connection was broken.

'Did you see that!' Tegné's excitement was a near shout.

'See what?' Tabata's voice was quiet, calm.

'The wolf! The wolf!' exclaimed Tegné, at a loss to divulge the deeper feelings of his experience.

'The wolf?' enquired Tabata, his voice remaining low.

Tegné calmed slightly. 'The wolf took the bait,' he answered, feeling slightly foolish. After all, Tabata had manipulated the lesson.

'And?' Tabata pressed.

'And we do not eat tonight . . .'

The answer was flippant, yet Tegné felt strangely defensive. Tabata smiled, nodding his head, looking at the boy. Then he bent forward and lifted the burning meditation candle.

'To begin. You saw patience, relaxation and perfect timing. That is what your eyes saw. I believe, however, that you also *felt* the wolf,' said Tabata.

Tegné's feeling of discomfort heightened as he shrugged his shoulders, cocking his right arm back, the fist tight to his side.

'Feel the wolf,' Tabata urged.

For some reason, the insistence on the words 'Feel the wolf' angered Tegné, as if they were somehow a violation of his privacy, an unwarranted intrusion into his inner self. His body tensed hard as he threw the punch. The fist contracted sharply in front of the candle flame. The flame did not waver. He looked up and believed he saw Tabata about to laugh.

'That's enough of this! I will not do any more,' Tegné growled, 'I want to learn to fight. This,' he said, looking at the candle, 'has nothing to do with fighting.'

Tabata's voice was stern, commanding, 'Fighting? This has everything to do with fighting. You *are* fighting. Yourself, the candle, your teacher. Because you are impatient, angry.' Tabata looked down at the boy; Tegné's fists had suddenly relaxed.

'Did you *feel* anger in the wolf?' Tabata asked. He did not wait for an answer. 'No, you did not . . . the anger is in yourself. You are full of anger,' he said, handing Tegné the burning candle.

'Stand back.' Tabata's voice was sharp.

Tegné held the flame a half-pace from Tabata's extended fist.

'Go back more,' said Tabata.

Tegné obeyed, moving the full pace backwards. Slowly, fluidly, Tabata pulled his striking arm back.

'If the wolf was like you, he would starve. Your mind and body do not work as one. You know this, the wolf told you – you felt it. And now, for some reason, you wish to ignore it. You must learn to listen, to see, to feel . . . concentrate, make this single act perfection . . . One punch . . . relax, flow like water, then *become iron*.'

With that, Tabata unleashed a fast, flowing punch – his hips pivoting towards the flame, as though the hips themselves were enough to extinguish the light. A *whoosh!* of air accompanied the technique . . . Tegné and Tabata stood in darkness as Tegné felt the last, stubborn, defensive wall of anger give way to trust.

'Forgive me, Sensei. May I try again?' he said, simply.

Tabata bowed, extending his hand and accepting the candle. 'Be patient. Wait for the energy in you to rise. One time. One chance,' he said quietly.

The boy's punch was fluid, graceful, beginning deep in the seika-tanden, allowing the ki to flow through the upper axis, through the arm, into the fist. Throughout the movement, Tegné remained aware of the earth beneath his bare feet. Whoosh! The flame extinguished.

Sensei and pupil stood for a moment in the still darkness. Then Tegné whooped, hopped and imitated the 'dance of the wolf'.

YEON 983
ZENDOW
VOKANE PROVINCE

The straight-stepping punch was basic, too basic. Zato's body was stiff, awkward, the tension constant as his right fist drove towards Renagi's throat. Easily, and with no waste in movement, Renagi caught the fist in his own mitt-like hand and simultaneously performed ashi-bari, sweeping Zato's leading foot from under him, sending the young man sprawling on the ground; then, without disrupting his flow, Renagi executed the 'axe' kick, heel extended. Down, down, the 'axe' descended towards the head of the young man. An instant before contact the foot snapped to a halt, hovering perilously close to the bridge of Zato's nose. A moment later, Renagi withdrew the technique, backed away and looked down at his son. Zato managed a tight-lipped smile.

His father bent forward, extended his hand and helped the boy to his feet. Renagi flushed with pride as they gripped, right hand to right hand, the Sign of the Claw on his own wrist seemed to wrap round and intertwine with the identical mark on the wrist of his son.

Zato was fifteen yeons, a strong, fine-looking boy. The Zendai woman chosen to produce the Warlord's heir had been superb; tall, large-boned, with glowing bronze skin and deep almond eyes. Her bloodline could be traced through ten generations of Zendai – she was pure, and now, although Renagi desired her less and less frequently, Natiro would occupy a place of power within the order of the Clan.

Zato brushed the dirt and gravel from his loose cotton combat uniform, faced his father squarely, and bowed. He knew that

Renagi scrutinized him thoroughly, so he made sure the bow was executed properly from the hip, eyes looking up, maintaining a continual awareness of his opponent. He felt relieved as Renagi returned his courtesy and acknowledged the end of their kumite. Zato turned to leave.

'No! It is not over . . . Now you must watch. Use your eyes and your mind – continue to learn . . .'

Renagi's words stopped Zato in mid-step. A wave of apprehension fell upon the boy as he sat down, facing his father.

'Now you.' Renagi's voice hardened as he motioned for the three trainee Warmen to face him.

Without hesitation, the men sprang to their feet, bowed, and faced Renagi in fighting stance.

At fifty-two years old, the Warlord had tapped the very source of the fighting form. He seemed to ingest the vital energy of the movements, becoming more powerful and deeply grounded with the passing years. His body weight had increased marginally, which added to the muscularity of his frame. He required minimal movement in his kumite, concentrating on subtle body-shifting and the use of his powerful stance. An aura surrounded him, an impenetrable field that required the young Warmen to call upon every ounce of their courage.

Menra stood close by, always attentive to his master. He noted the caution with which the three trainees edged forward, and he moved further to the right, allowing them ample room to shift and manoeuvre.

Although this sparring was performed as exercise, meant to build fighting spirit and technique, it carried with it a powerful element of fear. The Warlord was notoriously rough with his new men, and today the atmosphere was charged with danger.

Menra kept his eyes on the Warlord as he heard the heavy footsteps behind him. Finally Menra turned as the fully suited gate guard approached from the far end of the courtyard. He waved the man to a halt, chastising him with a stern look. The gate guard stood nervously on the outer boundary of the combat square.

What does he want? He knows he is interrupting . . . The thoughts passed with mild anger through Menra's mind as he turned back to view the combat.

The trainee in the centre position was clearly the most aggressive. He edged forward, preparing an attack. Menra studied closely as the young man tensed slightly, took in a deep breath and lunged, right leg extended, the ball of his lead foot aimed towards Renagi's solar plexus. The Warlord waited, waited until the fraction of a second before impact, then shifted to the left, stifling the kick with a downward palm-heel block.

Simultaneously, Renagi struck the attacker's jaw with a short, right, jabbing punch. The blow was deceptive, launched with less than one foot to travel, the power generated completely from the mighty counter-clockwise rotation of Renagi's hips. The attacker dropped heavily to the ground.

Menra shook his head, marvelling at the Warlord's ability to generate such enormous power with an absolute economy of movement.

The two standing Warmen moved in unison, quickly closing on Renagi from opposing sides. The Warlord did not evade their charge, instead he sank low into an open-toed sumo-style grappling stance, concentrating his eyes to the front, exercising his zanshin to gauge their distance.

Menra watched intently. Still he missed the subtle body shift as Renagi forced his hip into the right-side attacker, securing a strong grip on the man's thrusting arm and heaving him upwards and across, timing the throw to coincide with the forward lunge of the remaining Warman. For an instant, Renagi and the Warman seemed a struggling mountain of muscle and flesh. Then, in a masterful backwards slide, Renagi disengaged himself, pushing hard as he moved away from the two tangled bodies. The men struggled, trying to maintain balance, then collapsed in a heap on the ground.

Renagi remained motionless, eyeing the three prone Warmen. Then, slowly, he turned, caught Zato's eye and exploded with a full, deep laugh. His great white teeth flashed in the afternoon sun. Menra smiled and nodded his head. The Warlord was unquestionably a master.

From the corner, the gate guard noisily cleared his throat. Menra turned and grudgingly waved the man forward. The guard double-timed into the square and bowed low to his Warlord.

'Master.' His voice was anxious.

Renagi's 'Yes?' was clipped, impatient.

'There is a beggar in the Great Hall, he demands to see you,' said the guard, thoroughly embarrassed.

'A beggar?' Renagi repeated. 'A beggar who *demands* to see the Warlord?' His voice rose with indignation.

'He came this morning. We put him out, but he has come back. Four times he has come back,' the guard apologized. 'He is a very strange man; he claims to hold vital information, for your ears alone,' he added in explanation.

Renagi's face grew dark. He studied the gate guard. The Warlord seemed on the verge of explosion. Then, in a complete and pre-meditated reversal, Renagi bellowed with laughter.

'A beggar! A beggar! Well, why do you delay? Show him in.'

The gate guard exhaled audibly, relieved by Renagi's good humour, and, as he turned and exited the courtyard, Renagi looked towards Zato, then eyed the trainees.

'Sit down, sit down. We will have a bit of amusement,' he explained.

Sore from their encounter but enormously glad that the 'sparring session' had ended, the trainees bowed to Renagi, then moved into the cool of the courtyard. They were just sitting down when the gate guard reappeared, a haggard, bent, grey-bearded man in tow.

Zato and the Warmen suppressed their laughter as the beggar, a determined glint in his eyes, walked straight towards Renagi, his stiff, shuffling steps giving him an unintended air of pomp.

Amused, Renagi watched the old man approach. Less than two paces away he stopped, met Renagi's gaze, and bowed low before the Warlord. Renagi caught the flicker of light in the old grey eyes. *Probably insane*, he thought, as he performed an exaggerated, low bow before the beggar. Renagi could hear the muffled laughter from Zato and the Warmen; he enjoyed his audience.

'Well?' spoke Renagi, in his most dignified voice.

The beggar, undisturbed by the histrionics, maintained an air of gravity. 'I have seen him,' he said, his voice low and clear, 'I have seen your son.'

Renagi felt suddenly and without reason disquieted by this man. 'My son? My son is here,' he answered, indicating Zato amongst the guffawing group on the edge of the courtyard.

'The Ashkelite,' said the beggar, simply.

Renagi's sudden shift of mood seemed a complete contradiction to the still-laughing and cajoling Warmen.

'Ashkelite?' Renagi's pronunciation indicated the offence the word caused him.

'I have seen him. White skin, golden hair . . .' Before he finished the last word, Renagi caught the grizzled old neck in a vice-like grip, his fingers digging deep into the throat.

'Old man, do you know who I am?' he growled. Then, without waiting for an answer, 'I am Renagi, Warlord of Zendow. A Warlord *cannot have an Ashkelite son*.'

The words were final. Renagi's fingers encircled the windpipe, every instinct urging him to rip it from the neck.

Zato and the Warmen no longer laughed. Instead, they stared, stone-faced, at the bizarre scene. Although too far away to hear the precise exchange of words, they realized the 'game' had become deadly serious. The old man was beginning to choke, his eyes bulging from his head as he stared down at Renagi's right, grasping wrist.

'He bears your mark,' he gasped.

Slowly Renagi released his grip. 'Stand still,' he commanded, then turned and scowled in the direction of the Warmen, 'Out . . . leave me alone with him.'

For an instant the group stayed still, too frightened to move.

'Now!' bellowed Renagi.

In unison, they leapt to their feet and ran from the courtyard. Zato stopped, turned once to look at his father, then followed the Warmen through the gate.

Renagi walked four steps and halted, eye-to-eye with Menra. 'Many yeons past. The baby you took to the river. What happened?' he demanded.

'I did as you told me, Master,' responded Menra, his mind screaming the impossibility of the infant's survival.

'Did you watch the baby drown?' Renagi pressed, his eyes piercing, penetrating the other man. Menra lowered his head.

'I will not ask you again.' Renagi's voice was taut, insistent.

Menra grew calm as he looked up, full into Renagi's face. 'Master, I could not watch your son drown,' he answered, at last at peace within himself, at last free of the burden.

Menra saw the movement begin, the back-fist swinging up from Renagi's left side. He made no effort to defend against the strike, no effort to evade it. He had disobeyed his Warlord, harboured a secret, defiled a sacred trust. He accepted this retribution.

Renagi's rage erupted in a screaming ki-ai. The back-fist caught Menra flush on the right temple, driving the temporal bone inwards, cutting through the trigeminal nerve and compressing the brain.

Menra collapsed to his knees, his face contorting as he lost control of the fine, sub-surface musculature. He wanted to speak, to say 'forgive me', but his mouth would not be controlled. Now the blackness was coming, he could feel the dark, numbing grip. He let go.

Renagi stood above the fallen man. A sadness rushed through him, then the sadness turned to anger, the anger to a steely resolve. Renagi turned and walked back to the beggar. The old man was petrified; never had he seen such finality, and now, as Renagi stood close to him, he could sense the Warlord's fury.

'Where is he?' said Renagi, his tone icy-cold.

The beggar used every reserve of willpower to control his trembling. This was his chance, his only chance, his last. He pitched his voice low to conceal his complete panic.

'My name is Kenuke-Oyama.' He forced the words. Renagi remained stone-faced, showing no sign of recognition. 'When you came to this province, you drove me from my land,' the man pushed on. 'I was feudal lord of Western Shuree.'

Renagi nodded, coldly, as if to say, 'Get on with it'.

'You enslaved my only son.'

Now Renagi began to understand. This old fool had the audacity to believe he could strike a bargain.

'Yes?' said the Warlord, urging the man to finish.

'I am an old man. I have no need of land. But my son ... my son ...' The beggar's fear gave way to sorrow as his voice quivered, and he prepared to empty his heart to the Warlord.

Renagi anticipated the flood of emotion and stepped back. 'You wish me to re-unite you with your son?' he said simply, sparing himself the old fool's tears.

The beggar's face seemed to light from within. 'That is my wish, Warlord.'

'You have my word,' Renagi stated sincerely, solemnly.

The beggar began a low, thankful bow. Renagi's question halted him in mid-motion.

'Where is this Ashkelite?' The voice was business-like, firm; it left no room for anything but a straight answer.

'In Western Shuree, in the forest. This side of the Valley of Death. He lives in the lower cave region with a hermit monk . . .' The words spilled from the old man.

Renagi's eyes registered satisfaction. Keeping visual contact with the beggar, the Warlord walked to Menra's lifeless body and drew the katana from the dead man's belt. The midday sun sent reflections of light from the finely folded steel of the polished blade.

The beggar began to back away. Renagi held his eyes firm as he walked slowly, purposefully towards the cowering man. Finally, with less than one pace between them, Renagi extended the katana to the beggar, hilt-first.

'Show me exactly where he is,' the Warlord said, urging the old man to grasp the extended hilt.

With an involuntary sigh of relief, Kenuke-Oyama accepted the sword. Hurriedly, he began to cut a rough map in the earthen courtyard. He indicated the Valley, the surrounding mountains, and then scratched a series of crosses to show the caves at the base of the mountains. He finished his crude map with a large, deep circle. Pointing towards the circle he said, 'I have seen them here, an encampment. They live in the open, perhaps take shelter in the caves during the winter.'

Satisfied, Renagi took the katana. His thick, calloused fingers wiped the dirt and gravel from the blade. He looked silently into the old man's eyes. It was a burning, raging look.

'Your word, Master, you gave your word,' the beggar pleaded, backing away, his arms held up in defence. He hardly detected Renagi's sliding motion, in fact the initial entrance of the razor-sharp katana was absolutely without pain; only shock as he saw the blade buried nearly to the hilt, through the rib-cage beneath his heart.

'I will keep my word,' Renagi snarled, 'Your son died many yeons ago.'

Now the blade began its deep, intense burning. Kenuke-Oyama exhaled in spurts, the blood beginning to gush from his mouth. It was an agony he could never have imagined. In a final, instinctive effort, he gripped the exposed steel near the hilt and tried to push the blade from his body. He felt his hands grow slippery with blood as the katana cut the grasping fingers to the bone. He heard Renagi's growl, like a mad, rabid animal, 'Now you join him'. Renagi ripped the katana downwards, pulling to the left, disembowelling the old man. Then, slowly, he withdrew the blade, releasing the lifeless body. Kenuke-Oyama fell heavily to the earth.

Renagi dropped the cursed blade beside the dead man and walked briskly from the courtyard. His mind raced. *How much did they glean from what the old bastard said?* he wondered, desperately recalling the episode word by word. *Did they notice I was shaken, or would they think I was merely offended at the affront? Yes, naturally I would be mortally offended. An impostor, an Ashkelite impostor. An Ashkelite claiming to be my son. An impostor, that is what I will tell them . . .*

He pulled the thick hemp rope, sounding the assembly gong. Within seconds the Warmen began to gather in the Great Hall. Renagi scanned the faces, making sure the gate guard and the three trainees were in attendance. What he had to say must be heard by them, must be clear. He could leave no doubt, no room for rumours to begin, to undermine his absolute authority.

By now, nearly four hundred of the Warmen had gathered. Zato entered the hall from the left side, and Renagi noticed the three trainees grouped near his son. Finally, Renagi spoke. His voice was calm, clear and resounding.

'I have been informed this afternoon that a grave breach of conduct has occurred.' The room quietened, allowing the words to ricochet off the thick marble walls and vaulted ceiling.

'An Ashkelite, an untouchable, a slave, has risen to call himself . . .' Renagi paused dramatically, '. . . to call himself Zendai.'

A murmur rose in the crowd. Renagi continued, 'Not only Zendai, but this bastard claims to be . . . my son.'

The men erupted in outrage. Renagi met Zato's gaze, saw the stunned bewilderment on the boy's face. Raising his arms, he again quieted the Warmen.

'Naturally, it would serve their purpose to kindle such a lie, to cause insurrection amongst us. As I speak, this impostor is in hiding.' Renagi paused, scanning the faces. 'I will take six of you with me. We will rout him out, destroy him,' he concluded, eyeing the Warmen, studying each man. There was no doubt in any of their eyes; they accepted his statement as truth.

'Now line up in order of rank.' He was completely in control, matter-of-fact.

The gathering legion of Warmen formed into tight lines, structured according to seniority, shoulders squared, eyes forward. If Menra's absence was noted, it was certainly not apparent. It had been many yeons since Menra had ridden in a war party, and Renagi was fully aware that within this pecking order no tears would be shed on account of his attendant's 'sparring accident'.

Renagi pulled Tanak, the senior Warman, aside. 'Pick out five of the strongest,' he instructed, then waited as Tanak made the selection. The Warlord dismissed the remaining men, leaving only the six. Then he reviewed Tanak's choice. Satisfied, Renagi confirmed the time of departure.

*

Day-break, and the six Warmen sat astride their horses in the outer courtyard. Frost lay on the ground and thick, white breath billowed from the snorting stallions. The Warmen were dressed in their winter gear, the thick lacquered leather body armour clinging tight to them.

With a clatter of hooves, Renagi rode through the far gate and trotted towards them, his huge, white horse almost identical in appearance to Kano, his sire.

Tanak looked up as Renagi pulled firmly on the reins. 'All prepared and ready, Warlord,' the senior Warman said confidently.

At that moment another, unexpected, rider appeared from the adjacent courtyard. The Warmen turned to see Zato, fully suited, riding towards them.

'What are you doing here?' There was nothing friendly in Renagi's voice.

Zato was caught unprepared for his father's severity. 'I am coming with you,' he answered meekly.

The Warmen remained quiet as Renagi allowed a long, angry silence. 'You are *not* coming with us,' he said, then added scathingly, 'You are going back to your *mother*.'

The words held a belittling connotation, and Zato was desperate to save face in front of the Warmen. He eyed his father, his lips tight, face seething.

'I said *go back*!' Renagi bellowed, nearly shaking the boy from his horse. With this final command the Warlord turned, heeled his stallion and galloped towards the main gates. The six Warmen followed.

Zato sat motionless, watching the seven men vanish into the thick woods and heavy mist.

YEON 983
SHUREE FOREST
VOKANE PROVINCE

Tegné retained his half-lotus posture, not more than a single pace from Tabata. Their light, upper-level breathing was synchronized in the slight chest movement. Tegné had not reached the transcendental state, yet through this daily practice he had begun to feel traces of the freedom it held. Tabata had begun teaching the boy the classical asanas, stretching postures accompanied by breath retention and control. When Tegné's body reached a level of flexibility, enabling him to sit comfortably in full lotus for two or more hours, Tabata introduced the practice of contemplation. At first, objective contemplation; the quiet, focused study of nature. The study of a single oak leaf, the reason for its structure, the method by which the organism sustained life, drawing water and nourishment from the earth, transmitting the digested food throughout its intricate system of veins and capillaries.

Tabata used the objective contemplation to develop Tegné's powers of deep concentration. Then, when the boy had naturally begun to link the external world with his own body, when he had begun to understand intuitively his own part within the whole, Tabata had directed the contemplation inwards. He urged Tegné to feel the beating of his own heart as it sent blood, carrying nourishment, through his own veins. In time, Tegné realized he was also connected to the forest, and the forest to the Earth, a small part of this gigantic living organism. He recognized the nature of his human condition, the smallness of his self, and the greatness of the Earth's spirit. Tegné had begun to attain that most essential quality, humility.

Tabata had given the boy a simple mantra, a phrase which, when repeated continuously during the deeper contemplative state, led to the brink of true meditation. The mantra began with the boy's name, 'Tegné', repeated over and over until the name became merely a word without connotation, a single star in a galaxy of stars. As soon as this state was achieved the mantra was altered. 'I am a wave, make me the sea,' repeated until the mind was without thought or emotion, a flat, shimmering surface. Tegné hovered here, on this plane, feeling the beginnings of the transcendence.

> *They are the sacred circle,*
> *The Seven Holy Spirits,*
> *They are the Primal Virtue.*

Tabata was in Vakos, deep within the vision. He had come to know his dream men as the Protectors. Now he was able to commune with them, breaking the ties of Earth, to soar through the void and find them. Guardian spirits. They waited, guided, made him understand. Gave him the strength to witness the black, satanic body as it rose from the vapour. To gaze into the eyes of the Beast. Swirling chasms of darkness, windows which looked into the heart of evil; mirrors which reflected the hidden horror of every mortal soul.

One moment without form, the next a compelling fantasy. A woman, a feline. Exquisite in grace and movement. Captivating. Enticing. Drawing one closer. Encompassing. Deadly. And just as he could stand no more, just as he was willing to be drawn towards this dark power, to surrender, the Protectors were there. Encircling, shielding, helping him to accept the gravity of his own role in their ancient struggle. Making certain he realized the truth of the prophecy. For the millennium was near an end, and the Seventh Incarnation was imminent; the seed of the Beast was to be manifest on Earth. Manifest in the form of a female, a daughter.

Without sorrow, without attachment, Tabata felt his own frail mortality, realized his time was short, and understood more clearly than ever the importance of the young man who sat before him.

'I pray that I have taught him well, prepared him for what is to come,' Tabata whispered.

'I thought you had stopped breathing,' Tegné cajoled, as his Sensei's eyes opened.

'One day, perhaps, but not today,' Tabata answered, a fine warmth in his voice.

Tegné looked with love towards his teacher, feeling the deep calm produced by the two-hour meditation.

'Are you beginning to find the way?' enquired Tabata. Tegné

looked puzzled. 'Through your meditation and your practice of the Empty Hand,' Tabata said, becoming more specific.

'Yes,' Tegné said simply.

'And can you tell me the way?' Tabata asked, using this quiet, internalized state to build a firm intellectual understanding of his lessons.

'It is freedom from emotion. No anger, no passion, no violence. It is clarity; the same clarity in meditation as in Empty Hand,' Tegné explained, sure in himself.

Tabata smiled slightly and nodded, urging the boy to continue.

'The punch, the strike, the kick, each of the movements is an exercise in perfection, awareness. Each, when performed with an unclouded mind, leads directly to our centre, finding strength in our source,' Tegné continued, his understanding belying his youth.

Tabata listened, allowing the words of his pupil to fulfil him. 'And in Empty Hand, what is the meaning of victory, of defeat?' he asked softly.

'There is no meaning, Sensei, both are illusions, clouds before the eyes. The meaning of Empty Hand lies only in the perfection of self,' Tegné answered, retaining the calm of the meditation.

'Do you experience fear during your training, during your meditation? Are you frightened of death?' Tabata centred on the word.

Tegné sat still, quiet. Finally he replied, 'Yes, Sensei, I am ... Yet, I will not allow my fear to prevent me from pursuing my path. I will move on in spite of it, until fear, too, vanishes like the clouds of thought and emotion. The way is to rise above, both during meditation and Empty Hand.'

Satisfied, Tabata stood, motioning for the boy to join him. Together they walked to the centre of the clearing, and stopped in front of the unlit meditation candle.

'And do you understand, Tegné, that the same power, the same source which takes life, is also able to give life?' Tabata said reverently.

The Sensei drew his right knife-hand back far behind his right shoulder. He hesitated, allowing Tegné to ponder. Then, as understanding dawned in the young, blue eyes, Tabata brought the knife-hand smoothly, sharply across the wick of the candle. As quickly, he withdrew his hand and relaxed, smiling.

Tegné gasped, nearly disbelieving what he saw as the unlit meditation candle flickered into life, the flame finally burning full and bright.

*

They had been riding for eight hours. The horses were tired and the Warmen wondered if Renagi would ever call a halt to this journey. Since leaving the gates of Zendow, the Warlord had not spoken, had broken gallop only when the forest was too thick or the terrain too rough to push his stallion onward.

Tanak had never seen his master in such a state. He observed the tension in Renagi's neck and shoulders . . . *Surely, one pathetic slave claiming to be a Royal heir is more deserving of scorn than fury,* he reasoned, maintaining the appropriate twelve paces behind the Warlord. *The man seems possessed . . . God help the Ashkelite when he finds him . . .*

Tanak's thoughts were disrupted by Renagi's sudden slowing of pace. Swiftly he brought his mount to a trot, the five Warmen behind him doing the same. Renagi sat still, then turned in his saddle and with his gloved hand signalled them to approach.

'Tonight we will camp here,' he said, indicating the distinct fork in the road. 'In the morning,' he pointed roughly to the Warmen outside of his circle, 'you three follow the narrower, less travelled route. If you should come upon him, bring me the head, the right wrist and hand. I understand this bastard may be tattooed.' He extended his own wrist, displaying the Sign of the Claw. 'Do not fail.' Renagi's words were final.

Morning. Arton, Herok and Zanar were making little progress. They had departed at dawn, determined to find the Ashkelite, to fulfil their Warlord's bidding. Each knew their success would guarantee seniority amongst the Warmen. Yet, within two hours of beginning their ride west along the narrow dirt trail, barely wide enough to trot single file, the underbrush had become dangerously thick, the trees full and the stony ground impossibly uneven.

Zanar, the archer, Herok, the swordsman, and Arton, the grappling master, rode forward in silence. The trees were gnarled, thick; they stood proudly, as though the passing years had made them wise, and now they mocked these impudent human creatures who possessed the audacity to penetrate their darkness. The remaining leaves completely blocked the sun, creating an unnatural coldness to the air, and the trail was now little more than a narrow furrow created by the recent autumn rains, treacherous with sharp rocks and crumbling earth.

Finally, the three Warmen dismounted, and each led his horse forward.

An hour later, Arton spoke, breaking the long, tense silence. 'I say we turn back, catch up with the others, this is leading nowhere.'

'And how do we explain that to Renagi?' answered Herok. 'We were lost, the trail was too difficult?' he asked sarcastically.

'There will be *no* turning back.' Zanar's words settled the discussion; he was the senior Warman of the three and the responsibility rested with him. They would plod on.

Dusk came, and they were tired, hungry and cold. Herok had taken the lead, point position. The ground was soft and wet, and he had fallen twice within the last hour. Still he increased his pace, sighting the small area of flattened scrub less than twenty paces ahead. He pushed himself forward, tugging at the reins, dragging his horse with him in spite of its neighing protests against the knotted bark which scraped and bruised its flanks. Herok had just touched the outer edge of the small clearing when he stopped, bent down and picked up a small piece of timber.

'Someone has been here!' he said, excited, urging the others forward. He held the small, burnt log under his nose, sniffing the freshly charred wood. 'This fire was recent.'

Suddenly, all feelings of hunger and fatigue vanished. The hunters, having scented the prey, felt vigour return to their bodies.

'Tonight we stay here, no fire, no noise; in the morning we find them,' Zanar said.

Quietly, the three Warmen unsaddled their horses, then used the thick woollen saddle blankets to wrap around their shoulders as they unpacked their field rations and prepared for a long, cold night.

Less than five leagues to the west, Tabata sat in sei-za, tuned to the unsettled movement of the forest. Tegné lay close by, curled asleep near the rising warmth of the evening wood. Tabata looked at the fine young face. Tegné's waist-length golden hair lay across his upturned shoulder and then fell back, cascading on to the pine needles which lay upon the forest floor.

Still, he is so vulnerable ... thought Tabata, as he watched the boy's calm, even breathing, ... *and to know what is expected of him* ... Tabata allowed this moment of sentiment for the young man who had been his adopted son. Then he refocused his energy, entered the state of zanshin, and resumed his mental preparation for what lay directly ahead. He had sensed danger in the air for the past three days. It was not the instant, quick danger of a hungry wolf or prowling bear. This was danger of another kind, a dark foreboding, heavy with the finality of fate.

There will come a time; you will know in your heart and your soul that your work is complete. Prepare for this time, do not let circumstances catch you unawares, or all you have done will be lost. The Elder's words stayed with Tabata tonight. Again, he looked at the sleeping boy. *So much I would like to tell him, so much I can never tell him.*

As if he could sense Tabata's thoughts, Tegné stirred, nearly waking, then lapsed back into sleep. *Yes,* thought Tabata, *fate is the hunter.* Again Tegné stirred. This time, Tabata shifted his mind position, entering the peaceful void and allowing the young man to sleep deeply.

Sunrise ... not one Warman had slept more than three hours. The noises of the forest and the knowledge of human life so near kept their defence mechanisms high. They had waited silently and impatiently for the first break of day. The ground was cold, a frost had formed, and the thick horse blankets had been a poor substitute for a roaring fire.

Zanar was the first to speak. 'Not another night like that ... we find him today and we get out of here, then it is finished.'

Herok and Arton grunted their approval as each made off in separate directions to relieve their bladders and bowels.

'Definitely *not* another night like that,' grumbled Arton as he cleaned himself with a handful of cold, wet leaves.

Midday. The autumn sun was exceptionally warm, the frost had evaporated and the earlier, morning mist was gone. A light, westerly breeze drove the small, scattered nimbus clouds through the blue sky. Tabata had not slept, the feeling of danger was strong.

Tegné was an arm's length from him, leaning over, picking the bitter marjoram leaves from the tall, slender, pink-flowered plant. Tabata reached out, intending to adjust the small sack slung across Tegné's shoulder. His hand stopped dead as it entered the icy void surrounding the boy.

'Caw, caw ...' Instinctively Tabata withdrew his hand and looked to the sky. The huge black hawk, its wings spread, hung motionless, its body obscuring the sun. Tabata watched the giant bird circle once, twice, three times, then silently disappear, vanishing into the light.

A time when your work will be complete. Pay heed to the signs ...

'Tegné, come here,' Tabata said gently.

Placing the last leaves into the sack, Tegné straightened up and walked towards his Sensei. He had noticed a subtle change in his teacher these last few days. The change was difficult to explain; Tabata's manner had grown more serious, the twinkle in the old man's eye had been replaced with perhaps a touch of sadness. Tegné had wanted to ask if there was something troubling him, but he did not. If his Sensei wished to confide in him he would.

Tegné stood facing his teacher. He was nearly as tall as Tabata, and he looked searchingly into the deep brown eyes. For a long moment there was silence between them, then Tabata took the 'Sign of the Brothers' from his own neck and placed the leather thong which held the circular disc, with its silver quarter moon and single gold star, around the neck of his pupil.

Why is he doing this? I have never seen him without the Sign of the Brothers. The medallion is part of him ... Why? Tegné questioned, without voicing his thoughts.

At last, Tabata spoke. 'Many yeons ago I left the temple of my brothers. I came to this forest alone. I had a mission.'

Something in Tabata's manner, in the weight of his words, made Tegné pray his Sensei would stop, take back the medallion, wipe this moment from his memory.

'To save you from the river, to train you, to be a father to you ... Tegné, you were my mission ... now our path together is near an end.'

Tegné could hold back no longer. Sorrow burst within his heart, and the questions began to form again on his lips. The questions that had long burned inside him, the questions he could never ask.

'Why, Sensei? Why have you never told me of my parents or where I came from, why you have trained me? Why was I your "mission"?'

The words hung clear and motionless in the space separating the Sensei and the boy. Tabata stood completely still, his eyes locked on those of his student. An impenetrable wall surrounded him. Tegné turned his head down and away, ashamed.

Finally, Tabata spoke. 'I have not because it has been forbidden me to do so. You have been unable to ask because I have hardened my heart to you before the question could so much as leave your mind. Now, for this moment, my heart is open to you. And still I cannot reply. Yet I will tell you, there will come a time when you will know. And I command you, ask no one these questions. Trust. Wait. For time holds the answers.'

Tegné raised his head, saw the compassion in the eyes of his teacher. He recognized the love, yet there was more, much more inside those dark eyes. There was an acceptance, a final acceptance. *Is it death?* Tegné wondered.

'Our spirits will never part,' Tabata said simply, smiling, and then, as if in afterthought, he looked again at the medallion. 'Follow the Light of the Moon ... remember, the Light of the Moon.'

The trail had widened, allowing Arton, Zanar and Herok to mount and ride their horses. Still, they had moved slowly, cautiously, not wanting to give warning of their presence.

Arton was first to notice the trampled path branching off from the main trail and leading into the dense forest. With a shrill whistling signal he drew the attention of the other Warmen. Then, deftly dismounting, he pointed at the flattened grass and underbrush.

Now the strict military training of the Warmen took hold. Zanar, immediately in command, signalled for the horses to be tied, and the men to proceed armed and on foot, no voice communication between them. He crouched low to the ground and examined the footpath. It was well worn and about one pace wide, no clear marks of heel or shoe prints. Zanar knelt and looked up into the expectant faces. He used his hands and fingers to explain in sign language; the path had been used frequently and by two people. The grass was bent, yet not broken, indicating the bare feet and trained, sure movement. The most recent indentations showed the length of stride to be about one pace from toe to heel, probably two men of between five-foot-five and five-foot-nine in height and ten to eleven stone in weight.

Two men – exactly what we have come for ... he thought, as he motioned for Arton and Herok to follow him. Silently, in a state of alertness, the Warmen tracked their prey. The warm sun set, and the cool, full moon began to rise.

Tegné sat cross-legged, staring at the placid, closed eyes of the Sensei.

Time holds the answers ... The words danced and played on the still surface of his mind. The incident of the medallion had come and passed, and now Tabata insisted again on the usual ordered routine of meditation, Empty Hand training, rest, food, more training and meditation. *As if nothing of any importance has happened,* thought Tegné. Yet, the medallion hung around his neck, its fine metal alive in the light of the moon. And his teacher sat in front of him, close enough to touch, yet present in physical form only, for Tabata's mind and spirit had gone beyond. Finally, Tegné closed his own eyes and tried to control his drifting thoughts.

Tabata was in Vakos. The seven ethereal, white-robed and hooded men beckoned him, guided him and, as his finer astral form floated close to them, they urged him to gaze into the turquoise flux of their eyes, to gaze into infinity, allowing Tabata this final, calming preparation for what was to come. Only the thin, glowing, silver thread extending from the crown of his head prevented Tabata from forever leaving his coarse, restricted Earth body. Only this fine thread and the latent knowledge that his Earth karma was not yet complete.

Tabata's first awareness as he returned to conscious function was the unnatural stillness of the forest. He brought himself rapidly to zanshin. His eyes remained closed as he concentrated his energy on the sporadic warning cries of the owl. Then silence. Tabata opened his eyes and spoke in a low whisper, 'Tegné, Tegné.'

Tegné looked up. What was his Sensei doing now? He *never* interrupted a meditation.

Tabata anticipated the boy's reaction. 'Be still, don't speak,' he whispered.

Tegné kept his body motionless, allowing his eyes to search the perimeter of the clearing, looking into the dark, deep forest.

'Very quiet, like death,' Tabata's words were barely audible.

Tegné recoiled. In response, Tabata reached towards him, firmly and reassuringly gripping the boy's right forearm and wrist, the wrist which bore the mark of Renagi.

Tabata breathed in, a long, deep breath, as he moved his eyeballs high in their sockets, employing his night peripheral vision to scan the perimeter and surrounding trees. He made out the black silhouette of a man climbing upwards into the thick-branched beech tree about thirty paces to his left. He did not allow himself to linger on the man, but quickly shifted his focus to the rustling sound in the underbrush directly ahead.

The thought, *Keep the left covered, defend to the front* . . . flashed through Tabata's mind as Herok, his katana high above his head, exploded from the forest. In one sweeping movement, Tabata rose from sei-za, at the same time pressing down with his right hand, forcing Tegné lower to the safety of the ground.

There was a look of surprise, even shock, on Herok's face as he watched the old man flow like liquid before him. Then he felt the paralysing pain as Tabata's thrusting heel pushed deep and sharp into his groin.

Herok collapsed screaming, the katana still gripped in his left hand. Struggling, the Warman rose to his hands and knees, and just managed to shout, 'The boy! Take the boy!' when Tabata's instep crashed mercilessly into the upper ribs near his heart. His last image before losing consciousness was of Arton's lumbering charge, as the wrestler caught the old man and hoisted him into the air.

Drop him, drop him . . . give me room to shoot, willed Zanar, poised on the thick branch, his wide, steel-tipped hunting arrow loaded and drawn.

Arton could feel no movement in the body between his muscular arms. The old man was small, limp, and apparently dead. He was about to squeeze the lifeless flesh once more, to be sure, when he felt the burning heat, immediately so hot he could not bear Tabata's body near him.

Arton released his grip, and Tabata slid to the ground,

continuing the Dragon Breath as he rebounded, bringing himself up under the wrestler's jaw, driving hard, forcing Arton's head to snap backwards, momentarily exposing the vulnerable windpipe. With his right spear-hand, Tabata struck a percussive blow, breaking the larynx. Arton collapsed to the earth, choking for air. Tabata pivoted, his eyes searching desperately for Tegné.

The boy stood perhaps four paces behind him to his left. Tabata recognized the glazed look in Tegné's eyes; fear, paralysing fear. He was about to call out when Zanar released his arrow. The spring-loaded war-tip opened upon entry, fanning out against the flesh and gristle of Tabata's chest, thudding through his rib-cage below his heart. The Sensei's final command of 'Go! Run!', intended for the boy, was caught, blocked in his throat as if the unformed words were made of a solid, choking fibre. Tabata sank to his knees, the unspoken plea trapped in his eyes.

Tegné's legs carried him towards his Sensei while his mind screamed for him to run, to leave this nightmare behind. Yet he could not run, he must help. He must.

On the other side of the clearing, Herok had recovered enough to go for the boy. He lurched forward unsteadily, his arms raised high, the katana between his hands.

Tegné had just reached Tabata's crumpled body. Now he gripped his Sensei's shoulders, trying desperately to lift him. With a supreme effort, Tabata turned his head upwards, his eyes meeting the eyes of his student. Suddenly the Sensei's face was old, tired, the skin wrinkled and drained of colour.

'Please, no, don't die. No ...' The words fell from Tegné's lips. The tears had just begun when Herok began his final lunge, the katana held before him, the curved blade aimed straight at the centre of Tegné's back, between his shoulders. *Straight through and into the heart,* Herok promised himself as he reached full momentum.

As if in answer to his spoken prayer, Tegné felt Tabata's body tense, as if he was about to stand. Then, with an unexpected jolt, the Sensei swung his right arm in a cutting motion, slamming the forearm against Tegné's thigh. Tegné was flung to the left, in time to see Herok's sword sever the extended right arm and shoulder of his teacher. Blood spurted in a thick fountain of red, and Tabata groaned as he fell face forward to the earth.

Tegné turned on Herok, raging against him. The Warman

released his grip on the katana, leaving the blade buried deep in Tabata's flesh.

'I'll tear the fucking head from your shoulders!' Herok vowed, enraged that the boy was still alive.

Behind the Warman, Tegné was certain he saw Tabata move, attempting to crawl towards the Warman's black-booted foot. Tegné prepared for the inevitable charge, sinking into a low sochin stance. Yet as Herok fully faced him, his eyes wild with the intent to kill and the red Sign of the Claw on his body shield augmenting his invulnerable presence, Tegné felt his spirit give way. He stared at the Warman as a condemned man might stare at his executioner, accepting the inevitable outcome of their clash – death.

It was then that Tabata reached out his left arm from his face-downward position and grabbed Herok's ankle. Herok spun around on him. 'Yaaa!' the Warman shouted, kicking savagely at Tabata's face, shattering the old man's nose like a fly beneath a brick. The bloody sight caused the full force of Tegné's fear to break inside him. Overpowering him. He heard himself scream in a high, unfamiliar voice as he pivoted away from the carnage, away from his teacher.

He sprinted for the thick of the forest and into the night. His exposed skin was scraped and cut against the gnarled tree limbs and evergreen shrubs. Still he ran; his own screams continuing inside his mind.

Zanar fumbled with the arrow, cursing out loud as he watched the boy disappear. Quickly, he climbed down from the branch and walked into the clearing.

The swordsman could hardly meet Zanar's gaze, so great was his humiliation at allowing the boy to escape. Together, the Warmen examined Arton's lifeless body. Blood ran from his mouth, down his chin and across the black leather of his tunic; his windpipe had been crushed, the Adam's apple broken and displaced. Zanar looked once more at Herok, shook his head and turned towards the old man.

Tabata lay on his back, the single broken arrow embedded deep in his chest. Herok's katana lay on the ground beside him, next to Tabata's right arm. Herok stepped scornfully on the out-stretched hand of the severed limb, bending to retrieve his sword. Carefully he drew the blade between his thumb and forefinger, to clean it as he re-inserted the steel into the wooden lining of his scabbard.

Strange . . . There is no blood on the blade, he mused.

'We get the horses, find the boy,' Zanar said, interrupting Herok's thoughts. 'There is no going back!' he added, misinterpreting the question in Herok's eyes.

They had reached the edge of the clearing when something, some strange, inexplicable feeling, made Zanar turn and look back. His hand shot out, gripping Herok and spinning him towards the clearing. Both men froze.

How can this be? Herok's mind reeled.

'It is impossible,' Zanar answered aloud.

The decomposition of Tabata's body was already in its advanced stages, the skull and rib-cage fully exposed. Dumbstruck, the Warmen watched as the robes and skin flaked off, blew upwards, funnelling into a shimmering spiral, rising into the night sky. Within seconds, the spot where Tabata had lain dead was empty. No blood, no clothes, no trace of the Sensei. Herok stared, glassy-eyed. 'God of Light, deliver me from Satan,' he prayed.

Tabata's ki-ai broke the spell, rolling from the heavens like thunder, causing the ground to vibrate where the Warmen stood.

'Come on! Move! Now!' Zanar's desperate, instinctive command snapped both Warmen to their senses. They turned and ran from the clearing.

Tegné covered the first two vul easily. The running had dispersed the adrenaline inside his body and numbed his fear. He maintained a rhythmic pace, following the trail west. He knew the Warmen would pursue him, yet he still clung to the dirt path, not wanting to enter the forest and lose the guiding light of the moon. He remembered the fallen man screaming, 'The boy! Take the boy!' His mind searched for a reason; why, why did they want him? Enough to kill and to die. Yet on top of this another thought plagued him. *I have been a coward. A coward in the face of battle. I abandoned my Sensei to save my own worthless flesh . . .*

Mind like water. Mind like water. Tabata's words overrode his anxieties. Now, of all times, he must be clear, calm. *No negative thoughts. They will drain you, make you weak.* Again he heard Tabata's voice as he quickened his pace, keeping to the trail, following it down, down towards the low, treeless plain. He hesitated, looking ahead. He knew if he continued forward he would be completely exposed, an easy target.

Follow the Light of the Moon ... The words seemed to float next to him. He was running full-out by the time he hit the bottom of the trail and entered the open plain. Now the ground began to rise gradually and the fleshy bulk of muscles covering the front of his thighs started to burn.

Too fast, I am moving too fast, he told himself. Still, he knew they were coming. Closing. Mounted, riding ... he could sense the heartless beat of the hooves against the earth, as sure as the hammering within his chest. He could not slow down; he would push on until he found that place inside himself where no limits existed, no pain ...

Run ... run ...

Zanar checked the trail; he was relieved to find the footprints running in a consistent direction west, not varying in stride, giving no indication of intent to alter course. Herok rose in the saddle, trying to keep his bruised testicles from the uncomfortable contact with the hard leather.

Zanar remounted, looked once at Herok and spurred his horse. The stallion leapt forward, seeming to understand the urgency of its rider. Herok followed.

This was a chase, the road was wide, the ground dry, and the moon full and bright. Zanar and Herok raced along the western path. Minutes later they arrived at the wide, open plain. Zanar raised his open hand, signalling a halt.

Both men stretched high in their saddles, scanning the clear ground ahead. Zanar's lips parted in a satisfied smile, his heart began to pound. For, directly in front of them not more than six hundred paces ahead, he saw the small, running figure; the golden hair glowing like some incandescent halo in the light of the moon.

Now we have him, Zanar thought, as he turned, catching Herok's shoulder with a sharp slap, before pointing towards the boy.

It was then that Tegné looked back and saw the dark, mounted silhouettes; he watched the horses spring to life, surging towards him. Ahead, perhaps a hundred paces, a sharp rise led into a thick patch of woods. He willed his leaden legs to move faster, to climb the last hill. He was near the top, gasping for breath, pulling the grass and roots with his hands, pushing with his thighs, slipping, struggling.

'There! There!' Herok shouted above the thudding of hooves, pointing towards Tegné as the boy crawled into the thick underbrush. 'There's no way out, just the valley behind!' he continued, thinking aloud, as he viewed the high, jagged rocks on the outer edge of the patch of forest.

'Circle right, I'll go left, then we close on him,' Zanar commanded, taking charge.

Tegné lay face down on the earth, grateful for this moment of rest, hidden from the Warmen amongst the tall, thick trees. Slowly he pulled himself to his hands and knees, breathed in, filling his lungs, aware of the aroma of the dry, crisp autumn leaves. He felt them shroud him, protect him.

Hide until nightfall, hide, he reasoned as he rose to his feet and moved swiftly, quietly into the dense woods.

THE PLANE BEYOND
TIME: SYNCHRONOUS

The Protectors sat in a circle, legs folded beneath them, spines erect, hands joined. Father began the chant, a low hum originating in his diaphragm and filling the space before him with a dense, textured joining of molecules which grew visible to his eyes.

'Aoum, aoum, aoum,' the six joined in, concentrating on the centre point, causing the vortex to form. Father felt the dangerous drain of vital energy as the seven continued the 'aoum', forcing the vortex to harden, to take the coarse form of the first vibration, the Earth plane. Finally, as their shimmering, etheric bodies grew faint from this combined loss of prana, they saw the young, finely chiselled face materialize; tired, frightened blue eyes, long golden hair. The Protectors would watch Tegné closely now, as they prepared for their descent on to the Earth plane. Tabata had done his work; theirs was just beginning.

*

The patch of forest was thick, causing the Warmen to dismount, moving on foot from opposite directions, towards each other across the moist, uneven ground.

Herok's eyes adjusted rapidly to the limited light as the moon filtered through the skeletal branches of the tall trees. *Like hunting a rabbit,* he thought as he scanned the shrubs and underbrush for any sign of life, any movement. Then his mind jumped as he locked on the fresh footprints in the soft earth. He looked up; Zanar stood ten paces from him, on the opposite side of the ragged clearing.

Zanar had not yet seen him, and Herok watched as the other Warman crept slowly forward through the short shrubs. It was then that the idea formed in Herok's mind . . . *Concealment . . . patience. Let him come to us . . .*

Tegné moved quietly, hugging close to the thick, powerful trees. He breathed long, even breaths, calming himself, turning all senses inwards, listening. The forest was still, no birds, no animals. *Very quiet, like death,* Tabata's words warned him as he searched the trees and underbrush with his eyes. Nothing, no movement . . . then he noticed the flicker of light from beneath a bush ten paces away. The light flashed, then was gone, the bush flapping downwards. A fox? A rabbit? Tegné was uncertain but for one thing; the lair would give him protection, a place to hide until nightfall. He crept cautiously across the small clearing and bent over the thick, thorny bush. Gripping it below its barbed leaves, he pulled it towards him.

Herok sprang from his crouch, using the strength of his legs to propel his body upwards, driving his heavy right fist into the boy's frontal bone, below the forehead.

Tegné was unguarded, completely unprepared, and the punch caught him flush, sending him reeling backwards. He collapsed on to the ground as Herok jumped from the shallow hole, drawing his katana and rushing towards him.

'Wait! Wait!' Zanar shouted, leaping from the thick limb of the elm and running to the fallen boy. The archer squatted down, rolled Tegné over and pulled back one of the closed eyelids. A sarcastic smile parted his lips and caused his yellow, pointed incisors to dominate his mouth. 'You did not kill him . . . A perfect shot, and you did not kill him.'

Herok saw no humour in the observation. 'Then perhaps he will feel his right wrist as I cut it slowly from his arm,' he retorted.

Zanar backed away as Herok bent over the boy's body and pulled the arm out to the side, laying it straight on the ground.

Yes, he will feel it, thought Herok, aware of the dull, thudding pain in his own swollen testicles. He raised the cold, steel katana, allowing the blade to hover above Tegné's wrist. He turned towards Zanar.

Zanar nodded 'yes', and Herok brought the blade down, cutting slowly, lightly through the first layer of epidermis. Tegné groaned as the razor-sharp sword penetrated the outer shell of his unconsciousness. Again, Herok drew the katana across the wrist, slowly, very slowly, making sure the second incision was slightly deeper than the first.

The growl came from the rear, low and menacing. Herok looked quickly at Zanar.

'Finish, let's go,' Zanar said, acknowledging the growl and staring nervously towards the thick woods.

Quickly, Herok raised the blade high, preparing to sever the wrist in one final downward cut. This time the growl was loud and close. Both Warmen spun round.

She was directly behind them. Each saw his own death in her red, burning eyes. Black, magnificent, she glared at them; her white fangs, long and pointed, shining wet with drool.

Herok knew what was coming, yet he was unable to move, mesmerized by this evil incarnate. He felt a sickly hollow in the pit of his stomach, mixed, somehow, with an extraordinary sexual excitement as she moved purposefully towards him, singling him out of the two.

She paused an instant, her hot, sulphurous breath bathing his face. Then, in one simple motion, she drew back her unsheathed foreclaw and swiped his gaping head from his shoulders.

Zanar stood frozen, watching, motionless with horror. His mind screamed, *Use the katana, die as a Warman, use the katana!* Awkwardly and without purpose, he drew his blade. She waited, her eyes devouring him, then her huge, fanged jaws opened and closed, engulfing his head, shaking him, moving downwards and crunching through the bone of his sternum and ribs, tearing his body in half. For a brief flash Zanar knew he had entered the bowels of hell; then it was over, and his dismembered torso fell to the earth.

Now she concentrated on Tegné, gliding towards the boy,

gazing down into the vulnerable, unconscious face. At last she lowered herself to the ground, pushing close to him. She felt the desire build within her as she nuzzled him, licking him lovingly, her great, dry tongue massaging his soft, white neck. She heard him moan, felt him shudder as she took him gently in her jaws and carried him from the woods, down into the Valley.

It was in the Valley that the Protectors waited, using the last of their drained resources to take Earthly form. They stood, hands joined, as she carried the boy towards them.

She laid the body on the dry, sunburnt earth. Snarling, she held her ground, willing, at this level, to test their strength. Father stepped forward from the line; behind him, the six closed ranks, joined hands and chanted the 'aoum'. Father extended his right arm, the long, fine, ivory fingers stretching towards Tegné. The thin blue arc began to form.

The Cat snarled, drawing her huge mouth back, exposing the fangs. The beam inched forwards, the chant grew in intensity, as slowly the blue arc encircled the boy's body, weaving Tegné in the fine, warm, luminous cocoon. She watched as the healing shell formed before her hard, red eyes. She could attack, rip savagely at the fibres, tear the shell, take the boy. She knew that on this plane her power was superior. Yet she watched and waited, permitting these fading guardians a last, hollow victory. After all, it was not the boy but the man she wanted, the warrior – the fulfilment of this golden-haired child.

She looked once more as the last blue fibre wrapped around the pale skin. Then, howling in naked hatred and defiance, she turned and leapt upwards. The Protectors watched as the enormous black body vanished into the night sky.

Father walked forward and knelt beside the blue, glowing cocoon. Tegné lay, eyes closed, breathing slow, deep breaths. Father smiled, imagining the beautiful, multi-coloured visions that flooded the boy's dream mind as the protective fibres vibrated gently.

'He is the one?' Kusan's mind transferred the question.

'She has chosen him,' Father relayed.

'But he is a child,' Kusan protested, his face and mouth motionless.

Father concentrated on the gold and silver medallion, the symbol of the Brothers of the Moon. 'He will be trained. Then he will return. Yes, he is certainly the chosen one.' The pronouncement was final; the seven knew this was truth, simple and pure.

*

Renagi, Tanak and the two Warmen followed the trail west; they found no sign of human life. Finally the trail narrowed, leading them to the high, western precipice overlooking the desolate Valley. Nothing.

At this point, Renagi decided it was best to retrace their route, pick up the tracks of the secondary party and join them in hope that their search had been more fruitful. The deep hoofmarks were easy to locate. They led through the dense forest and into the encampment.

Arton's body remained where he had fallen. A thick cluster of flies and black forest ants were at work inside his open mouth and hollowed eye sockets.

'Bury him, quickly!' Renagi ordered the two younger Warmen, then he turned towards Tanak. Their eyes met; no words were necessary.

'Tanak and I will ride on. You can catch up with us when you have finished,' the Warlord said to the two remaining men.

The tracks led out of the forest and on to a hard dirt path. Due east. It was nearing sunset when Renagi and Tanak arrived on the outer ridge overlooking the wide, open plain. They sat a moment, surveying the land ahead.

'Use the magniscope,' Renagi said.

Tanak pulled the long metal tube from his saddle-bag; he sat high, pushing with his boot heels into the stirrups of the shining leather saddle, his back and neck straight as he snapped the scope open. Lifting the instrument to his right eye, he adjusted the calibrated handle to level four, and aimed the viewfinder at the horses' prints directly ahead. The locking device anchored and the thin, silver mercury in the lens below pointed towards the rise, a quarter-voll to the east.

Tanak snapped the magniscope shut and turned towards the Warlord. He was about to speak when the thunder of hooves caused both men to start.

The two younger Warmen galloped up the hard path towards them. Tanak waited until they reined in their horses, looking from face to face, settling on Renagi. Then he turned, raising his hand, the first finger pointing. 'There on the rise,' he said as he indicated the high mound of earth leading into the patch of wood, 'The boy must have tried to lose them in the bush.'

No sooner had he finished than Renagi spurred his stallion, galloping ahead. Tanak and the others rode close behind.

An uneasy, indefinable feeling gripped them as, cautiously, they dismounted and made their way through the giant elms and along the uneven forest floor. The red, setting sun was hidden amongst the dense branches, and a cold chill penetrated their body armour, adding to their shared sense of unrest. They formed a semi-circle, keeping visual contact as they spread out, moving forward.

'Master . . .' It was Nicon, the youngest Warman, whose voice broke the quiet. The group turned in unison to see him standing, frozen. He stared at Herok's severed head; it lay face down in the dirt. The skin where the head had been ripped from the neck was lacerated, the jugular vein hanging shrunken and white.

'Light a torch . . . Now!' commanded the Warlord.

Tanak struck the firestone, and ignited the thick sulphur stick. The foul, pungent smell filled the air as the group converged on the clearing.

The rest of Herok's body was six feet from the head, the visible skin a bluish-grey, drained of blood. The remains of Zanar were close beside it. He had been cut cleanly in half, and only the lower body could be found. Renagi sensed panic. 'Look for the boy . . . Look for the boy,' he repeated, stern, not allowing his own anxiety to surface.

'What could have done this, Warlord?' Tanak whispered, as the group, keeping close together, scoured the ground.

'A bear, a tiger maybe . . . Do not dwell on it, find him,' the Warlord answered, equally unnerved by the unnatural ferocity of the attack.

Five hours later, they had searched every inch of woods, pushing on until they reached the jagged rock edge, the sheer drop below them. It was nearing midnight. The full, yellow moon hung heavily in the sky, and the warm, dry wind blew up from the Valley.

Finally, reluctantly, Renagi turned to Tanak. 'Nothing, nowhere . . . he is gone. Gone.'

The senior Warman saw the terrible frustration, pain and

anguish etched deep into the Warlord's face. Renagi's eyes were vacant, his skin waxen in the moonlight. Then, something new and uncertain shone in the dark, slanted eyes.

Is it madness? wondered Tanak, as Renagi spoke again, low and guarded, 'But, by God, I will find him. He cannot hide from me forever. I will find him . . .'

5

THE TEMPLE

The ancient masters were subtle, mysterious, profound, responsive.
The depth of their knowledge is unfathomable.
Because it is unfathomable, all we can do is to describe their
appearance.
Watchful, like men crossing a winter stream
Alert, like men aware of danger
Courteous, like visiting guests
Yielding, like ice about to melt
Simple, like uncarved blocks of wood
Hollow, like caves
Opaque, like muddy pools.
Who can wait quietly while the mud settles?
Who can remain still at the moment of action?

(Lao Tsu)

Brothers Yon and Unsu found the young man lying unconscious at the edge of the Valley, below the twin-peaked mountains. The Elder had provided them with the directions, exacting and precise. Their instructions were to find the boy and to ensure that he arrived safely at the Temple.

Now, as they knelt beside the still body, both were fascinated by the long golden hair and the pale, smooth skin. For the province of Lunan was populated by a dark-haired, swarthy people, and the Temple was the frequent recipient of their unwanted children, placed outside the gates in hope that they would be accepted, adopted and raised within the Brotherhood.

'Blue. His eyes are blue,' Unsu whispered as he gently lifted the lid of one of Tegné's closed eyes.

'I can find no wounds, no serious injuries,' Yon concluded, discontinuing his superficial inspection and turning towards Unsu.

'What is this?' Unsu questioned, pointing towards the thin, pink scar which ran across the top of Tegné's right wrist, directly above the birthmark.

'An old incision?' Yon mused, then added, 'The scar is faded, the cut healed,' as he ran his thumb lightly across the line, which was slightly raised from the skin.

'And he is breathing quite normally, I just do not understand why he is unconscious,' Unsu continued, bending close to Tegné's left ear. 'Wake up, wake up. Can you hear me?' Unsu spoke quietly, so that if the words did take effect they would not frighten. 'Wake up, wake up,' he repeated the command.

Tegné's face remained placid, without expression. Nearly angelic.

'It is no use. I will prepare the litter,' Yon said, already beginning to unfurl the coarse hemp–cloth body sling. He inserted the twin wooden carrying poles and, together, they lifted Tegné on to the cloth.

'He is heavy,' Unsu noted.

'Well developed for one so young,' Yon agreed, looking down on to the hard flesh visible through the separation of the robe covering Tegné's chest. 'Perhaps the leather thong around his neck is causing him discomfort,' he added, as he bent and lifted the single braid of leather. 'How could we not have seen this?' he exclaimed, disentangling the medallion from where it had fallen to the side of Tegné's neck and been covered by the fabric of his robes.

Unsu knelt beside Yon and both men stared at the shining disc, identical to those discs worn only by the three senior Brothers of their Order.

'I do not understand,' Yon said, nodding his head and questioning Unsu with his eyes.

'Nor do I,' Unsu answered.

Then, without further speculation, they lifted the carrier from the ground and began the long trek down from the mountain rise and to the plain below where they had tethered their horses.

The ride from the Valley was slow, and Unsu and Yon stopped regularly to gauge the condition of the young man, still unconscious, whom they dragged behind on the low, flat-bedded cart.

'The Elder must have known of his condition, that is why he insisted we brought the litter,' Yon reasoned as he rolled easily in the saddle, over the bumps and ridges of the little-used dirt road. 'Surely, when we reach the Temple, he will tell us what is behind this mystery,' he concluded, wondering if it was not again time to rest the horses and pour another few drops of water into the mouth of their ward.

YEON 983
TEMPLE OF THE MOON
LUNAN PROVINCE

But the Elder did nothing to lift the shroud of secrecy which surrounded the strange young man who was carried through the gates of the Temple of the Moon on the seventh day of November, in the yeon 983.

Instead, Yon and Unsu were thanked sincerely and deeply for their arduous trip to the ridge of the Valley. Then the unconscious body was briskly lifted from the cart, covered with a warm cotton shawl, and transported to the far reaches of the remedial quarters inside the Temple complex.

No hint of explanation, not a word, thought Yon, as he walked from the courtyard. And he knew it would be in gross breach of etiquette to ever question the Elder as to these unusual circumstances, so 'not a word' was how it would remain.

'What is your name? Your name? Your name?' The voice was soft, lilting, washing over him.

'Tegné,' he answered, as gradually his eyes focused on the unfamiliar face before him.

'Tegné, Tegné ... From the raging water,' the voice replied, satisfied.

The face was a perfect oval, with small, deep-set brown eyes shining from smooth, bronzed skin. The head was without a trace of hair except for the single, thick, silver braid which hung down below the narrow shoulders. The nose was not protrusive, but rather flat, its width only marginally less than the full, pink-lipped mouth beneath it.

Not a single wrinkle in the skin, Tegné observed fleetingly. Yet it was not a young face, in fact the gentle eyes seemed ancient wells of wisdom. Somehow they reminded Tegné of his Sensei, Tabata, and in that instant the recollection of the Warmen and the death of his Sensei caused him to recoil; he pulled the white cotton sheet closer to him.

'Good! Good!' exclaimed the Elder, placing a dry, cool hand against Tegné's forehead. 'Release the cerecortex,' he instructed the attending physician.

The physician, a tiny man, his body swathed in a linen gown and his face masked in similar material, bent and removed the thin silver needle from the point on Tegné's forehead directly between his eyes.

Tegné felt something give way, something heavy but at the same time intangible. He actually was aware of the wetness of his eyes before he realized he was crying.

'Release the meridians,' the Elder ordered, never taking his attention from Tegné.

Through his tears, Tegné could see the thirty-six needles which outlined the periphery of his body and extended all the way to a point in the centre of each foot. Deftly, painlessly, the physician whisked the needles from his flesh, dropping them with only the slightest noise into a flat wooden box beside the mat.

'Acupuncture. Clearing the system. Allowing the ki to flow,' the Elder explained as he sat beside Tegné on the mat and cradled the sobbing young man in his arms. 'It is quite natural to have this emotional release. You have been through a great trauma. But you are quite safe now, quite safe,' he continued, his voice soothing.

Tegné felt foolish, small and humiliated at this open display of emotion in the presence of strangers. Still, he could not stop. Images of his Sensei, the love, the lessons, the patience, the compassion, flowed through his mind. He knew somehow where he was; this was the Temple, the original home of Tabata, and in that realization he knew at once that his childhood was past, over and gone. Gone with the Forest of Shuree. And now he was alone.

An hour later the tears subsided and Tegné sat up on the cot, the Elder, cross-legged, beside him. The physician had departed shortly after the onset of the tears, realizing his work had been successful and that privacy was the next requirement.

'Welcome to the Temple of the Brothers of the Moon. I am the Elder Brother.'

'Tabata, Sensei, is . . .' Tegné began.

The Elder raised his hand, halting the final word. 'I know, I know – no longer of this Earth,' he said.

'How can you know?' Tegné asked, awed by the serenity of this tiny man and by the grace with which he spoke.

'I know because you are here, because it is all in the correct order of events,' the Elder answered.

'Correct order of events?' Tegné repeated. *Does he also know that I abandoned him? That I am a coward?* Tegné wondered.

'Yes,' the Elder answered, as if reading his mind, his tone suddenly clipped, his eyes narrowing and his lips tight. His entire demeanour changed in that single moment, and again Tegné was reminded of Tabata, the stern teacher and disciplinarian. And Tegné understood immediately that this diminutive man was not a man to be questioned, that there was tempered steel behind the glowing eyes. Tegné nodded, silently.

'As soon as you are able, I want you to begin training in the

Dojo,' the Elder said, again warm and friendly. 'You will be an uchi-deshi,' he added.

Tegné had never heard the term 'uchi-deshi', and the puzzlement showed on his face.

The Elder smiled. 'Uchi-deshi means "special student". An inside student. You will live and breathe only to train in Empty Hand. You will eat and sleep within the confines of the Dojo and you will study with Yano Sensei. No distractions. One thousand days,' he explained, virtually beaming as though he were bestowing the absolute gesture of life on Tegné.

'Thank you, Elder.' Tegné accepted the gift, feeling uncertain as to its implications but aware of one thing; now was not the time to question or resist, now was a time to adapt, and move with the natural flow of circumstance. *The correct order of events . . .*

Yano Sensei was a big, gruff man, perhaps ten years younger than Tabata; he had, in fact, been one of Tabata's assistant instructors when Tabata was Grand Master of the Temple.

Tegné felt truly dwarfed as he bowed for the first time to his new Sensei. Yano nodded in return and extended his hand, indicating that Tegné should present him with the hand-written note of introduction from the Elder. Tegné stood just under five-foot-eight, and Yano was easily half a head taller, six-foot-two or three and seventeen stone in weight. His head was large, even for his enormous body, and as near a perfect square as was possible for a man's head to be. It reminded Tegné of an ironworker's anvil, dark, hard and unforgiving.

The eyes were mere slits in the flat face, and Tegné could barely discern their brown-black colour as Yano scrutinized the brief letter of introduction.

'Uchi-deshi, uchi-deshi.' Yano rolled the words off his tongue as if he found them particularly distasteful. 'You?' He looked up, giving a single, sweeping glance over Tegné's body. 'A gajiin, an outsider?'

Yano was making no secret of his aversion to the blonde-haired, blue-eyed stranger whom he had just been ordered to guide in the Way of the Empty Hand. 'Tegné,' Yano pronounced the name as though it were a fatal disease he had recently contracted, 'I will tell you now what you may expect in this Dojo, and what I will demand from you. You will report to me each morning at the sixth hour. You will be attired in a training gi, a white sash and bare feet. From here we will leave the monastery by the eastern side gate and run along the dirt road away from the Temple. We will run for one hour. You must never run ahead of me, but stay within a single body-length behind. If I set a fast pace, you follow. If I run slowly, you run slowly. Do you understand?'

'I do, Sensei,' replied Tegné, bowing.

'We will return to the Dojo where you will perform three hundred pressing-up exercises, three hundred sitting-up exercises and three hundred squatting movements. When I am satisfied with your progress in these simple forms, I will instruct you in the use of the power stones, the chikaraisha. Then we will begin basic blocking, striking and kicking. And each day we will practise sparring exercise.' Yano went on, the words coming in staccato bursts from his thin, stretched lips, 'There are three classes each day for students of the Dojo. Each class is two hours in length. You will attend every class. I will also expect you to train alone for a portion of each day. In all, at least ten hours every day. You will be personally responsible for the cleaning of this Dojo, the floor, the toilets, and you will be at my call for any other duties I wish performed.'

Yano took in another breath in order that he could continue. *He will never stop, never,* Tegné thought as he turned his head from Yano's piercing eyes.

'Face me, face me!' Yano barked, his voice sharp and coming from deep in his belly. Quickly, Tegné snapped his head up and met the burning gaze.

'Never move your eyes away from me when I am speaking,' Yano said. Then, without waiting for Tegné's acknowledgement, he continued, 'On the third, fifth and seventh day of each week you will, between the second and third training session, be tutored in speaking and writing skills. On the evening of the sixth day you will dine with the Elder in his private chamber. There you may discuss your training and your progress. One thousand days.' Yano searched his new student for the first sign of doubt.

One thousand days, Tegné repeated in his mind. The knowledge that he would be twenty yeons when he emerged fom this apprenticeship began to overwhelm him.

'One thousand days.' Again Yano said the three fateful words, observing that their weight hung visibly on his student's shoulders, 'and when you have completed your training, you will have accomplished what an ordinary student accomplishes in twenty-five yeons,' he finished, finally. Then, strangely, he bowed to Tegné.

Tegné instantly returned the courtesy as a thin, tight smile formed on Yano's lips.

'Now I am going to kill you,' Yano said quietly.

And as the sharp, unexpected mae-geri crashed sickeningly into his abdomen, Tegné was certain that Yano meant it.

*

Renagi waited alone beneath the cluster of stars cut into the domed stone ceiling of his pleasure room. It was the twelfth full cycle of the moon since his return from the ill-fated search-party.

He listened closely for the footsteps along the long wooden corridor which separated the main living quarters of Zendow from these private chambers. Finally, he heard the sharp clicking of the cleated heels which accompanied the soft, padded steps of slippered feet.

Renagi stood up from the bed. He could hear the muffled male voice outside the door; he could not make out the words but he heard the gentle female voice answer, then the cleated heels walked back up the passageway and their sound disappeared. Slowly, the brass handle turned and the thick door opened.

She stood a moment, framed by the light of the torches in the corridor, then her eyes adjusted and she focused on the Warlord. He remained motionless in the centre of the room.

She steeled herself, quieting the doubt and nerves which threatened to make her turn and run back up the passage and away from him. Then, in a movement that required all of her graceful theatricality, she let the shawl slip down, away from her shoulders, and at the same time removed the dark veil from her face.

She is good, very, very good, Renagi thought. He felt the first warmth in his testicles as the blood began to concentrate in his groin. 'Take off the dress.' He whispered the order.

She maintained her position in the far corner of the room, except now, confident of his acceptance, she closed the door of the chamber. Then, turning to face him, she slowly unfastened the crude ties of the heavy muslin dress and let the yellowed material hang open on her body. She wore nothing beneath.

She could see him clearly now in the centre of the room, his wide leather belt loose and his hands working to unbutton the front of his black leather trousers. He was already naked from the waist up, and his torso appeared solid and powerful.

She knew by instinct not to approach him; instead, timing her movements with his own, she removed the muslin dress, tossing it beside her, then kicked the red velveteen slippers from her feet. She looked directly at him, her wet excitement having little to do with his hard nakedness. No, her excitement was caused by her sheer ability to manipulate this great and feared Warlord, by her own inner strength and her capacity to overcome the initial terror of entering this pleasure chamber. She stood still, statue-like. She knew what would come next; she had performed this ritual-like routine ten times previously and always it was the same. Now was the critical time; she must not move.

Yes, look at her ... the whiteness of the hair, the pink of the skin, the full, rose-petal nipples ... Renagi thought as he moved his hand down along the line of his abdomen and into the thick hair beneath his navel. 'Turn, turn to the side,' he whispered, his voice deep with sensuality.

She turned, drawing her shoulders back slightly, raising her full, hanging breasts, giving them a jutting appearance. Her nipples were just beginning to rise.

'Good,' said Renagi, his hand now gripping his penis, rubbing slowly up and down the shaft. 'Now walk to the bed,' he ordered, his tone becoming dominant.

Walk to the bed, she repeated the command to herself. He had never asked her to walk to the bed before, she knew the body paint and false hair would not bear up to close scrutiny. And, Wang had assured her, this was only to be an exercise in fantasy.

'Come, Maliseet, come to the bed,' Renagi insisted. He was already sitting on the heavy quilt, waiting, caressing himself.

Maliseet? That was not her name. Who was Maliseet? What was happening?

Guarded, carefully, she walked to the bed, standing as far away from him as possible.

'Lie down,' he said, staring at her. She did as she was ordered, knowing that the thin layer of oil-based paint would stain the black quilt. She knew enough not to speak, not to voice the questions that had begun to fill her mind. Whatever spell the Warlord was under, she must not break it.

She tried to relax her tightening muscles as he crawled towards her on the huge bed and hovered above her spread legs. She affected a low moan of pleasure as he lowered his head between them and began the tentative licking of the now-dry orifice below the trimmed, bleached line of pubic hair. She pushed her hips up, forcing herself into his mouth as every fibre of her begged to pull away, to escape. It was as if he was tasting her, nibbling to see if he found the taste inviting. Then, he would consume her.

She wondered if the crudely fitted hair-piece had slipped or become dislodged from her head against the hard pillow, but dared not raise her hands to find out. She had begun to perspire from nervousness, and she could taste the grease from her face-paint as it rolled in tiny beads from her upper lip. She kept her eyes locked tight, willing her body to respond to his probing tongue.

'Maliseet,' he whispered.

She heard the strange name again as she felt his hot breath against her face and smelled the stale, heavy scent of red wine. Still she kept her eyes closed.

Now he was directly on top of her, his bare chest pressing into her breasts while his right hand fumbled between her legs, trying in vain to guide his suddenly flaccid penis into her dry opening. She reached down, finding him with her own hand, hoping to revive him and save this precarious situation.

'No! Maliseet would not do that!' he shouted, and the spittle from his mouth landed on her painted cheeks.

She opened her eyes. Even by the light of the moon she could see that the Warlord was crying. She withdrew her hand. She was trapped in this terrible moment and uncertain as to whether comfort or ignorance was the correct response. She remained quiet, still.

Awkwardly, Renagi disengaged himself from her and got to his feet. 'That will be all. Tell Wang I will not require your further visits,' he said, his voice calm and restrained, yet filled with a sad defeat.

Relieved, she rose from the bed, rushed to the door and picked up the muslin dress.

He did not watch as, quickly, she put the costume back on, wrapped the shawl around her body and up over her head, turned, and left the room. The door remained open, and the torchlight cast flickering shadows across the floor and on to the stained quilt.

Renagi left the palace by a little-used passage. He walked purposefully from the secluded grounds and towards the sector of private dwellings. For it was in this sector that Natiro lived, and it was this strong Zendai woman whom he sought.

The time was nearing the third hour when he climbed the low, wide stone steps which led to the leaded glass door of her elegant, two-storeyed dwelling. There were no guards in this private sector; there was no real necessity even to lock one's door. For there was no crime in the private sector of Zendow.

Renagi closed the door behind him as he quietly entered the entrance hall. A single torch remained lit, and he used its guiding light to find his way to the servants' quarters on the lower level.

The servant woman was awake, lying on her back upon the low, narrow cot. Her eyes reflected the light of the wall torch, and they reminded Renagi of a forest doe, caught in the beam of the hunter's flame; frightened, aware, yet protective of her young. It took only an instant for the old woman to recognize the Warlord, and when she did she leapt from the bed and on to her knees, kissing the bare boards of the floor.

Behind her, Renagi saw the glint of steel from the short-pointed dagger, left undisturbed beneath the bedcovers.

'Wake your mistress. Tell her I am here and wish to see her,' Renagi said, using the servant as intermediary and therefore giving proper respect to Natiro.

The old woman rose from the floor. She was clad in a coarse cotton nightdress, and the material dragged quietly against the wide oak boards as she shuffled from the room.

Renagi followed her as far as the staircase, then veered off into the large, panelled reception room. He sat down on the padded, high-backed seat with its two raised arm-rests. The seat was covered in soft, black, polished leather, and was ornamented with shining brass studs, each embossed with the Royal sign. It was a totally masculine piece of furniture and it reminded Renagi of the first evening he had come to be entertained in the new house.

All the surrounding furniture in the forty by thirty foot rectangular room was of a soft, feminine design. Exquisitely carved, hard black laquered tables and chairs, the work of the carver so intricately joined that it was impossible to imagine that each of the pieces was not cut from a single block of wood. Only in the far eastern province of Miramar could one find this craftsmanship, and the hard, shining wood from which it was created. The seats of the high-backed chairs were padded and covered in the palest of blue raw silk. The beautifully matched furniture surrounded a large, square, gold-and-blue silk-threaded carpet. It was instantly apparent that the black leather and brass-studded seat, although flawless in design and workmanship, stood out conspicuously from these more delicate furnishings. Yet Renagi had known at once that the seat was his own, placed in the house by Natiro, in honour of her Warlord.

He placed his right arm on the studded arm-rest and pressed his back into the fine, soft leather.

Natiro was soundly asleep when the quiet, careful voice called her name, using the proper formal pronunciation and adding the word 'Mis', thus offering humble submission.

'Natiro-Mis, Natiro-Mis,' repeated the soft but penetrating voice. Natiro opened her eyes, her body remaining still beneath the single feather-filled bedcover.

'The Master, Mis, the Master. He waits for you,' Darya continued.

'Now? The Master? Where, Darya, where is he?'

'He waits in the room below us,' Darya answered.

'Light the torch. Prepare my bath. Use the lemon oil, and leave my mauve robe on the bed. Do it quickly, Darya, then tell the Master I shall join him shortly,' Natiro ordered gently. 'Thank you, Darya,' she called after the small, white-haired woman as Darya scurried to prepare the bath.

Natiro rose from the bed and slipped the sheer nightgown from her shoulders. The gown fell behind her on to the floor as she walked across the room, to face herself in the full-length, silvered mirror. Her bedchamber was south-facing, and the light of the moon shone through three large, leaded windows.

Natiro was thirty-five yeons. She had been twenty when she had given Renagi his heir, Zato. A single child was the custom of

Zendai women; it was known that after one child the body would return to its former state. Three children, four children; that was for the lower caste of women, the breeders, who reproduced until their sagging, distended stomachs resembled the flesh of cattle.

Yes, Natiro was Zendai, dark and pure of blood. Her father, Rakeen, had been chief military advisor to Renagi's father. It would have filled Rakeen with pride to know that his daughter had given the new Warlord his heir, and that his grandson would one day be Warlord of Zendow. But Rakeen was gone, passed into memory.

Hard to imagine that I, too, will grow old and sleep away, Natiro mused as she viewed her naked body in the reflection of the mirror. In the soft light she could see no difference between the tight, bronzed flesh of the reflection and her recollection of herself as the twenty-yeon virgin who waited nervously, alone, in the chambers of the Warlord. Her breasts were not large, and that had proved advantageous as she matured, for they still sat high and firm on top of the delicately muscled rib-cage beneath the wide-boned, sculpted shoulders. The nipples were full and brown, and Natiro smiled as she remembered the Warlord's delight in their responsiveness to his warm. rough-skinned fingers.

Now she could hear the water running gently into the porcelain bath as she turned side-on to the mirror. Her belly was smooth, and ran flat down, protruding only slightly just above the pubis. The slight protrusion was, in fact, very much desired, as it displayed just the hint of opulence and again maintained the distinction between the Zendai women and the poorly fed working caste of female. The black hair of her pubis stood out long and thick. She ran her hand through it, drawing it further out and upwards. Zendai men loved their women to have a full thatch; it was the ultimate sign of fertility, and was known to cushion the ride to the heavenly plane. She had certainly not disappointed Renagi in that respect, for his ride was accompanied by deep groans of pleasure and, upon the release of his burning seed, she also had felt the rapid, unexpected contractions. She was certain then that she had conceived. And, true to her intuition, Zato was born nine months later, the Royal heir.

The bath water had ceased to run, and Darya was just emerging from the chamber, a thick, blue cotton towel in her hand. Natiro turned and accepted the towel as she swept past Darya into the bath-chamber.

'Will you require your back sponged, Natiro–Mis?' Darya questioned.

'No. No, Darya. I am going to be very brief. Our Warlord has been forced to wait long enough. Just place the mauve robe on the bed, then go to the reception room and attend the Warlord until I arrive,' Natiro said, already testing the warm, lemon-scented water with her hand.

Renagi had been an infrequent visitor to the private sector of Zendow since installing Natiro in this strong, stone-built house nearly fifteen yeons ago. Perhaps eighteen or twenty times he had appeared, usually in the depths of night. Yet, Natiro was always available to him, that was tradition. On his initial visits she had presumed as much as to insert the thin protective membrane into her vagina, offering a discreet protection from an unwanted pregnancy. Yet, with one exception, it had not been her sexual favours that Renagi sought; it was, instead, her considerate conversation and unpatronizing opinions as to matters of state and the general governing of Zendow. Natiro felt deeply honoured to be privy to this confidence.

The idea of the protective membrane did not so much as cross her mind as she wrapped the mauve robe around her body, glanced long into the mirror, then turned and walked from the room.

Renagi rose to his feet as Natiro entered through the arched door. He held a deep goblet of Miramese red wine in his left hand. Darya was quick to appear behind her mistress.

'May I bring Mis a glass of wine?' she asked.

'No, Darya, I will not be taking any wine. You may go back to your quarters. If we should require anything further, I will ring for you,' Natiro replied, with obvious affection for the old servant woman.

Darya smiled and bowed, then departed, leaving the Warlord and Natiro alone in the large room.

'How very thoughtful of you to honour me with your visit.' Natiro spoke the words sincerely, a polite yet formal gesture.

'It has been a long time,' Renagi said, avoiding her gaze.

She sensed his vulnerability; perhaps it was in his posture, somehow wounded, pleading. She moved closer to him, softly touching his arm and guiding him to his leather seat. He permitted himself the indulgence of her attention, yet instead of soothing him she seemed only to confirm his weakness.

'I am sick. Sick inside,' he confessed as he sat down, settling back into the soft leather.

Natiro sat beside him, gently touching his thigh. 'Sick? I do not understand. My master appears perfectly well,' she said reassuringly.

'It is a sickness of mind,' Renagi whispered, then turned towards her.

Natiro controlled her immediate urge to move back, to pull her hand from the Warlord's thigh. Instead she sat still, morbidly fascinated by the sunken black of his eyes. The eyes seemed to her, suddenly, to resemble the hollow, lifeless holes in the rough, elasticated masks she had known as a child; the masks that had once been used to cover the face of someone recently dead, prior to cremation. Their purpose was to frighten and dispel any evil spirit which might attempt to take possession of the Earth soul during its transition to the other side.

But the masks were of the past, and Natiro swore inwardly at herself for falling prey to this childish fantasy. The Warlord was here, now, because he needed her; she would certainly not deny him comfort in any form. Yet the look of death still showed in his hollow eyes as she lowered her head and moved closer to him.

Renagi sighed as she nestled under his extended arm. The arm folded around her and the hand rested gently on her right bosom. She felt his lips nibble the scented skin of her neck.

'Shall we go to my chamber?' she whispered, sensing his need.

'Yes,' he answered, feeling her will to comfort and heal him, and surrendering to it.

There was no urgency to the Warlord as he removed his clothing and laid it on the chair beside her bed. Naked and unaroused he stood as Natiro removed the mauve robes from her body. She did not excite him physically, yet at the same time he knew that she was the epitome of Zendai womanhood, and for this he admired her; for the breadth of shoulder, the long, almost muscular legs, the hirsute pubis, the high firm breasts, the cascading black hair, the strong, wide face and large brown eyes. His observation was becoming clinical when Natiro broke the mood by performing a perfect dancer's pirouette, spinning round in the moonlight and landing to face him with a wide, playful smile on her lips.

'Very good! You would have made a fortune in Wang's,'

Renagi said, suddenly joking. Already he was beginning to feel refreshed, and the memory of the tainted scene, earlier in the evening, began to release him from its grip.

Yes, this is how it should be. A Zendai man and a Zendai woman, he concluded as he stepped towards Natiro, brushing against her naked flesh. *This is proper, the natural order,* he confirmed as he felt the surge in his penis.

There will be no time to insert the membrane, Natiro realized as his hardness grew against her inner thigh. *I must not break the moment. Perhaps it is not my time of the month anyway . . .* she rationalized as he pulled her towards the bed.

He entered her caringly and the ride to the heavenly plane became a slow, steady joining of souls.

*

Tegné had integrated well into the formal classes of the Dojo. At first the other young men had stared blatantly at his golden hair, blue eyes and light skin, but within a few weeks of the exhaustive training no one so much as gave him a second glance.

Even Yano had come to like his gajiin uchi-deshi, particularly admiring the quiet, accepting fashion in which Tegné had endured his initial beating. The Dojo Sensei was equally impressed with the depth of knowledge and the level of technique that the young man already possessed.

Yes, Tegné is certainly a tribute to the former Grand Master, Tabata, thought Yano as he watched his uchi-deshi duck and shift below a face-level thrust during the closing moments of a kumite session. He smiled. Tai-sabaki, body evasion technique. That was his contribution to Tegné's mastery of Empty Hand. How often in their private sessions had he charged his student like an enraged bull? And once Yano started, he would not stop. It was speed, and speed alone, that saved Tegné from a severe battering. Until, finally, the young man had learnt the special methods of avoidance, to duck and weave, to spin and to slide.

As for Tegné, it was at first a matter of pride. Many times he felt like crying out with the anger and frustration of one who must confront an insurmountable objective day after day. At times he felt his spirit weaken, almost giving in to the spirit of this relentless teacher. Yet, he did not break, and eventually he realized that through his absolute and determined resistance he was growing, both as a disciple of Empty Hand and as a man.

And he realized that Yano Sensei was carefully and patiently ordering these changes within him.

That realization was the turning point, the point at which he halted his negative thoughts, heretofore directed at Yano, and began to work positively with his new Sensei. He began to love and respect this tough Dojo master, and through this changed attitude his Empty Hand took on a deeper level of meaning.

> *Achieve results*
> *But never glory in them*
> *Achieve results*
> *But never boast*
> *Achieve results*
> *But never be proud*
> *Achieve results*
> *Because this is the natural way*
> *Achieve results*
> *But not through violence*
> *Force is followed by loss of strength*
> *This is not the Way*
> *That which is against the Way*
> *Comes to an early end.*

(Lao Tsu)

Tegné had finally begun to overcome the anger within him; and accordingly his Empty Hand was fluid, without violence.

'The gonads play an extraordinary role in extracting and concentrating vital elements from the whole body. They produce the replica of the man himself, and they instigate the sexual urge through which the creative hunger of man is satisfied,' Master Goswami began amidst the muffled sounds of laughter coming from the back of the large, mat-floored lecture hall.

'The testicular hormone plays an important part in influencing muscular development and strength. It helps to maintain the heart and stimulates the blood-making organs,' Goswami continued, turning a sharp eye to the cluster of young men at the back of the room. Tegné was conspicuous on the far left of the line. Goswami temporarily halted his lecture.

'Excuse me,' he said, pointing a long, bony finger towards the general area of the disturbance. The thirty or so younger, preadolescent Brothers who occupied the mats towards the front of the hall sat stone-still, averting their eyes and praying that Goswami would spare them this humiliation. For Goswami hated to be interrupted during one of his lectures.

'You. Tegné,' Goswami continued, homing in on his target.

Tegné felt the first red flush of embarrassment as he cleared his throat. 'Yes, Master Goswami,' he replied, suppressing a perverse desire to laugh caused by a combination of pure discomfort and the secret nudge he was being given by a fellow Dojo disciple who sat on his left side.

'Perhaps you would be so kind as to step forward,' Goswami commanded, moving sideways in a dramatic gesture to indicate the space in which Tegné should stand.

There was another choked outburst of laughter from the back as Tegné rose from his cross-legged position.

'Now,' Goswami continued as Tegné slowly made his way through the quiet, seated students towards the front of the class, 'we shall continue our discussion on the topic of gonadal control.' Goswami hesitated, clearing his throat. 'The first stage of control is the process of ejaculation,' he stated, eyeing the class for any fresh signs of unrest.

By now, Tegné, still flushed, stood beside the tall, angular instructor and in front of the fifty apprentice Brothers. He was careful not to meet the eyes of his peers in the back line, knowing that a further show of misconduct would only increase his punishment.

'One of the first measures we must take in the control of both nocturnal ejaculation and our desire . . .' he hesitated again, scanning the guilty faces, '. . . for manual relief is to release pelvic congestion. There are no better exercises for this than the inverse act and head posture. Today, Brother Tegné will demonstrate the correct procedure for maintaining the head posture. In fact, he will maintain the posture for the duration of this one-hour lecture.'

Then, turning to Tegné, Goswami nodded towards the hard, straw-matted floor.

'Please assume the position,' he said, kindly.

Tegné knelt down, both heels raised, his body bent forward, fingers interlocked. Then, supporting his body on his forearms and head, he raised his trunk and hips until they were almost perpendicular to the floor. Finally, he lifted his legs until they were in a straight line with the raised trunk and hips.

'Fine, fine,' said Goswami, admiring the posture for a moment before turning back to address the attentive group before him.

'The main questions are these. Do the sperm cells retained in a living state within our bodies produce any substance which has a specific influence on the revitalization of our minds and of our bodies? And, after their death, are these sperm cells reabsorbed, thus supplying us with precious materials which may be utilized in the construction and reconstruction of the body? The answer, in both circumstances, is "yes".'

Goswami carried on, looking from face to face, 'Sexual control is the key to vigour. The spirit of continued struggle, the power to concentrate not only physical, but mental and emotional energy and the ability to awaken dormant powers; all these are directly associated with sexual control.'

With this, Goswami turned his attention to Tegné. 'It is not an easy matter to prevent the waste of the fluid. The fluid supplies certain chemicals to the blood. These chemicals provide a proportion of the sexual urge and desire, the other proportion being incited by imagination and association. And when imagination is strengthened by experience, it becomes extremely difficult to harness this creative force. Control can only be achieved through the combination of specific exercises and blood-purification regimes.'

Goswami knelt so he could look easily into Tegné's face. 'The exercises include the abdominal posture exercise, the spinal posture exercise, the pelvic posture exercise and the abdominal and pelvic control exercises. But first, as I mentioned earlier, pelvic tension must be relieved, and that is what brings us back to the head posture.' Goswami smiled, 'Do you feel a relief of tension, Brother Tegné?' he asked, noting the reddening in the pale skin of Tegné's cheeks due to the inverse flow of blood.

'Yes, Goswami Sensei,' Tegné answered effortfully, his head feeling positively crushed against the straw mat. The head posture was not new to him, but he rarely held the position for more than one hundred slow breaths. Today, he had already lost count of his breathing and was now just grimly maintaining balance in the uncomfortable posture. Goswami's face loomed above him and Tegné could detect, through eyes nearly forced shut by gravity, a faint smile on the kundalini Master's thin lips.

*

Goswami was not native to the Province of Lunan. He was, in fact, discovered by the Elder living in a tiny monastery nearly two thousand vul to the north of the temple, high in the Himilak Mountain region where the air was reputedly so fine and thin that travellers, unused to the altitude, would often succumb to seizures of the heart before their respiratory systems could adjust to the lack of oxygen. The Elder had visited this Himilak temple during a sojourn from his own monastery, and was so impressed by Goswami's display of absolute physical control that he at once beseeched the Yoga Master to bring his teachings to the Temple of the Moon. Goswami accepted the invitation, and shortly after his arrival in Lunan he provided the Brothers with a demonstration which had since become legend.

In the main courtyard of the Temple, before all its occupants, Goswami had assumed the position of the perfect lotus, his spine erect, his right knee bent and the foot in position against his groin, the left knee and foot in an identical corresponding position, both heels close to the abdomen. Both his arms were extended, his hands placed on his knees.

At this point the Elder had stepped forward and instructed two monks to assist him in blocking Goswami's nostrils with hardening wax. His mouth was similarly sealed, after those close enough to him had witnessed the retroversion of his tongue, thus completely blocking any possible breathing channels. The Elder and his assistants then wrapped Goswami in linen and placed him in a wooden box. The box was closed and locked for all to see. Finally, to the horror of the onlookers, the box was lowered into a six-foot hole, which had been dug into the soft ground of the courtyard. The space above the box was then refilled with earth, barley sown upon it, and the area enclosed by a wall of stone. The Elder ordered round-the-clock surveillance of the enclosure, two Brothers at a time, in six-hour shifts. No one disturbed the box.

There was a certain sardonic humour concerning this strange monk who had appeared after such a long and lonely trek from the Himilaks, lived amongst them for only seven days and then had himself buried in the courtyard.

On the fortieth day the Elder had sounded the giant brass gong, summoning all the Brothers into the courtyard. The box was unearthed and everyone present was encouraged to examine the lock and investigate for any signs of tampering. Satisfied, they opened the box.

Goswami, still clad in the linen wrappings, was found undisturbed in the lotus posture. Once the wrappings were removed, the temple physicians examined the body – there was no pulse, no breath, no external sign of life. Even Goswami's shaven face remained clean, no new hair had grown.

The Brothers were nodding sadly at the futile death of this peculiar man when the Elder walked from the crowd. Bending over the seated body he smacked Goswami soundly in the chest, below the heart. Again he thumped the patch of bare skin with the cushioned palm of his hand. Simultaneous with the second impact, Goswami's eyes snapped open and, like a newly delivered child, he gasped the breath of life.

The Brothers stood silent, believing they had witnessed a miracle, as the Elder massaged Goswami's limbs, enabling him to unfold from the lotus position. Finally, the Himilak monk stood before them.

'You have not seen a miracle,' Goswami said, facing them, reading their stunned faces. 'You have witnessed an example of the extreme endurance which my method of exercise and control has enabled me to perform,' he went on, then added, 'My teacher lived to be two hundred and eighty yeons.'

'Goswami's Miracle', as it came to be known despite his insistence to the contrary, had taken place nearly thirty yeons ago. Since that time he had remained at the Temple, teaching the Brothers methods by which they could awaken that vital energy, the kundalini, which, he promised, lay dormant within each of them.

The hour finally ended, and for the closing twenty minutes the entire class had maintained the strict head posture. At last, on the signal of Goswami's ringing prayer chime, the students had been permitted to return to a bent-knee position, and finally to rise and leave the lecture hall.

Tegné had remained on his hands and knees, resting, acutely aware of the dizzying rush of blood as it dispersed from his head and redistributed throughout his trunk and arms. Finally he stood up. He was alone in the Great Hall, except for Goswami.

'Tegné,' Goswami called, motioning from the far corner of the room.

Tegné approached, sheepishly, feeling a repentant fool for having been part of the disruption of the class.

'Sensei?' he said, stopping and bowing to his turbanned master.

Goswami smiled. 'Almost all young men your age find amusement in this facet of my instruction,' he said.

'I am sorry, Goswami Sensei,' Tegné apologized.

'There is no need for indulgence in sorrow or guilt. As I said, it is quite a normal reaction. But that is not the reason for my short talk with you now,' Goswami continued.

Tegné looked up, a question in his face.

'These exercises in self-control, in awakening your inner vitality, will be of particular importance to you,' he said. 'You were, at one time, a pupil of Shihan Tabata, is that not true?'

He must know the background of all his disciples, the Elder must keep records, Tegné thought before he answered. 'Yes, it is true'.

'To have a teacher such as Tabata is a great gift. A fated gift.'

'Yes,' Tegné agreed.

'There is no need for Tabata's teaching and guidance to be discontinued,' Goswami went on. 'There are many planes of reality. Many finer, less coarse, vibrational states. Upon the demise of our Earth shell, our bodies, our spirit consciousness passes beyond into one of these finer states. Do you believe this, Tegné?'

'I do,' Tegné answered without hesitation.

'If we harness our more basic and primitive desires, if we channel them internally, then we may, through deep meditation, form direct links in communication with those who have gone before us,' Goswami said.

For a moment Tegné stared silently at the Master. 'How long, how long until I am able to achieve such a state?' Tegné asked, finally.

'Sometimes this heightened level of awareness directly follows a trauma of the mind and spirit. That can occur at any time. Enlightenment is spontaneous ...' Goswami said, hesitating, studying Tegné, '... but rare. Practise diligently and you may reach this state in fifteen yeons.'

'Fifteen yeons?' Tegné repeated, incredulously.

'Practise diligently,' Goswami said, then turned and walked from the hall.

*

The Warlord now visited Natiro regularly. Perhaps once, even twice each month he would arrive at the elegant house and share food and wine with her. Renagi felt strong and centred when he was in Natiro's presence, and the recurrent attacks of anxiety which had plagued him until his renewal of their relationship had all but vanished.

It was during the fifth month of his visits that she told him she was carrying his child. She had been frightened to divulge this until now, fearful that it would make her less desirable or that somehow the Warlord would consider her pregnancy a device with which to draw him closer or control his feelings. And that she would never do, never want.

She was relieved, as if a great, oppressive weight had been lifted from her heart, when Renagi expressed his happiness at the coming of the child.

'A boy, a brother to Zato, that is what I want!' he exclaimed, alive with joy.

As for Natiro, the idea of a second child had never so much as entered her mind until that night, nearly six months ago, when Renagi had taken her to bed. At the height of their ride to the heavenly plane she experienced the same strange contractions that she had known at the time of Zato's conception. It was then that she knew. Yet, she had pushed the premonition from her mind, denying its possibility, until her time of the month came and there was no blood. At first she had panicked, considering numerous methods of aborting the pregnancy. But finally she had accepted her condition. And now that Renagi had not only endorsed but expressed joy at the possibility of a male child, she felt thoroughly justified. What did it matter if her body was no longer that of an inexperienced virgin? Surely, to provide the Warlord of Zendow with an heir, and now a second child, was ample compensation for a few stretch-marks in the flesh of her abdomen or a slightly loose bosom. And if only the coming child would be male, her life would be fulfilled.

Renagi, also, had changed during the term of Natiro's pregnancy. There was a growing warmth to his manner, a tangible care and concern for this woman who would bear him a second child. His visits to the private sector became more frequent. And, in the back of his mind, the question burned, should he not insist that, after the birth, Natiro join him to live in the palace proper. After all, were love and acceptance not one and the same?

The labour began at midday. As soon as Natiro was certain that the spasms were not going to abate and that the delivery was imminent, she summoned Darya and Anyo, the younger of her servants. Darya had, in fact, delivered Zato, and knew the exact procedures to follow in preparation for the birth. She could also foretell, by the length between the spasms, that the delivery would not take place until well into the night. Thoroughly and methodically she stripped Natiro's bed of its fine satin sheets and replaced them with several layers of thick, absorbent cotton towelling. Then she saw that Natiro was properly attired in a loose, comfortable nightdress and her body supported by three firm pillows.

'A pot of camomile tea,' she instructed Anyo, watching as the short, thick-legged girl ran from the room, anxious to perform admirably on this auspicious occasion.

'Are you in any pain, Mis?' Darya asked, turning again to Natiro.

'No, Darya, but I know he is coming. I can feel him moving inside me,' Natiro replied, already sure of the gender as if the gods above would not fail her in this gift to the Warlord. 'Darya,' she continued, adjusting herself on the bed, rising up so that one of the pillows would slip further down and support her lower back.

'Mis?' Darya was already beginning the gentle, kneading massage to the muscles of the swollen, exposed abdomen.

'I want the Warlord to know that his child is coming,' Natiro whispered, giving herself more and more to the warm, gentle hands.

'Of course, Mis. As soon as Anyo arrives with the tea, I will send her to inform the Warlord.'

'How long will it be until the baby is here?' Natiro asked, trusting completely in Darya's skill and knowledge.

'Ten, maybe twelve hours,' Darya replied. 'Now it is best if you relax completely, speak as little as possible and conserve your strength. I will take care of everything,' she added, her voice becoming dreamy-soft as Natiro began to breath in rhythm with the fine, caring massage.

Raine struck the two rough pieces of firestone, once, twice, and again until the spark caught, igniting the small, tightly bunched ball of hay. The sharp yellow flames rose from the earthenware heat dish. Now she lifted the tapering yellow wax candle from the wooden work-top and held the new greased wick above the flames. The fire took hold and the single flame burnt bright, dancing wildly at first and finally settling into a strong, steady pulse of light. The hay in the heat dish burned to a crisp red, then extinguished, leaving the candle as the sole source of light in the tiny front room of the hut.

Raine sat quiet and still before the flame, her eyes picking out each of the subtle spectrum of colours from the rising heat, her mind drifting on waves, beyond the sadness, beyond the pain.

Eighteen summers. Eighteen summers since she had awakened to that death-like emptiness. She remembered that morning as though it were her last; how she lay still on the hard, narrow cot, somehow certain that she was alone in the hut, yet too frightened of that reality to move. So she just lay and listened, hoping she would hear the sound of Maliseet's footsteps or the muffled whimpers of the hungry infant from the other side of the thin partition.

Finally, hearing nothing, Raine had risen and walked towards the dividing curtain. She hoped and prayed that she would find both mother and child peacefully asleep on the other side, yet she knew that it was not to be.

Maliseet and her baby were gone. The cot where they had slept for the four weeks following the birth was clean and orderly, the space around it swept, tidy. A single cotton dress hung on the last of the metal hooks which were mounted in the wall above the cot. The dress was unwrinkled, yet the eggshell white of its material had yellowed with age. It had been Maliseet's favourite dress, her special dress, and Raine recalled the delight in her daughter's eyes as she had folded and stitched the coarse fabric while Maliseet had slipped in and out of the garment to ensure its perfect fit. Raine had fashioned the dress for her daughter on the eve of Maliseet's fourteenth birthday.

The candle flame flickered, and with its flicker Raine's mind was pulled back from this past memory and into the present. She stood up from the table and walked into the vacant bedchamber. The dress was still hanging on the hook above the cot. She had never touched, never disturbed the tiny room. Yet each yeon, on this eve of her daughter's birthday, she lit a single candle and kept vigil until the rise of the morning sun. Eighteen summers; Maliseet would have been thirty-four yeons.

Morning. A knock on the battered wooden door. Raine rose up from the table and walked across the room. It would be Rawlin, checking on her, seeing that she had food and water. Rawlin was the same age as her daughter, she remembered them both playing as children in the dirt road, and later going to work in the fields together. At one time Raine had hoped a relationship would develop between Maliseet and this tall, kind man. A relationship which could have resulted in marriage, but it was not to be. And now Rawlin, as a token of his respect for the past, had taken it upon himself to look after Raine. She was no longer strong enough to work in the labour parties, and her tight, stretched skin, which had grown even more sensitive with the passing yeons, would tolerate only the minimum of exposure to the sun.

As Raine unbolted the door, she shielded her eyes with her free hand.

'Are you well?' asked Rawlin, stepping inside the hut and closing the door, blocking out the light behind him. He carried a large wooden bucket of fresh well-water and a small sack of new potatoes.

Raine nodded and smiled. Rawlin thought he saw a strange, animal shyness in her red, tired eyes. He placed the bucket and sack on top of the wooden work table. It was then that he noticed the still-flickering candle, the stem melted and spreading in a wide, thick oval while the wick, nearly spent, balanced in the last of the hot, clear wax. He turned and met Raine's gaze. He had forgotten the day, and now he understood why she had seemed particularly guarded. He had interrupted the last minutes of a very private ceremony.

'I am sorry, Raine, truly sorry. I just did not remember,' Rawlin apologized, softly.

She smiled and nodded in reassurance. No, he had not offended her. Then she stepped close to him.

'Stay. Eat,' she said, enunciating the two words very clearly, yet speaking in the spare, tentative style of one unused to conversation.

'I cannot, Raine. Perhaps later I will stop back. I have promised to work the double shift today. There has been a great deal of sickness amongst the men recently.'

Raine understood. 'A great deal of sickness' was a gentle way of describing the carcinogenic blisters which ate through and ruined the unprotected skin of the field workers.

Yes, I certainly know all about that, she thought as she glanced quickly at the soft, pink skin directly beneath Rawlin's eyes. *Nothing. He is still clean,* she noted, seeing none of the first signs of rawness and chafing.

She stepped away from him, turning, looking at the water and the cloth sack of new potatoes. 'Thank you,' she said, smiling again, releasing him with the two words, allowing him to leave her.

Rawlin fixed the blankers in place as he walked from the hut and up the narrow road towards the eastern fields. As he walked, he recalled the day those many yeons ago that he had stood in the door of the same hut, enquiring as to the condition of his friend, Maliseet. It had been common knowledge that Raine's child was unwell; in fact, she had been unable to work in the fields for over eight weeks. Most in Asha-1 were familiar with the story; she had been found wandering, delirious and badly over-exposed to the ultra rays. There were others, just a few, who spoke of a single Warman, one of the men from the Procession, who returned to the village asking specific directions to the hut of the girl, Maliseet.

On that day, Rawlin still only sixteen yeons and strong with the certainty of youth, had vowed to discover the truth. After all, Maliseet was a member of his work party, a friend, and, in his heart, much more. For Rawlin had hoped to couple with her, to build and share a hut, to parent children. And he knew that Raine would not oppose him. So it was with this resolve that he knocked loudly on the door of their hut. He still remembered the protective glare in Raine's eyes as she denied him admittance, saying that her daughter was recovering, resting, and could see no one.

'But it is me, Rawlin. And I love your daughter,' he had blurted out, voicing his true feelings for the first time.

Even then Raine had closed the door on him, but not before he saw the spill of tears from her eyes. He had remained in front of the closed door, thinking that somehow it would re-open, that Raine would reconsider. But the door did not open again and, finally, belittled and terribly saddened, Rawlin turned to leave.

It was then that he heard the distinct cry of a baby from within the hut. He spun round and, for an instant, intended to break through the thin wooden door with his shoulder. Again, the cry of a hungry babe. This time Rawlin revolted, running from the sound, back towards the fields, confused and somehow betrayed. And in his mind the voices began; the hushed gossip which he had ignored, the voices that claimed the girl had been raped, that the Warman who had sought her out was the attendant of the Warlord. Rumours. Maliseet was pregnant with the Warlord's child, an unpardonable transgression. The very rumours which, in their blasphemy of the pure state of Zendow, threatened every Ashkelite. And now Rawlin was recalling this deadly gossip, wondering, considering.

Two weeks later Maliseet had vanished, and the secret with her. For Raine would not speak of her daughter, never a word, until in time the conjectures grew faint and then, with Raine's continued introversion, all but disappeared.

But that was eighteen yeons ago, I was not much more than a child, Rawlin reminded himself as he neared the end of the dirt road. The path widened and grew less distinct as it merged with the sparse green of the low, rolling hills leading into the work fields.

*

'What is happening? I demand to know what is happening?' Renagi's voice was a gruff whisper.

He stood in the far corner of the bedroom. He had been there for nine hours, and now he watched the sweat bead and fall from Darya's forehead on to the padded white towelling, which was soaked and stained with blood. And still nothing. No child.

Natiro's eyes were closed and her head moved from side to side amidst her low, anguished moans. Darya worked frantically above the swollen stomach which was rapidly becoming bruised from the constant, no longer gentle, plying.

'The baby will not turn, Master, he remains sideways,' Darya answered, controlling the near panic in her voice.

'And Natiro? How long can she withstand?' Renagi asked, his tone anxious.

'I do not know, Master. It is already near daybreak,' Darya replied, glancing quickly at the glow of light from beneath the window-ledge.

The low, unconscious moans continued from the bed, yet the spasms from Natiro's lower abdomen were weakening, and the time between the contractions was beginning to lengthen. Darya had delivered countless children in the forty yeons she had lived in Zendow; she was the most experienced midwife amongst a host of such women. These women occupied an important place in a culture where midwifery was revered, for no physician could perform the birthing skills with such calm and dexterity. It was, in fact, these skills which won Darya her position as Natiro's personal servant, for Darya had delivered Zato.

Yet now, as she hovered over her unconscious mistress, a strange sense of ineptness swept over her. Her fingers could feel the child, the form outlined beneath the mother's flesh, yet there was something wrong, something unnatural in the shape and the position of the moving infant. And try as she might to manipulate its position, to turn the head downwards in an effort to guide it through the passage from the mother's womb, the baby resisted, still lying transversely.

'Give her more liquid, more tea,' Darya commanded the plump servant girl. The girl obliged by gently lifting Natiro's head from the pillow and pouring a tiny amount of the honeyed camomile and primrose mixture into Natiro's dry mouth.

Natiro's eyes opened for a moment and it seemed she was trying to form her lips into a smile. Then the muscles which had worked so hard in their efforts to free the unborn child began to relax.

And in that moment of relaxation the baby began its own desperate struggle. Tiny fists and feet pushed out against the strained flesh, causing undulating ripples in the abdomen. Darya tried with all her strength to turn the thrashing mass downwards as Renagi dashed forward to the bed.

'Tell me what to do, I will help!' he shouted above Natiro's renewed screams.

'Hold her legs! Firm!' Darya responded, and for a moment she forgot that it was the Warlord who obeyed her commands.

Midnight, eighteen hours later. They had failed, purely and simply. Natiro lay still before them, her dry, exhausted body breathing its last aching breaths. And, in watching her final struggle, Renagi came as close as ever he could to loving her.

Darya raised her face towards him, tears glistening in the old, tired eyes. She nodded. 'It is over.'

Then, with a heart as heavy as the stone walls of Zendow, Renagi drew his katana and sliced cleanly through the flesh of Natiro's stomach.

The unborn child lay still, on its side, next to the broken placenta. Darya bent down close to the tiny, motionless body, feeling with her fingers for the faintest beat of the child's heart.

'I am sorry, Master. The child, also, is dead,' she whispered, her uneven voice breaking with sorrow.

The room was illuminated by only two candles and Renagi's view of the child, lying amongst the blood and fluid of the open abdomen, was obscured by dark shadows. He stepped back against the far door, re-sheathing his katana in a single sweeping motion, his thick thumb pulling out on the scabbard, wiping the blood from the blade as it guided the curved steel into the wood-lined sheath.

'Is the child male or female?' he asked in a lifeless monotone.

Darya bent again over the gaping wound, her intention to free the baby from its mother. Her trained fingers cradled the tiny body as she lifted upwards. It was then that she saw the reason for the transverse lie, the cause of death. For the long, hardened umbilical cord had wrapped like a suffocating serpent around the struggling child's throat, strangling it as it tried to turn in the womb. She lifted no further, instead lowering the tangled infant back into the warmth of Natiro's flesh.

'Female, master, it is female,' she said, but Renagi was no longer there to hear her. He had seen the child lifted in the candlelight; he had seen the broken neck, the smothered face. He had seen that the child was female. He walked alone from the house, into the blackness of the winding alleyways and towards the palace, its high walls outlined against the full October moon. And Renagi felt his final chance for salvation as strangled and dead within his own soul as the infant had been within the womb of the woman who had reached out to him.

> *Knowing others is wisdom*
> *Knowing the self is enlightenment*
> *Mastering others requires force*
> *Mastering the self needs strength.*
> *He who knows he has enough is rich.*
> *Perseverance is a sign of will-power*
> *He who stays where he is endures*
> *To die but not to perish is to be eternally present.*

Tegné moved the one thousandth wooden bead from the left to join the nine hundred and ninety-nine others on the long wire frame which formed the abacus. He stood up from the rectangular straw mat, six feet long and two feet wide, folded the single woollen blanket and placed it neatly on the upper end of the tatami. The mat had been his place of meditation as well as his place of rest for the duration of his 'one thousand days'. And to-day, like every day preceding it for the better part of three yeons, Tegné pulled the rough cotton trousers of his training gi up over his waist, tying the twin cords tightly before he pulled on the matching jacket and secured it with the heavy white sash. Then he walked from the small, cold stone room and on to the shining, polished, pinewood floor of the main Dojo. He stood alone in the empty space beneath the oil portrait of Grand Master Tabata.

How much this old wood has taught me, he thought, feeling the dry, smooth hardness beneath his bare feet. *How many times have I picked myself up from this floor, how many punches, how many kicks, how many press-ups, sit-ups? All absorbed into its mirrored surface.* And as he remained still, he could again feel the power of the wood seep into him, sending its wonderful strength through his flesh and into his heart. Finally, he walked to the far corner of the training hall. In front of him were more than one dozen wooden buckets, each half-full with clean well-water. Next to the buckets stood a fresh pile of cotton rags, cut large and square, of left-over material from the Temple workshop. He took two of the rags from the top of the pile, placing one in the bucket nearest to him. Then, wringing the rag until it was merely damp, he turned and knelt upon the wooden floor. He had performed this cleaning only nine hours ago, following the last of the three daily classes, and, of course, the floor had remained spotless. But that was neither the point nor the lesson of this morning exercise. For the solo cleaning was also the practice of humility and a chance for contemplation.

Tegné began the slow, circular, clockwise rub with the damp cloth in his right hand while his left hand dried and polished in a faster, counter-clockwise rhythm. His forearms were thick and muscular where they emerged from the three-quarter-length sleeves of his gi: they seemed sure and strong, almost as if they belonged to someone other than himself, someone older and more powerful. Yet his whole body had developed in the same proportion, from the fine, smaller muscles which caused his feet to arch, able to grip the bare boards of the Dojo floor, to the more obvious pectoral muscles of his chest which added the breaking power to his hard-knuckled fists.

His body had matured and at the same time been educated. Even his natural way of movement had altered, his relaxed walk had lowered, his centre more in line with his natural axis, causing a sure, steady gait with no raising or lowering of the head. And with the continued help of Goswami, Tegné had grown in tune with the original teachings of Tabata, lessons whose meaning was only now beginning to blossom and bear fruit. Yes, Yano was his teacher, but Tabata was his source.

In the beginning, during his first months as a 'special student', he had resented being singled out, had even felt dishonoured and blatantly persecuted, as if he was being punished for his uniqueness, his skin, his hair, his eyes. It was only after a dozen or more private meetings with the Elder that he realized this was not the case, and he had accepted the merits of his situation. He recalled the first time the Elder had requested that he talk about the ambush, and the murder of his Sensei, Tabata. It was a subject his mind had buried, his sub-conscious hidden beneath layer upon layer of protective shield. At first it was as if he was re-telling a story he had read in a nearly forgotten book, the characters fictitious and vague in his memory. But the Elder had gone deeper, pushed, prodded and finally revealed the raw and open wound which festered deep within the young man.

The first tears were unlike those of the original awakening following the acupuncture treatment. For these were not the tears of release; these were the tears of terrible pain, suffering and terror. It was as if he had been forced back through the tunnel of time to what now seemed a distant life, and he was compelled to relive that single scene of his utmost anguish; the image of Tabata, the one person closest to his heart, standing alone in the clearing, his body suddenly bent, old, dying. And Tegné, unable to help, powerless, impotent, and yet somehow knowing that the death was intended for him. *A coward.*

'Continue, please. You are observing, you cannot be harmed,' the Elder had said, his voice soothing behind the steady click of the metronome.

And Tegné had continued, his mind recalling details which even he, at the time, had been unaware of observing. Gradually, over a period of many of these painful analytical sessions, Tegné was able to work the pain from his mind until, finally, the most relevant and lasting image was of an etheric body of his Sensei, rising from the earth.

'There is no death,' Tegné had said to the Elder at the start of a recent session.

'Good. Then you are free from the shock of the experience and there is no need to continue with our catharsis,' the Elder replied, turning off the metronome.

'But, Elder, I am still troubled as to the cause of the attack,' Tegné objected. 'You see, the men who attacked us, they shouted, "Take the boy, take the boy",' he continued.

'And you remember clearly how these men were dressed?'

'No, Elder. It was at night and I could not describe their exact costume. It seemed a type of war armour, all black, with an insignia, a red insignia,' Tegné answered. The Elder nodded knowingly.

Tegné observed the Elder's acknowledgement. 'Who were they?'

'Members of one of the warring clans,' the Elder answered, refusing to be precise. 'Perhaps they mistook you for a runaway slave. You see, the slave class bears a similar colouring to your own.'

'A slave? Are you suggesting I am the child of slaves?' Tegné asked, embarrassed by the notion.

'At one time, Tegné, before the influx of the clans into the east, the slaves you speak of were a fine, pure race of people. It was only when the aggressive, conquering hordes invaded the territories surrounding Shuree that these people were bonded into slavery,' the Elder explained.

'Without a fight?' Tegné persisted.

'Of course they opposed their oppressors,' the Elder answered, 'But they were not a militant group. They had never needed to be. And the first thing the clans did was to murder their strongest males, leaving the weaker ones to continue the line. Finally, through a continual process of separating and destroying their dominant offspring, the clan created a state of slaves.'

'And I am one of them?' Tegné asked again, barely concealing his revulsion.

The Elder smiled, nodding his head. 'Your eyes are blue, Tegné, your body is strong, and your skin can tolerate the sun. No, you are not a slave.' Yet there was something vague, inconclusive, in the Elder's tone.

'Then what am I?' Tegné asked, and as he did so he unconsciously formed his right hand into a loose fist.

The Elder glanced at the fist, noticing how the thick surface veins, inflamed even by this mild gesture, carried a surge of blood through the bellied muscle of the forearm and through the vivid, reddish-blue birthmark. Tegné, noticing the Elder's eyes upon his fist, quickly relaxed the hand.

'You are a disciple of the Temple of the Moon,' the Elder concluded.

Still the dissatisfaction in Tegné's eyes could not be hidden.

'Your awakening will take place in stages,' the Elder added. 'Do not rush, for nothing is gained by violent movement, whether it be of the mind or of the body.'

And that was that, the matter was to be continued no further. Tegné understood this, and he would abide by it, but in his heart he was certain that this wise Temple Elder knew more than he had offered.

Your awakening will take place in stages . . . Tegné was beginning to understand just what those seven words meant. For it was a statement that many times passed from the lips of Goswami following his private tuition in the more advanced body postures or the higher levels of meditation.

And at last, through the use of mantra and the concentrated release of his mind, Tegné had reached the transcendental state; that state in which he hovered in the peaceful freedom of the void, behind the attachments of his Earth life, far from the intricate and complex circuit of characteristics which formed his personality, making him individual.

It was in this transcendental state that his true renewal took place, for it was there that Tegné tasted the sweet nectar of the Mother Spirit, and it was there that he breathed in the vital prana, the energy of the source.

And it was there, in transcendence, that the seven Protectors monitored his progress, guiding him towards their light. It was there that they waited for him, just beyond the final veil, that last, thin shell of his understanding.

Goswami had been a powerful influence, and Tegné felt a deep sense of loss on the morning the Master told him of his intention to leave the Temple.

'But your place is here, with the Brothers,' Tegné had reasoned, looking deep into the strange eyes whose pupils seemed in a never-ending flux of rapid contraction followed by dilation.

'No, no, Brother Tegné,' Goswami answered gently, 'I was born in the high Himilak Mountains, and it's there I wish to be when I depart this Earth form.'

Tegné stood before the Meditation Master, his mouth wide with surprise, for in physical appearance Goswami seemed young and vital, his eyes clear and his skin smooth.

'Surely you cannot be speaking of death?' he asked.

'I have occupied this physical shell for one hundred and fifty yeons,' Goswami stated calmly, simply, as if there was nothing strange in the figure, 'And I feel it time to pass on to the next plane, to enlarge my knowledge before I choose my next incarnation. Perhaps in another ten lifetimes I shall return as an avatar,' he added, making a joke of his deification.

True to his word, Goswami departed on a clear morning, one month later. He was bidden farewell by only the handful of Brothers who had been made privy to his journey. Tegné watched, saddened but none the less amused, as Goswami, barefoot and carrying the lightest of bedrolls, smiled jubilantly, waved like a happy child and began the treacherous trip of two thousand vul as though he were taking a mere walk to the well.

*

'Are you ready?' The words came as a stark surprise, pulling Tegné from his reminiscence. He looked up from his kneeling position, both rags still held in his hands.

Yano stood alone, towering above him, not more than ten feet away. He was attired in the ceremonial hakama, the black divided skirt. His bare feet were a shoulder's width apart in the shizentai position and his fists were clenched tight, hanging like mallets on his relaxed arms in front of his broad-shouldered body.

As Tegné dropped the rags and rose, facing Yano, his eyes again caught on the thickly calloused first and second knuckles of the clenched fists. And just for a moment the recollection of Yano, standing side-on, urinating on the same bleeding knuckles flashed through Tegné's mind. It had happened after a two-hour session of continuous punching on the straw-padded striking-post, the makiwara. Two hours of repetitive striking, 'Seventy per cent impact on index knuckle, thirty per cent on second. Then the result will equalize on contact,' Yano had instructed. 'The urine disinfects the skin, then hardens the surface,' he had gone on to explain when he noticed Tegné staring at him on that afternoon.

Now Tegné brought his head up, his eyes linking with the thin, hooded slits below Yano's flat forehead. The whites of Yano's eyes barely showed.

'Oss, Sensei,' Tegné said, bowing low before his teacher, already aware of the taut, dangerous atmosphere in the Dojo.

'Today, last day in special training,' Yano snarled. 'Most important lesson,' the sinister voice continued in its clipped, broken sentences. 'Today I kill you,' Yano finished, repeating his promise of that first day, one thousand days before. Then he walked steadily towards his pupil.

Tegné looked long and deep into the wide, square face, drawn to the darkness of the eyes. There was no give, no compassion.

The first blow was a spinning backfist strike, started from the relaxed natural position and performed in a purposeful, slow motion, as if to defy retaliation or to test the level of fear in the intended target. Tegné watched the striking arm unfurl, in perfect time to the spin of the rear leg on the pivoting foot. He could have stepped back, evading the technique, or even struck with a counter-attack of his own. Instead, like some defenceless creature caught in the deafening, debilitating roar of a hungry lion, Tegné stood motionless as the backfist crashed into the muscle directly below his left shoulder, beneath the vulnerable collar bone.

The impact was strong enough to send Tegné reeling backwards, and Yano's sweeping right foot found an already unstable target as it ripped into the ankle, just below the calf of Tegné's forward leg. Tegné fell hard to the floor, his head snapping back and striking the wood.

'You have no spirit. Coward!' Yano bellowed the forbidden word from above as he ground the knife-edge of his lead foot into the soft tissue of Tegné's throat. 'Get up, coward!' he commanded as he removed the grinding foot and backed away from his fallen student.

He knows, Tegné thought, raising himself from the floor and regaining his feet. *Still, I must not attack him, I must not engage him further*, he reasoned, and glanced quickly towards the closed door leading from the Dojo and out into the adjoining courtyard.

Escape, flashed briefly through his mind as Yano, detecting the lapse in concentration, slid forwards and snapped a kizami-zuki easily into Tegné's unguarded face.

There was only a small, sharp, clicking sound as the entire left front incisor flew from Tegné's mouth and skidded like a stone across the polished pine. Stunned, Tegné lifted his hand to his open mouth and clearly felt the wide new gap left by the missing tooth. He looked at Yano.

I will not run, he willed, fully afraid and yet defying his fear.

Yano glared at him from a distance of less than two paces. *I cannot beat this man. No, there can be no victory, but perhaps I do not have to die*, Tegné thought as he settled into a sochin stance. And as he settled, regulating his breathing, his fear retreated, leaving him calm. Accepting.

Yano's next move was an example of perfection in distance and timing. Covering the gap between them with an apparent side-sliding thrust kick, Yano watched as Tegné moved backwards, his joined open palms held before him in an augmented blocking technique. Yano pulled the thrusting kick slightly short of contact with the block, then quickly the bull-like Sensei changed both the rhythm and the speed of his attack, performing a shorter, sharper version of the same kick. The knife-edge of his foot connected squarely with Tegné's stationary chest, pushing inwards against the rib-cage and knocking the breath from his body. Tegné was propelled upwards and backwards; he crashed hard against the solid, plastered wall of the Dojo.

Through glazed eyes, Tegné could see Yano line up for the final waza. The Sensei was being purposely slow, obviously setting up his blows in sheer defiance of his student's inability to block or counter.

'Oi-zuki, jodan!' Yano shouted at Tegné, announcing not only the intended front-lunging punch but the face-level target. Yano flew forwards, a raging ki-ai spilling from his drawn lips.

Yet this was not Yano, Tegné's Sensei, who screamed towards him across the glass-like surface of wood; this was death itself, fast and sleek and without conscience.

And Tegné met death with death. Shifting sideways, low and fluid, he barely needed to make contact with his left open-handed inside block. Yano's head was beside him now, still looking forward, in line with his failed punch. Tegné saw the naked, vulnerable flesh on the left side of Yano's neck, the area protected by the mastoid.

'Heeii!' Tegné ki-aied, and with every reserve of his heretofore restrained spirit he drove the foreknuckle punch into the exposed target. The flesh was soft, non-resistant, and the punch sank deep into the neck before Tegné withdrew the attacking hiraken. Then he shifted position and waited.

Slowly, Yano straightened from the low forward stance, stepping back out of striking range. Slower still, he turned towards his student. Yano's eyes were no longer the tight, hooded slits, those hateful windows of only seconds before. Now they were soft, brown and gentle.

A terrible feeling of remorse gripped Tegné as he dropped his guarding hands. He stepped towards his Sensei and as he did so Yano changed before his eyes, flowing and shaping like a crescendoing wave of water.

'Zanshin. You must retain mental alertness until your opponent is dead, or, if it is a sparring exercise, until the final bow. Then it is finished, not before,' Yano's voice castigated him through a cloudy haze as Tegné struggled to his feet. The Sensei's double palm-heel strike had sent him sprawling on to the floor, his head smashing again into the hard wood, knocking him senseless.

Yano stood smiling as Tegné finally assumed a semblance of the sochin-dachi stance.

'Now it is over,' Yano proclaimed, and bowed to his student.

'Thank you, Sensei,' Tegné's words rushed from him in relief as he straightened, feet together, and returned the acknowledgement.

Yano rubbed the left side of his neck. 'It was a good blow. You released your mind, and your spirit rushed forward,' he said as they walked across the floor. 'It was an important blow also, for it transcended our relationship of student and teacher. You came out from behind my shadow. You have shed a burden, a weight which has hung like a dark cloud around you since the day we met. Perhaps a grave self-doubt . . . You are a man now,' Yano declared, stopping and looking directly at Tegné.

Tegné was still struggling with the meaning of his lesson, caught in a myriad of confused emotions, for he also knew it was a turning point. Finally, he said quietly, 'Sensei, I was frightened I had injured you'.

Yano laughed, removing his rubbing hand from his neck and displaying the unblemished skin.

'Not even a bruise,' Tegné observed.

'There is still much for you to learn,' Yano stated, maintaining a hint of a smile. Then the Sensei bent forward and picked the long-rooted incisor from the floor. 'Take this,' he instructed, handing Tegné the tooth. 'Go immediately to the remedial quarters. If you are quick, the physician will be able to reset it into your jaw. You are lucky, very lucky. The tooth came out with the root intact!'

Tegné closed his hand around the tooth; he could not recall Yano Sensei ever appearing so jubilant.

YEON 994
ZENDOW
VOKANE PROVINCE

The knock on his door came at sunrise, as Renagi had requested. He had been awake for the latter half of the night anyway, and now he stood dressed and waiting as the cool daylight from his open window brightened the room behind him.

'Come in,' he called as he adjusted the front buttons of his black, square-shouldered tunic.

The door opened and Zato stood before his father. There was an undisguised expression of surprise on the young man's face.

'But are you not ready? Your war armour, your katana?' Zato questioned, closing the door behind him as he turned to approach his informally suited father.

'I am not going,' Renagi said flatly. 'I will join you later at the kumite and then, together, we will attend the feast.'

'But . . .' Zato began.

'No.' Renagi cut his son off, raising his hand as he stepped closer. 'You are old enough to lead the Procession. It is important that you begin to assert your presence,' Renagi insisted. 'Now sit down. There are things I must say to you.'

Zato walked towards the open window, turned and sat finally in the ornate, high-backed wooden chair. The long, carved dragon wrapped around the right arm and extended until its open, fanged mouth spat fire and flame on to the headrest. The dragon was carved into the actual wood of the chair, which was itself made from only three pieces of panouki, expertly and artistically joined together. It had been one of the few remaining treasures from the occupancy of the original monks, and Renagi had overseen its faithful restoration.

Zato settled on to its thinly padded seat, the base of his spine pressed firmly into the curvature of the wood and his arms supported comfortably on the carved rests.

'Built for contemplation,' Renagi said, noticing Zato's unspoken appreciation of the fine piece of furniture. Zato lifted his head to meet his father's eyes. 'Purity, that is what I want you to understand,' Renagi began.

'Purity?' Zato repeated.

'Correct thinking. Correct purpose. Proper speech. Proper conduct. Great effort, constant awareness. Concentration,' Renagi stated in an unusual, prepared tone.

'Have I displeased you in some way?' Zato asked, very unsure as to the reason for this discourse.

'Zendai,' Renagi continued, completely ignoring Zato's question, 'One who leads. One who lives by the strictest of codes, one who conducts himself impeccably in battle as well as in peacetime . . . A Zendai is the personification of purity. Do you understand me?' Renagi moved across the room, his eyes far away yet intense.

'Yes,' Zato answered, 'I am Zendai and I live by the Code of the Warrior.'

'Good, good,' Renagi said, his eyes re-focusing on his son. 'Since your mother died, I have lain with no woman. I will produce no other sons. That has been decreed by the Gods of Light.' Renagi's voice grew hushed as he stood directly above Zato, bending down, touching both hands to his son's shoulders. 'We . . . you and I, are chosen; the purest of Zendai. We are marked; we bear the Sign of the Claw. We must go forth and never stumble. Do you understand?'

Zato had begun to feel uneasy, a strange, physical revulsion. What was his father doing? What point was he trying so desperately to drive into him? Why, now, had he decided that Zato should lead the Procession? Zato began to rise from the chair but Renagi held him firmly.

'Say to me that we are pure,' Renagi pressed.

'We are pure. Pure Zendai,' Zato stated, studying the deep-furrowed, mask-like face above him.

'And in your thoughts, do you ever lose the way of pureness?' Renagi asked.

'Father, I do not understand,' Zato begged.

'Women!' Renagi nearly shouted, 'Have you ever found desire for a woman who was not Zendai?'

'Only for sport,' Zato retorted, making no attempt to disguise his distaste for this line of questioning.

'Yes! Good!' Renagi snapped, releasing Zato and backing away as his son rose from the chair. 'Then let them see you today. Ride tall and proud, . . .' he hesitated, again casting his eyes on Zato, '. . . ride through Ashkelan, let them learn to fear you, for they are the weakest, most loathsome of people.'

Zato held the Warlord's gaze as he walked across the floor, breaking eye contact only as he reached the door. 'Thank you for this honour, father. I will lead the Procession with dignity, I will uphold our family name,' he pledged, then turned quickly, opened the door and walked from the room.

Renagi stared after him, then he closed and carefully slid the metal bolt into position, locking the door. He could not see the concern and self-conscious embarrassment on Zato's face as his son walked through the long sombre corridor. The Warlord had already informed the selected Twelve that Zato would lead the

Procession; there had been no hint of opposition. In this respect, Renagi was satisfied, as, pensively, he walked toward the fine, high-backed dragon chair. He settled easily into the familiar wooden seat. 'No, he could not face another Procession. He could not endure the stares of those limpid pink eyes or the expressions on the white, translucent faces.' It was as if they knew, as if they were quietly mocking him. So he had made sure they were terrified. It was only last yeon that he had given the nod to one of his Warmen, and on that signal the Warman had drawn his sword and sliced an old, tottering field worker cleanly in two. *Only one yeon ago, in Asha–IV. Surely, they have not forgotten. One cut, clean . . .*

Renagi breathed in, smiling, feeling momentarily secure in the power of the katana. 'Purity,' he whispered the word softly. 'Unmixed, untainted, innocent,' he mused as he became aware of the familiar deadness within his groin. He placed his right hand against the cloth covering his crotch, his index finger unconsciously pressing on the head of his flaccid penis. *Yes, it is true that I have not been with a woman since the death of Natiro, yet I have not been without desire* . . . A desire that at once inflamed and disgusted him, a desire that he had at first tried to analyse on a physical level, only then realizing that the desire stemmed from his heart. For it was a particular purity he yearned for, a particular reflection of himself that he had seen only once, and that once was in the eyes of the Ashkelite girl.

The clatter of hooves shook him from his thoughts. He rose sharply from the dragon chair and went to the window. He could see the Twelve clearly as they rode out from the last of the winding roads which led from the stables and into the courtyard. *How clean, how precise*, Renagi thought, admiring the tightness of the formation as the group cantered from the main gates, spreading out as they crossed the demarcation line yet never once losing the cohesion of the unit. *One yeon past, twelve months, and I was holding that lead position*, the Warlord observed, watching as Zato widened his distance in front of the Twelve. As Renagi saw them disappear up the western road and into the Forest of Shuree he recognized the finality of his gesture. For, gradually, he had begun to relinquish his control of Zendow. Today Zato would lead the Procession, and soon his son would stand as Warlord. It was not the way Renagi had planned or foreseen it, but that was the way it would be. For the Warlord felt himself dying, day by day, night by night. His heart. His soul.

The class was small in comparison to the other groups of students practising Empty Hand, but it was his class – Tegné's. He was the Sensei.

He stood at the far end of the small Dojo which adjoined the larger, main training hall of the Temple, and watched as the twenty young Brothers, aged between ten and fifteen yeons, assembled. Their white gis were so new that the starch in the heavy cotton material caused the fabric to rub with the rough sound of wood against wood as they performed their warming-up exercises.

'First, learn to teach children. They will never lie to you; they are always an honest reflection of yourself,' the Elder had promised the day he assigned Tegné the position of Sensei to the junior novitiates.

The assignment meant that Tegné would be responsible for the introduction of Empty Hand to all the novice Brothers who chose the Martial Way as their path to enlightenment. Of course, his own tuition would continue; he was required to attend two of Yano's main Dojo classes per day in addition to spending one hour in the morning and one hour at the close of each day in the single meditation cells which lay in the massive vault below the Temple.

Tegné had been teaching this particular group for a little longer than three months, and already he could foretell which boys amongst the twenty would succeed in entering the higher ranks. For attitude, much more than natural physical ability, enabled the subtle learning process to continue. As soon as one of the young boys developed feelings of superiority, his individual learning would be slowed or completely halted. It was Tegné's task to sense these shifts in disposition and nip them in the bud. And in fulfilling his role as a teacher, in breaking down the simplest movements and postures so they could be understood and assimilated by this group of youngsters, his own understanding deepened.

He had already graduated seven of his older students to the lower ranks of Yano's class, and the senior Sensei had complimented him on their discipline and knowledge of basic technique.

Sensei, teacher; Tegné was beginning to understand the meaning of his position and the pride of fulfilment through his students.

It was towards the end of the one-hour session that the Elder silently entered the Dojo and stood watching from the back of the room. Tegné noticed the Exalted Brother and assumed he had come to oversee his work and would then quietly leave the training hall. But the Elder did not leave; instead he waited patiently while Tegné instructed in the stretching postures of the warming-down exercises, finally bringing the class to attention. After the traditional recital of the Dojo code he dismissed them. Still the Elder remained as Tegné rose from his kneeling sei-za position and walked towards him.

'Elder?' Tegné said, using the title as a gentle question.

'I trust all is well with you, Tegné? Your work progressing?' responded the Elder, pleasantly.

'It is,' Tegné replied.

'Good, good. Because I have a special task for you,' the Elder continued, 'A young boy, younger than you usually teach, but I feel if he is not taken in hand very soon, and very firmly, he will be lost.'

'And you wish me to admit him to my class here in the Dojo?' asked Tegné.

'Eventually, yes,' said the Elder. 'But first I would like you to take him on a one-to-one basis. Your own uchi-deshi.'

'And what age is the boy?' enquired Tegné.

'Seven,' the Elder replied.

Surprised, Tegné repeated, 'Seven?'

'Yes, he is very young. But at the same time, he is very wise in the ways of the world. You see, unlike the other boys here and very like yourself, he did not arrive as an infant. In fact, it was only nine months ago that he was brought into the Temple by one of our wandering Brothers. The reason for their meeting was that this little fellow had managed to remove the Brother's bo as well as his woollen shawl while the Brother was in meditation beneath a tree. When he was finally able to capture the little boy and recover his bo and his wrap, he discovered that the child was homeless, orphaned, and had been living by thievery for nearly two yeons. True to the spirit of compassion which we foster within the monastery, the Brother offered the child food and shelter inside our gates. I am sorry to say that the story deteriorates from there, for there have been a multitude of unexplained thefts and a series of minor disruptions amongst the very young novices. All instigated by our most recent admission,' the Elder concluded, opening both hands in a gesture of frustration.

Amused, Tegné nodded his head slowly, looking up to meet the twinkling eyes of the Elder. 'And I am to show this little one "the Way"?' he asked, with a slight play on the words.

'Yes. Exactly. That is correct,' the Elder answered, smiling broadly as if the problem had been instantly solved.

Rin stood dwarfed by the high plaster walls and vaulted, sky-lit ceiling of the Dojo. He studied his reflection in one of the four squared sheets of silvered glass which were mounted on each wall. His new gi was crisp and white, tied tight at the waist by an equally white sash which caused the rather large training suit to billow out at both top and bottom, giving the small boy an unintentionally comic appearance. Rin, however, found nothing humorous in his reflection. He saw only the stark beauty of the clean white cotton and felt only the great satisfaction of owning the new training suit.

He walked closer to the mirror, trying to move in the sure-footed, composed fashion of the older Brothers he had seen walking in similar suits across the small courtyard and into the training complex. He moved to within an arm's reach of his reflection.

I look like a girl, he observed with great annoyance, roughing up his jet-black hair so that it stood out at jagged, irregular angles and did not so softly frame the wide, almond-eyed face which ended in a nearly pointed chin; the chin which gave a slight, mischievous, elfin quality to the otherwise angelic countenance. Then he thrust his hips forward and squared his tiny shoulders. Still not satisfied that his appearance warranted the 'special training' with the 'great white Sensei' whom he had often seen in passing yet never had the courage to so much as meet eye to eye, Rin slapped his full brown cheeks just to give them a tougher, reddish quality. Finally, the little boy turned and marched stiffly across the floor and into the centre of the Dojo.

Tegné waited in the partially open door at the far end of the training hall. He had managed to watch the latter portion of the boy's private performance without breaking into laughter, but barely. And now, as he carried the heavy wooden bucket of water and the two thick rags towards the expectant child he fought to control his urge to smile.

Without a greeting or salutation of any kind, Tegné placed the three-quarters full bucket at Rin's feet. Then he dropped the two rags so the coarse material just covered the tiny brown toes which protruded from the folds of overlapping cloth which formed the bottom of Rin's gi.

'I noticed your interest in the mirror,' Tegné began, his voice purposely harsh and ungiving, 'This floor is also a mirror. It reflects the work and sweat which the students of this Dojo give in their training. But since you have walked upon it I can no longer see it shine ...' he continued, trying to give this prearranged speech the authority he knew it required. But he was rapidly falling prey to the frightened, waif-like eyes which stared up at him.

Finally, Tegné turned his head aside. *Do not smile, do not soften,* he told himself, beginning to feel ridiculous for these overbearing tactics, particularly when he was reminded that the recipient of his tirade was a seven-year-old child who stood not much more than three feet in height and wore a gi which would have fitted Tegné himself.

'Do you mean, Sensei, that before I walked upon it I could have seen my reflection as if I was looking into the silver glass?' Rin said in all innocence, quite amazed that he could have tarnished the floor so thoroughly and so quickly.

'What I mean, Rin, is that you will scrub and polish this floor until it shines,' Tegné ordered.

'But Sensei,' said Rin, lifting his arms to emphasize his bewilderment, "It already shines!'

'Enough talk!' Tegné snapped, shifting his attention to the bucket and rags. 'From this moment on, when I ask you to perform a task, you will respond, "Oss, Sensei", and nothing more. Do you understand?' Tegné picked up the nearest rag and dropped it into the waiting bucket.

'Oss, Sensei,' Rin answered, lowering his hands and staring into the clear water.

'Do not turn away from me when I speak to you,' Tegné continued, moving closer still to the quaking child.

'Oss, Sensei,' Rin nearly shouted in his effort to please this golden-haired tyrant who loomed above him.

'Now lift the rag from the bucket, wring the excess water from it, kneel upon the floor and with a circular motion of your arm, like this . . .' Tegné demonstrated the clockwise sweep, '. . . clean the floor. When you have cleaned a good-sized patch, take the dry rag, and with a reverse pattern of your arm, like this . . .' again Tegné demonstrated, '. . . polish the wood until it shines.'

'Oss, Sensei,' Rin answered, nearly devastated at the dismal reality of what he had anticipated to be his initiation into the mysterious order of the Empty Hand.

Tegné stepped back, away from the bucket, indicating with a motion of his head that Rin should begin. Rin bowed.

'Stop right there,' Tegné said. Rin froze, looking quizzically into the Sensei's eyes.

'The bow is the first sign of etiquette, and etiquette is the foundation on which our training is based. We begin with a bow and we finish with a bow. So you may as well learn to bow correctly,' Tegné stated.

Etiquette? Rin wondered what the word meant as he straightened more to attention.

'Now, on my command I want you to bend at the waist, keep your hips in, your hands outstretched, fingers straight and down at your sides – and keep your eyes focused on me.' Tegné instructed, remembering Tabata's insistence on retaining an awareness of one's training partner even when exchanging courtesies. *Consider your opponent's hands and legs as you would sharp swords. One strike. Finished. And always when you would least expect it,* Tabata had stressed during his early instruction in this aware form of etiquette.

'Rei,' Tegné said, using the formal command.

Rin stood frozen, unsure of the word and less sure as to the proper execution of the bow.

'Rei,' Tegné repeated the word, this time bowing correctly towards the child. 'Now you try it . . . Rei.'

Rin bent at the waist, his hips going naturally backwards, his chin tucking in and causing his eyes to point to the floor. Quickly but lightly, Tegné swiped at the top of the little boy's head with his open hand. Startled, Rin jumped back.

'Hips pushed in, arms and hands straight, eyes forward,' Tegné explained, and this time demonstrated as he spoke. Rin copied the movement, never breaking eye contact with Tegné.

*

'Rei,' Tegné repeated for the one hundredth time. And Rin performed the one hundredth bow, properly, even adding, 'Oss, Sensei,' as he flowed naturally into the forward bend.

'Now you may begin to clean and polish the Dojo floor,' Tegné said, satisfied that this first lesson in propriety had taken hold.

> *They stand like ivory gods at the gates of Heaven*
> *Loving all men. Understanding and open*
> *Bearing yet not possessing*
> *Working yet taking no credit*
> *Leading yet not dominating*
> *They are the sacred circle*
> *The Seven Holy Spirits*
> *They are the primal Virtue*
> *The Seven Protectors.*

The Elder read the words aloud.

'Are they real, Elder? Do such entities actually exist?' Tegné asked, looking up as the aged Brother turned the old, yellowed page.

'As surely and as purposefully as we ourselves exist,' the Elder answered. 'It is a matter of reaching out for them, recognizing their call, their will,' he continued. 'Find them through your meditation, beg them to come into your heart. For there may come a point in your life when only these Protectors can show you the clear path.'

The Elder stopped speaking and let his gaze rest on the man before him. *Five yeons, he has only five yeons,* he thought as he quietly assessed the clarity of the blue eyes, the discipline of the seated posture and even the unconscious control in Tegné's breathing.

'And have you seen them, touched them?' Tegné asked hesitantly, in no way wishing to offend this master teacher, yet needing to establish whether these spirits existed in a philosophically abstract form or, in fact, were tangible in a physical sense.

'I understand your question, Tegné, and if I may, I will answer it with a question of my own,' the Elder suggested.

'Please do, Elder,' Tegné urged.

'Have you been successful with your exercises in projected consciousness, successful in entering the astral state?' the Elder asked, referring to the practice of projection in which the practitioner shifted his conscious awareness from his corporeal Earth body to a much finer, less densely vibrating, astral body.

'I have made the separation perhaps half a dozen times,' Tegné answered.

'Illusion?' the Elder asked.

'No. A separate reality,' Tegné replied.

'And does your projected self "think"?' the Elder continued.

'Yes, but at a much greater level of detachment than my Earth body,' Tegné responded, beginning to follow the Elder's line of reasoning.

'Detachment from the possessive nature of our flesh and blood,' the Elder stated.

'Yes,' Tegné agreed.

'Well, if you can accept the reality of that first level of projected vibration, that first level beyond our flesh, then try to imagine a level of reality which is seven levels beyond, wich has no corporeal lust or need. Which is pure. The "primal virtue",' the Elder said.

'I cannot comprehend such purity,' Tegné answered.

'Nor can you hear the gentle beating of the silken wings of a single butterfly. Yet the butterfly exists. You see it, so you believe it,' the Elder said.

'And you have seen the Protectors?'

'Yes,' the Elder replied.

'And so the Protectors exist,' Tegné stated.

'Yes. Synchronous with our Earth plane. To help us, to guide us,' the Elder continued. 'And on the infinitely rare occasion that an Earth body becomes momentarily connected to this sacred circle, then that Earth body receives knowledge of a divine task or inspiration. And that Earth body must fulfil its mission.'

'What kind of Earth soul would be the recipient of such a connection?' Tegné asked.

'One who is pure of heart, free from corruption. A prophet, even a warrior,' the Elder stated.

'It would be an awesome experience,' Tegné said, then added humbly, 'A tremendous burden.'

'Yes. Most certainly,' agreed the Elder, consciously bringing his spirit in tune with the spirit of the man before him. *I must tell him without words, without betraying the trust, without breaking the pact. Five yeons; he will not be ready,* he worried, then quickly curbed the anxiety which threatened to force a reckless word, an untimely revelation.

'And are you managing to adhere to the teachings of our late Goswami?' the Elder asked, diverting the path of the conversation while at the same time keeping it within its spiritual confines.

'I sit in meditation for one hour in the morning, and at least two hours in the evening," Tegné replied.

'Transcending?' the Elder asked, as if the state was of trivial consequence.

'During both sessions,' Tegné answered.

'And the projection?' the Elder pressed, sensing a way to lead Tegné closer to the truth.

'In the evening before sleep,' said Tegné simply.

'Before we meet again, Tegné, I want you to combine the state of transcendence with your exercises in projection. In other words, I want you to attempt to project your astral spirit up and into the void. Invoke the spiritual aid of your Sensei Tabata; he will guide you. And remember our discussion today,' the Elder said, indicating that their conversation was over.

Tegné rose from the mat, leaving the Elder in the seated, half-lotus posture. 'I will listen for the silken wings of the single butterfly,' he said, smiling.

'And I believe you will hear them,' the Elder replied, acknowledging Tegné's bow with a slight nod of his own head.

6

THE SEVENTH INCARNATION

She is spewed from the bellows between
Heaven and Earth
Her shape may change but never her form
A woman
A cat
The Beast is born
Darkness
Evil
On Earth she is born.
(Book of Knowledge, Temple of the
Moon, Lunan Province)

'And when the power of the Seven shall diminish, the Great Snake shall rise in the East, blinded by turmoil and uncertainty. It is then that the state of Earth shall be vulnerable and weak, and it is then that the Cat shall join the Snake, guiding him with eyes of avarice, for she shall be the daughter of the Beast, sent to do his bidding on Earth. And she shall cry out for a pure soul with which to make union.

'The yeons shall number 999 when the Golden Son shall walk forth from the House of God: the Sign of the Moon as his ally. And this Golden Son shall endure the Test of the Heart.'

The Elder closed the ancient book, turned the iron key and locked the thick, wooden binding. He stood up from the small reading bench, lifting the book as he rose. Still deep in thought, he walked to the far corner of the private temple library and climbed the double-runged ladder. Carefully he placed the heavy volume back amongst the other sacred works, then stepped backwards on to the stone floor. Very slowly he raised his open right palm slightly above his bowed head and executed the circular Sign of the Moon.

He felt the rush of spirit as he drew the palm inwards, finally placing the open hand against his robed chest, above his heart. He remained like this, his eyes closed; he could feel Tabata close to him now as he recalled the wide, emotional eyes of the Senşei on the occasion of his single visit to this private library. And on that occasion the Elder had permitted Tabata the treasured privilege of reading the Book of Knowledge; a right rigidly withheld from all but the Patriarch of the Order. However, the Elder had judged this an exceptional time, realizing the Book's prophecy would be fulfilled within his charge of the Brotherhood, and knowing with all certainty that Tabata would play a critical role in the outcome of fate. And Tabata had indeed played his part; he had given his life.

Now the Elder remained motionless, feeling once again at one with Tabata's true, brave spirit.

*

The early summer sun rose just above the large, circular iron disc which was mounted high on the inner courtyard wall. The back-light formed a fine haze, highlighting the golden moon and single silver star which stood out from the black iron.

The Elder looked down from the tiny leaded window, three levels above the courtyard. By the position of the sun behind the Sign of the Moon he judged that the time was nearing the eighth hour. He could hear the echo of bare, hard-soled feet approach from the north gate, and watched Tegné walk on to the smooth stone floor of the large yard, remove the heavy black silk robes of the senior order, fold them carefully, and lay them on the far side of the wall. Now Tegné stood bare-chested, his loose, rough white cotton gi bottoms tied at the waist with a wide black sash, cross-knotted and hanging evenly at each end. Then Tegné began the warming-up exercise.

The Elder noted the spring in the knees as Tegné jumped lightly in place, at first up and down, then shifting from side to side. After a short time he stopped, stretching upwards, forwards and sideways. He rotated his hips, turning, twisting, pushing. The Elder could see the fine latissimus-dorsal development, giving the back a wide V-shape, tapering into the tight, well-defined abdomen. The chest was deep, the major pectoralis muscles full at both top and bottom range, creating a square, jutting appearance to the rib-cage.

A result of the chikaraisha, the Elder surmised, forming a mental picture of the power stones, each weighing eight kilograms and embedded on the end of a foot-long wooden stick. Each chikaraishi was gripped at the end opposite the weight, enabling any number of straight- or bent-arm strength exercises to be performed with the extended chikaraisha. The Elder could see the thick muscles in the forearms as Tegné snapped three relaxed punches into the air. Even from the height of the window the enlarged and calloused first and second knuckles on the punching fist could be distinguished.

Makiwara, the striking board. Punch the surface five hundred times each morning, both hands. One year and your hands will strike like hammers. Yano's words, and Tegné had followed them faithfully. In fact, Tegné felt most comfortable using his hands in combat, for his strength and reach were both extraordinary for a man of slightly less than six feet in height.

He completed the warming-up exercises then brought his feet together, hands to his sides, and bowed towards the eastern sun. Finally, folding his arms across his body, he allowed each fist to fall forwards and to the front, moving his left foot a comfortable shoulder-width from the right and assuming the natural, shizen-tai position. Then Tegné inhaled lightly, half-filling his lower abdomen. Exhaling, he brought his open right and left hands together, the fingernails of the right thumb and index finger gently covering the fingernails of the left. His body relaxed, pushing in slightly at the hips as Tegné brought the joined hands upwards, breathing in as his extended hands framed the morning sun.

The Elder observed the kata with intense interest, for it was through the traditional form that the physical and spiritual development of the practitioner could be judged. He was impressed with the relaxation and rhythm of the lighter circular movements, which contrasted to the sharp, linear attacks and blocks. He noted the controlled breathing and balance as Tegné performed the sixty-five techniques of Kanku-dai, – "looking at the sky". Satisfied, he turned away from the window and walked to the thick, arching door of the private library. He twisted the key and pulled the heavy, creaking door open. Closing the door behind him he listened as the lock turned once, twice, assuring him the double bolt was functioning and the chamber safely sealed.

One more session and the trial is finished. I shall be glad of that, the Elder thought as he moved silently down the twisting, narrow passage and emerged in the warm morning light.

Tegné straightened and bowed to the much-loved and learned Elder, watching the waist-length single braid of silver hair swing gracefully from side to side across the back of the fine turquoise robes. *He must be nearing a hundred yeons, and still his energy is that of a young man,* he marvelled as the Elder walked easily towards him. Tegné smiled, looking into the small, dark, glowing eyes. The Elder returned the smile as he extended his tiny, delicate hands to feel the newly repaired cartilage in Tegné's nose.

'No pain?' the Elder enquired.

'None,' smiled Tegné.

'Looks the same. No difference,' added the Elder, pleased with his manipulation. For barely three weeks ago, during the third phase of the 'Trial of One Hundred', a sharp, upward palm-heel strike had fractured Tegné's nose in three places. The Elder had reset the cartilage while Tegné lay unconscious from the strike. The senior Brother remained concerned for the appearance of the fine, chiselled face, and remembered his momentary distaste for this Trial. Then he recalled the deep-set blue eyes opening, looking up, as Tegné asked, 'How many, Elder? How many?'

'Twelve more and it is finished,' said the Elder, answering the question of three weeks ago. Skilfully, he examined the mild bruising above Tegné's sternum. 'And the knee?' he enquired, remembering the powerful and badly misdirected leg sweep which slammed awkwardly into Tegné's left knee during the last combat.

'The knee is fine, Elder,' replied Tegné, grateful for the other's deep, heartfelt concern as to his well-being. 'Thank you very much,' he added, straightening himself and turning towards the open North Gate.

Both could hear the muffled footsteps of the hundred participants in this test of body and spirit. Each yeon one senior Brother from the Dojo was chosen for the Trial. This honoured Brother would undertake full unarmed combat, excluding death blows, with each of one hundred of his highest-ranked contemporaries. The Trial was halted only when the chosen Brother was injured or unable to continue, then the number of successful, two-minute encounters was tallied and a rest interval granted. At the end of this interval, the Trial was reconvened and continued until the entire hundred Brothers had tested the chosen man.

The Trial of One Hundred had its origins in the ancient Jlon-Ji Temple, and the ritual, strictly adhered to since its inception, was now nearing three hundred yeons old. Yet recently several Brothers on the Council had spoken openly against its continuation, arguing that it was an obsolete and barbaric tradition. The Elder had, in his heart, understood their protests. Yet he realized that for the Brothers whose predilection was the Dojo – the Martial Way of Life – the Trial was invaluable. A test of courage, skill and endurance, it led its participants, both the one and the one hundred, along the path of insight and towards perfection of character.

And if there was ever one who needed strength, it is the one who stands before them now, concluded the Elder, as he watched quietly from the shadows of the courtyard. Tegné stood alone, facing the five lines of Brothers, their faces set firm, revealing no emotion.

In unison, the final twelve stepped forward and bowed to the Elder. Then they straightened, turned full face and bowed to Tegné. Tegné returned the courtesy. Etiquette, in this instance, was paramount.

The Elder walked four paces forward. 'Perfection,' he allowed the word to ring sharp and clear, 'Sincerity. Perseverance. Propriety. Control.' Each word was a lesson in itself.

After a respectful pause the first Brother ran from the line, halting smartly in front of Tegné. Again the bow, followed by the Elder's order to commence.

'Hajime!' The word ricocheted off the far wall ...

*

Rin's right hand shot out, the fingers relaxed, open. Quickly the hand withdrew as he stepped sharply backwards, clenching the large, ripe lemon. He stuffed the fruit securely down the front of his loose trousers; the trousers were tied tightly at the ankle for just this purpose.

That makes three – I'll try for one more, she hasn't even turned her head, he thought, studying the back of the short, mountainously fat village woman as she pulled the heavily laden fruit cart into the Temple's main courtyard. He shuffled close to the side of the cart, head down, his face hidden by the thick, brown cotton hood. He strained his eyes to the right, keeping his head forward.

Bananas, potassium. Yes, potassium for strength, he thought, just as the woman, sensing a presence behind her, turned and looked over her left shoulder. Rin just managed the grab as the cart handle was dropped and the heavy wooden stick careered towards his head.

'Stop, you! Thief, thief! Stop!' the hulk screamed as she pursued Rin through the arch leading to the inner courtyard.

God, she moves fast, thought Rin as, trousers bulging with stolen fruit, he evaded his pursuer by crawling beneath a stone ledge and through the damp, narrow crawl-space which led into the meditation chambers of the Temple. He paused to catch his breath; he heard her above him, the deep, rasping breaths intertwined with unyielding curses. Then, quietly, Rin removed his double-heeled wooden geta and, barefoot, entered the complex of small stone rooms.

Rin was the lowest order of novice, and he knew the penalty should he be discovered in these chambers. For the tiny vaulted cells were rigidly reserved for only a few of the senior Brothers. Still his excitement for the adventure and his curiosity at what, in fact, transpired in these rooms drove him forward.

He crept towards the first occupied cell; he could hear the deep, even breathing coming from the tiny, arched stone doorway. He inched forwards, timing his own footsteps with the rhythmic breaths. Rin was barely a yard from the entrance when the loud, reverberating blast stopped him dead.

No, it couldn't have been . . . He struggled to control his laughter as he dropped silently to his hands and knees. Again the sound, this time thin, loose, trill. *God, it is! A fart!* Rin bit his lower lip hard, holding back the snorts of laughter. *Control, control* . . . he commanded himself as he moved on. *Who can it be? Brother Randu?* The image of the corpulent astrologer flashed through his mind. *No, no, it has to be Minka, Brother Minka. He is forever lecturing on the value of lentils and other fibrous foods in the diet. 'Roughage, Rin, you need more roughage* . . .' Rin visualized Minka's skeletal, sunken-eyed face in front of him.

Varoomp! Another explosive blast cut the air. Now Rin *had* to know. Resolutely, he took hold of the cold, hard doorframe and pulled. Silently he slid the last few inches along the rough stone floor.

Brother Kao stood on his head before Rin. His long, thick, shining black hair was clumped and pressed hard into the small, square tatami mat, and his legs were bent inwards, forming a full lotus. Rin stared in amazement at the completely naked senior Brother. Kao's eyes were tightly closed; the rhythmic breathing and obvious relaxation of the sphincter indicated a deep meditation. Rin viewed the small, hooded penis and long, hanging, inverted scrotum with naive fascination. The sheer privacy of the vision, the act of viewing a senior Brother in such a personal, vulnerable state, held Rin transfixed. Only the flash of deep blue, to the right and slightly behind Kao, distracted his attention. The robe was neatly folded, beautifully clean, and the pristine old silk seemed alive with an inner glow.

Rin could not resist. He held his breath as quietly, stealthily, his small hand crept around the corner of the doorway. Without sound, he lifted Kao's precious robe, pulling it smoothly from the tiny cell. *It is not for me, anyway,* he rationalized as he got to his feet, clutching the heavy robe. He could smell the warm aroma of sandalwood as it wafted gently from the fabric. *He will look like a god in this,* Rin concluded, holding the new treasure close to him as he climbed back up the tight passage and into the light.

Randu backed away from the low, slant-surfaced astrological bench. He felt his heart pound as he stood and overlooked the table-sized chart. Its complex system of meridians and circles stared back at him.

'No, it cannot be,' he muttered to himself, bending to pick up the shining steel astralobe. Then he climbed again into the ridged, straight-backed chair and placed the instrument in position. Again the steel began to grow warm, vibrate, pulling Randu's hand along the smooth, oiled skin. This time he did not resist. He allowed the unseen force to guide him, to form the chart.

Twenty minutes later, Randu sat back in the bench, sweat dripping from his forehead, as he stared at the conjunction of planets before him. 'But the formation receives no major influence from any other house,' he said aloud to himself, 'It just does not make sense. Totally powerful, yet totally receptive without guidance.'

As if in answer, Randu felt his right hand jerk forward, the fingers in spasm, gripping the instrument. *Am I going mad?* he wondered, as the steel began to move towards the oilskin. The second ghost chart actually intersected and added to the original, Urak and Neptinis sat perfectly square to the unguided element of the first chart, the conjunction falling in the ninth house; the house of vision.

She will totally dominate him, take his raw, unpolished energy and direct it, Randu thought, then shuddered at the fact that he had given the second rendering a female personality. *Why? What is happening here? What force is using me?* Again he felt the urge in his fingers, but this time he held back, pushing himself up and turning from the bench; he walked from the room.

The Elder moved quickly to the centre of the circle. He knelt on one knee above the fallen, choking body. With a single, sure movement, he inserted his thumb and middle finger deep into the larynx and gripped the displaced thyroid cartilage.

The same power which extinguishes life is also able to give life. Tabata's words ran in Tegné's mind as he heard the desperate, choking breaths become clear, full, and finally at ease.

Thank God, thought Tegné. Still he retained the rigid sei-za position, his back turned in humiliation, staring at the wall, away from the fallen man. His sharp, spinning knife-hand strike had been an accident, a reaction to the powerful leg sweep which was intended to knock him to the ground. The Brother's ashi-bari had, in fact, succeeded only in sweeping Tegné's body in a counter-clockwise rotation and, as he moved, vulnerable and out of balance, Tegné had instinctively and without control flailed his left arm. The hand, in shuto position, had landed flush on his opponent's throat. Without the Elder's intervention, the knife-hand strike would have been fatal.

'Refrain at all times from impetuous and violent behaviour' – the first rule of the iron-clad Dojo code. To strike without control, to inflict injury with malice, to take life; these were the greatest affronts to the order, and today Tegné may well have walked alone from the Temple gate, forever to wander, a Ronin-monk, a man with no master, no temple. Control was of the essence, and this type of accident was simply not permitted.

'Continue.' The single word jolted Tegné from his thoughts. He stood and turned to see his Temple Brother standing, fully recovered, in front of him. There was no animosity, no blame in the fine grey eyes as the man bowed, turned, and ran back to the line.

Until the accident, Tegné had been fluid and well-centred, his timing sure and precise. He fought, as usual, from a loose, low sochin stance, shifting backwards and forwards, allowing his lead left hand to feint, snapping forward with frequent kizami-zuki. In this way, his right hammer-like gyaku remained relaxed but coiled to counter-punch. Rarely did a Temple fighter catch Tegné with a straight, single technique.

Now the twelfth and final opponent jumped to his feet, running forwards into the circle. He was younger, heavier and taller than Tegné, and he moved easily into the kiba-dachi stance, side-on, bouncing lightly on his toes.

The Elder stepped back and away from the combat. He was strangely nervous as he watched the two fighters close.

Ke-komi ... Tegné read the stance, noting the rear left leg taking most of the body weight, the right foot inching forwards. He anticipated the slide, the lead foot lifting and the foot edge thrusting towards him. He met the technique with a flat double palm-heel block. The augmented palms pushed down, negating the powerful kick, as Tegné maintained his forward momentum, lunging with a straight left punch. The heavier man dropped to the ground as the fist snapped into the air where his jaw had been, leaving Tegné momentarily extended. He had no time to recover as the scissor-grip clasped quick and strong against his shins.

For a split second there was only white light as Tegné's head cracked loudly against the courtyard floor. Sheer instinct forced the roll to his left and freed his legs from the closed grip. Tegné continued the roll, regaining his feet as he avoided the axe kick which was intended to finish him.

Now both men stood, facing each other, preparing for the next exchange. Psychologically, the younger man had the advantage, for Tegné was obviously exhausted, his legs heavy, without spring, and his stance was unsteady as a result of the sharp crack to his head. The two eyed each other, waiting. Then the younger man began his move.

Stop him straight on, Tegné reasoned desperately as he turned his left foot inwards, bringing the right leg up and aiming the heel of the back-thrusting kick towards the hard, flat abdomen. The pivot was too slow. The other man continued confidently forward, smothering the technique and hoisting Tegné off his feet and upwards in a powerful wrestler's grip, Tegné twisted within the strong, suffocating grasp, managing to wrench his arms free. He stared a moment into the cold, determined eyes, feeling his body crushed as it was heaved upwards. He could already imagine the hard throw to the stone floor, then the deadening impact of the final stamping kick or downward thrust.

Timing . . . . timing . . . Now! Tegné grabbed the sweating clump of coarse brown hair, gripped firmly with his left hand and pulled the head sharply back. The movement was just enough to break the balance of his opponent. He felt the large, struggling body buckle as he maintained the pull, using the hair to guide the heavy body to the ground. As they hit, Tegné remained on top, and before his opponent could twist or roll he applied the tiger-mouth hand. His fingers dug into his opponent's throat at each side of the windpipe. He did not apply pressure.

'Yame! Yame!' the Elder's voice rang out, halting the flow of adrenaline, putting a cold stop to the action.

Tegné maintained zanshin as he disentangled himself from the beaten man. He rose up, backing away, never once breaking eye contact. The twelfth Brother stood up slowly; he and Tegné faced each other and bowed, finally turning and bowing low to the Elder. Tegné could see the warm satisfaction in the Elder's eyes.

The Trial was over, and he began to feel the shared flush of love and gratitude rise within him. Close to tears, he straightened from the final bow and met the eyes of his Brothers. They stood quietly before him. A state of peace pervaded the courtyard, simple and empty. *Through the art of the warrior, Heaven and Earth become one.*

The sharp, rapid clapping of small hands shattered the moment. Tegné saw the Elder's brow furrow and his eyes become hawk-like. The long silver braid swung to the side as he spun towards the north gate, keen to spot the perpetrator of this breach of etiquette.

Rin stood, his eyes fixed on Tegné, clutching Kao's robe close to his body, under his arm, the baggy trousers swollen grotesquely with the stolen fruit. Every eye in the courtyard focused on the child, every ear awaited the Elder's furious tirade.

Randu's sudden, unexpected appearance averted the inevitable. His plump, corseted body, its moonlike head perched on the shoulders with no apparent neck, waddled past the panic-stricken imp. With irksome authority, and a look of sheer desperation, he bowed and walked straight towards the Elder. Rin seized the moment; he ran to Tegné, his small, shuffling steps made awkward by the stuffed trousers.

Tegné allowed the child to approach, waiting until he was close, then stopped him in mid-step with a stern, unforgiving glare.

'Tegné . . .' The thin, high voice trailed off in the face of the glare.

Tegné's voice was harsh, unrelenting. 'What are you doing here? You know this is not an open session. You know that no one applauds after a Trial . . .'

In answer, Rin dug frantically into his trousers, his hand running down inside the leg and rummaging around near the ankle.

'I thought you would be thirsty,' he sputtered, extending a shining yellow lemon in his small, grubby hand.

Tegné suppressed a smile. *Why am I always so close to forgiving this child?* he wondered. Then his eyes focused on the blue robe. 'Rin?' he began.

The child anticipated the question. 'Isn't it beautiful?' he said, pushing the robe towards Tegné. 'For you. It was made for you.' The long, ebony lashes enhanced the sparkle as Rin's huge eyes stared out from beneath the hood of his robe. The eyes pleaded.

Tegné did not touch the extended robe. He was, for the moment, at a loss for words. *Five yeons I have known this child, taught him, disciplined him. Five yeons and he is still a thief,* he thought, feeling suddenly angry, frustrated by his own apparent shortcomings. Finally he knelt down, so as to be face to face with the boy. He looked deep into Rin's eyes, seeing the unashamed cry for love and acceptance, and placed his hands on the frail shoulders.

'You have not done anything like this for a long time. Why now?' he asked, trying to remember himself at twelve yeons.

'Because it is a special day. The last day of your Trial,' Rin answered, still holding the robe forward. 'I had to bring you a gift,' he added.

Tegné nodded slowly, acknowledging the sincerity of the child's gesture. 'Well, I appreciate your thought. I am thirsty, and the robe is very fine,' he said softly, watching as the hope rekindled in the young eyes. 'But ... I cannot accept them.' Tegné's tone grew marginally less reassuring.

'Why?' said Rin, knowing the answer.

'Why?' Tegné repeated the question.

'Because they are not mine to give you,' Rin said, at last admitting his defeat.

Tegné waited a long moment. 'Now I want you to return the fruit ...' Rin's face rose up in horror, '... and go to Brother Kao. That is his robe, is it not?' Tegné continued.

'But ...' Rin began.

'Do it before you enter the Dojo again. You cannot live as a thief and a liar and expect to learn the true spirit of Empty Hand,' Tegné said sharply, allowing the first tones of anger to enter his voice.

Rin knew there was no reprieve. 'Oss, Sensei,' he said, then bowed before he turned to leave. Tegné caught him by the shoulder, holding him firm, as he bent close to the top of the small, covered head.

'One more thing – what is that smell? It is coming from beneath your hood,' Tegné enquired.

A faint smile began to transform the elfin face as Tegné lifted the heavy, drab cotton garment, pushing it back to reveal the dry, yellowed, bleached patch of hair above the child's forehead. Tegné stared in amazement.

'Cow's urine, Sensei. Two more days and my hair will be the same colour as yours,' Rin stated with renewed pride.

'No. No, you cannot do that,' Tegné managed, caught off-guard, backing away from the rising fumes. Rin looked mortally wounded. Tegné continued, 'God has given you fine black hair, you must not interfere with it.' Rin stood before him on the verge of tears.

'Now go,' Tegné added, regaining his command, 'Return what you have taken.'

The child sniffled, then began his shuffling journey towards the north gate.

'And no more cow's urine!' Tegné called after him, the words raining like missiles on Rin's downcast head. Tegné remained still, watching as the child disappeared through the high arched gate. Only then, as he turned to retrieve his own robes, did Tegné allow himself to laugh at the absurd comedy of Rin's performance. And only then, as he walked from the nearly deserted courtyard, did he notice the Elder and Randu, still deep in conversation.

YEON 999
WALLED CITY OF ZENDOW
VOKANE PROVINCE

Sixteen Celebres had come and gone. Zato was twenty-eight yeons, and this was the fifth time he had led the Procession. Renagi watched from the ramparts as the group of twelve galloped up the east road towards Zendow. He could hear the great iron-linked chains unwinding, their gigantic cranks being pulled round to lower the massive steel-reinforced gate. He moved resolutely down the steep, winding steps, timing his action to coincide with the Warmen's entrance.

The horses moved past him at a walk as each man raised his clenched right fist, the thin, black leather gloves punching straight up in unison; a salute to their Warlord. He watched from the mid-level sentry post which elevated him just above the heads of the mounted Warmen. He felt the surge of power as the Procession passed, yet the power was somehow distant, no longer his own. He studied Zato, the agile muscularity evident in his son's posture, his attitude, the tension of his thighs as he pressed them inwards, controlling the stallion. Renagi saw the thick, jet-black plaited hair which fell nearly to the top of Zato's high, brass-studded riding belt.

Did I once look that way? So strong, so proud? Renagi wondered as his gaze followed the Warmen until they turned from the main courtyard and proceeded in a single file towards the stables. The Warlord stood, looking after them, locked in thought. The matter of the Ashkelite had become his obsession, deep and private. He recalled Maliseet, her strange dreaming eyes, her silken white hair and seemingly poreless, pure skin. Many times during the last months he had awakened in the dead of night, to lie alone, trying to conjure the boy's face. Boy? No longer a boy, he would be a man now, two yeons older than Zato. But the face . . . he could not imagine the face.

During these sleepless spells he would grow furious with himself, his weakness of mind, his inability to control this grim fascination. Often he had risen from his bed and, in the single beam of moonlight from the small arched window, he would perform the most basic movements of the Morning Form. These simple, external exercises had the effect of solidifying his spirit, holding the demons at bay and winning him three or four hours' sleep before the rising sun. Then, when he awoke, he would brace himself against the day, assuming what had become the façade of Warlord.

He feared the rumours amongst his men, ever since the return of that first war party, sixteen yeons past. Rumours of the Ashkelite's escape and mysterious disappearance coupled with the unexaggerated descriptions of the slaughter of his own Warmen had proved a solid base for all forms of conjecture. Renagi did not hear Zato walk up behind him.

'They are waiting for you. The kumite is set to begin.' His son's voice was deep and rich with the promise of a prime soon to come.

Renagi turned, trying to conceal that he had, again, been far away. He placed his hand on Zato's wide, straight shoulders. 'Did you go through Asha-1?' he asked.

The same question, always the same question, Zato thought as he controlled his urge to be abrupt with his father, to cut him off, to tell him pointedly to drop this obsession, to let the past go. Instead, he looked at the bearded face, the distinct silver-streaked hair, and into the strained, questioning eyes.

'Yes, father. We went through Asha-1. Their production has been high since the Solstice, so there was no need to threaten them,' he answered, knowing that his father would not let the matter rest.

'Slaves! Filth!' Renagi blurted, 'My skin crawls at the thought of them. Do they still speak of him? Their saviour? The impostor!'

Zato stepped back as if the force of the words had pushed physically against him. He answered Renagi with a look of compassion, but there was impatience within the look. Renagi's eyes grew darker.

'Do they?' The Warlord's voice was rasping, harsh.

'I don't know!' Zato snapped, an edge of finality in his tone.

Desperately, Renagi's hand shot out, the open thumb and first finger wrapping round Zato's windpipe. The Warlord tightened his grip, momentarily raging, out of control. Then, suddenly aware of the twisted futility of his action, he let the fingers go limp. Zato stepped back and the hand fell away from his throat. Renagi looked suddenly pale, deflated.

'Shall we go to the Great Hall, father?' Zato's tone was flat, condescending.

Zendow had seen an influx of northern village fighters for the past three months. The young men had come purposely to enter this competition. Their chance to become Warmen far exceeded any opportunity they would find in their tiny, parochial villages. Zendai was, of course, a condition of birth, but the title of Warman could be won in combat. Although the northern style of rough grappling lacked the finesse of the fighting practised in the southern region, the big, strong northerners compensated for their naive skills with a level of courage and ferocity second to none.

Zato studied Renagi's face as the Warlord sat in the Velchar, overlooking the combat. He watched his father jerk forward, his eyes alight as the huge grappler in the centre square smothered a tentatively thrown back kick, and hoisted his opponent in both arms. Savagely, the stout, northern fighter head-butted the taller, slimmer man. Once, twice he butted him, all the while holding the now-unconscious man in his bear-like grip. Then, in a final and unnecessary move, the northern man bit deep into his opponent's throat. Even the hardened, more ardent spectators of the event murmured in protest, wincing at the accompanying sounds as the northerner held fast, wrenching his head fom side to side, effectively tearing out the other's jugular. The dying man hung limp in the bulging, veined arms, shuddering in the final spasms of death.

Zato was sickened, and he turned his head away from the bloodletting only to glimpse his father nodding with vigorous approval.

Finally, they had come to the last combat, and through his pure savagery the northerner had earned his chance to fight for the title of Warman. All eyes turned to his opponent; a tall, lanky, southern fighter. The southerner stood motionless on the outside of the square, his face staring down in horror at the last mutilated body as it was dragged unceremoniously in front of him and out through the main door of the Great Hall. The neck of the corpse was a raw, gaping hole. For a long, unsettled moment the southerner seemed lost, unaware of where he was, what he was expected to do. Then slowly he raised his eyes.

The northerner stood waiting; his only movement was the heaving of his enormous chest. Thick, semi-congealed blood smeared his muscular jowls, Then there began a slight twitching in his hands, just a flicker of the fingers, a faint taunt which seemed to beckon his opponent. The taller, less aggressive man remained frozen, trapped in time, all eyes upon him.

The sound of water broke the stillness, a thin stream hitting the stone floor. Zato looked closely; he could see the yellow stain begin to discolour the front of the white cotton fighting costume as the urine dripped from the southerner's calf-length trousers on to the floor. Then the voices began.

'FIGHT! FIGHT!' followed by the unified stomping of cleated heels against the stone. 'FIGHT . . . FIGHT!'

Still the southerner did not move. Renagi seemed twenty yeons younger as he rose from the Velchar, pointing to the guards on the outer perimeter of the combat zone. On his command, they approached from behind the stricken man, each gripping him under one arm, lifting him and bodily carrying him into the square. It was only in the last few yards that the southerner came to life, squirming, kicking, screaming. But the guards held firm and the chant of 'FIGHT!' was now a thunderous roar within the Great Hall. Closer, closer, until he was within an arm's reach of his opponent . . . then the guards dropped him to his feet.

'Fight! Fight!' the northerner joined in the staccato chorus, sneering at the southerner. But the man was beyond renewal, his energy dissipated, his courage lost forever. Futilely, he began a slow, wide, hooking punch. In sheer contempt, the northerner allowed the fist to land, grazing against his shoulder. Then he stepped forwards and, as he did so, he disdainfully shoved his opponent back, watching as the terrified man stumbled before falling to the floor. The southerner refused to rise.

Renagi sprang from the Velchar, both arms raised above his head in a signal for silence. Abruptly, the chant ceased and the hall fell deathly quiet.

'Mark him a coward,' the Warlord boomed, then remained standing, ensuring that his orders were carried out.

The two guards ran back into the square; they lifted the quivering man to his feet and held him firm. A third guard rushed from the far corner of the room. Drawing his katana as he moved, he brought the shining blade down, slicing the skin of the southerner's chest as the razor edge cut through the drawstring of the stained cotton trousers. Naked, the southerner stood before the jeers of the crowd. Then the guards forced him to bend forward, exposing his muscular, finely haired buttocks. The two men held him in this position while the third guard, his katana still unsheathed, turned to the northerner and urged him to take the sword.

The northerner hesitated, looking up towards Renagi. The Warlord nodded 'yes', and the northerner gripped the katana, raising it high above his right shoulder. He swung the blade awkwardly in a horizontal strike across the bare buttocks. It was the strike of a man totally untrained in the art of the sword. The gash was deep and uneven, and the blade embedded in the thick muscle of the buttock.

Now the southerner began to scream, to plead, as the blade was pulled free, hoisted up and swung again. The two wounds criss-crossed deep into the hips, severing the hamstrings and tendons. Finally, the guards released their victim and the southerner collapsed, sprawling, on to the floor.

'Get out of my sight,' Renagi growled, his voice low but easily filling the space between the Velchar and the fallen man. Slowly, the southerner pulled himself up into a seated position. He could rise no further without the use of his legs – and he would never use his legs again. Agonizingly, he bent forward, extending his trunk as he braced himself with his hands against the floor and began to pull himself towards the door.

Zato studied his father's face. An expression of strange, cathartic contentment washed over it as the Warlord watched the shamed man crawl from the Great Hall and into the night.

The Feast of Celebre was a loud, raucous affair. It was as though everyone, from Zendai to Warman, sought release from the horrific, undiluted images of the recent combat.

Renagi remained on a strange, edged high. He drank heavily, and often his rasping laughter could be heard above the general din of the revellers. Towards the end of the evening and the last of the traditional toasts, Renagi was vehement that the entire table should be quiet as Gazan, the newest Warman, stood to deliver his pledge of allegiance.

The resulting speech was fumbling and nearly inarticulate; the only memorable quality being the northerner's overwhelming conviction of his newly acquired self-importance. Still, Renagi led a hesitant and somewhat embarrassed table into a forced response of cheers and clapping that managed to grow, at the Warlord's urging, until the long, heavy dining table virtually shook beneath the pounding fists.

Zato looked on in continued amazement at his father's behaviour. He was at once repelled and fascinated. Finally, hours later, when the men had begun their traditional trek to the Willow World, departing in twos and threes, Renagi had wrapped a heavy arm around his son.

'Wang's. Madame Wang's ...' the Warlord slurred. Zato turned to meet the reddening, bloodshot gaze. 'Yes, tonight,' Renagi continued, turning Zato towards the door.

Thirty minutes later, Zato was supporting the Warlord's lumbering, drunken body as father and son staggered down the dark, unpaved streets and into the old part of the city, en route to the Royal brothel.

There had been little rain in Vokane during the last month, and the dry dust from the gravel and dirt streets clung to the polish of Zato's high black boots. Renagi's weight was beginning to bear uncomfortably against his shoulder, and Zato cursed himself for not summoning the Warlord's carriage for this unexpected journey. It was with great relief that he recognized the long, torchlit string of adjoining, single-storey dwellings which formed the front section of the Willow World.

Zato saw the freshly plastered white face of the brothel and noted that, aside from the plaster, little had changed since he had first seen it on the eve of his thirteenth birthday. These were the 'Rites of Manhood', Renagi had assured him on that summer evening nearly sixteen yeons ago. Since then, Zato had been an infrequent visitor to this rather pretentious building with its gold-framed, curtained windows and enormous polished mahogany double-arched doors, all of which seemed grossly out of context with the dirt streets and surrounding shop fronts.

Zato could just detect the dark eyes through the observation lens as he halted in front of the closed doors. The thin, wide double lens protruded from the wood at the base of the shining brass plate which bore the words, 'Madame Wang' inscribed in bold capitals. In fact, it was Wang who was viewing them through the lens, and it was Wang who opened the doors.

For all her sixty yeons, the Madame had changed little over the time Zato had known her. And he could see the warm glow of excitement in her face as she focused fully on her Royal patrons. Zato released his grip on Renagi and watched as the Warlord straightened, somehow composing himself in the outspill of light from the doorway. Wang beamed, throwing her arms up in appreciation for her guests.

Everything about the house mother seemed oversized and round. Her face was huge, flat, the large, yellowish, slanted eyes further enhanced by the surgical incisions made invisibly at the corner of each lid, permitting the eyes to open completely, thereby increasing their size. The luxuriously long black lashes beat a steady rhythm up and down as she used them to punctuate her frivolous patter. Her nose was wide and squashed, as if it had been constructed minus the septum and was merely a thick, pinkish flap of skin in the centre of the round face. Wang's mouth was narrow but full-lipped, the pouting quality augmented by the heavy red paint which extended above and below the lips in the shape of half-moons. Her jaw-line was non-existent, and several layers of chin pouched downwards, meeting the top of her chest, the effect being to obscure any indication of a neck. The mask-like visage was surrounded by thick, dyed, curling black hair, cascading down and encircling the fifteen-stone body. The hair stopped abruptly above the gargantuan hips.

Her arse always seems to have a life of its own, observed Zato, noting the rippling flesh bouncing in opposing directions beneath the synthetic jewels on her skirt as Wang turned to fill an empty goblet. He watched as she emptied the thick ruby port from the decanter, then spun back towards her more favoured guests. And as she turned, her billowing breasts followed her body movement, yet remained one beat behind, so as to make them appear somehow detached from the rest of her torso. It was true that Wang's bosom was legendary, and although it had been fifteen or twenty yeons since any Warman or Zendai had admitted to lying with her, tales were rife as to her ability to use these enormous, pink-fleshed mounds in the performance of startling sexual feats. Often, it was rumoured, she would take her partner to the heavenly plane with their use and manipulation alone, never needing to make any other form of contact.

Zato noted the oversized green, star-shaped gemstone mounted prominently above the fantastic cleavage. He knew that the stone, like everything else in the brothel, including the port and the crystal-like decanter in which it was contained, was a replica. Wang kept her original hoard of treasure locked safely in the stone vaults beneath the Willow World.

Zato could not help but admire the spirit and fortitude that had enabled Wang to control this group of drunken men and often temperamental young women over these many yeons. And now he watched as the fat, short-toed, sandalled feet moved towards him.

'I have something for you. I have kept them apart from the others, waiting. I knew you would visit me again.' Wang's tone was always conspiratorial, hushed. 'They are very special,' she added, then looked from Zato to Renagi. The Warlord's drooping eyelids parted slightly. 'Twins, virgins from the north. Former temple dancers.' Still not getting the desired response, Wang continued, 'They have both taken the vows of chastity. This will be a first . . .' Her tone remained hushed, but none the less managed to brim with anticipation.

Zato nodded, believing his father wanted this entertainment. He helped Renagi as they followed Wang beneath the ornate, pillared arches and along the corridor, through the reinforced door and into the steam which blew, heavy and warm, from the bath-chambers.

Wang moved quickly ahead of them, surprisingly nimble, as she turned to offer them clean, deep blue cotton towels and two matching plush robes. She motioned towards the small changing rooms, where the Royal guests were encouraged to shed their clothing in preparation for the soothing mineral baths.

Renagi seemed to sober instantly as he settled, naked, into the steaming pool. The baths were, in fact, a natural phenomenon, the waters rising of their own accord from the mineral-rich underground springs beneath the bath-chamber. Each bathing pool was cut square into the stone floor and was large enough to accommodate six persons. The frothing water swirled around them, entering through the large, phallic, black onyx spout and emptying through the iron-grilled drain at the far corner of the pool.

Wang had been careful to provide the Warlord and his son with the largest, most secluded bath, and now she allowed her guests time to relax as she held the two giggling sisters at bay, preparing for their entrance.

'Stop it! Immediately!' Wang's voice was modulated so as not to disturb the two men. Instantly, the sisters ceased their chatter and stood still as Wang gave them a final inspection. *They are so alike, they could be twins, it is possible,* she concluded as she opened the first girl's kimono, inhaling the delicate orange-scented oil which caused the firm, round, bronzed breasts to shine slightly in the torchlight. Wang could recall acquiring these two; she had paid a three-kon premium above the standard five for each of them. She realized then that the two, working as a team, could earn her a small fortune. They were indeed virgins, for in the six months that Wang had owned them she had permitted the sisters to be hired only for arousal and oral sex. She had preserved their tender hymens for a special occasion; an occasion such as this.

The Warlord will reward me handsomely, thought Wang as she parted the second girl's kimono and lightly, with her feather, touched the long brown nipple. The response was excellent; the nipple stood erect, a full fingertip in width and at least three-quarters of an inch in length. *I do think these provincial girls are more responsive . . . it must be the cross-breeding, produces a stronger stock,* mused Wang as she stroked the second nipple and considered having the girl visit her own chamber later in the evening. As a final gesture, Wang ordered each sister to part her legs. Then Wang employed her own hand to rub the full, black pubic hair upwards. The result was to give the pubis a high, wide crown, rising to just below the navel. Then, fully aroused herself, Wang closed the kimonos, inhaled a commanding breath and led the girls into the bathing chamber.

Zato saw at once that the two long-legged young women were not twins. He knew that Wang was actually incapable of speaking the truth, regardless of the circumstances. *Probably from thirty yeons of peddling re-stitched virgins,* he decided, as his eyes caught on the slightly taller of the two girls. Something in her attitude, the almost challenging manner of her walk, interested him.

Wang, her hindquarters doing their usual jellied dance, halted five steps from the pool. With a dramatic lift of both hands, she signalled for the 'twins' to halt behind her. There was silence, a dramatic gesture intended to build excitement, to allow the prospective clients to view the skilfully presented merchandise.

In this instance it was effective. Zato felt the first pulse of awareness thud through his member. The girl of his choice knew that she had inflamed him, and now she allowed her kimono to part slightly, revealing a hint of the large, jet-black patch of hair and a partial view of the soft, inside curve of her breasts. The other girl appeared less sure of herself, more demure; she kept her kimono closed and her eyes down, staring shyly at the floor.

'Would you like them to bathe you?' Wang asked, absolutely certain that the silence had done its work.

Zato was now gazing straight at the taller girl, his organ hard as iron. She was meeting his gaze and encouraging him with her eyes. He looked at Renagi, hoping his father did not desire the same girl, for, if he did, Zato would be obliged to give way to his father's wishes.

'I do not want a woman.' Renagi's words were deep, clear, and without any hint of inebriation.

'If these do not please you, I have more. Perhaps these are too coarse, common?' Wang said, suddenly sneering at the girls, ready to whip them, to drive them from the room if their presence offended the Warlord. 'I have many more for you to take as you choose,' she added, making sure Renagi was aware of her determination to satisfy him.

'I want no women. None,' Renagi's voice rose, becoming sharper, threatening.

'As you wish,' Wang said submissively, barely above a whisper.

'Hold on,' Zato stopped her as she prepared to take her offerings from the room. 'That one, I would like that one ...' he said, pointing to the embarrassed, taller girl, '... if my father does not object.'

Wang looked quickly at Renagi. 'If my son wishes a woman, I have no objection,' the Warlord said, his words slow and cold.

Zato held out his hand and Wang extended the blue robe as he rose from the steam. Wrapping the robe around himself, Zato stepped from the pool. 'Will you excuse me, father?' he said.

'Yes, of course. I would actually prefer to be alone.' Renagi's voice was tight, edgy.

'I will not be long,' Zato said, observing the sudden lack of expression in Renagi's face. *As if one moment he is charged with fire, the next drained of all life,* he observed, hesitating, suddenly concerned for his father's condition.

'Go! Leave me!' Renagi insisted, his voice taut as wire.

Zato stood for a moment, then finally turned, took hold of the tall girl's arm and led her from the room. Wang and the unwanted 'twin' followed.

Renagi closed the door to the chamber, locking it from the inside, and sat alone, quietly, in the hot bath. Steam rose from the water, filling the room, making it impossible for him to see more than a few feet in any direction. He was glad to be alone, and finally ready to confront the demons which stalked and tormented him.

I have been no more than a hollow shell, a frightened man, a beaten man. A man unworthy to be called Warlord ... His insight was scathing, but at last he would no longer turn away. *If what I feel is my own death, stalking, ready to leap, to take me, then I am ready.* Renagi breathed in, took the heavy, salt steam into his nostrils, and, breathing out, surrendered to the waters and to the strong, foreboding presence which surrounded him. His mind rolled back the yeons and again he stood outside the gates of Zendow, looking down into the blue eyes of his Ashkelite son, his first-born. It was at that instant the curse had begun. For he knew that this child was more than a breach of the sacred laws, more than a damning transgression, more than a dark secret to be swept away and forgotten. He felt it even as he took the girl named Maliseet, even as he released his seed within her. And now he grew frightened that his lust had been merely a superficial device of destiny, and the creation itself, the child, had been the true purpose of his act. *Fear? A Zendai, a Warlord, bowing in the face of fear?* He could not, he would not.

He was still deep in thought when he felt the soft, smooth hand against his inner thigh; he bristled, straightening his back, looking down through the steam into the water. Was it a reflection, a mirage? She seemed to be part of the water, a transparent form rising from the shallow depths of the pool, caressing him and, against his will, arousing him.

How did she get in? I heard nothing, saw nothing ... His mind raced as she broke the surface, smiling, reaching out with fine, long, graceful arms. The slender, delicately boned fingers extended towards him. Her eyes were like no eyes he had ever known; green, the colour of emerald, the iris not round but a thin diagonal which appeared to glow with a shimmering violet light. They were not the eyes of a woman. Renagi's rational mind searched for the meaning of this hallucination, for surely what he saw was not mortal. Then he heard the low, sensual purr as the full, soft lips pressed against his chest, the warm, rough tongue licking his nipples, lapping upwards as the arms entwined around his body, the fingers sending shivers through him as they kneaded the muscles in his shoulders and neck. He brought his own arms and hands upwards, fondling the full breasts which waited, warm and velvet-smooth from the wetness of the bath.

Every nerve, every part of him was alive, burning, screaming with the desire to be touched, caressed. He felt the tingling begin where her fingertips pressed gently behind his neck, sending a fine, needle-like current down the length of his spine, building, building into a bolt of lightning as it shot up through his shaft and hovered on the brink of explosion. His body jolted as the first uncontrollable pleasure of orgasm began ... It was then that she released him, allowing his intensity to subside while her knowing fingers maintained just enough contact to hold him within her spell.

'Master, may I guide you to my chamber?' The low, throaty voice was an extension of the purr, exquisitely female, completely submissive.

Renagi studied her from behind as she stood, walking the three wide, flat steps up and out of the pool. Her hair was a lustrous blanket, falling down her back, across her hips and stopping just above the slender, sure ankles and small, faultless feet. In response to his unspoken wishes she stood still, reached her right hand upwards and gripped the thick black hair, pulling it from the left side of her long neck and draped it to the front of her, permitting the Warlord to view the rear of her naked body.

Renagi inhaled with pleasure as his gaze fell upon the long, perfect legs, the calves gently rounded, tapering into the small, graceful knees, then blossoming again as the finely proportioned thighs rushed upwards to the hard, round hips. A hint of silken hair showed between the slightly spread thighs as she turned towards him, and Renagi felt the sheer strength which her body exuded. She moved closer to the pool, and in the small movement there was a visible sinew beneath her copper skin. Renagi sat, captivated, as she beckoned him. Her round breasts with their dark aureolas jutted out from each side of the bunched hair which ran down the front of her body, between her long legs, and concealed the core of her power.

Renagi rose from the steaming water. He was fully erect and her warm gaze upon his manhood drew him forward. He wanted to take her, to enter her there, on the steps of the bath, but she moved back and away from him. She controlled him with her eyes, yet he was unaware of her command. Instead he felt the promise, the wetness of her youth, the vitality which he had lost long ago and somewhere forgotten.

She turned, picked up the towelling bathrobe, walked towards him and draped it round his shoulders, guiding him to the heavy door which was still closed and bolted from the inside. Renagi slid the bolt and pulled the door open.

Madame Wang coughed loudly, waving her hands to disperse the steam as it rolled from the room and gathered before her wide, startled eyes. Zato stood beside her, equally astonished at the sight before him.

'I don't know how she got in, master! I swear I had nothing to do with it!' babbled Wang in a desperate apology. Then, before Renagi could speak, Wang moved closer, staring at the girl. 'Master, she is not even one of my women! I swear, I swear!'

'We were worried, father. It has been nearly four hours,' Zato said, cutting her off. Zato was controlled, calm, less concerned than Wang as to the origins of the strange young woman. Renagi did not answer. Instead he reached out and wrapped his right, robed arm around her naked shoulders, pulling her close to his body. Then, together, they walked past Zato and Wang towards the pleasure chamber.

Wang flew after him. 'Yes, now I remember! She is new. I found her just yesterday in anticipation of your visit,' she lied, trying to capitalize on the unexpected event. The Warlord's answer was to close the carved wooden door squarely in Wang's face.

*

VALLEY OF DEATH
LUNAN PROVINCE

The Elder had departed from the Temple gates at sunrise of the morning following Randu's disclosure. He had done his best to quiet and comfort the confused Temple astrologer, assuring the distraught man that the charts were not proof of possession but were, instead, a transmission from benevolent forces, a warning of impending events. Randu had pressed him for more explanation, but the aged Elder replied firmly and honestly that he was certain of nothing more. And now the Elder sought the answers that only one place could provide.

A journey of seven days on a single burro, no food and only

the pure mountain water to cleanse his physical body. Seven days and seven nights in which his resting moments were spent in deep meditation, in preparation.

And finally, on the morning of the last day, he could see the majestic twin mountain peaks in front of him, looming on the horizon like two gigantic breasts rising from the bosom of the Earth. The Seat of Power lay on the flat plain in the centre of these two peaks. It was a perfect, natural granite formation which was as old as the planet itself. A place known only to those who had experienced the height of spiritual evolution, revealed through the vision of the heart.

It was sunset when the Elder tethered his burro to the strong sapling at the base of the rock-face which formed the western side of these sacred mountains. Already he could feel the ancient energy stir within him. He began to chant the 'aoum' as he walked towards what appeared to be a sheer wall of rock less than fifty paces away. The setting sun behind him cast jagged shadows against the uneven mass of stone, and it was into one of these shadows that the Elder walked.

Only at sunset is the opening visible, he noted as he squeezed his body tight against the wall, turning in a counter-clockwise direction so that he actually faced away from the mountain, then turned again, clockwise. Now he stood at the base of a clearly delineated footpath which led up to the summit. The Elder inhaled a deep breath, filling his lungs with the chilled air which funnelled down along the path. Then he took the first in the series of nine hundred and ninety-nine steps which led to the Seat of Power. Up he walked, into the twilight.

By nightfall he had travelled three-quarters of the way to his destination. He stopped and rested, continuing his chant, building energy. He started again before dawn and, shortly after sunrise, the Elder had completed the journey.

The huge golden sun awaited him, sitting dead centre between the soaring mountain peaks. The cloudless sky was a glorious blue and the fresh, clean air brought the faint fragrance of wild hyacinth. The Elder experienced a weightless clarity as the divine energy began to fill him, making him ready for the impending communication.

He removed his geta and placed them aside before brushing

the dust from his robes. Then he turned and bowed reverently towards the crystalline, cylindrically shaped rock formation which rose three feet from the flat stone base. He walked forward and settled his hips slowly into the inwardly curved surface of the Seat of Power.

He felt the gradual interlock between his own swirling energy and the stable, deep-rooted vibration of the ancient stone. Physical life temporarily ceased as the stone drew him into tune with the ageless vibration of the mother planet. His body became a hollow vessel of flesh and bone, his heart suspended in time as his soul was propelled upward, departing the physical shell through the crown of his head, passing quietly through the fourth level of vibration, entering the fifth, then passing up through the sixth plane, outwards and beyond.

The Elder's soul hovered a moment above the external subtle vibrations of the planet, still drawn by a slight magnetic attraction. Then it flew free, up towards the Light . . .

It was there, within the supreme radiance, that the Protectors awaited him. It was there that their astral souls merged with his own and basked for an endless moment in the mother warmth. Then they began their slow spiral down, down through the single point in space which provided the opening for their life energy to come into the material world. The contact was complete.

The Elder opened his Earth eyes. The Seven formed a half-diamond, facing him, their brilliant auras swirling, encompassing the Seat of Power and bathing the Elder in their warm, green and golden light. The Elder directed his thoughts towards the central figure. The fine, vibrating beams extended outwards as the Father Protector received them, allowed them to penetrate him and establish the communication.

I have heeded your warning . . . is it true? Is she now amongst us, on the Earth plane? the Elder questioned.

Father's reply was a solemn nod in the affirmative.

And she is, at this moment, with the Great Warlord? The Elder kept the flow of his initial contact, now confirming his own interpretation of the astrological events.

Yes. The seventh incarnation has taken place. The prophecy will be fulfilled. Now the Cat plays with the Snake, teases him, tempts him, but soon she will command him. Father's thoughts were crystal clear, the communication penetrating, imprinting the Elder's mind-source.

Then it is time? The Elder echoed a sense of reluctance from deep within his Earth nature. Father detected the attachment and concentrated his mind, shattering the Elder's thin shell of possession and restoring the state of emptiness.

Have you trained him, prepared him? The question was quick, to the point.

We have, Father, we have, the Elder confirmed, once again in perfect tune with his host.

And you did not violate our trust? Father's aura vibrated less brilliantly as the six held close to him, their energies fuelling the last moments of their contact.

He knows nothing of his origins, the Elder responded.

Good. Then you will know what to do when his moment comes . . . Now, we shall make ready for him. Father was growing faint, the brilliant colours now a dim flicker as the strain of function on this physical plane taxed the resources of the Seven.

Renagi lay stretched on the canopied bed. The early morning sun was just beginning to send its warm beams through the small, star-shaped openings in the vaulted ceiling. The Warlord was at peace, his body sated and his mind relaxed.

She knelt above him and massaged his tired shoulders. Then she bent closer and playfully, gently, licked the small, oval wound on the side of his neck where she had bitten him during the peak of their love-making. As her warm, rough tongue made contact with his skin, Renagi closed his heavy lidded eyes and allowed the memory of her purring whispers to wash over him, rekindling his desire. Never had he known such passion, such strength and such fury as she had coaxed, urged and finally torn the seed from his loins. Three times she had taken him to the place of Supreme Bliss and now he lay beside her . . . *Reborn, yes, I am reborn . . .* he thought as his lips parted, awaiting the stem of the pipe, its sweet elixir burning in the dark, carved bowl, the tiny red coals sending the pure smoke spiralling like silver ribbons into the air.

'Deeply, draw deeply,' she whispered as the Warlord drew the smoke into his lungs. His eyes remained closed as he drifted, watching the brilliant colours swirl round and round inside his mind. Now the colours began to form, shaping, creating a bright, moving picture . . . He was there, close, absorbed, watching as the blue-white water bubbled and splashed before him. He could see the bundle, carried by the water, rushing towards the cascading fall. It travelled easily, buoyantly, on top of the surface, bouncing happily up and down as, unrestrained, it moved with the current.

Renagi inhaled a full, deep, new breath, intensifying the effect of the elixir as he smiled at the sheer joy of his dream. For although he did not know exactly what he saw, or its meaning, there was an innocence, a wonderfully naive quality to the vision.

Renagi exhaled as the bundle turned over, rolling gracefully, and he began to see more clearly. It was a child, a baby. The skin was pale against the blue of the water. Renagi wanted to touch the infant, to lift it. He raised his arms, and as he did so, the full face flashed before his eyes. But it was not the face of the infant; it was the face of a man. The face he had tried to imagine, the face which had eluded him. Deep, intense blue eyes, wide, full lips, a hard, angular jaw and long golden hair. The eyes seemed to focus, to lock on to Renagi.

'No!' the Warlord screamed, punching wildly at the vision.

Quickly, quietly, her warm hands gripped his shoulders, immediately releasing him from his horror. 'My master is upset?' Her voice calmed him, brought him back. He stared at her, speechless. 'A matter which was never resolved, a man–child who was never found,' she continued as she refilled the long-stemmed pipe with its disproportionately tiny bowl.

Renagi stared at her, his eyes desperate. 'I have knowledge of this Golden Son, half-Ashkelite, half-Warlord . . .' she went on.

How can she know these things? No one can know these things . . . Renagi's mind raced, his fear growing.

'Yes, I know him. The one they call . . . Tegné.' She gave the name a space of its own, a clear, final ring to the last syllable.

'Tegné, Tegné . . .' Renagi repeated the name, reluctantly attaching it to the face in his vision.

'He threatens eternal shame upon you, upon your house, upon your family,' she said, drawing him closer to her.

So I have not been insane. I have known. Known all these yeons that the child was mine, that he lives, that he will destroy me, he thought, already doomed in his heart.

'You must find him,' she said, anticipating.

'Where?' Renagi's voice was quiet yet demanding, as he tried, even now, to maintain control.

'To the west. Beyond the Valley,' she replied, waiting for the impact.

Renagi reeled backwards, his worst suspicions confirmed. 'The Valley of Death? My Warmen cannot cross that Valley. There is no water, no shade, no shelter,' he answered, near explosion.

'Shhh . . . shhh,' she whispered, stroking his shoulders, bringing her naked body close to his, rubbing her breasts against his chest – not to excite, but to calm him.

'And who are you? Why have you come here, how do you know these things?' Renagi bristled, withdrawing from her.

She followed his movement, never allowing their physical contact to be broken. 'I am called Neeka, and I have come from beyond the Valley. I have come for you. I am your ally, your new strength. This knowledge I have is your knowledge. It is your heart that I read. Trust in me,' she continued, pressing close to him, 'Because I am yours. Yours alone.'

Slowly, gently, he cradled her. She picked the pipe up from the soft sheets and blew upon the tiny, smouldering coals inside the bowl, rekindling the elixir. 'Take the dreams, they will be our dreams,' she said as she held the stem to his lips. Finally, secure in her spell, Renagi drew slowly from the pipe.

'The dreams will guide you,' she purred. And as he permitted the thick smoke to enter him, he saw only her eyes before his face and he was lost within them.

7

THE DOMINATION

If one desires to weaken something,
  he must first strengthen it;
If one desires to destroy something,
  he must first raise it up.
If one desires to take something from others,
  he must first give them something.
This is called the 'subtle-but-clear'.
  The soft and weak subdue the brittle and strong.

(Lao Tsu)

It was spring, and the hills surrounding Zendow were alive with the small, bright-red leaves of the tiny hapaver plant. Their appearance seemed to herald the joining of the Great Warlord and the secretive, veiled woman who remained constantly by his side.

The highest Zendai advisers and Warmen quietly resented the intrusion of this new concubine, particularly since her origins seemed untraceable and shrouded in mystery. Yet it was undeniable that she had fully rejuvenated the failing Warlord and restored him to his former vigour. It was also true that because of her expertise in the gleaning of the thick, clear sap from the seed pod of the hapaver, a product was created which drew foreign buyers from as far east as Yusun and Miramar. Drew them like a magnet, causing them to trade irrationally with their horses, precious stones and kilo weights of silver and gold.

Questions arose as to how this woman, who had been no more than a creature of the Willow World, could have acquired the skill to extract the bitter sap of the hapaver and transform it into the dark, tender brown squares which were worth ten times their weight in gold. The questions remained unanswered.

Even Madame Wang, as crafty a businesswoman as any brothel in any province had ever known, bartered greedily for the new 'elixir'. She replaced the old, less-desirable mixture, made from the bark of the myristica tree, in each of her most expensive pleasure chambers. So desperate was Wang to possess a stock of the magic substance that she traded from her jealously guarded underground vaults of rubies and emeralds. *After all*, she told herself, inhaling a long pipeful of the bitter smoke, *if the harvest of hapaver should suddenly fail, I will become the sole suppliers of 'dreams'.* The new elixir was used everywhere, from Wang's Willow World to the finest bedchambers of Zendow.

'As always, I have saved the very essence for you,' Neeka said softly, holding up the tiny, sparkling crystal bottle with its amber liquid content.

Renagi lay naked on the heavy spread of the wide, canopied bed. He remembered the Celebre of their first meeting, yet the memory seemed clouded, distant, long ago. It was as if he had known Neeka always. He studied the fine, aristocratic features of her young face, marvelling at how youth could so belie profundity. For he knew she had resurrected him, given him strength when he was weak, courage when his courage had faltered and had, in fact, pulled him from the very brink of obsession and insanity. *Yes, this beautiful creature has been my anchor, my very salvation,* he acknowledged.

'Shall we try just one drop?' she said, teasing, coming close so he could smell the sweetness of her perfume.

Renagi smiled, leaning forward as she slowly drew the thin glass stopper from the neck of the bottle. Then, tilting the bottle, she allowed a single, glistening drop of the fluid to gather on the slender tip of her first finger. Re-inserting the stopper, she moved close to Renagi and slid the fingertip into his mouth, massaging his gums gently with the bitter-sweet moisture.

Renagi closed his eyes as the warm tingling began in his gums and worked inwards, lulling, soothing, yet awakening within him a deep longing. It was more than a physical passion; it was a desire to possess, to envelop.

'Come here,' his voice was full and low as he lifted his arms towards her.

She sat beside him, pouring another drop from the shimmering bottle into the palm of her open hand. Then, reaching down, she rubbed the oily warmth into the crown of his semi-engorged penis. The Warlord moaned as his organ came completely to life, growing huge in her small, soft hand.

'We do well together, do we not?' she teased, gripping the circumference of his shaft and beginning a gentle stimulation. He reached for her as, playfully, she pulled away from him.

'Zendow is prospering as never before,' Neeka said, then waited, timing her next sentence. 'Even Ashkelan is producing twice its usual harvest.' She felt the blood cut off sharply inside him at the mention of Ashkelan. Now she moved closer, but allowed the hand which gripped him to relax as her fingers perceived his fear, his vulnerability.

'The older Zendai still talk. Rumours ... rumours,' she repeated, allowing the words to settle. 'And now, with Zendow so strong, you must maintain control. For your sake, for the sake of Zato, for the sake of your lineage.' Neeka whispered, manipulating his emotions, studying his eyes, watching her words take hold. 'Now, of all times, you cannot afford insurrection.'

Renagi pulled back, his organ becoming limp. She followed his movement, gently caressing his thigh with her long, flowing hair, licking along the top of the musculature with her warm, rough tongue, bringing him, in spite of his fear, back to life.

'The time is right for you to erase the final doubt,' she continued, hesitating before she spoke the name. 'Tegné,' she whispered.

'Tegné.' Involuntarily, Renagi repeated the name, the name he had refused to speak since the eve of their first meeting. 'Tegné'; it sounded strange as he rolled it from his tongue. Somehow less threatening. The Warlord was completely hard by the time her lips reached his centre. 'Yes, now is the time,' Renagi agreed.

The war party was five strong, including Gazan, or 'Animal', as he had come to be known. At first the men had been reluctant to volunteer, but the promise of promotion plus a full kilo weight of the fine, cured hapaver provided adequate incentive to attempt the crossing. Besides, Renagi had assured them that he had plotted their course and could guarantee water and shelter from the blazing sun; the sun which burned in the Valley for eighteen of its twenty-four-hour cycle.

Neeka was mounted on a huge black stallion; she cantered ahead of Renagi while the Warmen remained only a few paces behind. She led as they travelled along a path which cut through the sheer rock face and down towards the forsaken Valley. Suddenly she brought her horse to a halt. Renagi reined in behind her, raising his hand to stop the Warmen.

They had arrived at a slight clearing, wide enough to group their horses. Neeka nodded to Renagi.

'This is the place,' she said, motioning out over the vast, spreading vista. The Warlord dug deep into his leather saddlebag and produced a single metal compass. He handed the instrument to Tabar, the senior Warman.

'Keep to the compass, due west. Do not alter a fraction of a degree. You have water enough in your canteens to travel for five hundred vul.'

Renagi turned, looked at Neeka. She nodded her head, confirming his words, her hair blowing like a black banner in the gusting wind. He continued, 'At five hundred vul you will find a lake. The water is clear, drinkable. Rest there, the cactus plants surrounding the lake are edible, so cut the leaves, clean them thoroughly and store a supply of them in your saddlebags. Refill your canteens and continue west for another five hundred vul. At this point you should find yourselves at the western rock face. Look upwards from the base; you will see two high-peaked mountains. They stand alone; there should be no trouble recognizing them'. Again Renagi stopped and looked at Neeka. She picked up the direction from Renagi's last word.

'At the centre-point of these peaks, at the base of the rock face, there is a small passage,' her voice rang out, clear and commanding. The Warmen, realizing their single hope rested upon these instructions, listened intently.

'The passage will be high and wide enough for you to enter and ride in line for approximately a half-voll. You will emerge in the Province of Lunan. Continue to ride west. There are several villages in Lunan, and one monastery. The monastery is called the Temple of the Moon,' she concluded.

'Search everywhere, thoroughly. Spare no one. Find him, and ...' Renagi hesitated, faltering as he looked towards Neeka. She nodded her confirmation. 'I want him brought to me alive,' he concluded, his voice strained in an effort to disguise his inner turmoil.

Use him as your consummate show of power. Banish all fear, all doubt. Display him openly as an impostor and you will forever silence the dangerous tongues which speak against you. They were Neeka's words and, reluctantly, Renagi had accepted their wisdom.

The candle burned bright on the waist-high wooden plinth in the centre of the Dojo.

The line of twenty-four novice Brothers stood in front of the flickering flame, their white cotton gis saturated with the sweat of their exertions. Last in line was Rin.

Tegné had saved the exercise of the candle until the end of the session, leading the novice Brothers first through the basic forms and then through the prearranged five-step sparring. They had been training for over two hours, and Tegné felt that they would welcome this variation. He often incorporated Tabata's lessons into his own teaching, and now, after so many yeons, he had gradually come to understand the depth and subtlety contained in his own early training.

'We are going to practise gyaku-zuki,' he began, looking from face to face as he demonstrated the flowing counter-punch. 'I want you to aim at the flame of the candle. Do not hit the flame, stop a half-hand in front of it. Focus your fist and send the flow of energy up from your centre, through your striking arm, allowing the air caught between your fist and the candle to push forward and extinguish the flame.' Tegné slowly performed the technique, stopping his fist a precise half-hand from the candle.

'Oss, Sensei,' the small, excited voices chanted in unison.

'Remember,' Tegné continued as the first novice took a low sochin position, 'Relax your body, relax your mind. Do not "try" and punch the flame out. Try to perform a perfect gyaku-zuki. The flame will go out naturally.'

The first child punched, putting his entire body into the movement.

'Too much tension. Too much concentration on victory. Relax, be natural.' Tegné recognized his own paraphrasing of Tabata's words. Again, the small fist shot forward, with no result.

'Once more. Three times each,' Tegné said.

One hour later, the novices stood tired, frustrated, and somewhat less determined before the dancing, defiant flame. Tegné knew their tiredness was good, for through fatigue of the body the mind and spirit became strong, willing the exhausted muscles through one more movement, less intent on success and more on the mere performance of the technique. It was at this stage that true understanding took place.

'Not once has the flame even wavered,' Tegné said, smiling, looking from face to face. 'Now I want you to try an exercise with your mind,' he continued, singling Rin from the others and placing the puffing, sweating boy in line with the candle. 'First let us be sure that the position is correct,' he said as he helped Rin into the forward stance, making certain that the child's extended fist was the required half-hand from the flame, then guiding the same fist so that it cocked back, drawn in tight to the right hip.

'Now, close your eyes, grip the floor with your feet, your hips turned clockwise. your body relaxed,' he said, gently leading Rin through the correct form. 'Think of your fist as a weight, a stone on the end of a string. Throw the stone by rotating your hips towards the flame. Relax your arm, throw the stone.'

Tegné watched as Rin twisted his hips, The fist moved easily, fluidly.

'Good, good. Now open your eyes.' Rin opened his eyes and looked with dismay at the burning flame. Tegné caught the disappointment in Rin's face.

'The technique was fine. The feeling was perfect. This time you must keep the same feeling, the same flow, except open your eyes and concentrate on the flame. Allow your body to work by itself,' he explained.

Rin cocked his right arm back. The other young Brothers watched closely, each sure that Rin was on the verge of mastering the mysterious ki – that energy which flowed up from one's innermost source and made impossible feats such as this possible.

Rin could feel the eyes of his brothers upon him. He knew full well that the flame was expected to go out, and he realized that his Sensei, Tegné, had chosen him to perform this magic. Rin was determined that he would not fail.

Tegné noted the tension in Rin's body, watched his mouth tighten, and recognized the desperate glint in the wide eyes.

'In your own time,' Tegné said calmly.

Rin's arm shot out, the fist pushed hard by muscle alone, the hips and their rotation forgotten in his effort to defeat the flame. Tegné watched as the fist reached its full extension. Then the small hand snapped open and the fingers stretched the final distance and flicked the candle wick. Rin and the falling candle hit the Dojo floor at the same time.

Tegné towered above the child, his deep-set eyes concealing none of his dissatisfaction at Rin's blatant attempt at deception. Finally, Tegné stooped and picked up the obstinate candle, its flame miraculously still burning. Rin lay where Tegné had swept him.

Ignoring the child, Tegné placed the candle back on its base. As the class watched, he assumed a low, loose sochin-dachi stance.

'Relax, be patient. One time, one chance. Flow like water,

then become iron.' Tegné spoke softly, almost as if he spoke to himself, yet every ear in the Dojo was attentive. He moved easily, gracefully, straightening his back leg as he punched. His fist stopped a full hand in front of the flame. 'Whoosh!' With a rush of air the light was extinguished. Then, gently, Tegné turned to the young Brothers.

'It is easy. Every one of you can do it. There is no magic, no trick. It is a matter of finding the gentleness within you; relaxing and allowing the stream to flow.'

'Oss, Sensei,' the twenty-three students responded, their voices joined.

'Now line up,' Tegné said, before turning to the fallen boy. 'Line up with the rest of the class. And you, Rin, lead the Dojo code.'

'Exert oneself in the perfection of character . . .' Rin's voice was shrill, self-pitying. The class, speaking as one, echoed his words.

'Be faithful and sincere. Cultivate the spirit of perseverance. Respect propriety. Refrain from impetuous and violent behaviour. Shomen-nei. Rei.'

The class, including Tegné, bowed to the oil portrait of Tabata, which hung in the centre of the wall, overlooking the Dojo. 'Sensei-nei. Rei.' The young Brothers bowed towards Tegné. He returned the bow and dismissed them.

Rin had nearly reached the door of the changing room when he heard Tegné's voice.

'Rin.'

The child turned and walked back across the hard, polished floor.

'Did you think I would not see what you were doing? Do you think I do not know that trick?' Tegné spoke softly, searching the sheepish eyes. Without waiting for the boy to answer, he continued, 'I do not want to see you in the Dojo for seven days. Instead I will arrange with Brother Minka for you to work in the pottery kilns. I believe Brother Minka will put your inventiveness to good use. If, in seven days, he tells me you have worked hard, I will test you myself. We will see if you are ready to return. Do you understand?'

The large, single teardrop ran unfettered down the child's quivering cheek.

'Seven days, Rin,' the Sensei said firmly.

The Warmen travelled carefully, conserving both their horses and the precious supply of water in the canteens. They had used the light, cotton-net tents to shelter from the relentless, burning sun, keeping speech to a bare minimum. They had not wasted a single calorie of the tightly boxed field rations. The Warmen had been fourteen days in the Valley.

Groton lay very still, stretched out on his back, the soft red cotton scarf wrapped loosely around his head, flapping down over his eyes, shielding them from the rising sun. He felt the first pangs of hunger gnaw at his empty stomach; he thought instantly of the dried, tasteless, leathery meat in his field kit and then remembered Neeka's instructions regarding the cactus plant. He pulled the scarf away from his face, rolled over, and crawled head-first from the one-man tent.

It had been a hard, hot ride from the east, and now he could hear the heavy snoring and deep, even breaths coming from the tight cluster of sleeping Warmen. He looked with satisfaction at the glistening, still water of the lake. So far they had been successful, travelling five hundred vul due west by the compass, and Groton silently congratulated himself, for he was amongst the first Warmen ever to attempt this crossing.

Quietly, with his short sword in hand, Groton walked from the encampment towards the giant cactus, its arm-like leaves outstretched towards him. As he drew close he noticed an elegant cluster of tiny, pearl-shaped mushrooms. They grew in a perfect diamond formation at the base of the larger plant. There was a strange, sweet aroma surrounding them. He knelt down and skilfully sliced the first button from the small stem. He brought the cream-coloured mushroom up under his nose, inhaling its scent.

Nectar, like honeysuckle, he thought, as he bit into the button lightly, just breaking the surface of the soft flesh. *No bitterness, no poison,* he reasoned as he began to chew. He waited as the mushroom entered his stomach. There was no nausea, no burning, simply a warm, satisfying feeling as his system went rapidly to work digesting the small morsel.

Then Groton cut the buttons from the remaining mushrooms. There were fourteen of the pearls in his hand by the time he had finished. He ate half of them and carried the remainder to his tent.

His fellow Warmen had remained asleep, and Groton crawled back inside the cotton net and lay upon his own thin blanket. He felt content, at peace with himself, and the warming sun induced a dry euphoria as he replaced the scarf around his head and drifted off.

Groton was just entering the most blissful of dreams when he heard the beautiful, high female voice singing a plaintive song, somewhere far away. The song trapped him, lured him; he could very nearly make out the words.

Singing to me, she is singing to me, he thought, and, lifting the scarf from his eyes, he seemed to float from his tent and into the sunlight, hovering above the crystal-clear water. The sun appeared to reflect at odd angles from the shimmering surface; bright flashes from every quarter, as if there were four suns moving upwards to converge as one. And from the rapidly distorting reflection of the water, the odd, convex shape suddenly reminded him of the old, bleached white begging bowls he had so often seen carried by wandering temple monks.

He knelt down; the lovely singing seemed to envelop him. He stared into the shining glass surface. He met his own eyes, and marvelled at the clarity of his mirrored image. He bent closer, cupping his hands in the water, bringing the wet coolness to his face, tasting the chill. And as he stood to remove the garments he had slept in, he was certain he could see his own face smiling as if the image had remained in the water, independent of its source.

Groton felt the coolness lap gently against his skin, drawing him inside its calm. The singing was now a fine, high-pitched whine as, naked, he dipped below the surface. The lake was deep, and his body submerged slowly into the cooling depths. He breathed in, amazed that he could derive such pure oxygen from the water. And for a moment he was certain he saw an exquisite, ivory-skinned face in front of him. The blue, swirling eyes of the face were part of the lake itself. The eyes knew him.

'Over here! Over here!' Gazan called, motioning for Tabar and the two other Warmen. They ran towards the single tent, the only tent that remained standing on the shore.

Groton lay naked inside the tent, face down, his nose and mouth pushed into the wooden bowl from his field kit. The bowl was full of water. Something was clasped tight in his right hand.

Tabar hauled the dead Warman from the tent and roughly rolled him over. Gazan noted the strange, beatific smile which seemed frozen on Groton's lips.

'In the three yeons I knew him, this is the first time I ever saw him smile,' remarked Tabar, as he pried open the clenched hand and let the seven mushrooms fall to the earth.

'Let it be a lesson,' Tabar continued, matter-of-fact, 'Drink the water from the lake, eat the leaves from the cactus, nothing more.' Then he saw the tiny golden butterfly. It flew from the tent and alighted gently on the mushrooms as Tabar added, 'Leave the mushrooms to the insects.' With that he turned to Gazan and motioned towards Groton's carcass. 'Bury him, fill the canteens; it is time to move out.'

Tegné sat alone in the small meditation cell. His back was straight, unsupported, his concentration centred within the eighth chakra. He took in a slow, deep breath, drawing the energy up through the pineal gland before guiding it down and into the seventh chakra. He swallowed to stretch his throat slightly, making a hollow and relaxing the muscles. He continued the breath, feeling the pulse run down and into his heart. He held the count for ten beats.

He became aware of a faint building of tension within his body; he relaxed and felt the tension drift away. As he exhaled, he kept just enough air inside his lungs to maintain the sense of expansion, then he inhaled a second time, drawing a more powerful, surging current inwards, through the open passage.

Tegné willed the current to do its work, to unblock the centre and allow the dark feelings which had plagued him for these last days to surface, to make themselves known to his conscious mind. He felt a sharp rush of anxiety which hovered below the level of his consciousness, just outside his rational grasp. Then as he slowly exhaled he sensed the dissipation of this negative field, again leaving him aware of its existence yet unable to subject the feeling to his own rational examination.

What is this foreboding? Like a black cloud within me, Tegné thought as he deepened his breathing, taking in the air in rapid, successive bursts. His body temperature had begun to climb, and he recognized the warmth as the first sign of the Dragon Zone.

He continued the breaths, pushing against his own rational fear, towards the place where all ki is unblocked and conscious function surrendered. For the Dragon Zone was the supreme state of introspection, and if the mind was in turmoil the Dragon Zone was the supreme hell. Tegné felt the perspiration drip from his body.

You can still stop; regulate your breathing, his conscious mind made a final plea. Tegné ignored the plea and increased his respiration, cutting through the last threads of fear.

The village was called Zacatec. It was the last inhabited region before the final hundred vul west which led to the monastery. The search of the six previous villages had been fruitless, and all but Gazan were satisfied that the simple dirt farmers knew nothing of the Ashkelite.

Zacatec, however, was a different story. There was an assured opulence to the row upon row of adobe houses, their sun-dried bricks forming varied and individual shapes, some octagonal while others were square in structure and painted white with a thick, plaster-like outer coating. There was definite pride here, pride and purpose.

Tabar was first to note the complex, above-ground irrigation system, connecting three main wells to six cylindrical water tanks which were attached to each of the visible dwellings by a network of reddish-brown terracotta pipes. *Running water, plumbing . . .* he surmised as his eyes followed the road directly ahead of him.

At the far end stood a fine, bleached stone building, perfectly round with a shining domed copper roof. *A chapel? But what form of worship?* Tabar mused, finally acknowledging the three Zacatecan men who had come forward, anxious to be of assistance to these imposing, out of place strangers.

'Have you lost the main road?' The voice was gentle, genuinely concerned. Tabar looked down on to the dark-haired, bearded man. He noted the fine quality of the brightly embroidered cotton tunic and the well-made leather-strapped sandals. Two other men stood beside the bearded speaker and Tabar detected a striking similarity in the prominent, hooked noses and wide, thin-lipped mouths.

Probably a father and two sons, he thought as he purposely remained silent, allowing a texture of foreboding to fill the space between them.

Finally Tabar spoke. 'Listen to me very carefully,' he began . . .

Within half an hour every man, woman and child had, as commanded, fallen into formation; opposing lines at the sides of the main, earthen road. Still, the Zacatecans were a non-violent group, and the Warmen's black-lacquered body armour with its tight, hard leather and distinctive red Sign of the Claw, aroused as much curiosity as fear within them.

This apparent complacency irritated Tabar. He drew himself up, sitting squarely in the saddle, determined to imitate, both in his posture and his resonating voice, the manner in which he had seen Renagi address his minions in yeons past.

'We have come from the west, from the Clan of the Great Warlord,' Tabar began. 'We travel in search of an Ashkelite. A slave. An impostor. A man who claims to be the son of our Warlord. He is a liar and a fugitive. We intend to arrest him, to take him to Zendow; there he will be punished.'

At this point, Tabar paused dramatically, turning in the saddle of his enormous horse, searching the wide, puzzled eyes of the people below him. Gazan and the other Warmen positioned themselves along the two lines, allowing gaps of twenty paces between their horses. Tabar could feel the frustration and tension in the three men. The ride through the Valley had extracted every bit of their courage and fortitude. Water had run out, the field rations had been spoiled by the constant heat, and the horses were virtually exhausted by the time they reached the western rock face. That, coupled with the vacant eyes and babbling, nonsensical denials of the inhabitants of the preceding villages, had fostered an explosive atmosphere.

Tabar realized that to keep order amongst his men something concrete, something that would at least validate their journey, was vital. Reflexively, the fingers of his right hand feathered lightly on the cold, hard hilt of his katana. He eyed the cluster of faces in front of him. Their curiosity had passed and now each Zacatecan lowered his head in submission. Finally, Tabar focused on the last man in the group. The man met his gaze. There was no hint of challenge in the eyes, but perhaps a spark of self-righteousness.

That will do, thought Tabar, maintaining the contact, his nostrils beginning to flare as his lips parted in a scornful sneer.

'You! Step forward.' Tabar's voice was edged.

The man took two steps towards Tabar. The senior Warman studied the stocky, middle-aged man. He noted the first sign of nervousness as the dark eyes wavered, decidedly less sure than they had been moments before.

'Please! Please, he is a priest,' the shrieking voice rose from the crowd as the small elderly woman ran to the man's side.

'I am not a priest, Mother,' he said, putting a comforting arm around the woman and looking again at Tabar.

'A priest? From the monastery?' Tabar asked. Then, without waiting for an answer, 'Does the name Tegné mean anything to you?' Tabar's voice was already assuming a positive reply.

The man remained silent. Tabar turned, looked towards Gazan and gestured for him, the Animal, to approach.

'My men and I have travelled very long and very far,' Tabar said, as Gazan dismounted and walked towards the man. The Warman glowered down at the mother and son.

'It makes no difference to us if we kill all of you, every man, woman and child,' he continued, then nodded to Gazan.

Instantly, Gazan hauled the old woman off the ground. She screamed as he suspended her by her long grey hair. Her son reacted quickly, and the short front kick caught Gazan sharply between the legs. The instep snapped loudly off the shining, hard leather groin guard. The kick had no effect other than to enrage the Animal.

Gazan's half-gloved free hand shot forward and the long, powerful fingers gripped the desperate attacker's face in a vice, squeezing so hard that blood ran from the man's nose.

'Enough! Enough of this! Tell him, Yung, tell him!' an old man urged as he lurched from the line.

'Free them . . .' Tabar commanded.

Gazan reluctantly released his grip on the man while setting the frail, frightened woman on the ground. The old man stood, staring at Yung, nodding vigorously, pressing him to speak.

The alleged priest turned to the senior Warman; his body trembled and his voice was a jagged monotone. 'I know of him.'

Every ear tuned to the unsteady voice.

'Sixteen yeons past, I was a novice at the Temple of the Moon. It was during my first term there that the boy was brought into the monastery.' Yung's voice had begun to settle, his nerves to quiet, as he continued. 'He was unconscious, carried on a litter. They took him to the remedial quarters. I saw little more of him, I never even spoke to him, but I do remember his name. "Tegné" – an unusual name, "Tegné".'

Gazan looked up, hoping that Tabar would be dissatisfied with this information, for nothing would have pleased him more than to slowly wring the neck of this insolent bastard. Tabar kept a steady eye on Yung, allowing the moment to hang ponderously, wanting him to feel the full animosity in the Animal beside him.

'How long did you spend at the monastery?' Tabar asked, finally breaking the silence, as the first sweat broke out on Yung's brow.

'Four yeons, until I withdrew,' Yung said. 'I did not take the vows,' he added, as if this additional information would somehow excuse his association with Tegné.

'And you never spoke to the Ashkelite? Not in four yeons?' Tabar snarled.

Yung could feel Gazan's breath on him; he could sense the Animal's desire to maul, to kill.

'No, never. He was kept isolated from the other novices, trained in the Dojo, tutored privately by the senior Brothers.' Yung spoke quickly, freely, trying hard to satisfy his interrogators.

'Is Tegné at the Temple of the Moon? Is he there now?' Tabar pushed, allowing no room for indecision.

'Yes, I believe so,' Yung answered, unsure and yet certain that this would be the only answer to protect his mother, himself, and the rest of his people.

'Right!' Tabar snapped, then turned to the waiting Warmen. 'Gather every man in this village. Group them and bring them here,' he ordered.

A cry cut the air; a teenage boy broke from the far end of the line and ran, frightened, towards one of the houses. Instantly, the closest Warman spurred his horse. Within seconds the Warman was on top of the running boy, kicking down with his armoured foot, sending the youth sprawling unconscious to the ground. Then, dismounting, the Warman attached a thick, tough rope to the boy's legs, remounted and dragged the barely conscious body into the centre of the road.

Two hours later, every Zacatecan male above the age of puberty lay hog-tied in the far corner of the village. Thick lengths of rope formed tight nooses around their necks, anchoring them firmly to the two rigid stakes which had been driven deep into the ground.

Tabar wiped the sweat from his brow, remounted and looked down on his prisoners. Then he pointed to Yung, who sat bound on Gazan's horse.

'Pray that your "priest" has spoken the truth,' Tabar said, loud and clear, 'for he will guide us to the temple. If we find the Ashkelite we will return and free you. If we do not . . .' Tabar hesitated as he let the fear sink deep into the submissive Zacatecans, '. . . I will instruct my Warman, who will remain as your . . . guest, to indulge himself upon the flesh of these men,' he finished, looking directly at the bound prisoners.

Then, with a final, confirming glance towards the Animal, Tabar reared his horse and galloped from Zacatec. The two mounted Warmen, with Yung firmly in tow, followed him from the village.

The quiet of the evening floated on the spring breeze which blew gently through the stone window, bringing a sense of rebirth to the small, austere bedchamber. Tegné's gold and silver medallion lay on the low oak table in the centre of the room, within arm's reach of the single tatami mat and its thinly upholstered cotton mattress.

Tegné sat up on the mattress, his back resting against the white-plastered stone wall. Almost unconsciously, his fingers outlined the claw-shaped mark on his right wrist.

For three days Tegné had been unable to transcend during meditation and equally unable to continue his exercise in projection. Instead, his mind remained locked on the succession of ever-changing images which had swept through and over him during his ascent to the Dragon Zone. A kaleidoscope of black and red, ominous silhouettes which had nearly formed, nearly crystallized, yet, within this introspective dimension, remained a breath away from his inner vision.

Something black, something red. Something I have seen once and forgotten, or suppressed. Something that unconsciously motivated me, something that will turn the final key, provide the final answer, his thoughts raced and collided, his rational mind arguing the illogicality of a quest for a 'final answer'. Yet he had come to a most definite impasse and, recently, had begun even to question his role amongst the Brothers, his position within the Order. A teacher of children? A monk? No, something else called to him. The voice was distant but, nevertheless, the call had begun.

And now, more than ever before in his life, Tegné felt the need for spiritual guidance. *The Elder? Surely the Elder will help me,* he thought as he rose from the mat, placed the medallion around his neck and walked towards the closed sliding door.

He stopped as he heard the faint, irregular knock. Again the knock, this time louder. Tegné twisted the round wooden handle of the frame and slid the panel open. Rin stood in the fading light of the corridor.

'I have finished my seven days, Sensei,' Rin said with the tired voice of true repentance.

Tegné looked into the hopeful round face, still dusty from the kiln. He had thought long and hard about Rin since the last episode in the Dojo. *Why is he still given to these outbreaks of misbehaviour?* A stolen piece of fruit, a small lie; trivial misconducts but enough to force Tegné to reassess his own worth as a teacher. *Perhaps he is a born thief?* The thought crossed Tegné's mind as he studied the apparent and genuine sincerity behind Rin's eyes.

Influencing a person's being is not unlike finding the combination of a safe; each advance and retreat is a step towards the final achievement. Perseverance. Tegné maintained an air of detachment from the child forcing Rin to break the silence.

'I have come to ask you to re-admit me to the Dojo,' Rin said simply.

'And Brother Minka is satisfied with your work?' Tegné questioned.

'Yes, very satisfied,' Rin confirmed.

Tegné nodded his approval. 'Then you will recall that I promised you a test of my own when your seven days had ended,' he added.

'Yes, Sensei, I do remember,' Rin replied, while executing the low, exaggerated bow he had practised in the kiln. Tegné noted the overstated form, the open hands pressed tight to the sides of the hips, the eyes forward and upwards, and the head lowered well beyond the waist.

'Very good, Rin. Now let us go to the Hall of Light . . . Brother Kao is expecting you,' Tegné said, suppressing a smile.

'Brother Kao!' Rin gasped, the memory of the stolen robe fresh in his mind.

The Hall of Light was a wondrous cavern; a long white stone room with a low, vaulted ceiling and seemingly endless rows of chest-high burning candles.

Each newly initiated Brother, having sworn the sacred vows and having been fully accepted into the order, was given a single candle to carry to the Hall of Light. The enormous candle remained lighted, replaced only when the wax had melted and the wick burned down, a symbol of the new Brother's commitment to the Order and of his eternal loyalty to the Temple of the Moon.

Rin's eyes grew wide as he entered through the ancient arch and beheld the sea of light. Brother Kao, upon their approach, struck a firestick, touched it to the wick of a new, conspicuously positioned candle, and stood back as it ignited.

'I see you are ready,' Tegné said to Kao, acknowledging the new flame.

'I am, Brother Tegné,' Kao replied.

Then Tegné turned to Rin, 'You should be honoured,' he said to the astonished boy. 'Most novitiates must wait until formal acceptance before they are permitted to enter this hall. You, on the other hand, are not only privileged to be here, but your candle is here also.'

Rin stared at the imposing candle; it was very near his equal in height. Then he looked again at Tegné, knowing there was more to come.

'However,' Tegné continued, 'until your formal initiation, your light must be extinguished.'

'Extinguished?' Rin repeated.

'Do you remember our last lesson in the Dojo?' Tegné asked, already beginning to adjust Rin's posture so that his pupil stood in a forward stance in front of the candle.

'I do, Sensei,' Rin replied as Tegné aligned the small fist with the billowing flame.

'And will you repeat for me the third line of the Dojo code?' Tegné asked, stepping back, away from Rin.

'Cultivate the spirit of perseverance,' Rin answered.

'Good. Good. Because if you wish to re-enter the Dojo you must learn to live by that code,' Tegné stated. 'Now; relax your body and . . .' Tegné hesitated, looking at the smiling Kao, '. . . persevere.'

'All night if necessary,' Rin heard his Sensei's final words as he threw the first punch towards the flame.

Tegné did not need to look back; he knew that the candle still burned as he walked through the arched doorway, up the stone staircase and out into the moonlit courtyard. Tomorrow he would visit the Elder. Tomorrow.

The morning sunlight fell upon the great iron disc which hung above the main courtyard gate. The single silver star and golden quarter moon were radiant in its glow. The powerful emblem seemed to revolve in space as the rising sun gently warmed the precious metal. The ritualistic morning chant echoed from the Temple, built into a single voice, hung harmoniously in the clear, chilled air and washed over the influx of village people as they entered with their full wooden carts of fruit, grain and raw cotton fibre.

The Elder stood in the centre of the courtyard, smiling and welcoming the traders, his silken robes resplendent in the warming sun. Morning, his favourite time of day. Morning, a new beginning.

Suddenly the harsh, loud clang of the huge brass warning gong shattered the tranquillity of his thoughts. The Elder looked up towards the high arched temple roof.

The sentry-monk stood straight, staring out over the trees. 'Armed riders approaching the main gate.' His voice was sharp, certain. Silently, without question, the courtyard cleared; the traders with their carts, horses and donkeys, along with the few Brothers who had come to exchange finished product for raw material, pulled back beneath the shadows of the slanting roofs.

The Elder hesitated, taking a full, clear breath of air. Then he carefully adjusted his robe as he surveyed the empty courtyard.

'Open the gates, admit them,' he ordered, an air of expectancy in his voice.

The leading stallion seemed huge, black, and the man upon it blacker still. And with each of its slow, measured steps, the Elder fought his own desire to move backwards, away from these dark intruders, to lose himself amongst the shadows and the observers. It was a desire inspired not by fear but by a desperate wish to avoid the inevitable. For he knew why they had come.

Still, the Warmen rode forward, looming large and out of place against the austerity of the scrubbed cobblestones and high yellow brick walls.

Violent men, girded for battle . . . The description stayed in the Elder's mind as he studied the bearded face of the Warman closest to him.

Tabar was watchful, wary, his eyes flashing with the sharpness of a predatory hawk, assessing the surroundings, searching for potential danger. 'Leave the gates open,' he commanded, as the two trailing Warmen, their prisoner in tow, followed him through the heavy wooden entrance. The Elder's eyes flickered, a mere hint of recognition as they rested on Yung, then he turned again to meet Tabar's intense gaze.

'We want water, food for ourselves and for our animals,' Tabar said slowly, drawing his horse to a halt.

The Elder bowed, standing only as high as the stirrups on the great black stallion. 'You are welcome here and you will be given all that you ask for on condition that you lay down your arms. This is a temple of peace.' The Elder's voice was quiet but strong.

'Lay down our arms?' Tabar challenged, 'We are Warmen of the Zendai Clan – we will not lay down our arms.'

'I know who you are,' the Elder answered, noticing the surprise cross Tabar's face.

'Then perhaps, old man, you know why we have come,' Tabar pressured.

'Perhaps,' the Elder responded, willing himself to relax, to accept this confrontation. He turned towards the edge of the courtyard and clapped his hands once. Within seconds, two Brothers, carrying large jugs of water, walked towards the Warmen.

'We have been informed, and, we believe, reliably,' Tabar

began, dismounting while he looked back at Yung, 'that you, or rather, your temple, has given shelter to an Ashkelite, a fugitive from justice.'

The Elder appeared puzzled. 'We have no fugitive from justice within these walls,' he said.

Tabar grabbed the clay water jug and lifted it to his mouth, drinking deeply, allowing the overspill to run down his neck, inside his leather uniform. Then he concentrated again on the fragile old man who stood before him.

'Tegné.' Tabar pronounced the name bitterly, distinctly, studying the Elder's eyes, awaiting their reaction.

Kao sat in half-lotus posture at the base and slightly to the right of the enormous candle. Rin lay curled asleep beside him. Above them the flame burned brightly. Kao kicked out with his top foot, and it thudded firmly into the boy's hip. Rin remained still, pretending to be asleep.

'Let your body flow . . . your fist is a stone . . .' Kao yawned, then continued, '. . . on the end of a string.'

Rin's lifeless voice completed Kao's line of wisdom, 'Throw the stone.'

'Come on, Rin, the flame is tired. It has been awake all night,' Kao continued, as again he prodded the novice.

Rin rose to his feet and looked hopelessly at the candle. The burning flame seemed as large as his fist. He positioned his body before it. He could feel Kao's eyes upon him, suddenly and genuinely curious as to the movement, the balance, and the distribution of weight in the stance.

'What is it called?' Kao finally asked.

'Gyaku-zuki,' Rin answered, making sure that his front leg was approximately thirty degrees to the side and twice the width of his shoulders forward. He bent the knee, allowing the leg to bear sixty per cent of his body weight, pointing the toes of the leading foot slightly inward while keeping both feet flat on the ground.

'And how long have you practised?' Kao asked.

Rin pulled his hip back, clockwise, so that he was half-facing towards the flame. 'Two yeons in the formal class,' he answered, drawing his right, striking fist into position just above his hip.

With Kao attentive to his every move, Rin's concentration was totally absorbed in performing the technique properly. *Seek perfection*, he repeated to himself as he inhaled.

The flame was now merely a focal point, no longer an adversary. Rin exhaled as he executed the reverse punch.

'Whoosh!' The light extinguished, leaving only the smoking black wick. Rin remained still, staring, hardly believing his accomplishment.

Kao was already on his feet, examining the result of Rin's 'perfect' punch.

'I did it, I did it,' Rin whispered, incredulous, looking at Kao, then bowing to the senior Brother. 'I can go back to the Dojo!' Rin's excitement was contagious, and Kao found himself beaming happily.

'May I leave now, Brother Kao?' asked Rin, a new respect for himself and for his fellow Brothers awakening within him.

'You may,' answered Kao, still smiling.

'I will come back one day,' Rin vowed as he lowered himself into the sei-za position, touching his forehead to the floor. Then, jumping to his feet, he turned and ran from the Hall of Light, in search of his Sensei.

'Tegné! Tegné!' Rin shouted.

'Tegné! Tegné!' The piercing voice echoed through the silent arches as Rin ran towards the courtyard.

'Someone here is most familiar with the Ashkelite,' Tabar said, listening to the shouts. Slowly, he drew his katana and rested the razor-edged blade against the Elder's throat.

Suddenly Rin burst from the last corridor into the bright light of day. He sensed the danger, but it was too late.

'You, boy, come here!' Tabar called. Rin stopped, staring with disbelief at the scene in front of him. 'Now! Or this old man dies,' Tabar commanded, a deadly menace in his voice. The boy was about to obey when he heard footsteps behind him.

'Stand with your Brothers, Rin.' It was Tegné's voice, calm and sure. He turned to see his Sensei and a dozen or more senior Brothers from the Dojo walking towards him.

Tabar saw the long golden hair, the pale skin, and he knew that at last their journey had found its meaning.

'You!' Tabar called, pointing at Tegné, 'Come alone,' he ordered.

Tegné held up his right hand, halting his Brothers, and continued by himself towards the Warmen and his beloved Elder.

Tabar was sure he could see the mark on the Ashkelite's wrist. *This bastard is tattooed*, he thought as he observed the low, centred walk and compact, solid body of the approaching man.

Tegné studied the three Warmen, making careful mental note of the two swords each of them carried. If he was to be effective, he must first remove the Elder from danger, then disarm the Warmen. His breathing was deep and even, his energy centred low in his seika-tanden. He was twenty paces from the group when his eyes focused on the blood-red Sign of the Claw which was etched into the Warman's black chest shield. Unconsciously, the key began to turn ... the missing piece began to fit into place. He knew that sign; he had seen it before, on the armour of the Warmen who had murdered Tabata. At first a rekindled fear hung like a red mist before his eyes, the fear of a child. Then a raw hatred began to fill his man's heart. A sudden heat enveloped him, finally centring in his right wrist, as if a blade of burning steel was being drawn slowly across the flesh, and for a moment his spirit was lost.

Tabar watched the Ashkelite stumble, not more than ten paces from him. *Good, he is frightened*, the Warman thought as he pushed the tip of his katana deeper into the old man's neck; a thin scarlet rivulet ran from the wound.

Tegné drew close, less than a body's length away. *The Sign of the Claw; it is my sign*, his mind reeled, *it is the mark on my wrist*. Tegné knew, but he did not fully understand.

'Tegné.' Tabar spoke the name, but the Warman no longer needed confirmation.

Tegné stopped in front of him. 'You should have no further need for our Elder,' he said, barely controlling the tremor in his voice. The Warman ignored his words.

'Get rid of that one, we need the horse,' Tabar ordered, turning his eyes towards the mounted prisoner.

The movement was too fast to anticipate. The katana was drawn and sheathed, and within that split second had come the horizontal strike. Yung's headless body sat a moment on the horse, as if it were poised, somehow, to escape, to gallop from the gates. Then, twitching, the body fell and lay beside the head, its wide eyes staring up from the dirt. The blood came in spurts, gushing from the headless neck, as if the heart had continued to rail with anger against this injustice.

Tegné felt the pull in his stomach, the urge to move, to act. Still he remained motionless. The two Warmen dismounted and walked cautiously towards him.

'Tie him to the horse,' Tabar commanded.

'He is marked,' the younger of the two said, noting with surprise the birthmark on Tegné's wrist.

'It is a forgery, bamboo and ink. The man is an impostor, a filthy, Ashkelite impostor!' Tabar stated, then added, with bile, 'A bastard who calls himself the son of our Warlord, the son of Renagi.'

'He is the son of Renagi,' the Elder's unexpected words rang like two swords clashing in the still air, cutting the final cord, the last hope.

'For that you die,' Tabar snarled.

Tegné lunged towards him. Too late, for the Warman's blade had already cut deep into the Elder's throat. The Elder slumped to the ground.

He has killed our Elder, killed him . . . The realization exploded in Tegné's mind as his right fist connected sharply with Tabar's nose. Tegné felt the cartilage break on impact; still he pressed the punch inwards, driving the broken gristle, like a splintered sheet of glass, up into the Warman's brain. He left no time for retaliation as he pivoted in a continuous, fluid motion, the same right hand forming the haito, and with a wide, spinning movement, the hips driving the ridge hand on an up-sloping, forty-five degree angle, Tegné attacked the second Warman's neck, penetrating deep into the mastoid. The blow caused an instant blockage of blood to the heart, and as the Warman was seized in cardiac arrest, Tegné stepped in, grasping the falling head. With a pull of his left hand he snapped the spinal column. Then he turned on the last man.

The Warman unsheathed his katana, more as a warning than as an intended weapon. He raised the sword above his head.

Tegné moved with violent contempt for the blade, sliding, inching closer. Now he could feel the Warman's fear, and the fear drew him on, making him more intent on destruction. Tegné feinted once, noting the downward, defensive move of the katana. Again he feinted, and then, with a roaring ki-ai, he unleashed the powerful, side-thrusting kick. The knife-foot caught the exposed chest beneath the blade; driving inwards, focusing directly below the sternum, catching the lower, attached xiphoid cartilage and smashing it up and into the chest cavity, puncturing the heart and lungs.

The Warman collapsed with a final intake of air, a choking scream, mortally wounded. Tegné moved on top of him, punching down, over and over, into the unguarded face. The face turned to pulp beneath his fist.

'Tegné! Tegné! Tegné!' Somewhere he could hear his name; he felt strong arms pull him back and away from the face. He heaved a breath, regaining a low level of control, as his eyes focused on the carnage around him. In the background he could hear the sobs of the village women, the low wailing of the Brothers. Then all sounds began to merge into a mournful chant.

He saw two monks cover the Elder's lifeless body with a wide, shining black cloak, and finally he met Minka's eyes as Minka stepped towards him, carrying the Elder's blood-stained robes in his outstretched hands.

Tegné remained transfixed, locked in the horror, as if he had entered a timeless vacuum where all action was eternal. No words were exchanged. Tegné felt the tears well within him, saw them run down Minka's face. He knew that Rin had watched, had witnessed the killing, had seen his Sensei frenzied, responsible for death. A murderer. A killer.

Unworthy. He withheld his tears, turning the sorrow, shame and self-loathing inwards. The hellfires already began to consume his soul as he turned away from the bare faces of his Brothers. He walked alone towards the open gates; the gates which led out and away from the Temple of the Moon.

> *Awakening,*
> *The lotus flowers*
> *The leaves unfurl*
> *Running red with blood*
> *The beauty is tainted.*

8

THE SHAPING OF THE BLADE

Weapons are not instruments of
the superior people
Only when there is no other choice
will they be used.
Regarding tranquillity and peacefulness
As the highest good.
In victory, there is no elation.

(Lao Tsu)

THE PLANE
BEYOND
SYNCHRONOUS TIME

The Seven Protectors maintained the vortex through which they had witnessed the pre-determined act of violence; the act that forever separated Tegné from the Brothers of the Moon. And in its aftermath they felt the hollow of his heart, felt his rage, his shame. They knew its purpose but could not enlighten him; not yet.

*

Seven days and seven nights; he had taken no food, sleeping only in fitful spurts, waking to the screams of the Warmen and the sad, knowing eyes of the Elder. Thrashing out with his arms and fists, keeping the demons at bay, yet knowing that the true evil was within him, its malignant stamp etched upon his skin. His robes were torn, dirty; his body unwashed, his long golden hair matted with sweat and filth.

The forest, which as a child had loved and sheltered him, now loomed above like a dense, suffocating cloud. He was a stranger, alone, alien. He could feel it, hear it in the animal cries and the warning calls of the birds. He did not belong, all unity was lost and his soul was splintered.

Tegné stumbled into the clearing, a natural barren patch amid the full forest. He was weak now, and the thought of death calmed him. His only desire was to lie down and forget, to sleep and never wake. His eyes searched for a place to settle.

Facing him he saw the giant, a redwood standing alone on a solitary patch, somehow defying the cluster and congestion of the lesser, surrounding trees. The long, deep roots and full, magnificent branches extended like strong, protecting arms from the thick, gnarled trunk. The green leaves danced proudly in the fresh breeze of spring.

Tegné stood beneath the tree, looking up, dwarfed in size and spirit. *Yes*, he thought, *I will die, and you will be my opponent, my executioner*. For he knew he could never defeat such power, such perfection. He bowed before the redwood, then lowered himself into the 'immovable stance', pulling his tightly clenched fist back to his rotated right hip.

His first ki-ai came from a vast reservoir of self-hate and pity. The hip twisted violently as it threw the arm forward, smashing the fist mercilessly into the waiting bark. He felt his flesh rip and his bones break as he repeated the movement, striking with all his strength. Slowly, his spattered blood began to cover the birthmark.

THE PLANE BEYOND
SYNCHRONOUS TIME

Time and again the fist slammed into the bark of the tree, seeking to merge, to become whole, yet unconscious of its own intention.

And through the swirling funnel the Seven Protectors watched as the tiny Earth figure drew his energy from the ground source, through the leaves, into the vortex and up through the spiral, allowing their own delicate and ethereal bodies to act as conductors for this violent charge. And as the thudding waves pulsed through them and outwards, they concentrated the converted energy upon the block of shining silver which jumped and undulated like liquid mercury before them.

*

Night was falling, yet time held no meaning. The pain of the broken fist had given way to cold numbness. The blood from the raw, open wound dried and caked on the birthmark.

Over and over again. Tegné punched into the bark, his hips rotating on their axis, driving his swollen hand with a force that had nothing to do with muscle and flesh; for he had become a part of the Earth, drawing his strength from its source, as deeply rooted as the tree which gradually and lovingly surrendered to the man. For the tree was also with purpose; to be the anvil on which this warrior's heart would be forged.

THE PLANE BEYOND
TIME: SYNCHRONOUS

When the block is carved it becomes useful. When the sage uses it, he becomes the ruler. (Lao Tsu)

And with each rush of energy from the pounding fist, the shining silver, at first white hot, folded in upon itself, turning red, forming, becoming wide and flat. Finally the metal tapered to a point. Cooling. Hardening.

*

The moon remained hidden behind dark clouds, and only the steady, incessant thud of the fist against the bark drew Rin's attention; he cautiously entered the clearing.

He had remained ten days in the monastery. Ten days, and his heart could stand no more. Without Tegné, his Sensei, the boy had no light, no guidance. He needed his Sensei and, he believed, Tegné needed him.

As he crouched low, hidden by thick bushes and trees, Rin could make out the silhouette. He stared as, in the darkness of night, both man and tree seemed to move in unison, the man punching, the tree bending, absorbing the blow.

Quietly, Rin moved closer, until he could recognize the figure; it was Tegné, his Sensei, yet the far-away, vacant expression on the face and the empty, flowing motion of the body made Rin unsettled, confused.

Empty mind, empty body ... empty mind, empty body ... Tegné could hear the words. It was Tabata's voice, fresh and clear, as if Tabata were standing next to him.

Tegné punched after each command, barely conscious of his body, aware only of the blissful breath of life which filled his lungs and carried him on silken wings, high above the plane of Earth.

You are a wave; become the sea. The words were fulfilment in themselves. *I am a wave; make me the sea ...* Tegné answered, feeling his spirit soar.

The fist was broken, the wrist splintered, the blood dried and congealed. Rin was close enough to see the damage as he watched through his streaming tears.

The child no longer made an effort to conceal himself; he stood only paces away from his Sensei. Tegné's punches appeared heavy, as if the motion were slowly grinding to a halt. The forest had grown dark beneath the thick layers of cloud, and somehow Rin understood; death was approaching.

The sound began at the base of the redwood, a low groan which came from the roots and rose up through the tree. Tegné ki-aied with every punch, a ki-ai of such intensity that his entire body appeared to vibrate as the rush of air was forced up from his diaphragm and augmented the weight of his blows. Rin listened as the groan from the tree increased with each of Tegné's ki-ais. Soon the combined sound was so great that the child covered his ears with his open palms. Still the ground shook, and Rin's sorrow and compassion were replaced by cold fear. He stared, the tears dry in his eyes, as the redwood buckled, giving way at the point where the fist impacted against its bark.

'Hee-aa!' Tegné's ki-ai broke through the barrier of Rin's tightly closed ears. Slowly, the tree strained backwards, bending away from the fist. A deep, splintered indentation was visible in the thick bark.

'Hee-aa!' Again the ki-ai, like a roar, loud and demanding. Then, in a splendid moment, the clouds parted, and a cascading burst of bright sunshine shone down upon both man and tree. And in that moment the proud trunk split open in a mighty chasm. Rin shuddered as the earth moved beneath him and the tree began its slow, majestic fall. The thick, heavy body of wood bounced once against the forest floor, coming up, trying to rise, to stand once more before the man, as if, perhaps, its work was not complete. Then, finally, the redwood settled, quiet and still upon the ground.

THE PLANE BEYOND
TIME: SYNCHRONOUS

The sacred blade was finished. A shining, perfect creation. Shaped by the Protectors, forged by the Warrior, waiting for him to grasp it, to give it life. For in its singular beauty was the mirror of Tegné's soul.

*

Tegné knelt before the broken redwood, bending forward, kissing the earth. Now the rain began, washing him, cleansing him, mingling with his own tears. He felt the cool, gentle fingers upon his wounded hand; he was not startled, nor did he move quickly. All quickness, all passion, was momentarily erased. Slowly, Tegné raised his head.

Tabata smiled down upon him, the wonderful twinkling brown eyes, the fine, full, round face, the thick grey beard.

'Is this death?' Tegné asked, responding to the coolness of Tabata's touch.

The old Sensei smiled. 'No, this is awakening, the beginning of your journey,' he answered.

'Journey?' Tegné questioned, calm, accepting.

'The journey of the Warrior; your journey,' Tabata replied.

'And my purpose?' Tegné asked.

'To understand the source of dreams, the nature of illusion, and the meaning of reality,' Tabata answered.

'Dreams. Illusion. Reality,' Tegné repeated, a discernible edge below the surface of his voice. 'You speak to me in riddles. Please, Sensei, I am no longer a child.'

Tabata held him long within his gaze. 'Then beware you do not fall prey to the enemies of a child. Anger, passion, fear,' Tabata said.

Tegné bowed his head before his master.

'And strive to know inner peace. For inner peace is the true resource of the Warrior. Discipline your human nature, conquer it, use it, become fully awake. It is only then that you will know the path of your heart,' Tabata continued, strength bursting from his full voice. 'Learn to see, to accept, to understand the difference between passion and love, between purpose and desire. For, without purpose, the Warrior is a hollow, wasted man.'

'I must go to my father,' Tegné stated, as if the decision was without choice, irrevocable.

'Travel east, through the Great Valley,' Tabata answered, finally releasing Tegné's hand. Then the Sensei rose and walked towards the forest, turning only once to bow to his student.

The redwood stood full, renewed, above him. Tegné lifted his right hand, examining the fingers, the wrist, the birthmark. The hand was perfect, healed, the birthmark clear and, in its way, beautiful. He breathed the clean morning air as the sun warmed his back through the heavy silken robes.

The barking howl came from close by, jolting him to full consciousness. He turned to see the wolf walking towards him, a familiar twinkle in the brown, flickering animal eyes. There was no fear between the wolf and the man, and Tegné bent forward, intending to stroke the rough fur. As his hand drew near, the wolf looked up, its face shy, expressive.

Tegné hesitated a moment, then touched the coarse fur on top of the hard, bony head. At that instant the sound of light, running footsteps came from behind them. The wolf backed away, suddenly timid, wary. The footsteps came closer.

'Sensei! Sensei!' It was Rin's high, familiar voice.

The wolf spun quickly and bounded into the forest, disappearing amongst the brush and trees. Tegné stared after the animal for a moment, then turned to face the wide-eyed youngster. Rin carried fruit, robes and several canteens of water.

'I am so glad you are alive. It was a terrible dream! The tree, you were punching the tree!' Still frightened, Rin motioned to the redwood, then dropped his cargo at Tegné's feet, leaning forward to examine his Sensei's hand.

'Yes, yes, it was a dream. Because ... your hand; you had broken your hand!' Rin exclaimed, relieved.

Tegné bent down and looked into the pleading eyes. 'Why have you followed me?' he asked, cutting through the flood of emotion.

'I am coming with you. You are the son of a Warlord. You will need these things,' Rin answered, pointing out the supplies he had brought. 'And you will need a servant.'

'Thank you, Rin. It is true, I will need the food and water. But, Rin, I cannot take you with me. It is impossible.' Tegné said sadly, wishing at that moment that, in fact, he could take the child, for Rin represented the security of his past.

'Impossible?' The small voice mirrored the deepest hurt.

'Your life is at the monastery, among the Brothers,' Tegné explained, knowing his words would fall upon deaf ears.

'I have renounced the monastery. I am free, free to serve you,' Rin said, firmly.

Tegné nodded 'no' as he stood, stone-faced, looking down at the child. 'Thank you for the water. Thank you for the fruit, and I thank you deeply, Rin, for your concern. But now we must say goodbye,' Tegné said, a forced severity in his tone. Rin's mouth opened in protest, but Tegné stopped him before he could speak.

'I do not need a servant, I do not need a companion ... I want to go alone.' The finality of the words left the child no recourse.

Rin's eyes filled with the tears of loss and frustration. Finally he turned and ran from the clearing.

*

The Warlord and his concubine sat quiet and alone in the small antechamber adjoining their private dining-room. At last, Renagi spoke.

'Five weeks and nothing; not a sign, no word,' he said, his spirit low, teetering on the edge of defeat.

She looked up at him, her eyes reassuring. 'They have found him, he is coming. Trust me,' Neeka answered, 'I can feel it,' she added, remembering that night, nearly three weeks ago, when she had lain restless, unable to sleep. Finally, as Renagi slumbered, drugged and snoring, she had risen from the bed and walked to the arched window. There, in the clear, full moon, she had seen his face; his deep eyes, his long, golden hair. She had experienced a yearning, an exquisite warmth which filled her loins. She had wanted to cry out in ecstasy at what she knew would happen, must happen. For, finally, she would be complete. And that night, as she turned back towards the bed, she understood her utter loathing for the Warlord; for his corpulent body defiled her bed, their bed – the bed she would share with the Warrior.

Tegné reached the crossroads and looked up, raising his hand to his forehead, protecting his eyes from the bright sun. The road to the east pointed away from the lush forest and towards a dark column of smoke. The smoke rose in the blue sky and hung heavy and black, disturbing and out of place. He followed the eastern road, into the heat and towards the smoke.

As he approached the far boundary, less than a single voll from the village, he noticed the sickly-sweet odour which rose with the smoke, thick in the air. An odour which he could not identify.

Tegné stopped in front of the faded road-sign, bolted tightly to the high, wooden stake.

'Zacatec,' he said, reading the name aloud. He had heard of the village, and was familiar with the fine weaving and woollen rugs which its natives produced. He continued to walk up the wide road towards Zacatec.

One hundred paces in front of him he saw a child running forward through the haze of smoke and sun. Her long black hair hung loose to her waist, contrasting with her fine, white embroidered silk and cotton dress. Her skin was lightly tanned and her small bare feet were covered in dry dust from the road. Tegné smiled as he watched her approach.

'Better not come into the village . . .'

Her voice was sweet, shy. Tegné allowed himself to be charmed by this little princess as he squatted down and met her grey-green eyes.

'And why is that?' he asked, gently.

'Because there is a man, a giant man, and he will burn you on the fire,' she answered, still timid, but obviously earnest in her plea.

Tegné saw the tears begin to form in the beautiful eyes. He placed his hands on her delicate, narrow shoulders. 'Please, do not be frightened. I have come to help you. Just show me where the giant man is,' he requested.

The child turned, pointing towards the dark, pungent smoke. Tegné followed the line of her finger as the realization gripped him. *The odour was the smell of burning human flesh!*

'Maona! Maona!' The screams were desperate, shattering. The village woman ran towards them, her arms outstretched. 'Please, please do not hurt her!' she continued, sweeping the child up and turning pitifully towards Tegné, 'She knows nothing . . . Please!'

'It is all right, I am not going to hurt her,' Tegné said above her sobs.

'We do not know him, really. We do not know where he is,' she carried on, unconvinced by Tegné's words.

Tegné reached out and, before the woman could pull away, gripped her firmly by the arm. 'You must believe me. You must trust me.'

His voice was strong, solid. She recovered, focusing on his face, his eyes, then she saw the medallion hanging from his neck.

'They say he is from the monastery.' Her voice was more controlled as she stared at the medallion. 'They took one of our men with them.'

'To guide them to the temple?' Tegné asked, now suspecting the truth.

'Yes,' she confirmed, 'But they have not returned with the Ashkelite.'

'Ashkelite?' the word took Tegné by surprise.

'The man they seek is an Ashkelite. A slave – who claims to be the Warlord's son. They believe he is hidden at the monastery,' she said, her words growing slow as she looked from the medallion into the extraordinarily blue eyes of the stranger. 'For a moment I thought you could be the one, the Ashkelite. Your hair, your colouring, but it is not possible,' she added, apologetically.

'Why?' Tegné asked.

'Because of your eyes. Ashkelites have pink eyes, eyes without pigment; they cannot bear the light of day. But you ...' she hesitated, holding his gaze. 'Your eyes have the colour of lapis.' Suddenly self-conscious, Tegné turned from her.

'And what, exactly, is going on in your village?' he asked, looking towards the smoke.

'A Warman has remained behind. Every day until they return, or until we give up the Ashkelite, he throws one of our men on to the fire. They are burning alive!' she cried, finally breaking down.

Tegné moved closer to her. 'Come, we will take Maona, leave her safely inside,' he said, touching the woman's cheek. 'Then I will go and put an end to this killing.'

Gazan stood straddle-legged in the centre of the rough clearing. He wore a tight black leather hood, concealing his head and giving him an evil, terrifying countenance. In his right, gloved hand he carried a long-handled, double-edged steel axe.

Tabar and the others had been gone nearly twelve days and, as instructed, the killing had begun. Gazan turned, his breathing like the loud hiss of a snake through the leather mask; he viewed the prisoners. A sudden surge of power ran through him as he saw the fifty men cowering, some crying, before his gaze. They lay, bound, in a heap; humiliated, defeated, their clothing fouled from the twelve days of captivity. He walked amongst them, occasionally rolling one over with his heavy boot, checking the knots of their bindings, making sure they were secure, unable to break free. He said nothing, uttering only low grunts as he kicked out, breaking their spirits as well as their bodies. Gazan enjoyed this work, the feeling of total dominance. In fact, he hoped Tabar would not return for another day or so; by then he would have burned more than a dozen men.

Gazan looked up. He judged the time by the position of the sun in the late-morning sky. He circled the mound of living flesh and stopped in front of the pyre. Bending down, he tossed another heavy, dry log on to the blaze, and watched as it caught, the orange flames weaving up into the dark tunnel of smoke.

He knelt and pulled the charred rabbit from the outer edge of the blaze, waving it in the air to cool. Finally he laid it on the ground, chopping the legs and tail free with his axe. Then, lifting the small body, Gazan bit greedily into the hot flanks, devouring the animal's unskinned flesh before washing it down with the cool water from his canteen. Finished, he wiped the grease from his mouth and turned his attention to his prisoners.

'Time to die,' he muttered, walking towards them. 'Time to die.'

Gazan's eyes settled on a tall, thin Zacatecan. *He still has the gall to look at me,* thought Gazan, noting the man's upturned face amidst faces too terrified to do anything but stare at the ground.

'You,' he said, standing directly above his captive, 'Would you like to burn?' The man did not answer, but neither did he avert his eyes.

'Good,' said Gazan, bringing the axe sharply down, slicing cleanly through the rope which connected the prisoner to the others. He hauled the man to his feet, then let him go, delighted as the Zacatecan fell awkwardly, his legs seized from the days of cramped binding.

'Get up,' Gazan ordered, and was surprised when, by sheer strength of will, the Zacatecan struggled to his feet and stood before his executioner.

'Move,' Gazan commanded, pushing the shuffling man towards the pyre. He saw that the prisoner's wrist bindings were worn, nearly broken, as he walked close behind the Zacatecan towards the flames. He made a mental note to check the wrists of the other prisoners after he had disposed of this one.

They were now close enough to feel the heavy, stifling wall of heat as it pushed outwards from the fire. This was the moment Gazan cherished, the look upon his victim's face at the time of entry. Gazan watched as the man came to a trembling halt before the burning wall.

'Well? Why do you hesitate? Move forward,' Gazan snarled, placing his war axe on the ground to ensure his two free hands for the final push.

'ENOUGH!' Tegné's voice boomed from the far corner of the clearing.

Gazan turned to see the blonde, bare-footed man approach. He knew instantly who it was; the hair, the pale skin, the mark on the wrist. *All the better*, thought the Animal. *I will take him myself; I alone will have the honour of presenting him to the War-lord.* Gazan forgot completely about the Zacatecan as he turned and walked towards Tegné. The bound, beaten village men strained their eyes upwards as the two men closed.

Gazan crouched, his fists moving in a slow, circular pattern. *As long as he is alive ... Alive but crippled ...* the Animal concluded as he beckoned Tegné to advance. 'Come on, little man, come to me,' he growled, a sneer parting his thin lips.

Tegné studied the Warman, caught for a moment by the sheer aggression in his posture, and the absolute confidence in the dark eyes which glowered through the slits in the black hood. Tegné watched the forward somersaulting roll begin, but did not recognise the movement or its purpose. His slide back and away was a moment too late as the massive, muscled body bunched up and tumbled towards him. Then the rough, cleated boot heel of Gazen's right leg extended, kicking out, catching Tegné mid-solar plexus, pushing in at the umbilicus. Gazan completed the roll, landing, balanced, on his feet.

Tegné was hunched over, winded; a dreadful nausea filling him as Gazan leapt forward and gripped him, pulling him close. He felt Gazan's hot breath an instant before the sharp incisors broke through the skin of his neck. The Animal's head twisted from side to side, ripping at the yielding flesh. Surprise and indignation buffered the pain, and Tegné heard the echo of his own ki-ai as he brought his right fist upwards, the fore-knuckle extended, pounding into the soft temporal bone at the side of the Warman's head. The jaw released its bite, and Tegné gripped the leather of the black hood and again drove the fore-knuckle into the soft target, then once more into the nose beneath the mask.

Gazan staggered backwards, surprise flashing in his clouding eyes. Then his vision blurred and he saw five Ashkelites, not one, standing before him. *I will kill him . . . Now, I must kill him,* Gazan willed. He forced himself to attack the small man who suddenly seemed so sure, so relaxed, in his strange, low stance. Tegné waited, timing his movement to Gazan's advance.

Another step and Tegné brought his left foot up sharply, then retracted as his instep made contact with the rough leather groin guard. The mae-geri was well timed, perfectly focused, and Tegné felt the leather guard break inwards against Gazan's testicles. The Animal buckled, collapsing on the ground. Tegné watched, alert, as Gazan tried once to rise, then fell heavily, unconscious.

'God in Heaven! Thank you!' The woman's voice rose, high and emotional. Tegné turned to see mother and daughter, tears streaming down both their faces.

'It is over. I promise you, it is over,' Tegné said, walking towards them. As he walked, he raised his hand to the bleeding wound on the side of his neck, castigating himself for being taken unawares. He saw the sudden change on Maona's face – without breaking rhythm, he pivoted towards the fallen Warman; Gazan was again standing, staggering forwards. Suddenly, the sun flashed on the blade of the axe as it swung down and dug deep into the Warman's shoulder. A dull thump accompanied the impact, and Gazan bent, lurching, falling. Blood poured from both sides of the blade.

The Zacatecan stood defiant behind him; it was the man Gazan had intended for the fire. Again the Warman struggled to his feet, looking first at Tegné, then at his attacker. He hesitated, unsure. Then, with his last failing reserve of strength, he ran for his tethered horse, pulling himself clumsily into the saddle.

Gazan glared down as Tegné came closer. With a pained cry, the Warman tore the axe from his shoulder, waving it murderously.

'Come another step and this blade finds a home in that pile of flesh!' he snarled, looking at the bound Zacatecans as he pulled the leather hood from his bloodied head. Then he turned back, staring at Tegné. His eyes burned like hot coals. 'Remember my face, little man, I will not forget yours.'

Gazan used the axe to cut the leather strap which held his horse to the post. He galloped from the clearing, up the dirt road and away from the village.

Tegné turned to the Zacatecan. 'Thank you,' he said. The man acknowledged the thanks with a faint smile as Tegné shifted his attention to the mother and child. He spoke softly to the woman as, gently, he stroked Maona's silken black hair.

'Get a knife, cut their bindings. Bring more of the village women, massage their arms and legs before they try to walk,' he instructed, turning back, looking at the captive men.

'And you will not stay with us?' she asked, pensively.

'I cannot. I must go on,' Tegné answered.

'It is you – it is true,' she said, looking down at the mark on his wrist as he stroked the child's hair.

'If any more come, tell them the man they are searching for is travelling east. Tell them I am going to Zendow,' he replied. 'Goodbye, Maona, take good care of your ...' he hesitated a moment, looking once more at the child, then again into the woman's eyes, 'Take good care of your mother.'

Tegné turned and walked from Zacatec.

Renagi sat at the head of the oblong mahogany table. Neeka sat close to him, in the chair to his left. She wore the ninjinka, the traditional Zendai half-mask which veiled her eyes and nose. The ninjinka marked its female wearers as 'taken' and, from the moment it was worn, only the Zendai male, in this case Renagi, could lift the veil and lay eyes upon the wearer.

Zato's empty chair was positioned to the right of Renagi. Yanon and Zakov, the highest-ranked military advisers, sat in line with the sixty Zendai men and the three visitors who occupied the rest of the table.

The feast had been a necessity of business, a polite formality to display the opulence of Zendow to the three northern merchants who had come to trade their precious blue lapis lazuli stone for quantities of processed hapaver. The evening had been a long one, and now Renagi discreetly eyed the three merchants. He noticed their slurred speech and awkward movements.

The Warlord was glad the evening would soon be over. For the last hour his mind had been on Zato, hoping that his son would bring news of the original party of Warmen.

After all, Renagi thought, quietly unhooking the buckle of his thick leather belt and releasing the pressure on his engorged stomach, *Zendow is already rich beyond measure. It is not riches but purity which I seek. Purity ...*

He relaxed in the wide, padded, throne-like chair. *Zato, Zato's children ... Yes, that is my goal, my task. To ensure that the Royal lineage is extended, multiplies. The lineage of the Warlord Renagi, the ruler of Zendow, the most powerful clan in the history of mankind.* Renagi's thoughts were interrupted by the light, warm touch of Neeka's hand upon his own.

He looked into her veiled eyes. 'You have been far away, my love,' she whispered.

Renagi smiled, inhaling the musk of her body oil.

'Your son has returned,' Neeka continued, her voice like thick velvet.

'What? Zato? I have not seen Zato; he has not been here, I am sure.'

'He awaits you in your chamber,' Neeka insisted, gripping his hand.

Renagi rose abruptly from the table, holding his silver goblet in his outstretched hand. Both Zendai and guests quietened instantly, attentive to the Warlord.

'I am sorry to say that a family matter requires my immediate attention. However, the evening is young, and I implore you to relax and enjoy yourselves.' Renagi hesitated, looking from man to man, stopping at the coarse, raw-boned faces of the visitors. 'Naturally, we have arranged entertainment for you, and we would be delighted if you would avail yourselves of our gifts.' With that, Renagi nodded to the guards who attended the huge, arched wooden doors.

The doors were ceremoniously pulled open to reveal twenty of Wang's finest. Barefoot and giggling, they swept into the room. Behind them, two drummers and a string player launched into a sensual, festive rhythm. The girls moved forwards, swaying easily to the beat.

Renagi emptied his goblet, then the Warlord and the Royal concubine walked from the Great Hall.

Zato sat on the hard, high-backed dragon chair beneath the window. He was prepared for a long wait. He knew his father was hosting the northern merchants and he anticipated the evening would stretch into the early hours. He was somewhat startled to hear the two sets of footsteps outside the chamber door, and he stood, his hand on the hilt of his katana, as the brass knob turned and the door opened.

'Zato, my son ...' Renagi's voice broke the tension as he approached through the open door. Neeka followed, keeping a respectful distance behind Renagi.

Zato did not like his father's concubine, nor did he trust her self-contained, elusive quality. Yet, like the other Zendai, he acknowledged the stability and renewed strength that was apparent in Renagi, and he could only attribute this to the woman.

'Is there any news? Have you found them?' Renagi asked, clasping both arms around his son in a strong, affectionate embrace.

'Father, I have ridden as far as the western summit, located the place you described,' Zato replied, acknowledging the precise directions which Neeka had provided.

'And?' Renagi was anxious.

'And I have been through every Ashkelite village, including Asha-1,' Zato continued. Renagi bristled at the mention of Asha-1.

Zato's voice was slow, tentative; 'There is no trace of the Warmen, but in Asha-1 I spoke to the people.'

'Yes?' Renagi said, backing away.

'Perhaps it is better if we speak alone,' Zato responded.

'I have nothing to hide,' Renagi snapped. Zato hesitated, then began.

'There is the story within the village that many yeons ago a young Ashkelite woman was kidnapped and brought to Zendow.' Zato grew hesitant, then continued, 'She returned pregnant. There was a child.'

'Yes, yes, the Saviour, the legend,' Renagi pressed. 'But no one has ever seen this man.'

'They claim the woman left Asha-1 directly after the birth. She took the infant with her. They say her mother is still alive,' Zato answered.

'And did you see the mother?' Renagi asked.

Zato shook his head, as he answered, 'She is a recluse, mute.' Renagi stood quiet, waiting.

'Father, for yeons I have heard of an impostor, an Ashkelite who claims Royal blood. I have never believed in his existence,' said Zato, as if confessing. 'But now . . . now . . .' he broke off the sentence, not wishing to continue.

'Now you begin to understand my obsession,' Renagi stated.

Zato looked directly at his father, a question in his eyes. 'There is more to the legend,' he said, still hesitant.

Renagi swallowed hard. 'Well?'

'The young woman was abducted by the Warlord's personal attendant. Your attendant, Father,' Zato finished.

Renagi used every reserve to remain in control, to present an impenetrable front. 'They lie, and they will pay for their lie,' he said, his voice strong with sincerity. 'Our blood is pure, Zato. You are my heir, my only son. In time you will become Warlord, you will rule Vokane, as will your son, and his.'

'Then let me cross the Valley. If an impostor exists, I will rout him out – I will bring him back to Zendow. Then we are free, clear,' Zato replied, relieved of his burden.

'My son,' Renagi said, moving close to Zato and placing his hands on the broad shoulders, trying to reason with him. 'Not one Warman has yet returned.'

'But Zato is your finest, Master.' Neeka's voice broke the link between father and son. They turned towards her as she spoke. 'It would bring great face to both of you,' she persisted.

'It is true, Father. It is certainly true,' Zato said, augmenting her words.

Renagi was caught in the middle, every instinct urging him to forbid his son the journey. Yet the combined will of Zato and Neeka prevailed. He looked deep into his son's eyes, considering. Finally he spoke. 'Pick four of my best Warmen to go with you.' There was a sad resignation in his tone.

Zato's mouth tightened as he nodded in agreement. Then he bowed to his father and walked from the room.

Tegné knelt beside the wide, flowing stream. Patiently he baited the wooden hook, using the earthworms he had soaked overnight in the moss-based mixture of radium, juniper and cedarwood oil.

With a fat, wriggling worm securely in place he sat on the dirt bank, letting his bare feet touch the cool mountain water, and tossed the line into the stream, watching as it sank slightly below the water's surface. The lively current caused the stream to babble gently as the water ran across the jutting rocks and fallen logs. He could just make out his distorted reflection.

'Ashkelite.' He said the name as the gold of his hair flashed briefly in the rippling water. From his geographical studies at the temple he had been vaguely aware of this isolated, inter-bred race of albino slaves. He knew of the stigma attached to them, yet he had never laid eyes on an Ashkelite. *Until now,* he thought, looking at the lightly tanned skin of his arm as he drew gently back on the fishing line. *So that is my heritage; half-Ashkelite, half-Zendai,* he mused, not quite understanding why the Elder, or indeed his own Sensei, had never told him of his origins.

You will know in time . . . The phrase played over and over again in his mind as he caught the first glimpse of the giant silver-bellied trout. The fish swam up from darker, deeper water and cautiously approached the baited hook.

Acceptance. Inner peace, he thought as he played gently with the line, pulling the bait towards him, then slackening off, allowing it to drift. The trout followed, nibbling, but not committing itself. *A time for patience, a time for action,* he said as he teased the beautiful fish. Once, twice, Tegné tugged on the line, causing the worm to break the surface, then slide backwards. He believed he could see the fish make the final decision an instant before he felt the strong, sharp pull on the line. Tegné responded as quickly, snapping the line back, firmly hooking the catch.

The trout was strong, and struggled tirelessly against the hook. Tegné released more line, allowing the fish a short run, then pulled the line back and drew the trout closer. Again and again he repeated the movement, until finally he could feel the fish weaken, growing less active against the line.

Now Tegné squatted on the shore, an arm's reach from the shining silver trout.

'Fate is the hunter . . .' He spoke another of Tabata's phrases as he gripped the dorsal ridge of his catch, his fingers holding it firmly beneath the heaving gills. He lifted the struggling body from the stream as he used his free hand to seize the heavy, fist-sized rock. He laid the trout down, holding it secure as he raised the killing stone high above his head. 'Fate,' he said again, as he hesitated, then lowered the rock, unwilling to slay the captured fish. Carefully, he disengaged the wooden hook from the open mouth and tossed the gasping trout back into the water.

Tegné stood a moment, watching as the silver giant floated, stunned, beneath the surface. Then, at last, the fish began a gradual, tentative movement, testing its fins, seeming to grow aware that it was still alive. Finally its tail broke the surface in one strong, sharp snap and the trout swam for the deeper, darker depths of the stream.

'Free?' Tegné asked, as he watched the fish disappear, somehow knowing that if he threw the baited hook back in the water, he would catch the same trout again.

'Free!' he laughed, then turned and walked towards the eastern trail which led to the Valley.

By nightfall Tegné had arrived on the high, rocky precipice. The fine white mist obscured his view down into the Valley of Death. The cold mountain air caused him to pull his robes tight as he gathered kindling to begin a fire.

Within an hour the seven logs were placed so that the ends nearest the burning kindling began to smoulder as they dried. As the fire grew stronger, Tegné pushed the logs closer together, feeding the blaze with a little tinder, ensuring that it would burn throughout the night and leave a good supply of embers for the morning.

He sat peacefully by the fire, gazing into the dancing flames. He had consumed only the pure mountain water for the past three days and, with the exception of the trout which he had thrown back, he had had no desire for food. *Perhaps that is the proper way to enter the Valley*, he thought as he looked out over the moonlit vista. He breathed in, filling his lungs. He felt clear, clearer than at any time in his life, his body strong and part of the Earth, part of its spirit, clean and unafraid. He exhaled the breath and sat quiet, motionless, listening to the dry crackle of the thin branches which burned in the centre of the logs. Tomorrow he would survey the precipice, search and find a way down the rock wall and into the Valley. But now he would sleep.

He stood to unfurl the heavy woollen blanket. It was a small sound, like the yelping of a young puppy ... it came from the bushes on the perimeter of the clearing. He moved quietly towards the sound, stopping above the short, full shrub ... Nothing. He pulled the thorny branches back.

The tiny, torn piece of cotton cloth clung to the innermost

branch. He pulled the cloth free, examining it, listening. Far away he heard light, running footsteps.

Tegné rose before the sun, warmed himself by the burning embers and performed the six basic asanas, relaxing and stretching his body. He folded his bedding, packing it into a tight roll, slung it across his shoulder and walked along the ridge of the Valley.

The gulf stretched as far as his eyes could see, and the fine, white mist of last evening was nearly transparent in the morning sun. Tegné followed the ridge into a northerly, downward slope and by early afternoon he stood below the mist, overlooking a rocky but negotiable passage. He began the descent, at times having to cling precariously to the jagged masses of stone; yet, slowly, he made his way down.

Mid-way, and he was uncomfortably aware of the radical change in temperature. The heat seemed to rise in waves from the white desert floor, which was still fifty body lengths below him. He paused, sipping water sparingly from one of three full canteens. Looking up, he watched the mist as it parted for a moment, allowing the radiant, multi-coloured beams of sunlight to break through. His eyes caught briefly on a dark speck moving high above on the rock wall, then the mist covered his view, and the speck was gone.

A burro? A wild dog? he wondered, remembering the running footsteps of last night. He turned and continued his descent into the suffocating, dry heat of the Valley.

Two hours later, Tegné stood on the white, sun-baked earth. He reckoned it to be late in the afternoon, near sunset, and still there was little sign of the sun having shifted position in the dazzling blue sky. He squinted as he looked up, shielding his eyes with his open palm. Even through his closely held fingers, he could bear no more than a second's glance. He realized that protection from the powerful rays was vital if he was to survive within this inferno. He pulled his robes tight to his body, using his wide silk sash to wrap around his face and up over his head. He took the zori from the sling bag and placed his feet in the tough rope sandals.

Again he looked up, not directly at the sun but to the left of it. He hoped he was correct in speculating the westward movement of the great orange ball, for this was his sole means of direction. Then he turned and walked directly away from the sun.

The heat reflected in heavy, relentless waves from the hard, burnt earth. There was absolute stillness, not a sound within the Valley, just the steady clack of his rope soles against the ground. Giant cactus grew in sparse, sporadic patches, their thick, spiked leaves jutting out like ferocious, clawed hands. Yet Tegné knew that the moisture contained in those leaves could sustain him, and their flesh nourish him. And in this empty, lifeless space, the great cactus was indeed his ally.

He walked on, losing all track of minutes and hours, sipping his water sparingly and searching through the ever-rising heat mist for any sign of life. The sun hung in the sky, moving slowly towards the wide horizon.

It was the stillness which was most disconcerting, so still that he could hear his heart beat within his chest, so quiet that his thoughts became voices. *'Travel east, through the Valley, the Valley of Death . . .'* Yet it was less than death he felt around him, for death must be preceded by life, and surely there could never have been life here, inside this inferno. *Yes, less than death* . . . He had entered the void.

THE PLANE BEYOND
TIME: SYNCHRONOUS

Yet he was not alone. For they waited for him on the other side, as if the Valley, its heat and rock, were simply a mirror, and he would walk through, travel beyond his own reflection and find his true self, his soul and his purpose. That was the desire of the Seven Protectors, and now, as they watched through the vapour, they prayed his test would be decided in a single moment; yet within their prayers there was doubt. For he was mortal, with a mortal heart, and the task which he was required to perform must transcend mortality.

So they watched, and waited.

No fatigue, no thirst, no hunger . . . The realization gradually dawned on him. *Why? What property does this Valley have that could erase these human needs?* he wondered as he looked right, then left. The terrain had not changed, and for one desperate moment he thought that he had not gone forward but had, in fact, been walking in one place ... but no, that could not be, because finally the sun had set and the bright, full moon risen. So time had passed, even though he was unaware of it passing.

Before embarking on this crossing, he had planned to travel by night and during the early morning, resting in the heat of the day. Now everything had changed, he would just keep moving; he had no need of rest. In fact, the more he walked, the greater his energy.

THE PLANE BEYOND
TIME: SYNCHRONOUS

The Seven Protectors formed the sacred circle around him, chanting the 'aoum', filling him with prana. They willed him forward, guarding him from the dehydrating heat, viewing him with love and with hope. For although they would never fully understand the complex nature of his Earth soul, the attachment, the possession, they could feel within this man the God-self trying to fulfil.

'*Be at one with the dust of the Earth; this is the primal union.*'

*

Renagi was fraught with anxiety. Had he been wise in risking his only son? Should he not have waited until he had, at least, some sign from the original Warmen? Neeka responded by soothing him, flattering him, and plying him with hapaver.

And now she felt warm and wonderfully alive as she meticulously mixed the fresh-cut flowers of the primula veris with the familiar red poppy buds, kneading the mixture into a fine, sticky blend. Then, carefully, she placed the resulting paste into the waiting pot of boiling water, allowing the essence of the combined plants to infuse into an aromatic tea. She breathed in the sweet fragrance and her mind began to drift ...

Tonight ... yes, tonight. Finally I will touch him, test his Warrior's heart, feel his clean, Earth soul surrender ... Tonight I will be victorious ...

> *The Valley spirit never dies*
> *It is the woman, primal mother*
> *Her gateway is the route of Heaven and Earth*
> *It is like a veil barely seen ...*
> *Lift the veil.*

He was walking, yet he was not walking, the feeling was more of gliding. His consciousness seemed to hover just outside and above his body. *And what is my body?* he asked himself in an internal dialogue which was at once lucid and abstract. *A conveyance, a shell, discarded at death, dust to dust ... And my father? A Warlord; my mother? A slave. How absurd, the human drama. No anger, no shame, simply compassion. Compassion for ignorance, for ignorance is the human condition ...*

Tegné walked all night and through the day, alone yet not alone. *Yield and overcome. Bend and be straight. Empty and be full. Wear out and become new. Have little and gain. Have much and be confused.* He understood 'The Way'. Time had dissolved; sunlight, moonlight, all was illusion.

The lake shimmered before his eyes. A mirage? *Heat against earth.* He walked towards the water. Water? *Inside the water is my true self ... Tegné ... I have come from the water ...*

His thoughts collided and merged, and finally the dialogue ceased.

The tea had done its work; lulled the Warlord, pacified him, and sent him into a deep, dreamless sleep.

Neeka lay far away from Renagi in the wide, flat bed. Far enough that she could not feel the touch of his skin nor the heat of his body. How she loathed him and how she would enjoy the moment of his destruction.

But for now, she lay still, quiet, in the soft sea of silk, alone within herself as she began the projection. She could feel her body grow numb as she became conscious only of the minute jolts of energy that ran like pins and needles through her spine and played delicately inside her womb. She breathed the cool air into her lungs and exhaled, giving no resistance to the short, sharp spasms which began and continued at ever-decreasing intervals. The feeling seemed to originate in her belly, expanding and filling her. She placed her soft, open palms on her navel and felt a subtle warmth which grew rapidly into a fine, encompassing heat. She controlled her urge to moan in the exquisite agony of its embrace.

Now Neeka became aware that her consciousness was shifting, centring within her abdomen, and finally she relaxed, arching her back, closing her eyes, as the projection was born. Floating

easily down the black tunnel and drifting out, over the abyss . . .
Flying into the crystal night . . .

Tegné rested on his hands and knees, looking down into the glass-like water. Never, in any mirror, had he seen his own reflection so clearly. It was as if he was studying the face of someone he was meeting for the first time. The hard, high cheekbones, the deep-set blue eyes, the proud, defined jaw and full wide lips. His golden hair was now nearly white, bleached from the constant sun. His skin, in spite of the scarf wrapped round his face, was tanned, near golden in colour. He looked deeper into the face, into the eyes, and as he stared, hypnotized, the eyes began to grow dark, swirling in tight, spiralling circles, until finally they were still. Magnificent eyes, alive and glowing.

He bent closer to the water, watching in amazement as a new face formed. A beautiful, feminine face, yet the shape seemed to materialize from his own reflection. The violet eyes held him as the rich, full mouth smiled up, and the long, jet-black hair lay flat on the water's surface.

Tegné felt the first waves of pure physical attraction envelop him as she rose from the water, naked and warm. Gently, he accepted her extended hand and walked forward into the clear, cool Lake of Dreams.

He was vaguely conscious, on the outer edge of peaceful sleep, his eyes closed. He felt the soft, light fingertips trace the outline of his mouth, travel upwards over his cheeks and gently caress his forehead. There was such trust and contentment within the fingers that he relaxed, unaware and unconcerned as to where he was. Finally, almost reluctantly, he opened his eyes.

She sat on the bed, leaning towards him. 'Tegné.' Her voice was low, purring, velvet.

He smiled as she wrapped her arms around him, pulling her body closer, nestling into him, kissing him softly on his parted lips. He breathed her intoxicating scent.

The chamber was octagonal, blinding white, the colour of pure, driven snow. The ceiling was high, its sloping sides meeting in an apex. In the centre of the hard, white floor lay a flat, smooth stone slab, three feet in height. The six Protectors stood, surrounding the slab, while Father Protector knelt before the small altar at the far end of the chamber. Incense burned in the ornate brass dish, filling the air with the delicate aroma of pine.

The sacred blade lay upon the altar, glowing and powerful, awaiting its master. Father rose from his knees, turned and locked focus with each of the six.

'Ready?' he asked.

All wore flowing white robes with full hoods, exposing only their eyes.

'We are.' The answer came in unison.

Father nodded once and walked towards the solid wall. Without altering his movement he passed through the wall and out of the chamber.

Tegné lay cradled in her arms, completely satiated, soundly asleep. The bright, full moon shone through the leaded glass of the window, the thick red curtain pulled tight and sashed to the side. The huge door was closed and bolted, completing the sense of total security within the bedroom.

She listened to his quiet, even breaths. He had been all that she had hoped for; innocent yet strong, naive but wonderfully physical. She re-experienced the warm, sexual rush as she recalled the moment she had guided him inside her. He had filled her, completed her, and now she had found him she would never release him. They had become one, inseparable, a single soul, and in time he would come to realize that, through her, he would live, grow, rule an empire, produce a son.

She turned slowly, gently, so as not to disturb him. She studied the face, and somewhere in the recesses of her primal memory she remembered the helpless babe, thrown into the river and left to drown. She blinked her eyes and saw him again, this time as the youth, alone and unconscious on the forest floor. She had saved him, guarded him, guided him, held the power of fate over him and now, finally, he had returned.

'Love me. Love me,' she whispered the simple words softly in his ear. He moaned and cuddled closer to her as she felt the wetness grow between her legs.

*

Father entered the room through the heavy oak door, his ethereal form passing noiselessly through the coarse, slow vibration of the wood. He stood above them, next to the bed, then reached out with both arms and gripped her tightly by the shoulders.

She knew this moment must come and she was prepared for it, confident of the Warrior's heart.

'Tegné! Tegné!' she called into his dreaming mind.

He awoke and saw her being dragged, helpless, towards the closed bedroom door.

'They must not do this to me!' she pleaded, appearing to resist her captor as they passed miraculously through the heavy wood.

Shaken and confused, Tegné rose from the bed. To his amazement he was clothed in a soft, white, loose-fitting garment similar to a gi, but without the stiffness or weight. He ran quickly to the door and pulled it open.

He stood in a grand, mirrored corridor. He functioned by instinct alone. Something dear to him, close to him – indeed, a part of his soul – had been stolen, and he would fight to reclaim it.

He ran down the corridor of mirrors and towards the darkness at the end of the hall. Faster and faster, his image becoming diffused as his own reflection converged inwards, giving him the feeling of headlong flight. The solid wall was directly in front of him.

'Do not stop; go through, go through . . .' The message entered his mind as surely as if the words had been spoken.

He continued his rush forward and met no resistance. At first the purity of the whiteness blinded his eyes, causing him to blink, trying to focus as he came to a halt. The scene before him seemed enclosed in a veil of gauze.

She lay naked on the stone slab, held firmly at the wrists and ankles by the six white-robed and hooded figures. The tall, broad-shouldered man rose from the altar, the shining blade extended in his open palm. His voice was soft and rich.

'We have waited for you. The blade is yours.'

Tegné stood still, staring, frozen. His very heart and soul lay with the raven-haired girl upon the stone, yet there was something of such trust and purity within this man's turquoise eyes and fine, melodic voice. Something so familiar . . .

Father stepped towards him. Tegné did not move. The blade glowed warm.

'Pierce her heart. It is your purpose. Pierce her heart,' Father urged. The chant began; the low, rhythmic 'aoum . . .'

Tegné wanted to touch the blade, to hold it; for, as much as he knew that she belonged to him, he also knew that the blade was his. Slowly, decisively, he extended his open hand. The chant magnified in volume. As he touched the warm metal, a charged flow of energy surged through his body.

Now he turned towards the raven-girl. The gauze-like veil dissolved before him and he saw the black, demonic shape of a huge creature. A devil? A cat? The image of the Beast locked in his mind. He lifted the blade high above his head, his heart beating in rhythm to the 'aoum', his intent true. He would pierce her heart; that was his purpose, pure and simple. He could hear the low, guttural growl as he approached the creature. All else in the blinding whiteness had disappeared. He was alone with the Beast, the silver blade his only salvation. The 'aoum' filled him, gave him clarity, gave him power. Then, through the chant, through the vibration, he heard her voice. 'Tegné, Tegné . . .' The words were like music.

'Love me, love me.' It was the voice of the raven-girl, crying, pleading. He stopped dead, the blade held back by the strength of his arms. For the blade had already begun its descent; still, Tegné was its master.

The chant was soft now as the veil again fell before his eyes and the raven-girl lay naked on the slab. Father stood behind him, close. Tegné turned and held the blade outwards, returning it to Father, A single tear formed in the turquoise eyes as the blade was accepted. Tegné looked away from the tear, away from the eyes, turning, bending, and lifting the light, feminine body from the slab. There was no resistance. The 'aoum' ceased abruptly. He placed the raven-girl on her feet and leant towards her waiting lips. As their mouths met, the roar exploded inside the chamber. It knocked him backwards, pushing him like a bellowing, gusting wind hard against the wooden altar. He held up his arms to protect himself from the onslaught. But there was no onslaught, just the black vision of death as the Beast reared on its hind legs. The long, pointed foreclaws lashed savagely before him and the fine white robes dissolved in a rush of blood and flesh.

Tegné sat helpless, staring, as the roar turned into a mocking howl. The Seven lay dead, mutilated, strewn about the chamber.

Now she turned and faced him. Slowly, silently, the Beast approached. He felt the futility of resistance. Closer, closer she came, until he looked into the red, bottomless eyes. He felt the sickness within his soul. Her breath was hot, deathly sweet, as the rough, warm tongue licked his neck, causing the skin to chafe and bleed beneath it.

Then she turned and leapt. He watched the black shape vanish into the white of the apex.

'My son, my son . . .' The voice came from Father. Tegné rushed to the dying Protector.

'There is no blame,' Father whispered.

Tegné felt the first rush of emotion as the tears gushed from his eyes and fell to the floor.

'Take up the blade. You have seen her. You know her heart,' Father continued, his words coming painfully through dying lips.

Tegné knelt, cradled the fine ivory head, searched the swirling turquoise eyes, saw the life-force ebb. Finally, the body relaxed in his arms, and he lowered Father gently on to the floor.

The blade lay still in the ivory hand. Carefully, Tegné lifted the glowing metal from the long, cold fingers.

'Tegné! Tegné!' The voice was familiar, but far, far away, like the rolling of waves on some distant shore.

'Tegné! Tegné!' Again his name was called, insistently, urgently. Slowly, painfully, he opened his eyes to the burning sun.

Tabata stood in a haze above him. Tegné drew himself to his knees, averting his face from the glare.

'Tegné!' Tabata shouted.

He looked up and saw the smiling face beneath the large parasol. Tabata seemed somehow mischievous in his demeanour. He bent down and rubbed his open hand lightly over the raw chafe mark on Tegné's neck.

'I see you have been with her,' the Sensei said.

Tegné was taken aback. 'A dream, it was a dream,' he answered.

'You are quite correct, yet in a way which you do not yet understand,' Tabata agreed, assisting Tegné into a comfortable seated position. Tegné looked quizzically into Tabata's eyes.

'By that, I mean you do not yet understand the nature of dreaming ... illusion,' Tabata said. Then, before Tegné could respond, he continued, 'Let us begin at the beginning'.

'I was looking into the lake. This lake,' said Tegné, turning and indicating the glass-like water. 'She came up from the water.'

'And you got on well? She liked you?' Tabata enquired. Tegné turned away, embarrassed.

Surely he cannot know my dreams, he thought, as he turned back towards the Sensei.

'A cat is a sensuous creature, am I not correct?' asked Tabata, pressing him.

'She was beautiful,' Tegné said as if he had not heard Tabata's last remark.

'The Cat?' Tabata pushed.

'The raven-girl,' Tegné stated.

'And ... She has taken your purity. Be careful,' the Sensei's voice grew more serious.

'Purity? I do not understand what happened to me?' Tegné responded.

'You have looked into the Lake of Dreams,' Tabata explained.

'Lake of Dreams?' Tegné repeated.

'You have touched the daughter of the Beast,' Tabata stated, 'For a moment you saw through her veil of illusion but, finally, she was too strong for you, and too strong for the Protectors.'

'The Protectors? They were the Protectors ...' Tegné sputtered, a terrible feeling of despair overcoming him.

'Theirs is the light within your soul. They are the guardian spirits of this Earth,' Tabata answered. 'And they have chosen you, just as she has chosen you. And soon, Tegné, you will make the final decision.'

'Final decision?' Tegné queried, his mind beginning to swim.

'To accept the task which the Protectors have given you, to take up their blade, to break through her veil of illusion ... or to fall prey to the weakness within your own heart, to be seduced by the power which she will offer you. To join with this woman in an unholy union. To father her child, a child which would be the very son of Darkness, of human flesh and blood yet possessed with the soul of the Beast.' Tabata studied Tegné as he spoke, gauging his reaction.

'Sensei?' There was undisguised fear in the voice.

'This truth has been prophesied for one thousand yeons. The Elder was made aware of its imminence, as I was, before your birth . . . We could not tell you,' Tabata said.

'Why?' asked Tegné.

'Because the knowledge must come from the Warrior's soul, not his heart or his mind. It must be your single purpose and you must recognize that the superficial drama of your Earthly life is no more than a means to carry you to its end. You must be able to see in the deepest sense of the word, beyond dreams, beyond illusion,' Tabata stated.

'And Renagi, my father? Must I not go to him? Face him?' Tegné asked, confused.

'Yes. You must,' Tabata agreed.

'But . . .' Tegné began.

Tabata reached towards him, touched his arm, calmed him. 'Tegné, trust in what I say. All the paths of your life will lead you to only one place.' Then Tabata stood, raising the parasol high above his head. 'Keep your soul free from the thoughts and emotions of the Beast. Become the sea. Give his daughter no place to grip with her fierce claws.'

Tegné rubbed his face as if he was finally waking from a deep, heavy sleep. When he looked again, Tabata stood on the far side of the lake. He stared straight at Tegné, his brown eyes penetrating. His voice seemed close, as if it was displaced from his standing figure.

'Remember, you must not dream her dreams.' With these final words Tabata folded the parasol. There was a sharp, cracking sound as both the Sensei and the lake disappeared, leaving Tegné alone, lying on the hot, burnt earth.

He sat up, opened his canteen and gulped the warm water, splashing it recklessly on to his head, rubbing his eyes with the overspill.

Dreams. Illusion. Reality? his mind questioned, but already the memory was less vivid. *The tree, the lake; what is happening to me?* he wondered, then he glimpsed a flash of silver. He turned to see the blade lying next to him; wide, unique in its simplicity, shining, perfect. Tegné reached out, touched the warm metal.

Dreams, illusion, reality . . . the words danced again in his mind as he lifted the knife from the ground. *All paths lead to only one place* . . . He remembered the words.

The blade was his; he knew this beyond doubt. And in some way this finely honed creation of silver was the last turn of the key; he was complete. He breathed in, attuned to the stillness of the Valley.

The whimpering voice was faint, barely audible, as it drifted up from behind the slight rise, perhaps one hundred paces to the left of Tegné. It was the single sound in a void of quiet. Cautiously, Tegné stood and walked towards the rise.

Rin lay on his side, his skin burnt and dry. He had followed his Sensei, tracked him through the forest, asked after him in Zacatec and finally caught up with him on the ridge of the Valley. He had injured his leg during his descent, scraping it on the rocky wall. Still he followed his master, never losing sight of him as he weathered the heat and sun of the desert floor. But now his canteens were empty and the child could feel the certain fingers of death. His feet were blistered and his legs had given up. He wanted only to lie down. He could feel himself grow light, dizzy, and he knew death was close as his wide, vacant eyes beheld the Angel of Light. The brilliant white, glowing halo came close and the fine blue eyes looked into his soul while the sure, strong hands began to free the spirit from his expired shell.

'Rin! Come on, Rin. Come on!' The angel spoke to him as he bathed his head with the holy water. Then blackness . . .

Rin knew he had sinned in his brief time on Earth. There was the stolen robe, the freshly baked bread from the hearth, the fruit, the books from the library that had gone undiscovered, but he had atoned for all these. Surely he had not transgressed enough to end in hell? But here he was, without light, lost in darkness.

'You are going to be all right. Just hold on,' he heard the angel's voice from far away. *Perhaps all is not lost, at least someone is fighting for my soul.* He could feel the strong arms pick him up.

'Rin! Talk to me, talk to me . . .' The angel's voice was somehow familiar and he knew that if he wanted to enter the gates of pearl, now was his last chance.

'I am sorry, God. I will never sin again,' Rin generalized, thinking that to be specific now he risked omitting something he had perhaps forgotten.

Tegné removed the dark, wet cloth from the child's forehead.

The light was blinding. *I am in heaven*, Rin thought as the face of the angel became gradually more clear.

'What are you doing here?' Tegné's voice dragged him back to Earth.

Rin's answer was spontaneous. 'I am following my heart.' Painfully, to give credence to the words, he extended his small right hand. The knuckles were cut and bruised. 'I have punched the tree and found my way,' he declared, before falling limp in a dramatic gesture.

Tegné lifted the child's body in his arms. His eyes searched for shade, and finally rested on an enormous cactus, less than fifty paces away. Its long arms cast shadows in the setting sun. He carried Rin to the cactus, realizing that he would now have to take the boy with him, at least as far as Shuree.

*

Zato and his Warmen camped on the ridge overlooking the Valley. They woke early. From far away, the barely discernible sound of a single horse drifted on the parched wind. Zato stood, looking out to the horizon, searching the scorched earth for the origin of the sound.

'Magniscope, medium power,' he ordered. Quickly the partially extended metal tube was placed in his waiting hand.

Zato lifted the scope to his eye and began a slow scan of the Valley below. The thin line of magnetized mercury in the viewfinder formed an arrow, indicating a speck to the north-west in the upper corner of the lens. Zato adjusted the scope, pulling it to full extension and maximum magnification.

The figure was clear in the lens. The rider was hunched forward in the saddle, the black lacquered body armour dusty and torn. The red Sign of the Claw stood out sharp and certain. The clickety-clack of the trotting hooves came closer and closer.

'Gazan! The Animal!' Zato recognized the hard, uneven face hidden behind a thick black stubble of beard. He watched through the lens as Gazan rode directly below him and entered the low passage which cut through the rock face.

Thirty minutes later, Gazan's exhausted stallion climbed up the last of the rocky trail to their encampment. Zato ran towards him as the injured, sun-blistered Warman began to dismount, then fell from his saddle. His black hair was streaked with yellow, sunburnt patches, his face was puffy and distorted, and the skin below the socket of each eye was blood-raw from over-exposure. White, sticky pus oozed from the torn padded leather of his right shoulder.

Zato knelt beside him and examined the deep, festering wound, then pulled back and stared questioningly into his face. An ugly black bruise ran from his temple, down across his left cheek and broken nose.

'Water . . .' The single word dropped heavily from the split, swollen lips.

Zato grabbed a full, fresh canteen. 'Sit . . . sit,' he said, using his right arm to support the Animal as the injured Warman lost his balance. 'Bring me a blanket,' Zato called, then offered the canteen, taking care that Gazan did not guzzle the water and cause his empty stomach to seize.

'What happened?' Zato asked, staring into the dark, clouded eyes.

Gazan sat motionless, silent. Zato took the blanket and wrapped it round the broad shoulders. Finally Gazan looked up.

'He is coming . . .' The weighty, foreboding words accompanied his sideways stare out over the Valley.

How long have we travelled? Ten days, twenty days? More? Tegné wondered as he began to count his every step, seeing each of them as an individual bead on Yano's abacus, and somehow imagining, as in his early yeons as an uchi-deshi, that when he reached one thousand he would be free.

Time had dissolved, its hours and minutes melting into a burning pool beneath the relentless sun. Still Tegné moved on, the weight of Rin upon his shoulders seeming to double with each new step. Finally, tired and discouraged, he stopped.

'We must find out if you can walk,' Tegné called to his tightly wrapped passenger. Rin's legs straddled Tegné's neck, hanging down over his chest.

'Oss, Sensei, I am ready,' the boy replied, feeling the full guilt of his actions.

Tegné lifted the small body up and over his head, then brought Rin down, placing him lightly on the ground. Rin stood, uncomfortably.

'I am healed, I feel fine,' Rin assured him, despite the sharp pain of his blistered feet through the padded cloth. He took two tentative steps forward and landed in a heap.

'It will take at least another two days,' Tegné said, bending down and hoisting Rin back on to his shoulders. Then, tired and dry, Tegné continued the slow walk across the hard, unforgiving earth.

He walked on through the heat of the day, away from the setting sun.

Twilight in the Valley was strangely beautiful, a glowing half-light of gold and blue. The hazy incandescence lasted hours, shadowing the barren earth with a peculiar tranquillity. Tegné felt his mood lighten as the walking grew easier now that the sun had set. Even his constant thirst had somewhat abated, making their regimen of one litre of water a day seem nearly tolerable. The cactus buds were a nourishing, if somewhat bitter, food, and Tegné bit into one as he walked, passing another to Rin. He was estimating the amount of ground they had covered when he saw footprints. Quickly, he lifted Rin down.

It cannot be, he thought, as he ran towards the single set of prints. Kneeling beside them, his worst suspicions were confirmed: the footprints were his own.

He looked back at the last strains of daylight. 'We have come in a circle.' The words carried the weight of utter futility. Slowly, he looked up at the child.

Rin stood very still, hs eyes wide, frightened, and staring directly behind Tegné.

She stood not more than fifty paces from them. Tegné's hand went instinctively to the hard, knurled silver grip of the dagger. At this moment he was thankful that the boy was with him, if only to confirm that the enormous black cat was real, and not an hallucination.

His eyes linked with the eyes of the Beast. He felt his heart pound as the blood surged to his temples. All his energy converged at the centre point of his forehead. He held back the cry of pain as the first beam of thought penetrated him.

Tegné. His own name flew forward from the red, glowing eyes. Then the second thought formed in his mind; *I have come for you.*

Who are you? he questioned before his lips could form the words.

I am your soul ... she answered, and he felt the shadow of darkness cross his heart. The fatal attraction ... *Come* ... The final rush washed over him as the Cat turned and ran beneath the huge, rising moon.

She led them into the night, the black body, the flowing eyes before them, ever present. And when, finally, near daybreak, Tegné and Rin lay down to sleep, she remained close by, watching over them.

Tegné awoke before the child, called from his dreamless sleep by her compelling presence. He turned towards the rising sun.

She stood with her back to the early light. He faced her and walked slowly forwards, listening to her deep, low breaths as she watched him approach.

How delicate he is, she thought, studying the lines of his clearly defined abdomen and the strong, lean hips. *His hair is like gold,* she observed, as he came within the last three yards.

Touch me . . . touch me . . . she willed. She sensed no fear as he stood beneath her. She lowered her head and Tegné raised his arm, his open hand extended as he touched her, at first tentatively, then growing more sure. The hand was ecstasy as it stroked her, kneading the sleek muscles of her neck. She bent her head towards him, allowing his fingers to rub deep into her shining black fur.

'Sensei! Sensei! Sensei!' The child's scream ripped the still surface of the morning.

Tegné's movement was sharp, abrupt; she felt his moment of fear, of guilt, as he withdrew from her. Rising to her full height, she towered above him. Her heart blazed and her giant mouth pulled tight back, revealing bone-white fangs as they grew wet and glistening.

It was the child who came between us. The child must die! she vowed as she crouched low, preparing to spring.

'No!' Tegné's shout was charged, powerful. 'No!' Again he cried out. He stood squarely before her, the boy behind him. The sun shone on the drawn silver blade.

It had been their moment, and now their moment was gone. She backed away. There was only her sorrow as she turned and leaped into the sky, leaving the man and the boy staring after her, alone in the Valley. Then, in the wake of her disappearance, Tegné and Rin beheld the fading of the morning mist as the eastern rock-face grew clear before them.

*

The heavy iron-mesh net was spread its full four paces square, hovering above the clearing, supported and partially concealed by the leafy branches of the surrounding oak trees.

Zato squatted down, hidden behind the thick tree at the far corner of the net. Gazan, his face wrapped in white cotton bandage and his right arm in a crude sling, knelt beside him. The four other Warmen were in position at opposite corners of the clearing.

The trap had been set for two days, and now, after much faith and patience, the Warmen knew their prey was close. Zato had spotted the man and child through the magniscope, nearly six hours ago. He had watched with fascination as they approached the rock-face, finding and entering the passage which led into Shuree. He had strained to pick out the details of the face, the blue eyes, the golden hair. And now, at any moment, their wait would be over.

Tegné inhaled the clean, cool forest air. A rush of memory overcame him, and he stood still for a moment, letting the memories pass. It had been more than half his lifetime since he had breathed this air and felt the soft brown earth beneath his feet. He watched as Rin moved on ahead.

He could feel the deep fatigue within his own body and now he noticed how thin the boy had become. *As soon as we come to a village I will see that Rin is looked after, and then go on alone,* he resolved as he increased his pace, overtaking the youngster. The trail before them was of fine, broken stone and gravel. Tegné saw the deep hoofmarks.

'Rin!' he called, halting the boy. Rin turned and walked back.

'Sit quietly beside me,' Tegné said, calm but firm, as he knelt above the prints, breathing in, sensing danger. 'I want you to stay well behind me. Keep me in your sight, but no closer,' he continued. Rin looked at his Sensei, fighting the first, dull twinges of fear.

'The men that came for me at the temple – there are others from the same clan. They are close, I can feel it,' he told the boy, looking at him closely to make sure he understood. 'If we should separate, you must follow the path of the rising sun. Travel east,' he continued as he pointed Rin in the right direction, 'There are many villages in the east, one will surely take you in.' Tegné paused, then stood up, 'Now I will go on up the trail, and you follow. But keep plenty of distance between us.'

To ensure that the boy would be safe, Tegné took the medallion from his own neck, Tabata's medallion, and placed it carefully around the neck of the child.

'If ever anyone should ask where you have come from, show them the medallion, tell them of the Temple ... Do you understand?' Rin nodded, doing his best to control his mounting anxiety. 'Do you understand?' Tegné repeated, insistent.

'Oss, Sensei,' Rin replied, his voice quivering.

Tegné smiled at the child, suddenly aware of how it must feel to have a son, an echo of one's own flesh and blood. He leaned forwards and touched the small shoulders, drawing Rin close and embracing him. Then he stood, his facial expression hardening as he turned and began his climb up the steep trail.

The Warlord had awakened before dawn, sensing the strange emptiness in the wide bed. He turned, relieved to see Neeka lying peacefully on her back beside him. Slowly, gently, he reached out to her, letting his fingers rest above her naked shoulder. Then he brought the fingers down upon the ice-cold, waxen flesh.

His heart jolted as he rolled over, coming up on his hands and knees above her closed eyelids. 'Neeka! Neeka!' he called. There was no response, nothing except the mask of death.

No, it is not possible! his mind screamed as he massaged the skin of her arms, working frantically with his fingers, squeezing, pulling, trying to restore warmth to the cold body.

'Neeka, Neeka,' he cried as, at last losing control, he fell forward, gripping her, cradling her, lifting her to him. His tears spilled into her hair and down upon the silk pillowcase.

'No! No! No!' he sobbed.

She watched from above the bed, her astral form hovering, vibrating, ready to re-align with her Earth body and once again occupy its shell. She recognized the irony of the scene below; the old Warlord, weeping with grief over a soulless bit of flesh and bone.

Why do they attach such sentiment to this transient state of physical life? she pondered, listening to his sobs as, finally, he prostrated himself on the bed beside the body. She finished the re-alignment and began her descent, the finely vibrating astral form entering perfectly into the corporeal shell.

She experienced the uncomfortable numbness in her bloodless limbs as she re-adjusted to the limited state. Now she could hear him beside her. She listened to his sobs, as gradually, she regained the feeling in her hands and feet.

Renagi's back was towards her and slowly, painfully, she inched closer to him, her movements light upon the bed. Finally she was behind him.

'Is something troubling my Warlord?' she asked, her voice quiet, nearly teasing.

Renagi was instantly still, his heart missing a single beat. Then he turned to her, the tears dry in his wide, disbelieving eyes.

It was not the danger of death that whispered to him on the warm breeze. A different sort of tension clung to the thick branches and dense foliage of the forest trees.

An ambush, a trap ... His mind relayed the message to his body, warning it to prepare. He deepened his state of zanshin, maintaining a slow, steady pace as he walked towards the clearing.

Zato could see him clearly now. *He is not so big, quite strong-looking, but not big,* he noted randomly as he knelt lower, concealing himself behind the trunk of the oak.

Tegné was at the perimeter of the clearing, The breeze came from the south-west, blowing the smell of the iron net away from him. Still, he felt the danger, knew this was the place of ambush, yet his body movements did not alter. *Do not draw the dagger. Give no indication of preparedness* ...

Two steps. Three steps. Four steps. He heard the snap as the short sword sliced through the taut rope, releasing the net. The dark shadow descended from above as he dived forward, tumbling, landing free of the heavy-meshed iron.

'Take him! Take him!' the rough voice commanded. Tegné heard the *whoosh!* of air and ducked beneath the six-foot bo as, pivoting from a crouch, he rose up and grabbed the smooth wooden pole. He twisted away from the Warman as he executed an ashi-bari, sweeping the man's legs from under him and wrenching the bo from his grasp. The Warman attempted to rise, and

Tegné thrust the tapered end of the fighting-stick into his solar plexus, dropping the man again before pivoting to face his next assailant.

Zato remained at the side of the clearing, studying the Ashkelite as the three Warmen closed. Gazan stood next to him.

'He has been trained with the bo,' Zato observed, watching as Tegné warded off the first vicious, horizontal strike of the twin rods which were connected by a short iron chain. The Warman wielding the nunchaku stepped back from Tegné's block and began swinging the weapon in a whistling figure-of-eight pattern. Tegné stepped forward, within range of the weapon.

He will certainly go down, Zato thought as the Warman suddenly changed to an aggressive motion. Tegné studied the hands which gripped the nunchaku, not the weapon itself. His timing was precise. At the moment the nunchaku began the overhead, downward swing, the striking rod no more than a blur before Zato's eyes, Tegné brought the extended end of the bo sharply upwards. The smooth, hard wood caught the Warman beneath his chin. Tegné stepped into the movement, using the full forward thrust to push the man's head backwards. Then, in a circular swing, he attacked the vulnerable muscles which protected the carotid artery. There was a sharp *whack!* as the bo connected with the Warman's neck, sending the man reeling dizzily to the ground.

Tegné half-turned as the third Warman slipped his calloused fingers into the iron-pronged tekko. He moved back and away as the metal fists began a double circular motion. Tegné remained just outside of striking range as the Warman moved forward, bouncing easily on the balls of his feet. To gain full advantage of the iron fists, Tegné reckoned that the man would attack using a lunging, driving punch. He positioned the bo straight to his right side, parallel to the earth, guarding against a rush from either the front man or the one behind him. For a long moment there was only stillness, and Tegné concentrated his awareness into slow, even exhalations, allowing his body to react by trained instinct. The tension was broken only by a hissing, sucking sound from his far right; the sound of steel being drawn quickly against hard wood and leather.

'Stop! Enough! Enough!' Zato's voice cut the air. 'I said enough!' Zato repeated, and Tegné sensed a break in concentration from the Warman behind. Still he maintained zanshin as, finally, the fighter using the tekko backed cautiously away. Tegné pivoted slowly.

Zato stepped out from behind the oak tree, his short sword unsheathed and pointed at Rin's throat. Gazan stood next to Zato, holding the child secure; his right hand extending from the sling and pressing over Rin's mouth, forcing his head back, while the Animal's huge left arm squeezed the boy's body close to his own. Tegné met the cold, piercing dark eyes which stared from the bandages wrapped around Gazan's head. Then he looked at the smaller, more handsome man.

'You,' Zato said, motioning towards the standing Warman, 'Tie him to the sled.' Without a word, the Warman pushed Tegné roughly to the flat wooden bed which was attached by harness to Zato's stallion.

'Tie him securely,' Zato ordered, as the thick, rough ropes cut into the skin of Tegné's wrists and ankles. Tegné remained silent.

'Blindfold him. Gag him,' Zato continued, sliding the foot long blade back into the lacquered sheath as he walked towards his captive.

The heavy cloth scarf tasted of salt and smelt of sweat as it was drawn tightly across Tegné's mouth and knotted behind his head. Tegné looked up to see Zato above him, and noticed the alarm in the wide eyes as Zato studied the birthmark, now visible on Tegné's bound right wrist.

A tattoo? Surely it is a forgery, but how? Zato wondered, looking furtively at the identical mark on his own wrist. Then his eyes caught the dagger which was buried in the waistband of Tegné's trousers. *I have never seen such a fine blade,* Zato thought as he withdrew the knife, cradling it a moment in his own hand, noting its superb balance. Then he tucked it neatly in the obi which held his katana. He turned to Gazan.

'Release the child. We have no use for him.'

Gazan hesitated, a question in his eyes.

'I said let him go!' Zato repeated, his voice sharp and clipped.

Reluctantly, the Animal released his grip. Rin remained still for a moment, then slowly began to rotate his head, trying to ease the stiffness and pain caused by the powerful lock. From the corner of his eye he could see Tegné, tied and helpless. He turned towards the sled, his mind racing desperately.

'Go on! Get out of here!' Zato snapped.

I will help, or die trying, Rin promised himself an instant before he began his sprint towards the sled.

The boy's sudden movement was all that Gazan needed. Quickly, he stooped and grabbed the pistol-bow from the small pile of field supplies. He pressed the alloy frame against his body, cocking the mechanism while, with his free hand, he engaged the bolt. In a continuous motion he aimed and fired.

The short, deadly bolt flew forward, entering the child's leg, burying itself in the muscle behind his thigh, just below the left hip. Rin sprawled on to the ground. The pain was white-hot, searing.

'No!' Zato screamed, moving angrily towards Gazan, as the bandaged Warman began to load a second steel bolt into the hand-held pistol-bow.

Tegné could see nothing through the dark cloth, yet from the sound of commotion, from the voices, he knew that Rin had been injured. He strained, cutting his wrists on the rope, choking on the gag as he tried to free himself.

'That was not necessary,' Zato spat the words at Gazan, snatching the weapon from his hand. 'Mount up! Do not make another mistake, or so help me . . .' he added, leaving the threat open.

There was the hint of challenge, an unmistakable insolence, in the dark slits behind the bandages. Reluctantly, Gazan obeyed his superior.

Zato bent over the child. The bolt was lodged in the thick of the hamstring muscle. It was a clean entry, and the spring-loaded war-tip had not opened. Rin lay still on the ground, whimpering softly.

Quickly, with assurance, Zato pressed his open left palm against the injured thigh; he positioned the bolt in the space between his thumb and first finger. Rin held back the scream as Zato gripped the four inches of extended steel and pulled it free from the leg with a single motion.

'Give me some alcohol, rope, bandages,' he ordered.

Within five minutes, the wound was clean and bound, the rope used as a tourniquet, tied high up on the thigh to diminish the flow of blood from the heart. Then, gently, Zato lifted the child's thin body, cradling him in his arms.

'What are we going to do with him?' asked one of the mounted Warmen.

'Take him as far as Asha-1; we will leave him there,' Zato replied, carrying Rin towards the horses.

'Asha-1?' came the question.

'Asha-1,' Zato confirmed.

The tiny, windowless cottages stood in the baking sun. It was midday, and the Ashkelites had, as usual, returned from the fields to take shelter from the ultra rays.

Zato raised his arm, halting the Warmen. He looked back at the sled; Tegné was cut and bruised from the constant contact with the rough ground, his golden hair filthy, matted. Zato studied him for a long moment, willing himself to despise this man who had caused Renagi such pain. Yet the doubt rose again within his heart, and he turned his head away. *Why? Why do I feel such an affinity with this prisoner?* He straightened in his saddle, looking ahead through the north gate of Asha-1. *Perhaps I can answer my question here,* he hoped, riding through the gates, for he knew the welfare of the child was only a small reason for this journey.

Inside the gates the single dirt road widened, leading towards the two uniform lines of thatched cottages. The six horses moved at a slow walk, now only a short distance from the first dwelling.

Not a sound . . . a village of ghosts! Zato observed as he pulled gently on his stallion's reins. Dismounting, he looked at the boy. Rin was seated in front of the nearest Warman. Zato walked closer, stopping to examine the bandaged leg. For the first few hours of the journey they had been forced to a near standstill by the necessity of loosening the tourniquet every fifteen minutes, allowing the blood to flow freely through the child's leg. The blood had finally stopped pumping from the wound and the bandages were changed and fixed more permanently. Now, four days later, the leg was bruised and mildly swollen. *Gangrene?* Zato wondered as he pressed gently on the swelling below the cotton wrapping. Rin winced, but did not cry out.

'Lift him down,' Zato ordered. The attending Warman climbed down from his horse, turned, and took the child in his arms.

As Rin was carried past the sled, he stared at Tegné. He saw the bloodied wrists and ankles, the torn, filthy robes and dark bruises which rose from behind his Sensei's shoulders and wound around his neck.

The child turned to Zato. 'Why? Why are you doing this?' he pleaded. Zato ignored him, looking instead at the Warmen.

'You men wait here. I will take the boy into the village,' he said, transferring Rin into his own arms, then turning to walk the final stretch into Asha-1.

Zato stopped in front of the first cottage, placed Rin on his feet and knocked at the thin wooden door.

The look of shock and surprise in Rawlin's pink eyes lasted only as long as the eyes took to focus on the red Sign of the Claw. Then the look changed to one of terror.

Zato watched the thin, barefooted man back away from the incoming sun. The fear remained in his eyes as he stood in the shadows of the hut. Zato supported Rin as he guided the boy inside.

'He is injured. We will leave him with you.' Zato spoke as he saw the two pale children and their frightened mother peer round from behind the curtain which divided the single room into eating and sleeping quarters. 'I want you to see that his wound heals. Give him food, rest, and in return you may employ him in the fields when he has recovered,' Zato said, an edge of authority in his voice. 'Here, take him,' he commanded, pushing Rin towards him.

'Yes. Of course,' Rawlin responded, stepping forward while motioning for his wife to attend to Rin.

'And there is another matter with which you may help me,' Zato said, looking sharply at the Ashkelite.

'Yes, Master, anything you ask,' was the instant reply.

'I suppose you have heard the rumours, which I believe are lies, regarding an Ashkelite sired by the Warlord?' Zato asked, a forced bitterness in his tone.

'Yes, I have. The story is many, many yeons old,' answered Rawlin.

'And what was the name of the woman who had this supposed union with . . .' Zato hesitated, '. . . my father?'

The disclosure came as no surprise to Rawlin. He had immediately recognized Zato, for Zato was the leader of the Procession. 'Her name, Master, was Maliseet,' he answered.

'And am I correct in saying that Maliseet's mother is still alive and living in this village?' Zato pressed, yet the threat had dissipated from his voice.

'You are. But I fear she will be of no assistance. She has hardly spoken a word for over thirty yeons,' Rawlin answered, relaxing as he spoke, sensing, somehow, that the man before him meant no harm.

'I want to see her,' Zato said simply.

'Now?' asked Rawlin.

'I am going to bring someone with me. I would rather we did not draw any attention. It should take no more than a few minutes to bring him here, then you can take us to the woman.' Zato stopped, looking into the pink eyes.

'Certainly, Master,' Rawlin answered, meeting Zato's gaze.

'A few minutes,' Zato repeated, then turned and walked from the hut.

The blood rushed into his hands as the first ropes were cut. Then Tegné was pulled roughly from his reclining, head-downward position on the sled. He breathed a long, deep breath, letting the oxygen revive him. The scarf was ripped from his face.

A blast of bright sunlight blinded him and he lowered his head, shutting his eyes, and opened them again, squinting as the pupils contracted, adjusting to the light. His first clear image was the birthmark on the wrist of the man who stood before him.

Brother? The question crossed Tegné's mind as his eyes traced the mark up the bronzed, sinewy arm and looked into Zato's face. He believed, for an instant, that he saw the same question in Zato's deep brown eyes. Then the eyes hardened.

'The boy is all right,' Zato said, 'And to ensure his safety I advise you to co-operate.'

Tegné nodded in silent agreement.

Two Warmen flanked Tegné and pushed him along while the short rope which bound his legs together forced him to shuffle behind Zato. Tegné guessed where they were; he had read of these tiny, enclosed slave villages. And now, looking down the dirt road, the sight of the small but immaculately kept thatched cottages filled him with a strange sadness.

Could it be true? Could I have come from such a place? Tegné wondered as he stumbled towards the door. His eyes widened as he saw Rawlin standing, waiting, inside the hut. It was the near-translucence of Rawlin's skin that astounded him; he stared a moment at the fine paths of veins beneath the white epidermis.

Like a leaf, like a pale forest leaf, he thought as Rawlin walked up to him.

The Ashkelite stood a full hand below Tegné in height, perhaps five feet six or seven. His face was finely boned, as were his long, narrow hands and feet. His shoulders, visible beneath the cotton tunic, reminded Tegné of the shoulders of a young, fragile woman. There was, somehow, a frail beauty to this man, yet a dignity in the high, wise forehead, and a resigned strength to the square, clean-boned jaw and pale, wide lips. Tegné looked into the liquid pink eyes.

'The boy will be safe. He is with my wife and children,' Rawlin said as he turned and pointed towards the thin cotton screen which separated the room. 'We have given him the bed.'

'Thank you,' Tegné replied. It was as if he and the Ashkelite were alone in the room, so strong was the link between them. Rawlin seemed completely unaware of Tegné's bindings and even of the three Warmen guarding him.

Zato studied the interaction; he was quietly amazed at the ease between the two men.

'Do you recognize him, do you know who he is?' Zato asked, looking hard at Rawlin.

'I see that he is your captive, but no, I do not know him, Master,' Rawlin replied.

'He is the one who claims to be the Warlord's son,' Zato stated. 'He is the Ashkelite.'

'Master, I beg your forgiveness, but this man is not Ashkelite. No Ashkelite has such skin or such eyes,' Rawlin said, looking straight into Tegné's face.

'Then you will guide us to the house of the woman ... the woman we spoke of,' Zato ordered.

'Of course, Master,' replied Rawlin, then turned and took his blankers up from the rough wooden table.

'First get me a large bucket of water,' Zato demanded.

Rawlin moved quickly to the stone work-top and grabbed the metal pot containing the family's cooking water.

'Outside,' Zato ordered. The entire group, including Rawlin, assembled in the sun outside the cottage. 'Now, a cloth, I want a large cloth,' Zato said.

'Marin! Bring us a sheet from the bed!' Rawlin called.

Within seconds, the thin, pale arm handed a sheet from the door of the cottage.

'Pour the water on his head,' Zato commanded, looking at Rawlin.

'Master?' queried the Ashkelite, unsure of the command.

'On top of his head!' repeated Zato.

Rawlin lifted the huge pot and let the water spill down, soaking Tegné's hair and running down over his body.

'Now clean him with the cloth,' Zato ordered.

Rawlin rubbed Tegné's hair vigorously, scrubbed him, removing the dust and dirt from his skin. Tegné's hair grew golden-white as the hot sun completed the process of drying. Finally Rawlin began rubbing Tegné's right wrist. Slowly, the caked dirt dissolved, revealing the birthmark.

God, he is the one, it is true, it is true . . . Rawlin's mind reeled, his heart bursting inside his chest. Still, he revealed nothing as he looked up at Zato.

'Fine. Now let us go to the woman,' Zato said, studying Rawlin, searching for his answer.

Raine's cottage was at the far end of Asha-1, one of the last dwellings on the right side along the road. The walk through the village was slow, and several of the thin doors opened slightly as the occupants peered out to see the strange group pass by. Finally they stood in front of the hut.

It was a building not dissimilar to the others, unusual only in that the thatch of the roof was in need of repair and the wooden door was old and dry.

'Raine! Raine!'

It was Rawlin's voice she heard through the door. *But why does he call for me now?* she wondered as she made her way from the bench beside the ventilation shaft to the door.

'Raine, please open the door,' the voice called, a certain urgency in the tone.

She drew the locking bolt sideways and pulled the door open, standing well back to keep the sun from her eyes. Brusquely, the men entered the room, closing the door behind them. Raine breathed in sharply as she saw the black lacquered leather and the Red Sign of the Claw. Only once before had anyone wearing that sign crossed her threshold. *Now what do they want of me?* she despaired, keeping her face lowered towards the floor.

'Look up!' Zato snapped.

Raine kept her face averted, willing them to go, to leave her alone.

'Is she deaf as well as mute?' Zato asked.

'She is frightened, Master,' Rawlin responded, then walked to Raine and touched her gently on the shoulder.

'Raine, it is important that you see the man who stands before you. It is important for all of us in Ashkelan.'

'That's enough!' Zato cut him off, wanting to give away no hint of his suspicions.

Slowly, her eyes closed, Raine raised her head.

A flood of emotion filled Tegné as he looked upon the tiny woman. She was painfully white, and the single, pale layer of skin stretched like a dried membrane across the fragile bones of her tired face. Her colourless hair had grown thin, and hung in fine, single strands from the soft, ashen scalp. There was a drained, beaten look in the eyes as they gradually opened.

The pupils dilated rapidly, causing them to flicker as if they were afloat on a clear pond of water, unanchored. She squinted as she struggled to focus on the vision before her.

Akid, my husband! Have you returned from the fields? Raine wondered, her mind awash, past and present blurred as one reality. Through the haze of her vision she could see the golden hair, like a bright aura surrounding the strong, square jaw and high, defined cheekbones. She walked nearer to him, her frail, stick-like arms extended. Involuntarily, Zato moved backwards, repelled by this feeble, emaciated slave woman.

Tegné bent to her, allowing her outstretched fingers to trace the lines and structure of his face. He felt his own tears begin, and he steeled himself, preventing the moment from overcoming him.

She could see him now, the deep blue eyes, the lightly bronzed skin. *No, it is not Akid. But I know him. I know him,* she thought as the silent, inviolable wall began to crumble. For, glowing through the blue of the eyes, she recognized the spirit of her beloved Maliseet; she felt her child's soul reach out to her. It was a memory that she had kindled, nurtured with her own silence and finally locked away forever. Now the memory was alive before her.

The word began slowly, as if it was forming for the first time from the lips of an infant. 'Ma ... Mal ... Maliseet,' Raine cried, her body going limp, the legs giving way beneath her as a lifetime's sorrow began its warm, cleansing embrace. Tegné knelt beside her, touching her gently with his bound hands.

Zato stared, awkward, uneasy, wanting to avert his eyes. Yet something compelled him to witness this open, unashamed emotion, Something within him was touched, made aware; a deep, closeted yearning. He thought of his own mother, Natiro. He could not remember ever having held her, touched her. *It was not the way of the Zendai*, he told himself as he moved closer to them.

'Cut the bindings on his wrists,' he whispered to the Warman.

'But Master, he . . .'

'Do it,' Zato hissed, leaving no room for argument. A fast, downward cut freed Tegné's wrists.

Now he cradled Raine in his arms, rocking her gently, allowing her tears to run on to his cheeks and down his face. Still he held back the waves of his own emotion, yet through the tears of his mother's mother he found peace. Finally he rose, helping Raine to rise with him, holding her within his soft gaze.

'Your name?' Her voice was a quiet whisper.

'Tegné,' he answered.

A faint, proud smile parted her lips. 'Tegné,' she repeated, reaching up and lightly touching his cheek. He took her hand, held it for a moment, then turned, looking at Zato.

'I am ready,' he said simply.

'Cut his ankle binding,' Zato ordered the Warman. This time the order was obeyed without question. Raine watched from her hut as Tegné, surrounded by Zato, Rawlin and the Warmen, walked slowly up the dirt road of Asha-1 to the waiting horses. It was late afternoon and the work parties were emerging from the shelter of their cottages.

These are my people, my people ... The thought repeated over and over in Tegné's mind as he looked upon the tired, undernourished bodies and into the docile but inquisitive faces, their eyes hidden behind the small, circular lenses of the blankers.

Was it conclusive? Was an old woman's breaking heart the proof of legitimacy? Is the birthmark real, or some finely crafted counterfeit?

And if it is true, if Tegné is indeed my half-brother, the product of an illicit union between my father and an untouchable, what will become of my family? The questions burned in Zato's mind as they rode through the outskirts of Zendow.

They had dispensed with the sled and tied their prisoner to the rear of the youngest Warman's horse. Tegné's wrists were bound in front of him, and his head concealed by a sack cut into a crude hood. Zato looked back quickly.

Gazan rode behind him, his face bandages dark with grime and perspiration. Zato was well aware of the Animal's wishes. He let his eyes rest only a moment on Tegné. *Maybe I should let Gazan kill him and be done with it,* he thought. Then Zato recalled his father's firm orders. *But why? Why keep him alive? Why bring him into Zendow? Why take such an enormous risk?*

'Because it is your duty as Warlord. To yourself, your family. Expose him. Truth is power,' Neeka concluded, having had this conversation innumerable times with the Warlord.

Yes, and if only she knew the truth, Renagi thought, looking into the eyes behind the golden openings of the ninjinka. *Or perhaps she does,* he speculated, studying her veiled face. She had been somehow estranged from him since that morning he had supposed her dead. It was a subtle change, a pulling away, and the pulling away only caused him to become more desperate, more grasping of her affection. He sensed her awareness of this, felt her quiet manipulation, yet he was powerless to oppose her. For now, more than ever, he knew he would be lost without Neeka.

They sat in silence at the small chestnut table in the private dining-room. The heavy crystal decanter of Miramese claret stood full and untouched between them.

The meal had been meticulously prepared; the carcass of the young roebuck had been properly rubbed with the mixture of flour and pepper and hung in the dry, cool food cellars for four days, then the fine meat had been marinated for three weeks. Finally, the Zenchef had taken the loin and roasted it gently on the spit as he cut the meat into wafer-thin slices. And now the beautiful dinner, with its steaming bowl of boiled yellow beans and jellied redcurrants sat cooling, uneaten, on the fine porcelain plates before them.

*

Zato entered Zendow through the small concealed passage, wide enough only to ride the horses in single file. The group emerged from the torchlit tunnel and rode into the tiny rear courtyard beneath the high stone walls of the fortress.

The gate-guard recognized the Warmen instantly and issued no challenge. Instead, the iron-slatted door leading to the recesses of Zendow opened before them. They rode beneath the spiked slats and entered a square stone enclosure. In each of the four walls was a large, wooden door.

Zato raised his hand and give the order to dismount. The heavy sound of feet hitting stone echoed in the high, ceilingless square like a solitary clap of thunder. Only Tegné remained alone on the stallion. Gazan moved towards him.

'I will do it,' Zato said, moving quickly between Tegné and the Animal. Then, turning, he pulled Tegné from the horse, allowing him to land roughly on the hard floor. Zato squatted down and re-tied the rope binding Tegné's ankles. Then, rising, he looked from face to face.

'I know each one of you,' he said, hesitating as he stared into Gazan's dark eyes, 'And I am ordering your absolute silence. Should I hear anything regarding our captive, anything at all, I promise that I shall find out which one of you has spoken and I shall have the tongue burned from his mouth. Am I understood?'

Each man nodded a solemn 'yes' as Zato maintained his fixed gaze.

'Gazan,' Zato said, addressing the Animal.

Gazan straightened. 'Oss.'

'You and I will take him to the cells ... and you ...' he said, turning to the remaining Warmen, addressing them as a single entity, '... use the inner tunnel, take the horses to the stables.' *I will show no feeling, no concern for this man,* Zato promised himself as, roughly, he shoved Tegné towards the wooden door. *Give away nothing; no fear, no emotion,* he vowed, looking at Gazan and motioning with his head for the Animal to follow. They walked close together as Zato pushed Tegné forward. *Then why can I feel no hatred for him?* he questioned, in spite of his efforts to silence his doubts.

'Hold him,' Zato ordered as he pounded three times on the steel-reinforced door.

Gazan gripped hard, employing a pinching finger-vice to squeeze the narrow trapezius muscle which joined Tegné's head and shoulders. Gazan found no difficulty in unlocking the vast reserves of hatred for this prisoner as he used every ounce of his massive strength in trapping the sensitive nerves of Tegné's shoulder.

Tegné fought against the pain, prayed the door would open. Again Zato's palm slammed against the dense wood. One, two, three times. Tegné breathed in as Gazan dug deep into the soft muscle tissue. He could spin, use his leverage and body weight to attack, yet he knew he must not. He knew that a struggle, a violent reaction, could result in his death, and death, now, would be selfish. His purpose lay within these walls.

'Come on, come on!' Zato muttered beneath his breath. Bang! Bang! Bang! His gloved hand beat against the door.

Tegné's eyes began to water and a fine line of perspiration broke on his brow, gathered and ran down his face. The pain was concentrated, intense, like a hot burning fork driving inwards where the Animal's thumb wrapped round and under the muscle fibre. He felt his body give way as the pain began to generalize, filling every limb, every space.

'What are you doing? Get away from him! Away!' Zato's shout broke through the red haze. At last the Animal released him, leaving his right arm and shoulder paralysed. Zato's strong hands lifted him from behind, guiding him through the open door and into the darkness as Tegné's gasping, hollow breaths caused the heavy cotton material of the hood to fill his mouth, nearly choking him. He smelt the mildew and felt the cold damp as, gradually, he regulated his breathing, and his legs moved, carrying him forward.

He was vaguely aware of the hollow eyes staring from the bars to the left and right of him as he moved awkwardly down the dimly lit passage. A single torch burned on the wall in front of him.

'Only six in this one, Master,' the gaoler's dry laugh accompanied his words and cracked though the morbid silence. Tegné heard the jingling of the key-ring, then the sound of the single key entering the old, worn lock. An empty, hopeless sickness filled the pit of his stomach as the hands pushed him forward. He stumbled across the hard, bony limbs of a prisoner lying silently in the dark and landed on the wet, thick straw which covered the floor. The cell reeked of urine and excrement. Tegné pulled himself forward, reaching the wall, and in the darkness struck his head on the fixed wooden bench.

'He will be safe in there . . .' The same voice, the same cackling laugh, then the sound of the iron key turning in the lock. Tegné crawled up on to the bench and finally, mercifully, felt the blackness wrap round and protect him.

Zato found his father standing alone, high on top of the eastern ramparts of Zendow. He mounted the steep brick steps quietly, unobserved by Renagi. He remained silent, studying the profile of the Warlord. Renagi's face had fallen with time, and the eyes had become narrow slits beneath the slightly protruding forehead. The nose was long, the bridge straight and close in to the cheekbones. Renagi's lips were tight, and reminded Zato of a desperate, clenched fist, as the Warlord stared out, over the tree-tops and into the distant sky. Zato took two steps forward and Renagi spun, his right hand already beginning to draw the katana. Zato held up his hands in mock surrender.

'Zato, Zato my son! When did you come back?' Renagi's voice was gruff, strained, yet filled with the relief of seeing his son alive and well.

'One hour ago,' Zato answered.

'And no one alerted me? That is not possible,' Renagi protested.

'We came through the eastern tunnel, straight in through the cells,' he explained, walking closer to his father.

'Through the cells?' Renagi was quick to grasp the implication.

'We found him in Shuree. There was no need to enter the Valley,' Zato said flatly.

'Tegné? You have Tegné?' Renagi stuttered, fear and relief waging a battle within his voice.

'Yes. He is below. No one saw us enter and my Warmen are sworn to secrecy,' Zato replied.

Renagi grasped his son by both shoulders, hugging him, genuinely moved by his success. Then he stepped away from Zato, holding him firmly at arm's length. His voice became hushed, conspiratorial. 'Take me to him.'

Zato looked closely at his father, measuring his own silence before he spoke.

'I took him into Asha-1,' he said with a slight taste of bitterness.

The words cut into Renagi, straightening him, moving him backwards. 'You did what?' His voice was near rage, sensing betrayal.

Zato grasped the moment, aware of his father's weakness. 'Is it true? Is he your son?'

Renagi did not answer. His eyes raged and for a tortured moment Zato believed his father would draw his katana and lash out at him. Then Renagi grew calm and, finally, he spoke.

'Think very hard and carefully, my son. Try not to allow the self-righteousness of youth to destroy us both.' His voice had somehow mellowed, and the hardness in his eyes vanished. 'Look around you,' Renagi continued, using both arms in a grand gesture to encompass all of Zendow. 'Now, look out there. Vokane ... Shuree ... Ashkelan ... Miramar, Yusun, the Valley beyond. I am Warlord of all this, and you ...' he hesitated, moving closer to Zato, '... you are my successor.'

Zato knew exactly where his father was leading and he well understood the logic. 'Is he your son?' he repeated, his voice soft and low.

Renagi faced him, looking directly into his eyes. 'He cannot be my son.'

Tegné lay on the hard wooden bench. He had entered the first level of waking sleep, his eyes closed, his mind drifting, yet his consciousness was in control of his deep, even breathing. The presence had been close to him for at least ten minutes, and now he listened as the stealthy, shuffling footsteps drew near. He opened his eyes.

The huge, domed head loomed above him while the single torch in the adjacent passage created a flickering back-light. Tegné could barely make out the distorted features of the face as one eye stared down at him. The other appeared to be stitched crudely in its socket. A heavy brass earring hung from the extended lobe of the right ear, while the left was torn and severed at the middle. The toothless mouth parted in a demented grin as the hulking prisoner bent over the bench.

Tegné remained motionless, acutely aware of the bindings on his ankles and wrists, the cumbersome canvas hood, and the nearly incapacitating pain in his right shoulder. The face was now less than an arm's length from his own and he could smell the sickly, rotting breath. The single open eye studied him as the damp fingers traced a pattern across his chest through the open robes. The nausea began in his stomach as the fat, open palm rubbed his exposed nipple with a slow, circular motion. All the time, the grotesque single eye monitored his reaction, as the prisoner's breathing grew heavy with excitement.

Slowly, surely, Tegné brought his bound wrists up, pressing them against the caressing hand and prohibiting its movement. An annoyed grunt came from the toothless mouth as the powerful hand pushed Tegné's wrist away, and again began the circular rubbing pattern. Tegné pulled back on the bench, bringing his arms once more to bear against the hand.

'No . . .' Tegné said, as if he were speaking to a disobedient animal.

'No . . .' the deep voice mimicked. 'No?' Again the deep voice repeated the word, and now the single open hand encompassed both of Tegné's hands. Gripping strongly, the giant pulled Tegné to his feet. Tegné did not resist as he was dragged awkwardly across the cell. He could see the wretched, crawling prisoners pulling themselves through the fouled straw to burrow safely against the walls, their flashing eyes caught in the half-light like the eyes of hunted beasts.

Tegné began to withdraw his hands from the tightening grip, twisting his wrists away from the clenching fingers. The grip increased, and the pressure against his knuckles became painful. He relaxed, apparently giving way to the force. In reaction, the toothless mouth hissed as it formed a conquering smile, then the grip eased slightly as though to test his victim's submission.

Tegné used the moment to roll away, freeing himself. Midway through the counter-clockwise roll the two thick arms encircled him, pulling him close to the bare chest and lifting him upwards. He felt the other man's hard excitement through the filthy, ragged cotton trousers. Now he was head-high with his tormentor, the chugging breath hot on his exposed neck beneath the hood and the powerful arms crushing the air from his body. He leaned back within the grip, extending his neck, twisting his head to the right. He saw the brass earring, alive with the light of the flickering torch. He bit hard into the earlobe, above the ring.

The scream erupted from the head beside him, it was a scream as much of surprise as of pain. Now Tegné contracted his abdomen, lifting his legs, throwing them hard at the ceiling, allowing the binding on his wrists to catch beneath the grizzled chin and break his momentum. His body curled backwards and down, the binding held firm by the massive neck as Tegné forced his knees into the lower back of the hulk and pulled. The sound of gurgling, of choking, came before the body went limp.

Tegné rode the man to the straw floor, exerting more and more pressure against the throat.

'What goes on there?' The shout came from outside the bars. Then a second voice, deep and bellowing, 'Open the cell! Now!'

Tegné relaxed the stranglehold, disengaging his bound wrists before jumping back and away from the unconscious man.

'Go in. Get him out.' Again the deep, grainy voice. Tegné looked through the iron bars and saw the gaoler searching nervously through the large, jangling ring of keys. Zato stood behind the gaoler, and next to him was another, bull-like man. Finally the gaoler found the key and opened the lock, then shuffled swiftly into the cell.

'Come along, come along,' his nervous voice urged as his bony fingers took hold of Tegné's arm. The hood had come up during the struggle and the bottom half was bunched tight beneath Tegné's nose, causing him to regain his breath by gulping the dank air through his mouth. The gnarled hands pushed him through the cell door. It clanged shut behind them, leaving the rat-like inmates in a crawling circle, surrounding the barely conscious hulk as he lay silent, face down, upon the floor.

'Bring him to the interrogation chamber,' the deep voice rasped.

The interrogation chamber was a high, square stone room, not large enough to lie down in and barely wide enough for Tegné, Zato and the Warlord to stand. The two faced Tegné, who stood with his back pressed hard against the cold wall.

'Leave us,' Renagi ordered the gaoler, noticing the man lingering curiously outside the iron-grilled doorway. The man spun and hobbled rapidly down the dark corridor.

Renagi moved close to the hooded figure, staring, silent. He looked hard into the blue eyes, then stepped back as far as the narrow chamber would allow.

'Do you know who I am?' he asked, venomously.

Tegné remained quiet for a space, amazed at the facial resemblance between the two men before him. Finally he replied, 'You are Renagi, Warlord of Zendow.'

'Yes.' Renagi's voice was flat.

'And . . . you are my father.' Tegné barely finished the sentence when he saw the tightening of the Warlord's right shoulder. The movement began with the sucking *whoosh!* of steel against raw, untreated wood. The blade whipped past his left eye in the downward cut, then continued in a single, flowing motion, and was returned to the scabbard. Tegné stood, the crude hood sliced cleanly in half, his face bare before them.

'Pull the hood from him.' Renagi ordered.

Zato reached out and threw the cloth to the floor.

'Now cut the ropes from his wrists.'

Zato moved forward with his short sword. 'He is marked, I have seen it,' he said as he severed the thick bindings.

Renagi grabbed at the freed right wrist, pulling it to him, running his rough fingers over it, examining.

The birthmark was deep blue and its shape resembled the front leg and foreclaw of a wild mountain cat, the leg running several inches down the natural line of the wrist. At the lower end, where the mark joined and lay upon the back of the hand, it opened outwards, stretching into what appeared to be four jagged claws.

Renagi stared at the mark, rage and fear building inside his silence. Finally he released the wrist, stepping back against the iron door. Zato studied his father's movement; he saw the moment of indecision as Tegné remained impassive before them.

Truth is power, Renagi thought as he looked up into the blue eyes. *And it will be his power, not mine,* he reasoned as his right hand twitched nervously. *Do it now, finish it,* his mind willed as his fingers moved towards the hilt of the katana.

Tegné saw the hand move sideways across the wide leather belt. His wrists were free, the cell was tiny; he could attack, perhaps kill both Renagi and Zato. Now the hand rested on the hilt of the katana; the filigree of gold and silver sparkled through the braided binding. *Another breath,* Tegné thought, centring himself. *First the Warlord, then his son,* he resolved as he focused on Renagi's middle chest. The hand tightened on the sword.

Now, now! Tegné's instinct for survival screamed, urging him to attack. Yet a stronger, more dominant intelligence held him back, forbidding the first movement.

Kill him, be done with it. Then it will be over, Zato thought, relieved somehow to see the first inch of steel as the blade began its ascent.

'Renagi!' Neeka's scream came from directly behind the Warlord. The hand froze, leaving only the slight glimmer of the exposed blade. 'What are you doing?' Her voice punished, the tone seeming more appropriate to an exchange between a mother and a disorderly child. Then the golden-masked face appeared through the grille of the iron door.

'How did you know we were here?' Renagi growled, never taking his eyes from Tegné.

'Do not be naive, the men are already talking. Soon it will be all over Zendow,' she answered.

Renagi swung his gaze towards Zato, who moved away, his back pressed against the wall. 'That is impossible, the Warmen were sworn to silence,' he said, although the doubt was there, below the surface of his voice.

'And you actually thought that no one would see you enter Zendow, not one person in all of Vokane would notice your masked prisoner?' Neeka asked, a gentle mockery in her tone.

The voice, the eyes behind the ninjinka, the soft demeanour of the woman – it was as if Tegné was being summoned by the echoes of some forgotten dream. *The blade, the blade* . . . For the first time since his capture he remembered the shining silver. The blade was his connection and, the blade had been taken from him.

'Please, my lord, allow me to speak to you privately,' Neeka said, changing her tack, sweetening.

The Warlord looked into the emerald eyes, then at Zato. Finally, his face set firm in resignation, he nodded, 'Yes.'

'Gaoler! Gaoler! Let us out of here!' Zato called through the grille.

Tegné was alone in the tiny interrogation cell. Aside from the far-away flicker of the single wall-torch there was only darkness. He sat in the centre of the square stone floor, noting how like a meditation chamber the cell was.

Your true spirit cannot become manifest while you are in a state of turmoil. He remembered Goswami's teaching as he breathed in the dark, cold air, quieting his mind. The bitter, astringent taste of adrenaline still clung to the roof of his mouth as he assumed the full lotus position and began the long, suspended, low abdominal breathing. He listened to the inner sound of his heart and allowed all thoughts which entered his mind to drift gently away without examination. He was mildly aware of the soreness beneath his trapezius muscle, a result of Gazan's thumb, but he did not move or adjust his position. Soon all distraction vanished and he was totally passive, receptive to the powerful flow of energy within him. He breathed a long, full breath, allowing the vital ions to move and circulate.

I am a wave; make me the sea . . . his mind repeated the beginning mantra. Soon he was in the alpha state and flying forward above the smooth glass-like surface of his consciousness. Automatically his breathing rate increased, taking his body temperature higher. The perspiration flushed the impurities from him as the electric serpent began its undulation, uncoiling, rising up from his sacrum, taking him into the Dragon Zone.

Red heat, mist . . . *a black form rising. Emerald eyes* . . . *Four suns. A mirrored lake. Ivory men. A silver blade. Her face. The raven-girl. 'Love me, Love me* . . .' *The frenzied roar, overpowering, consuming. Flesh. Blood* . . . The sounds and images converged. His breathing became shallow, rapid, chugging as the intensity of the vision multiplied, increasing the pressure at the point between his eyebrows until he entered super-consciousness.

Then . . . Crack! The sound of bones breaking, muscle tearing, and he was free, his projected self tasting the sweet honeysuckle nectar and soaring without constraint. He looked down, saw the sprawling stone fortress below him. The fine, needle-thin, shining silver thread unfurled; his sole connection to the Earth plane. For a moment he floated, then he lifted up and into the spiral.

Tabata sat smiling, basking in the single ray of sun. His skin possessed a golden inner light, his hair spread outwards. Swirling colours of yellow, blue and green emanated from each strand.

His robes were of the purest, whitest silk and his face had grown young.

Tegné wept at the feet of his master; his tears were the dust of diamonds, shimmering, alive, tiny prisms of supreme colour.

'*You know and yet you cannot remember . . .*' Tabata's voice was a song, rhythmic and lyrical. '*You remember and yet you cannot awaken. I call to you, the Protectors call to you, yet she draws you to her, the Beast who hides behind the veil of maya.*'

The voice came from behind him, caressing him, tantalizing. '*Love me . . . love me . . .*' Tegné clung to his vision of Tabata, holding the contact, sure that if he allowed himself to succumb to the gentle, drifting voice he would be lost. '*Dream my dreams. Dream. Dream . . .*' The words washed over him, gentle and soothing. '*We are one,*' she continued, lapping against his consciousness like a quiet wave. So easy to listen to, the words like music, so easy to let go, give up all resistance . . . So easy.

'*She is the daughter of the Beast. The Devil Cat. You are the Warrior. It is your duty to break through this wall of illusion. Tear away the veil!*' Tabata's voice resounded, commanding him.

'*I am yours . . .*' the silken voice continued, seemingly aware of Tabata's words and countering their logic. Tegné felt her strong presence. If he turned from Tabata, broke the contact, he knew he would find her waiting. The struggle would be over. The temptation manifested itself in a deep suffering within him. He wanted to turn towards her, if only to see her once more.

He heard the sharp snap as he experienced the tug against his seika-tanden, pulling him down and away. He watched the brown eyes become distant as the face of his Sensei grew smaller.

'*Look at me; I am yours . . .*' She beckoned, tempting him, torturing him. Still he held back, maintaining his vision of Tabata as his etheric body was drawn down, through the dense slate roof and again into the tiny stone cell of Zendow. He felt the deep, throbbing pain in the centre of his Earth heart, burning within the anahata, and he realized his true test was beginning.

Renagi sat on the carved single-seated chair, his back to the room, his eyes gazing out, up into the night. He studied the solitary star which hung in the northern sky below the moon.

Behind him, on the side table, a single lighted candle burned beneath a suspended brass cup. The sweet scent of lemon permeated the air as the aromatic oil warmed above the candle.

Silently, on bare feet, she walked across the room to the Warlord. She watched his naked shoulders rise as he inhaled, then lower as he exhaled a deep, pensive breath. Now she stood above him, dipping the fingers of her right hand into the heavy, warm oil. Lightly she drew her fingers across the line of his shoulders and slowly up to the back of his neck. She repeated the exact movement with her left hand, first anointing the fingers, then barely touching the skin; she ran her hand across from the opposite side.

Renagi sighed, relaxing beneath the fingers as she increased the pressure and began a deep, penetrating massage. Rhythmically she stroked his neck, repeatedly dipping her fingers into the brass cup and applying the oil. She could feel his anxiety give way beneath her hands and for a long time there was only the stillness of the night and the long, satisfied breathing of the Warlord.

'Now is the time for you to be strong. You must show no fear.' Neeka's words came within the rhythm of her fingers, disturbing neither the quiet of the moment nor the focus of his thoughts.

'I have no fear,' Renagi replied, secure in her grasp.

'Good. Good. That is how you must be,' she answered. 'And what will you do with your prisoner?'

'Kill him.' Renagi's voice was crisp, sure, his mind set.

'Yes, yes, naturally he must die. But the true art lies in the nature of the execution,' she said, pressing deeper into the acupoints below the base of his skull.

'And have you a suggestion?' Renagi asked, a mild irritation in his voice. Neeka did not answer immediately; instead she bent close, her mouth behind his neck, her warm, slow breath caressing his skin. 'If you allow me time with him, I will have an answer,' she whispered.

'What? What are you saying?' Renagi bristled.

'Permit me to visit him in the cell. To take him food,' she replied.

'That is out of the question.' Renagi answered flatly, beginning to rise.

'Please, let me finish.' Neeka said, countering the upward movement with her warm, firm hands. The Warlord settled back into the chair.

'Right now we know very little about him. His strengths, his weaknesses. I could gain his trust, then . . .' she hesitated, feeling the Warlord weighing her wisdom. 'Then we will dispose of him in the most effective fashion.'

Renagi sat in silence as Neeka moved slowly to his side, bending to look into his eyes. She sensed his reluctance.

'There is absolutely no way of getting rid of him quietly. It would be your admission of guilt. You must make the matter known and open . . . that is your way to absolute power.' The words rang with finality.

'Fornication with an Ashkelite? For-nic-a-tion . . .' Yanon exaggerated the words, staring drunkenly into Bakov's eyes.

'Atira was in Zato's party at the time of the capture. He saw the mark on his wrist. And his eyes, his eyes are blue.' Bakov added, building the case.

Yanon leaned forward, grasping the neck of the heavy decanter, pulling it towards him, sliding the smooth, velveteen-lined base along the low lacquered table. He looked at the half-full vessel, studying the thick ruby port, pondering, almost forgetting his intention to refill the two empty goblets. Finally, Bakov hoisted his long-stemmed glass and held it out to Yanon, urging the other to pour.

'Fornication with an untouchable. Punishable by death.' Bakov said as Yanon lifted the mock crystal and tipped the warm liquid into the extended glass. 'And if the Royal family was deposed,' he continued, sipping pensively at the port, which remained glistening and wet upon his fat, wide lips, 'Zendow would be governed by a military junta.'

'What are you suggesting?' Yanon asked, suppressing a hard smile as he leaned closer to his senior adviser.

Bakov remained silent, eyeing the tight, round face in front of him, judging whether the man would be an ally or an opponent. *It does not really matter. One word of this and I can have him discredited and destroyed,* he thought, then smiled broadly at Yanon.

'I am suggesting nothing!' Bakov said, lightening his tone, throwing his open hands up in front of him in a gesture of innocence. Then, as quickly, his smile vanished and he looked straight into the eyes of his under-adviser. 'But I do think we must pay careful attention to the situation of this . . . Ashkelite. We may be on the cusp of a crisis, and a crisis creates opportunities – do you follow me?' he said, putting a particular emphasis on the final four words.

Follow you? I am not so sure of that. But understand? Yes, most certainly! thought Yanon, nodding his head and holding his senior's gaze as he filled each of their goblets with the heavy fortified wine.

Madame Wang took her ear away from the paper-thin partition separating her from the secluded portion of the reception hall where the two men sat drinking. *An Ashkelite son? A military junta? Would I be better or worse for a shift in power within Zendow?* she wondered as she padded her way towards the main reception room. *What would it be worth to Renagi to know of a potential plot against him?* she pondered as, silently, she reached the end of the long hall. She could hear the muffled giggles cease as she entered the room and pointed authoritatively at two of the newer, fresher girls.

The two had returned only yesterday from a visit to Doctor Ow, the Willow World physician. The process of having the delicate, wafer-thin dorsal membrane of the monkuno fish stitched two fingers deep inside their vaginal passages was not pleasant. Nor was it comfortable when the fine vegetable fibre cross-stitches tore away during sexual entry, but it was lucrative. Usually a working girl could have the procedure performed two or three times during her professional career. The operation took less than one hour and was accomplished under a local cocoa-rub anaesthetic. Minimal bleeding, twenty-four hours' recovery, and the 'virgin' could earn a year's wages in one evening.

Tonight Wang would supply these new virgins to Bakov and Yanon. *I will throw in the port and elixir for free,* she decided as she led the girls up the warm corridor towards the pleasure rooms. *It will do me no harm to stay in favour with these two,* she concluded as she swept into the antechamber, the girls close behind.

Yanon and Bakov looked up simultaneously, their eyes by-passing Madame Wang and eagerly assessing the evening's entertainment.

'Virgins,' Wang stated proudly, stopping and turning to the

smiling, scantily clad females. Bakov looked first at the girls, then at Wang. His eyes revealed his satisfaction.

'Naturally,' he said.

Neeka stood in absolute silence, observing him through the tight iron slats of the tiny window in the interrogation cell.

Tegné sat with his back pressed straight and firm against the stone wall, his eyes closed and his legs folded easily in the relaxed half-lotus.

So singular, so complete . . . she thought as she rested her gaze on his placid, expressionless face. She read the vulnerability in the full, slightly parted lips and the fine bones which formed a proud, angular structure beneath the pale skin. *A good face, a kind face,* she mused. Yet this face was much more than the simple product of genetic inheritance. *His face bears a distinct countenance, a dignity, an honour; it is a brave face, a warrior's face* . . . she concluded as her gaze shifted to his open hands, his folded legs and bare feet. There was a certain gracefulness to these hands and feet, just a hint of femininity in their proportion when compared to the broad, spreading shoulders and square, muscular chest – as if the musculature had been created as an armour to protect an inherent gentleness. The way he was positioned, with the deltoid muscles drawn back, caused his rib-cage to pull upwards and gave the defined chest and flat abdomen the look of a hard, protective shield.

A shield to guard his heart, Neeka whispered to herself as her eyes fell upon the smooth skin surrounding his nipples. It was pale, yet contained just enough pigment to effect the faint hue of gold. Fine, silken hair surrounded the breasts, while the only other visible body hair was the short, silken strands which adorned the forearms and calves and the darker, reddish trail which led from the navel down over the lower abdomen, widening as it disappeared beneath the heavy magenta band of the torn muslin trousers. It was a sensitive body that had been carefully and faithfully disciplined, giving the final appearance of great strength. A body and face which glowed with the soul within it; a body she had known, a soul she had coveted. *I will rule with this man, make a child with him,* she vowed as she felt the warmth begin inside her womb. She remained still for one more moment, allowing the warmth to wash over and bathe her.

*

Tegné had found the place of peace, of tranquillity, inside his heart, a reservoir from which he drank strength and purpose. He rested in its cool waters, his thoughts drifting easily, slowly, in the clear space surrounding him.

'Tegné. Tegné,' the voice called to him, as if it were carried on the very air he breathed. Slowly he opened his eyes. In the dim light he could barely see through the window, yet he could detect the beautiful glow of violet and the warm smell of musk. He heard the slow twisting of the iron key in the rusty lock, watched as the door creaked open and she entered.

She wore the ninjinka, and the violet light came from inside her eyes, the fragrance of musk from her bare shoulders. A sari of rich silk, its blended colours of blue, red and gold, wrapped loosely round her body, while soft, pale leather sandals protected her fine, slender feet. She carried a tray of food in her hands.

The door closed behind her. She stood a moment, smiling down on him, then, disregarding the filthy floor, she hoisted her robes and sat cross-legged, facing him. The aroma of the steaming rice with its thin, sautéed pieces of marinated sandafish rose up from the bone-white porcelain bowl.

'Please, eat,' she said, smiling as, carefully, expertly, she lifted the small tea-cup and warmed it above the lighted candle on the edge of her serving tray. As she warmed the fine ivory china she ceremoniously wiped the pristine cup with a white cotton cloth. The almond tea steamed from the ornate, single-handled pot, and at no time did Neeka take her eyes from Tegné.

He sat quietly, enraptured by the grace of her movement and the dexterity of her fine, perfect hands.

'Are you not hungry?' she asked quietly, noticing his reluctance.

'Yes, I am hungry,' he replied, still making no move towards the rice. Gently, she placed the warmed cup down beside an identical cup on the wood and brass tray. She lifted the china spoon and dipped it delicately into the rice, bringing a small portion to her own lips. Taking a few grains into her mouth, she nibbled at the rice, then smiled faintly as she swallowed. Now she reached out, extending the spoon to his lips.

'It is delicious,' she said softly as Tegné opened his mouth and accepted the offering. Finally, she placed the spoon down beside the bowl, gesturing for him to continue, as again she picked up the cup and began to warm and clean the vessel above the flame.

'I understand you come from the Temple of the Moon?' Neeka asked, quietly continuing her work. Tegné nodded, slowly chewing the rice, then taking another spoonful. 'And does that mean you are an ordained priest of the Temple?' she continued, her voice maintaining a soft, easy pitch.

'I am not a priest,' Tegné answered, lowering his eyes, 'And I am no longer a Brother of the Order.'

'And that is upsetting you?' she enquired, watching as he raised his eyes to meet her gentle gaze.

'My purpose was never to be a Brother of the Order,' he answered, his face placid and his voice matching hers in its soft timbre.

'Your purpose?' she asked.

He looked into the warm violet, somehow believing that he knew the face behind the ninjinka, remembering the Lake of Dreams, and for a long moment there was a quiet sense of uncertainty between them. Then, slowly, she reached out to him, touching his wrist so lightly that it seemed her hand merely lay upon the fine golden hairs of his arm. Her warmth soothed him as she smiled. 'I understand your purpose.'

At that instant his heart was touched and his love for her began to cloud him. She stroked his arm gently, closing her eyes. Finally she whispered, 'You must trust me – I am your ally.'

Tegné felt the choking of emotion, his Earth heart wanting her, his Earth mind desiring this trust, this union. And yet he felt the wrenching grip of conscience twisting him, holding him back, warning him. She noticed the subtle shift of expression in his eyes, felt him pull away from her.

'You are his son, are you not?' she asked, removing her hand, strengthening her voice, changing direction.

'Yes, I am,' Tegné answered.

'And your mother?' Neeka continued.

'My mother was Ashkelite,' Tegné stated, a slight defiance in his voice.

'I need not tell you the consequences for the Warlord if his transgression became public knowledge,' she said. 'He would be executed and his family discredited,' she continued, studying Tegné's face, waiting for his reaction.

'That is my intention,' Tegné answered.

She remained silent, handing him the full cup of tea; the soothing aroma of almonds rose from the liquid. Tegné accepted the cup.

'Do you hate this man ... Renagi?' she asked.

He sipped the tea, searching her eyes, then said, 'No man has the right to violate another human being, to rape, to kill. I do not know my father, but I do know what he has done.'

'And you have never sinned? Never?' she asked, her voice hushed.

Tegné lowered his head.

'And there is no dark side to your own nature?' she continued, feeling the contact between them strengthening.

Now he looked at her, his eyes clear, concealing nothing. 'Why have you come here?' His voice had an edge, a coldness.

Neeka met his gaze. 'Because I am as you are; hungry, incomplete. Searching for something intangible, something which will make me whole. And uncertain whether to love or fear, to embrace or destroy it,' she answered, her voice also cold. Then she stood and walked to the iron door. She pushed it open; it was not locked. 'I will see you again,' she said. Then, closing the door, Neeka was gone.

The invitation to dine with the Warlord came as only a slight surprise to Bakov. After all, it was nearing the end of the third trading quarter and, no doubt, Renagi wished to discuss the military budget. In fact, Bakov expected the entire staff of advisers to be in attendance as he knocked three times on the outer security door to the dining hall, hesitated and knocked twice more.

Instead, the door was opened by Yanon, who appeared anxious and alone within the windowless room. Seven bottles of vintage Kanton Red stood open in the middle of the highly polished, oblong mahogany table. Fluted crystal glasses sparkled in the warm light of the five burning candles which adorned the silver centrepiece. The table was set for three, and the bone-handled, serrated knives indicated that the main course would be a meat dish. There was an ominous quiet to the room.

'We seem to be the only ones invited,' Yanon said, breaking the silence, looking questioningly at his senior.

Bakov surveyed the table before he answered. 'Apparently,' he agreed, nodding slowly, his voice, unlike the other man's, giving away none of the anxiety he felt.

'But why? you don't think . . .' Yanon began.

Bakov's hand shot out, his index and middle fingers pushing flat and hard against Yanon's lips, halting his speech. 'I think that we have been invited to a quiet dinner with our Warlord, that is what I think,' he stated, finally taking his fingers from Yanon's lips.

Both men spun round as the heavy doors parted and Renagi entered the hall. The Warlord walked straight to Bakov, smiling broadly as he embraced him with both arms, then turned and repeated the greeting to Yanon.

'It has been too long, far too long, since we dined together,' the Warlord said, nodding and smiling at each of them in turn. 'My two senior advisers, my two most trusted advisers,' he added, motioning for them to take their seats at the table. 'And tonight I must beg your absolute confidence, your loyalty, your support and, above all, your advice, in a most personal and delicate matter,' Renagi continued as he pulled the high black chair out from the table. He rubbed his fingers over the embossed red Sign of the Claw which stood out from the velvet at the very top of the arched back. The red lacquered leather seemed to shine beneath his hand as, satisfied, he sat in the chair, resting his arms on the table before him.

Yanon relaxed, the tension in his body replaced by a secure confidence as he returned the Warlord's smile.

'But before we talk, I think we should drink, then we will dine, drink some more and then . . . yes, then we will talk,' Renagi said, as he indicated with his head that Bakov should pour the wine.

It was a heavy, rather sweet wine, aged for a single generation in the humid cellars below Zendow.

'Exquisite,' said Bakov, nosing the beverage, then sipping and rolling the warm liquid on his tongue before closing his eyes and swallowing.

They emptied three of the amber glass bottles within the first hour. There was very little conversation, but a mutual trust pervaded the small dining hall.

'Food? Hungry? We must be hungry,' Renagi said, his voice just beginning to slur as he poured the last drop into Yanon's glass. Without waiting for a reply he leaned back, reached behind him and pulled the tasselled cord, signalling the servants.

Yanon gasped audibly as, ceremoniously, the double doors opened and the huge rhandoconda was brought in, its entire body skewered, marinated and, now, rotating above a burning bowl of coals. The serpent's head remained intact, the mouth drawn back and a small, stewed plum artistically impaled between the two long, bent fangs. One servant turned the handle of the spit while another pushed the entire wheeled serving tray to the table. Renagi laughed aloud at the horror on Yanon's face, noting at the same time Bakov's strained control.

'A delicacy, I assure you, but so very difficult to prepare that I serve it infrequently. Generally reserved for my immediate family. Tonight is an exception!' Renagi exclaimed, making no secret of his amusement at the reaction of his guests. 'Difficult to prepare,' he repeated, then looked directly at Yanon. 'You see, the serpent must be skinned while still alive, then boiled slowly from the neck down. The head must always remain above the water. In that way the venom is excreted through the pores and diluted. The water must be changed at least three times during the process or the flesh is unsuitable for consumption. Here . . . here!' he said, stabbing his fork into a section of the snake and ripping the flesh from the spit. 'You must try a little,' Renagi insisted, holding the loaded fork towards Yanon. 'I promise it will melt on your tongue.'

It is a test; everything this man does is a test, damn him, Yanon thought as he forced a smile and intercepted Renagi's fork with his own, lifting the meat from it.

Renagi settled back, watching as Yanon brought the rhandoconda up under his nose, sniffing tentatively.

'Go ahead,' the Warlord commanded, yet the command was not unfriendly. Yanon placed the meat on his tongue. His face expressed pleasure as he tasted the fine, spiced sweetness of the flesh.

Rather like chicken but sweeter, fuller, he thought, relieved, as he chewed the first bite and swallowed. Then he turned to his host. 'Delicious, absolutely delicious!' he proclaimed, smiling broadly and lifting his glass.

Bakov's explosion of laughter was a mixture of acute nervous relief and genuine humour as he kept his eyes on Yanon, still half-expecting his fellow adviser to fall face forward, dead on the table. After all, the venom of the rhandoconda was legendary, causing its victims an incapacitating muscular paralysis. Tales of men lying in the fields, unable to move, while the carnivorous serpent ate the eyeballs from their sockets or the tongue from their mouths were legendary in Vokane Province. Bakov had been aware that it was possible to eat the meat of the serpent, but the process of cooking was exacting and known only to a few. A single error in the distillation and the first mouthful would be fatal. Still, Yanon seemed perfectly well and, in fact, enjoying the delicacy.

Bakov pulled two of the thick, sinewy ringlets from the skewer as it was passed to him. He purposely avoided the stare of the dead serpent's eyes. Somewhere, in the underlayers of his now clouding mind, the eyes reminded him uncomfortably of the eyes of his Warlord.

The meal progressed easily, and the serpent was consumed completely with the exception of the head, which was finally and thankfully removed from the centre of the table. The sweet was a superb mixture of crushed Yusun grapes and plums, soaked in honey and blended into a thick bread pudding. The men were well into the last of the heavy red wine when Renagi changed the tone of his conversation.

'I do not need to inform you that I am holding an Ashkelite in the cells below Zendow,' he said, looking slowly from Bakov to Yanon. Neither man responded. 'Come along, come along,' Renagi urged, 'I am not telling you anything you do not already know.'

Bakov cleared his throat, holding Yanon in his gaze, willing the under-adviser to remain calm. Then he turned his eyes to Renagi. 'Warlord, of course we have heard of the man's capture. We understand him to be an impostor, subject to trial and death.'

Renagi rose slightly from his chair, then settled again. 'I want you to be honest with me. Hold nothing back. If I cannot rely on you, then who can I rely on? I want to know what the men are saying, do you understand me?'

'Yes. Yes, of course we understand,' answered Bakov, hedging for time, realizing the double edge of the situation and wanting to give away only enough to ensure his indispensable value to the Warlord. 'There are those who claim he bears the Royal mark,' he continued.

'I want a list of those men,' Renagi ordered, a growing edge in his voice.

'But Master, they are few, and even they believe the mark to be counterfeit. The work of a man skilled in ink and bamboo,' Bakov countered.

'And you? What do you believe?' Renagi asked, suddenly shifting his attention to Yanon.

Now was the moment and Bakov saw the flicker of fear in Yanon's eyes. He wondered if Renagi had also seen the involuntary shift of expression.

'Master, I would never question the truth of your words,' Yanon answered, holding his gaze firm on Renagi and praying the Warlord could not read beyond his lie.

Renagi relaxed, his entire body seeming to expand to fill his chair. 'Good, good. I knew I could rely on your support,' he said, then leaned forward, his arms spread wide on the table, as if he intended to take both men within his grasp. His voice grew hushed. 'I have a horse carriage and a driver waiting in the courtyard. I would be honoured if you would accompany me to the Willow World.'

Surely with his new vixen he has no need of the Willow World, Bakov thought as he smiled and nodded at Renagi.

'I know what you are thinking,' said the Warlord, 'But occasionally even the owner of a thoroughbred desires the excitement of an unbroken mount . . . even if it is only a cart-horse!' he added, then laughed boisterously and rose from the table.

Wang peered nervously through the convex lens which allowed her a complete view of the winding, cobbled street leading to the brothel. She had expected them for over an hour, and the muscles in her calves had become cramped from the continual raising and lowering as she stood on the tips of her toes to look through the lens.

Nothing! Where can they be? The girls cannot stay like this forever, she grumbled to herself as she stood flat-footed, resting against the locked door. *And if they do not come! God, the business I am losing!* she continued, muttering, as she calculated the loss of closing the brothel for an entire evening. It was then that she heard the sharp clatter of hooves and the clickety-clack of the metal carriage wheels. She raised herself to the lens and smiled as she saw the Royal carriage pull up directly outside, the dark curtains drawn to conceal its occupants. She watched the driver open the door and saw the Warlord climb from the seat to the single step and down on to the cobblestones. Bakov and Yanon followed. She noticed the slight nervousness in both men in spite of the intoxication which was apparent in their unsteady footsteps. Renagi turned and instructed the driver to wait before he guided his guests towards the door.

Wang hesitated another beat, then unbolted the entrance and swung the gigantic door open. 'Master! I am honoured,' she exclaimed, throwing both arms up in a sign of welcome. Graciously, she stood aside as the Warlord, followed by his two advisers, entered the reception hall of the Royal brothel.

Wang followed them in, excused herself and disappeared momentarily through the curtained entrance to the inner chamber. Yanon nudged Bakov as three girls were led from the adjoining room. They were tall, dark beauties, and Bakov surmised them to be of pure Yusun stock, judging by the richness of their skin and the large, widely spaced ebony-lashed eyes. There was a dignity to the women as each walked slowly forward and offered a soft hand to her predetermined partner for the evening. Wang experienced a brief moment of anxiety as the tallest girl moved cautiously in Renagi's direction.

No, you fool! the Madame thought, then breathed a sigh of relief as Lemar turned at the last and smiled gently at Yanon.

'The first three pleasure chambers on the right have been made ready for you,' Wang said, satisfied that each of the girls had made the appropriate choice. 'As much hapaver as you like,' she added as Bakov made the first move towards the lamp-lit corridor. Yanon followed, turning only once to offer a token bow of gratitude to his Warlord.

Renagi smiled broadly, standing between Wang and the last of the girls. He listened as the doors of the adjacent chamber were closed and bolted, then waited another minute to be certain. Finally, he motioned with his head for the girl to leave them. Silently she obeyed. Now he looked expectantly at Wang.

'This way,' she whispered, taking him by the arm and quickly leading him to the narrow passage which ran the entire length of the rear of the chambers. Renagi nodded his head in quiet appreciation of Wang's devious ingenuity. *I wonder how much more this fat old cow has heard through these walls,* he pondered as his ears grew attuned to the sound of heavy breathing and the low moans which filtered through the taut cloth partition separating them from the rooms.

Wang held her plump hand up near Renagi's face, smiling and respectfully signalling patience. The Warlord nodded in agreement and both waited in the darkness, listening to the growing sounds of passion which seemed to build in perfect synchronization from the two chambers.

Several minutes passed, and Renagi looked at Wang. She read the beginning of doubt, mixed with anger, in the hooded eyes. The entire scheme had been her idea, and she had no intention of incurring the Warlord's wrath or, indeed, losing the kilo weight of hapaver, the one hundred golden kons and the immeasurable gain of face that would accompany its successful conclusion.

She had laboured for days getting the exact measurements of each of the girls' pleasure passages, moulding the wax, shaping it, fitting and refitting the artificial canals. It had taken twenty kons each and no end of convincing to assure the two that the jagged-edged razors would do them no internal damage. Finally, the razors were skilfully inserted into the hardening, rubber-based wax. And now Wang prayed that the men would be sufficiently intoxicated by the hapaver to take no notice of the slight difference in feel as they entered the warm, oiled passages.

Another minute passed, and Wang reached inside her small, jewelled purse and produced the thin brass finger cymbals. Renagi watched as she slid her thumb and middle finger through the leather strap on the back of each cymbal. Then, noiselessly, she walked directly behind the partition of Bakov's room. The two humming rings of the cymbal were nearly inaudible.

Wang listened a moment as the sounds of passion coming from behind the partition seemed to intensify. She smiled sweetly at Renagi and then tiptoed the twenty feet to the back of Yanon's chamber. There was a practised artistry in her movement, even an air of theatricality as again she raised the hand wearing the cymbal and twice brought the fingers together.

'Zing! Zing!' Yanon was certain he heard the 'Bells of Bliss' as he prepared for his ascent to the heavenly plane. He hoped that the hapaver, combined with the red wine, would give him the staying power of youth as he parted the long legs beneath him on the bed. Looking down proudly at his hard, fat penis he prepared to drive the shaft inwards, burying it in one explosive thrust. *That should make her scream a bit,* he thought as her light fingers held him gently below the testicles and guided him to her warm opening. He clenched his buttocks as he drove forward, penetrating her fully. She gasped, a strange, expectant gasp, and he opened his eyes to gauge the expression on her face.

She stared up at him from the pillow. He withdrew and drove in again. Now there was a look of horror in the eyes below him. It was then that he began to feel the white, searing heat at his very core. He looked down to see the blood exploding from between his legs as his mind raced to make sense of the icy numbness which spread from his organ. He pulled away from her just as Bakov's agonized scream reached him from the next chamber.

Renagi listened a moment to the anguish on the other side of the partition. 'Stay here,' he ordered Wang, drawing his katana. With a single downward cut he sliced the thin cloth which separated him from Yanon's chamber.

Yanon lay writhing on the floor, doubled up, holding himself, sobbing, begging. The girl stood frozen, watching from the corner.

'Out!' the Warlord commanded. She obeyed with an awkward, shuffling step and disappeared into the corridor. Renagi hovered above the bleeding man, his katana raised high.

'An Ashkelite son? A military junta!' The Warlord screamed the words as they had been repeated to him by Wang. 'A time of opportunity!' he continued, allowing the man to suffer beneath him.

'Bakov . . .' Yanon barely managed to whimper his senior's name.

'Yes, I understand,' answered the Warlord. 'And for that I will give you the gift of my blade while your "superior" will die dishonoured.'

Yanon turned his head to face Renagi, meeting his eyes. The blade seemed to flow in slow motion as it fell towards his neck.

Has it been two days or three that I have been here? Tegné wondered as he stared into the hopeless darkness of the cell. Slowly he unfolded his crossed legs and stood, stretching his arms up, then down, placing the palms of his hands flat against the stone wall and breathing in as the long hamstring muscles relaxed, allowing him to grip his ankles and pull his head down to touch his upper thighs. He held the position, regulating his breathing and letting his mind flow with the surging of blood as it pumped from his heart.

Far away he could hear the awkward, limping gait of the gaoler as the man carried out his rounds, dispensing the watery gruel made from beef bones and stale, soggy bread. Only once since Neeka's visit had Tegné been offered the slopping bowl through the small, diagonal opening at the base of the door. He had attempted to eat the cold, stinking broth, but his belly, unused to animal flesh, reacted with nausea and vomiting.

The footsteps seemed to come closer as he released his grip on his ankles, stretching upwards once more and squatting down, pulling his arms tight around his bent legs. Then he lowered his hips to the floor and sat again in the resting half-lotus.

Now Tegné could hear the disgruntled noises which accompanied the uneven footsteps as the gaoler turned the final corner and approached his cell. He expected to hear the sound of tin sliding across stone and see the sickening gruel as it was pushed through the door, but instead he heard the iron key twist in the old lock, and for a moment the thought of escape swept over him.

'You are very lucky, my friend,' the gaoler said, looking down on Tegné, his small, pitted eyes as dead as the stone walls which had surrounded him for the thirty yeons he had been in charge of these cells. 'She says you are to be moved. A larger cell, a toilet, a bed,' he continued, genuinely impressed with Tegné's prospective accommodation. 'A cell of your own, no one to trouble you,' the gruff, tired voice added as he dropped the heavy leg-irons at Tegné's feet.

'Put them on,' ordered the gaoler. Tegné clamped the circular iron restraints, attached by the heavy, foot long chain, to his ankles. The gaoler nodded as Tegné snapped the last clamp shut. 'Good. Good . . . now walk ahead of me.'

Tegné walked from the door and turned down the dim corridor. 'That's right. That's right, keep moving,' the voice behind him said as the gaoler maintained a respectful distance, remembering the fashion in which Tegné had disposed of his fellow prisoner just five days ago. 'Now to the left,' he ordered, seeing

Tegné hesitate at the point where the corridor ended in a T-junction. Tegné turned left and moved along the bars which enclosed a series of adjoining cells. He could see the sallow, wasted faces, their hopeless, hollow eyes staring at him as he passed. He reached the end of the cells and the passage narrowed, leading him on a slight downward curve. The floor grew damp and cold beneath his feet.

'Stop. Stop,' the gaoler nearly shouted.

Tegné stood motionless as the gaoler hobbled up to him, then the man turned and looked at him; the eyes now bore a bare hint of expression. Tegné could see nothing but solid grey walls on each side, the passage now so narrow that he stood sideways in order to avoid touching the cold stone with his shoulders. The gaoler studied him another moment, then took his right hand from the hilt of his katana and smacked the heel of his palm hard against the stone.

Twice, three times he repeated the dull, thudding blow, then broke into a muffled, strangled laugh as the sound·of heavy chains and pulleys came from behind the thick stone. Tegné watched as the grey panel closest to him slowly rose, coming to a grinding halt nine feet above the floor. A series of evenly spaced gas torches cast wavering shadows on the ascending steps.

'Go ahead,' said the gaoler, urging Tegné upwards. He tried to take the first step, but the chain binding his ankle locks would not permit his right foot to reach the plateau. The gaoler stood a moment, contemplating their predicament then, nodding in quiet agreement with himself, he cleared his throat and spat the result on the floor.

'Jump!' he commanded.

Tegné obeyed, clearing the first step and landing with a clank as the chain hit the rock between his bare feet.

'Again. All the way,' the voice behind him pushed.

Twenty minutes later, Tegné stood in front of a solid wall at the upper end of the staircase. He was drenched in perspiration, his legs leaden and his hard-soled feet had begun to blister. Behind him the gaoler cursed and wheezed as he climbed the last of the three hundred steps.

'Move aside, move aside,' the voice rasped as he squeezed along-side Tegné on the top, wider step. *Whap!* His palm slapped against the slight indentation in the wall facing them. This time the action was smooth and oiled, and the panel rose without sound.

It took a moment for Tegné's eyes to adjust to the strange, glowing light cast by the moon as it penetrated the star-shaped openings cut into the high domed ceiling. A bed was positioned in the centre of the room, soft and canopied. The gaoler stood at the door, mouth agape, as if he was staring into the gates of some dreamt-of distant paradise.

'Get out!' Neeka's voice was sharp, clear, breaking through the spell of the moonlight and causing the bent, hobbling man to snap to attention. Neeka rose from the chair which sat to the left and slightly behind the huge bed. She moved quickly and menacingly towards the still-stationary gaoler. Before she could reach him he turned and scurried from the landing, jumping down the first two steps before catching himself by spreading both arms out against the narrow passage, thus preventing a headlong fall.

She stood a moment looking after the fleeing man, then turned, smiling, to Tegné. Her eyes rested on him as if she could communicate her deepest thoughts by their use alone. Then she bent down, kneeling by his feet, running her exquisite, cool hands down the sides of his calves and resting them a moment on the rusty iron manacles. Again she looked up into his eyes, then tugged gently on the lock of the clamp. He felt his left leg grow light as the restraint fell from his ankle to the floor, and she repeated the small, deft movement, running her hands down his right lower leg and with the same motion released the second iron. Then she stood, rubbing her body softly against his.

'Come. Come,' she said, touching his naked shoulder and directing him to the bed. He walked across the moonlit room, the sweat dry upon his body and a strange, comfortable warmth rushing over him, making him feel vigorous and whole. He sat on the edge of the black-quilted bed.

She sat beside him, a long-stemmed pipe in her hands. He watched as she struck the firestick and held the thin yellow flame above the small silver bowl. The flame was drawn downwards as she inhaled, igniting the tiny, deep red brick of hapaver. Finally, a winding ribbon of blue-grey smoke floated lazily towards the ceiling.

'Here, it will give you strength,' she whispered as she offered him the stem. He hesitated, looking into the eyes behind the ninjinka. He knew her, he knew what he must do, yet he longed for her, longed for the heat of her body. He ignored the pipe and instead reached for her, his fingers extending towards the ninjinka.

I must see her face, I must be certain, he thought as he began to raise the mask.

'No, no,' she said, pulling back, knowing his intention. 'The time is not right. Not yet.' He withdrew his hands, and she continued, 'Please, share the pipe with me. Share my dreams.' She moved close again, placing the stem between his parted lips. Tegné inhaled the bitter-sweet smoke.

'Yes, yes ... hold it within you ... close your eyes,' she purred, nestling into him, sipping the smoke which escaped through his nostrils and mouth.

The first rush of the elixir sent a warmth flooding through him, extending down his arms and into his fingertips. The sensation was unlike any he had known before, and he tried to control the ripples of energy as they played on the still surface of his mind.

'Relax, let the smoke take you, guide you ...' Neeka's words floated to him from far away. Now he smelled the sweetness of the smoke as Neeka drew in from the pipe and blew gently against his face. He lay back on the bed, his eyes remaining closed as her warm, rough tongue licked the skin around his nipples, tasting the salt from his dried perspiration before moving lower. The silken-soft lips kissed and caressed the area below his navel where the fine golden hair thickened and spread. He felt her untie the sash which held the rough cotton pants on him and he arched his hips upward as she slid them down, her hands working quietly as the rough tongue and full lips kept contact with his skin. Now the long, fine fingers touched him as lightly as a single feather and she exhaled her warm breath along the sensitive skin of his manhood. The core of him begged to her, pleaded to be held, touched, and at last she gripped him gently with both hands, bringing her mouth down to him. He shuddered as she licked, slowly, circling the head of his full, hard penis.

Now she held him in the grasp of a single hand as she threw off the scented robes which covered her. Naked, she straddled him, pulling him towards her, rubbing his penis against the dark wetness of her vagina. Tegné opened his eyes, marvelling at the sleek sinews of her body, the strong fluidity of her movement. He raised himself up, burying his face in her neck, breathing her, licking her skin, seeking her lips. He felt a power he had never known, a fulfilment, a totality. Yet behind the feeling of his body was a deep, shivering guilt, a knowledge of doom, of betrayal. And the conflict angered him. He listened to her moans as he lifted her up on the arch of his own body, penetrating her, enslaving her, as in a single movement he rolled on top of her without breaking their connection.

Now their tongues entwined, as his body thrust into hers time and time again. Still she seemed to devour him in her heat, and with each thrust his rage increased. Was he loving her or killing her? The thoughts tore at his mind like claws against flesh until finally he pulled his lips from hers and looked down into her open eyes.

The eyes seemed to mock him, then in an instant they filled with love, pleading with him. He bent his head, inhaling the scent of her body, and kissed the fine skin; then again the anger rose inside him as he felt her urge him on, challenging him with the pumping rhythm of her loins, forcing him to surrender. He opened his mouth and bit down, hard, into the flesh of her neck, sucking, biting, devouring.

Her animal scream crashed through his senses, ripping through his consciousness like a scorching, single rush of flame. Tegné jumped up, away from the burning bed, his body covered in sweat, his heart thundering in his chest. He took a deep, lower breath, trying to shake the fear from his soul.

He stood alone in the quiet of the room. The leg irons clanked against the wooden floor.

Dreams. Illusion. Reality . . .

He heard the twist of the key in the lock, heard the gaoler clear his throat, watched the inner door open and saw the tired eyes staring at him across the room.

'You are very lucky, my friend. She says you are to be fed,' the gaoler said as he carried the steaming bowls of rice, fish and vegetables to the low table beside the bed. Sunlight streamed through the starred dome above him as Tegné sat up, instantly hungry for the food.

The gaoler salivated as he arranged the teapot, cup and saucer on the outer edge of the matte-black table. 'You are very, very lucky,' he repeated, straightening himself as he prepared to exit. He looked down for one last time at the succulent portions of fish in the bowl, wiped his mouth with a swipe of his sleeve and walked to the inner door. He halted a moment, locating the correct key on his jangling key-ring, then placed the key in the lock and twisted.

Tegné caught only a glimpse of the black-tiled marble floor and the fine, gold-trimmed cornices as the door opened and the gaoler walked from the room, then he turned to the bowls of steaming, aromatic food. He was suddenly aware of his ravenous hunger and he shuffled to the table and sat down, facing it, on the side of the bed.

He devoured the rice, fish and vegetables and was sipping the blended, honeyed tea when Neeka entered through the wooden inner door. She wore the gold ninjinka and her white silk robes clung to her body as she swept across the room.

As she came closer he became aware of the sweet scent which hung delicately in the air surrounding her. It was her perfume which brought the images of seduction rushing back to his mind. He felt his body tighten as she drew near to the bed.

'These must be very uncomfortable,' she said, kneeling down and running her hand along his left calf and on to the leg-iron. He wanted to pull back, escape from her spell, yet he felt the sure, quiet warmth begin to fill his loins. His body shivered as she rose and sat beside him. She placed a calm, warm hand on his neck.

'Why? Why are you troubled?' she asked. 'Was the food not to your liking, the tea not satisfying?' she continued, a tantalizing challenge in her tone.

Why does she so unnerve me? he wondered as Neeka moved closer to him on the bed.

'I dreamed of you last night . . . a lovely, lovely dream,' she said, smiling as if to one who shared a deep secret.

He remained silent, but now a slight smiled played on his own lips as he saw the violet shimmer of her eyes.

'Have you never dreamed of me?' she teased, moving her body towards him, nestling.

'Yes, I have,' Tegné answered, his voice no more than a whisper. She rested her hand on his upper thigh, savouring the heat of his body, stroking him gently in a slow, circular motion. She watched as he grew hard, his manhood straining against the cloth of his cotton trousers. She knew that she could take him; that his will was as nothing against her own.

Neeka heard the footsteps from far away; the sharp clicking of boot heels against marble. She knew her ears were many times more sensitive than his, and estimated another ten seconds before Tegné would become aware of the approaching men. She bent to lick his neck, his cheek, and finally kissed him full on the lips. She tasted the sweetness of the honeyed tea as her tongue penetrated his mouth and she pressed her palms flat against his ears as he wrapped his arms around her. His awareness was lost in passion.

The key twisted in the lock. She held him a second more, then released him, pushing him away from her. Renagi stood, stunned, in the doorway.

'What is going on in here?!' he bellowed as he stormed towards them across the room. The gaoler remained at the door, hoping secretly that his Warlord would take the head, not only of the Ashkelite, but of the surly bitch beside him.

'Nothing, Master. Nothing at all,' Neeka said, rising, knowing full well that Renagi had witnessed the embrace, for that had been her intention.

'Nothing? Nothing!' Renagi shouted, his mouth twisting grotesquely in a mixture of pain, humiliation and sheer loathing.

'Yes,' Neeka said, firmly placing her hand on the Warlord's heaving shoulder. 'Nothing,' she repeated.

Tegné watched as Renagi calmed, his breathing becoming relaxed, choosing to believe her lie, even against the proof of his own eyes.

She is in complete control of him, Tegné thought as he began to understand the woman's power.

Finally, Renagi turned and looked down at Tegné. There was the beginning of fear in the Warlord's eyes. 'Take him back to the cells,' he commanded the gaoler, then, looking at Neeka as if to ask for her approval, he ordered, 'At daybreak put him in the cage.'

Tegné looked once at Renagi as the sliding stone panel rose to reveal the torchlit steps leading down. Renagi looked old and bewildered as he stood beside the bed and Tegné felt a wave of compassion before he turned and walked through the arch and into the dark passage.

Neeka had broken the Warlord completely, her last, dramatically timed scene injuring him beyond repair. For a long moment silence filled the room. She knew he was open, his inner wounds raw and vulnerable. Finally he turned towards her and she saw the hint of tears in his eyes.

'Sit down beside me, please,' Neeka said, her voice soft and loving. He obeyed like a lost, sad child.

'I did what I had to do to find out about him,' she began in a plot to ease and erase the pain, whilst keeping him unsettled. He turned to face her fully, wanting to embrace her, to love her, and at the same time to smother and destroy her.

'And what did you discover?' Renagi asked, his voice unsteady and small.

'That it is time for him to die,' Neeka said flatly, studying his face, watching the hope return to his eyes. 'He does intend to discredit you,' she continued, watching the Warlord bristle, gaining confidence as each of her words reassured him as to her love and loyalty.

'Tomorrow. I will do it myself. Then it is over, finished,' he concluded.

'Why? When you are so close to victory?' Neeka countered his impatience.

'Because I am threatened,' Renagi answered, the final layers of his psychological armour falling away. 'Last night I executed Yanon and Bakov, my two senior advisers. I have a list of half a dozen more. They are plotting against me.'

'A list? Half a dozen? So tomorrow you kill the Ashkelite, then what? Go through the list, one by one?' she questioned, intending to goad him. Renagi nodded 'yes', a vacant commitment in his expression. Neeka continued, 'And the result will be more lists, more conspiracy, more executions, until finally Zendow will turn against you. You will have confirmed not only your guilt but your inability to rule,' she stated, then considered before she spoke again.

'What you must do is find people you can trust. Forget the Council of Zendai; they are old, obsolete. Inject new blood into the hierarchy. Replace Yanon and Zakov with military men, men who are loyal, men who would give their lives for you and for Zato,' she said.

'Military men in the Council?' Renagi retorted.

'Why not? A great leader is always the one who institutes reforms,' Neeka countered.

'But the Council has governed Zendow for two generations, it is a succession of blood,' he answered.

'And now that succession has turned against you,' Neeka stated.

Renagi stood silent.

'What better way to restore order and loyalty than to implant military men – men who understand the meaning of blood,' she continued. 'Who are your oldest, most trusted Warmen?'

Renagi remained quiet, his mind working, considering. *There is Kein ... and Miyaz ... No, no, Kein would not be suitable. A fine Warman, perhaps, and loyal certainly, but illiterate. No, he would command no respect, not in the company of the twelve men who oversaw such fastidious details as the balancing of the trading budgets and the tax paid by Wang's brothel. Kein is definitely out ... but what of Kase? He has been with me for nearly thirty yeons, risen through the ranks of the Warmen ... and he is educated ... Yes. Miyaz and Kase ...*

'Well?' Neeka urged, studying the Warlord's eyes.

'I would trust Miyaz and Kase with my life and the life of my heir,' Renagi said slowly.

'Good, good. Then it is done,' Neeka stated.

'The Council will resist,' Renagi said, still uncertain.

'Not if you move quickly while they are in a state of unrest; they will all be badly shaken when they learn of Yanon and Bakov,' Neeka reasoned.

Renagi looked into her eyes, taking strength, before he nodded, 'Yes'.

'Then, once they are in place and the situation settled, you can convene the trial,' Neeka continued, following her plan through.

Renagi drew away. 'A trial?' he questioned, a reluctant plea in his voice.

'Yes, a test of honour,' Neeka answered grandly, 'Combat. In front of the people of Zendow, in front of your "revised" Council,' she went on, hesitating only long enough to allow the words to sink in. 'From what I have learned of the Ashkelite, he has been trained at the temple in the Way of Empty Hand,' she said. Then, noting the resistance in Renagi's eyes, she added, 'Enough anyway to make a plausible appearance in the arena.'

Renagi watched as Neeka rose from the bed, her eyes burning, her gestures large and inspired as she elaborated. 'Yes, that is the answer. The perfect answer. A trial beneath the eyes of God. A trial for all to see. The man who claims to be Zendai pitted against your chosen Warman.'

Renagi sat upright, his spine straight, a nervous energy beginning inside his stomach. He recalled the first incident in the cells. *Did Tegné not beat another prisoner while his own hands and feet were bound? And Zato, did he not speak of the Ashkelite's fighting ability? Plausible? Tegné is more than plausible . . .*

'Too much of a risk,' he stated flatly.

Neeka threw her arms up, nodding her head in genuine amazement.

'Risk? There is no risk! You have ordered him to the cage at daybreak. You have told me yourself that no man has ever survived more than four days in the cage, let alone emerged to fight in the arena? We will plan it; make the announcement, organize the event, choose the Warmen. It will be perfect, a spectacle, not a denial but an open display of truth!' she said, her voice rising dramatically as she punctuated the words with her raised hands.

'Yes . . . Yes, but they will know he is weak from the torture,' Renagi said, his mind now working in conjunction with Neeka's.

'No one need see him. Close the inner courtyard – it is rarely used anyway. The gaoler will not speak, particularly if he feels the touch of the heat-prod against his tongue. The hour before the event we will bathe the Ashkelite, clothe him in a fresh combat uniform, drug him. Believe me, it will work. Believe me,' Neeka said smiling, moving closer to the Warlord, holding his upturned face between her hands.

They were the highest walls he had ever seen, ten times the height of the monastery. *I will never get out*, Rin thought, trembling, as he pulled the heavy burlap up around his shoulders and over his head. He limped forward, joining the other beggar children. Each carried a box of sugar-candy, chewing molasses, or thin, badly made firesticks, anything that could be sold for a mili-kon or even less inside the looming, walled city of Zendow.

The children formed a narrow, ragged line behind the two hundred or so market traders with their donkey-drawn carts and haggard, worn-out horses. It was a sad, spiritless mass of people who waited each Thursday for sunrise and the gigantic twin armoured gates to swing open on their greased steel bearings. Rin stared upwards as the mechanical crackle sliced the morning air and the generator cranked energy into the speakers of the voice-enhancer.

'Stand back. Stand back. Wait until the gates are open. Do not crowd the gates. Stand back. Stand back.' The voice was thin, cutting and metallic. A hush fell over the milling crowd as again the speakers came to life.

'All grain and carts will proceed to first in line, horses and vinegar kegs will follow. Adults on foot will fall in behind. All below the age of sixteen will enter last.' The piercing command was exactly the same in words and phrasing as it had been for as many yeons as any of the older traders could remember, but still there was the inevitable reshuffling in position as the late-arriving carts drew close to the demarcation line.

'Stand clear, stand clear,' the voice echoed as the enormous iron-wood and alloy gates began their outward swing, revealing two cast-iron inner gates which moved simultaneously in the opposite direction, their spiked corners parting like the jaws of some gigantic, predatory beast. Rin took a sharp breath as the city of Zendow opened before him.

His only frame of reference, his only comparison to its grand myriad of stone courtyards intersected by flat, wide, paved avenues, was the pen-and-ink illustrations of fantasy cities he had seen in the story collection in the monastery library. *Except this is even bigger*, he thought as he fell last into line, behind a particularly foul-smelling boy of about his own age. The boy carried two small yellow birds in a tiny, crudely crafted wooden cage. Rin noticed the method with which the boy held the cage out in front of him, his arm stiff. Rin imitated the movement with his own small, perforated box. He was not even certain what type of animal he had captured and contained in his box-trap. He had constructed the trap only last night, and felt immeasurably lucky that anything at all had taken the bait of stale cheese which he had stolen from a dozing trader. Now, as he held his arm out straight and walked slowly, in single file, towards the entrance, he could see the pointed brown nose and dark, beady eyes peering angrily at him from one of the larger holes in the box.

Two armed guards flanked the wide opening. They questioned and checked each person upon entry. They were now beginning the long line of children, and Rin watched nervously as one waif-like girl was turned away, her barter of dried, lifeless flowers deemed unacceptable to gain her access.

Rin watched as the boy ahead of him was summoned to the entry guard. He strained to hear the low, matter-of-fact voice ask about the contents of the box, the type of birds and the proposed value of the trade.

It is a game, just a game, Rin surmised as he saw the bored guard nudge the boy through into the main courtyard. Then the guard motioned for Rin to approach.

Holding the cage stiffly in front of him he shuffled forward. The guard paused dramatically, suspiciously eyeing the burlap bag which Rin had fashioned into a hooded robe. Seemingly satisfied, the guard turned his attention to Rin's outstretched arm.

'What is in the box?' the guard asked, not really curious but merely performing his duty.

'A gotja,' Rin replied, already cursing himself for the flippancy of his reply.

'A what?' the guard said, running his hand across the top of the closed lid.

'A gotja,' Rin repeated, this time augmenting his sincere tone with a slight, respectful bow.

'I do not believe I have ever heard of such an animal,' the guard said as he slowly raised the lid and placed his outstretched third finger beneath the nose of the four-legged prisoner. He moved the finger closer, nearly touching the cowering gerbillion.

'What did you call it?' he asked again, allowing his finger to dangle into the box as he looked at Rin.

'Got-ja,' Rin's answer coincided with the guard's quick, high-pitched yelp as he shook the sharp, clinging teeth from his finger. He glared furiously at Rin.

'Get out of here!' His words snapped at Rin's heels as the small boy ran through the gates, dropping his box and losing himself among the thick cluster of children, animals and the host of Zendow citizens who curiously awaited this weekly ritual.

*

'What is the meaning of this?' Zato challenged as he burst into the private dining-room adjacent to the Warlord's chambers.

Renagi stared up from his chair, anger in his eyes, as Zato threw the large white scroll down on the table. The torn end of the paper dipped into the serving-bowl of dark, thick gravy which sat beside the enormous portions of char-broiled lamb. Renagi eyed the announcement carefully before clearing his throat to speak. His voice was certain and controlled.

'It is quite correct. I am holding a selection. Three Warmen,' he said, confirming the accuracy of the scroll.

'Three Warmen for what purpose?' Zato pressed, already assuming the answer from the excited talk circulating in the Zendow barracks. Neeka watched quietly, amused at the frustration in Zato's voice.

'One of the three will kill the Ashkelite in combat,' Renagi answered flatly.

'And I suppose that is intended to prove the supremacy of our Royal bloodline?' Zato replied, making no disguise of his sarcasm. Renagi tried to control his growing agitation.

'Exactly,' he said.

Neeka noted the angry quiver in the sub-musculature surrounding Zato's mouth. She contained her satisfaction as, slowly, she lifted her goblet and sipped delicately at the wine.

'And would it not give this event true meaning if I . . .' Zato hesitated to drive his words into the old man, '. . . your only son, was the Royal champion?'

Involuntarily, the Warlord withdrew, pulling himself backwards, tight against the high, padded chair.

'It is out of the question,' he said, his voice sharp, centring his gaze on Zato's insistent eyes. 'Out of the question,' he repeated his words, this time relaxing, allowing his son to feel the warmth and concern within his heart.

'But it is a matter of honour,' Zato countered, his own intensity now rapidly dissipating, for he realized Renagi would not be swayed.

The Warlord placed a hand on his son's wrist. 'We are alone, you and I, and I will not take a risk with your life.'

Does he think I am not equal to Tegné? Zato wondered, containing the question.

'Now, please, dine with us. Let this matter be forgotten, at least for one evening,' Renagi insisted.

As Zato sat in the chair closest to the Warlord, he felt Neeka's gaze upon him. Finally he looked up.

Your father shames you! The thought projected from her eyes. It was as clear, as undeniable, as if she had spoken the words. Zato lowered his head, unable to look at her again.

Alone, Renagi walked slowly down the winding steps and into the dark, dank corridors of the prison. He would take Tegné to the cage himself; after all, it was the only way to ensure security! Yet there was another, deeper, hidden reason for his insistence. He had never been alone with Tegné, had never fully faced the fear that had obsessed him and driven him for the sixteen yeons that he had been aware of the Ashkelite's existence. And now, if he was to be truly strong, truly able to control the destiny of Zendow, he must conquer the uncertainty and dread which churned and twisted in his heart.

He turned the final corner and saw the narrow door of the interrogation cell less than twenty paces ahead. He heard the hobbling steps of the gaoler behind him as the man, having seen the Warlord enter the passage, struggled to catch up with him.

'Shall I open the cell, Master?' The voice came from close behind and as Renagi turned, the gaoler lost his balance and stumbled forward, falling into Renagi's arms.

'Sorry . . . sorry,' the gaoler said, pulling himself back, straightening his rumpled cotton tunic and attempting to stand at attention.

'Just give me the keys,' Renagi said, extending his open hand, unamused by the other's lopsided posture and awkward attempt at decorum.

'Shall I not accompany you to the prisoner?' the gaoler added as he handed over his coveted key-ring.

'I will see him alone,' Renagi answered, his stomach tightening and the first acute twinges of nervousness beginning to heighten his sense of awareness. 'Now leave me, I will call when I want you,' the Warlord added. The gaoler nodded, a slight look of dejection in his eyes.

'Go!' Renagi said sharply, watching as the man turned the corner and disappeared.

He walked the final distance to the cell. He hesitated only a moment, composing himself, feeling the hard steel of his katana pressing warm against his right side. Taking a deep breath he exhaled slowly as he twisted the key and pushed the creaking door inwards.

Tegné sat against the far wall; he looked up, making no effort to rise or change his position. Renagi entered the tiny cubicle, standing directly over Tegné. The door clicked shut with an ominous finality and father and son were, for the first time, alone.

There was absolute stillness in the cell. Tegné could feel both fear and indecision in this man who stood glowering down upon him. He studied the dark, hooded eyes, the wide flaring nostrils and the tight, full lips. The black, silver-streaked hair framed a face that had once been strikingly handsome and now still retained a distinct but pained pride. The deeply etched lines descended from the nostrils to the upper edge of the lips and continued beyond, cutting into the bronzed flesh. Renagi's forehead furrowed as he tightened his mouth in a mask of hatred, causing his eyes to sink low within their sockets. Tegné could hear the sound of angered breathing grow more intense as the Warlord glared at him. Yet Tegné felt no fear. Instead he was aware only of the sorrow which welled within him, hovering on the brink of expression.

Renagi read the compassion in the deep blue eyes, and for one moment he saw his reflection within them.

He spun away, avoiding Tegné's gaze, overcome with shame. Then Renagi hardened himself against the sob he felt rise from his tortured soul. The Warlord stood, head bowed and vulnerable, before the man he had despised, denied, and now would kill.

'Why?' Tegné's voice was soft, somehow naive, and in its naivety reminded Renagi of the Ashkelite girl, Maliseet.

Why, why? The word repeated in Renagi's mind as he turned again to Tegné.

'It is a matter of survival.' Renagi forced the sentence, giving it an anger which was not intended, for in his heart was only apology. 'Now stand,' he ordered, backing away, his hand hovering close to the hilt of the katana.

I will not weaken. I will see this through, Renagi commanded himself as he found his eyes searching the fine, pale face for a resemblance to his own.

*

The cage stood in the centre of the small, enclosed courtyard. At first sight it appeared to be a simple iron barrel, half-buried in the floor of the yard, but as Tegné walked closer, his leg-irons clanging noisily against the stone, he saw the full horror of what lay ahead. On top of the hollow barrel was what appeared to be the inside metal frame of a war helmet. Two padlocks held the face shield in place at the front of the helmet. Welded to the top and to each side of the frame, pointing inwards, were three sharpened metal spikes.

Tegné hesitated a moment as he and Renagi approached the device.

'Your first test of strength,' Renagi said, his voice low and determined, as he pushed Tegné towards the cage.

Tegné looked up and around the courtyard. He could see no escape from the high, barbed compound, and although the morning sun had barely risen above the western wall, the enclosed yard was already uncomfortably warm. Renagi eyed him cautiously as he unlocked the front of the iron barrel, pulling the two heavy metal sides outwards and open. Then with the same key he freed the bottom padlock and lifted the gridded face mask. Now he turned and faced Tegné.

'I am going to remove your leg restraints and cut the rope binding your wrists. You will climb into the cage. You have my word that if you do this you will be given a small but fighting chance to live. If, on the other hand . . .' Renagi said, drawing his short sword with a single sweep of his arm, '. . . you make a single move against me, or a single motion to escape, I swear to you that I will have your head, here and now.'

Tegné's expression did not alter as he bent down to retrieve the key that Renagi threw at his feet. He fitted it into the rusty lock of the leg-irons, turned it once and stepped free of the restraints.

Renagi backed a half-step away, his short sword in his left hand and his right ready to draw his katana. *If he moves towards me I will have no alternative,* he thought, almost hoping for a final confrontation. Tegné remained passive, still.

'Get in,' Renagi ordered, indicating the open metal doors.

Tegné walked forward, his wrists still bound, and awkwardly climbed into the metal barrel. The cage was hollow, as if he was stepping into a well. A thin, round metal bar ran across the emptiness below him and his bare feet perched painfully on it as Renagi walked closer.

'Hold your wrists out,' Renagi ordered.

Tegné extended his bound arms and Renagi hooked the blade of his short sword beneath the rope and cut it. 'There are two iron handles, one each side of the barrel,' Renagi explained. 'You will last longer if you hold on to them. If you do not, your body will hang free in the shaft and you will strangle,' he said as he closed the metal doors.

The sun-heated metal enveloped Tegné like a suffocating furnace. He breathed a long breath inwards, already attempting to control his respiration in an effort to limit his fluid loss.

Renagi pulled down on the face mask and the thick steel locked into position, the spikes pushing close to his head, permitting no movement. A sharpened half-plate closed in on the front of his neck and the locks secured the face mask.

Tegné's hands quickly found the twin handles and he shifted his bare feet so the pressure of the lower bar bore evenly beneath his arches. He stared out through the grid of the face mask and his eyes met the hard, fixed gaze of the Warlord.

'If you should survive I will allow you the privilege of death in combat,' Renagi said, his voice set and firm. Tegné did not answer.

A test of will, Renagi thought as he turned and marched away from the cage, looking back only once, yet somehow he was sure that Tegné would, indeed, survive.

The great white stallion reared on his hind legs as Renagi dug his boot heels into the bulging flanks and forced the horse forward, up the ramp and on to the newly constructed platform.

Zato followed, entering the yard at a canter as he rounded the far corner of the north gate. Then he slowed his mount to a walk and smoothly climbed the wooden ramp.

Father and son sat side by side on their horses, high on the raised floor. Renagi remained still, allowing the nervous tension to descend upon the waiting Warmen like a steel curtain. He scanned the faces, noting the effort his soldiers made to maintain a perfect, straight posture. For each Warman understood that the test was under way the moment the Warlord's eyes met theirs.

Zato saw Gazan standing last in the back of the four lines.

The Animal looked even more forbidding than Zato had remembered, then he noticed the wide, broken nose which had set flat and crooked against the broad face. Even from this distance Zato read the determination in the dark eyes and he observed the new and distinct twitch in the ridged muscles behind the jaw.

How on earth did Tegné beat him? Zato wondered as he held his eyes on the massive Warman who stood at least a head taller than any of those around him.

Renagi cleared his throat and Zato turned, intent, waiting for his father's opening words. Once more Renagi dramatically scanned the faces before him.

'My finest, most courageous Warmen! You!' Renagi began, and Zato relaxed slightly in his saddle, acknowledging that the passing yeons had taken none of the authority from the deep, rich voice.

It is a voice which drives, inspires, Zato observed as he watched the chests swell and the eyes harden in the men standing before him.

'You all know why you are here. You have all chosen to be here,' Renagi continued, looking from man to man. 'And from you I will choose three; the finest, the fastest, the strongest.' He hesitated, letting the words grip, already able to pinpoint the real contenders by the look in their eyes and the attitudes of their bodies.

'You will bring your Warlord great honour ...' he paused again, '... and you will gain great face ... heroes of Zendow!' Renagi boomed, his voice having built in subtle rises so that now it echoed through the exercise yard.

'Oss!' The single word reverberated from the lips of the forty Warmen, the word which meant, *We will push ahead. We will never give up*.

Renagi looked down on them, his eyes glowing, his shoulders drawn back so that he sat perfectly square in the saddle of Kano. He breathed in; a long, slow breath.

'Now, form one line. Facing me!' he ordered. Quietly, quickly, the Warmen obeyed.

'Back up. Leave plenty of room before the first man and the wall,' Renagi instructed, motioning for the leading Warman to move back, away from the wooden platform. Now the line was formed and the men waited expectantly for the 'test' to begin.

Wisely, Gazan had taken a place at the back, preferring to see what form the trial would take, to gauge the difficulty of the test. He watched as the less experienced, more exuberant participants grabbed positions near the front. He watched as the Warlord rose slightly in his saddle, his head turned to face the west gate. Then Renagi raised his left arm and, with a sharp gesture, signalled an anxious, waiting servant.

The servant walked forward, straining to hold the body-sized wicker basket at arm's length. His steps were small and precise, his head pulled back from the top of the basket, which was roped shut.

Whatever is in the basket, he does not want to disturb it, Gazan thought, studying the servant's tentative approach.

Zato craned his head sideways, his curiosity fully aroused.

'You will like this,' Renagi whispered, enjoying his son's interest.

The servant and basket were directly below them now, the servant breathing laboriously with his nervous exertion. Zato's horse shied, jerking backwards on the platform. Quickly, he tightened his hold on the reins, squeezing his thighs, controlling the stallion. The Warman standing first in line tensed, his eyes riveted on the wicker basket.

Renagi looked directly at the man, holding his gaze, until the Warman looked up.

'First test – speed,' Renagi stated, the barest hint of sarcasm in his voice. Then he turned to the uneasy servant.

'Now!' he commanded.

The servant tipped the basket away from him, simultaneously pulling the rope attached to the lid. He jumped backwards, then turned, dragging the empty basket, and sprinted towards the west gate. The thick, tightly coiled rhandoconda hit the ground with a resounding thud.

The three Warmen at the front of the line gasped in unison as the eight-foot serpent lifted its flat, flaring head. Hissing, the snake bared its long, curved fangs. The sharp black tongue darted in and out of the gaping mouth; a mouth which could easily envelop a man's fist.

The rhandoconda was angry, its body pressed tight to the rough wooden wall of the platform; the fear and nerves of the men standing before it only added to its feeling of capture, of containment.

Every Warman was familiar with the large, diamond-shaped, orange and black markings on the shining skin of the monster. They knew the rhandoconda had no natural fear of man and was, in fact, the single member of its species that would aggressively pursue and attack with no provocation.

'Catch the snake!' Renagi bellowed from the platform, his booming voice shattering the glassy window of terror through which the leading Warman viewed the long, carnivorous predator. The snake slid directly towards the first Warman in the line.

'Catch the snake! Now!' Again Renagi shouted, as the rhandoconda closed to within a body-length of the Warman. The line of men pulled back, out of range, as the Warman crouched, using the spring of his legs to bounce lightly on the balls of his feet, his right hand cocked and extended, the fingers pressed together while the thumb opened in the tiger's mouth position.

Zato watched as the man moved counter-clockwise round the snake. He was impressed with the physical control the young Warman exhibited, in spite of the obvious fear which had threatened to immobilize him just seconds before.

The rhandoconda remained still, the anterior portion of the tube of swollen muscle arched high, the head flared and facing the Warman as he drew closer, his sure, muscular feet gripping the stone and gravel floor. All eyes followed his movement, every stomach tight, waiting, wanting him to snap the hand forward, to grip and break the thick neck which had begun to sway ever so slightly . . . willing him to succeed in this test, if only to save themselves from an identical fate.

The serpent and the Warman stood eye to eye, the man's low, crouching stance causing them to be adversaries of equal height.

Zato sat stone still, his breath suspended as the moment of truth approached. He watched the extended arm as it drew back, readying for the strike. The serpent's head seemed to mirror the movement, drawing slowly away from the hand.

Yes! thought Zato as the hand flew forward, the full weight of the Warman's body behind it. The rhandoconda's head moved only slightly, the mouth appearing to open and snap lazily shut.

Yes, he has him! Zato was convinced, seeing the Warman grasp the long, heavy body with his left hand and attempt to lift the rhandoconda off the ground. His attacking hand remained intertwined with the serpent's head.

'Aaaah-eee-ahhh!' the spasmodic screams began as the Warman released his left-handed grip on the snake's body. He was already beginning to convulse as he pulled back, trying to escape from his enemy.

Zato could now see exactly what had happened, for as the Warman strained backwards, his right arm stretched out, the splayed open hand remained in the grip of the huge mouth. The twin bone fangs pierced and tore at the soft flesh between the thumb and first finger. Gradually the sheer weight of the serpent dragged the paralysed Warman forward until he dropped, face flat on the ground. Within a single beat, and before anyone could intervene, the rhandoconda let go of the hand, reared back, and bit once into the exposed neck. Renagi looked at Zato, nodded and grimaced as the venomous serpent held firm, twisting its head from side to side. Finally, the snake released its death bite. Then, as if through some instinctive intelligence the creature was conscious of its task, the rhandoconda rose up, its head once again flared, ready for the next man in line.

9

THE TEST OF THE SPIRIT

Those whose courage lies in
tenacity are usually killed.
Those whose courage lies in
diffidence usually remain alive.

(Lao Tsu)

The sun hung in the clear sky directly over the enclosed court-yard, beating relentlessly on the iron barrel and the attached steel cage. The metal simmered, sending its baking heat inwards.

Tegné maintained an even footing on the lower bar while balancing the bulk of his body weight with his wide-armed grip on the side handles, forcing himself into a straight-backed, cruci-fix position.

He inspirated through both nostrils with a soft, sobbing sound, then held the breath, counting a full sixty heartbeats before exhal-ing very slowly and silently by slightly retracting his abdominal wall. His head remained rigid, the sharpened spikes positioned perilously close to his forehead and temples. It would have been possible to let his mind go, allowing himself to drift into super-consciousness, but Tegné understood that to sustain the life of his physical body it was necessary, now, to remain cognisant of its condition. Already there had been a dangerous amount of fluid loss caused by the oven effect of the iron enclosure. Perspir-ation ran from every pore, a quantity gathering high on his upper chest and running in a thin, single stream down between his pectorals and over his abdomen.

His thoughts drifted with the pulse of his heart. *If you should survive . . . If you should survive . . .* The Warlord's words caught and repeated on the quietening surface of his mind.

I will survive, he resolved, without anger or sentiment. *Thirty days without food, six days without water . . .* He had learned at the temple that these were the maximum periods the deprived human body could sustain life. *But that was in the cool tranquillity of the mountains. How many days here, in the heat? In the cage?* He remembered his first survival fast; he had been barely twenty yeons when he had endured the initial exercise in self-preservation. Ten days alone in the forest, permitted only the juice of the seasonal fruits and vegetables. How clever he had thought himself when he had located a grove with full, rich oranges on the trees.

Yes, he could live the entire ten days on oranges alone. For the first two days he felt vital, pure and bursting with energy. Yet, by the evening of the fourth, his urine and faeces had taken on a distinct change in colour and the corners of his mouth seemed slightly sore and blistered. On the fifth day his stomach grew unsettled, his bowels loose and irregular. Still he had continued, sure that his system was merely purifying itself. On the sixth day he began the first mild cravings for fresh, clear water, anything other than the juice or flesh of the orange.

On the seventh day his mouth was tender to the touch and even the movement of his tongue along his gums was sore and irritating. By the evening of the eighth day he was certain the aroma of oranges exuded from his pores and even his skin seemed a yellow-gold colour. After nine days his scalp hurt and the mere action of rubbing his fingers through his hair caused shooting, needle-like pains in the top of his head.

His throat had swollen sufficiently by the tenth day to make the ingestion of the flesh of the fruit impossible. His body had become too weak to search for a source of fresh water and he was certain that he would die. Only then had his senior Brothers emerged from their places of hiding and given him the wonderfully cool, clear water to drink whilst chastising him gently for not paying heed to the warnings of his body. 'Better to have taken no food, no liquid, than to have unbalanced the yin and yang reserves of your system.'

And yet he remembered thinking that his ordeal had been nearly worth the discomfort if only for the near-ecstasy he experienced as he sipped the sweet, fresh mountain water. So chilled against his swollen throat, so light in his stomach. 'Water of life' – it had been his water of life.

Water, water, his mind focused dangerously. *Water, water* . . . His body cried out for the sweet, wet coolness.

And now the sweat that had initially poured from him had stopped, and a damp, clammy film covered his body. The sun perched high behind his stationary head.

'Get rid of the snake, it is unnecessary,' Zato said, his voice low, yet making no attempt to disguise his disgust for what was taking place below the platform.

Twice the rhandoconda had veered away from the line of men,

its own predatory urges overcome by its instinct to escape and survive. Each time Renagi had called a halt to the trial while two terrified servants were summoned to net the fleeing creature and drag it back to its position in the courtyard.

Three Warmen now lay dead before the rhandoconda. Still Renagi held firm, determined that one of those in line would defeat the serpent.

'Is there any point in destroying your own soldiers?' Zato hissed, sickened by the futility of the ordeal.

'Ask them. Go ahead, ask them if they wish to leave. Ask them if they wish the trial to be abandoned. Go ahead!' Renagi intoned, never taking his eyes from the new Warman who crouched and moved slowly towards the snake.

'I will, Father, I will,' Zato promised. Then he also turned his attention to the man below the platform.

Gazan had stayed well back in line, and now he complimented himself on this foresight as he watched the wiry, bandy-legged Warman move in measured half-steps towards the rhandoconda.

This man seems different, or perhaps the snake is tired, noted Zato, withholding his promised protest until the challenging Warman was either dead or victorious.

The flared head was up, swaying rhythmically back and forth. Instead of tensing in preparation for the strike, the Warman grew more relaxed, moving in a steady, even rhythm with the snake. Zato studied the man's cocked right arm, watching as the open hand, thumb and forefinger held wide apart, moved in a graceful, mesmeric motion, forwards, then backwards. Zato found himself captivated by the grace of the hand and whereas, in the beginning, the mood and motion of the rhandoconda had dictated to the Warmen, now the dominance had shifted; the rhandoconda moved in unison with the man.

Simultaneously with the motion of his hand, the Warman began a soft, high-pitched whistle, a lilting flow of music to which his outstretched hand moved. Gradually, almost imperceptibly, he drew closer to the serpent. The remaining men were silent, and the weight of anxiety which had hung so heavily in the air had vanished; every man watched, fascinated. The large, wide, flattened head was within a fingers breadth of his hand, the swaying motion in both serpent and man had ceased. For a moment Zato imagined the two as fine, beautifully carved statues, perfect, still, yet full with the potential of sudden life. He hardly noticed the toes of the Warman's bare feet as they flexed, securing a firm grip on the dirt and gravel of the floor of the exercise yard. Nor did he notice the man's slow, even inhalation as he readied himself for the final movement.

There was no lunge, no sudden strike. Instead the Warman slowly, smoothly, brought his hand below the serpent's head and easily, almost caressingly, rubbed downwards, gripping the narrowest part of the muscular neck.

'Yes!' Renagi shouted triumphantly.

In that instant the snake came alive, jolting as it began to open its mouth. But too late, for the Warman was already wrapping his leg around the massive neck as he pushed the thumb of his gripping hand into the soft white hollow beneath the rhandoconda's lower jaw. The thumb broke through the smooth, vulnerable skin and punctured the creature's windpipe.

The Warman held the serpent strongly, with both hands and one leg. The rhandoconda struggled a long moment, then with three desperate, hollow gasps the huge body went limp and lifeless.

The Warman looked up at the platform; Renagi's clenched fist was already high in the air.

'Yes! Yes!' the Warlord shouted again, emphatically, then turned to Zato. 'That is what I am looking for,' he said.

'What, a snake charmer?' Zato replied, but the sarcasm was directed at the superciliousness of his father, not at the awesome display of nerve and control he had just witnessed.

'Get the two geldings ready. Harnesses only. No saddles,' the old stable-master ordered. 'Come on, move!' he added, shaking his long-bristled sweeping brush at Rin.

Rin looked along the two parallel lines of stabled horses. *Two geldings? Where are the geldings?* he wondered.

'Geldings! Geldings! Last in the line on the left!' the grating voice shouted, although the tall, wizened man was only an arm's length from the boy.

It had been relatively easy, once inside the walled city, to separate himself from the others and find his way to the working heart of Zendow. There were many boys his own age labouring in menial positions; feeding wood to the giant kilns, stoking the forges, carrying bread and pastry from the stone ovens, and generally attending to the innumerable Zenchefs, smiths and weapon-makers who were the cogs in this mighty city.

Although far more grand and complex in its winding alleyways and multi-storeyed buildings, the nature of Zendow's inner workings reminded Rin of the Temple.

I can easily lose myself in here, he had thought as he found his way to the stables and observed the cluster of boys busily going about their tasks of cleaning, feeding and grooming the horses. He remained in the shadows of the adjacent grain holds while he ascertained the seniority of the workers. Finally he watched as a gaunt old man stepped into the centre of the straw-covered enclosure, looked impatiently at the surrounding boys and gestured with his hands.

Immediately the two closest to him snapped to attention, then the larger of the two lifted the pitchfork from the ground and disappeared into the stable while the other ran to fetch a wooden watering pail.

So that is the head man, Rin concluded as he walked into the enclosure. It was only when he walked close to the stable boss that Rin noticed the dull, nearly opaque eyes.

Cataract? Yes, that was the word he had heard the temple physicians use to describe this strange condition of the eyes. *I can use this to my advantage,* Rin thought as he stopped in front of the tall, stooping man.

'Sir? What would you like me to do now?' Rin asked, allowing his voice to give the impression that he had just completed one assignment and was anxious for the next.

'What? What did you say?' the stable boss questioned, bending his head and bringing his ear close to Rin's mouth. 'I do not believe I know your voice,' he added before Rin could speak again.

Rin took a full step back, tempted for a moment to turn and run, then he regained his composure.

'No, sir, you do not. I have been sent to you from the kilns; they have no more work for me,' he said, fabricating the story as he spoke.

'No more work? What? What?' the stable boss muttered, confounded by Rin's statement.

'No more work, sir,' Rin repeated, giving his voice a boost of authority.

'No more work? No more work?' the stable boss echoed, then considered. 'Well, good. I can always use you here.'

That had been five days ago. Now Rin was ensconced with the dozen other boys who worked in the stables and spent their few leisure hours talking of recent events in Zendow. All were aware that an impostor parading as the Warlord's son had been captured and confined to the cells, but the current excitement and talk centred exclusively on the imminent trial. A trial of combat in which the impostor would face the Warlord's chosen Warmen. A trial which would establish the supremacy of the Royal blood. A trial that everyone in Zendow was entitled to witness.

'Pssst! Hey!' the hushed voice persisted.

Rin turned to see the filthy face staring at him, the two brown eyes the only bright, sparkling spots amidst the grime.

'Stump?' Rin asked, hardly recognizing his new friend beneath the dirt. Stump hunched against the weight of the heavy bag of manure bearing heavily against his shoulder.

'The geldings,' Stump said, his voice low, secretive. 'The ones you are going to harness. Do you know what they are for?'

'No,' Rin answered, turning in time to catch a whiff of the manure as Stump hoisted the sack down from his shoulder. He held the heavy weight extended for a moment on his disproportionately muscular right arm, then let the burlap strap slide down over his wrist, across the joint where his hand had once been and on to the floor.

Whap! Another dense blast of manure made Rin reel away. Stump laughed, then inhaled deeply. 'What's the matter, ruin your appetite?' he said, wiping his nose with his blunt wrist.

Rin glanced at the point on his friend's lower arm where the limb had been chopped and the skin folded. He winced as he thought of how the remaining arm would have been held above the burning coals to seal the wound. Stump claimed to have lost the hand in a savage battle with a pack of timber wolves, but Rin guessed the truth: his friend had been caught poaching and the hand had been axed as punishment. Such was the law in the less-civilized northern provinces and Stump was, in fact, a northerner.

'So? What are they for?' Rin asked, turning his attention back to the geldings.

'Right now, while we speak,' Stump said, emphasizing the urgency of the moment, 'they are testing the Warmen.'

'Testing?' Rin asked.

'To select the man who will fight the Ashkelite,' Stump answered.

'And the geldings?' Rin pressed.

'The geldings are part of the test. I have seen it before, once during the Feast of Celebre. They hitch a man behind the horse, then they whip the horse to drive it forward. The man holds the horse back! I have seen it!' Stump went on, excited by his recollection.

'No!' Rin said disbelievingly.

'It is true, I swear,' Stump continued, emphatic.

'Do you think we could watch?' Rin asked, reasoning that a closer proximity to the Warmen might enable him to discover something as to the whereabouts of Tegné.

'Yes, if we can convince old Marble Eyes to let us deliver the geldings to the exercise yard,' Stump answered.

The servant stood poised on the platform, the small wooden cage held before him. In front of him stood Zanu, the Zendai swordmaster.

Zanu was the only Zendai participating in the selection. So skilled was he in the use of the katana that the Warlord had insisted upon his presence. His performance now was merely a formality.

'Blindfold him,' Renagi ordered.

Zanu stood alert, relaxed; the divided, skirt-like trousers of his black, square-shouldered hakama flapped easily in the light breeze. A second servant approached from behind and carefully placed the scarf in position, covering Zanu's eyes.

As many times as Renagi had witnessed Zanu's art with the katana, he again found himself eagerly anticipating another display. It was his kisagake which differentiated Zanu from the other resident swordmasters; the ability to unsheathe the blade and strike decisively with no pause in the acceleration of the blow, creating a lethal whipping action that was the mark of a true master. To draw, cut and resheathe, leaving no room for escape; that was the essence.

The Warmen stood, relaxed, forming a semi-circle around Zanu as the servant holding the cage readied himself to respond to his Warlord's command. Renagi studied Zanu, trying to perceive the swordsman's short, shallow breaths.

If I can just catch him on the out breath, Renagi thought, reasoning that it would then take perhaps an extra beat for the draw. He concentrated, waiting. Then, suddenly, he detected the slight bulge in the heavy silk of the hakama above Zanu's abdomen. 'Pull!' he shouted.

Instantly the wooden door of the cage snapped open.

Through the blackness of the scarf, Zanu sensed the subtle change in the vibration of the gentle wind. He pushed from his lower stomach, drawing the blade, increasing its momentum, raising the steel high, slicing down, then crossways and to his left before resheathing. His scabbard was still warm from the friction of the blade's exit. The entire movement had been a blur before Renagi's eyes.

The exercise yard was quiet as the servant removed the scarf from Zanu's forehead. Before him, three thumb-sized hummingbirds lay on the ground, each divided cleanly in half.

The Warlord looked down, nodded, then smiled. 'Three. Very good. Very good – you missed only one,' he said, maintaining the challenge.

Now it was Zanu who smiled; his oblong, olive face displaying a gleaming set of large white teeth. Then he extended his clenched left hand, palm upwards.

'Number four, Master,' he stated, opening his hand to reveal the severed bird.

'Make yourself dead.' How many times had Tegné heard those three words during the day-long sessions of concentrative meditation? *'Make yourself dead ...'* Goswami had repeated as he walked amongst the Brothers with his long bamboo stick, smacking mercilessly at any dozing novice.

'Make yourself dead.' All awareness of self, of action, of thought, had been dissolved. His eyes were closed and the cool, full moon hung suspended in time at the centre of his consciousness. Somewhere, far away, he heard the mantra, *'I am a wave. Make me the sea.'*

'Make yourself dead.' The red, shimmering ball of fire dropped lazily behind the western wall. The cage stood alone in the shade of the courtyard and, finally, the heavy corrugated iron began to cool.

*

'Wait a minute! Hold on,' Rin called, halting Stump on the outer edge of the exercise yard.

'What are you doing that for?' Stump questioned as he watched Rin pull the wrinkled hood up and over his head, then tie the dirty cloth loosely around and over his mouth, securing the hood in place.

'Sunstroke. I am very susceptible,' Rin answered, having already spotted the huge, shirtless Warman in the corner of the yard. 'Those eyes . . . I know those eyes,' he thought as he became suddenly aware of the nagging pain in the back of his thigh where the bolt had entered.

Stump frowned sceptically as Rin led the gelding forward.

'Nervous?' he asked as he crossed the perimeter.

'Yes,' Rin admitted. Both he and Stump could see the Warlord and his son mounted high on top of the twelve-foot platform. *Like some great, almighty god,* Rin thought as he took in the full grandeur of the older man; the gigantic white stallion, the shining black leather of his uniform and the wide, padded shoulders. The Warlord was positively glowing with the last light of day. The boys hesitated.

'Come forward!' Renagi's full voice beckoned. Slowly they approached the platform.

'Fine, fine!' Renagi said, stopping them within the last few yards. 'Take the horses from them,' he ordered, and instantly two servants ran from the edge of the yard and took hold of the harnesses.

Rin and Stump, empty-handed, stood looking up, attentive to the Warlord.

'Move over to the side. Stand with the servants. You will take the horses back when we are through with them,' he said, accompanying his words with a sweeping, left-handed gesture. Obediently the boys ran to the far corner of the platform.

The geldings were pulled so that they stood side by side, facing out from the Warlord. A clear, deep line was cut into the gravelly dirt a full body's length behind them. The harnesses were extended by the use of leather straps so that they reached back and overlapped the line. A group of a dozen Warmen gathered near the horses, removing their shirts, flexing and loosening the muscles of their naked torsos.

'First two . . .' Renagi said, lifting himself in his saddle so he could view the proceedings directly below him. Two Warmen ran from the group, took their positions on the line and allowed the servants to adjust the harnesses and straps, wrapping them round their shoulders and making certain that the wide flat straps lay evenly across the Warmen's deltoids. The two Warmen arched back, away from the horses, as they dug their boot heels deep into the soft gravel.

'Ready!' Renagi commanded. The men crouched slightly, bending at the knees and flexing their thighs.

'Now!' shouted Renagi.

Simultaneously, each of the attending servants brought his hair-whip down on the haunch of his assigned gelding. Both men held firm as the horses strained forward. Rin sensed the enormous exertion as he watched their bodies shudder and quiver with the effort not to be pulled across the line.

'Ahhh! Ahhhh!' the Warmen cried.

'Again!' Renagi commanded, and again the hair-whips were brought to bear on the muscular horse flanks. Rin heard what sounded like the single crack of stone hitting stone, then watched as the Warman nearest him went limp, his body lurching forwards as the gelding charged ahead.

'Stop him!' Renagi shouted.

A single Warman caught the harness and brought the runaway horse to a standstill. The contest had lasted only a few seconds, and as Rin watched the loser's body being carried from the exercise yard, the head twisted strangely where the cervical vertebrae had broken, the boy was reminded of the quickness and finality of death.

'You stay,' Renagi ordered the victor, then looked at the dwindling group of challengers. Gazan stepped forward. Rin could not take his eyes from the mountainous man; never had he seen such muscularity, the thick arms with their rope-like veins twisting down to the gnarled wrists and huge-knuckled hands. Gazan turned to the gelding, challenging the horse with his eyes, his face set and committed. The servant carefully aided him with the harness and strap.

Rin stood off to the side, behind Gazan. From his vantage point the Warman's back seemed to billow outward from the tight waist until the latissimus muscles spread the entire width of the massive shoulders. As Rin watched, the Warman competing against Gazan glanced over, a look of defeat already in the deep, shadowed eyes. Now they were both ready, and sank into their crouch, their toes tight on the line.

'Now!' Renagi shouted, and the sound of hair-whips cut the tense air. For a long, effortful moment, both men held the line. 'Again!' Renagi ordered.

Snap! The whips came down on the hard horseflesh. 'Whoa! Whoa!' Gazan shouted, seemingly on the verge of losing his footing. Then in a slow, bending motion, as if the gelding was pulling him forward, Gazan leaned across the line, bent at the waist.

Rin expected to see the huge Warman toss the harness straps up and over his shoulders, freeing himself from the contest and escaping the chance of injury. Instead, Gazan slid his hands along the flat leather straps on each side of him. Then, screaming through clenched teeth, he straightened, pulling on the straps, heaving upwards and back. Rin was certain the coursing blood would explode through the veins of his pumping biceps.

'Yaaaa!' Gazan yelled, rising to a standing position and straining to pull back more.

'Yes! Yes!' It was Zato's voice that cried out, moved by the display of sheer brawn, urging the Warman on. Now the gelding was beginning to give way, losing ground, its sinewy legs buckling as the metal horseshoes cut into the gravel. Still Gazan pulled, breaking the gelding's spirit as the hindquarters lowered to the ground, the rear legs relaxing, giving up, and the horse was dragged backwards to the line.

'Enough! Enough!' Renagi boomed, just as Gazan's competitor lost his footing and toppled headlong, his body beginning a dangerous skid across the gravel. Renagi turned his head in time to see the sprawling man rise to his knees as with a lightning reflex he pushed the harness and strap from behind his shoulders, throwing them away from his body while the gelding continued its charge, dragging the empty rigging behind. On any other occasion such a quick, well-timed move would have gained the Warlord's attention, but today the man was left to stand and recover with the aid of only a single servant. All eyes were on Gazan.

'Are there any other challengers amongst you?' The Warlord called out, his voice proud and easily commanding the entire yard.

'For any of these three?' he continued, his tone deepening as he looked down on the snake charmer, the swordmaster and the Animal.

The men responded with silence. 'Then I say, these shall be my chosen Warmen!'

'Oss! Oss! Oss!' the cheer echoed, unifying the ranks as the clenched right fists punched skywards.

'Well? Are you satisfied that we will be properly represented?' Renagi asked Zato, having observed his son's excitement during the testing and now, finally, expecting him to concede to his father's superior wisdom.

'That is not the point, Father,' Zato responded. 'They are not of Royal blood, and with the exception of Zanu they are not even Zendai,' he finished, his voice heavy with the weariness of one whose reason would never be acknowledged.

'They will carry the Sign of the Claw,' Renagi snapped, then without waiting for a reply he turned, heeled the white stallion and clattered down the wooden ramp.

Zato followed, catching his father at the base of the platform directly in front of Stump and Rin. The boys stood quiet, unobtrusive, waiting for the servants to bring them the two geldings.

'And what, after all this, if Tegné defeats our chosen Warmen?' Zato asked bitterly, although aware of the near-impossibility of such an event.

'Never!' Renagi replied, confident. 'There will be no chance after the Ashkelite has spent three days in the cage!' he added, letting his secret slip in bitter retaliation for Zato's persistence.

'The cage!' shouted Zato angrily.

Renagi turned in his saddle and looked hard at Zato, satisfied that his revelation had taken effect.

'Yes, the cage,' he said flatly. Then he dug his heels into his horse's sides and galloped towards the gates, leaving Zato to stare after him.

'The cage . . .' Rin whispered to himself, already fearful of the image it created. *Where is the cage?* he wondered, growing desperate.

Night, and time drifted on a smooth, cool sea, mid-way between sleep and wakefulness, as if Tegné's open-armed body sailed through a black void while images formed in his mind like the converging shapes inside a kaleidoscope. The symmetrical figures created faces then, breaking up, they swept past before being caught again in the whirling tide of his consciousness.

For a second Tabata's face hovered in space before Tegné's closed eyes. The Sensei's face evoked instant emotion; love, trust, and a filial loyalty to uphold all that was pure and honourable. Tegné felt the clarity which the image produced, a clarity which he struggled to maintain as Tabata's face fragmented against the blackness, the composite pieces splintering before, gradually, drawing back together.

This time it was the raven-girl who smiled from the ether, and this time the rush of emotion was centred in his heart, a longing, a yearning, a promise of what could be if he would put aside his purpose and become merely a man of flesh and blood, a husband, a father. And as rapidly as this thought passed through him her image split apart, replaced by the face of the Elder and the feelings of guilt. *Guilt? Why am I not freed from this guilt? Everything in my past ... is it not part of the divine plan, the divine purpose? Surely that was the point of my instruction, my meditation. Self-knowledge. Or is my meditation a trick of consciousness, a figment of my imagination? Self-deception ... Perhaps there is no divine purpose, no leap of faith. The Warrior ... I am the Warrior. Or is that some fantasized façade behind which I justify my existence?*

His mind raced back, creating distorted images of his childhood; *Abandoned, chased, hunted ... Alone ... alone ... An outsider at the Temple, a destroyer of life. All paths lead to one place – here. Imprisoned, trapped like an animal, sentenced to death. My very existence is a crime against nature, the result of an atrocity committed by my own father. A father who denied me. Indulgence, self-pity; the enemies of a warrior ... But am I really a warrior? Am I not simply a tired, dying man?* A lifetime of training had made him strong but now his strength gave way. His tears were dry; he had no body fluid left with which to cry, but they were none the less sobs of sorrow. *Why? Why am I entangled in this dreadful nightmare? I have done nothing. I am a victim, violated, humiliated. I do not hate anyone, why am I so hated? Why can I not die?*

Finally, mercifully, sleep took him in its grasp and the suffering blurred, then dissolved into darkness.

He awakened as the warm, rough tongue touched him through

the iron slats, moving across his forehead, down over his cheek and against his dry, cracked lips. He kept his eyes locked shut as the tongue probed further, penetrating his mouth, licking his sore gums, transfusing him with a sweet nectar. He sucked, taking the tongue and its liquid down inside him. The tongue dissolved into a full stream of water as it slid along his throat and into his stomach. Then he felt the tongue on his face again, massaging his tightly closed eyes, adding blackness to blackness. Finally it retracted, and a warm, full breath dried the moisture from his skin. The breath cooled and became a rush of chilled air, blowing along his body, reviving him and giving him strength. Then the breath was gone.

He opened his eyes. The moon above was three-quarters full and the stars hung close in the clear sky. He looked straight ahead through the slats of the cage.

She stood only a few yards away, her enormous black body resting back on her sleek, muscular haunches. He knew her from the lake, from the desert, from his heart. She had always been with him, and now her gaze soothed his anguish.

She remained until the first light of day. Then, as his eyes adjusted to the early morning glow, he could no longer see her.

Awake. Asleep. *Dreams. Illusion. Reality.*

Zato stood alone on the landing, staring down from the open window. The cage was directly below him, solitary in the midday sun as the heat baked the ground of the courtyard, quiet and relentless.

Zato studied the device with a morbid curiosity, finding it difficult to comprehend that a man – indeed, his half-brother – was confined inside the ugly structure of rusty iron and steel. Again he felt the compulsion to move closer, to watch, to observe. *Why do I attribute such nobility to this suffering? Would I trade places with the man in that cage?* he wondered as he backed away from the window, growing disgusted with himself for his display of voyeurism. *If I need to see Tegné, surely then I could walk down the steps, out into the yard, and face him?* he thought before he turned and began the climb down, slowing his pace as he reached the bottom of the staircase. Finally he stood before the bolted wooden door leading to the courtyard.

He braced himself. It was hate he must feel, pure and unadul-

moon and the single silver star. But Rin was already far away in thought. The announcement had set Julin 22nd as the day of combat.

'How many days can a man last in the cage?' Rin asked.

Stump was taken aback by the question. He hesitated a moment. 'Two, maybe three,' he finally answered, his eyes fixed on the medallion.

Two, maybe three . . . Rin considered. To the best of his knowledge, Tegné had already been in the cage two days, and the combat was still two days away.

Renagi stood in the centre of the Great Hall as the labourers, servants and builders worked tirelessly around him. He watched as the giant sheets of silvered mirror-glass were wheeled into the room on the low, flat trolleys, then hoisted by pulleys attached to scaffolding until the entire northern wall was covered with the reflection of the working multitude.

'Good! Exactly what I want!' Renagi shouted his approval above the din of the building works.

The construction engineer in charge of the grand mirrored walls looked up and bowed quickly to the Warlord in acknowledgement of his praise, then turned and waved the next enormous silver sheet forward. Soon the entire hall would be encased in the shining mirrors, causing the already vast room to appear infinite in size and to multiply the ten thousand expected onlookers by a hundredfold.

Flat, bench-like wooden seats were being constructed to take care of the lower orders of Zendow inhabitants while the high, more elaborate stone seats would be padded with velveteen cushions to accommodate the Zendai and the various advisers and administrators. Renagi, of course, would occupy the Velchar, Neeka would sit to his left and Zato on his right. Miyaz would occupy the seat closest to Zato and Kase next to Neeka.

The appointment of these two Warmen had met with far less resistance than Renagi had anticipated. Again, Neeka had been astute in her judgement, the Council of Zendai were far too unnerved by the demise of Yanon and Bakov to offer more than token objections against two 'commoners' assuming seats of power.

And Miyaz and Kase had rewarded Renagi's faith by instilling a loyal practicality into subsequent meetings of the Council. The Warlord had heard nothing more in the line of gossip or damaging rumour. *Yes, everything is working according to plan,* thought Renagi as he inspected the semi-circular row of banked seats which had been arranged for his black-armoured Warmen. He could see it now; he could already feel the power build inside him as he looked at his proud mirrored image against the northern wall. He straightened, adjusting the line of his loosely belted, knee-length jacket, the red embroidered Claw distinctly visible against the matte blue of the silk.

Neeka was right; she has always been right. This will be my moment of absolute power; a purging, a process of purification. I will banish all doubt, all fear. I will stand almighty, Neeka by my side, Zato as my successor. I will bask in the glow of Zendow, solid and sure . . .

Again he looked into the wall-length mirror. He would be sixty-eight yeons this year, yet still had the stature and bearing of a soldier. His right hand shot to the hilt of his katana, drawing the blade enough from its scabbard to see the flash of steel in re-flection.

'Very good, very good. Why bother with the Warmen?' The voice was warm, if somewhat sarcastic.

He watched in the mirror as she glided across the floor, her low-centred movement so still in comparison to the hauling, hammering and building which took place all around them. Her shoulders appeared to remain in one line as she came forward; there was none of the ordinary up-and-down movement to her steps.

Neeka was dressed in white, the finest of the Yusun-spun cotton, and her long, tight-waisted skirt was so thin that Renagi could make out a hint of her silk undergarments as she came up beside him. He took a long look as they stood together in reflection; her head reached only to the level of his broad, padded shoulders, yet her total demeanour was so radiant, so vital, that it was as if, by standing next to her, Renagi became merely a shadow.

He turned from the reflection. 'Magnificent,' he said, opening his arms expansively, seeking her appreciation of the Great Hall and the works in progress.

'Yes, magnificent,' she agreed, but withheld a crucial level of enthusiasm.

'Is there a problem?' Renagi queried, aware of her distance.

'There will be a great problem if, after all this extravagant preparation, you are left with only the corpse of an Ashkelite on which to prove your honour,' she stated, suddenly reducing his fantasies to rubble.

'It will go as I have planned,' Renagi countered, his voice brusque.

'Then perhaps you should take a closer look at your prisoner. I have just come from the courtyard and I can tell you that he will not last until the combat. He is barely breathing,' Neeka said. 'Do you intend to wheel him in here propped on wooden supports?' she continued, motioning with her head towards the carpenters who were constructing the lower seats. Renagi stood stone-faced, lost for an answer.

'It will be a sham, a total travesty!' Neeka concluded.

The two glared at each other in silence as the builders continued their construction, no one daring to glance at the Warlord and his concubine. For a moment Renagi thought he glimpsed a spark of hatred in the violet eyes behind the ninjinka.

No, no, it is only her anger that I see, he reassured himself, recoiling and softening in one involuntary exhalation. 'I cannot take any risks with him,' he offered, his voice quiet and containing the trace of a plea.

'It is no risk to have him bathed and properly clothed. Remember, he was a Brother in a Martial Order. Give him the outward appearance and his training and sense of propriety will guarantee us a good, albeit hollow, performance. But let him enter this arena ragged and filthy and you diminish everything this trial stands for,' Neeka reasoned.

Renagi did not answer, but there was clear reluctance in the set of his jaw. 'Leave him in the cage tonight, even through the heat of tomorrow, but please allow me to have him bathed and dressed when he walks from the cells to the combat,' she said, then continued, 'I will give him the hapaver tea. That will fortify him temporarily. Anything to make him appear equal to your Warmen. That is the only way all of this will be effective.'

Renagi silently weighed her words. She had never failed him; indeed, he had come this far because of her strength, her guidance. *Yes, Neeka is right; she has always been right.* He looked again into the soft, violet eyes, seeing only love and devotion.

'Tegné does not come out of that cage until midday before the combat. Then you may bathe him, clothe him, give him enough hapaver to enter the arena. But no more . . . nothing more,' the Warlord stated, somehow feeling that he had initiated the entire plan.

Neeka bowed demurely to the Warlord, turned and walked away. Renagi watched the low, gliding steps, admiring her once again before he looked up, noting the placement of the second wall-sized mirror. Then the Warlord reviewed his reflection from a new, different angle.

'I do not want to go back,' Tegné said.

'I am sorry, but you must. Your work is not finished,' answered Tabata.

'I would prefer to begin again,' Tegné insisted.

'You cannot begin again until you complete the circle in its entirety. Then it will be decided if you shall begin again,' Tabata continued, his voice rising and falling in soothing waves.

Tegné turned from his Sensei and searched the other bright, glowing faces which surrounded him. There was sympathy and compassion in all of them.

The white robes of the Seven Protectors shimmered in the golden light. Their faces smiled and the swirling turquoise of their eyes reached out to him, forgiving.

The Elder stood directly before him, his face full and peaceful, He nodded slowly as he reached out his small, gentle hand and touched Tegné's naked shoulder, urging him to look to his left.

There, beside his Sensei, stood a beautiful young woman. Her white skin was flawless, exquisite, pulled like fine porcelain across the high, chiselled cheekbones. Her large, wide eyes were golden amber, accentuated by the long white lashes and fine, curved brow. Her lips were pink, like a delicate, full-petalled rose, her face framed by long flaxen hair which hung below the waist of her azure robes. It was the face his heart had yearned for, the face of his mother.

'Maliseet . . .' he whispered her name as he stepped towards her. She opened her arms to him, the soft, weightless fabric of her robes brushing his skin. He closed his eyes, and he could hear the beating of the silken wings of a single butterfly.

'Tegné . . .' she said his name and the syllables trickled like spring water, dissolving into a fountain of light. 'Tegné, you must turn from me. You must see, you must know,' she said, stroking his hair. He felt the warmth behind him even before he obeyed her.

The Being of Light stood before him, a spirit different from the others yet loving and familiar. The Being of Light had no face, no discernible features.

Look ... look at me ... The command was gentle, non-verbal. Tegné looked into the light.

He watched the images form, the pictures vivid, colourful, rolling before his eyes. He recognized himself; the baby plunging over the falls, rescued by Tabata, chased by the Warmen, saved by the Beast, taken by the Protectors, sheltered in the temple ... hunted by the Clan, wandering alone. He revisited the Lake of Dreams, saw his naivety, his own seduction. Watched himself as he accepted the blade from the Protectors. He viewed his capture, saw the look of recognition in Zato's eyes as the birthmark was revealed. He saw Neeka's face, waiting behind the ninjinka; always waiting. He saw his own body, unconscious inside the cage, hanging limp in the iron barrel ...

He understood the absurdity of this death. No ... he could not die. His Earth life must have meaning, resolve – death, now, was futile. He would not die.

Now Tabata stood before him. 'Breathe the breath of life,' Tabata ordered, inhaling, filling his own lungs, then with a cool, whistling sound he exhaled.

Tegné took the air into his own body; once, twice, three times.

'Breathe the breath of life ...' He could still hear Tabata's words as he felt the rough hands lift him from the inferno. Then muffled voices reached him; 'Is he dead?' 'Maybe.' 'No, I think he is breathing.'

They carried him up, up the winding stairs, along a corridor, their feet clacking against the wooden boards. Finally, they laid him down; a cool, dry hand rested on his forehead, then peace ... blackness ...

'Tegné ... Tegné ...' It was Neeka's gentle voice which woke him from the heavy, dreamless sleep. He opened his eyes.

The room was large, square, and the late afternoon sun streamed in through the open window.

'You have slept nearly eight hours. I have been worried,' she said as she carried the tray supporting the steaming pot of tea across the room to him.

Tegné pushed himself up against the pillow. He was naked beneath the light summer quilt. He used his eyes and his hands to take stock of his condition and was amazed to find his body clean, his hair washed and combed, and his face smoothly shaven.

'How do you feel?' Neeka asked, placing the tray on the low bedside table and sitting close to him.

He thought before answering. Somehow the memory of the torture seemed distant. He remembered the heat, the never-ending heat, sucking the moisture from him drop by drop until his skin felt like a thin layer of parched paper which would wrinkle and peel away from the bones. He had tried to control the dehydration using long, suspended breathing, reducing the beat of his heart, staying close to consciousness. Initially his discipline had kept him alive, for two, perhaps three days. But finally his body would stand no more and at the point of his greatest distress, in the early morning of the fourth day, he had begun to hear a loud, uncomfortable buzz, as if a giant wasp had somehow entered his hollow skull. The buzzing continued, building in volume until the level was intolerable. Simultaneously he had felt himself moving rapidly down a long, dark tunnel, and finally he was outside the cage, yet able to see his Earth body within it. He had recognized this as a state of projection, yet the detachment from his Earth form was so distinct, so clear, that he knew he had entered the first stage of physical death. Then he had seen the light and heard Tabata call his name.

'Alive,' he said simply.

Neeka was already in the process of warming the cup in preparation for serving the tea.

'I have brewed this especially for you. It will restore you, give you strength,' she said, all the time working the cup and cloth in a circular motion above the candle's flame.

'Why?' Tegné asked, yet somewhere remembering Renagi's promise that if he should survive the cage he would be granted the privilege of death by combat.

'Because tonight, in the arena, I want you to be victorious,' she said, a solemn sincerity in her tone.

'Tonight?' Tegné reacted, 'I will never be able to fight . . .'

'You will, I shall see to it. Believe me,' she said, cutting him off. 'Now sip the tea. Do not swallow it immediately, hold it in your mouth,' she instructed, lifting the cup to his lips.

The bitter-sweet aroma reached his nose before he sipped the hot liquid. He held the tea without swallowing, circulating it beneath his tongue and around his gums. He marvelled at how the mixture numbed the inside of his mouth and seemed to chill almost instantly.

'Now swallow,' she coaxed, studying the pupils of his eyes for the first dilations.

Tegné swallowed, and the coolness entered him, settling only a moment in his stomach before spreading its calm, sure fingers into his extremities. He felt the new, fiery strength rekindle the sleeping muscle fibres of his arms and legs.

She watched, satisfied, as the pores of his light skin began to tighten and a visible energy entered his face.

'Better, much better,' she said, offering him the cup again. 'This time, drink the tea rapidly, empty the cup.'

He took the cup from her hand, lifted it, tentative at first, to gulp the steaming brew.

'Do it,' she urged.

He tilted the cup, allowing the liquid to spill into his open mouth. There was absolutely no sensation of heat.

'Drink it! Quickly!' Neeka's voice suddenly contained an edge of authority.

Tegné downed the tea in one continuous, open-throated swallow. He handed her the empty cup, a half-smile on his face. His eyes questioned her. At first he felt nothing.

It happened all at once; the powerful rush made the first sensation of the tea seem mild, insignificant. His skin positively tingled, every nerve ending alive and vibrating, his muscles virtually exploding, begging to be used, exploited. All doubt, all fear, was instantly erased from his mind. He stared into Neeka's smiling, knowing eyes. He felt a sudden wildness, an unfamiliar violence. He wanted to take her. Now.

He reached up and gripped her arm, drawing her towards him on the bed as he pulled the cover from him, exposing his aroused nakedness, wanting her to see him. Unashamed, unafraid.

'Yes. Yes. You will do well,' she said, admiring him, yet not succumbing to his desire. Then she reached out with her right hand and placed the cool, open palm on his forehead. He closed his eyes.

I have waited for you. You know me. We are one. Her thoughts entered him in a clean charge, crystal clear in his mind, and with them came the vision of darkness, the Black Cat.

He knew the Cat was his ally, his strength, restless, stirring inside him. He drew her closer, looking up, imagining the face hidden behind the ninjinka.

'When the time is right you shall know me. Completely,' she said. And for a moment he was certain she bore the eyes of the Cat. And then the certainty passed.

'I want you to turn over, on to your stomach. It is important that you do as I ask,' she insisted, removing his hand from her. And, as if the removal of the hand caused the electricity to subside, Tegné became instantly calm, his mind lucid and the overpowering sexual energy which had dominated him only moments before vanished, replaced by a heightened sense of physical awareness.

Her fingers traced the vertebrae of his spine, working, kneading, liberating the vast reservoir of coiled energy at the base of his sacrum. He recognized the tingling pulses as the serpent began its rise. But this was different; she was controlling the energy, holding it longer in the lower chakras, allowing the nerve-centres to open fully, activate totally. Gradually he felt his heart and lungs respond.

He hovered on the edge of the Dragon Zone, knowing that through her manipulation she could push him forward or hold him back. She held him back, and finally his mind entered a slow, drifting pattern where all thoughts were one thought and the river flowed surely to the sea.

'Tonight, Tegné, you enter the arena,' she began, yet the sound of her voice was far away, coming from the other side of the dream. 'You will fight with the quickness of a panther, your claws like razors. One strike. You will not be touched, you will not be harmed, for you are protected. You will look into your adversary's eyes and he will see only blackness, only death. One strike and you will take his heart ... Tegné, there is death in your fingers. One strike. One strike ...' The words echoed, trailed off, floating towards infinity.

*

Rin stood among the milling crowd. It was well into the twentieth hour and still the doors of the Great Hall remained locked. His shoulders were stooped, his eyes downcast, his heart heavy with sorrow and guilt. Too late he had learned the location of the cage, and only then on hearsay from another stable-boy. Then he had filled a cumbersome wooden bucket with water and dragged it, slopping, through linking courtyards and finally to the supposed location.

There he stood below the high, impenetrable stone wall. He had placed the bucket on the ground and searched until sunset for a way past the thick grey stone. Finally he had knelt down on the sharp gravel and used his bare hands to dig, trying to reach under the foundation until, exhausted, his hands cut and bruised, he sat, absorbed in his own futility, and sobbed.

'What's the matter with you? You look like you are going to cry,' Stump said, coming up beside Rin and nudging him.

'Nothing ... nothing. I am just tired of waiting and I hate crowds,' Rin answered, looking around at the growing number of anxious faces.

'It will not be long now. They will bring him through, then we can go in,' Stump replied.

'Bring him through?' Rin repeated, questioning.

'The Ashkelite. He will be paraded before the crowd. It is all part of the trial,' Stump confirmed.

'How do you know?' Rin asked.

'I have seen one other trial like this, two yeons ago; a military adviser, accused of plotting against the state. They executed him publicly. Not here – it was not this grand, but they let everyone see him first. Part of the humiliation,' Stump continued.

'But this is not an execution, it is a trial by combat,' Rin countered.

'Trial by combat. Execution. Believe me, they mean the same thing. The Ashkelite will not stand a chance. You have seen Renagi's Warmen,' Stump said, shaking his head as he remembered the day of the selection.

As Rin stood, meeting his friend's eyes, the image of Gazan, with veins bursting through the massive, bare chest, filled his mind.

Tegné woke at the twenty-first hour. The sun had fallen like a red, fiery ball, below the horizon, and the after-light cast warm, familiar shadows into the room. Death seemed a long way away.

The black silk hakama with its heavy, shining sash, sat beautifully clean and perfectly folded on the table beside him. A thin, black leather half-glove lay next to it. The air was still, peaceful, no breeze, no moisture within it.

Tegné rose from the bed, stretching his joined hands upwards, breathing in, then exhaling as the fingers parted and his arms stretched wide to each side and downwards in a circular motion. Three times he repeated the movement, each time expelling all thoughts and doubts from his mind. Then he walked to the steps in the far corner of the room, mounted them and entered the small bath-chamber.

Squatting above the sewage hole in the corner of the room, he evacuated his bowels and bladder. He felt the tight-coiled muscle in his thighs as he rose from the position.

Finally he entered the bath, letting the icy water surround him, feeling it tighten his lungs as he breathed in against the contraction. He took the pumice stone from the marble surround and rubbed the skin of his face and neck, working down across his shoulders and chest until his entire body felt alive and clean.

He threw his head back, submerging himself completely, running his fingers through his long hair, pulling it to his head. When he surfaced he held the hair, rolling and knotting it so that the bulk hung like a pony's tail behind him.

He walked, wet and naked, into the main room and sat down on the wooden floor, bathing in the last glow of sunlight from the window as he crossed his legs in full lotus.

Death seems a long way away . . . That was the illusion of life. Death was close, always. In the warmth of the sun, in a breath of air. Sitting beside him now on the wooden floor. Death was his discipline, his teacher.

Tegné opened both arms, breathing in his death, accepting. For a moment he imagined the Warmen. Black, ominous. He saw them move, their huge padded bodies dancing in silhouette before his closed eyes, their fists and swords cutting towards him. He imagined the thudding fists against his skin, their steel weapons burning his flesh. He opened his arms, breathing in, absorbing the pain. Then he breathed out, pushing the pain from him. Separating. His mind was calm, certain, alert.

Every lesson he had learned, every fighting form: the candle, the wolf, the Trial of One Hundred, internalized, assimilated, giving birth to a true spontaneity. He floated comfortably, empty, without obstruction. Free of desire, of attachment. One strike. His intent was pure, true. All his being centred. His only course was action. He had borne his moment of doubt and weakness, and banished it. Now he was sure, confident, ready.

He stood up. His body was dry, his hair clean and smooth. He took the hakama from the table, placing his left leg into the corresponding side of the divided skirt, then his right, pulling the hakama upwards. Drawing the heavy, quilted top to his body, he tucked the waist down inside the belt, pulling the ties tight and securing them.

Finally the shining sash. He wrapped it around him, beginning on his left side and doubling the heavy material so it sat in two layers at the back of the hakama, never letting the silk touch the floor. Then he pulled the left end under and over to the front, bringing the right end from beneath, tying left over right to form a square knot. Finally, he lifted the soft leather half-glove from the table. He inserted his hand into the smooth leather and pulled it over his knuckles. The glove was cut perfectly, allowing him complete freedom, his fingers bare while the birthmark was covered.

He hesitated, looking at the glove. *Renagi is taking no chances* . . . he thought. A moment later he heard the soft gliding footsteps as she entered the room.

'Water. Clear water,' Neeka said, offering him the cup.

'Oss,' Tegné responded, turning towards her, his voice curt, distant. He walked the five steps between them, took the cup and drained it of the precious liquid. He returned the empty vessel to her hand and watched as she turned and exited.

The door had not quite closed when the four Warmen entered.

'Are you ready to . . .' the sarcastic tone died in mid-sentence as the leading Warman's eyes focused on Tegné. Something in his presence, his demeanour, demanded respect. A hush fell as the four gathered round, keeping a measured distance from him. No words were spoken as they walked from the chamber.

Boom-bom . . . Boom-bom . . . Boom-bom . . .

At first it sounded like the heavy beating of a single heart, the reverberation causing the thick, steel-reinforced wood to vibrate as the sound rolled from the double-arched doors of the Great Hall.

Boom-bom . . . Boom-bom . . . Boom-bom . . . The crowd quietened.

'Shhh,' Stump said, silencing Rin before he could speak as Stump moved closer, whispering in his ear, 'It is time, they are bringing him now.'

Boom-bom . . . Boom-bom . . . Boom-bom . . . The beat was joined, doubled, increasing in intensity.

Drums, they are drums, Rin realized.

Then the crowd seemed to turn as one unit. The muffled footsteps, walking in counter-time to the rhythm, echoed from the north yard.

'Make way!' the sharp command came from the Warman leading the small group. Rin could not see them yet; he fought forward as the crowd split, falling naturally into two halves, the walkway between them.

Part of the trial . . . Humiliation. He remembered Stump's words and expected to hear the jeering begin.

But there was no jeering, just the heartbeat of the drums and the sound of the approaching footsteps. Rin strained forward, looking to the right, down the tunnel of people. Now he could see the leading Warman.

The man was tall, and his high, black lacquered boots seemed to reflect the gaping faces of the crowd as he marched, his knees drawn high before smacking his feet down into the stone and gravel of the courtyard. His head was enclosed in an alloy war helmet, its leaden face-shield pulled down, permitting vision only through the single diagonal opening at the level of his eyes. On the top and to each side of his helmet were the twin tusks of a wild boar. Like a machine, void of all human quality, the black-suited, gloved Warman advanced. To his left and right two identically clad men moved in perfect synchronization. They were close, not more than fifteen paces from Rin, and now he could see Tegné, in the centre of the group, an equal distance from each of the three preceding guards and the same again from a Warman who took up the rear position.

Rin stared, expecting to find his Sensei worn and bedraggled, chained and gagged. He had dreaded this moment, doubting his own self-control, afraid that he would not be equal to the sight of his friend being led like an animal to the arena, frightened that he would somehow add to his Sensei's degradation, perhaps collapsing into a violent flood of tears. Over and over again he had imagined himself as a grown man, faced with an identical situation, and over and over again he had found himself shuddering in fear. But now the time was at hand, and Tegné was walking towards him. Rin gasped as he beheld his Sensei, for Tegné was neither chained nor cowed. Instead he appeared the embodiment of everything he had tried to instil in his student; self-reliance, courage and dignity. His long golden hair was fixed straight back, knotted, and fell down on to the radiant fabric of his hakama. His face was clean and angular, his blue eyes clear and intent, focused straight ahead as he walked.

It is as though I never truly saw him, never understood him, never knew what he was, Rin thought as Tegné approached. And suddenly Rin straightened, his inner trembling quelled by a sense of duty and belonging. For in one revelation, Rin understood what he was seeing. *It is the final acceptance of death,* he realized, *and it is that acceptance which causes the human spirit to shine, to triumph.* He felt tears come to his eyes, but they were not the tears of fear or pity, they were tears of humility.

Now the Warmen were level with Rin and he could almost touch Tegné. The boy's move was without premeditation as he lifted the medallion from his own neck, bunching the leather thong against the gold and silver disc in the palm of his hand.

With the hand extended he lurched forward, his unexpected action catching the left-flanking Warman unaware. For an instant his hand touched Tegné's; Tegné turned, his eyes showing no recognition, yet he accepted the medallion, snapping it cleanly and secretly from Rin's extended hand just as the boy was caught by the negligent guard and tossed roughly back into the crowd of onlookers.

Tegné concealed the medallion in his clenched fist, continuing his walk with no break in rhythm. The great doors swung open as he and the Warmen mounted the steps; the clear, throbbing heartbeat of the demon drums spilled out of the hall and into the night.

*

Be still while moving, like the moon beneath the ever-rolling waves . . . this is clarity. Tegné was met by the enormous bank of mirrored walls, the myriad of reflected faces and the echoing voices of the eight thousand pre-seated spectators. One hundred paces straight ahead of him he recognized Renagi as the Warlord stood up from the Velchar.

Even from this distance Tegné could detect the shimmer from the pleated crimson ceremonial robes. Beside Renagi, in a lighter, radiant shade of red, stood Neeka, the gold of her ninjinka sparkling in the reflected light of one thousand torches. Zato, his long black hair running down the back of his stark white hakama, remained seated to his father's right.

Tegné was bombarded with this collision of sound and vision, yet now a lifetime of preparation held him like a safety net from the disconcerting grip. His mind was calm, empty, and the staring faces and excited voices passed through him like wind through the leaves of a tree. He walked forward.

The twelve drummers formed a single line at the base of the wooden benches to the left side of the hall. Two men for every one of the huge zelkova drums, each hollowed from a single log and weighing close to three hundred kilos. Each pair of drummers crouched in a low, forward stance at opposite ends of the double-headed drum. The player to the right of the drum beat the simple, basic rhythm while the player to the left improvised freely, hitting the taut cowhide with ever-increasing intensity until all twelve players locked into a throbbing synchronization, at one with the sound and the rhythm. The effect was of the beating of a single heart, powerful yet somehow tranquil in its predictable simplicity.

Tegné saw the drummers in the periphery of his vision, their oiled, sweating, naked torsos moving in flowing, mechanical motion. He kept his eyes forward, allowing no distraction. Behind him the crowd from the courtyard entered the open doors and were directed to the lower wooden benches. Within minutes the Great Hall was full, every seat occupied, the anxious excitement building with the crescendo of sound from the incessant drums.

Now Tegné stood directly below the Warlord, gazing up through the sea of faces. He saw the dark commitment in the snake-lidded eyes and tasted the first bitterness in his own dry mouth.

Renagi raised both arms before him, palms open, fingers tight together. Instantly, as though the entire mass of people were attuned to this solitary gesture of orchestration, the Great Hall stood silent. And, as surely as if the throngs had vanished behind this curtain of silence, Tegné and Renagi faced each other, alone.

'Tegné,' the name rang clear through the hall, 'You have come forward to shame my house. You. You who claim to be my son,' Renagi began, the words focused on Tegné yet resounding through the hall.

'Tegné, you are not my son. Your blood is not my blood. You are an Ashkelite, a product of an inferior race. A slave,' Renagi continued, the passion building in his voice. 'Your trial will serve as an example to all who would attempt treason and insurrection against the State of Zendow and the family of Renagi. You stand accused, a liar and an impostor,' the Warlord stated, building towards the climax, 'Let the people of Zendow and the Powers in Heaven witness your hour of reckoning. And if there is truth in your heart, may that truth give you the strength to survive,' he finished, standing completely still, holding the moment.

Tegné stood silently absorbing the Warlord's glare. 'I am your son,' he said finally, the words whispered, as he turned towards the arena.

Rin watched from the far corner of the hall, squashed next to Stump on the crude wooden bench. His eyes scanned the room and stopped on the door which was situated between the two foremost sets of stone seats. Slowly the door opened.

Gazan stood framed in the grey stone opening. Then the massive Warman began his walk up the narrow passage and into the cordoned square. He wore only the black, heavy cotton trousers of his combat suit, his chest bare, and the mighty swelling pectoralis muscles seemed to roll in rhythm with his walk, their striations visible in the overhead reflected light. His head was shaved, with the exception of a single narrow band of black hair which began at the peak of his forehead, extended across the top of his head and down towards his back. His hard, close-set eyes spat hatred as he approached Tegné, and his huge head, with its oversized lantern jaw, seemed as invulnerable as the trunk-like neck and wide, sloping shoulders which supported it.

Renagi's was the first fist to rise as Gazan set foot inside the combat square. 'Hei!' The Warlord's cry erupted, sending shivers down Rin's spine.

'Hei!' Kase rose from his seat at Neeka's side, augmenting Renagi's war-cry. 'Hei! Hei!' the Warmen, Zendai and spectators joined in, standing, punching their right, clenched fists into the air.

'Hei! Hei! Hei!' the war chant began, boot heels colliding with the cement of the floor and the huge drums pounding until there was only one thundering staccato beat.

Just when it seemed the Great Hall would explode and the mirrors shatter on the walls, the Warlord lowered his fist and again raised his open hands. As if by magic, the hall was suddenly and absolutely silent.

'Begin!' Renagi bellowed the command.

Gazan moved forward immediately, his thick, bunioned feet gripping the stone and pulling him towards his prey. Tegné did not move backwards; instead he met his attacker in a relaxed half-facing stance, staying light on the balls of his feet.

Gazan had been informed that his opponent would be weak, that he would only recently have been released from the cage. He was therefore to make a show of it, demoralize, humiliate, kill.

He studied the blue eyes in front of him. He remembered Zacatec and vowed not to misread this little man again.

How to despatch him effectively yet dramatically, he wondered as he crouched, feinting with his hands and moving closer, gauging his own kicking range. Then it dawned on him.

A reverse spinning roundhouse kick ... A big, impressive technique which would easily break the Ashkelite's neck yet leave Gazan enough time to claw-hand his throat and rip the larynx free in a final, spiteful gesture. He would have to get close for the claw-hand, but by then the Ashkelite would be dead on his feet, Gazan reckoned as he began clapping both hands in a sharp, percussive snap, intending the noise to disturb and provoke his opponent. Yet Tegné would not be provoked, and Gazan thought he discerned a strange lifelessness inside the blue eyes. *The spectre of death; his own death,* Gazan told himself as he stopped all movement, freezing his body in a high, functional, forward stance.

Tegné sensed the split second of tension, knowing the waza was coming and read the nearly imperceptible twitch in the hammer-like big toe of Gazan's leading foot. He exhaled as the giant began his spin, moving close and into the big man's wide-arcing leg. Tegné continued forward, timing his movement down and under the kick, rising inside the technique and, for a single moment, stood balanced before the Warman's bare, unprotected chest.

Tegné's ki-ai utilized the last of the contracted breath from his diaphragm as he drove his straight, rigid fingers into the soft, cartilaginous area to the low centre of the Warman's thorax. There was a sharp snap as the cartilage gave way, pushing up before his spear-hand; the pointed, broken gristle entered and punctured the soft, muscular tissue of the Warman's heart. Tegné held the spear-hand in place, momentarily buried in the heaving chest. Then he curled his extended fingers, pulling down slightly and gripped the third of the upper seven ribs.

He held Gazan suspended, watching as the life drained from the Warman's surprised, frightened eyes. Finally, Tegné withdrew his attacking hand, stepping back and away, retaining zanshin as the limp, muscle-bound body fell heavily to the stone floor. He saw the pained, glazed look in the open, lifeless face as thin rivulets of blood began to trickle from Gazan's ears, nose and mouth.

Tegné turned and looked up. He met Renagi's cold, stunned gaze. The crowd remained still, shocked, afraid.

'Move! Do something!' Neeka whispered urgently, inaudible to all but the Warlord and Zato.

Renagi rose from the Velchar, appearing stiff and awkward, as if he had suddenly been transformed into a wooden marionette and the puppeteer had momentarily forgotten how to manipulate the strings.

'This proves nothing!' he shouted, his usually modulated voice an octave too high, 'It is not over!' the Warlord added. Tegné stared dispassionately as Renagi looked out over the crowd. Then, remarkably, the Warlord recovered his bearing.

'Get him out of here!' he ordered, pointing with disgust at the bleeding corpse lying on the floor.

Two guards rushed into the square. Each gripped one ankle of the twenty-stone carcass and effortlessly dragged Gazan across the floor, up the narrow passage to the open door. A wide smear of blood spread outward from the open-mouthed head and trailed their path.

'Quickly! Quickly!' Renagi commanded, pointing towards a third guard. The man ran into the square, a large, wet cloth in his hand. He leaned forward, his legs bent, his rear end in the air, the cloth in both hands before him. In this way he pushed the wet cloth along behind the body, removing the blood from the floor.

One chance, one strike ... The words floated in Tegné's consciousness as he deepened his state of zanshin, empty, allowing neither thought nor emotion to separate his mind from his physical movement. *Pristine purity*, the removal of all psychic obstruction.

Zanu looked down on Gazan's corpse as it was dragged past him into the antechamber leading to the rear exit of the Great Hall.

'Bad luck,' he said, looking up, half-smiling into the assured, fixed eyes of the snake-charmer. 'Ready?' Zanu asked.

The snake-charmer nodded 'yes', and Zanu led as both men walked from the small room, through the door and towards the bright light of the arena.

Renagi's spirits lifted as he watched Zanu, the Zendai, step lightly into the combat square, his orange robes gathered tight at his waist where the sheathed, three-foot katana was thrust, cutting edge upwards, through the red, thickly knotted obi. Renagi saw the wiry, bandy-legged Warman enter behind Zanu, and remembered the lightning quickness of the calloused hand that had choked the life from the vicious rhandoconda. *Yes. He had prepared for a situation like this. An accident, a mistake. One chance in a million*, Renagi told himself as he breathed a long, deep breath, exhaled, and relaxed into the thick cushion of the Velchar.

Zanu and the Warman stood together, bowing once to the Warlord before turning to the waiting opponent. Renagi looked left, then right, amazed at the continued silence of the crowd. His gaze rested a moment on the impassive eyes behind the ninjinka, then he glanced at Zato.

Zato sat rigid, his face tight and his lips pressed hard together. Renagi rose from the Velchar and looked down into the combat square, satisfied that his men were in position.

'Hajime!' he yelled, using the more formal, clipped command.

In an instant, Zanu unsheathed the katana, raising the sword in both hands, elbows bent, above and behind his right shoulder. Tegné held Zanu in his sight, allowing the smaller, unarmed man to circle round and take up a position to his rear.

This is going to end quickly, thought Renagi as he watched Zanu shift forward. The Warlord leaned out of the Velchar, his hands gripping the ledge in front of him, his stomach knotted with anticipation.

Zanu and the snake charmer advanced with a distinct yet broken rhythm, one moving forward while the other shifted laterally to the rear. They seemed of one mind as they drew within striking range of the man in the centre.

He is too straight, too much target. Why is he standing so straight? Rin thought, staring at Tegné, desperate and on the verge of shouting to break the thick spell of silence which clung to the crowd. But the child remained quiet.

Tegné studied the slight flutter of the swordsman's robe, observing the shallow, lower abdominal breathing. Concentrating, waiting for any subtle change in the pattern of the breaths.

Behind him the snake charmer crouched, preparing to launch his tight right fist in a focused, unobstructed thrust to the coccyx. He would use a counter-punch, leading with his left leg while pivoting his hip to the left and forward, thus driving his right fist home. This simple gyaku-zuki was his favourite technique, and he had always wondered what effect it would have on an unguarded human body. *It will at least paralyse him,* he surmised, realizing the nervous response would reach the tip of every limb. *Then Zanu can take the head,* he concluded, preparing for the assault. He looked up once, contacting Zanu with a slight flicker of his eye.

Tegné saw the swordsman's minute break in breathing. His reaction was to straighten even more, maintaining only a slight bend in the knees, presenting a full target. Then the flicker of light from the katana's blade . . .

Renagi lurched forward as the snake charmer unleashed his strike, the fist relaxed yet ready in an instant to become a deadly battering-ram. Zanu exhaled, loving this moment of freedom, his mind, his body and his sword locked in one cosmic pulse.

Enlightenment. Zanu felt the slice, the cut, saw the gush of red. His katana was nearly back in its scabbard before the swordsman became aware of the burning pain in his groin where the snake-charmer's fist had entered him. He fell forward, his stomach seizing as the other's severed head skidded across the floor to his front.

Then, from the corner of his eye, Zanu glimpsed Tegné rise from a sidewards roll. An instant later the hard sole of a foot came down once upon his face before Tegné's second, more accurate stomp crushed the swordmaster's head, smashing the temporal bone and compressing his skull against the stone floor.

The silence of the crowd broke with a mighty roar. 'Tegné! Tegné! Tegné!' the screaming chant erupted from the lower benches, from the working class of the city. 'Tegné! Tegné!'

Tegné turned towards them, a look of astonishment and disbelief in his face. Rin watched through eyes awash with tears. Now he could see the shining silver and gold medallion hanging high on his Sensei's chest.

'Tegné! Tegné!' Rin's voice rose, joining the chant. Several of the spectators on ground level rushed forward, arms outstretched, towards Tegné. Rin moved with the surging crowd.

Suddenly a score of black-clad guards swept from the mid-level seats, assuming a wide formation, spreading out, pushing, shoving the people back. Rin was caught in one huge gloved hand, hoisted from his feet and thrown on to a vacant bench.

Tegné spun round, searching the faces, finding the Warlord. 'Tell them to stop!' he shouted above the mayhem.

'Enough!' screamed Renagi. 'Enough!' His voice boomed louder and more clear than the disorganized din below. 'This is not over,' he continued, climbing down from the Velchar, moving clumsily through the mixture of spectators, some standing, some sitting. The crowd quietened, falling back of its own accord as Renagi and Tegné stood, facing each other, in the combat square.

'If this is how it must end, then so be it,' Renagi vowed, loosening his robe. 'I am prepared to die for my name, for the name of my only son, and for Zendow.'

Tegné backed away, his open palms held up in a gesture of peace. 'I want no part of your empire, no land, no name of Warlord. I ask you only to stop the persecution that is taking place in my name, to make amends for the slaughter, to free the Ashkelites.'

'You make demands of me?' Renagi asked incredulously, angrily. 'You will *not* make demands of me. I am Warlord of Zendow,' he snarled, moving closer, his fists clenched.

Now Tegné stood his ground, watching as the old man closed

the distance, wary of a sudden rush. Another step and Zato's hand came from behind, gripping Renagi's shoulder and halting him. Then Zato walked forward and faced Tegné.

'No. You will not kill my father, but so help me, you will fight his son,' Zato said, resigned, staring into his half-brother's face. 'One son. One heir. One Warlord. That is the law and that is how it must be,' he finished, knowing that the Zendai, the Warmen, the Military Council and the hungry crowd would settle for no less.

Tegné weighed Zato's words, then turned to Renagi. The Warlord's face was frozen with apprehension.

'That is how it must be . . .' The soft, penetrating voice came from the Velchar. Neeka stood above them, in front of the throne, confident, poised, her shoulders arched high as she gripped the stone railing. Renagi looked up, past the anxious faces of Miyaz and Kase, and met the cold violet behind the ninjinka.

'Hei! Hei! Hei!' The chant began to build as the smack of metal heels against stone filled the hall. 'Hei! Hei! Hei!'

Ten thousand voices, twenty thousand stamping feet. The demon drums. The collective will. Tegné was unprepared, his mind and his body no longer at war. His intent confused, diluted, feeling once again a pawn in this unsolicited drama.

Zato came forward and Tegné could read the desperation in his brown eyes. Tegné shifted back and away, doing what was necessary to avoid an attack. He studied the mid-level of Zato's hakama, saw the broken, anxious breathing, the low, open hands and the unguarded face.

'Fight! Fight! Kill him!' Tegné heard the voice. It occupied a space of its own within his mind. 'Kill him!' It was Neeka's voice, rising above the roar of the crowd. 'Kill him! Kill him!' Distinct, penetrating, commanding. And for a moment her face flashed in his thoughts and he knew, more certainly than ever, that it was she who was the architect of this tragic scene, the dreamer of this dream, the creator of this illusion.

I will end it, I will walk away. The thought entered him as Zato began a tentative advance. *I must find the power to break her will,* he commanded himself, desperate to exercise this ultimate control of his destiny.

He stopped his backward slide, standing in the low, immovable stance as Zato crept forward. At last they were eye to eye.

'Brother, it is over,' Tegné whispered, quietly so that only Zato could hear him. Then, slowly, Tegné relaxed his guard. He watched the tears begin to well in Zato's eyes; tears of sorrow, frustration, indecision. The tears of a warring conscience. And for a moment Zato also relaxed, his shoulders dropping, the tension falling away.

'It is over,' Tegné repeated.

'No!' Tegné heard the scream an instant before his brother's fist pounded into the mastoid region of his neck, then dizziness and what seemed the crashing sound of an enormous stone wall, disintegrating inside his skull.

'No!' Again Zato's scream and again the thudding fist.

Kase and Miyaz rushed from their seats, down to the floor, joining Renagi at the side of the combat square. Tegné doubled over stumbling backwards. The Warlord could feel the crowd turn, their excitement building. He straightened, squaring his shoulders.

Renagi. Warlord of Zendow. Zato, my only son, my heir. Yes, this is how it should be. My testimony.

'Finish him!' He shrieked the command at Zato, then, drawing his katana, he stepped forward into the square. Miyaz moved to stop him, but Kase intervened, catching the other man by the shoulder.

Zato stood a full two paces from Tegné, hesitating as Tegné heaved, reeling from the last blow.

'Take it,' Renagi hissed, pushing the hilt of the katana towards Zato. 'Take it,' he repeated, pressing the cold grip into his son's hand.

Tegné looked up as Zato raised the ancient, balanced sword. Its grooved gutters ran evenly down each of its sides, ensuring that the enemy's blood would be dispersed so as not to soil the katana's cutting edge. Zato breathed in, focused his mind, holding the weapon.

'Yaaaah!' he screamed, rushing forward, already beginning the flowing, horizontal cut; the movement intended to sever Tegné's head.

The sheer instinct of survival saved him as Tegné dropped beneath the blur of steel, feeling the rush of air in the weapon's wake. He hit the floor and, as Zato began the downward cut, he rolled away from the arc of the sword. Simultaneously, he scissored his legs against Zato's shins, using the power of his roll to break his brother's balance. Zato's head slammed against the floor as the katana slid from his grasp.

'Kill him! Kill him!' Neeka's voice rose free from the mounting din. Tegné sprang to his feet, moving behind Zato, gripping his head in a tight, wrapping lock.

'Kill him!' Again the voice, unmistakable, dominating. Tegné began to pull the jaw with his left hand while pushing the head in sequence with his right, listening, listening for the crack of the cervical vertebrae.

Suddenly, breaking the spell, Tegné felt strong hands grip his shoulders. He heard the deep, pleading voice.

'Please. Please, I beg you. Stop. Please!' The voice became a full-throated sob.

Tegné halted the breaking technique just as Renagi dropped to the floor, weeping openly on his bended knees. Tegné stepped away from Zato and turned to face his father. A confusion of hatred and compassion flooded his heart.

Slowly he removed the black half-glove. He raised his right fist; the birthmark was visible to everyone. The Great Hall quietened.

'I am your son,' he said simply, softly.

Renagi stared up, helpless, then slowly he stood. He removed the fine, pleated crimson robes; his torso was soft, fleshy, the patch of hair between his breasts coarse and grey.

'Never,' he whispered. Then, defeated, he dropped the robes at Tegné's feet, the crimson falling like blood against the stone, his power disintegrating before the eyes of his minions. Only Kase and Miyaz stepped forward to assist him. Then, bending, Renagi lifted Zato's unconscious body from the cold floor. Carrying his son, cradling him against his bare chest, Renagi walked through the parting throngs of people.

Neeka pushed forward. She stopped in front of Tegné, stooping to gather the crimson robes. She draped the pleated silk around his shoulders.

The chant began, throbbing, beginning low and building louder and louder, 'Tegné, Warlord of Zendow'.

'Tegné. Warlord of Zendow,' she said, fixing him with the soft violet of her eyes. The drums lifted and the gathering Zendai walked towards him. Rin joined the surging crowd, converging on the golden-haired, crimson-clad figure in the centre of the square . . .

'Tegné, Warlord of Zendow!' the voices continued, growing, in unison.

Tegné turned from the swarm of faces. He could see Renagi still carrying Zato in his arms as he walked through the wide door at the far end of the hall. He felt Neeka's gentle hand take his own and begin to raise it above his head.

'Warlord of Zendow,' she repeated the three fated words.

'No!' Tegné shouted, his anger finally erupting as he threw the robes from his shoulders and walked towards the door.

Rin struggled through the crowd, running, stumbling, finally overtaking him, reaching up, touching him, calling, 'Sensei! Sensei!' At last Tegné stopped, turned and looked down at the boy.

Rin stood motionless as he saw the pain etched in the face, distorting the features, causing his Sensei to appear worn, beaten. And within his teacher's eyes Rin discerned a silent plea, as if the eyes belonged to a wounded bird, caught lame and unable to fly.

'Rin,' Tegné spoke the name softly, 'Thank you,' he whispered, touching the medallion which hung from his neck. Then his blue eyes hardened like pools of freezing water. Tegné turned and walked quickly from the boy, out of the Great Hall.

It must not end this way. There can be nothing gained from violence. My father . . . My father must understand. He must accept what has been done. I will convince him . . . His thoughts reeled as he entered the long passageway, stretching away with doors on each side. His father and brother had vanished.

10

THE TEST OF THE HEART

*One should cleanse his motley thoughts
   and eliminate wanton considerations from the
   reflections of his mind
But can he be without imperfection?*

(Lao Tsu)

Renagi knelt before the small, raised altar, the symbol of his Zendai Clan carved with minute detail into the polished walnut. Breathing in, he studied the carving, finding peace within the intricate swirls of the wood.

Miyaz and Kase guarded the locked door of the tiny chamber. Zato had recovered and now he stood, absolutely still, to the right of his father. Both knew what was required; there was no alternative. The shining tanto lay before Renagi on the altar, its snakeskin hilt ornamented with the graceful, painted figures of swallows in flight.

Slowly, carefully, Renagi took the sharp, pointed dagger from the altar, cradling it in his open palms. Then, gripping the hilt with both hands, he turned the blade inwards.

'Why are you running?' Neeka's voice followed him along the passageway. 'Tegné, can you hear them? They are calling for you. They want you. Everything. It is yours. Take it,' she continued, walking towards him, smiling, her arms extended. As she reached him he took her extended hands. Gripping them, he pulled her closer.

'My father, where is my father?' he asked.

'Come, I will lead you to his room,' she replied.

The thick, carved door to Renagi's chamber opened on smooth, silent hinges. Inside, the full moon hung centred in the arched window, shining its light on the blue embroidered quilt which covered the canopied bed. There was a faint aroma of hapaver in the air.

Two ornate Miramese chairs, a tall mahogany chest and a single bedside table stood upon a red, silk-threaded rug. The room was simple yet elegant. Rich in its own memories, it was a room which would never be empty.

Neeka turned to face him, aware that the back-light from the window framed the outline of her body.

Tegné looked away, averting his eyes, yet already he could feel the force of her will.

'Why? Why do you turn from me?' she asked softly, as if he had wounded her. 'You who have had the power to defeat the Warlord, to earn your right to rule, to stand proud before the people of Zendow. And now, even now, you turn away from your truest prize – my love.'

'And Renagi?' Tegné asked, but the veil was already beginning to form, clouding his conscience.

'Renagi is past. Gone. Dust in the wind. You, Tegné, you and I are now. Our son is the future.' Her voice rang, like truth, full with promise.

He lifted his eyes and she felt him drink in the swell of her breasts, the curve of her hips and the darkness of her mound. She felt his desire as he walked forward, and before he could speak she wrapped her arms around him, pressing the thin silk of her crotch against his groin, feeling his warmth. She moved only enough to create a mild, sensual friction. His body began to respond, his penis growing hard as she rose up on her toes and placed his hardness closer to the wetness of her opening.

'Take off the ninjinka; it is your right,' she whispered. Her breath was hot against his neck.

He lifted the golden mask, pulling it out and away from her face; the face from the Lake of Dreams.

'You. It is you,' he said as she began a light, circular movement with her hips, riding up along the length of his shaft and then lowering, pushing slightly harder, controlling the movement of her vagina so that as she came down the tip of his penis rubbed against her point of ecstasy.

'Yes. I have waited. You are the one,' she whispered. Then she pulled away from him, just enough to slide her warm right hand inside the front of his hakama while loosening the ties with her left. She ran her fingers down between his legs, gently cupping his tightening testicles, then released them and stroked up, along the sensitive skin of his penis, finding the single drop of moisture, gently gripping the throbbing head while she used the soft, cushioned surface of her thumb to rub the slippery fluid into the hot, throbbing crown.

Slowly, she stepped back, releasing him. 'Would you like to see my body?' she teased, already beginning to part the red robes.

She let them fall away from her, and she stood before him wearing only the high rope sandals and the pale silk thong.

Her nipples were dark and erect, jutting forward from the full breasts. Yet it was her abdomen and pelvis that fascinated him. Even in the semi-darkness of the room he could see the delicate, clearly defined muscles beneath the fine, bronzed skin. The waist so clean, tight, tiny, and the navel perfectly round and deep. A thin line of jet-black hair ran beneath it, widening into a full diamond pattern which remained visible beneath the sheer silk covering her crotch.

He reached out and touched her through the silk. She was wet, and the ebony hair was as thick and soft as velvet fur. He knelt before her, gripping the tight, round buttocks and licked, high up against the smooth inside skin of her thighs. He tasted her sweetness.

She guided him to the bed, sitting down as he unlaced the sandals, taking them from her feet. She lay back on to the blue quilt, then arched upwards as he pulled the silk thong down and over her thighs, taking the garment from her, leaving her naked.

He inhaled the natural musk of her body, falling deeper beneath her hypnotic spell. She reached up for him as he dropped his hakama, kicking it free as he bent towards her, climbing upon the bed. He straddled her for a moment as she parted her legs, opening herself wide to him. His hard, unyielding penis found her with no guidance, rubbing between the soft, hot lips of her womanhood, entering the smooth, wonderful passage and penetrating deep, pressing against her womb

Renagi did not gasp or cry out, and no sign of the white, searing heat told upon his face as he pushed the pointed steel of the dagger into the left side of his belly. Slowly, he drew the tanto across in the long cut. He kept his eyes concentrated in front of him, focused on the carved wooden Claw. Yet it was not the carving that he saw, not the sign of his Clan nor the spiralling swirls of the polished wood; it was the clear amber eyes of the Ashkelite girl, Maliseet. And within her eyes there was peace and forgiving.

Blood and muscle spilled from the widening wound, seeping down and soaking the front of his white cotton undergarment. Zato watched, his face set, his heart aching, his katana raised over his right shoulder, the razor edge of the blade high above his head and aimed downwards. It was almost time.

'Hei!' Renagi screamed. It was the last ki-ai of a dying warrior as, with his final rush of strength, Renagi ripped the tanto in a sideways motion. His entrails flooded from the gaping wound.

'Yaaaa!' Zato yelled, pulling the whistling blade downwards, surprised for an instant that the katana met no resistance as it entered the sheet of muscle at the base of Renagi's neck; the sword severed the third cervical vertebra, cutting the head clean from the shoulders. For a moment the headless body remained kneeling, twitching, as the blood came in synchronous spurts, timed to the final beats of Renagi's heart. Then the body pitched forward, landing beside the head on the small, bloodstained carpet, the eyes fixed and open, the mouth forming a sad half-smile.

Zato stood still, maintaining a two-handed grip on the katana, as if preparing to use the weapon for a second strike. Then gradually, he relaxed, shaking the blade as he lightly tapped the base of its hilt with his right palm. Renagi's blood fell from the polished steel, falling like warm rain upon the floor. Finally, Zato drew the blade upwards between his thumb and index finger, cleaning the metal thoroughly before guiding the sword back into its scabbard. He turned to Miyaz and Kase; they stood solemn-faced at the door, studying him, waiting for a reaction. He could feel the terrible sadness trying to escape from inside him. He held it in check, tightening the muscles of his abdomen so hard that it affected the set of his jaw and the thin line of his lips.

A display of grief now would bring the ultimate loss of face, a dishonour to my father. I will show no grief. I will show only pride for his final act of courage, Zato vowed as he squared his shoulders and walked from the chamber, leaving the Warmen the task of wrapping the body and cleansing the floor.

His mind raced as he walked through the long, dim passageway towards the seclusion of his father's room. He had watched Neeka during the initial combat; he had seen the satisfaction in her eyes, heard her scream against him. It was as he had always suspected. He had never trusted her and in the end his instinct had been confirmed. But what was her purpose? As he drew closer to the room a sense of doom settled upon him. Now, more than any other time in his life he needed to be alone. To mourn. To heal. To think.

'Be still, be still,' Neeka whispered, wrapping her long legs around Tegné's waist, maintaining a counter-rhythm to his slow, deep thrusts, gradually controlling his body.

'Yes . . . yes . . . Just let me feel you inside me,' she continued, settling the roundness of her curved hips into the warm palm of his open right hand, bringing him down, deeper still, into her. 'Kiss me,' she moaned, and as he did she began the strong, undulating contractions against his hot, smooth shaft, sucking on his tongue, matching the rhythm of her vaginal muscles with the rhythm of her tongue and lips. She stretched back on the bed, opening her eyes, watching him in the glow of the moon.

'This is our beginning,' she purred as he began to swell inside her, nearing his climax.

Now she could hear the footsteps coming slowly along the hallway. She recognized Zato's steps; she had expected him. The door was not locked.

Tegné wanted to raise his hips and thrust into her, but the strong legs wrapped around him would not permit his movement.

'Yes, my love, yes,' Neeka whispered, sensing his urgency, holding him tighter, her right arm pulling him closer to her breasts as her left hand moved silently to her side, beneath the pillow, finding the knurled hilt of the silver blade. Her contractions increased, gripping him, running in spasm along the sides of his phallus.

She pulled the blade from beneath the pillow, turning the point downwards as she lifted it above his bare shoulders. The metal was already beginning to burn her flesh; still she held on, withstanding the pain, absorbing it as the first hot rush of his semen began to fill her.

'It is done,' she said softly, feeling the warmth fill her womb.

Zato stood outside the thick oak door, his right hand frozen on the brass handle. From beyond the door he could hear the muffled yet unmistakable sounds of love-making. Slowly he drew the katana, then he turned the handle and pushed against the heavy wood.

The moon through the arched window bathed the room in light. His eyes focused quickly, centring on the two naked bodies which lay upon his father's bed. He recognized the long blanket of raven hair as it fanned out on to the blue quilt. Neeka's legs extended towards him, her knees raised, her feet flat on the bed. Tegné lay nestled into her breasts, positioned between the elegant legs, secure in the aftermath of his passion.

The scene sent a shudder of revulsion through Zato as he took the first step towards the lovers. Neeka was already meeting the cold steel of his eyes as Tegné turned towards him. Zato raised the katana, holding the flat surface forward.

'This sword bore the blood of my father. Dead. Because of you. You,' he spat the words eyeing them hatefully, 'you who defile his name,' Zato finished in slow, bitter fury.

Tegné felt the strangely familiar heat of the metal as Neeka pressed the silver blade into his hand, the entire motion concealed from Zato by the position of their bodies on the bed.

'Use it,' she said, directing her words at Tegné while effectively challenging Zato by the contact of her eyes. Her unrepenting defiance enraged him as Zato turned the katana, raising the cutting edge in the two-handed grip, moonlight glinting off the graceful curvature of the steel.

First the bastard son, then the betrayer, he vowed, lowering his stance, centring, inching forward.

Tegné rolled from Neeka's relaxed embrace, finding the floor, standing naked before Zato. In his right hand he brandished the silver blade. Zato lifted his katana higher, its cutting edge so clean, so sharp, that a leaf pushed against it by a stream's gentle current would split cleanly in two.

One strike, one chance, Tegné knew as he crouched, resting lightly on the balls of his feet, waiting for Zato's rush, preparing to counter with a straight thrust. *One strike, one chance ...* Tabata's voice spoke the words as surely as if his Sensei stood beside him. And suddenly he could see Tabata's face shining in the reflection of Zato's eyes. And the face was heavy with sorrow.

This man I am facing now is my brother, my own flesh and blood. Yet there is murder in my heart, and murder in the very blade which binds me to virtue. The realization fell upon him like a cold, deadening weight, and it was then that he felt the medallion which hung from the narrow strip of leather around his neck.

The spell was broken; the dream shattered. Tegné dropped the blade to the floor, the metal ringing with the clarity of a temple bell. He stood defenceless against Zato, knowing that in the end, in the final test, he had failed, fallen prey to the lust and greed of his own mortality, entrapped by its deception.

He watched the katana rise, ready to begin its sweeping, downward cut. *Now it is over*, he thought as he met his brother's gaze.

'Forgive me,' Tegné said, quiet and soft, surrendering. Zato hesitated, and for a moment there was a death-like stillness in the room; then the sound of panting and a low, guttural growl. Tegné watched as his brother spun towards the sounds, bewilderment and horror twisting the fine features of his face.

The bed seemed bathed in a subdued yellow light and the white secretion of saliva and perspiration which covered the black, ragged fur of the four-legged creature appeared to glow with a nauseating inner heat. This was not the beautiful Cat from the desert, nor the Cat from the Lake of Dreams. This was something infinitely more malevolent. Pure evil.

Zato held the katana in the high, ready position as he retreated from the Beast, his body losing its fluidity, tightening with uncontrolled fear. The creature strained forward, its oozing, fanged mouth gaping in a deafening howl. It seemed to be labouring against some invisible chain, the stinking sweat of its body flying in thick globs from its raging, shaking muscles. Yet there was a power to the creature, a captivating power.

Tegné stared, seeing finally, clearly, completely. For it was this power which had called out to him, touched the darkness within his own heart, planted the seed of avarice, weaving inside him a web of illusion. For this Beast was the manifestation of evil, and Neeka was its child, its projection of flesh and blood.

'Take your eyes from it! Turn away!' Tegné shouted, bending down to grasp the blade. But Zato was lost beyond communication, his eyes locked on the furious creature which rampaged before him, devouring his seeping energy.

The sound was like the explosion of shattering glass as the creature leapt from the bed, spreading its taloned feet, knocking Zato helplessly against the wall.

'No! No!' Tegné screamed, running forward, throwing himself on the mauling Beast, wrapping his left arm around the grizzled neck, pulling back on the head and driving the blade into the hard surface of the slippery hide.

The blade slid sideways, unable to penetrate the thick sinew. He raised it again, high above his head.

'He-ai!' Again he brought the blade down, focusing his spirit, yet again it glanced off the horny flesh and the Beast rose beneath him.

Tegné rolled, regaining his feet, the blade gripped desperately in his right hand. *The heart, pierce the heart . . .* It was the voice of the Father Protector which came to him as he stood before the creature. *One chance, one strike . . .*

Tegné sank low, his hips pushed forward, his right arm cocked back, the blade held tight in his grip, his left, open hand guarding to the front. The Beast stalked towards him, yet Tegné would not retreat. He felt the hot, burning breath, as if it would incinerate the flesh of his body.

Now the black, shining, animal lips stretched back, revealing the long, glistening fangs. Yet there was no attack. He looked deep into the wild fire of the eyes and saw the shimmering trace of violet. A sudden, overwhelming sadness consumed him.

'Neeka! Neeka!' he called her name, 'Neeka! Neeka!'

A shroud of blackness fell before his eyes. Then, gradually, the blackness lifted and he was bathed in the cool light of the moon.

'Why? Why are you doing this? We have everything, you and I. We are one, One mind. One heart . . .' Neeka's voice floated on the still air of the night. She stood before him. Beautiful. Naked. Alone. 'Love me. Love me,' she whispered and walked towards him, unafraid. It was just as her soft, delicate fingers touched the skin of his shoulder that he drove the silver blade inwards, burying the metal in the soft, warm flesh below her left breast.

Neeka did not scream, nor did she resist as he forced the blade into her heart, twisting, relentlessly twisting. She half-smiled as he looked into the fading violet of her eyes. Then her body grew limp, falling before him. Still he held the blade firm, lowering himself on top of her, watching the fading violet give way to the grey, dead stone beneath. Finally her eyelids closed and there was only the feeling of emptiness below him. His tears fell against her quiet flesh. Earth tears.

At last he rose, leaving the blade buried in her heart. Suddenly cold and conscious of his nakedness, he lifted the blue quilt from his father's bed and wrapped it around him as he walked across the floor to his brother.

Zato sat with his back pressed against the wall, his body bruised and the jagged, open wound seeping blood through the torn fabric of his jacket. 'Is it over?' he asked, staring at Neeka's body, his words disarmingly direct, simple.

Tegné looked once more at the body, then again at Zato. Zato saw the fathomless sorrow in the deep blue eyes. Then came the growl, distant yet distinct. Both turned towards Neeka's body.

The flesh had begun to undulate like some swelling cocoon of molten wax. Rising, distorting; the growl came from within it. Tegné lurched forward, attempting to grip the blade once more, Too late; the waxen cocoon split open and the blade fell, embedding itself in the hard wood of the floor. Zato trembled as he saw the dark vapour rise from the chasm in the broken, melting shell. Slowly the vapour took shape, form, and for a terrible moment the looming shadow of the Beast hovered above them. Then the vapour grew thin as it dispersed and drifted towards the open window.

Out. Out into the night sky.

'Now it is over,' Tegné answered, his voice firm, his passion dissolved. He reached down with his right hand, the birthmark strikingly visible in the light of the moon.

Zato accepted the hand and by the time he had risen to his feet, Neeka's waxen shell had disappeared.

Only the silver blade remained.

*

Renagi's head looked large, as if it had expanded in death. The ashen grey skin was drained of blood and the open brown eyes resembled flat, clouded glass. The mouth had frozen with rigor mortis, and the strange half-smile gave an eerie, distant quality to the overall demeanour of the face.

There was no gore and, in fact, the flesh which had once attached the short, thick neck to its torso was cut in a perfectly clean line, as if the incision had been made with some finely crafted surgical instrument. In all there was no horror, simply a conclusive dignity as the Warlord's head was held respectfully in Kase's gloved hands.

Kase stood in front of the Velchar. Renagi's body lay below him, wrapped in the great black and red banner of his Clan and placed in an open, carved chest which served as his coffin. Miyaz stood to the right side of the coffin.

A cloak of silence hung over the crowd, broken only by an occasional muffled cry of anguish. Finally, Kase spoke.

'In the yeon one thousand, on the twenty-second day of Julin, at the twenty-fourth hour, Renagi, son of Volkar, and past War-lord of Zendow, commited the act of Seppuka. His death was courageous and honourable, attended and seconded by his son, Zato.'

The Warman's voice enveloped the ten thousand as each realized in turn that they were witnessing an indelible entry into the annals of history. Then Kase raised the head high, holding it still, with outstretched arms, above the people.

'May Renagi's soul be purged and his spirit made pure. And may he rest in peace . . . Long live Zendow!' His voice rose, deepening; 'Long live Zendow!' Kase repeated, virtually shouting the three words.

'Hei! Hei! Hei!' The voices of the people responded as one, and a multitude of clenched fists punched into the air. And for a moment, the spirit and strength that had been Zendow lifted the Great Hall, and courage returned to the people. Then the head was lowered, wrapped carefully in a cloth of scarlet silk, and laid gently to rest beside the body. And as quickly as the collective spirit had soared, a hush fell again upon the hall.

Rin could feel the swelling wave of anxiety beneath the quiet. For Zendow was without a leader, a gigantic ship adrift without its captain. And through this trial of blood the line of succession had been broken.

Will anyone step forward to assume control? And if someone dares, shall I stop him? What is my position now? wondered Miyaz, as he gazed into the throng of faces. Still, the people remained quiet, yet the lull was filled with an expectant energy.

Should I say something more? Kase pondered, growing anxious, self-conscious in the combined gaze of the people of Zendow. It was an eerie, awesome silence, alive with the potential of a burn-ing fuse and yet miraculous, in that every tongue remained in check.

Waiting, we are waiting . . . Rin realized, trying to define this singular, disquieting feeling.

The sound of the wooden door scraping against the stone walkway travelled amongst those gathered like a charge of electricity. Rin turned towards the door.

There, silhouetted against the back-light from the hallway, his figure ghostlike in the white hakama, stood Zato.

Rin stared, wide-eyed, as Zato determinedly scanned the faces closest to him. Then, resolutely, the Warlord's son walked forward.

The great dyke of silence finally began to break and shrill, excited voices cut the air.

Where is Tegné? What has happened? Rin despaired, watching as Zato turned to the steps which led up to the Velchar. Then he saw the ripped cloth of the jacket, exposing the ugly, open wound which began at Zato's right shoulder and ran down the torn front of his padded chest.

Could there have been more violence, another fight? Could Tegné be . . .

'Rin.' The familiar voice halted the desperate speculation. The boy turned to see Tegné walking towards him from the door. 'Sensei!' Rin cried, rushing to meet the wide open arms.

Zato was already on the first landing, midway to the Velchar. He stopped, turned, and looked out over the people, finding Tegné, beckoning for him to follow.

But now, after all that has happened, will the people accept him as their leader? Tegné wondered, listening to the building voices increase in volume with each of his brother's steps. He felt a sudden, anxious concern as he watched Miyaz and Kase close ranks, apparently guarding the stately chair. Still Zato continued to climb, again turning to wave Tegné forward.

'Stand to the side, Rin. Use the door if the crowd becomes violent,' Tegné instructed, walking quickly away from the boy and towards the steps.

'Oss, Sensei,' Rin replied, yet there was a strange sureness to him, as if he was aware of something which Tegné was not.

Tegné increased his pace, trying to overtake Zato, to protect him if necessary. It was as Tegné mounted above the level of the onlookers that the pitch of the voices grew and the tension finally broke within the hall.

By now Zato was exchanging words with Kase and Miyaz, who stood directly in front of the Velchar; Renagi's body lay unguarded in the open casket at their feet. Tegné was close, and he studied their hands, wary of the fingers which hovered above the hilts of their katanas.

A moment of indecision . . . Tegné began to sprint. Suddenly the Warmen stepped aside, leaving the Velchar open, unprotected. Zato stood before the cushioned seat, his face creased into a wide, welcoming smile. Tegné ran forward.

'Turn, look,' Zato said, gripping his brother's shoulder, urging him to look out, over the ten thousand people.

Tegné turned. The vast collage of faces gazed back at him, their eyes meeting his. Zato punched his fist skyward, as his cleated heel slammed against the stone floor.

'Hei! Hei! Hei!' the massed voices seemed to explode as the huge drums resumed their beat. Behind the faces of the people of Zendow, Tegné could see his own reflection. A myriad of mirrored images; his golden hair streaming on to the black silk of his robe, his shoulders set, squared. He felt an overwhelming power, his heart pounding inside his chest, building with the strength of the drums.

Somehow Rin had manoeuvred himself to the very front of the crowd. Tegné could see him clearly and, as he listened, he was sure he could distinguish Rin's voice from those around him.

Zato raised his arms. The chanting ceased and the drums became quiet. Then Zato took a long, deep breath.

'My flesh and blood!' he began, and in that moment his voice was the voice of Renagi. 'My brother, Tegné!' He called the name, loud, clear.

'Warlord of Zendow!' Zato's words rang, and with them the faces of Tabata, the Elder and the Protectors filled Tegné's mind. A strange, disquieting feeling entered him. A warning? Then the faces faded, like haze against the sun, and Neeka was there, smiling. But only for a moment, as, at last, his mind cleared, and he stared out on to the sea of people.

'Warlord of Zendow!'

EPILOGUE

*Better to stop short than fill to the brim. Oversharpen the
blade, and the edge will soon blunt. Amass a store of gold and
jade, and no one can protect it.
Claim wealth and titles, and disaster will follow.
Retire when the work is done. This is the way of heaven.*

(Lao Tsu)

GLOSSARY

Ajna	The seventh chakra, also known as the third eye, located in the centre of the forehead, equidistant from the physical eyes
Anahata	The fifth chakra, the centre of the heart
Asana	Any of a number of basic yoga postures which are designed to stimulate the chakras and control the flow of vital energy
Ashi-bari	'Leg sweeping technique' – used to unbalance or throw the opponent
Avatar	Descent of a deity to Earth in incarnate form
Bo	'Staff', 'stave' or 'stick', approximately six feet long. One of five weapons systemized by the early Okinawan practitioners
Body length	A measure of approximately 6 feet
Chakra	Centres of energy. The eight principal chakras are along the axis of the spine, each associated with a different group of bodily functions and a different level of consciousness
Chikaraishi	'Power stone' – a wooden stick of approximately one foot embedded in a round stone weighing about ten pounds. Used to develop strength in the upper body
Chudan	Middle level of the body, often used to designate a target area for techniques

Dojo	'The place of the Way' – a training-hall in which martial arts are practised
Empi-uchi	'Elbow strikes' – chiefly used in close-quarter combat
Finger	A measure of approximately $\frac{8}{10}$ of an inch
Foot	Lineal measure of approximately three hands
Gajiin	Foreigner or outsider
Gedan	'Lower or lower level' – the lower trunk area of the human body
Geta	'Clogs' – Japanese wooden shoes
Gi	'Uniform' or 'suit' – traditional costume worn while training
Gyaku-zuki	'Reserve punch' – a punch executed by the hand opposite the forward leg
Haito	'Ridge hand', thumb-edge of hand
Hajime	A command, 'begin'
Hakama	'Divided skirt' – traditional garb of the Samurai class
Hand	Lineal measure of approximately four inches or five finger widths
Hiraken	"Flat fist' – a technique in which the fist is semi-clenched, using the second knuckles of the four fingers as the striking surface
Jion-ji	A famous Buddhist temple, from which many of the 'classical fighting forms' are thought to have originated
Jodan	'Upward level' – face and head level of the body

Karma	Actions which determine the soul's progress. The law of karma is that we reap what we sow, that everyone must suffer the consequences of every action and every thought, though the effects may not be immediate
Kata	'Formal exercise' – a series of pre-arranged manoeuvres executed against one or more imaginary attacking opponents. The forms through which traditional martial arts are passed from generation to generation
Katana	'Sword' – a Japanese sword with a curved, single-edged blade, two or three feet in length
Ke-komi	A thrusting kick
Ki	Mental and spiritual energy that can be applied to accomplish physical feats, the 'animating force of life'
Ki-ai	'Spiritual meeting' – expulsion of air from the diaphragm; it reinforces the strength of a striking or blocking technique, both physically and mentally. 'Pushes the spirit forward' – usually a loud yell or shout
Kiba-dachi	'Horse-stance', 'straddle-stance' in which feet are parallel and extended approximately twice the width of the shoulders
Kime	'Focus' – the act of concentrating complete mental and physical force into the split-second at the completion of a technique
Kisagake	A whipping action of the sword as it is removed from the scabbard in an attack
Kizami-zuki	Short, jabbing punch
Kumite	'Sparring' (*Jiyu-kumite* – a free exchange of blows, blocks and counter-attacks)

Kundalini	Latent power at base of spine, often depicted by a coiled, sleeping serpent. Most asanas of hatha yoga are intended to 'awaken the serpent' and guide it upwards through the chakras, with the ultimate result of super-consciousness
Lotus position	'Place each foot on the opposite thigh.' The classic yoga posture for meditation
Mae-geri	Front kick
Makiwara	'Straw-padded striking post' – designed for toughening various striking points. Usually made from a piece of timber seven or eight feet long, three feet of which are buried and cemented in the ground, the top four feet bevelled so that the very top is only half an inch thick. The top foot is wrapped in straw rope and provides the striking surface
Mantra	Sacred symbolic sounds, the repetition of which leads to transcendence of normal consciousness. The sound 'auom' is the supreme mantra
Maya	The physical world, sometimes translated as 'illusion'
Nanchuku	A fighting weapon comprising two wood or metal rods separated and attached by a twelve-inch chain
Nihon-nukite	'Two-finger spear-hand'
Obi	'Belt' – knotted sash through which scabbard of katana is carried
Oi-zuki	Lunge punch
Pace	A distance of approximately eight hands
Prana	The life force, the cosmic energy, that which gives life to all things

Rei	'To bow' – a command
Seika-tanden	'Lower abdomen' – seat of the soul and centre of ki
Sei-za	'Correct sitting', a full kneeling position, hips resting on the heels of the feet
Sensei	'Teacher'
Seppuka	Formal word for ritual suicide practised with short sword. An honourable death (*Hara-kiri* – 'belly cut')
Shizen-tai	Natural stance
Shihan	'Master teacher'
Shuto	'Knife hand', 'sword hand' – the edge of the hand
Sochin-dachi	'Diagonal straddle-leg stance'
Super-consciousness	Simultaneous knowledge of all things – state of supreme 'oneness'
Tai-sabaki	'Body movement' – turning, evasive action of the body
Tanto	Japanese dagger with a blade of eight to sixteen inches
Tatami	'Straw mat' – usually measuring three feet by six feet and three inches thick
Tekko	Iron-pronged fists, similar to modern 'brass knuckles'
Transcend	To rise above all egocentric thoughts and emotions
Uchi-deshi	'Special student' – selected for individual training
Ushiro-mawashi-geri	'Reverse roundhouse kick'

Vakos	The 'supreme state of inner vision', a complete subjectivity, often entering the realms of the unconscious mind
Voll	A distance of approximately one mile
Vul	Plural of voll
Wakan	A spontaneous merging of souls, the deepest rapport
Waza	A single technique
Yeon	A period of 380 days
Zanshin	'Perfect posture' – a state of perfect mental awareness
Zenkutsu-dachi	Forward stance
Zori	Rope sandals

ABOUT THE AUTHOR

Richard La Plante was born in Pennsylvania in 1948. He has travelled extensively throughout the United States and Mexico, at one time living alone for nine months in the Mexican Sonora desert. In 1976 he moved to London, and in 1978 founded the American rock band, *Revenge*. He has studied with Masters Keinosuke Enoeda and Teriyuki Okazaki and is ranked Sandan – Black belt, third degree – by the Japanese Karate Association. He lives with his wife, author Lynda La Plante, in Surrey.

Warlord of Zendow is his first novel, and the beginning of the *Tegné* trilogy.

SIGN OF CHAOS

ROGER ZELAZNY

METHOD IN THEIR MADNESS . . .

Merle Corey, son of the great Prince Corwin of Amber, has been pursued through Shadow by unknown enemies and left trapped in an Alice in Wonderland world – a bar with the Mad Hatter serving and the Cheshire Cat grinning malevolently. In a dramatic escape from a monstrous Jabberwock, Merle embarks upon a fantastic adventure, leading him back to the court of Amber and finally to a confrontation at the Kepp of Four Worlds. And here he learns the strange secrets of the Courts of Chaos and their role in his destiny . . .

'The Amber series is daring and magnificent'
SCIENCE FICTION MAGAZINE

Also by Roger Zelazny in Sphere Books:

0 7474 0097 0   FANTASY   £2.99

The mighty warrior stares death in the eye . . .

THE RENEGADE

LEONARD CARPENTER

In rebellion-wracked Koth, Conan of Cimmeria sells his sword as a mercenary and finds himself deep in deadly intrigue. The Prince plots against the King; the Baron plots against the Prince; the Wizard serves any master who furthers his own dark designs; the Queen loves Conan, yet will send him to his death for the good of her land; the warrior woman allows no man's touch, yet desires the muscular Cimmerian. And in the mountains that legend says will rise to destroy any invading army, the scene is set for thunderous and bloody conflict. For Conan to survive when there is no hand to trust, when the whirlwinds of treachery and death arise, he must become

CONAN THE RENEGADE

0 7221 2237 3   FANTASY   £2.75

A selection of bestsellers from SPHERE

FICTION

JUBILEE: THE POPPY CHRONICLES 1	Claire Rayner	£3.50 ☐
DAUGHTERS	Suzanne Goodwin	£3.50 ☐
REDCOAT	Bernard Cornwell	£3.50 ☐
WHEN DREAMS COME TRUE	Emma Blair	£3.50 ☐
THE LEGACY OF HEOROT	Niven/Pournelle/Barnes	£3.50 ☐

FILM AND TV TIE-IN

BUSTER	Colin Shindler	£2.99 ☐
COMING TOGETHER	Alexandra Hine	£2.99 ☐
RUN FOR YOUR LIFE	Stuart Collins	£2.99 ☐
BLACK FOREST CLINIC	Peter Heim	£2.99 ☐
INTIMATE CONTACT	Jacqueline Osborne	£2.50 ☐

NON-FICTION

BARE-FACED MESSIAH	Russell Miller	£3.99 ☐
THE COCHIN CONNECTION	Alison and Brian Milgate	£3.50 ☐
HOWARD & MASCHLER ON FOOD	Elizabeth Jane Howard and Fay Maschler	£3.99 ☐
FISH	Robyn Wilson	£2.50 ☐
THE SACRED VIRGIN AND THE HOLY WHORE	Anthony Harris	£3.50 ☐

*A black con man in
South Africa*

"Dugmore Boetie . . . stole, lied, cheated,
conned, maybe even killed. But he survived,
at least long enough to write about his life.
He had a rare talent, this small black South
African with one leg and a con man's audacity and a storytellers' eyes. . . .

"How much of this self-biography is true?
Who knows? . . . It is not, finally, of any
consequence. . . . The book is a beautifully
told story of growing up black in a hellhole
of inhumanity, written by a human who grew
up black in South Africa. That's fact—all
that counts.

"*Familiarity Is the Kingdom of the Lost*
is the best factual account of black life to
come out of South Africa. But even more
than that, it is artful."

—*Book World*

"A wild and antic vision."
—*Saturday Review*

FAMILIARITY
IS THE KINGDOM
OF THE LOST

by DUGMORE BOETIE

edited by Barney Simon

preface by Nadine Gordimer

A FAWCETT PREMIER BOOK
Fawcett Publications, Inc., Greenwich, Conn.

PREFACE

Although I, a white woman, introduce this book, and
Barney Simon, a white man, provides the epilogue, the
writer was nobody's tame black crow. A thorn in the
flesh, yes. Barney Simon gave him as much succouring
kindness as any human being can give another, and he
showed no gratitude. Asked him for his confidence and
received deception. Asked for the truth and received lies.
How could it have been otherwise, if Dugmore Boetie
were to remain true to himself? What should he know of
gratitude, the South African black man who must take off
his hat and say Thank you, *Baas,* not for what comes to
him as of right—for nothing comes to him of right—but
for the tithe of the white man's abundance handed out at
the back door? What should he know of confidence who
must daily accept to be the dupe of the white man's
"innate superiority"? What should he know of that truth
of those who can afford to acknowledge concrete reality,
the facts as they are, because for them these facts refer to
a positive state of being, one that contains always the possibility of self-realisation—what meaning could *the facts
as they are* have for the black man for whom they provide
only the bolts and bars of his negation? They serve merely
to define all that he is not, cannot have; the positive truth
of this, for him, is the fantasy that deprivation gives rise
to. A feast dreamt of on a hungry stomach is more wildly

5

sumptuous than any actual feast; yet it conveys better than any objective description the actual pain of hunger.

This was Dugmore Boetie's truth. In time, place and deed, much of this autobiography never happened. What does that matter? His fantasies of power, revenge, bravado, absurdity are a revelation of the mean and degraded condition of living that bred them. His cruel, funny, savage narrative is the autobiography not of one individual, but of every black child grown old in the cunning of survival in lawless segregated townships, every black man swallowing his gall and playing the sycophant to the white while making a fool of him behind his back. Such a man—black man—was not even allowed to carry a gun in the white man's war; and so even Dugmore Boetie's loss of a leg (amputated in childhood, it seems) provides a dream of unattainable glory: the honour accorded the returning hero of the right colour.

If this book tells better than any factual document what life on the dark side of the colour bar really is like, it also gives a picture, honest in the way that Pop Art is honest, of the qualities with which the black man in South Africa contrives to stay alive and kicking. They are not virtues, according to a moral code laid down by any establishment. But then one must remember that it is the moral code of the South African establishment that has made its own virtue out of depriving the black man of any possibility of ordering his own life according to his conscience. He must live, learn, work, eat, evacuate and procreate in areas specified by white law, and if he thinks what he pleases of this, he may not say so, certainly not in so many words. Therefore all becomes a paradox, the paradox of this book: the man of the majority (coloured population of South Africa, 16 million, the white, 3½) cultivates the survival qualities of the outsider; the truth emerges in fantasy. Dugmore Boetie lies about himself and the lies give back a faithful image of a society of trick mirrors, a society based upon what is perhaps the biggest lie man ever told—that what a man is, is ordained by his colour.

Baudelaire spoke of the accusation that the ruling class

might read in the drunkenness of the people. There is an accusation to be read in the fantasy of the people, too. Dying, still lying, Dugmore Boetie produced his "true, hot book" that nothing could kill inside him.

NADINE GORDIMER

*FAMILIARITY
IS THE KINGDOM
OF THE LOST*

ONE

"Say 'mother'! Go on, say 'mother', you son of a bitch!"

Wham! Wham! went the leather strap.

"Say 'mother', damn you! Louder, you little bastard, louder!" she shrieked.

The strap went wild all over my face, head, and neck. It was as if she was suffering more than me.

My mouth opened, and instead of the word "mother" a clot of blood rolled out. It was followed by a distinct "Futsek!" She shrieked and swung a frying pan, cracking four of my ribs. I pushed and her skinny body fell to the greedy flames of a healthy fire-galley.

Maybe I had broken her back, or maybe she was just too exhausted to lift herself. Anyway, my mother just fried and fried and fried. . . .

"Where is he?"

"We've got him in bed thirteen."

"How is he?"

"Oh, his ribs are coming on fine and we took the stitches out of his right thigh this morning. It's the cut above his eye that seems to worry him. He'll soon be out of here."

"You're a social worker, aren't you?"

"Yes, Nurse."

"I wonder how old he is?"

"Between seven and eight, I'd say."

"God," said the nurse.

"What's going to happen to him when he gets out of here?"

They were many now, all ringed around my bed dis-

cussing me as if I had fallen from heaven and had broken
a wing. The one not in uniform shrugged her shoulders
and said:

"These cases are many; they might be different, but the
pattern is the same. Take this one—he's too young to be
sent to a reformatory and too old to be placed in a crèche.
Children of the gods above and the gutters below. One
day, with God's help, the Government will build a home
for them."

My ribs were not fully healed when I ran away from
hospital. I walked back to Sophiatown where I got myself
a job at the Good Street bus depot. It was more voluntary
than fixed.

I worked without asking permission from anybody. I
busied myself sweeping stationary buses with an improvised rag broom.

At night, I would wait for the last bus to come in. It
had to be the last bus because you never knew which one
might pull out first. The last bus would come in between
eleven thirty and twelve midnight and then I'd coil myself
on the back seat and sleep.

When the first bus pulled out at four a.m. I would get
up and stand at the corner of Good Street and Main Road
to wait for the baker's horse-cart. Right on time I would
hear the clop-clop echoes of the horses' hoofs on the tar
road as they galloped towards Newlands. This was a daily
routine. They were delivering fresh-baked bread to the
white inhabitants of Newlands.

I would stand hidden behind one of the shop pillars
and watch the driver till I was sure that all his attention
was centred on the road before him, then I would dart
swiftly out of my hiding place and without hesitation jump
lightly on the back step of the van. Sometimes I would
just sit there with my bare feet dangling while I enjoyed
the ride.

One morning I was too hungry to brag. I pulled at the
thick wire loop to swing the door open, but nothing
happened. Then I noticed that the van was freshly painted. The paint made it difficult for me to lift the loop; it

needed stronger hands. Hands that materialised right out of the tar road. Or so it seemed. One minute I was struggling with the wire loop and the next I knew, a different pair of hands appeared mysteriously and lifted the loop without effort.

"Jump!" was all he said.

I did. We retreated up Main Road with four loaves of fresh-baked bread under our armpits. When we came to the spot where he had so mysteriously appeared, he stopped and eyed me speculatively.

"Where's your home, boy?"

I shook my head. "No home."

"Where d'you sleep?"

"At the bus depot in Good Street, on the back seat of the last bus."

He had a big dent in his forehead and it was throbbing violently as if it was inhaling and exhaling. He was very much undecided about something. What made him come to a quick decision was the shouting we heard from the still-receding baker's cart.

We had forgotten to close the back door of the van. The door was flapping wildly in the wind and someone was hailing the driver, hoping to draw his attention.

"In here," said my new-found father. He threw himself on to his stomach and, sliding crabwise, vanished into the gutter.

I was still undecided when I felt his fingers closing around my ankle in a powerful grip. That decided me. I went flat on my stomach and slid in after him.

I felt him crawl, and I followed. We had crawled for only a few yards when suddenly he wasn't in front of me anymore. If he hadn't grabbed me, I would have blundered head-first into a larger tunnel.

Here it was blacker than the inside of a devil's horn. You couldn't see your own hand in front of you, but at least you could stand upright.

"Follow me, and trail with your hand against the wall," he said.

I did. We travelled this way for about a mile, and then we stopped. He groped for my hand and led me up four steps. Up here, he was forced to stoop, while I still remained upright.

That was how I first met the man who was responsible for my future life. It was a dog's life, but nevertheless a life.

I heard him going through his pockets, then I heard the rattle of matches. He struck one. The flame nearly blinded me. He got a lamp from somewhere, and lit the wick.

I gasped. I was looking at the cavern of Ali Baba and the forty thieves. Only that was fiction and this was real.

The walls were plastered with pictures of Tom Mix the cowboy. Strewn on the floor was what must have come fresh from a washing line. There were bed-sheets, pillow-cases, ladies' bloomers, men's underwear—all were still damp. There was a wheelbarrow, a gramophone and records, a stale wedding-cake, a police helmet, a pressure stove, pots, a red battered money-box, a guitar with three strings, and a horseshoe nailed to the entrance to keep away evil spirits.

But above all the prizes, my eyes kept straying towards the gramophone. He must have noticed this, because he went straight to it and started playing some records.

I looked around and saw that this part of the tunnel was V-shaped. Water couldn't come through here because he had placed a thick slab of cement to block the outlet that runs through to the main tunnel. One tunnel was then forced to share the water of the other. What really helped a great deal was that we were about three feet above the major tunnel.

After enjoying some of the records, we had our breakfast. Then my father started schooling me on the numerous small tunnels that start in and around Sophiatown and end up here in the big one.

I was taught when and how to take advantage of them, which one to use, and which one to avoid, where they led to, and what to do in case of rain. It was like a game of snakes and ladders with the ladders crossed out. We didn't need the ladders because they led up. All we needed was the snakes. The snakes swallowed us, and when we crawled out of their bowels we found ourselves back in our underground home with arms heavily laden with stolen goods. And no tail behind.

I looked with awe at my father when he was through explaining. He was an unusually short man. Because of this, it was difficult to determine his age. He could have been anything between twenty and forty.

He told me that his real name was Ga-ga, but because of his bandy legs, people referred to him as Kromie, "Crooked" in Afrikaans. When I begged him for permission to refer to him as Ga-ga, which was his real name, meaning not to remind him of his bandy legs, he refused. He told me that in the American comic strips ga-ga means mad; he wasn't mad.

The dent in his forehead was frightening to look at. It was so big that you could fit a tennis ball into it. He told me that it was caused by the hoof of a farmer's horse. I started hating horses until this very day.

Kromie was bad through and through. He was more mischievous than troublesome. He could without effort cause a highly religious person to use vile words. Wherever he went he left grief and chaos behind. I honestly don't think that he could walk past a dry field of grass without setting fire to it. His pocket money came from children sent to the shops by their parents. My teaming up with him did not improve my relationship with the young population of Sophiatown nor the Main Road shop owners. There was a verbal prize hanging on our heads.

Take Honest Charley, for instance, from the Chinaman shop next to the bioscope. He was named Honest Charley instead of Black Market Charley. This Chinaman kept a big pocket watch in one of his waistcoat pockets. The watch was attached to a chain.

I must have made a note of it unconsciously. One morning, after oversleeping and missing my usual bread supply on the road, I went into the shop to buy myself a tickey's worth of bread. I was suddenly struck by a mischievous brainwave.

"Charley," I said, leaving out the Honest part of his name, and holding out the bread in my hand, "will you please push this bread down the back of my neck? I'm afraid the other boys will snatch it and run into the bioscope with it." Charley grinned, showing a row of golden teeth.

While Charley was busy pushing the bread down the back of my neck, I lifted the watch.

It was more through fate than anything else that I bumped into Ga-ga, my gutter father, as I was leaving the shop. Outside, I showed my father the watch. He whispered fiercely into my ear, then he dragged me back to the shop's entrance. He called to Charley who was busy scaling sugar into six-penny bags.

When Honest Charley looked up, Ga-ga said, "Look, he's got your watch." Honest Charley dropped what he was doing and grabbed a meat cleaver. If I had known that the watch meant so much to him, I wouldn't have pinched it. Maybe he had come all the way from Chinaland with it.

I wanted to run for my life, but Ga-ga held me fast. The cleaver was being brandished with murderous intent. I tried to pull free from Ga-ga, but he held on. It was only when the cleaver was lifted for the fatal blow that Ga-ga let go. I ran down Main Road as if the Devil was after me. Maybe he was, at that.

Then Ga-ga went into action. He darted into the empty shop, jumped over the counter, and emptied the till. . . .

I was lying flat on my stomach, another morning, with my cheeks resting on the palms of my dirty little hands. A gramophone record was playing.

The voice in the record belonged to Jimmy Rodgers. He was singing a song called "Waiting for the Train" with guitar accompaniment. The first time I heard that record, I took to it like a drunkard takes to drink.

I must have been really dreaming. Of what? Only my ancestors know. But what I do know is that I was dreaming, because Kromie had looked up from his comic strip and said,

"I'm talking to you!"

"What?" I asked.

He pointed a fat jam-stained finger at the comic strip. "Do you think the Red Indians will catch him?"

To shut him up I said, "Yes, he doesn't stand a chance."

My Daddy chuckled gleefully at the plight of the pony express rider. As long as you agreed with him, nothing went wrong. I didn't want anything to go wrong. Not while I was listening to that record.

But something did. Good things don't last. My father trampled on my favourite record by accident.

A nightmare search for the record started. Every time I stole a record, it would turn out to be the wrong one. You see, I couldn't read. If I could, I would have saved myself a lot of trouble and the Jew a lot of grief.

It went on so long, that I was beginning to think that the old Jew at the bicycle shop didn't have that record.

But my will was as obstinate as the cracks on my mud-caked feet. I was in and out of that Jew's shop as if I owned it. At last I got the right record and six months in the reformatory. The youngest convict there.

When I came out, I was bitterly reprimanded by my father for stealing records instead of food.

One morning I went out as usual for our daily bread. When I came back, the gramophone was missing. My father had sold it during my absence. He claimed that it was spoiling me.

I felt as though my back was broken. My bowels wanted to work. I packed my guitar and left the tunnel for good to wander again in a world of uncertainty.

I didn't wander long. I soon found myself working for a circus, washing elephants' feet. Sometimes I wondered which feet needed to be washed most, mine or the elephants'. But seeing that I wasn't getting paid to wash mine, I didn't bother with them.

I traveled with the circus to Cape Town where for the first time I saw the sea.

In Cape Town I was mostly with a Coon Carnival group known as The Jesters. There was a guitar player that I greatly admired. He played almost like my Jimmy

Rodgers. We were inseparable; I trailed behind him like a
devoted young pup.

He sent me everywhere. I went daily to town for him
to pick up cigarette stubs and empty wine bottles. Eighty
empty wine bottles landed him a full one at the liquor
store. In turn he taught me a few chords on the guitar.

I was so busy running errands for my friend that the
circus left without me. I didn't care much. I was fed-up
with the elephants' feet and getting tips instead of wages. I
felt that if I kept on washing elephants' feet I'd never get
around to washing my own.

I liked Cape Town because sleeping accommodation
was no problem. I just slept where I felt sleepy. In corridors. On stairs. Balconies. Anywhere. I just lived, and
lived, and lived.

My life was so free that I was just beginning to be
convinced that this nice town had no reformatory. Then
they arrested me for trying to steal a bus conductor's
money bag.

My knife was too blunt, otherwise I would have gotten
away with it. I had his money bag, which was hanging
from a leather strap, with my left hand, while my right
was slashing at the leather strap which was buckled to the
bag. The damn-fool knife wouldn't cut the strap in one
stroke. The white conductor tried to grab my knife hand.
That made me forget the leather strap. Instead, I sank my
knife through his hand. It's funny, the knife wouldn't cut
the strap but it sank through his hand as if it was made of
reformatory soap. That got me two years in Tokai, the
Cape Town reformatory. The kind of work they gave me
in the reformatory got me out of the reformatory. We
were weaving fishing-nets. My nimble fingers were so good
at it that in a year they gave me a "hat" as promotion. I
was now a monitor.

It was while I was a monitor that I learned about the
fish train. The fastest train on the track. It travels non-stop
from Cape Town docks to Johannesburg, with one water
break at Bloemfontein so that the fish it carries shouldn't
get rotten. The non-stop journey plus the chunks of ice

with which they line the coaches keep the fish still fresh all the way to Johannesburg.

Maybe the fishing-net business was beginning to bore me. Or perhaps it was the fish train knowledge. I don't know. All I know is that I found my hands manufacturing a rope ladder instead of a fishing net, while the corner of my right eye kept straying towards the prison walls. It's a long time ago, but I can still hear the echoes of police whistles in my ears whenever I recall what I now refer to as the Tokai Break. They behaved as if I was forty instead of eleven.

Seven days after my escape from Tokai, a policeman was saying,

"Jump over his head and get to the other side, then work on the fingers of his left hand while I work on the right."

A crowd of onlookers had gathered on both sides of the fish train. I was perched between two coaches. The white policeman on my right was grumbling and swearing as he struggled to release my frozen fingers from the wire cage of the coach. He was hurting me. The other policeman on my left was more gentle.

"Can't we light a fire and melt the ice around the little devil's fingers?"

"No, he'll get frostbite."

"I wonder how the devil the little bastard got himself into such a mess."

He gave one quick unexpected pull and my right hand was jerked free. Blood dripped from my fingers and tears spurted from my eyes as I examined my bleeding hand. The nail on my little finger was missing.

"Better do the same with that left hand, we can't afford to waste any more time with this little brat."

"Hold on, I'm only left with the thumb."

Pulling the baton from his belt, he knocked it several times against the wire cage. The ice cracked and fell away, and my thumb was free.

They hauled me off the train. At first, my knees

wouldn't let me stand upright, but after the police gave them a good rub I was able to stand unaided.

"Pikannin!"

"Yes, baas."

I looked up at the policeman with a dirty, tear-stained face.

"What on earth were you doing on that train?"

"I was trying to get loose, baas."

"Yes, yes, I know. What I don't know is how the hell you found yourself hemmed in between two coaches and half-frozen to death?"

"I was coming home, baas."

"Coming home from where?"

"From Cape Town, baas."

"You mean," spluttered the other policeman, "you travelled a thousand miles from Cape Town like that?"

"I come from Cape Town with this train, baas."

"Where do you stay, boy?"

"Sophiatown, baas."

"What street, boy?"

"Good Street, Baas."

"What number?"

"No number, baas."

"You mean there is no number at your house?"

"No number, baas."

"Why?"

"Is not a house, is a bus garage, baas."

"You mean, you sleep in a bus depot?"

"Yes, baas. On the back seat of the last bus."

"The back seat of the last bus, heh?"

"Yes, baas."

"This is a case for the social workers. . . ."

"Not social workers, please, baas."

"Why not social workers?"

"Long time ago, they say I'm a head sore."

"A what?"

"A head sore, baas."

"You mean a headache?"

"Yes, baas."

"How old are you?"

"Leben."

"Eleven!" they echoed in unison.

As I was led through the gaping crowd, I fished out a half loaf of stale bread from inside my shirt and started biting into it.

I didn't care what they were going to do with me as long as I was back home. Familiarity is the kingdom of the lost.

They locked me up and only released me when they felt that I was old enough to look after myself. I could, too, if the police would only stop interfering.

TWO

After four years I was out.

A rasping kind of sound came from my new khaki prison suit as I walked away from the Auckland Park Reformatory towards Westdene. I drowned the monotonous sound by jingling the money that was in my pocket. Reformatory wages—two shillings a month for four years. Four pounds sixteen shillings.

My mind was dwelling on the parting words of our convict preacher: "Son, once you come to the outside world, teach yourself to look upon problems as the wheels of progress. Go forward with them and you won't go wrong. Reverse, and you end up here."

The people who preach most about reform are found in prison. When you're free, you wonder where the hell they are. When you go back, you find them there. You don't dare ask them why they didn't follow their own advice. They go on like a whore that tells every man in bed with her, in all seriousness, that she has never had it so good before.

Lying to yourself is the biggest sin of all because you

end up the sufferer. Why fry your own carcass? Why stand in judgement on yourself? Clear your conscience by elbowing the blame. You have as much right on this earth as the next man. My advice is: keep the blood-pumper out of it and give the reins to the brains. But in this country a hungry stomach takes the place of brains. Use it. Take or be taken. The home of the timid is the grave.

If you want to get rich quick, take the road that leads to prison. There's a steel door at the end. As you go to it, don't go in, turn sharp right. Then you're on your way.

I came to the first gate that led into Newclare Township. The gate I call "Weaklings turn back". Instead of making the sign of the cross because I was just about to enter into hell, I took out a bag of strong prison tobacco. It's a Xhosa tobacco commonly known as Ndanya Ndanya—"I shit, I shit".

Newclare Township lies five miles west of Johannesburg City. In those days it was an African township, encamped right round with an iron spiked fence. Whoever thought of that giant-size cage must have thought it proper to place the inhabitants of this township on the same level as wild animals; because in all my born days I've never seen a township frequented so much by police vans, except, perhaps, its opposite neighbour, Sophiatown.

There were four legal entrances to Newclare, each closely guarded by hefty Zulu policemen armed with heavy knobkerries. The knobs of their kerries were covered with spiked buttons of steel.

In spite of these security precautions, the rough elements of the township tampered with the iron fence that so jealously guarded them and you could always find man-size holes at convenient points.

The first entrance led directly into Ballendine Avenue. This was the only tarred street in the whole township because it led to the superintendent's home and office.

Turn right or left at any street you came to. If you were black, you'd see life. If you were white, life would see you.

The streets were divided by ox-cart-wide alleys. If you stopped at the mouth of any alley and shot a glance either way, you were sure to see the bent form of a woman hauling skokiaan from a drum that lay mouldering in the ground.

Right where you were, if you knew what to look for, you'd see someone, male or female, resembling part of the surrounding scenery.

Immediately after the skokiaan queen rose from her undignified position and disappeared into one of the back yards, the inconspicuous figure would also disappear. There was nothing mysterious about this. The party just happened to be scouting for police while the skokiaan queen hauled her brew.

If you kept on along the avenue, you came to the tramlines and the football grounds. Then you turned right. You were at another gate, the second entrance to Newclare. The biggest and busiest of the township.

First thing that I looked for here was the gutter that led to the tunnel where I lived as a boy. Next, the "Prisoners Corner" near the public lavatories. Here you'd see Africans—as many as fifty to a hundred—sitting miserably in a long queue. Closer inspection revealed that they were handcuffed in pairs. Pass-law victims.

The familiarity of such a scene hardly warranted a second glance, unless you wanted to invite enquiries about your own pass.

You turned your eyes away from those bundles of misery to the elderly women sitting in half-circles selling fried corn cobs. They worked over fire-galleys made out of four-gallon paraffin tins with holes punched into them. Some sold pork trotters and sheep trotters in pots blackened by wood and coal smoke. There were coffee carts where you could get a quick cup of coffee in the open or a shilling's worth of skokiaan on the sly. Some women sold hard-boiled eggs, and right next to them a Coloured woman also sold eggs. Hers went much faster because the insides contained brandy mixed with tobacco juice.

There was a little waiting-room built by the Johannesburg Municipality Transport Company to shelter tram passengers from the rain. The only patrons of this little waiting-room were a gang of unruly teenagers waiting to

pick the pockets of passengers as loaded trams rumbled in
from the city.

Written inside the waiting-room in bold red letters were
the words: BENZINE GANG. Next to the waiting-room stood
the skeleton of the township's only telephone booth, long
since out of use.

I crossed Main Road and left Newclare to mingle with
the pawns on the Devil's board—Sophiatown.

My beloved Sophiatown. The skeleton with the permanent grin. A live carcass bloated with grief and happiness.
Where decency was found in filth and beauty hidden
behind ugliness. Where vice was a virtue and virtue a
vice. A black heaven glowing with sparks of hell.

From its feverish womb crawled many of the country's
finest black doctors, teachers, sportsmen, businessmen,
musicians and intellectuals. Also its best-dressed criminals.

Sophiatown mothered all races. That's why her apron
was always dirty. Without blushing she could produce a
Timbuctoo Swahili with the same ease as she would a
Zulu flat-boy. She looked upon them all with the equal
affection of a long-suffering parent.

Here, four hundred miles inland from the nearest
coastal town, American influence ran thick. Because Sophiatown was the first black town in the whole of Africa
that could boast a cinema as far back as the early twenties. As civilisation advanced, so did the evil life of Sophiatown. I saw the turnover from the traditional stick fights
to fist fights, and then to the buckles of heavy scout belts.
From there, it was knives, and then guns. Sophiatown
became a slum jungle of here-today-and-dead-tomorrow.

Just across the main road from Newclare was Good
Street and the notorious and one and only bus-rank.
Whoever named this street must still be wriggling in his
grave. This street was no damn good. It was hell's own
highway. Bad through and through. It was nearly impossible to go from one side to the other without paying a fine
in broken ribs or a busted head.

Saturdays and Sunday afternoons were sheer hell. The
Pedi gang used to have fist fights in shebeen backyards

just to see which one of them was strong enough to lead the pack. Then they'd storm down Good Street towards the bus-rank, leaving pedestrians screaming and cursing as they painfully picked themselves up from the ground. A cyclone gone mad.

Then there were the Zulu gangs. Their undying belief is that they represent the bravest and strongest black race in the whole of Africa. Me, I think they are just plain stubborn. They would come in groups from the beer halls, waving and hitting the air with their heavy sticks, fighting an imaginary foe. Often the foe was not imaginary, especially when they reached the bus-rank at Good Street where they were sure to come face to face with the Basutos. The result was always a free-for-all, with a few scattered dead and badly maimed bodies. Mostly Sothos.

The Sothos also moved about in groups. They wore cone-shaped straw hats, and bright blankets covered the top half of their bodies. Underneath those colourful blankets, they carried dangerous sticks. If you saw Sothos coming towards you in a group, you got the hell out of their way. Their way of fighting was first to cover the victim with their blankets and then to beat him to death. If they detected movement under the blanket, they justified their blood-thirsty act by suggesting that the victim was fighting back. If they hit you and you fell, they said you were picking up stones. If you screamed, you were calling your brothers to come and kill them.

Those were a few of the playmates you could find at the corner of Good Street and Main Road.

At night time it was even more jazzy. Then you could always meet up with true, cultured gentlemen like the Black Caps. They were a gang of more than fifty. Here's a typical operation: A man takes a stroll with his wife. He's smartly dressed in his own way—brown-and-white shoes, grey flannel trousers, black blazer, cream straw hat. The fool is swinging his wife's handbag like it's a briefcase. His bragging ways make the Black Caps jealous. So one of them says, "Look at that romantic bastard. He must be a real black Clark Gable to be able to own such a beautiful brown doll."

Then another one of them says, "I'm going to show that bum that the fact that I don't own a cow doesn't mean that I don't like meat. He thinks it's only people with baskets that can go to market."

So they strip him of his clothes and his wife. His wife he gets back the next day.

A little further up Good Street was the untidy bus depot where I made my first job and slept as a child. You were always sure to find a circle of men gathered on the pavement nearby shooting dice.

These gamblers were the real hard cases of Sophiatown. My reformatory wages needed increasing. I decided to go and try my luck. When my turn came to pick up the dice, I dropped a ten-shilling note and made my challenge. I bent half-forward and shook the dice, waiting for my challenge to be answered. I didn't wait long before four half-crowns came spinning down from above.

On my first throw, up came the winning number. It was number eleven. I reached out with my left hand to pick up the money, when I heard a voice growl. It was just that, nothing else; just a growl like an animal imitating speech.

I looked up. What I saw made me take a step back. The money was completely forgotten. In all my life I'd never seen such a frightening brute! His head was clean-shaven, showing many brutal scars that brought to mind bicycle chains, heavy belt buckles, knives, axes—you name it. What was fascinating was that there were no stitch marks on any of those swollen scars. They must have healed with no outside help. They looked like criss-cross pieces of rope.

He grinned at my blatant stare. That made him even uglier. He had a huge scar that started just above his left eye and ended below his chin. His lips were badly scarred too. Everything expanded when he smiled.

"Throw again," he said. "Can't you see the dice is not sitting straight?" He sounded like a leaking organ in B flat.

I gulped and picked up the dice again. It wasn't necessary to shake them because I was shaking already. I threw, and another winning number came up. This time it was number seven. As I reached for the money, the gorilla growled again.

I threw so many damned times that I felt my back ache. At last I threw a double six, a crap. The losing number. "Aaah," beamed the son-of-a-bitch. "Now you lose." With bile and disgust in my mouth, I threw the dice in the middle of the school and walked away.

I sat in the back yard of a Chinese grocer's shop drinking bath-tub brandy and related my grim crap game experience to some fellow drinkers. One of them looked at his friend and grinned as if enjoying a secret joke.

"This, my friend, is Sophiatown. Here you must look before you leap. Last night I was enjoying myself at a friend's party way up Gold Street. At eleven o'clock I decided to call it a night. I went into the bedroom and I took off my clothes until just my underwear was left. My friend asked why I was going to sleep so early when the party was just getting hot.

" 'Sleep?' I said. 'I'm not going to sleep—I'm going home!'

" 'How the hell can you go home in your underpants?'

" 'You wait and see,' I said. They all thought I was drunk or mad.

"I opened the door and began to jog home at a nice dignified pace. Just when I came to the Newclare fence, I heard a voice coming from a dark shop doorway:

" 'Leave that one alone. Can't you see they've already stripped him?''

"Hell, I smiled to myself. You see, I wouldn't have stood a dog's chance and I knew it. When I leave here, I'm going straight to my friend's place to collect my clothes.

"Yes, my friend, Sophiatown is becoming a real hell town. The police are not improving it either with their pass laws and their liquor laws. Now they have passed a new law known as 'Lekker Loop'. It's really 'Drunken Noise'. The fine was ten shillings or ten days. Now it's fifteen pounds or three months.

"Man, now they are arresting us left and right. Even if you're not drunk, they'll claim you *are* drunk! Day before yesterday, no! It was Monday morning at the corner of Victoria and Bertha Street, I found a white policeman arguing with an elderly man. The policeman said the man was drunk. The man said he was only on his way to work. 'Then,' said the policeman, 'if you're not drunk, why the hell do you eat fish and chips in the street?'

" 'I'm hungry, baas, that's why.'

"The policeman clipped handcuffs on his wrists and said, 'Come on, only drunkards eat in the street. Besides, you're shivering.'

"As he was being led away, I heard the man say: 'I'm shivering because I'm angry, not drunk.' " The speaker sighed, then took another deep breath as though he was going to launch into a new yarn.

"Do you know this ugly ape who did me down there?" I interrupted quickly.

"That, my friend, is Number Nine. He is called that because of that ugly scar like a nine on his face. Keep well away from Nine, he's dangerous. He fights like hell, but what's so bloody unfair is that he doesn't seem to get hurt. Fighting him is like fighting grinning rubber!" Everyone nodded in agreement.

There and then I decided to spend all my reformatory wages on Nine. I'm going to make the son of a bitch drunk, I said to myself, and when he's nice and drunk, I'm going to beat him half to death. Either I get Nine, or he gets me.

THREE

It was either the bitter taste of bile in my mouth, or the stench seeping through the broken window of the latrine that woke me. Maybe it was both.

The taste of bile was so thick that I wouldn't have been surprised to see a purple face in the mirror. And Christ! did that lavatory smell! Imagine one bucket-latrine catering for a whole yard of people. It was being used inside and out. I needed to vomit.

I got out of the bed without studying my surroundings. I went straight to the water bucket without bothering to look for a mug. I picked up the four-gallon bucket and drank a quarter of its contents. I looked about for a basin and saw one. I didn't care what kind of basin it was—a dish-washing basin or a face-washing basin. I went down on my knees in front of it and pushed three of my fingers down my throat in the hope of drawing the bile out.

It worked. When I was through, the basin was filled with green stuff. It was as if some evil had just snaked out of me.

I took the basin out and emptied it in a blocked drain. I went back to the little room and sat on the only bed, my head resting between my hands. I was trying to review the events of the night before. Much as I tried, I couldn't recall a thing. Thinking only increased the pain in my head, so I gave it up and studied my immediate surroundings. There was nothing to study. The room was bare, except for two benches and the bed I was sitting on.

Suddenly I jerked upright as I thought of my reformatory wages. Hastily I ran through my pockets and uncovered four shillings. I went through them more carefully, emptying everything on the bed. Everything meant prison tobacco, matches, pieces of brown paper that I used for rolling the tobacco and finally, my prison discharge papers. I looked at the brown pieces of paper, half willing them to turn into pounds, then the room turned dark. I looked up, and there was the large figure of Nine blocking the door.

He was grinning from ear to ear. Hell's chief stoker. Whatever decided me to try and fight that brute I'll never know. I had as much chance of winning as David would have had if he had fought Goliath fair.

"How you feel?"

"Never mind my feelings, where's my money?"

"You dranked it, Little Brother."

"All?"

"You told the shebeen queen to decorate the table and count the empties."

"Then what happened?"

"Drinks make you brave, Little Brother. When you were drunk you took a swing at me. I caught your fist over my shoulder and hanged your body there instead, then I carried you home."

"Just like that, heh?"

"Just like that." He grinned.

I groaned and fell across the bed. When I again looked up, Nine was busy cooking thick porridge on the pressure-stove. When the porridge was cooked, he produced a thick slice of beef steak. The steak was still dripping blood when it joined the porridge. I thought that surely somewhere the cow was still alive.

After feeding he said, "How much money you got?"

Instead of telling him to go and shovel the bones in hell, I heard myself saying, "Four shillings."

"Gimme," he said, just as rudely.

"On the bed," I said listlessly. He took the money and left.

I lay back and stretched myself. I was unused to strong liquor, it was playing hell with my nerves. As for my four shillings, I didn't give a damn what was going to happen to them. I had just made the painful discovery that I was incompetent to look after myself. I was here to serve humanity. My gutter father. Then the circus population. Then the Coon Carnival guitarist. Then the reformatory authorities. Now Number Nine.

The worst feeling was inside me. A depressed feeling of human oppression that caused my insides to shake like raw eggs, leaving me mentally, physically and spiritually in a funk. A frightening feeling of self-pity, the foundation of disaster.

I must have slept, because when I came back to the world without pity, the sun was just going down in the west.

I got up and lit the piece of candle that was perched on

the bottom of an empty jam tin. Its feeble light revealed bloody stripes of long-dead bed bugs on all four walls. I closed my eyes again.

"Wake up, Little Brother," came the hateful voice. "It's Christmas for you and me. Your four shillings got me eight pounds—three for you, and five for me."

He threw the money on the bed and grinned. I wished that he wouldn't grin so much. Somehow, that grin made me feel lost, like I was intruding in a man's world. It made the reformatory look like a much safer place.

"Put on your jacket, Little Brother, we're going out tonight. First, we're going to Sisinyana's shebeen where we'll drink a few mugs of skokiaan until the clock strikes twelve. That's when our lives will begin, Little Brother, at midnight."

As we crossed the deserted main road of Sophiatown, I saw someone lying in the middle of it. I told Nine. I wish I hadn't.

"Let's go and see, Little Brother. This is going to be a lucky night." I followed reluctantly. Nine turned the still form over. The man was covered with blood. You couldn't even see the face.

"Dead?" I asked.

"Yes, Little Brother, hit and run."

There was a smell of skokiaan oozing from the dead man. I felt like becoming sick.

"Let's go, before they blame this on us," I urged.

"Not before you search him, Little Brother."

"No! No!" I protested. "It's bad luck. Besides, I'll only get my hands full of blood. It's bad luck to steal from the dead. I've never done it before."

"You're not stealing, you're taking, Little Brother." Everytime he referred to me as "Little Brother", I got the impression that he was mocking me.

"Look," I argued, "this dead man might be our blood brother, for all we know. Why molest him?"

"Money, Little Brother, is never enough. And if the dead man is our blood brother, remember, blood is only thicker than water when it runs in our veins. Once it spills, no brother wants it. So make use of the dead while you're alive. The dead die so that we may live. They have no need for money where they are going."

Nine's philosophy. I suppose he had a point. If you read the Bible right, you'll find that Cain only started living after he had spilled Abel's blood. The only thing he hated about Abel after killing him was his blood.

"To hell with you, you heartless bastard," I said, as I went on all fours. I searched and vomited at the same time. Then I dragged the body to the gutter, so that cars could pass.

When I stood up from my revolting task, I was shivering. There was a tobacco bag dangling from my fingers. As usual, Nine was right about it being our lucky night. The tobacco bag contained seven single pound notes and some loose change.

When we came to our room at Bertha Street, Nine counted the money on the bed. Then he went on all fours and dragged a plank suitcase from under the bed. From it he took a black money-box. The insides of the box were empty except for a tiny nickel-plated revolver.

My eyes must have bugged because he smiled crookedly.

"Like it?" he asked. I picked up the fire-arm, handling it like you would a poisonous snake.

As I examined it, Nine said, "I prefer a knife to that. I once shot a man in the head with it at Prospect Township, and he ran all the way down the street shouting my name at the top of his voice before he dropped dead. Lucky for me nobody heard him." He said this and dismissed it as if he'd just told me that the skokiaan we had drunk last night was too weak.

FOUR

Sisinyana, biggest, and most respected shebeen queen of the early twenties, catered for all the subversive elements of Sophiatown. At her headquarters you found all forms of gambling from dice to the Chinese numbers game known as Fafi.

The first time that Nine took me to her place and she peeped around the door, I could only stare and stare. Man, she was beautiful! She laughed at the way I gaped. When she laughed her whole face brightened up, including the gold filling that sparkled between two sets of pearly-white teeth. What laughed most was her eyes; they were baby-blue and they twinkled with all kinds of pleasant suggestions. The very sound she emitted had the tinkle of music. One look at that breathtaking face made you swear never to patronise another shebeen house.

She then opened the door wider and walked in. I very nearly screamed foul! The Maker had played a dirty trick on that woman. A deliberate blunder—a kitten with the body of a rhinoceros. I once saw her embracing and kissing a man who weighed well over a hundred and fifty till he went insane with desire, then calmly she picked him up and threw him bodily through a closed door. "That's for taking advantage of the weaker sex," she called after him.

Her shebeen house was about one brick cottage and two zinc shacks from where me and Nine lived. We were practically neighbours. I went there with Nine or to look for Nine. It was the only place where he hung out.

One Friday I went alone. Three quaver knocks on Sisinyana's door, and I heard a rustling sound coming from within. The door opened partly, and I saw a hole-digger concealed behind it. I pushed it open and it revealed an ill-lit passage.

I waited for the hole-digger to close the door, then followed after him down the dimly-lit passage. The passage was long and narrow. Both walls had long stripes of black soot caused by the strategically placed candles. A globeless electric cord dangled from a narrow black ceiling. In gone days, it must have been a pretty house.

On both sides of the passage, facing one another, were door frames without doors. They led to what were known as Skokiaan Drinking Rooms. These rooms were bare of furniture except for four long benches placed four-square around the room.

Whenever the police made a raid on the premises, Sisinyana would deny all ownership of them. Besides being used as skokiaan bars for skokiaan drinkers, they were also used as sleeping quarters for the cleaners, hole-diggers or barmen.

In the midst of all this squalor there was one room that was furnished like the inside of a palace, and that was Sisinyana's own room. She called it the Holy Spot because of the numerous religious pictures that were hanging from its walls. When we came to the door that led to the Holy Spot, the grave-digger, I mean hole-digger, knocked.

A voice not without melody bade us enter. As the hole-digger turned the knob, his behaviour reminded me of someone who was about to enter a sacred place. I didn't blame him, because I felt the same.

"Ah! Little Brother!" she exclaimed with genuine joy. Since my friendship with Nine, I was respected throughout Sophiatown.

"Tell me," she said, "is Little Brother your real name? Nine is always calling you that."

"My name is Duggie," I stammered. I was forever uneasy in the presence of this woman.

"Duggie?" she repeated. She rolled the name over her tongue as if fearing it would drop out of her mouth. Dreamily she said: "Mmmmmmm Duggie, that's a nice name."

I didn't tell her that I got the name through the circus

elephant that I once looked after. The elephant's name was Duggie. Everytime the circus population called that name, me and the elephant would turn our heads in unison. That's how the name got stuck on me. My second name, which I'm using as a surname, was supplied by the Tokai reformatory authorities. They called me Kaffir Boetie. In the Afrikaans language it means "little kaffir brother". That's the name I must have given Nine the night I wanted to beat him half to death and became drunk instead.

"You know, Duggie," said Sisinyana, "I'm feeling low. A customer just died owing me skokiaan money. Still," she shrugged her shoulders helplessly, "it can't be helped, if the man had to die, he had to die. All I know is that when I die, I'll collect a fortune in hell and pay my way to heaven with it. I talk too much, I nearly forgot to give you your message from Nine. He wants you to meet him at the Johannesburg goods shed first thing in the morning, come rain or snow."

"Isn't he here?"

She shook her lovely head. "No! He said his loins were bothering him and the only person who can relieve him is his girl in Moroka." After a slight pause, she said, "I pity the girl. Let me get you a drink."

Moroka! Nine once took me there, and I hated the place. A city of mud and sack. It made Sophiatown look like a dream place; a difficult township to describe, or understand. A flat heap with countless alleys. Smoke from thousands of fire-galleys. The reddish-brown mud buildings looked like anything but houses. It was as if the builders had had to finish before the sun went down.

The latrines were built at a distance from the dwelling-places. As a result, when you were at a skokiaan party, and you felt the urge to relieve nature, it was best never to leave your hat behind but take it with you. The precaution was very necessary. Not because your hat was in danger of being pinched or something like that; the danger lay in the fact that you might never be able to find your way back to the same house from the latrine.

I wasn't surprised when Nine once told me that his

girlfriend's neighbour used to experience considerable difficulty in finding his own house whenever he came from work. Until Nine sold him an idea. The man took a long pole and tied an old cap on the one point of the pole, then he planted the pole in front of his house. Every time he came back from work, all he did was look for the pole with the cap on.

I wasn't surprised that Nine left without me. He knew how I felt about the place.

Sisinyana, appearing with my six-inch mug of skokiaan, caught me studying a picture that was hanging over the fireplace. It was the picture of Jesus Christ on the crucifix. I thought this picture was as out of place here as it would be if it was hanging in the heart of Prince Lucifer's domain.

She looked at the picture then said: "Oh, Him. He's Jesus Christ our Saviour, the only man I pay protection money to."

"What kind of protection?" I asked.

Lifting her lovely eyebrows she said: "Does it matter what kind of protection as long as I'm protected?

"You know, Duggie, I once paid protection to a white policeman and the bastard kept bleeding me even when it wasn't necessary. So I fixed him by framing him. Now he's no more bother. In fact all the police of Newlands Police Station are giving my place a wide berth."

She frowned. "Ever framed a policeman, Duggie?" When she saw me looking stupid, she said, "Sergeant van der Merwe was the worsest among all the police of Newlands. I say was, because he's been transferred.

"One morning I was short of money to buy my stock when the bastard came in and demanded his usual cut. I tried explaining but he just wouldn't listen. Instead of understanding and coming back on Monday—because this happened on a Saturday morning—he decided to search my place. Under the mattress of my bed, he found four bottles of brandy. He wanted to take me to the charge office, but I begged off. I told him that I was still waiting for my weekly customers to come and square the books. I promised to join him later on at the charge office. He agreed because he knew I was a woman of my word. That was one time I didn't keep it. I never followed him.

"Monday morning when the court-room opened, I was there. I went in and made myself comfortable among the spectators. When the clerk of the court called my name, I stood up. The magistrate read the charge. He didn't even look up. On the desk in front of the prosecutor stood the four bottles of brandy. I hadn't even had time to doctor them. My heart went out to them. Next to them stood the cheerful van der Merwe.

" 'Sisinyana,' the magistrate said, 'you are charged with being in possession of four bottles of brandy. How do you plead, guilty or not guilty?" He waited for the interpreter to put it across to me. Meanwhile I had heard and understood every word.

" 'Four?' I said.

" 'Yes, four,' he said, looking directly at me. I shook my head slowly, then frowned like someone who doesn't comprehend.

" 'Four,' he repeated as he pointed at the four bottles of brandy on the desk. There followed a 'Well?' He waited for me to say they were two or even less.

" 'Your Honour,' I said, 'the bottles were not four, they were a dozen.'

" 'A what?'

"The interpreter was forgotten. It was man to man. 'A dozen, Your Honour.'

" 'Then what the he ... I mean, what happened to the other bottles?'

" 'I don't know, Your Honour, better ask the policeman who raided my place.'

"He turned to van der Merwe and asked: 'Is it true what the accused claims, Sergeant—that there were twelve bottles and not four?'

" 'No, Your Honour, there were only four bottles of brandy under the mattress.'

"I shook my head, 'Your Honour, would I want to pay for twelve bottles when I can hardly afford to pay for four? I had to search the bottom of the barrel besides running to friends and relatives for the money I have here. Money for twelve bottles.'

" 'How much money have you there?'

" 'Knowing, Your Honour, that the fine for one bottle of brandy is fifteen pounds—and I'm going to stop selling it as I'd rather stick to skokiaan because the fine is only five pounds per four gallons—I brought along with me, Your Honour, a hundred and eighty pounds for the dozen bottles.'

"The magistrate said to the prosecutor: 'Count the accused's money.' The prosecutor counted.

" 'A hundred and eighty pounds, Your Honour.'

"The magistrate then turned to Sergeant van der Merwe. 'Where are the other eight bottles, Sergeant?'

" 'I told Your Honour that there were only four bottles!'

" 'Come now, Sergeant, are you seriously trying to tell me that this woman, or anyone for that matter, would prefer paying a fine of a hundred and eighty pounds to that of sixty? Let's not waste the court's time, where are the other eight bottles?'

" 'I swear, Your Honour, there were only four bottles.'

" 'When you found those bottles, assuming there were four under the mattress, what did you do with them?'

" 'I took them to the charge office, Your Honour.'

" 'Where was the accused?'

" 'She was left behind, Your Honour.'

" 'Is that general procedure?'

" 'Well, no, Your Honour, but seeing that there were only four bottles, and the accused looked to be a woman of her wor . . .'

" 'Yes, yes, go on, Sergeant, you were saying?'

" 'Well, Your Honour,' stammered the sergeant, 'she looked to be a woman of her word . . . I mean . . .'

"The magistrate just ignored him. 'Sisinyana,' he said, 'I find you guilty of being in possession of four bottles of brandy. Your fine will be sixty pounds. You, Sergeant Johannes Andries van der Merwe, I find you guilty of failing to produce the other eight bottles of brandy. Corruption in the police force will never be tolerated. You will be dealt with accordingly. Next case!'

"So you see, Duggie, the only person I pay protection to is the man you see hanging there. I offer him my prayers every night before going to bed."

I nodded, then took a deep drink from the mug of skokiaan. I gagged because of the merciless beating that my empty stomach was taking from the strong brew.

Sisinyana said: "Easy, Duggie, don't go head-on into that stuff, try sneaking up on it." I blinked the tears back and nodded dumbly. An old man once told me that he had once been so drunk from Sisinyana's skokiaan that he fell into a bath of cold water. The next day when he woke up, the water was lukewarm. Take it or leave it.

I fell asleep, not in a bath full of cold water, but right where I was sitting. When I woke up the following morning, it was to discover that someone had taken the trouble to cover me with a blanket. I got up, and went to the back yard in search of a water tap. I badly wanted to gargle, to stop my throat from behaving like a sewer pipe.

It was Saturday morning. The sun was shining. The air smelt clean, even in this back yard. The only sign of last night's storm lay on the ground in the form of mud, dangerous, slippery mud. Otherwise, it was a beautiful Saturday.

As I said, me and Nine were as thick as thieves, and I mean just that. When you saw Nine, you saw me. Our living came from goods trains that were parked on lonely sidings during weekdays. On Saturdays, we stripped the goods shed. The shed was big and well-provided.

Weekdays, we went to lonely sidings after dark, then I checked on the cards that were stuck on the coaches. The kind of goods that are to be found inside the coaches are tagged on the cards. The railways can be very obliging.

Mostly we found cartons of assorted cigarettes, cases containing whisky and brandy, or bales of all kinds of material. All I did was to read what was written on the cards because Nine couldn't read without glasses. Not that he ever had any.

After deciding on the required goods, Nine would swing

his fifty-pound hammer, handling it as if it was a shaving machine. All he'd say to me was, "Guard my back, Little Brother." Then he would carry the goods to our waiting car. We hired the car from a well-known racketeer on the understanding that if we were not back by eight in the morning, he would report it stolen at the Newlands police station so that the law wouldn't confiscate the car if it was found with stolen goods. This manoeuvre wasn't bad; it saved us the trouble of really having to steal a car. The one snag about it was that if we got caught we would stand trial for two charges: theft and car theft.

We were so damned expert in this, that at times we would take orders from our Chinese customers before invading the sidings.

I made the goods shed in good time. Then I parked myself at the usual place. After waiting for a quarter of an hour, I decided to go in and see if Nine was not roaming inside. At the entrance I stopped. Something unusual was going on in the yard.

Police of both races stood in a circle excitedly discussing something that their bodies hid.

An unwanted feeling started nagging me. It touched at all my nerve centres, like the feelers of an octopus. Feelers that were getting ready for what? All I could say was that this feeling wasn't doing my kidneys any good. It kept saying, *Nine is in trouble, Nine is in trouble*.

Then I saw a lone African policeman standing at the extreme end of the yard guarding the small gate. Brushing off my troublesome feeling, I strolled up to him. As I neared him, I made as if to pass, then suddenly I pulled up short, making as if I'd just remembered something. At the same time I noticed the round corks that were hanging from both his ears. They told me the policeman belonged to the proud Zulu race.

I greeted him in the best Zulu traditional way. According to the Zulu custom, when you want something from them, never rush them, be extremely patient and annoyingly polite.

He responded. Then I asked after his health, as if it mattered. After that, there was a long pause. I waited patiently for what seemed an age. Then the bastard took out a snuff box, tapped it three times with his middle finger and said, "To whose house do you belong?"

"I belong to Butelezi's house, Father."

"Where?"

"At Dundee Natal, Father. We get our drinking water from the Blood River."

"Mmmmmmm, I see, Butelezi. I'm glad to know you. I am from the house of Kuzwayo, at Eshowe Zululand. We drink from the Umvolozi River."

"I'm happy to know you, Father." I was lucky that he didn't give me a synopsis of the house of the Kuzwayos beginning with his great-grandfather and ending up with himself.

At last he said: "What can I do for you, boy?" Christ! What a price to pay for a little information.

I said: "I was just wondering at seeing so many policemen at the goods yard, Father. I'm working on the other side of the street and it's the first time for me to see so many police. Could something be wrong?"

"Yes, my son, something is very wrong here. They have at last caught the mouse that has caused the railways so much headaches. He sits in yonder circle waiting for the police van. It's a pity, my son, for the man is a warrior, a real warrior. If the two labourers and the one policeman were here, they would have agreed with me, but an ambulance carried them away. It took all those men you see standing there in a circle to subdue him, and they don't dare move away. All they did to him was daze him." Taking a pinch of snuff, the policeman said, as if talking to himself; "Yes, the man is a warrior."

If the policeman had not pushed me aside, the police van would have backed into me. The van backed up until the open back door covered the little entrance neatly. They aren't taking any chances with the prisoner, I thought. I still didn't want to believe that it was Nine.

The human circle opened and a blood-covered figure was roughly pushed forward. There was no doubt about it. Blood-covered or not blood-covered, it was my Nine. The famous grin was replaced by flaring nostrils and a heaving chest. His shackled figure was being roughly pushed from behind. When he saw me, he stopped dead. The whole dozen couldn't seem to move him. Like magic the grin came back. He lifted his manacled wrists in a farewell gesture and said: "Look after our room, Little Brother." With that he stepped into the van. I walked away feeling sick.

No need to tell you how I felt after the arrest of Nine. The world suddenly became a place without walls to lean on to. Like wobbling in trousers ten times too big. I had depended too much on him, now I was on my own.

FIVE

There was a certain gang that patronized Sisinyana's shebeen. This gang always seemed to be loaded with money. They were always well-dressed and neat. Heads were shaved prison-fashion. Clean.

What I didn't like about them was that they seemed to regard going to prison as part of daily experience. A life of one year in, and the next out. They had no special speciality. They took anything that came. When they went into town, like they did every morning, they went there to take whatever the town had to offer. Handbag-snatching and pick-pocketing were their by-the-ways. Their tactics were often daring if not ruthless. One thing about them was their total indifference to consequences. Their conversation was always about their daily escapades in and around town. The first day I drank with them, I found myself listening and watching them like a dog fascinated by the activities of a bunch of snakes in a hole.

In Sophiatown we had many short cuts that could lead you from one street to the other without you having to look for a crossroad. That is, if you knew where to look for them. These short cuts were more like jigsaw puzzles because you had to go through one yard and out the other, jump a fence here and there, mind a disused skokiaan hole, and, more important, look out for human waste lest you tramp on it.

My new friends and me were using one of the short cuts. We numbered eight in all. Among the eight, I was the only one with hair on my head. The heads of the others were all clean-shaven.

As we emerged into Gerty Street from Bertha Street, a number of African women were chatting noisily. If only one would stop and listen to what the other was saying the noise would have been much less. But they would have none of that. If one spoke the other answered or put in her own words before the other could finish. Like assorted birds in a cage. These women were runners, or agents in the Chinese game of Fafi.

They were all waiting for the Chinaman to pull the day's winning number out of his hat, then they would disperse and go and pay out or report the winning number to their clients.

This gamble has thirty-six numbers. What you have to do is guess the right number. Each number has a name. Number six, for instance, means "Cow". Seventeen will get you "Diamond Lady", twenty-four, "Big Mouth", and so on. A tickey got you six shillings, a sixpence twelve.

This is a dream game. People's dreams are responsible for the Chinaman's riches. If someone dreams he's drowning, the first thing he does in the morning is look for a Fafi agent, then place a bet on number thirteen which is "Big Fish", he'll cover it with number three which is "Sea Water", just in case the Chinaman draws the water instead of the fish. If you dream of silver, play "Small Change"; a funeral means "Dead Man". It's a hell of a racket. All the Chinaman hopes for is that we go on having sweet dreams.

How's this for a story that went around the townships? A woman once dreamed a strange dream. The day following, she scraped every penny in the house to play a certainty. The money amounted to ten pounds, rent money and all. This she took and placed on one number.

When her husband came home from work, she told him about her strange dream and what she had done with the money. The man was dog-tired from work, but he felt he wasn't too tired to strangle her. He did. He killed her. The irony of the thing is, as her breath left her body, a car door banged outside and a voice came through the open window from the street saying: "Hey, Bengu! Your wife broke my bank—she won!"

Anyway, we ducked into the next yard, nearly upsetting a fire-galley. Through an open window came the strains of blues music played on a gramophone, while behind a tall zinc fence someone was banging and yelling for another shilling's worth of skokiaan.

One by one we squeezed ourselves between the walls of two houses. We had to move sideways. As I brushed the dust from my front and back, dust caused by the tight squeeze of two walls, the din around me told me that we were in Good Street.

It was as busy as ever. Buses were lined from one corner of the street to the other. They came in different shades; red, green and blue. These buses belong to different companies. As a result, loading competition was fierce. A conductor would try to force a passenger into his bus, while the other conductor would work just as hard at dragging the individual into *his* bus. A voice would shout above the other, "Don't go into that bus, can't you see it'll never reach town?" The other would come back with: "Your mother will never reach town, you get in here!"

Then the hair-raising journey to town would follow, one bus trying to get there first, so as to be first to load again.

We entered a Syrian café. I was surprised to see Jeegar, the undisputed leader of our gang, cutting right through the shop and going through a back door as if he owned the place. We followed him through. I found myself in a room with a long table and two benches.

Jeegar ordered breakfast. Fried steak and eggs. Not knowing how to handle a fork and a knife, I asked for a spoon. I don't remember ever having had such tasty food in my life. I made a mental note to frequent this place whenever I found myself in the money. This was no thick-porridge-and-meat café, this was a place for the real upper class.

After breakfast, we crossed the street and caught the first bus into town.

In town, we got off at the Diagonal Street bus terminal. On that same side of the bus terminal were rows of shops, mostly barber shops. We entered one of them. It was owned by a Rhodesian who went under the name of Black Mischark because of his blue-black complexion.

Before having my head shaved so as to be in uniform with the rest of the gang, I was introduced to Black Mischark. He didn't wear a shirt. His protruding stomach was covered by a soiled undershirt. Mischark, I was told, harboured whatever goods we brought in from town.

While Mischark was shaving my head, the boys entered some cubicles that stood like telephone booths in the shop. When they emerged, they were dressed in khaki dustcoats. The dustcoats had red letters printed on the shoulder blades such as K & B, S & C, and so on. By all appearances they looked like city workers. My admiration for them increased.

Jeegar and Madaku were going to take the top part of town. Twala and Mabongo would concentrate on the centre, while me and Tiny looked after the bottom half, near the post office and also part of Johannesburg Station. T-Boy and Thabo had the Indian market. A dangerous place because it's always crowded. Only the night before I heard Jeegar say, "When you are being chased at the Indian market, never forget to run with your knife open."

Me and Tiny crossed Frazer Street, heading towards the other side of town. We were going to start at the top, then work our way back towards the bus-rank. At the corner of Bree and Loveday Streets, I saw a group of people, white and black, standing in a semicircle looking at one black man who sat with his back against the wall. Closer inspection showed the man sitting on his haunches fanning three playing-cards at his audience, daring them to find the red card amongst the two blacks.

This form of gambling is known as the Red Find. The gambler throws three cards face-down on the ground; all you have to do is place a pound note, or even less, on the card you think is red. If it is, you win an extra pound.

"Duggie, watch." It was Tiny. He elbowed his way to the front. I followed. From his pocket he extracted a tiny roll of pounds. Publicly he selected one, making sure that the gambler saw the roll.

The man picked up the cards. With one twist of the wrist the cards lay face down. I noted the red card, so did Tiny. In fact, so did most of the crowd, because they all pointed excitedly. Tiny was about to place his bet when a man standing next to him blocked him with his foot at the same time saying: "I saw it first." He placed three pounds on the card. The gambler opened the card; it was red. The crowd applauded. The lucky man won three pounds. I think I saw Tiny grin, but I'm not sure.

Down came the cards again, I thought the man next to Tiny was going to block him again, but he didn't. Nor did Tiny place a bet. A black, fat, grinning woman came forward and placed a pound on a card. When the gambler turned it up, the card was black. There were cries of "Shame" from the crowd.

Down went the cards again. I noticed Tiny watching the foot of the man more than he did the cards. As soon as the cards were settled face-down, the man tried lifting his foot, but Tiny's right foot was resting firmly on it.

Tiny placed five dirty-looking single pound notes on a card. The gambler swallowed hard as he looked up. He was sweating. I could see the white behind his eyeballs.

"Open up!" shouted the crowd gleefully. "Open up!" He did. The card was red.

Tiny lifted his foot. I saw the gambler looking daggers at the man next to Tiny.

After counting and pocketing the winnings, Tiny said, "The bloody Shangaan bastard—he only came to Joburg yesterday and he thinks he can con me!"

"Why didn't you stay to press your luck, Tiny?"

"Luck?" scoffed Tiny. "That would have been inviting trouble. There's no such thing as luck in that game, Duggie. You get back there you'll see so many black cards that you'll really see red—and I don't mean the red card,

I mean the man's blood. Putting your money on the red card is like supporting a child that's not your own.

"You saw the man that was standing next to me?" When I nodded, Tiny went on: "That man is a decoy. There are two others and a girl. If you spot the right card, either the girl or that man will block you. Place your bet on the wrong card, and they won't interfere with you. That's a no chance game, Duggie, that's a sure game. Because the right card is like looking for a needle in the wrong haystack."

Tiny changed the subject by saying, "Duggie, have you ever picked pockets before?"

"I've tried my hand." I shuddered, remembering Honest Charley's meat cleaver.

"O.K., let me tell how we go about it. The trouble is, we are only two instead of three. It's all right if we are going to do ordinary pickpocketing, but when we go 'square' hunting, we need three. The square is the small purse inside the big one. When we are three it's one of the easiest things to take. Even if the bag is clipped. But when we are only two it's a bit risky.

"First, never try lifting a square on the pavement. Always check on the robots before you make your move. If the robot shows red, we close in on the woman. One of us will be on each side of her on the kerb. The 'square' man will be slightly behind her. The 'jolter'—I mean the man who distracts her attention by elbowing her in the ribs—will be on her left side. The 'pincer'—he's the one who opens the bag—will be on her right. Coming from the opposite direction towards us will be the 'square-puller'. When the light shows green we move. Never take the victim until you are in the middle of the street. You see, her nervousness about motor cars helps.

"The jolter will jolt, she'll look up only to be met by a 'Sorry, madam'. This gives the 'can-opener' a chance to unbuckle the bag. At the same time the square-puller will come in between them and lift the square. We never miss, because there's no stopping, no hesitating, no pausing, it's just one smooth movement. Clear, straight and neat."

I was still mulling over what Tiny had told me when we

arrived at Von Brandis Street on the side of the General Post Office.

Suddenly Tiny stopped dead. I followed his gaze and was in time to see a white man emerging from the post office entrance. The man was busy stuffing a fat-looking wallet into his jacket inside pocket. Tiny looked around wildly, then said as he dashed into the post office yard, "Don't let him out of your sight!"

When Tiny came back, he was breathless. In his hands he held a cardboard box. This he trampled flat by stamping on it with both feet. He gave me the feeling that he was losing his reason, but it couldn't be, because he had been talking sense only a few minutes before.

"Here," he said, shoving the now flat board towards me. "Take this and hit me on the head with it. Hit hard, don't be afraid that it'll hurt—it won't. It's only cardboard. Now go on and hit me." I hesitated. It's hard to play at being mad when you know damn well that you're sane.

"Go on, damn you, you're wasting time!" he shouted. Half-heartedly I lifted the cardboard.

Wham! The blow was clumsy. Tiny ran. Wham! Wham! He screamed. Not knowing why, I started beating him earnestly. He zig-zagged towards the white man who had emerged from the post office and was now walking towards Small Street. Tiny was drawing a lot of attention to himself by screaming "Hey! Heh!" at the top of his voice. Wham! Wham! Everybody turned and looked as I rained murderous blows on Tiny's clean-shaven head. I managed to get in two more blows just as Tiny reached the white man.

I was beginning to enjoy myself, even though I didn't know where all this was leading to. Wham! went the cardboard. Wham! Wham! Wham! almost with rhythmical precision.

"Please help me, my baas," sobbed Tiny. "He's hurting me!" Wham! There was real fear in Tiny's eyes as I continued my assault.

The khaki dustcoat, with the letters S & H printed on the shoulder blades and the red dust rag sticking out of one of his pockets, gave Tiny the appearance of a hard-working African, while I had the look of a loafer. There was also the determined look in my eyes, as I hailed blow after blow on Tiny's unprotected head.

Tiny held the strange white man from behind. He was vainly trying to use him as a shield. He was handling the man just as you would handle the steering wheel of a get-away car in heavy traffic.

Wham! went the cardboard as it glanced off the shoulder of the bewildered white man. Face reddening with embarrassment, the white man said, "Hey! Boy! Leave this boy alone!" He was helplessly trying to look at Tiny over his shoulders. He said to Tiny, "You, too, leave me alone!"

Wham! Another bull's-eye. It landed squarely on Tiny's head. Wham! Wham! Wham! Tiny couldn't take any more. "Yooooh!" he screamed as he let go of his only protection and ran down Jeppe Street. Behind, the white man sighed with relief as he straightened out his jacket lapels. Then slowly his mouth opened as if his lips were gummed together.

"My wallet! My wallet!" he screamed. Wham! Wham! echoed the cardboard box as we raced across Von Brandis Street, completely disregarding the red light, in the direction of the Indian market and the Sophiatown bus-rank.

This market is one place where I like to be. I could wander about it the whole day and never get tired or bored with it. Here there's never a dull moment. The fruit stalls with their crafty-looking owners, their high-pitched voices forever urging passersby to examine and buy their fruit. This place is a symbol of life, guile and greed.

Later, as we walked along Diagonal Street looking for something to eat, Tiny nudged me. He pointed to a small car that was parked next to the pavement.

A European woman was sitting in the driver's seat behind the steering-wheel. Lying negligently next to her was her handbag. That was not the real attraction, the real attraction was the window beside the bag. It was open.

Sitting in the back seat and looking lost, was her African servant. I made a bee-line for the opened window, while Tiny walked directly towards the woman. "Lies, lies, that's all you told me! I told you one day we'll meet and I'll mess you up! When you are at the missus' yard you tell a lot of lies. You got a lot to say, all lies! Come out of there!"

"What's the matter? What has he done to you? Leave my boy alone!"

Ignoring her, Tiny continued threatening the boy, who, because of fright, started working his jaws and saying nothing.

"What has he done to you?" asked the madam indignantly.

"I'm not talking to you, missus."

"But I'm talking to you! What has my boy done to you?"

"I told him one day he'll get hurt." Tiny made as if to open the door.

"You leave my car alone . . ." I lifted the bag.

As we walked back to the bus-rank my hunger was completely forgotten. Tiny said, "Serves her right for not allowing him to sit next to her."

SIX

At Sisinyana's place the skokiaan bubbles were floating pleasantly up and down my stomach. Every time I belched, one would pop, spreading heavenliness throughout my body.

I was in high spirits. The white man's wallet had yielded forty pounds and the woman's bag, twelve.

When Jeegar came in, heavily laden with two suitcases, my happiness knew no bounds. The straps around the cases told me that they belonged to a commercial traveller. Jeegar was followed by Marfaku, who was likewise burdened.

I asked a foolish question, because I was very excited. "What's in there?"

"How the hell should I know?" growled Jeegar, at the same time giving me a dirty look. I didn't care, I was far too happy to feel offended.

I never liked Jeegar. When we first met, it was hate at first sight. He was a brutal bastard. I once saw him stab a girl for spilling some skokiaan on him.

I helped to open the suitcases. Jeegar groaned. First I didn't understand his dismay. The suitcases were full of gent's shoes. All different designs. Then I added my groan to Jeegar's. The shoes all belonged to the same foot, the right. The second suitcase had ladies' one-sided shoes, the suitcases that Marfaku had were crammed with boys' and girls' one-sided shoes. Jeegar cursed. "Bloody samples!" he growled.

From that day onward, I never had a dull moment. Tiny was the perfect partner. We were a faultless team. It was as if I was born for nothing but this kind of work.

We ravaged the town. Our success lay mainly in what the brain doctors call telepathy. We never asked questions or discussed a situation while on the job. One always seemed to know what the other was thinking. Our timing was perfect. We didn't plan in advance. We thought on the spot. The word hesitation was considered a deadly enemy.

Jeegar was a good pickpocket, but Tiny was the best. If Jeegar picked a pocket and the victim found out, he beat hell out of the victim. Not Tiny. Tiny went about it with an elastic sense of humour.

He once pinched a purse and, finding it empty, walked up to the victim and said: "Lady, here's your purse. Next time don't decorate the inside of your bag with an empty purse—keep something in it. Think of all the risks I have to take."

He surprised me once as we were walking down Plein Street. I wasn't even aware that he had made a pinch when he suddenly stopped short like someone who had forgotten or just remembered something.

"Wait!" he said. He ran back in the direction we had come from. After a few minutes he was back.

"What's up?" I asked.

Grinning, he said, "I forgot to close her bag."

Me, I still have to discover my true talent. Because I discovered painfully that picking pockets is not one of them.

This happened at von Weilligh Street. I was about to cross it when I saw an elderly Jewish woman also about to cross. I knew by her hawk-like features that she was Jewish, and where else do you find the biggest egg if not in a hawk's nest?

After nudging Tiny, I went for her. I was going to take her in the middle of the street like I was taught. Tiny veered off to the left to divert while I took her.

All went well, but I bungled by being too damn curious. I couldn't control my patience, I wanted to see how much money was in the damn purse. I was itching all over. My breath was hot with excitement. So right there where I took it I stopped and peeped inside while cars hooted. I was pocketing it when I felt a heavy hand gripping my shoulder.

I didn't turn. I just took a quick look at what was pressing so painfully into my collar bone. I saw hairy fingers as big as corn cobs. What was frightening was the colour of the fingers. They were a pinkish white.

My first guess was right. The hand belonged to a white man. I dislike guessing, because I ususally guess right when I'm doing wrong, and wrong when I'm doing right. What caused me to look up behind me for the second time was the silver star I saw on the helmet. It held my gaze more than the hostile blue eyes that were boring into me.

Miserably I guessed again. My second guess was that this was a policeman. Another bull's-eye. If only I could guess like that when I played the Chinese numbers game then there would be no point in me picking pockets.

"Madam!" shouted the policeman after the woman. "Is this your purse?" He lifted my hand still holding the purse high above my head. I felt the tips of my toes helplessly scraping the tarmac. I wondered whether he was more interested in severing my arm from my body, or in giving the purse back to the owner. I concluded he was interested in both.

Much against my will another unpleasant guess escaped. This guess caused me to moan. I guessed that his hand was bigger than a cow's bladder. I was right. Police all over the world are chosen mainly for their size, not for their brains. God doesn't give a man brains as well as size; I have never known Him to be so generous.

"Madam! Your purse!"

I hereby swear to do my duty, to my God, my King and my country, the son of a bitch, I thought.

"Madam, your purse!" I couldn't even struggle in this man's hold.

The woman looked around, then cursed in a strange language. Frantically she started rummaging in her bag, rummaging and talking at the same time. The only sensible word that invaded her strange dialect now and again was the word "Officer".

It's funny, when you're frightened or angry beyond control you learn a lot about your origins. That's how I discovered to what black race I belong; something I never used to take notice of before. When I use strong language, Xhosa comes easier, so maybe originally my ancestors were Xhosas. Not that I care a damn. I remember when I first saw myself in a long mirror at a chemist shop. I was passing and suddenly there I was; ragged and dirty, yet getting a kick at what I saw. In Sophiatown all the boys of my age looked like that. Rags were our uniform. With a smile and giggle I hopped away from the mirror.

Looking up from her fruitless search, the white woman snatched the purse from my grasp then opened it with fingers that shook uncontrollably. All this told me that I had just lost a fortune because of a good Dutch Samaritan bastard.

Looking up from counting the money, she said, "Thank you, Officer; the money, it is all here." Next, she turned and elbowed her way through the curious onlookers.

"Hey! Wait!" yelled the policeman, still holding on to

me. "You've got to come to the Marshall Square police station to lay a formal charge against this kaffir."

"Sorry, Officer," came from the woman. "I'm in a hurry; besides, I'm not missing a penny." With that, she turned and disappeared through the crowd.

The crowd, most of it black, started laughing and jeering at the policeman. I didn't like that, especially when I saw what anger was doing to his complexion; it was beet-red.

Then lightning struck in the form of a fist. It landed on the side of my head. I wanted to drop and cover my face, but couldn't. How could I when I was dangling six inches from the ground, a rag doll in the man's hands? He chopped me on the bridge of the nose with the cutting side of his hand. The stars I saw were unlike the one on his helmet; they were tiny and numerous and they glittered in a sort of liquid transparent blue. What was maddening about them was that they couldn't seem to keep still, when one popped another moved in. Then through a bemused brain I heard a voice say, *"Gee him vir my konstabel—give him to me!"*

A right that must have broken my jaw sent me flying into the hands of another obliging son of a bitch. I was not unconscious. I should have been, but I was not. Because dimly I could hear a crowd of people shouting, "Lock him up! Don't beat him up, lock him up, you bloody cowards!" I didn't agree; being locked up in jail after what I was going through was unfair.

I found myself lying under a car. I must have crawled in there for sanctuary from the cruelty of the world in general. Tiny's voice came faintly to my ears as if from another world.

"Come out, Duggie, they're gone. God knows they're gone! Come out, man!"

"Bugger you, leave me alone!" Opening my mouth nearly caused me to pass out.

"Look, Duggie," he said. "Here's my cross." He had gone down on all fours. Awkwardly he pushed his crossed fingers under the car for me to see.

The sign of the cross to us blacks in South Africa is a

sacred symbol. The dirtiest liar uses crossed fingers to show sincerity by crossing both his first fingers from the thumb. A sign that he means what he says. After moving my jaws sideways twice, I decided to ignore Tiny's crossed fingers and to stay right where I was. A crossed jaw is more painful than crossed fingers. It was only when he said that the owner of the car was coming to move his car that I saw the sense of crawling from my sanctuary.

Instead of leading me home or to the hospital, Tiny led me to a place known as Malay Camp. This area rubbed elbows with Johannesburg City. It was a semi-slum, and metropolitan in a way like Sophiatown. Where Sophiatown had shanties and mud buildings, Malay Camp boasted wooden double-storey buildings. Here you could buy a woman of any colour. It was your money that counted. Take away the tar roads and the electricity and you had one of those American Wild West towns that we see so much of in the bioscope. Only here, wine bottles flew, not bullets.

Tiny insisted that all I needed was a drink. If I could have moved my jaws I would have argued, but you can't argue with a broken jaw. The pain made me walk like a man in a trance. Talking was out of the question, hearing was annoying; feeling only meant additional blinding pain, and thinking was outright misery. Shit, I was sure I was dying.

Before we could reach a shebeen, Tiny became conscious of the seriousness of my condition. If passersby hadn't stopped to stare at me, it's doubtful if he would have done what he did. He hired a taxi, bundled me in and rode with me to the General Hospital. I was fitted with wires around my jaws to keep them in place.

After spending three weeks at home drinking soup through a straw, I went back to the hospital where they removed the wiring.

This part which I am about to relate is the only part in my life which I can't seem to believe myself, because history doesn't repeat itself so soon; at least, not just after three weeks of broken jaws. But if the truth has to come out, then I have no alternative but to set down on paper all the events that took place, even if there might be a ring of fantasy in them.

"How do you like the town, Duggie, after three whole weeks at home?"

"I don't."

It was Tiny talking, we were walking down Bree Street in the direction of Doornfontein. There was a bitter feeling in me. I don't know whether it was caused by failure to prove myself, or just plain fear.

Tiny was penniless. I had a shilling piece somewhere in one of my pockets.

He interrupted my troubled thoughts by saying, "Give me one of your cigarettes, Duggie."

Shaking my head, I said, "I wish I had some, Tiny."

The tips of my fingers went into the top small pocket of my jacket where I kept stubs. They came out empty. I went through all my pockets with the same results. Then my fingers met with the shilling piece.

I looked around and spied a tea room. I went inside.

In the shop, lined next to the counter, stood five Africans, all dressed in blue overalls. In their hands were empty jam tins for tea-buying purposes. Daily customers, I thought. Just behind sat European customers having their lunch.

I took a place next to the first African. I didn't want to waste time. I rapped the shilling piece on the glass counter to draw the owner's attention. If you irritate them that way, they quickly get rid of you by serving you first.

"Packet of ten Lotus, please." He gave me the packet. I handed over the shilling. He was about to give me my four pennies change and there the matter would have ended. But fate took a hand. Just before he gave me my change, he was urgently beckoned by one of his servants. Instead of giving me my change he answered the summons.

Then I saw it. I didn't see it before because his body had been screening it. A roll of pounds as thick as my wrist lay just within arm's reach. It was tied with a rubber band.

I must have been a born thief. A real stranger to hesitation, with impulses that work overtime. Without thinking or looking around, my hand shot out like the tongue of a deadly cobra. At the same time I sensed rather than saw Tiny inspecting the window display just outside the shop entrance.

It was fast. Too damn fast, especially for the naked eye. One minute the roll was in my hand, the next it was sailing through the air towards Tiny, who caught it expertly and without thinking. Then he slowly made his way to the opposite pavement.

I was about to bolt through the door after Tiny, but when I looked at the African next to me, I saw to my amazement that he wasn't a bit concerned with me. Instead, he was grumbling to his fellow worker about the slowness of the Greek. It was unbelievable, yet it happened. NO ONE SAW ME!

I decided to wait for my change.

When the Greek came back, the first thing he noticed was that the money was missing. Next, he looked at me. The look he gave me made me curse myself for still being where I was. What kept me rooted to the spot still disturbs me right up to this day.

Without a word he went around the counter and bolted the door, surprising everyone in the cafe. Then he told the Africans to point out the one who took the money. They all denied having seen the money, let alone having stolen it.

After carefully searching each of them, he told them to go. Then he turned to me. Before touching me he told me to give back the money. I told him I didn't have any money. As always when I'm truthful he just didn't believe me.

"Look," he said as he released a long-held breath. His body bent sideways and he leaned with his elbow on the glass counter. "I know you have the money even if I didn't see you take it. Now let's be sensible; if you give me the money of your own free will, I promise to let you go and there the matter will end. But if I search you and find it on you, I'll make you suffer."

"Go to hell! I haven't got your money, but you got mine, you got my fourpenny change."

"Listen, for the last time, give me the money." I stood my ground.

Then he searched me. He didn't find anything, of course. How could he when the money was on the other side of the street?

"Now give me my change," I said, full of confidence.

"You stay right there," he said.

He was picking on me because those other Africans were his daily customers, also, I was nicely dressed, in a way. My clothes alone made me suspect number one, also the fact that it was my first time in his bloody shop. He was bright, but in a dull way.

Again he searched me. This time he was more careful. When he didn't find anything, he went to the phone and rang for the police. While we waited, he kept on pestering me about his money, promising to let me go if I showed him where it was.

I told him I didn't know anything about any money. That the only money I knew of was my four pennies change. And that still had to come to me.

I was more sure of myself. My only prayer was that they wouldn't send the same policeman who broke my jaw the month before. The Greek could go to hell. He wasn't going to get any money from me even if he borrowed it.

There was a sharp rap on the door and in they came. I mean the police. It wasn't the same one as before. This one was even bigger. With him was another one with a young pink face.

"Where is the kaffir?" he asked. The Greek indicated with his head towards where I stood.

He turned to me and bellowed, "Where is the money, kaffir?" I told him too that I didn't know anything about any money except for four pennies change. The child policeman came nearer me and started jabbing me in the ribs with his baton. I kept facing the burly one who kept repeating the question. I was about to repeat that I didn't know anything about any money when they started working on me.

Suddenly, I heard a female voice scream, "Stop! Stop! Can't you see you're killing him?"

The burly policeman said, "Keep out of this, lady, it's none of your business."

"Where's the money, kaffir?"

"No money, baas, only my change."

"You'll talk, you black bastard."

My face was so numb, it didn't seem to hurt anymore. It lost all sense of feeling.

He was throttling me with the front of my shirt by screwing it into my Adam's apple.

I heard the lovely voice again, now more furious, "Of course it's my business. I was sitting right here when this whole filthy business started!"

"Lady, for God's sake," said the policeman impatiently. "Will you for God's sake keep out of this?"

Squinting, I saw a white woman glaring at my tormentors with bared teeth, hair drooping over eyelids and arms resting palm-down on the table. She was spitting out words faster than a green snake could spit poison. And the words were just as venomous. The way she went on, it was as if she was suffering more than I was. A lovely bundle of fury.

"The fact that I was sitting right here when this whole thing started makes it my business."

"Lady, for the last time, mind your own business." I began to wonder if those were the only words he knew.

"To begin with, that boy didn't take the blasted money."

"How do you know?" scowled the policeman.

"Because it's a logical if not a physical impossibility for him to have taken the money."

"Lady, you're not telling me anything."

"If," continued my guardian angel, "God did not use some of your brains to give you a bigger backside, you would have arrived at the same conclusion. Stop behaving like a third-rate bully and start using your head!"

"Madam, one more word out of you and I'll run you in for obstructing the police in the course of their duty."

"Since when does duty mean beating up a man who

hasn't been formally charged, and on private premises for that matter? In fact you are so brainless that I believe you would make a fool of yourself in front of your superiors by locking me up for trying to help you!"

As the man straightened up, I saw that his trouser at the knee was wet with my blood.

"All right, lady," he said harshly. "You tell us what happened to the money."

"I can give you a hundred reasons why it is absurd to think that this poor boy could have taken the money. But three should be enough for a brain like yours!"

Then she went into detail. It was like a school teacher explaining a simple subject to a sixteen-year-old pupil who had no business in the third grade.

"That boy was searched twice yet the money was not found. If, as you say, he took the money, then where in heaven's name could he have hidden it? Because," said my lady with great emphasis and spacing every word, "he never once left the shop, nor did he move from where you found him! Tell me, now," she was almost begging, "do you for one minute think that if anyone could steal a roll of pounds he'd be so stupid as to stand and wait for a measly fourpence change when the door was wide open and he had every chance of running away? I," she spat, "would give everything I possess—and I can assure you it's considerable—" (Chancer, I thought) "if that boy is guilty of theft." I stole a glance at the other customers and saw most of them nodding their heads in agreement.

The burly policeman said, "Then who the hell has stolen the money?"

"That's the first sensible question you've asked since coming through that door! Now kindly direct that same question to the man who phoned for you. For all we know, he might not have lost a penny, it's just his word against this poor boy's."

The law turned his eyes from the lady to the Greek and there was fury in them.

The shopkeeper said to the lady, "Do you think I would have gone to all the trouble of searching the natives and calling the police all for nothing?"

"There! You have done it!" said my lady triumphantly.

"Did you really lose money?" asked the policeman facing the shopkeeper.

"Of course!" spluttered the man indignantly.

"Show me the spot where the money was." The man pointed at the spot behind the counter. The policeman released his hold on me for the first time, leaving me to sway with the tide. Examining the spot, the policeman asked, "Was he the only kaffir that was standing next to the counter at the time?" Worriedly the shopkeeper shook his head.

"There were four or five others," he added hastily, "but those were my daily customers. They would not steal from me."

"What!" barked the policeman, throwing his hands in the air in a hopeless show of disgust. "Are you standing there telling me that kaffirs don't steal when they were born for nothing else? Why did you let the rest of them go?"

There was a note of anger in the shopkeeper's voice as he said, "I tell you those other natives are my daily customers, and this boy, well, you can see for yourself how he's dressed, he's a skellum."

"Now you're judging the man by his clothes!" came the voice of my guardian angel.

"If I remember right, those boys that were here were in a much better position to have made off with the money! They were all dressed in overalls—right! And in their hands they carried jam tins—right! Jam tins full of tea bought from this shop! It's my guess that the roll of pounds—if he did lose a roll of pounds—is safely reposing at the bottom of a jam tin of tea!"

The big policeman started to say something, when an eager voice from the cradle said, "Should I lock up this kaffir?"

"No, better let him go. What will we charge him with? We've already messed up his face."

Turning to me, the policeman said, "Scoot, kaffir." I slowly shook my head and stood my ground. Glaring at me he said, "Well, what the hell are you waiting for?"

Through bloody, swollen lips I said, "My fourpenny change."

Turning to the Greek he asked, "Has he got change coming?"

"Yes, he gave me a shilling for an eightpenny packet of cigarettes."

From his pocket he selected four pennies and threw them at me. I picked up the pennies and counted them carefully before pocketing them.

SEVEN

If my brains were not as dry as the marrow in a witch doctor's fortune-telling bones, I would have gone and joined the queue at the Labour Exchange Department with a view to getting myself some honest employment, instead of listening to what Tiny was saying. Something told me that one day Tiny was going to get me into a lot of trouble.

I was two days out of hospital, after three months there. What kept disturbing me was what the doctor said just as I was preparing to leave. His actual words were, "From now on, and for a good long time to come, know that there is very little difference between your jaw and a piece of cut glass, because that's what your jaw has become, and that's what it's going to be for a very long time."

Tiny was saying, "What you need, Duggie, is a . . ."

"Good steady job," I interrupted.

"No! No! Man, I didn't mean that."

"Well, I meant it," I said, giving him a mean look.

"You want to go and work for twelve shillings and sixpence a week, Duggie?"

"Yes!"

Ignoring my answer he said, "What I was going to say

is that what you need is a good witch doctor with a strong medicine. You see the monkey's skin that's tied around Jeegar's right wrist? He got that from his witch doctor; it's powerful stuff. It brings him luck."

"Is that why he stole two suitcases full of one-sided shoes?" I asked.

"Aw, Duggie, don't talk shit, man. You're bitter, that's all." Brightening up, he said, "Look, I got one, too. Only mine hangs around my neck."

"If I'm going to hang anything around my neck, Tiny, it's going to be a rosary, and not a piece of juju that's going to explode in my face."

"You can't hang the work of Christ around your neck and expect him to help you in devil's work, Duggie. Stealing is devil's work. You got to have him around your neck if you want him to protect you."

"What I intend doing, Tiny, won't need the Devil's protection or a monkey's skin around my wrist."

Stupidly he asked, "What are you going to do, Duggie?"

"Work my fingers to the bone."

"Look, Duggie, just give me one chance to prove to you that this stuff works. Tomorrow we'll go to my witch doctor and I'll ask him to prepare one for you. After that, you'll see, nothing will ever happen to you."

Nothing did happen to me, that is, if nothing means going in and out of prisons as if prisons had back doors.

Me and Tiny started again. That is, after I had made it clear to him that I didn't want to have anything to do with picking pockets. Lucky charm or no lucky charm, I was going to go through life openly, no sneak-thief stuff. Not even elbowing the victim so that Tiny could go to work. My cut-glass jaw came before a dirty little bag around my neck.

"Johannes," said the white man loudly as he got out of his car at the noisy Indian market. He was talking to his African servant who was sitting next to him in the front seat because the back seat was crammed with suitcases. "Look after the things in the car while I go into this building."

"Yes, baas," said Johannes.

Tiny heard the white man. So did I. Dressed in his khaki dustcoat, Tiny followed the white man into the building.

A second later, Tiny appeared. He shouted, "Johannes, your baas wants you! Come, hurry!" Without waiting to see what Johannes' reaction would be, Tiny turned and walked back towards the building's entrance. Johannes, fearing that he might lose Tiny in the crowd, followed. He didn't suspect a thing. If his baas didn't send Tiny, then where the hell did Tiny get his name from?

Johannes was just about to enter the building when I sprang into action. I emptied the back seat of all the suitcases at the same time, praying that they did not contain one-sided shoes. I was putting the last one on the pavement when Tiny joined me.

As we were carrying the suitcases towards Black Mischark's barber shop, I said, "What happened to Johannes?"

"I took him into the building, there was an elevator, but it was written 'Europeans Only,' so I showed him the stairs. I left him climbing to the fourth floor."

The white man of South Africa suffers from a defect which can be easily termed limited intelligence. The cause of this mental handicap can be safely attributed to a frustrated background of poor beginnings.

I say this because no man, no matter how dense, will allow himself to be taken in twice by the same trick. They don't learn by mistakes, for the simple reason that they'd rather die than talk about their mistakes. Me, I learn by my mistakes because human beings make mistakes, and I'm a human being. Their pride is based on colour, and it's on this pride that we blacks feed ourselves. Call him "Baas" and he'll break an arm to help you.

He takes advantage of his white skin, we take advantage of his crownless kingdom.

"Baas, can you please tell me where this address is?" That would be Tiny, showing a crudely-written address under the nose of a railway truck driver, while we hovered at the back like a pack of hungry wolves waiting for the kill.

It was either difficult, painful, or degrading to have to admit to a black man that he couldn't read. Whatever it was, I'll never know. What I do know is that he'd turn that envelope round and round, and make senseless sounds through his blocked nostrils, while we unloaded the trailer at the back.

Finally he'd say to Tiny, giving back the envelope, "Tell your baas to write better or go back to school." If Tiny didn't hear the all-clear signal from us, he'd go on making conversation with the driver.

"Doesn't this look like an 'E,' baas?"

The driver would take the envelope back from Tiny to have another look, then he would give it back to Tiny with a "Yes," adding with some finality, "Now go back to your baas and tell him to write better."

"But . . ."

"Go! Can't you see I'm busy?"

The all-clear whistle would come floating to Tiny's ear. Tiny would shrug his shoulders muttering, *"Dankie,* baas."

The driver speaking to himself would say, "Poor kaffirs, wonder what they'll do without us." Sometimes I wonder, too.

Knowing the white man, we never bothered to change our method. They were not going to talk, and we were not going to change.

We were hitting the railways so mercilessly that they decided to hire a second white man. One that sat on top of the goods at the back of the trailer.

Another mistake. They should have given the look-out jobs to black men, men who have long discovered that only sticks and stones break bones, not abusive words. When we saw our first trailer with a guard behind, we couldn't help laughing. The guard scowled. The scowl gave Tiny an idea.

Tiny's body was small, I doubt if he weighed more than a hundred and ten. That must be the reason why he was named Tiny. I could give him a hiding with both my hands tied.

What Tiny did was to go up to the guard and volubly describe his mother's anatomy. The guard would go beet-red. He'd jump off the trailer and chase Tiny down the street with murderous intent while we off-loaded.

We did this every day, though sometimes the results were not a hundred per cent successful. Tiny would meet a watchman whose abusive language was equally good. So, instead of giving chase, he would fling the words right back.

Then Jeegar started something. Something so good, that it never failed. All Tiny had to do was to go up to the guard and spit in his face. Christ! Then he ran. Not just for the sake of running, but for his very life.

After disposing of the goods at Black Mischark's place, we used to go to Babes's car park for a drink of good pure brandy. Sisinyana's brandy was becoming more poisonous as she became richer. She had long stopped using cigarettes for mixing purposes. She was using pipe tobacco instead. She claimed that cigarettes were too expensive.

Babes worked as a car attendant at a parking lot. He collected parking fees. As a sideline he sold back-door brandy for Shamba. "Back-door" meant something you took out through the back door where you worked. Shamba worked at a liquor store just opposite Babes's car park.

Unlike Sisinyana's, Shamba's brandy was pure, because there was very little time to doctor it. Besides, it came from directly opposite.

When we got to Babes's car park, he took us to a beautiful black sedan car. The owner must have been very rich. Babes opened the back door, and me and Tiny climbed in.

From the cubby-hole of the expensive car came a sealed half-bottle of brandy, and from the pockets of his white dustcoat he produced a tin mug. He left us to go and guide a small car in. While we were drinking, we heard Babes scolding a female driver.

"Madam!" came his voice. "Can't you see you're reversing into someone's car? You'll damage that head-lamp. What do you use for a driving licence—the rent receipt of your flat, or did you buy a licence?"

Just then I saw Shamba's dwarf-like body dodging be-tween cars, and making for ours. His head appeared at our car window. He was a tiny, grinning man with a crinkly goatee, dressed in oversized overalls. He looked like a circus clown.

He opened the back door of the sedan and seated himself next to Tiny, grinning from ear to ear. His goatee was bobbing up and down.

"Where's Babes?" he asked breathlessly.

"Scolding a white lady," grinned Tiny.

"Look, Tiny, help me with this bottle of brandy, it's hanging between my shoulder blades. Quick! Before the baas misses me."

After Tiny got the bottle out, Shamba opened the door and scrambled out. Before re-closing the door, he said, "Give it to Babes, he knows what to do with it." With that, he was gone. We could only see the top of his head as it weaved and bobbed through cars.

When Babes came back, Tiny gave him the bottle of brandy. Babes took the bottle to an old battered car and hid it. After joining us, he said, "I use that battered car as a store-room, and all these posh ones," he said, waving his hand carelessly around, "I use as sitting-rooms for my customers.

"You know, Duggie," said Babes, "if Shamba can go on at this rate for another year, he'll damn well buy his own car. He steals six to seven bottles a day, and when the store is busy, he steals up to a dozen."

"What's the risk like?" asked Tiny.

"Not much risk, the way Shamba handles it. The fun-ny-looking beads around his neck and the oversize over-alls does the trick. Him being short also helps. You know all short men love clowning. There are days that Shamba leaves the baas and the whole staff roaring with laughter.

"His baas once asked about those strange beads around his neck. Shamba told the baas that it's a family custom. Meanwhile the necklace really acts as an anchor for the bottle that's hanging between his shoulder blades. The overalls hide the bulge. Every time they send him out, a full bottle goes with him. His baas once suggested he cut the overalls down to his own size. Shamba nearly fainted. 'Baas!' he said, 'my father will disown me! He didn't give me the overalls to cut, he gave them to me to wear. Besides, these overalls bring me luck.' After that the white man didn't worry Shamba. He took him to be a little mad, otherwise a hard, solid worker."

After the drink in the car, we left the car park, determined to go back to Sophiatown and to steal nothing on the way. To ensure this, we rammed our hands into our pockets and kept our eyes glued on to the pavement before us. As we crossed Main Street, someone in a khaki dustcoat with a duster rag in his hand paused from cleaing a shoe-shop window and greeted Tiny.

After walking on for a few yards, Tiny said, "Will you believe it, Duggie, if I told you that the man we just saw cleaning the window back there doesn't work at that shop?" I nearly stopped in my tracks. Tiny said, "Don't stop, man, walk on. . . . He works all the blocks in town dressed as he is: dustcoat and red duster. His name is Victor. He's what the Americans call a confederate trickster."

"A confidence trickster," I corrected.

"When he sees a likely victim admiring what's in a window, he'll move and start cleaning that window. After a few strokes with the duster he'll move in and say, 'If you like that, I can get it for you. You see, I work here. If you want I can get it for you back-door at half price.' It never fails, Duggie. Victor goes to the back of the shop. When he comes back, he'll be carrying a neatly-wrapped shoe box. The victim won't open the box for fear of getting Victor into trouble with his employers. Money will exchange hands. His victims are mostly domestic servants. When they reach wherever they're going, they find that they've just bought themselves something like a pair of old useless shoes. I don't care for such a profession, Duggie— it's too slimy for my liking. I prefer the open game. Like the gangster, the shop-lifter, even the smash-and-grabber.

A life with no strings attached, no conscience-pricker. Something that needs no brains, you know what I mean, something like jazz that goes in the one ear and out the other. No regrets, no nothing. Like food you ate the previous day.

"But Victor's game, it's too classic. It has to be because it lives with you forever. It sticks to the subconscious mind like meat in pie. A future of 'Brother, look over your shoulder!' The danger in this game, Duggie, lies in injured ego. Not the deed, but the principle will get you in the end. What greater provocation is there on earth than when you enter a human being's mind and start misplacing things? No living soul wants to be made a fool of.

"The success of every confed ... I mean, confidence trickster depends upon cleverness. Cleverness that oozes from a brain that gets its stimulants from the vitamins of an empty stomach. It's like a game of snakes and ladders; the victim usually prefers the rungs to the ladders instead of the long and safe way around. Only to be swallowed by the snakes, emerging from its bowels with nothing to show but grief and misery.

"The seekers of manna from heaven are responsible for the con man's bulging waist-line, Duggie. If they ignore the shortcuts of life, they won't be touched. They should let the perspiration of their brows tighten their purse strings. Be deaf, and he'll never reach you, let alone touch you. Remember, his life depends upon explaining."

"Tiny," I said with awe, "I didn't know you got education!"

After listening to Tiny, I started thinking deeply. I was mulling over what Tiny told me. Like Tiny, I didn't care much for such a game. In spite of that, that confidence trickster gave me an idea. An idea that could be made to work. All it needed was guts and brains. And I think I had them both.

The following day I went to the Indian market alone. I didn't want to tell Tiny my idea, in case it back-fired. At the market I bought a second-hand khaki overall. I took it to an Indian tailor shop. I instructed the Indian to sew the letters "A.B." on the shoulder-blades. The letters should be red. This is the uniform of the African staff at the A.B. Bazaar.

This bazaar is big. It boasts three storeys and a basement and about two to three hundred African workers. It's always packed with customers of all races, so it's only natural to see African labourers carrying goods about the place.

I spent one whole week studying the place from the inside. When I was sure of all angles, I donned my overalls and went to work. I wasn't a registered employee, but that did not worry me because I knew it.

I took advantage of two facts. One: to all whites, a black man's features don't count. Only his colour does. To them, we are all alike; when you're black, you're just another black man. They don't even bother about your real name. To them, you're just John, Jim, or Boy. Your Daddy spends nine months thumbing through a dictionary for a fancy name to bestow on you and then some white trash comes and calls you what he feels like without even bothering to think or look at you. If that isn't contempt, then what is?

The second fact—and I like it best—is that they have a total disregard for our mental efficiency. That's why they couldn't dream that anyone, especially a black man, could be capable of doing what I did in this big bazaar.

If I took from the third floor, the staff there thought I was from the second floor. If I looted the basement they thought I was from the ground floor. A white assistant actually said to me in the basement department, "Boy, leave that and help me here."

If I carried the goods across town to Black Mischark's barber shop, the police thought I was a delivery boy. I was the only one who didn't think. It wasn't worth it. Not while everyone else did the thinking for me.

As time went on, things became even easier for me. I was getting accustomed to the place. I learned where to take and where not to take. Best of all, the staff, both black and white, took a liking to me. Hell, it looked as if I was going to get promotion. A few white sales ladies would send me out for sandwiches and cigarettes. I was a

John-do-this, and a John-do-that. The only place I kept well away from was the pay-master's office. Hell, I'm not greedy. Fridays, when the boys queued for their pay, I was gone.

Good things never last, and they always seem to stop lasting on a Saturday.

"Stop thief!"

I froze. At last, I thought. When I looked back, I saw one of our European female workers frantically pointing at an African who was hurrying away with four boxes under his armpits.

"Stop thief! Stop him, John!" She was looking directly at me. When I hesitated, she said, "Hurry, he's getting away." I cursed the thief under my breath and made after him with every intention of letting him get away. Just as I was about to veer away at one of the entrances, two interfering white men caught him just as he was about to sprint through the street door.

"Here, boy, we got him for you." I was going to ignore them when I became conscious of someone breathing down my neck. Looking back, I saw the floor manager breathing flames like a dragon; with him were two African workers. I was hemmed in between the floor manager and the thief catchers. There was nothing I could do. So I did the next best thing. I grabbed the thief.

There was fear in the African's eyes; he was shaking badly. I was shaking just as badly, but they must have thought that it was because I was holding him.

As we led the thief back to the manager's office, I sought for a way to get out of this awkward situation. I felt certain that once I entered that office my doom would be sealed.

Desperately I reviewed my position, but everything looked hopeless. I stole a quick glance at the floor manager and saw him angrily grinding his teeth as he led the procession toward his office. Clearly this was no time for me to ask one of the African workers to hold the thief for me. Spectators made way for us and as we moved on our number swelled with officials and curious onlookers. You'd have thought we'd just caught a dangerous maniac.

I saw my chances of getting away slip with every step we took.

As he opened the office door, he looked at me and growled, "Don't lose him, or you lose your job." I didn't mind. You can't lose what you haven't got. I just hate prison.

I pushed the thief roughly in, meaning to retreat, but someone pushed me in from behind and heeled the door shut. It was the second white man.

Putting up a bold front, I went to the closed door. My hand was closing around the knob when the floor manager paused, phone in hand, and said to the second white man, "Don't think we didn't know."

Oh God! So all the time he knew.

Turning to me he said, "You stay right here and guard this kaffir." The kettle and the pot are on the same stove, I thought. All sizzling equally. After that I was completely disregarded. It was as if me and the thief didn't exist.

There's nothing so gnawing and nerve-racking as uncertainty, especially if you're guilty. It's like hanging in midair with nothing holding you up. You know you're going to fall and break your neck. That's all right, you've half expected it. But what produces mental agony to a point of madness is this unseen thing that's holding you up. You wonder when it's going to snap. I was fast becoming a total nervous wreck.

There was a light tap on the door. Me and the thief both stiffened visibly. Instead of the expected police, the lady who served at the counter where the goods were stolen came in. She gave me a dazzling smile and the thief a dirty look.

"You want me, mynheer?" she asked, addressing herself to the floor manager.

"No, Miss Smith, you go back to your counter; I'll send for you when the time comes." She turned and left the office, but not before flashing me another smile.

I was changing my weight to the other foot when my jaw itched violently. Before I could guess again, they came in. I don't know whether it's imagination, but every time I see a policeman, my jaw begins to itch violently.

They didn't even knock, and I didn't have to guess their size. They were there. I felt my skin crawl.

"Boy!" the floor manager had to call me twice before I could swallow my fear.

"Boy, will you go and tell Miss Smith that the police are here."

"Heh? Yes, baas."

"Then come back here with her."

I walked out of that office stiff-legged, as if I was leading a funeral procession. I couldn't believe such luck.

Then come back here, the man had said. What kind of fool did he take me to be? In pirate stories, once they make you walk the plank, you don't walk it twice. Why should I? Once through that door, they never saw me again.

The day following that narrow escape, a white policeman riding a motor bike with a side car, called at Sisinyana's place looking for someone by the name of John. He was accompanied by an A.B. employee. When I heard this, I nearly left town. What kept me rooted was the fact that I was terribly short of money and Jeegar had a railway job lined up.

EIGHT

Me, Tiny and Jeegar were driving to the other side of Randfontein, where the lonely siding was situated. A distance of about forty miles lay ahead of us. Our road passed through Newlands where the biggest police station was situated. It was built just at the tail end of Sophiatown, buffering Sophiatown from Newlands.

The humming drone of the engine soothed my nerves, making me feel strangely elated. As the car drove on, I caught myself humming with the engine. Tiny was saying, "Did you have trouble getting the car, Jeegar?"

Jeegar shook his head without taking his eyes from the road. He was the only one who could drive a car. Then without turning his head, he said, "That Chinaman is too greedy to refuse. He'd sell his life for money."

"What do the Chinese do with all the money they make?" asked Tiny. When nobody replied, he said, "You'd think they live for nothing else but money, money, money." To satisfy himself, he said loudly, "Send it to China, I guess."

"How could he refuse us his car after what we've already done for him?" Jeegar said, his eyes glued on the road. "Besides," he added, "the agreement between us safeguards the bastard while we stand to fry both sides!"

"What do you mean by saying we fry both sides?" I asked, not realising that it was the same deal as Nine and me had organised. "I hate burning."

"Ask Tiny," suggested Jeegar. I turned to Tiny.

"What does Jeegar mean by saying we fry both sides, Ti . . ."

"Look!" said Tiny excitedly.

From the side window of the car I saw a figure run out of a street crossing. It turned and raced in the same direction that we were travelling, keeping well on the side of the flat and straight road.

I tried to focus my eyes on the feet of the running figure, but found it almost impossible. The feet were moving too fast for the naked eye to follow. They were just a blur. I've never seen such fast-moving feet. Maybe there were wings attached to the ankles. They were just not touching ground. From the same crossing shot the nose of a pick-up van, nearly crashing into us. Jeegar cursed as he swerved to the right, narrowly avoiding an almost certain crash with a tramcar whose bells were shrieking ear-splitting warnings.

The police van was gaining on the winged figure. In all fairness they should have abandoned the chase and given the benefit of the doubt to the runner. The man was too damn good.

"Christ!" said Tiny, awed. "You ever seen anything like this, Duggie?"

"No, but I'm seeing it now."

"Know who that is?"

I nodded, I had recognised the ugly king-size pimples on his face as he took the corner at the crossing.

"It's brother Ortell, he sometimes patronises Sisinyana's shebeen. He specialises in H.B. (House Breaking). Remind me to buy him a scale of skokiaan when next we meet," said Tiny.

"If he sticks to this straight and narrow road, it will be a long time before you can buy him that scale," prophesied Jeegar.

"Can't we pick him up?" I asked apprehensively, as I fingered my jaw.

"No," said Jeegar. "Definitely no! This job is not going to be spoilt by any gallant actions! Crime and chivalry don't mix."

I lay back and continued to enjoy the ride. We were not going to hit the place until well after dark. To kill time, Jeegar left the white suburbs of Randfontein and drove the car to one of Randfontein's meanest-looking African townships. Guarding the gate at the main entrance of the township was a municipal policeman heavily armed with a spiked knob stick. Next to the big gate was the township superintendent's offices. We left the car and walked up to the offices where we were issued with twelve-hour visiting passes. These passes would shield us from arrest while in the township.

Jeegar nosed the car along the rutted streets. The streets were muddy and slimy because they were without gutters. They were strewn with dirty dish-water. The air reeked with overflowing latrines. Naked children with bloated bellies stood lined up, staring at us with mouths hanging open at this glimpse of glitter from the outside world. Now and again, braver ones would steal a ride on the back bumper of the car.

Jeegar turned a corner and stopped in front of a rain-rusted cottage. As we filed out of the car, women that were sitting long-legged on woven grass mats screamed with joy as they saw Jeegar. We filled ourselves with thick maize porridge and drank it down with a brew known as

Black Courage. There's very little difference between skokiaan and Black Courage. The only difference lies in the name. To me, the stuff tastes the same, and both are equally sinful.

This Black Courage not only made us a little drunk, it also ran true to form. It gave us the necessary courage for the job ahead.

The goods train was emptied without a hitch. Jeegar drove back to the cottage at Randfontein. We didn't think it wise for us to proceed to Johannesburg at that time of the night as we were almost certain to run into the night patrols. So we decided to pull out of Randfontein at the first light of dawn.

That night the zinc cottage vibrated with noise as we celebrated. There was a four-gallon tin of Black Courage, plus a bottle of Tambo Lenyoka ("Snake Bone"), a colourless liquid made from the vapour of boiling corn. I don't remember leaving the cottage or being carried to the car.

The wind cutting into the side window and the painful hunched position that I found myself in must have been responsible for bringing me out of my drunken stupor.

My shirt smelt of vomit. I moved my legs, and felt a wetness. God, I had wet my own bloody trousers.

The taste in my mouth was revolting. It was as if I had been feeding on rotten intestines. My tongue felt thick and scurvy. I wanted to open my mouth to let it hang out, it was taking up too much space. My fingers were shaking uncontrollably, while disgust and loathing for myself mounted by the minute. God! What a hangover!

"Don't you think we should abandon the car?" It was Tiny talking. There was anxiety in his voice.

"No!" came from Jeegar. "Not after all the trouble we've gone through. We might still make it."

"But you yourself have admitted that time has run out on us, that we overslept."

"We might still make it!" insisted Jeegar irritably.

After that, there was silence in the car except for the

steady drone of the engine and the ceaseless hammering pain in my head.

Suddenly Tiny shouted with an unusual trace of panic in his voice, "No! No! Jeegar, look at the time, we'll never make it, man! Stop the car and let me out—you can have my share of the goods. Only for God's sake stop the car and let me out!"

"Shut up and sit still, and keep your hands off the steering wheel—do you want to kill us all?"

I looked around for the first time and wondered about Tiny's sudden outburst. It was not like him. Besides, nothing seemed to have gone wrong. Our car was still packed to capacity. Through the small back window I saw no sign of approaching trouble. Why should Tiny run up a sweat? The answer wasn't long in coming. As if by magic, we found ourselves sardined between two squad cars.

I looked through my side of the window and saw a red face grinning at me. The other squad car signalled to Jeegar to pull up. There was nothing he could do. The cards were up. They had us cold. Tiny was shouting, "I told you! I told you! Damn you! I told you!" Right on the car's floorboards I bent my head and was violently sick.

It's very vague, but I recall being driven into the yard of Newlands police station and pushed into the charge office. A charge was read but I was too dense or dazed to understand. Then we were ushered through a passage that led to the cells at the back. As the turn-key opened the iron gate, he said to Tiny, "This one stinks like the crevices of a witch doctor's buttocks after an initiation ceremony. What's the matter with him, is this his first lock-up?"

That night in the cell, Jeegar was cursing the Chinaman with every foul word that he could lay his tongue on. I didn't think it right. After all, it was just our bad luck that landed us here. Jeegar was cursing the Chinaman, Tiny was cursing Jeegar and I was cursing my weakness for drink.

"When we awoke at the Randfontein cottage, you told

me yourself that time had run out on us. Go on, deny it, go on!"

"Shut up, Tiny," Jeegar said.

"I won't shut up, Jeegar! The trouble with you is that you are born greedy. Always was, and always will be. I'm saying it here and now, and I'll always say it—if you had listened to me and not your greed, we would have jumped the fire and remained with our freedom. We wouldn't be here. No! Never! I repeat, we wouldn't be here."

I wished Tiny would shut up. He was putting more strain on my strained nerves. Didn't he realise I was dying?

"Tiny," I said at last, "will you for God's sake shut up?"

He ignored me and continued to revile Jeegar, who was now engaged in the task of carefully turning his pockets inside-out in the hope of finding cigarette waste. All our possessions had been taken from us, including our cigarettes and matches.

"You knew the rules," went on Tiny. "But you ignored them."

Nursing his find carefully in the palm of his hand, Jeegar said, "What would you be saying if we had made it?"

"Don't talk shit, Jeegar. The Chinaman was to report his car stolen to the police at exactly seven o'clock, and where were we at that time? Right in Randfontein under dirty blankets!"

Jeegar cursed. "I still think that bloody Chink could have waited for another hour."

"What! And run the risk of losing his car?

"Wasn't the agreement that he lends us his car for the job and if we were not back by seven o'clock he reports the car stolen to the police? If he had given us that extra hour that you're raving about, and we were found with the goods, he would have been taken as an accomplice and his car would have been confiscated. Besides, we promised to abide by the rules, and an agreement is an agreement, even if it's made with a Chinaman."

"You'll never make a successful criminal, Tiny," growled Jeegar.

"Not if I tag along with you!" Tiny yelled.

"What we should have done was to hide the goods and abandon the car at the stroke of eight, like that Cinderella picture."

"I still say . . ."

"Shut up, Jeegar, you make me sick! You heard what that charge sheet read. Instead of one sheet, there are two.

"One reads, 'Theft from the railways', instead of just plain theft. Do you know what that means? To them, this is special. They are going to charge us with every undetected crime that ever took place on the railways in the hope that we were the gang responsible. That alone's worth a five- to seven-year sentence—they are going to throw the book at us, Jeegar!

"The second charge sheet reads . . ."

"Shut up!" screamed Jeegar, getting to his feet.

Tiny jeered and went on, "The second charge reads, 'Car theft'. It should read 'car theft by arrangement', but it doesn't, for the simple and logical reason that the Chinaman will never admit his part in the deal. In fact, to him we just don't exist! So stop clenching your fists and spilling those cigarette grains and tell us about the penalties that go with car theft. Let your previous convictions be your guide!" Then Tiny did a surprising thing. He sat flat on his buttocks and cried bitterly.

While all this was going on, I was listening with a detached mind, then my brains started revolving slowly. I wanted very much to detach them again, but what Tiny said about two charges when I only knew of one made it difficult. I could excuse the railway charge, but it also said car theft. I knew nothing about that. I didn't steal any car, nor did I know about Chinaman arrangements.

That night I slept very little. The cell was lousy with lice. I thanked the Almighty when the first signs of daylight filtered through the cell window. I studied my surroundings. The first thing I saw was the sleeping figure of a man, covered from head to foot with these foul blankets. He slept as if he was in a nursery. Must be a bigger louse, I concluded. My hangover was much better, in fact it was almost gone. I felt that I might live. Even if I stank like a Zulu warrior's armpits.

Jeegar got up. He went to all the prisoners in the cell, about fifteen in all. He started kicking, cursing and pulling the blankets roughly from them. The lion is back in his jungle, I thought. A guard peeping through the iron bars grinned his approval.

He went to the prisoner who was covered from head to foot, and whisked the blanket off. The figure groaned.

"Hey, Duggie," yelled Jeegar. "Know who this one is? It's our friend with the flying feet—Ortell! Just look where that straight and narrow road led him! Look at him!" He laughed. "They've buggered him up good and solid. He's all bruised and bashed up—he can't even see!" I took a look at Ortell. He was mumbling unintelligible sounds.

The iron gate clanked open. Tiny said, "Fall in next to me, Duggie. We are on the way to Number Four."

"What about him?" I asked glancing at the inert form of Ortell.

"Forget about him," said Jeegar. "He's not going anywhere. They won't take the chance of making him appear before a magistrate or doctor while he's in that condition! He'll lie here until he's fully healed before they lay a charge against him."

Number Four. The Fort. A prison dug out of a mountain as far back as the turn of the last century. It's a mile from the heart of Johannesburg City. Its bold, hideous structure makes the surrounding suburbs look ugly. Like a septic boil on the face of a beautiful girl.

As I shuffled through the giant gates, a ghoulish feeling started engulfing me. A feeling you would get when you invaded the bowels of an ancient tomb. A cracking sound that could only have been produced by a pistol or whip in the hands of an expert made me forget all about ghouls and tombs. But neither whip nor pistol was responsible for the cracking sound. It was the palm of an open hand landing with force on an unprotected face.

The smack was dealt out by a Blue Jacket convict trustee. A Blue Jacket is a convict who served indefinitely.

It may be seven, it may be fifteen years. It all depends on the prison board members.

Criminals are in dread of this sentence, because it doesn't terminate. The least you are expected to serve is seven years if your behaviour is good. I'd like to see the results of good behaviour if a man finds himself locked up in a cage with a pack of hyenas. Besides, I don't see how anyone can be good in jail, when he's there because he's been bad. . . .

Smack! "Answer fast, you black bastard, where do you think you are? In your mother's womb?"

The newcomer stood naked while his belongings were checked.

"One trouser, baas, one shirt, one pair boots, no socks, one cap, baas, no money, no watch, no nothing." Smack! "Move, dog!" He recited all this in one breath.

"Next! Name!" Smack! "Don't stammer, you dog! Father's name? Which river do you drink from? Which tribe do you belong to? What's the name of your chief?"

You've got to answer fast, be bright and awake all the time. If you are dull-witted, you enter the big cell bleeding. The Dutch clerk sitting behind the counter took all this down without lifting his head.

After three months waiting trial, while they were searching for our previous convictions, we were hauled in front of a magistrate. Tiny was right. He threw the book at us. I got five years' hard labour plus ten strokes; Tiny got the same. Jeegar was sentenced to seven years' imprisonment because of his previous convictions.

NINE

I was in a span of forty; each of us had different sentences, ranging from twenty years to five. Not one of us was a fourteen. A fourteen is a convict who serves one to two years or even less. We were leaning on the handles of our pickaxes, resting from the gruelling task of having to drive a pickaxe into hard, rocky earth. We were making tar-road gravel. I had long stopped trying to fight the sweat that was running freely down my face.

"Chocholoza!" Chocholoza is the song that South African blacks sing under hardship. Especially by long-term convicts when engaged in hard labour. Chocholoza is like a child with no parents. Nobody knows when or where it originated from, but what everyone knows is that when there is some kind of deep-rooted ache in the heart the first thing to visit the lips will be "Chocholoza". The song with no beginning and no end, as old as misery itself.

This mystery song of dark ages was passed down to us by our ancestors through generations of hardship. Its sound rises from the very depths of a tortured soul. It encourages faith to take up when hope threatens to leave off. The word *Chocholoza* means "Go forward" or "Make way for the next man".

"Chocholoza!" The convicts in the first row were beginning to sing in high-pitched, almost soprano voices. This was the cue for the rest of us to lift our pickaxes high above our heads in one smooth motion and hold them suspended in mid-air. The more experienced convicts would twist the handles of the picks with one deft movement of the wrist, causing the two sharp points to blur as one in the air. Then they held them poised for the earthward drive.

The bass voices repeated: "Chocholoza!" The signal to strike. The pickaxes came down swiftly in one smooth motion like conducted lightning bolts piercing the stubborn ground with a forty-in-one sound.

"Kwezantaba!" (At those far away mountains). Up went the axes to remain poised in the air, waiting for the bass voices to repeat the word "Kwezantaba" before coming down in rhythmical precision.

I wished they wouldn't hold the song out so long when the pickaxes were in mid-air. My arms couldn't carry the weight too long. Clearly this was no place for weaklings. I wondered how Tiny was making out.

The singing went on: "Wena uya goloza" (You're a cheeky man). The bass voices would echo the words. "Goba uya baleka" (Because you're running away). The bass voices would repeat . . .

"Chocholoza!" God! Is this how I was to spend five years of my life?"

"Chocholoza!"

To hell with the song, it was doing nothing to help my aching muscles. As for my heart, it was about to stop beating and no amount of singing was going to stand in its way. I checked around at my immediate surroundings. I didn't know why I was doing it, but what I did know was that it wasn't with the intention of escaping. That was out of the question.

This was no reformatory. This was the real thing: prison; ten rifles, fifteen assegais, all placed strategically on high ground. Each convict was under direct focus. These Afrikaner guards didn't smell green. One stood spread-legged directly above me, cradling his rifle like it was his only child. He kept throwing abusive language in the short-cut Zulu language known as Fanakalo. His words were very discouraging. He kept saying, "Ten years jele no skuff two week, faka lo nstimbi lo pick lo shovel"— Ten years prison life with no food for two weeks, put you in irons with a pick and shovel. "Three months kululute pikanin skuff, zonke lem tondo yena fele hazeko lom fazi, nyansi nkosi pezulu"—Three months in the kulukutes. The kulukutes are the small torture cells. Pikannin skuff means food fit for a small boy. *Zonke lom tomdo yene fele* means "all the sexual organs will be dead through lack of womanly comforts, true as there is a God above".

As he came to the part of deadly sexual organs, I couldn't help grinning. Not when one long-term convict had already tried his luck on me. I had an uneasy feeling that I was going to have to fight like hell to keep these romping sexual organs out of my thighs. If they used direct methods, it would have been easy to fight them off. But those dogs were sly. To make you a "boy", that's the prison term for woman, they first tried the direct ap-

proach. That meant asking you outright. If you show
bared teeth, they began to bribe you.

The convict who favoured you would first give you a
much-needed puff from his rolled tobacco. He'd see to it
that you were well-fed, he'd make sure to get you the best
prison garb and regular pieces of meat. By meat I mean
pork fat.

If you were a fool, you'd think he was being friendly.
There's no such thing as friendship in prison. Nobody
comes to prison for the purpose of making friends. Here
only survival counts. The only sure way to survival lies
on top of the shoulders of the next man. Here dog eats
dog. The prison-wise ignore such clock-precision gifts. A
time will come when you can't do without these regulari-
ties. Then the old-timers move in and you are ready to be
slaughtered. You become a regular mistress. Your morals
are torn to shreds. You need all the physical strength you
have to protect your morals. You have to fight till you
drop. Mother Nature can always rebuild your physique,
but morals you have to shape yourself. That all takes
will-power, something I'm sadly in need of.

There was a newcomer in my cell, nice plump and
juicy-looking—the way I like my girls to look. His buttocks wobbled under his short pants when he walked, his
fat thighs shone as if smeared with fat.

The convicts took one look at the boy, then started
tearing at one another. Not me.

The hooter blasted, giving out a shrill sound that drowned
out my guard's abusive ravings. We were through for the
day. When the hooter sounded off, it meant we had at
least worked off one day of our sentence. One after the
other the convicts would yell, depending on their sentences. One who had served two years of his twenty, would
yell, "Woza eighteen years!" (Come eighteen years); the
one who had served three out of his ten would yell, "Come
seven years!"

It was heart-breaking to hear them urging the years to
come nearer. Somehow, it helped. I drew courage from
those that still had a long way to go.

"Come five!" I shouted. Unlike the other convicts there wasn't much heart in my shouting. It sounded faint and feeble. I'm sure there was a kind of sob in it. Anyway, I was the last to admit to such weakness.

My five came, hard.

After my visit to the Fort, I was in and out of prisons as if I had a share in them. The place becomes a magnet once you've graced it with your presence. With the records I piled up, I was a regular prison fan. All theft records!

The funny thing is, I didn't for one minute think that there could be any other kind of life for me except this kind. I just accepted it. Stealing to me was—well, just living.

Three months out of Cinderella Prison and I was hauled before a magistrate again. He took it upon himself to look at me with disgust. I didn't care. After all, the man was not my redeemer.

He actually stood on his feet as he declared me society's number one pest. A habitual criminal with slimy ambitions, something that should be stamped out, and if he didn't send me away for a long time, he'd be failing in his duty not only to society but to God as well. I wanted to tell him that the trouble with him was that he took his job too seriously. But the man was too angry. It would only have made him more dangerous and mean. He looked at the pile of documents before him, then he pushed them aside as if they'd contaminate him. He drummed his fingertips on the desk. He seemed to be pondering. This man was overworked.

He picked up the first document and after studying it, looked at me. I was feeling hungry. Speaking almost as if to himself he said, "Five years at the Fort. Theft!" Throwing it aside, he picked up another, "Nine months Leeukop Prison, theft! Eighteen months Bobbejaan Spoor, theft! Six months Cinderella Prison, theft! Eighteen months Sonderwater Prison, theft!" He snorted.

Thinking that he was wasting his time by going carefully through all the documents, he hurriedly thumbed through them muttering. "Theft, theft, theft—*Got*!" There was saliva at the corner of his lips, "What kind of a creature are you?"

"It was all for food, my baas."

"Food?" There was contempt in his voice. "I'm going to send you to where you are going to get it three times a day, and if you do not come back, it will be God's will." Grinning, he looked skywards as if whispering secretly to God. I didn't like that. God knows.

"How long have you been outside?"

"Three months." The prosecutor interrupted, whispering something to the magistrate. Two against one, I thought.

He looked at me and smiled. There was irony in the smile. The same kind of smile landed Napoleon on some island.

Clearing his throat he said, "I was going to give you an indeterminate sentence, but you can thank the prosecutor for suggesting something quite different and worthwhile. It so happens that there's a war on. I don't think you knew, did you?" I didn't. How could I? I had a private war of my own, the fight for existence.

"This country needs soldiers. You can choose between joining the army or being sent to prison indefinitely."

Blackmail sprinkled with justice, I thought. He knew damn well that the scars of Blue Sky were still fresh in my mind, and here he was threatening to send me back. "Blue Sky" is the unofficial name for Cinderella Prison, because that's all you see. The sky and nothing else.

"The army!" I almost shouted, but held myself. It should be easier to run from there than from the "Sky".

TEN

The year 'forty. The white men were desperately in need of soldiers. They were recruiting black men foul or fair—mostly foul—forcing them to go and put out a fire they didn't help kindle. Unemployment flourished on purpose; not that I wanted to be employed. It became a matter of join the army or starve. Every morning men would go looking for work, only to come back carrying long faces. Homes went to pieces. Women had to leave them to go and whore in order to maintain their offspring.

In the Native Military Corps there were two things that disgusted me. First, the kind of food they gave us; it wasn't fit for a dog. Second, we were not allowed the use of rifles. Not even to clean. They armed us with assegais. There's nothing wrong with the assegai provided the nation we were going to fight—they referred to them as Germans—were also going to use spears. Bringing down an aeroplane with the aid of a spear, was something I was going to live for. Even the cotton wool in my head told me that there was something terribly wrong with this assegai business.

This was my third month in the army plus one week A.W.O.L. I was lying low in Sisinyana's shebeen wondering how to escape punishment. The military police were all over the place. I'd long since discovered that getting out of the army and staying out for good was next to impossible. Not with a magistrate waiting for me in civilian life.

I was drinking skokiaan with two other soldiers, all deserters. One was a Coloured in the Cape Corps.

Victor the ex-con man was saying, "You worry about being absent without leave for one week only? Why don't you do what I once did—play dumb! I once stayed away

87

from camp for three weeks, sleeping with another soldier's wife. When I finally got back, I purposely went to the wrong camp and made myself at home there. The next morning, after dismissing roll call, I went up to the sergeant and asked why he never called my name after roll call. He gave me a scornful look and demanded my name. Respectfully I told him my name, number and rank. After going through all the names on his list, he frowned.

" 'Why the hell isn't your name here?'

" 'I don't know, Sarge.'

" 'Where the hell are you from?' he barked.

" 'This is my third week here, Sarge.'

" 'I don't want to know how long you've been here, what I want to know is, where were you stationed before you came here?'

" 'I was stationed at Welgedacht, Sarge.'

" 'How did you come here?'

" 'By train, Sarge.'

" 'You mean you were not transferred to this camp officially?'

" 'I don't know what you mean by the word officially, Sarge, but seeing that all soldiers are the same, and therefore brothers in arms, fighting the same enemy and for the same cause, I didn't see anything wrong in coming to this camp, so I just chose the nearest camp and came to it. You see, I didn't have enough train fare to go to my original camp.'

" 'Where's your kit?'

" 'Back where I was, Sarge, that is if it's not already stolen. I thought you people will issue me with a new one.' "

Wiping the skokiaan foam from his thick lips, Victor continued, "The sergeant's face swelled up right in front of me. I never knew human beings could produce sounds like dying frogs. In the meantime I had sold boots, bush-jacket, great coat and ground sheet to Sisinyana. She had bought the stuff for one of her hole-diggers."

"What happened to you?" I asked Victor.

"Nothing," he said, belching. "The sergeant hauled me

before the commanding officer and did all the talking for me.

" 'Look at this bloody block-headed private,' he howled. 'Will we ever make good fighting soldiers out of these black idiots? You haul one foot out of the bush and the bastard puts in the other. He's been lying in this camp for three weeks because he thought that it didn't make any difference in which camp he was as long as it's a soldiers' camp. He's originally from Welgedacht!'

"All the O.C. said was, 'Take him to the adjutant's office and have them make out a report then send him back to his camp with the first mail truck!' "

I grinned. I wasn't grinning at Victor's experience. I was remembering something about him.

The reason why Victor joined the assegai force is because he suffered from bad memory. It's bad for a con man to have a bad memory. He told me so himself. He complained that he was looking too much over his shoulder, that his memory was so bad that it was difficult to remember who his victims were. A good con man should have a camera mind, so as to spot before being spotted.

Victor had conned so many flat-boy Zulus, that it was dangerous for him to walk the streets without meeting one of them. And Zulus have a habit, call it dirty if you like, of fighting at the drop of a hat. They never forgive a wrong.

His last job was what made him hurriedly put his name on a recruiting pad. He was selling a perfume to the Zulu flatboys.

His perfumes were guaranteed to make any white housewife fall madly in love with her black servant. The master was in danger of losing the madam to his native servant. One whiff, and her parachute won't open. She'll just fall, and fall and fall. No need to go into detail about how the flat-boys queued for this ninth-wonder-of-the-world perfume. Victor in the army was enough proof of that.

But I had my own worries. How to get back to camp or how to get out of the army for good. Victor told me one way of how to beat the guard room and escape pack drill, but that was one man's meat, it might not have worked out that way for me.

"Duggie." It was the Coloured soldier. "Are you people really being issued with assegais instead of rifles?"

I nodded miserably. "That's nothing, you should see the food they give us. Potatoes, pumpkins, carrots, tomatoes—not one of them peeled! All dumped into the same pot with the meat. The pot is lined with motor-car grease—it must be car grease because that's how it tastes! Hell, I'm not going back there! And what really boils my bile is the speech I heard over the wireless! The General said we natives are not going to be rewarded with money after the war because we don't know the use of money. Our reward will be cattle. I've long given up trying to think of what use a cow will be to me! They say you Coloured soldiers will be given money because you know what to do with it. I happen to know that the only money a Coloured knows anything about is liquid money—and that's a fact!"

The Coloured soldier laughed.

"In the C.C.," he said, "we get good food, good uniforms, and we are issued with rifles. We even get more money than the N.M.C."

"That's because they're your uncles," I cut in bitterly.

Then something Jeegar once said came to me. His actual words were, "If you are in trouble and want to disappear from the police or anyone, never leave town or run. That's what any fool would do. The wisest thing is to blend with the local colour. Become part of the surrounding scenery."

At first I didn't understand him, nor do I think anybody would have. Surely the best way to look after yourself is to run or keep out of sight? Now here was Jeegar telling me that in order to lose yourself you should look belonging, like one of the babies in the row of cots. It was only when he explained a little further that I began to understand.

Jeegar once got an indeterminate sentence, and while serving it at a place called Barberton in the Eastern Transvaal he eluded his guards and escaped. They searched for him all over the place, including Johannesburg, until they finally gave up.

Meantime, he was in another jail under a different name serving a six-month sentence for a minor offence. Who would have thought of looking for him in prison? Jeegar wasn't in the shade, he was in the branch that provided the shade.

The following morning I was in front of the Coloured Recruiting Office dressed as a civilian. I hardly had any trouble getting in. My Afrikaans is flawless, and my surname didn't need changing. Boetie means anything; mostly it means nothing.

While the military police were looking for me all over Sophiatown, I was speeding towards Kimberley, my first Coloured base camp. The days of the spear went out of date with the last Zulu war at Blood River. Even then the damn things were no good. If I was going to fight any war, it was going to be with real weapons.

It was the biggest blunder of my life. I might still have been home drinking Sisinyana's skokiaan instead of inhaling desert sand into my throat through my nostrils as a transport driver in Garawi. I got there and back so fast that the thought still sends me reeling. It was Kimberley, Durban, then North Africa. Somebody was in a hurry for me to die.

The first night, a Friday, I was standing awed by the beauty of the desert. A soft breeze was blowing from the east, across sand dunes that stretched as far as I could see. In the moonlight they looked like a dead white sea.

On that Sunday, me and Private Penny Myburgh had to fetch the camp's weekly supply of rum. The drive in the merciless heat made us wish for all kinds of drinks.

The heat made Private Myburgh say, as we were driving back to camp with the supply, "Christ, Duggie, my throat is dry."

"Mine, too," I affirmed.

There was a pause, then, "Can't we pinch a little of the rum at the back?"

I shook my head. "No chance—no tools. The barrels are heavily sealed."

I stole a glance at Penny and saw his eyebrows screwing up, almost meeting the hairline. Heavy thinking, I thought; he's not going to get much opposition from me, not with Sisinyana's skokiaan uppermost in my mind.

"Stop the truck, Duggie." He was wetting his lips by rubbing them together. His Adam's apple behaved like a yo-yo.

I ground to a stop. We got out of the truck and made for the back. One look at those formidable barrels told me that no race on earth could open them without the necessary tools. But I hadn't reckoned with the Coloured race: he's many races all in one. Nothing short of a wall of flame was going to stop Penny from getting a drink from one of those barrels. He raced to the dashboard of the truck and reappeared with a hammer and a nail. Without a glance at me he punched a hole in the side of the barrel.

The rum pissed out.

"No cup," I said.

"Hell, who wants a cup?" he said as he threw himself flat on his back, mouth open.

I gave him a few seconds then kicked him aside and went under. Then he kicked me aside, then I kicked him aside, then he kicked me aside. . . .

Then I remember being behind the wheel, doing a crazy zig-zag and laughing my head off with old Penny screaming beside me. Then there were all kinds of other noises and all kinds of other things all over the show. Hot lead noises, hot lead things and mushrooms of white sand shooting up around us. I remember Penny and me screaming together, but not with laughter anymore.

And then there was burning and blackness and silence. A long blackness and a long silence.

Nobody ever complained about the rum.

ELEVEN

Three months later, after my neat weekend stint as a desert rat, I was hanging on a pair of crutches like wet overalls on a washing-line. I was sailing home from the port of Aden. There were premature grey hairs on my head. My left leg was amputated above the knee, leaving a five-inch stump. But when I disembarked at Durban Docks, my stump had grown to below the knee. There were a dozen Belgium brownies reposing in my stump sock, my winnings at a dice school during the voyage. A man has to live.

By the time we got to Durban, my stump was paining me. It had taken a terrible beating from the artillery that was stored there. My first problem was to find a hiding-place for my winnings. It wasn't difficult. After wrapping them in a respectable-looking parcel I took them to the Methodist Institute for Soldiers at Grey Street, where I gave them to the reverend to keep until I called.

After getting rid of my armoury, I saw that my stump was bruised and swollen. This worried me. I reported it to the M.O. and, instead of going through with the troop train to Johannesburg, I was admitted to the Addington Hospital. It was through the social workers that I was fitted with a metal leg. The Army was all for giving me a wooden peg leg, but the social workers pointed out that such a leg would be too heavy for a five-inch stump. So I got a shiny new metal one, which I nearly lost.

That happened at Umbilo Park, after the orthopaedic people had fitted me with it. They advised me to take the leg to a place where there was a lot of grass to try it out, so that, when I fell, the grass would cushion me. I did. I chose Umbilo Park. I was giving myself a rest from the trying task of having to learn to walk all over again. It was painful work. My stump was getting all bruised up again, so I took the leg off to relieve the ache; and then I must have dozed off. When I woke up, the leg was gone. At first I thought the leg had walked off, but I ruled that out. It still couldn't walk properly. After searching fruitlessly for it, I decided to report the theft.

I was just hopping out of the park gate when I saw a one-legged hobo running away with it. The funny thing was that his right leg was amputated, as opposed to my left. Under his armpit dangled my artificial leg. The fool was going to end up having two left legs. I tried to give chase, but saw the uselessness of it. The bastard had the advantage of a crutch. I had none.

A few hours after that, the social workers drove me back to the scene of the crime. There, on the park bench, lay my immortal leg. A note was attached to it. On the note was written: "Wrong side leg". I could have told him, the son of a bitch.

Anyhow, after mastering the shine out of my brand new leg, I entrained for Johannesburg, armed with a letter from the social workers of Durban to those of Johannesburg. But not before collecting my armour from the reverend. Even priests can sometimes be put to good use.

I decided to give up my past life of being lean and free. I wanted to be fat and chained. I wanted to be an honest-to-God hard worker.

At Johannesburg the social workers got me a clerical job. If putting letters into envelopes can be termed clerical.

We were driving through the streets of Johannesburg in the firm's van. I was sitting at the back of the van while the white driver occupied the driver's seat. He was taking me to the pass office where I was going to get my first pass. Without the white man's company it could have taken me as long as three weeks to get fixed up. And without the necessary pass, you were not allowed to work.

"Name?"

Just like Number Four, only here an Afrikaner asked the questions with rudeness equal to a convict trustee.

"Duggie," I told him.

He paused to look at me. Then, "From which fish-tin label did your father copy that name?"

The Afrikaans driver who had come with me doubled over with laughter. I swallowed and transferred my weight on to my artificial leg. I was getting tired of standing.

When he was through, he directed us to another office upstairs. We went into so many offices that my head whirled. In the last office we came to, a young clerk was chatting gaily to a European lady. When he saw us he became all business. I passed my papers through to him.

"Name?" It was right there in front of him.

"Duggie," I said thickly, fearing another wisecrack.

"Ooh!" cooed the lady. "That's my father's name."

The devil came up in me. I couldn't, oh no, I just couldn't miss this chance. This was a coincidence that happens once in a million. To hell with the consequences.

Straightfaced, I blurted, "From which fish-tin label did your grandfather copy that name?"

Knuckles like motor-bike ball-bearings crashed into my ribs, doubling me up. My balance stick fell; blindly I groped for it. I straightened up and started sucking great gulps of air into my tortured lungs.

"Know who you're speaking to, you black bastard!" It was my driver. I didn't look at him in case he might see what was in my eyes. Back in the van, I studied my black-stained fingers. I had been fingerprinted so many times that it would take days before the stuff could be removed.

Through the mirror the driver saw me inspecting my stained fingers. He laughed outright, the one-sided humourous bastard.

I was serious about my job and stayed that way for about two years. I loved it. Then one day that devil came up again. It was the end of the month, one of our European female clerks called me into her office; an elderly lady with a nice homely face.

"Duggie," she said, "I'm lunching out today. Please have this packet of sandwiches."

There was a big piece of ox-tongue reposing in my stomach. I was filled to the brim. Still, I felt it would be rude if I refused this kind lady's offer. And one day when there wouldn't be any ox-tongue weighing me down, she might not take it upon herself to help me out. I thanked her and took the packet to my office. I checked on my wrist-watch and saw that it was five minutes after one. Unconsciously I picked up the lunch packet and made for the street door. To get there I had to cross a big hall of working desks.

On my left was the secretary's office. It had a glass partition. You can see in from outside. I looked, and there was the secretary, Mr. Groenewald. He was busy with the morning paper, both his feet were on his desk.

Without a thought, I knocked and went in.

"Mr. Groenewald," I said, placing the packet of sandwiches on his desk. "Here's some sandwiches for you. I don't feel like anything today."

With that, I went out. I didn't think a reply was necessary. The dials on my watch were on two-thirty when my internal phone rang. It was Colonel Pringle, head of the department. I was wanted upstairs.

What I saw when I entered his office made me uneasy. There, sitting like stone marble, was Mr. Groenewald. My eyes travelled from him to the large desk.

Then I saw them. I was reminded of old times in court rooms. The exhibit, I mean the packet of sandwiches. There was black anger on Mr. Groenewald's face.

Then someone coughed, or rather cleared his throat. It was the colonel.

"Duggie."

"Yes, sir," I stammered.

Again he coughed. "Eh . . ." he started. "Well—" again he coughed. He gave me the impression that he didn't know where to start. "Well, damn it!" he exploded. "Why did you give Mr. Groenewald a packet of sandwiches?"

"Did I do wrong?"

"Well, damn it, no, but . . ." he coughed again as if his throat wasn't already cleared. "You are not supposed to give a white man your food."

"But . . ." I started. With a wave of his hand he shut me up.

"You should have taken the sandwiches upstairs to the building boys instead of giving them to Mr. Groenewald. You have made him feel small."

"Doesn't Mr. Groenewald eat sandwiches?" I asked innocently. Hell, at war we used to eat out of the same dixie.

"No! I mean, yes, he does eat sandwiches, but not when they come from a . . ."

"Kaffir!" put in Mr. Groenewald.

Indignantly I said, "The sandwiches did not come from me, they came from Mrs. Surge. I didn't feel like eating either, so I passed them to Mr. Groenewald. What is wrong in that, sir?"

"Plenty," growled Mr. Groenewald. "Who the hell do you think you are that you should come to my office and give me sandwiches? Do I look hungry to you?"

"No, I merely looked upon it as a gesture of humanity."

Soothingly the colonel said, "You should know, my boy, that it is not correct for a black man to give . . ."

"Not correct, sir?" I asked aghast.

"All right, damn you, get out of here."

God! What a race! Unlike the black man, they are supposed to have had the advantage of a civilised environment, yet their barbarism is as thinly veiled as the prison lash strokes on my buttocks. I should have resigned on the spot, but determinedly I kept on. Then Mr. Groenewald took it upon himself to make my life so miserable, that I was forced to resign two weeks after my misplaced kindness.

In 1948 the Nationalist Government came into power.

There was a big new building at 80 Albert Street. It was simply known as Influx Control. A beehive of black misery. They should have named it Liberty Control. This is where you had to report without the slightest delay after losing or resigning from a job. Failing which, you risked being charged under the Section 29 law, a law carrying a two-year jail sentence.

The trouble with this house of lawful humiliation is that

here you are made to take any job they offer, whether it suits you or not. Here, black man must take work, not choose work. Remember, never talk back to your employer; you are not indispensable. You're in orbit around town. Don't accept employment twelve miles out of town, even if there's no work to be found where you live; you can lose, or forfeit, all right to live where you've always lived. Do not marry a girl who comes from a similar distance because she is regarded as a foreigner; they won't allow you to live together. If you want to visit relatives, see that your pass is properly stamped. Also, if you want to make some sort of celebration at your home, do not buy live-stock to slaughter without getting a special permit from the superintendent. Most important of all, before going to bed at night, make sure that your pass book is either in the pocket of the trousers or the jacket you're going to wear the following morning.

Influx Control was my destination. I was going there with the hope of getting new employment. As I approached the place, I nearly turned back. Queues a half-mile long were snaking around the four-block building. The Africans were moving in pairs at a snail's pace. Misery was written on every face, as if they were walking the last mile. Maybe we were, who knew. Most of us were either going to be given twenty-four hours to leave the urban area of Johannesburg, or sold to potato farmers for failing to renew work-seeking permits in time.

In time? Look at that queue! By the time I reached the small gate so as to get the necessary rubber stamp in my pass book, it would be four-thirty, time for them to close, making me twelve hours behind schedule and liable for arrest by any street policeman who demanded to see my pass.

There's a tall tale about the trees of Canada. They say the trees are so high that if you look straight up, it will take you three weeks to see the top. Right here in Johannesburg is a queue like that. Every time you came to that gate, it would be four-thirty. Then they closed it in your face. If you tried to get back by five in the morning, you'd find that hundreds had had the same idea. If you spent the night there so as to be first in the morning, you risked arrest for Night Special.

Instead of joining the queue at the tail end, I made a beeline for the side-entrance. Imagine having to stand in a queue the whole day with only one leg to support you. Clearly this was no place for cripples, respectable or otherwise. The side entrance was guarded by two municipal police, commonly known as Black Jacks because of their black uniforms. You were not allowed to stand on the pavements. The pavement was for Europeans only. Europeans who were looking for servants, or those who were trying to get their servants' passes in order.

"What do you want? Why don't you join the queue?" asked the Black Jack glaring at me.

"I'm not here to put my pass in order. I'm here to see the social workers."

"What is social worker?" he asked aggressively.

"They are on the third floor. They are the people who help cripples."

"You mean the doctor?"

"No! The social workers." Not knowing what social workers were caused him to let me go through. I was seven years old when they called me a headache, I suppose I just had to go on being one.

Inside was a hall with a giant horseshoe-shaped counter. Behind the counter were divided cubicles. In each cubicle sat a white clerk. On the hall side, opposite each cubicle, were bar-room stools where black interpreters sat. An iron grille divided the interpreters from the white clerks. Nowhere in this vast arena was there a place where the job-seekers could sit. This is where the queue ended.

The interpreter would hand your pass through the grille to the white clerk who would take his time studying it. If there was an irregularity, he'd give it back to the interpreter with instructions.

The interpreter would hang on to your pass which you didn't dare leave without. He'd then shout, "Escort!" Two police would appear and escort you upstairs to the interrogation room.

If you fail to give satisfactory answers about why your

work-seeking permits are not in order, they conclude that you don't want to work. You are then given twenty-four hours to get out of Johannesburg. Failing which, they charge you under Section 29. Two years' imprisonment. And after serving your sentence you still have to get out of Johannesburg.

If you tell them you were sick and couldn't come into town, they demand a doctor's certificate. Africans who have money go to private doctors and buy certificates. The best excuse is out. It doesn't work anymore because too many Africans have used it. It was to tell the authorities that you were mad in the township and that you were treated by a witch doctor. Witch doctors don't issue certificates.

The procedure is to give you a first job. If you find you don't agree with your employer because of the wage, or because the work is too strenuous or because your baas is just plain mean, as is often the case, they'll give you a second and third job. If you don't accept them, they declare you a vagrant by refusing to give you a fourth work-seeking permit.

The best thing to do is to take any work they give you and stick to it no matter what the circumstances are, while you keep your eyes open for a better job. You are bound to get it. The black man is not indispensible. We are a rotating labour force. Here, there are no middle-class Africans. Whether you're educated or not, you are looked upon as an illiterate and treated as such. In this building the worse sufferer is the educated African. If you've been a teacher you'll be offered a job as a grave-digger, or coal-heaver, or a domestic servant. They hate the sight of an educated African.

I know an African teacher who was married to a senior nurse. The nurse worked at Coronation Hospital. The teacher resigned from his teaching post because he flatly refused to parrot for the Government. He didn't believe in channelled "Bantu" education. His beliefs lay in western education, not in "Bush" education, as he put it. This teacher, or ex-teacher, found himself a clerical job with some private enterprise until he heard of a better-paying job in Germiston, some eleven miles out of Johannesburg. He used to travel in and out by train to his new place of employment. He had only worked there for about a month when he had an argument with the foreman, who fired him on. the spot. Back to Influx he went with the view of finding another job, only to be told that he was no longer permitted to seek work in the urban district area of Johannesburg. He was told to go back to Germiston.

When he pointed out to the authorities that his house was in Johannesburg, and that his wife was nursing in a local hospital, and also that he was born in Johannesburg, he was told that it was none of their business. They pointed out that he had violated the rules of Influx by having gone and worked outside Johannesburg, and that if he was found in the city, he was liable to be arrested.

Which he was. He was sold to a potato farmer. When he came back, he found that his wife had misbehaved. This was apparently too much for the ex-teacher. He cracked up.

I was limping up the stairs to the social worker's offices, when I heard the voice of an angry African shouting, "Why do you tear up my J.C. certificate, baas?"

Then the voice of the black interpreter yelling, "Escort!"

A social worker escorted me personally to numerous counters. After that, I was shown the way to the doctor. Before getting your first work-seeking permit, you are required to see the doctor. Not your own, but theirs, so as to be declared fit.

As I walked into the consulting room, I mean, hall, a degrading sight greeted me. Grandfathers, middle-aged men, teenage boys were made to stand naked in rows while a doctor gave their parts a sweeping glance. If he doesn't see a septic pimple on your penis you get a clean bill of health.

I could see old men hurriedly picking up their clothes from the floor and trying unsuccessfully to hide their nakedness by tying the sleeves of their shirts around their waists before putting on their trousers. They would then hurry out to get their work-seeking permits. Father was

made to stand naked in the presence of son. The last layer
of human dignity was being peeled off.

I made my way to the von Weilligh Street beer hall. It
has since been removed. It was feared that we may one
day run wild and harm the whites on our way home
through the town.

As I turned left into von Weilligh Street, I nearly
bumped into a well-dressed African woman who was having an argument with a European who was collecting
money for charity. The African girl wanted to know
whether she was collecting for black cripples or white
cripples. I walked on.

As I came to the beer hall which was fifteen minutes
walk from the Influx Control for a one-legged man and
ten for a normal one, I saw the queue. A black man's life
is a life of queues, I thought.

I don't care much for this kind of legalised corn beer. I
say legalised because we were not permitted to drink or
make our own. We were only allowed to drink in municipal beer halls. What I don't like about this beer is that it
takes a hell of a long time before it affects you. You've got
to fill your stomach with the stuff first then do a lot of
talking before you can get it going. There are times that I
stop to wonder what makes us drunk—the noise in the
beer hall, or the beer.

My reason for being here was to see if I could find
some of the boys and be brought up to date with the latest
local news. While I was working I hadn't paid them
much attention. The beer hall used to be our regular
meeting place.

At the time I was staying in a Hillbrow backyard with a
girl who loved me strictly from a financial point of view.
When she found out that I'd left my job, she would
without hesitation replace me.

"Excuse me, my friend, could you please make a place
for me?"

"Why should I make a place for you? I don't know
you."

"I've got one leg and I can't stand for a long time. This
queue is too long."

"I didn't make you one leg."

"I know, I . . ."

"*Ag*, let him through, man." The words came from a voice behind me. "Can't you see he's sick?"

"All right, but these cripples worry me. They make the beer halls look unclean. Some crawl, some are . . ."

To hell with you, I thought, as I sneaked in front of him.

I stood inside the beer hall and looked at the familiar sight. To describe the noise is difficult, but if you've ever stood around a moody volcano you'll know what I mean.

Right there, at the entrance where I was standing, sat rows of dirty old men making business by straining the chaff from the beer with sieves. They charged a penny on a shilling mug.

The bastard in the queue outside was right when he said that the place was crawling with all sorts of cripples. They were everywhere, begging for a drink or for grains of tobacco. As for the mental cases, they could have filled a hospital.

It was a large cemented yard with rows and rows of long benches. The benches were filled to capacity with corn beer drinkers. On these benches sat the Bandlas (fellow drinking members). There was no law that said you couldn't sit where you liked, but the code of the beer halls said that you couldn't occupy a place that belonged to a Bandla, unless you wanted to be bashed.

The dealer—he was the one who didn't have a shilling piece to contribute—was responsible for dishing out the beer. He'd fill up a shilling mug, the mug would be passed around and each member would take a deep drink before passing it on to the next.

This beer cannot be hurried. It's filling. If you drink it in a hurry, you take the gamble of vomiting. While it's being drunk, fights, domestic troubles, thefts, and life in general are discussed.

Picking their way carefully, so as not to spill or tramp on the drinkers, were the salesmen, the con men, selling cheap watches with expensive tags on them.

I stood wondering where the hell to look for my crowd

in this ant-heap. There, beating on a drum was a mad man. He stopped beating the drum and started preaching. I moved nearer so as to hear. As I craned my neck, he moved away and started beating on the drum again. I kept on moving around.

"Duggie!" I spun around, nearly losing my balance. Sometimes I forget I've got one leg.

"Duggie! It's me, man!" It was Tiny. I hadn't laid eyes on him for months. He looked shabby, on the down and out. Life was making a mess of him.

"Come and join us, man. Where's your shilling card? You know you can't share or join our Bandla unless you have a shilling. Give me the card and I'll go and get your drink for you."

I studied Tiny's friends and didn't like any of them. Maybe I had reformed.

"Where've you come from, man?" It was Tiny holding an overflowing mug. His fingers were dripping with kaffir beer. He wiped his brow with the crook of his arm without relinquishing the scale. "I'm out at Orlando now," he said. "I'm boarding there. Hell, things are bad now, man, everything stinks, especially my pass. Nothing is like before."

"Why don't you go and live in a hostel?"

"Shit, man, who wants to go and live in a compound with thirty other kaffirs? No privacy, no nothing. Gramophones, pressure stoves, concertinas, farting, vomiting and no women allowed. No, Duggie, that's not for me. I'm strictly a steak-and-egg man."

Suddenly Tim, a trumpet player I knew, was beside us. In his hand was a sixpenny mug. That meant he was in a hurry, he wasn't going to sit with us long; otherwise he would have bought a shilling's worth. I made a place for him.

"How's the trumpet, Tim? When we going to start our band?"

"Haven't touched music for months, Duggie."

"What's the matter? You're looking low, man."

He took a deep drink from the mug. "I've just been potato-farming."

"How long?"

"Long enough."

"Sorry. What's the story?"

"Usual. You know. I'm in bed, Sunday morning, reading the Sunday comics, when the cops come in. They want my pass. I shout to my wife to give it to them. She goes to the wardrobe, opens the proper drawer. No go. So she starts feeling all over her apron pockets. Still no go. I just lie there watching her. I can't move a muscle. She turns back to the wardrobe and starts flinging my clothes around. And she still doesn't find a damn thing. Now she's sweating, man! So she rolls me out of bed and starts flapping the blankets around. Not a sign!

" 'Well,' says the cop, 'we haven't got all day.'

" 'Please, baas,' I say, 'she'll find it; she had it in her apron-pocket this morning.'

" 'Why does she have to carry your pass?'

" 'I gave it to her yesterday when she went for permits to buy corn beer and to slaughter a sheep, baas. All our relations are coming, baas. We've just finished six months after her mother's death, baas.'

" '*Lieg*,' he shouts. 'It's a lie! I can see you're one of those kaffirs who wants to make themselves Europeans! You sleep with pyjamas and read comics like a white man. Come along, your wife can bring your pass to the charge office. You say you've got one—I say you haven't!'

"Next thing, I'm standing in a line of handcuffs outside the police station. Then my wife's there, waving the pass book like a red flag. She gives it to the cop in charge. He looks at it, says it's in order . . . but it's too late! She must report with it to the Fordsburg police station next day.

"She starts screaming, at them, at me. 'It was our baby!' she screams. 'Our little baby boy! He was playing with it in the backyard!'

"The cop shouted, 'March!' and I marched with the rest.

"Apparently, next day she was at Fordsburg with the pass book like the man said. But again, no go. I was gone, boy. Potato-farming. It took a lot of time, a lot of trouble, a lot of money to bring Daddy home again. And for now, Duggie, all I want to do is—nothing!"

As Tim picked up his mug to drink, I heard one of Tiny's friends say, "Shezie here wanted to stab him. I said to Shezie, 'Why stab him? Why kill the porridge and meat? Let's just take his money and clothes and let him go. This way we are keeping him alive for the next time. Killing him is like biting the hand that feeds you.' Shezie here, he . . ."

I moved away. At the door I heard the voice of the mad man shouting above the din.

TWELVE

Walking, to a one-legged man, is like hard labour to a convict. That's what messed my pass up. The idea of walking to the Influx Control every day, just to be told that there was no work, became so tiresome that I stayed away.

I was sitting with my real leg resting on the bent knee of my artificial leg in a shebeen house, exhausted from begging the woman of the house to give me a scale on credit. Her refusal made sense. She wanted to know where was I going to get the money to pay her.

Right next to me sat a lone drinker. The man was mean, he wouldn't give me a drink. He kept taking a sip, then resting the scale on the floor between his legs.

"Pass!" It was the police, I didn't see them come in because I was facing the wrong direction.

"You!" they said to the lone drinker. "Where's your pass?" He gave it to them. After scrutinising it, they gave it back.

"What are you sitting so quietly for? Produce!" Reluctantly I took out my pass and gave it to him. He looked at it, then hung on to it. That told me that I was in trouble.

One policeman was opening pots, and the door of the cold stove, while the other was peering under the unmade bed and up the chimney in search of skokiaan.

A voice behind me said, "Hey, you, pick up that scale and let's go." I looked at the man next to me, expecting him to pick up his scale, but the man sat tight.

"I'm speaking to you," said the policeman, as he poked me in the ribs with a stick.

"Me?" I said truthfully, "I haven't got any scale."

"I say, pick up that scale and let's go!" continued the policeman aggressively.

I looked between the lone drinker's legs where his mug was kept. There was no scale. My eyes travelled slowly from his legs to mine, and there, next to my artificial leg, only half drunk, was the skokiaan scale. This wasn't magic; the bastard must have seen the police in the yard, before they came in, because he sat facing the window while I sat facing him, mutely begging him with my eyes to give me a sip. When he saw them, he must have pushed the scale right up to my artificial leg, I couldn't feel the scale touching me because the thing's got no life. I once did the same to someone. Maybe that's why I wasn't mad at the man. He gambled and won.

My man was sitting and facing me like I was facing this damn fool. (Funny calling a man a fool when he's just gone one up on you.) Anyway, I was chatting with the scale in my hands, taking my time, when through the little broken window I saw the yard crawling with police. I looked around the room where we were sitting, and saw that nobody else was aware of what I was aware of. I hurriedly took a deep drink then nonchalantly passed the scale on to the man next to me. He was just lifting the scale to his lips when a voice said, "Hold it just where you've got it!" After giving me a dirty look, the man got up and departed with the police.

Now the same thing was happening to me. But I was not going to give in as easily as the man I had sent up. Not when I hadn't even got a drink from this man. Besides, the fine for skokiaan was five pounds or three months. If I went with them, it would be because my pass was out of order, not because of a skokiaan scale that didn't belong to me.

"Baas," I said heavily, and with truth, "this is not my scale." But one look at him told me that no amount of pleading was going to change that wooden face. I looked around for the woman of the house but, as expected, she was nowhere to be seen. As for the man, he was already going through the door. The hopelessness of my situation made me pick up the scale. I prayed that we wouldn't tour the whole of Sophiatown before going to the police station.

Outside, I drew a sigh of relief, when I saw the men prisoners. It meant we were not going to roam much. Some of them had scales in their right hands, while the iron cuffs glittered on their left wrists. Most of them were just cuffed. That told me they were pass offenders. They didn't bother to cuff me, but I was told to walk right at the tail end so as to be under the direct eye of the police. At Anadale Street we halted, while another string of prisoners joined us.

All the time I had been praying for something like this to happen. If I had belched then, the stuff would have come back. Luckily, I didn't. I was having trouble with my eyes, I was trying to blink the tears back into my head. In all my life I'd never emptied a mug of skokiaan so fast. Now all that was left for me to do was to get rid of the scale. The bastard didn't even see me. It was too depressing to labour for something that didn't belong to me.

We were crossing the tram-line when I got rid of the empty mug. If it wasn't for the fact that they had my pass, which is something no man can do without, I would have tried to steal away at the first busy intersection. But without my pass, I was just as securely shackled as these prisoners.

After a louse-bitten night at Newlands Police Station, I appeared at the Fordsburg magistrate's court. It wasn't a question of guilty or not guilty, I was as guilty as hell. It was all there in the pass book, written in black and white. The only thing that they couldn't hang on me was the skokiaan, not when there was no exhibit. The magistrate must have taken pity on me, because most of the offenders received six months to two years imprisonment. I got off with three months.

Again the gates of Number Four closed on me. But this time I was a fourteen, not a long-time offender. Those sentenced from six months to one year, were forced to have the one side of their heads shaved clean, thus giving them a comical look. Black Red Indians. Only those with long-term prison sentences were given the privilege of having their heads shaved clean.

I was marched to cell number eight, known among the inmates as the Prison Market. It's where the farm labour convicts are kept. I was in cell number eight for three days before being auctioned off. The farmer paid cheap for me because I had one leg. He wanted someone who was disabled but who still had the use of his arms to cook for his convicts.

The well-guarded lorry ride to Bethal somewhere in the Eastern Transvaal was uneventful. It was when we turned into a muddy track that I became a little apprehensive. The track led to some farm buildings.

I saw a large, rain-rusted zinc cottage and guessed it to be our sleeping quarters. Hanging from paneless windows and blowing gently in the breeze were potato sacks. To keep out the cold.

Sitting on the plank veranda of a large farmhouse was the farmer. Four dogs were keeping him company. One look at those saliva-dripping fangs told me that this farmer wasn't putting on any floor show for our benefit. These dogs were real mean, and so was their owner. These dogs reminded me of a picture I once saw: *Hound of the Baskervilles*. One look at them and any idea of escape became void. Something told me that they were not only vicious, but that they were also well-trained.

A driver at the firm where I once worked told me that once he was driving from Durban with the firm's car. When he came to a village known as Howick he lost his way. Alongside the lonely road, he spied a beautiful white-washed farmhouse with a long drive-in road leading to it. After parking the car alongside the road, he walked up the well-kept driveway, meaning to ask for the direction that would put him back on to the Durban-Johannesburg highway. As he approached the house, he was relieved to see the owner of the house sitting on the veranda, newspaper in hand and sucking a pipe. Next to the master, and resting on its haunches, was one of these same vicious-looking dogs. Hat in hand, the driver approached the master, who he now saw was reading an Afrikaans newspaper. The newspaper supplied him with the clue on which language to use.

"*More, mynheer.*" (Morning, sir.) No reply. Only silence. Silence that made him feel he didn't exist. The master's eyes were glued to his paper. He cleared his throat and tried again, a little louder this time in case the master was a little deaf.

"*More, mynheer.*" Silence. The driver became uneasy. The atmosphere made him move. He took a step back. Then the hound growled, exposing merciless fangs. The driver stood pillar-stiff. The hound relaxed. The master kept on looking at his paper. Sweat streamed down the driver's face as he grinned vacantly at someone who wasn't even aware of him.

He wanted to transfer the weight of one foot to the other, when the hound growled again. He knew damn well the hopelessness of trying to run for it. He'd only be ravaged to death. Fear got the better of him, he started shaking visibly. "Please, baas, *ek vra die regte pad.* Please, baas, I'm asking for the right road."

Slowly the master looked up from his paper. The veins on his forehead were throbbing.

"Look," he said in Afrikaans, as he pointed the stem of his pipe at the driver. "In future, never refer to a white man as *mynheer*. To you a white man is a baas. Not *mynheer*. Understand? *Mynheer*, coming from a kaffir, means a kaffir preacher. You hear?"

"Yes, baas," stammered the driver.

"Now, get your arse out of my sight."

The driver went on to tell me that after the master had

opened his mouth to speak to him, the dog didn't growl when he moved. When he neared the gate, he stole a look back. The man and his dog were sitting in the same position that he had found them earlier. That just goes to show how educated a country dog can be. As long as the owner doesn't open his mouth to you, you are regarded as an enemy. My new baas on the veranda wasn't saying a word.

As I prepared myself to get off the lorry in front of our sleeping quarters, I saw three labourers garbed in potato sacks. A hole was cut out at the sewn part of the sack for the head to go through, and two holes on the side for the arms. Uniforms, I thought. Another way of making escape impossible. Who wants to be seen wearing potato sacks in the streets?

The following morning we were all up at four a.m. I was warned to get up earlier so as to have breakfast ready for the convicts. Most of the convicts were made to dig for potatoes in the fields with their hands. Some were draining disused stagnant wells, while the rest cleared weeds.

It was difficult to keep count of how many we numbered because we all looked alike in these potato sacks. But there were three shacks like mine, and I was bedded down with about twenty prisoners. The only furniture in the shack was the potato sacks we used for blankets, and sleeping mats and the two improvised latrine buckets. These were emptied every morning by prisoners who were not strong enough to fight back.

The menu consisted of potato peels and thick porridge. Sundays, the diet was the same except for a piece of pork fat to remind you that it was a Sunday. Pork trotters would have been acceptable, but pork fat! As each week crawled by, I grew tired of it. When I get tired of a thing I get real tired of it. But just getting tired of it is not good enough. So I decided to do something about it. Life has proved to me time and again that a hungry stomach is a far better thinker than a skull full of brains. I started to plan, but I stopped planning, because to plan is merely an excuse to waste time.

The next day, I gonged the dinner gong. While the

prisoners were busy looking as if they were enjoying the shit I cooked, I stole away to the nearby tool-shed where I busied myself with looking for the instrument that would serve my purpose. As luck sometimes favours the unlucky, I found what I was looking for. It was a piece of thick steel wire about twelve inches long. I filed both ends until they were dangerously sharp. Then I hid the weapon in the hollow of my artificial leg. We have a name for this kind of weapon, we refer to it as the "chumenchu". After you are stabbed with it, it leaves no visible marks; you bleed to death slowly from the inside; then Africans jump to the logical conclusion that you've been bewitched.

Me, I set out to bewitch all those lambs in that kraal and put the blame on snakes. The bastard would never find out as long as the marks looked reasonably like snake-bite marks. One thing I was sure of: he wouldn't dare eat poisoned meat, nor would he risk the lives of his four pets.

Some people have patience; I have none. Not with the thought of roast lamb orbitting in the hollow of my stomach. I was softly whistling "Chocholoza" as I made my way towards the sheep kraal. Christ! To think I used to live on cow's intestines twice a week, and maybe a quarter pound of beef on Sundays; yet here I was eating mutton left and right on a prison farm.

The only thing that the farmer said to me about his sheep that were dying systematically at the rate of one a week, was, "You kaffirs are certainly courting death by eating meat poisoned through snake bite."

"Baas," I sighed, picking mutton from the crevices of my teeth, "all I can say, baas, is that the devil looks after his own."

Good things never last. I was beginning to look upon the farm as my home, when my three months came to an end.

THIRTEEN

As I jumped off the farmer's lorry at New Market, I felt heavy. As if my weight had increased. If it had, then it can be attributed to the mutton. Only my clothes gave me away. They were old and worn out. I resembled a real down-and-out crippled beggar.

Instead of going straight to my girl friend's place in Hillbrow, I went searching for a drink. When I finally did get to her place, it was late. I knocked, and a male voice told me gruffly to enter. Inside, I saw a burly, blue-black African sitting on the bed. The top half of his body was naked. And what a body! It was rippling with muscles. His bare feet were dangling inches from the floor. There was a long knife in his right hand. He was using it to clean the finger-nails on his left. The long nails were bluish with dirt. Not that I was thinking that that knife display was for my benefit. He didn't need it. Not with all those boulders and hills on his torso. Besides, I can tell if a man is trying to frighten me, and this one certainly wasn't.

Behind him lay my girl. The bitch was reading a newspaper wrong side up. She gave me one look, then completely ignored me.

"What for you want?" he growled. I made him north of the Limpopo because of his complexion and broken English. These Kalangas—that's the name we use when describing Rhodesians—brave the wilds of Bechuanaland and the Kalahari Desert to come to the Golden City in search of work, but mostly to get our light-complexioned girls. They have no family ties here; they are irresponsible, therefore dangerous. Imagine having to die at the hands of an illiterate.

When they get here, they find that they have walked

right into road-blocks of language difficulties, because they know neither Zulu or Sotho, let alone English or Afrikaans. So the first thing they do is to lose themselves in white men's kitchens, as plain cooks or garden boys. This gives them four advantages: food, a place to sleep, a few shillings a month and the master's old clothes. They become domestic servants, something that we, the owners of Johannesburg, regard as work for females. We look down upon it.

Now the only way for Jackson here to get a light-complexioned girl, seeing that he can't speak her language nor she his (I might add that neither of them is prepared to learn the other's language), is to buy her, i.e. give her money and buy her clothes. Something Sophie must have been praying for all her life, the bitch.

Have you ever tried taking a woman away from a man who has braved lion-infested country, and is at the same time faithfully bestowing her with the sweat of his brow each month? Try it. It's not listed on the Suicide Method List, only because the man who drew up the list hasn't come across this sure method of dying. I can assure you, brother, it's just as deadly as throwing yourself under the wheels of a fast-moving train.

"What for you want?" he growled again. I inspected the six-inch knife in his hand, then gulped. The bloody knife made me say,

"Doesn't Mary work here?"

"Who Mary?" he asked. I didn't know either. With the knife in his hand, I couldn't very well tell him that I was looking for Sophie, the bitch that was lying behind him.

"No Mary, baba." The bastard was calling me *baba*, which means father, when he was far older than me. Mock politeness, I thought. Hopelessly, I feigned dignity and slipped into the familiar bathroom where I spent the rest of the night.

I went back to the beer hall in the hope of meeting some of the boys. Perhaps they could put me up until something better showed itself.

I was in luck. Tiny. Still looking like the dark side of

the moon. Still, the pot shouldn't call the kettle black; there I was looking like the letter W on a worn-out Welcome mat.

That night, after convincing his landlady that Rome wasn't built in a day, and that every dark cloud is lined with sixpences and tickeys, Tiny told me about Jeegar's death. Horrible as it was, this was one death I didn't mind hearing about. Jeegar was no favourite of mine. It's one of those take-it-or-leave-it stories again.

The thing that killed Jeegar was the promise of a life sentence. That's what a Judge promised him if he ever got himself into trouble again. The Judge's words were hardly cold when Jeegar found himself lying in hospital under heavy police guard. He was shot while trying to run away from a railway trailer. While in hospital he begged and cried for his friends to help him escape. If it wasn't that he had some goods hidden, I doubt if Tiny and the rest of them would have bothered about him. They decided to try after the bullet had been removed. Jeegar would still be under chloroform; that way, he wouldn't feel any pains while he was being carried.

That night, dressed as hospital orderlies, they managed to wheel him away under the noses of the two African police guards. They were just placing him in the car when they heard a police whistle. Their car shot forward, taking the turn at the hospital gate on two wheels. They gained speed with every lamp post they passed. Two cars gave chase. "Make for Orlando Township," Tiny said. He was sure that they could lose them there. It was easier thought than done.

Their driver did his best to lose the two cars. He turned into every street that they came to, but the two cars stayed behind as if they were being towed. At last their driver saw his chance and took it. There was a taxicab coming from the direction of Orlando Station. The driver pressed his foot down hard on the gas pedal, causing their car to shoot out like a police bullet. The tyres of the taxi screeched as its driver brought his foot down on the brakes. They missed a hell-bound train by a fraction of an inch. The car behind wasn't so lucky. It went bonnet-first into the taxi. Man, the crash was terrific!

They turned two blocks and were about to take the third, when their car stalled and the engine went dead. They tried to restart their car, but there wasn't a breath left in the engine. "Let's carry Jeegar out of the car and try to lose ourselves," someone suggested.

As they carried the limp form of Jeegar out of the car, they noticed that he was bleeding freely. The wound must have opened during the chase. They were trudging along a dark alley when they heard a police whistle for the second time that night. This time the sound came from the direction of the abandoned car. They got rid of the white orderly uniforms and lost precious time.

At the back of them, at no great distance, they saw the lights of torches coming directly towards them. Frantically they looked around and saw a field of long, dry mealie-stalks at the back of a house. You could just make out the house in complete darkness. Without hesitating they lifted the unconscious form of Jeegar over the fence. They were about to carry him deeper into the dry stalks when one of them slipped. With a thud, Jeegar fell face down. They heard a deep groan.

"Leave him!" Tiny whispered frantically. "They can't see him. We'll come back for him later."

In single file they made their way to the front of the house. When they came to the gate, they saw a number of people running up the street. They joined them. Everyone was running to the scene of the accident. From the crowd they learnt that the driver of the taxi was killed instantly, and the ambulance driver who gave chase was badly hurt.

Then a policeman elbowed his way through the crowd and whispered something to the sergeant. Tiny saw them moving away. They turned into the alley where Jeegar was stored. The one that led the way suddenly stopped and shone his torch on their white orderly garments. Then he saw the blood spots. With an oath, he followed them. They led him to Jeegar who was lying face-down in a pool of blood. He turned Jeegar's body and the first thing that the light showed was the horrible expression on Jeegar's face. The policeman gave three short blasts on his whistle and in no time the alley was filled with police and curious onlookers.

A doctor pushed his way through. He bent over Jeegar and then straightened up and said, "He's dead. He died in agony."

The police sergeant said, "You mean the wound he was operated on opened up and he bled to death?"

The doctor wiped his forehead with a spotless white handkerchief and shook his head, "See that corn-stub? Whoever was carrying him dropped him face-down, and by some freak chance the corn-stub stabbed him through the cut he was operated on. It went right through his gut. You can see the toe-marks of his bare feet—he was wriggling in agony! God!" the doctor said heatedly, "this poor boy died horribly. I wouldn't wish the murderer of my own mother such a painful death!"

"God, Duggie," shuddered Tiny. "It was horrible. I mean the expression on Jeegar's face."

"Still," I said, "his worries are over, and ours, at least mine, are just beginning." If I had known just half of the truth of what I had just said, I would gladly have exchanged places with my left leg that lies buried somewhere in the Sahara Desert.

"What are your plans, Duggie?"

"At the moment, nothing."

"It's a pity," he said ponderingly. I looked up.

"What's a pity?" I asked suspiciously, without really wanting to know.

"It's a pity you've only got one leg."

"What's my leg got to do with the pity?"

"I can't drive a car, and you can't drive a car, yet all we need is a car."

"Leave the parables to Jesus Christ, Tiny, and tell me what's on your mind."

"There's nothing on my mind, Duggie, except lots and lots of money, plus clothes to tide both of us over the winter. I know where, and I know how."

"Tiny," I said heavily, "I was a transport driver in the army. I can do anything with any car, including locked

ones. All I need is for you to press in the clutch if I tell
you to."

Tiny sat up with a jerk. "No, man!"

"Yes, man!"

"Look, man . . ." He began to whisper furiously.

FOURTEEN

We were sitting in the stolen car. It was packed to capacity with stolen goods. Then we both heard it. The wail of a
squad-car siren.

"Stop looking over your shoulder, and press in the
clutch, damn you!"

"I'm not pressing in any clutch, I'm getting out of
here!" I tried to grab him but he was gone.

The police found me sitting helplessly and resigned
behind the wheel of the stolen car. . . .

When the dirty thought passed through my mind that I
should mess up my pants so that the stench would make
these prison warders leave me alone, I knew that I had
just about reached the end of my endurance. The mara-
thon beating-up had been going on for about three days.
Again the thought passed through my mind, but I dismissed it. How can there be anything in your bowels when
you've been three days without food? A baton hitting me
on the side of the jaw rudely jarred such intentions from
my mind.

Only half-conscious, I foolishly wondered what the hell
two tasteless sweets were doing in my mouth. Then it hit
me! These were not tasteless sweets, these were my front
teeth. The bastards had knocked my teeth out.

"Are you going to use it now, kaffir?" The million-
dollar question, I thought. I felt like screaming, but you
can't scream through swollen lips.

"No!" I managed to croak the million-dollar answer. "It's my property, not prison property."

Again the baton flew. This time it landed on my ribs. Barely conscious, I heard the chief say, "This is beyond me. I looked it up in all the prison rule books but I can't find anything that says that this convict is not right. After all, they did arrest him. And his artificial leg should be regarded as his property and not as part of himself. If he refuses to use it in prison, well, we'll just have to see where we can fit him. Maybe that's why he was sent to us. They didn't know what the hell to do with him at the Fort!"

"But," said the warder exasperated, "I can't have him hopping all over the damn place with one leg—besides, this bloody kaffir had his artificial leg on when he was arrested! Why shouldn't he use it in prison like he used it in that stolen car?"

"Wrong!" I thought. "My artificial leg is innocent. It was Tiny's leg that was supposed to press in the clutch."

"Don't forget," said the chief, "he also had his clothes on, a wrist-watch, a cigarette-case, a wallet, and small change that we are keeping as part of his property. Why shouldn't we keep his leg?"

"How in hell," said the resourceful warder, as he pushed the peak of his cap to the crown of his head, "is the bastard going to work if he's not prepared to use his artificial leg? I'm not running a jail for cripples!"

Nor did I ask to be arrested, I thought.

"You know the rules, Chief. They don't allow us to issue crutches as they may be used as dangerous weapons; now this black bastard has the gall to tell me that his artificial leg should be regarded as property and stored with the rest of his property. No, Chief!" pleaded Ambitious. "Give me three more days and I'll make this kaffir wear his leg."

Fort Glamorgan Prison, East London. My home for the next three years. Where I was drafted from Number Four. A prison within a prison. Home of the lost. Inmates have a name for it. They tag it the Shit House. The Afrikaners call it a *Straf Tronk,* jail of punishment. A prison where they confuse you for life in less than a year.

The warder got his wish. He dragged me to the segregated cells where the beating continued. He beat me in the morning before he started work, and in the evening when he was about to clock off. Hell, this man didn't even get a day off. He worked from Sunday to Sunday.

Whenever the door clinked shut on me, and I found myself alone, a depressed feeling clouded over me. I tried to laugh it off, as is my habit. Sometimes I would make jokes about my disability just to keep up my spirits, but the depressed feeling wouldn't go away. If I didn't have myself to blame, I would have cried. But I found it hard to pity myself because nobody was to blame but me.

Sometimes I felt like pacing the floor with my hands behind my back. But you don't pace the floor with one leg. You've got to hop, and hopping only jarred my brains. It also made me appear ridiculous. Imagine someone hopping up and down with his hands behind his back in the hope of trying to think out a solution. I had to try to preserve my energy. To try by all means to stay fit so as to be able to absorb the man's punishment. Because me, I'm not prepared to use my artificial leg in a prison. If it gets damaged, nobody is going to give me another one. I need it, it's my life. Without it, I might even sink lower in the outside world. Besides, it's too damn expensive.

The white man issues us blacks with wooden peg-legs. Only Europeans get legs that can be fitted with shoes. In fact, now that the war is over, they don't want to see a black ex-serviceman. They even go on to say that we blacks didn't fight, that all we did up north was to clean army boots. This makes me wonder whether it was a tin of shoe polish that fell on my leg, or a piece of shrapnel from Moaning Minnie's navel. So I was damned if I'd waste my leg in that rat-hole.

The following morning my cell door was rudely flung open. Instead of receiving my daily breakfast of moans and groans, I received a guest. A cell mate. He looked like an undernourished herd boy until you got to looking at his eyes. There and then I decided that this was no boy, nor had he ever been one. Not with those eyes. Milestones of hell. They were mud-red and deep-sunken. They told of a black past, a black present, and a blacker future.

One thing that stood out like the sharp points of a Zulu maiden's breasts was that this man-boy was ill. You could tell by the wheezing sound in his breathing, as if someone had punctured tiny holes in his lungs with a knitting kneedle, or as if he had swallowed a policeman's whistle. Brother, I thought, your days on earth are not as many as the fingers on your hands!

The Dutch bastard was bawling at the cell door. At first I thought he was talking to me, but what he was saying told me different. . . .

"You not only mucked your bloody cell with the shit from your bucket, you even plastered the walls with it, you dirty black swine! Sit on that bucket and empty your guts! The stomach-wash I gave you will produce those eight half-crowns you swallowed! When I come back in thirty minutes' time, I want to see that money lying at the bottom of that bucket—every penny of it!"

The cell-door clanked shut. The convict didn't even hear the guard. He was far too busy coughing his life away.

He was a shadow. You couldn't think of him as walking dead, because when you're dead and you walk, you walk because you don't want to stay dead. But when you're alive, and at the same time behave as if you're dead, then you have no respect for the living. When you added all this up, you got only one answer: waste. This man was nothing but a bloody waste.

At first I didn't understand what the prison warden was talking about, then I got it. The shadow had swallowed eight half-crowns. Now they were trying to get them out of him. The boys out at Number Four once spoke about stomach banks. This was it. To break the money-box, the prison guards give you a stomach wash with a syringe hose. Then they follow it up by forcing Epsom salts because the salts are as big as hail-stones. You are then placed on a toilet bucket and told to empty your bowels. Christ! I never thought I'd see the day they broke a stomach bank. Then something happened that very nearly made me scream foul! The shadow was playing foul. The bastard was re-swallowing the half-crowns as fast as they came out of his bowels. He wasn't even looking at them, let alone cleaning them. He gave me Zulu courage.

If this puny little man could openly defy his tormentors for so long—and it had been going on for days because I could hear them beating him up in the opposite cell—why should I give in to them so easily? They could go to hell and back and I still wouldn't use my leg!

And I did not. The morning after spending two days with my foul-smelling guest, I was made to hop to the prison yard where all the prison inmates gathered for their morning breakfast and daily orders. In this cemented yard that was surrounded by four formidable-looking walls, lay the heart of Fort Glamorgan. Whoever chose this particular spot for a prison must have had an intensive dislike for criminals. It is situated between the Buffalo River and the Indian Ocean. It's cold to freezing point throughout the year. There's a permanent visitor that frequents the prison every morning at six-thirty a.m. This visitor is so punctual that you could set your watch to it with dead certainty and never be wrong. Inmates have a name for this unwelcome visitor: The Mad Dog of the Ocean. Actually, it's a cold wind that blows from the sea. It has a mournful wailing sound like a dog that's being ill-treated by a cruel master.

When this mournful sound bounced off the four walls, it left us clouded in echoes of frozen misery. Our clean-shaven heads would be bleached with sea mist, our teeth would chatter, and our hands shake with uncontrollable spasms of hatred for this ill wind which has been responsible for many a convict's death.

One of the minor rules that added discomfort to misery at Fort Glamorgan was that when the convicts were gathered for their daily breakfast, which consisted of thick maize porridge, plus hot water dyed a dirty black and given the blessed name of coffee, it was an offence to sit flat on your buttocks. You were only allowed to rest on your haunches. Haunches! Hell, how can you sit on haunches with only one leg to support you? I sat flat! The convicts next to me giggled. After painfully forcing down the last lump of porridge that somehow got stuck in my throat, because coffee was only served to those who were serving sentences ranging from five years upwards, we were told to get up and line up.

Convicts working the East London harbour were first to be checked by the chief warden then marched out of the big gate escorted by six rifles and eight assegais. Then followed by the quarry span, then the plantation span, etc. At last my name was called. I was assigned to a platoon of twelve. Twelve bloody old men, I thought with disgust; these Dutch bastards have little respect for me.

As I understood it, we were to pick weeds out of the chief warden's garden. A nice and easy job. That is if you like picking weeds—God knows I don't! The only snag about this job was that the chief warden's house was situated on the other side of the prison, quite a distance from where we were.

"March!"

We marched. At least, I hopped. All went well as we passed through the big gate. It was only when we reached a newly-repaired gravel road that the soft sole of my one and only beautiful light-complexioned foot began to complain. From complaining it went to objecting. From objecting it started suffering. From there it was outright rebellion. I sat flat causing a minor disformation. In spite of the disruption, the platoon marched on. I thought I caught a gleam of amusement in the eyes of one of the old convicts. I couldn't care a damn. I was suffering, not him.

There I was, sitting flat on my buttocks in the middle of the road, busy massaging the sole of my foot. If they had given me one old shoe, all this wouldn't have happened. I might have made better progress. But now they know better. I suppose they do, otherwise I wouldn't have been there.

What was surprising was that my platoon guards hadn't missed me yet. Hell, I wasn't missing them either. But if those old convicts thought they could walk out on me, they had another thought coming. I looked around at my immediate surroundings, playing about with the idea of escape. Then I remembered that my leg was still locked up back there. Hastily I dismissed the idea.

Clever, I thought. Keeping my leg as security. They needn't have bothered, I'll never run out on any part of myself, not again. I've already left my real leg in the Sahara and I'm damned if I'm going to leave this one at Fort Glamorgan, whether it's real or not.

The thought of losing my artificial leg made me hop with renewed vigour after my platoon of convicts who now looked like the twelve disciples to me.

Ever tried hopping a long distance on one leg? Maybe you never had cause to. Well, I have. When you hop on one leg, you don't look where you're going. No. You watch the ground so as to see just where to place your foot on the next hop. This way you won't sprain an ankle. I was doing just that when I went charging after my squad.

When I looked up, it was too late. This was one collision that could not have been avoided. Not when I saw the guard's shiny boots right where I intended planting my next hop. I looked up too quickly, I shouldn't have. The back of my head got him squarely on the point of the jaw.

The contact was sickening. It jarred my brain, nearly causing me to black out. The only reason why I didn't lose consciousness, was the pain that seemed to spread like the tentacles of an octopus through my brain. An impact like two trains meeting headlong. I lost my balance and sat heavily on my buttocks, blinking the tears back into my eyes.

As for the prison guard, he was sitting directly opposite me. In fact, we were facing one another. The only difference was that his rifle was missing. Bashfully, I smiled at him, knowing quite well that what had happened was entirely his fault.

Then I noticed his glazed eyes. My God! The guard was out cold! I wanted to scream for a lawyer because I knew quite well what was going to happen to me.

Without a glance at me, the other guard went over to his unconscious companion and stood looking at him. After shaking his head once or twice, he sat on his haunches, it seemed to me, for a closer look. Then he pulled the skin under the glazed eyes of the guard. After that, he did a strange thing. He laughed. Christ, did he laugh! He laughed until he sat flat on his behind. I didn't like that. He was only going to make the unconscious guard more mad at me.

After what seemed an age, he got up, still laughing, and glared at me through tear-stained eyes. Then he looked about for his friend's rifle which he found lying four yards from where the incident had taken place. With the help of two black policemen, they got the injured man back on his feet. There he stood, swaying on rubbery legs, as if he had drunk skokiaan on an empty stomach.

Dazedly he looked for his rifle. His friend gave it to him. Then he squinted at me like someone who was looking directly at the sun. I just sat there waiting for them to help me up like they had helped him up.

"What do we do? Do we go on or do we go back?" It was the laughing hyena speaking.

"We go back, we'll never reach the chief's place with that thing along. I told the warder before we left the prison that I don't want that cripple convict in my squad. He told me that if we make this black bastard hop all the way to the chief's place, he might change his mind and use his leg. Cripples are bad luck; all cripples are bad luck, and as for this one, I'm going to make it my personal duty to escort him to hell and leave him there!"

In spite of the pain that was threatening to split my head into tiny atoms, I wanted to laugh at him. Because a missionary once said, all cripples are going to heaven, no matter what they do. He said it was better to enter the kingdom of heaven with one leg than with two.

"*Got!* I feel sick," complained the guard. Who doesn't? I thought.

"When I reach the prison I'm going to book off and go home." Good for you, I thought.

"About turn!"

"What about that convict?" asked the hyena.

"To hell with that convict!" came the fiery response.

When I saw that nobody was going to help me up, I got

up painfully from the ground and started the painful hop back to prison. I was the last to go through the big gates. Everyone was waiting for me. Even the chief warden. This made me feel important.

For knocking the guard unconscious, and for refusing to use my artificial leg, I was placed in solitary confinement on half rations.

That didn't change me. I looked the same when I came out. I could have told them that I'd been living on half rations all my life. In fact, the advantage was mine because, through lack of sunshine, my complexion was lighter.

By now I should have been a hardened convict that nothing could move. But every time I thought of Majola, I became unhappy.

Majola was in the segregated cells with me. He was from the outskirts of Pietersburg, somewhere in the Northern Transvaal. He was sentenced in Pretoria and landed here at Fort Glamorgan, protesting his innocence every inch of the way. He was fifteen years old and sentenced to fifteen years' hard labour. Only his youth saved him from hanging. According to Majola's lamentations, and he lamented every minute of the five years that he'd been there, he wept for nothing else, thought of nothing else than his unfair arrest.

At first I didn't pay him much attention because there isn't a convict I know who's not suffering from unfair arrest. We are always innocent. Especially men like me who are found red-handed behind the wheel of a stolen car packed with stolen goods. Every Sunday after exercise they would bring Majola into my cell while the other convicts cleaned his. He had long ceased to use the sanitary bucket, and no amount of beating would induce him to.

Majola's diagnosis was simple. Majola was mad. But the authorities wouldn't believe this. They said he was shamming.

Majola's story went like this. He was a herd boy for some sheep farmer. Sheep are no good. They are stupid animals, quite capable of getting any man into trouble.

The only good sheep is a dead sheep. I'm thinking of mutton.

One late afternoon while Majola was busy looking for a lost sheep, a storm broke loose that threatened to drown everything, himself included. Drenched to the skin, Majola vainly searched for shelter until finally, through sheets of rain, he saw a lonely hut. Relieved, he went to the hut and shouted a greeting from outside. A shrill voice from the inside said he could enter. Typical of all country huts, he had to go on all fours to get in. Inside, on a grass mat next to a roaring log fire, sat the oldest woman that Majola had ever laid eyes on. To him, this *go-go* (old woman) looked ageless.

After exchanging polite greetings with the ancient and explaining why he was there, Majola begged for shelter till after the storm. As he stood drying himself in front of the fire, steam emitted from his soaked clothes. The old lady said, "Take all your clothes off, son, and hang them on the nail you see there. That way, they'll dry quicker."

As Majola seemed to hesitate, she said, "Don't mind nakedness in front of me, my child. I'm an old woman and only fit for the grave."

There he stood, stark naked, enjoying the fire. He was oblivious of everything, especially the old lady. After all it was she who said that he shouldn't mind her. As the heat melted the cold in his bones, it also brought alive his sexual organ, but that didn't bother him, because he didn't feel any kind of urge. All the time the old lady was watching him covertly. She just couldn't pull her eyes away from the youthful figure of Majola. Maybe that's why her Adam's apple was bopping up and down in her wrinkled throat as she swallowed saliva after saliva.

"Son!" Majola stiffened, and the hair on the nape of his neck started to rise.

"Son, please, son, let me taste," begged Eve in her last days.

"No! *Go-go*, no!"

"Just this one last favour, my boy, so that I can leave this world happily. Please, son, no one need know."

After the act, the poor old darling sighed happily and

died. It was as if she had waited for nothing else but that.

Fearful of what had happened, Majola dressed hurriedly in his clothes that were now dry. He was buttoning the front of his trousers when the old lady's great-grandson came crawling through the opening, dragging a bag of wood after him. One look at his grandmother whose private parts were still exposed, one look at the fear-stricken face of Majola, and he was convinced that his grandmother had been raped to death. In spite of the wrinkled smile on the dead old lady's face, they didn't believe Majola's story. He was dragged before a judge and charged with raping an old woman to death.

You might not believe Majola's side of the story, but I do. No one on earth would repeat the same story time after time for five years until he went mad and not be telling the truth. Anyway, Majola went to heaven to go and look for the old bitch with every intention of choking her to death. I know I would have done the same.

Majola died one morning. What remained of him was found in his cell. He bled to death after cutting chunks of meat from his own body with thick pieces of glass that he managed to break from his cell window.

Once again I found myself in the prison yard of Fort Glamorgan. Still without friends. Only with guards whose eyes glared naked hatred at me.

I didn't give a damn. I might have lost a lot of weight, but I certainly didn't lose my pride which was very important if you were going to be a successful cripple all your life. Besides. I'd won the Battle of the Leg. Because here I was assigned to the task of cleaning mugs in the prison-yard.

The prison was jinxed. I just couldn't seem to stay out of trouble. One night when all the prisoners were safely locked up for the night, I was somehow overlooked. I found myself sitting very lonely in the yard. You see, the prisoners' sleeping-quarters at Fort Glamorgan are located upstairs. Three storeys above the ground. The only buildings found on the ground floor, are the hospital, the kitchen, the prison offices and a special cell for the monitors.

If anybody thought I was going to risk my second leg by hopping up those steep-looking stairs, they had another thought coming. They could have gone right on thinking. I wasn't born yesterday. It might be better to have one leg, but it certainly isn't good to have no legs.

Though it shouldn't have been so frightening, it was. I mean to hear the same guard that I once had the fortune, I mean misfortune, to knock out cold, scream, "Eeeeee!" in C sharp, when he saw me sitting on the bottom of the steps that led up to the prisoners' quarters.

He must have thought that he had locked up all the convicts for the night, yet there I was, sitting very lonely like the orphan I am. He sounded like someone who'd been knifed between the shoulder blades. Maybe he thought he was seeing a ghost.

"You!" he screamed, as if it wasn't me.

"Yes, baas," I stammered. It was the first time I had addressed a prison guard by the title of baas since I had entered the gates of Fort Glamorgan. I did it because I felt sorry for this boy who didn't know what to do with me. I think if I hadn't had less than a year to serve he would have resigned from his job. He clouted me with the bunch of cell-door keys on my clean-shaven head, leaving tiny dots of blood on my skull. Then he grabbed me by the scruff of the neck and started up the stairs at a running gait with me dragging behind in a sitting position. Each step hit me on the kidneys just above the buttocks. I was going to lose my manhood. I would never be able to produce children.

"You people don't seem to like me," I moaned.

"That's a bloody understatement!" he said.

"Then why don't you let me go?" I asked hopefully. He was panting when we reached the door of my cell.

"Let you go? I'll see you in hell first, you one-legged bastard!" With that he banged the cell door in my face.

The next morning I was carried down the stairs by two convicts who accidently caused me to fall on my face as we reached the prison yard.

I was painfully picking myself up, when I felt, rather than saw, someone standing over me. Looking up, I saw the same guard of the night before. I braced myself for whatever was coming and groaned in advance. Instead of the expected rifle butt, I heard him saying, "Report to the warden's office." This man amused me when he talked, he couldn't pronounce the letter "r"; he went *ghhhhh*.

When I entered the warden's office, the starch went out of my knee. It buckled, causing me to go down on all fours, I mean all threes. I had reason to. For sitting on a long bench directly facing me, were six of the biggest Afrikaners I had ever seen.

I wondered if they were real. When I last saw such big people it was out at the Church Square of Pretoria. They were standing around good old Paul Kruger, the father of Afrikaans history. Still, they were only statues. Now here I was seeing the same old bearded men. Only these were not statues, they were real flesh and blood.

Boers don't grow that big anymore. Sometimes I seriously wonder why. Now take these overgrown grown-ups of the ancient days, one look, and they reminded you of the playmates of "Mad Dog" Chaka, bulldozer of Africa and Lion of the South. These were the originals. The true illegitimate children of Africa. Men who could haul a covered wagon from a muddy river without consulting any cows. Christ! I was due for some real trouble.

"Get up!" said the guard behind me. I stood up, holding on to the wall.

"This is the convict, mynheer." They glared at me until I felt like a black piece of fat on the floorboards of a well-scrubbed cell.

One of them cleared his throat and it sounded like suppressed thunder.

"The members of the board of Fort Glamorgan have decided to set you free even if your sentence is not quite finished yet. We find that you are a worthless embarrassment to the authorities and a bad example to the convicts of this prison. It is felt that if you are kept here much longer, you will contaminate the convicts of Fort Glamorgan with your behaviour and give the prison a bad name."

He looked around at the others, and they all nodded their heads in agreement. "Dismiss!"

"Excuse me, sirs," I said. "This looks like an unconditional expulsion. If it is, how do I get home without a penny in my pocket or a jail warrant from you? You can't just put me out like that! Johannesburg is hundreds of miles away from here—besides, I didn't ask to be brought here."

"That's your look-out." The guard was dragging me away when somehow I got a few words across.

"When I get outside," I shouted, "I'm going to try and steal money for my train fare, and that might land me right back here!"

The words hit home. The results were instantaneous. The six giants turned blood red and the guard behind me gagged, I've never seen a rail warrant produced so fast. It was like magic.

When I got off the train at Johannesburg Station, it was raining in sheets. I stood undecided on the platform. I was wondering whether to take a bus to Sophiatown, or to squeeze my rail warrant to the end. Back at Fort Glamorgan I had made the authorities stretch it as far as Westbury Station just south of Johannesburg, near Newclare.

The crumpled piece of rail paper in the pocket of my old Army great coat decided me to go by rail. There was no point in wasting Government money. Besides, the station was right there. The bus-rank was some distance away.

I crossed the bridge and made for platform three and the Randfontein train. I hadn't been exposed to the rain yet, so I wasn't wet like most people around me. I was dry inside too. There was only one thought in my head, and that was for Sisinyana's skokiaan. It was as if I was possessed the way I was drooling at the mouth. Like a sex maniac in front of a nude statue. After forty-five minutes I dropped off from the Randfontein train at Westbury Station.

There's a big difference between Johannesburg Station

and Westbury Station. Johannesburg is far too big, Westbury is far too small. But that's where the difference ends, because as far as the rain was concerned they are equal. It was raining just as hard here as it did back there. I pulled up the collar of my great-coat to shield my neck from the rain. I was about to walk through Newclare and get into Sophiatown from the direction of the second gate.

I passed through the station's entrance to begin the long walk. Nobody took any notice of anybody. The rain saw to that. When I asked somebody for the time, all I got was a look that said, "Why don't you buy your own?" Instead of walking on the pavement under the shelter of the verandas, I chose the tar road because of its rough surface. I thought it better to suffer the onslaught of the downpour than to slip and fall on the smooth sheltered pavement. Past experience had taught me that an artificial leg doesn't agree with smooth wet pavements. The second reason why I was braving this storm rather than waiting it out under one of those shelters was because I was trying to get my clothes as wet as possible. If you think I was stupidly courting pneumonia, then I can tell you off-hand that were you in my shoes, you would have done the same! Have you ever had your clothes tied roughly in a bundle, dumped unceremoniously into a canvas bag and kept for three years in some hole they call a storeroom? That's what they did to mine at Fort Glamorgan.

I sighed with relief when I spotted the tram-line. It meant that I had less than a quarter of a mile to walk before reaching the big entrance that led to Sophiatown. I was walking with my head bent forward to keep the onslaught from getting me full in the face. When I reached the entrance of the second gate, I looked up.

Then I forgot everything. Past, present and future. Heavy raindrops lashed freely at my eyeballs, threatening to knock them out. I ignored them. You see I was staring. I didn't even blink. I closed my eyes tightly to drain the rainwater out of them. Also to make sure that the next time I opened them I'd see different. But it was not to be. I wasn't seeing things, I was seeing right. I blinked them again, then I started licking the rain from the tip of my nose and around my lips. The water tasted salty. I knew why. I was crying shamelessly.

Sophiatown was flat! A ghost town of grass and rubble. Slowly I crossed Main Road and stood stupidly at the spot where I had once waited for the baker's horsecart and helped myself to my daily bread. I looked up Good Street and could almost see the other end of it. Everywhere I looked, I saw nothing but grass and rubble.

I felt defeated. Like a king returned from war to find his kingdom smashed to dust. Worse even than that day in the tunnel when I came back home to find my father had sold the gramophone.

How I came to find myself at the corner of Victoria Avenue and Good Street, I'll never know. But there I was, standing forlornly at the deserted cross-roads of a black ghost town soaked in rain and despair. As I walked down Good Street, my artificial leg started to squeak. It was as if it felt the pain more than me.

Fort Glamorgan taught me one thing, and that was that crime was not for cripples. There was only one thing for me to do, and that was to look up Tim the trumpet player. First for a place to rest my head. . . .

Tim got me a job playing guitar for a jazz band known as the Black Crows. The Black Crows got me to Cape Town. No work, no food, too much booze put pay to the Black Crows, so I got me a job on a sugar boat as a potato peeler. This coaster did the runs between Durban and Cape Town, carrying cargoes of sugar.

When I got off at Durban, I liked what I saw. One look at the town and I decided that it was my kind of town. I was convinced that here a jazz band would prosper. Wrong again. . . .

FIFTEEN

"Let's try that number again."

"Try it yourself. I'm so bloody hungry I couldn't blow my nose, let alone a trombone!"

"Look, Duggie, why don't you give it up? It's no use, man, we've been in this cursed town for more than six months now, and what's the score? V.D.'s got our vocalist for life and our buggered-up pass books are going to take care of the rest of us. These Zulus don't know a damn thing about jazz. They make me feel like going into the jungle to play for the monkeys! At least monkeys clap!"

"Fana, are you trying to start a mutiny?"

"Mutiny, shit! I'm just trying to get you to understand—remember your own words when you first recruited us at Johannesburg? You said that Durban was jazz-hungry. You said—oh, you bastard, you said—Durban's money bags were all tied up in melody, and all we had to do to untie the strings was drop a few blue notes. And look at us! Not only have we dropped blue notes, we've dropped every colour of the rainbow and still no damn money! You want us to keep on playing until we're blue in the face? To hell with you, man!"

"Wait, Fana."

"What for? My pass is all crapped up because of that sweet tongue of yours."

"Gentlemen, I think we should all get together and talk this situation over."

"Situation, my arse! Look, Duggie, if you didn't have one leg, I would have beaten hell out of you. Why don't we just break up and let each one see his own way home? Why don't we, heh? Why don't we? Hell, man, that way we stand a better chance of reaching Joburg."

"Fana, stop raving."

"Better chance!" screamed a female voice very near hysterics. I turned; it was Zani, our vocalist. "Duggie, don't listen to him! If we split, what's going to happen to me? Don't forget that it's through all of you that I've got syphilis. You practically pushed me into whoring with those foreign sailors just so you big brave men wouldn't die of malnutrition. Now that I'm practically rotting away, you talk about splitting up and deserting me! We . . ."

"You enjoyed every minute under those sailors!" interrupted Fana.

"Now . . ."

"Shut up! Fana, you want her to go on, and on, and on?"

"Yes," continued Zani. "As I was saying, we all came from Johannesburg together and we'll all go back together or else each one of you will see his mother!"

I left them to fling words at one another. This was our only daily bread. . . .

We were all sprawled on the floor, far too listless to get up, when in came Brother Joe. Joe was our bouncer and handyman. Just how handy he could be, you'll soon learn. I found him in Durban when he was on the down and out, having escaped some criminal charge up Joburg way. He came into the room that morning with his arms heavily laden with parcels. Sleepily I watched him as he unloaded the parcels on the unsteady little table. As each parcel was being unloaded, my eyes grew wider.

I nudged Fana, who lifted his head and looked. Fana turned right round and resumed his interrupted sleep. He must have thought that he was dreaming, because I heard him whimper. Then he suddenly jerked, knuckling sleep out of his eyes so as to see better. He shook me roughly without shifting his eyes from the little table, as if afraid that what he saw might disappear. Well, it did not. It was food, and it was real. Six loaves of Jewish bread, six bottles of fermented milk and four tins of beef. After the feast everyone blessed Brother Joe.

As usual we had all prepared to go our different ways. There were no rehearsals. I was getting into my jacket when I heard Fana asking nobody in particular if they hadn't seen his shoes. No one seemed to be taking any notice of him. Then Fana turned to me with the same question. I shook my head. The formidable-looking form of Brother Joe was fast asleep in the corner, both his hands resting on his protruding stomach.

"Try Brother Joe," I suggested. Fana went to Brother Joe. Usually it was dangerous to rouse Brother Joe when he slept, but this was an emergency.

After carefully waking Brother Joe, Fana said, "Brother Joe, I'm sorry, but have you seen my shoes?" Joe blinked, then yawned. Fana repeated the question.

Then Joe nodded. "I sold your shoes this morning and bought food with the money."

When Fana continued staring stupidly at Brother Joe, his mouth hanging open, Joe hastened to add, "I didn't hold anything—honest, Fana. If you won't believe me, I can take you to the rickshaw shed where I sold them."

First, Fana looked like he was going to vomit. Instead he sat down heavily and cried. Brother Joe looked at him, shook his head, turned over and started snoring. It's not pretty to see a middle-aged man crying. There's something awful and sickening about it, especially if he's bearded.

"You—you—you sold my shoes, Brother Joe? Why, man, why?"

Without turning his head, Brother Joe said, "Number one, I didn't want you to die of hunger. Number two, I could have done it to any of you, only your shoes happened to have been the best." Fana went out into the back yard, his tears rolling into his beard. From then on, it was dog eat dog. Every man slept with his belongings clutched tightly to his bosom.

When we first came to the cottage at Victor Lane some seven months before, the Indian landlord had agreed to let it to us for seven pounds a month. We paid for the first month all right. The second month, our shows went bad. We suffered a string of flops. Most times there wasn't even enough money to pay for the hall after the show.

Secretly, without the knowledge of the landlord, we hired out one of the rooms to a Zulu washerwoman.

Whenever our pangs of hunger reached an unbearable peak, we would force this woman to pay her rent in advance, or threaten her with eviction even if she had paid only a week before. We would point out to her the importance of paying the rent in advance. Now she was a year ahead in her rent, so that dried up our only source of income.

You could ask why we didn't look for work. Work was out of the question. In the first place, we were looked upon by the authorities as illegal immigrants. If the Durban police found out that we were citizens of Johannesburg and not of Durban we were sure to be arrested, even if Johannesburg was only four hundred miles away. Our pass books carried the Johannesburg stamp, not the Durban one.

The more I thought of our situation, the more hopeless it seemed. Christ! It was as if we were marooned on another planet with only one wish: to come back to earth —I mean Johannesburg.

Listlessly, I opened the door to one of the bare rooms and there was Timothy's lean black body. Tim, our first trumpeter—you could actually count his ribs. He was trying to keep his balance with one foot while he pushed the other into the sleeve of an old, worn-out, navy-blue jersey. He lost his balance and his bony buttocks collapsed on the floorboards. Sweat streamed down his face.

He was so intent on what he was doing that he wasn't even aware of me. It was only when I coughed and said, "Tim, if you want to make that jersey underpants, why don't you cut the sleeves a little bit higher to make allowance for your thighs? Or aren't your thighs bigger than the top half of your arms?"

He looked searchingly at me as if trying to determine whether I was mocking. After satisfying himself that I was quite serious, he said, "They are my last damn trousers! The seat is so full of patches that I'm damned if I know where to put the next one." Broodingly he added, "It's a sin for a man with no wife and no children to wear trousers like these."

"We were talking about the jersey, not the trousers," I reminded him helpfully.

"Yes, yes, the jersey." He sighed, looking down at his knee where the sleeve of the jersey was stuck. "All the same, it's through the trousers that the jersey is suffering."

I didn't get it. As far as I was concerned, Tim was the only one who was in trouble and suffering. Still, I allowed myself to ask, "What do you mean, 'it's through the trouser that the jersey is suffering'?"

"The way you play your guitar, Duggie, convinces me that all your brains are in your fingertips. There's nothing up here," he said, pointing with the scissors at my head. "Look," he said, with patience that I never dreamed he possessed, "we agree that the seat of my pants has so many patches that it looks like a cabbage, right?"

I nodded my head, and with the corner of my eye searched for a place where I could sit. I was getting tired of standing.

Diplomatically, he said, "If we want to camouflage the hole that's going to get me arrested for indecent exposure, without adding another patch to the batch of patches, what do we do?"

"I don't know. You see, my trousers haven't got a hole."

"I know, damn you! I wasn't talking about your trousers, I was talking about mine. Who wants to hear about your bloody trousers?"

"Sorry."

"Well," he said, "where was I?"

"You said something about your buttocks getting you into prison."

"Not my buttocks, man! I was trying to teach you what to do if you ever found yourself in such a predicament." Hastily I made the sign of the cross, but he caught me.

"What the hell you making a cross for?"

"Nothing," I assured him. He scowled.

Pointing at the jersey, he explained, "I was going to camouflage my buttocks—I mean, the hole in my trousers, by putting a patch directly on my buttocks—I mean, by wearing this jersey as underpants. But now," he looked morosely at the jersey, "the damn sleeves are too small for my thighs."

"Look," I said, as an idea hit me, "why don't you tie the sleeves around your waist with a pin and let the bottom half of the jersey hang over your behind, and then wear the trousers on top?"

He brightened up. "Maybe I made a mistake about your brains being in your fingertips."

"Yes," I said, and there was a sarcasm in my voice. "My brains only come to my fingertips when I play the guitar. Most times you'll find them in my head." Then suddenly I laughed. I laughed until tears streamed down my face. Tim looked at me, then slowly nodded his head. Something like this had to happen after the way we'd been living these past few months.

"Don't worry, Dug," he said. "I assure you I'll stick with you. I promise I won't desert you—just as long as you don't become violent."

"What the hell are you talking about?" I asked wide-eyed.

"I thought your brains were going the way of your leg."

"Nonsense, Tim. You know what I was laughing about?" He shook his head. "Cape Town. The Black Crows in Cape Town."

He didn't look any the wiser. How to explain?

Durban is only four hundred miles away from Joburg, and if we had the strength and clean passes we could have walked it in less than a week. But Cape Town is nearly a thousand miles away from Joburg. You travel on that train until you come to think that the driver is either going in circles or that he's on the wrong track. In Cape Town The Black Crows had it bad—we ended up without musical instruments. Without anything. But what had really made me laugh was remembering our second trumpeter. He was a lot like Tim.

I once found him sitting quietly on the doorstep of a house in District Six. He looked so troubled that I found my heart going out to him and I went up to find out what was eating him. He just stared and stared, ignoring me.

After a time, he said, "Duggie, my shoes are so worn-out that it's just through habit that I put them on every morning. I'm telling you, Duggie, I walk alongside them and both the shoes and myself know it. Yet our pride won't let us part, or admit the fact. Only common decency keeps us together. My shoes are dead, Duggie, but it's hard, my friend, very hard to part with something that has walked the lonesome road with you without a single complaint. As I say, Duggie, my shoes are late but we won't admit it. But that's not my real worry. I only notice them when I happen to look down; and that's not often, because I don't have to look at what I don't want to see. The thing that's giving me real hell, the things that're threatening to drive me out of my senses are really my trousers."

I must have looked confused, because he continued, "If your trousers are torn at the back, Duggie, it doesn't matter so much because you can't see it except maybe when the wind blows in and you feel a draught. But when your trousers are torn at the knees, Duggie, it's pure hell, brother. Every time you sit, the very first thing you see are your dirty knees. They don't only remind you that your trousers are torn, but that you need a bath badly, too."

Cape Town. I hated the bloody town and all the people in it. The coloureds for instance.

You know what my introduction to Cape Town was? I had got off the train at Cape Town Station and started looking around for the toilet. I found it next to the station's entrance. I passed through the door marked "Non-Europeans". Inside, I was confronted by four closed doors; written on each of these four doors were the words: "Insert Penny To Turn Slot." You have to pay to relieve yourself.

Standing in front of one of these closed doors and discussing women were two rough-looking Coloured characters. Just as I approached the first door, it opened and someone came out. Without breaking my stride I went in and closed the door behind me.

Man! I never heard so much abuse thrown at me in all my life! These characters have got no pennies of their own, so they wait for someone to come and use the toilets, and when he comes out they block the door before it locks itself. This way, they get a free shit. I've never in all my born days heard such swear words. They started with my great-grandmother and ended up in the maternity home where my mother was the leading lady. Then one of them suggested that I should be shaved. That meant they were going to go over me with cut-throat blades. Hell, there was only one thing to do, and I did it. I took a handful of loose change from my pocket and sprayed the coins over the top of the door. While the swines scrambled for the money, I opened the door and sneaked out. But not before I heard one of them say, "You're lucky, kaffir Yank." That's the name they use for blacks who are smartly dressed.

But that's not the real reason why I want nothing to do with the Coloured race. The real reason started just when I crossed the parade grounds into District Six, the Coloured man's domain. I was suffering from a hangover that nothing short of foaming skokiaan could fix. It was threatening to drive me dog-mad. After racking my brains for a substitute, I decided on brandy. But the trouble was, we blacks weren't permitted to enter liquor stores, so I was forced to look for a shebeen.

Just off Castle Bridge I saw a Coloured man who looked like he could help me out. After chatting a bit, I asked him if he knew of a place where I could buy some brandy. He thought a while, and then he said, "I know a friend who knows of a place where you can get fixed up." He led the way and I followed happily.

In a few minutes we were at his friend's place. His friend said after we told him what we were looking for, "That's easy. Come along—I know of a friend who knows a friend that knows the spot." I should've smelt a rat then, but I didn't.

When we reached the friend that knew a friend who knew the spot, that friend said, "You shouldn't have gone to all this trouble." Subconsciously I agreed with him. Because, he went on, his friend's friend knew of a friend that actually has a friend whose only friend owned the best shebeen. . . .

I ended up entertaining more than a dozen Coloured bastards. When I finally joined the rest of our band members, I had a lousy two-shilling piece to my name out of three whole bloody pounds!

Do you want the Coloured in a nutshell?

When God said to the Afrikaner, "What is your major wish?" the Afrikaner answered, "All I want, Lord, is strength and fertile soil." The Englishman, when God asked him, replied, "Education, Lord, education!" When He turned to the Jew, the Jew tapped his head and said, "Brains." Before God could say another word, the black man said, "I'm a simple man, Lord. All I want is a pick and a shovel." Then God turned to the Coloured man and said, "Well, what can I do for you, my good man?" His hands in his pockets, the Coloured man turned and looked at the black man. He shrugged his shoulders and said, "I was just keeping him company, Lord. . . ."

To get back to Durban. . . . At last, one morning, I was able to call a meeting. Thomas was the last to come in.

"Is everyone here?" I asked.

Thomas nodded. "Except Alpheus. It's his turn to do guard duty."

"Never mind, get him. I'm beginning to think that it's not necessary. That Indian landlord was just bragging when he said he was going for the cops.

"Where's Zeblon?"

"He's scared to put his foot in here since he pinched the washerwoman's boss's shirt from the washing line."

"How does she know he pinched it?"

"How couldn't she, when that's about all he's wearing?"

"All right, all right. Just get the rest of them in here. This is important.

"Early this morning," I told them, "I spoke to an Indian by the name of Hadjee. He owns a café-night club. Hadjee has agreed to sign us on for Saturday night on a fifty-fifty basis. We don't pay for the use of the club and he doesn't pay us a fee. Whatever money we make, we split fifty-fifty with him. I also checked on the ships.

There'll be at least four American cargo-ships in the harbour on Saturday night. So no matter which way the dice roll, we must come out with something."

Sunday morning, as we came back from Hadjee's nightspot, everyone was in high spirits. Even Zani had forgotten the sores on her feet. The show had been a near-success. I was the only one who felt depressed.

They all gathered in the room. "I'm happy to tell you that we've scored exactly ten guineas. Enough to get five of you to Johannesburg." They all beamed. The bastards. Not one of them was interested in knowing what was going to happen to me. To hell with them, I thought. The sooner they get out of my sight, the better.

After giving each his two pounds one and six, which was a single third-class fare to Johannesburg, I was left with a half-crown.

"Now, Fana, Tim, all of you. Before we part I'd like to thank you for sticking with me so long.

"In Joburg you are going to have a lot of trouble straightening out your passes. You haven't renewed your work-seeking permits. If you say you were sick, they'll ask for a doctor's certificate. To go to a private doctor for one is asking for trouble; they know that private doctors can be bought.

"So your best bet is this: go to the address on this piece of paper. You'll meet a friend of mine there. He goes under the name of Zuluboy. Zuluboy will put you in contact with someone who will get you prisoners' discharge papers. They'll be quite genuine; it will be written on them that you have been released from Leeukop prison—that's where they keep the vagrants. Those papers are the only ones that will save you from a six- to nine-month prison sentence. Don't be ashamed of carrying such papers. In this country it's not a disgrace for a black man to have been to prison; prison to us is just a break from monotony. So if such papers can be of some use, why not make use of them? Me, I know of no other way, and I should know.

"Another thing, go to Singh's Billiard Saloon. There you'll find Hakkeltjie, the Coloured drug smuggler from

Cape Town. Ask him to go and buy your rail tickets for you. We blacks can't buy long-distance train tickets without the proper travel documents."

When everyone had gone, I looked around the bare room and felt a lump in my throat. Legal or illegal, everything I touched turned black.

I took my last crumpled cigarette from my pocket and made myself comfortable in one of the corners of the bare room, to wait for darkness. I didn't dare venture out this early. Not while I owed all the shops in Grey Street food money.

One thing was certain, I'd have to change my sleeping quarters. But where to go to? Durban stank of one problem. All the domestic servants were men. In Johannesburg we have women. You could always make love to one of them and live with her in her room at the back of the master's house. No rent, free food and one or two of the boss's shirts while he imagined that they were in the wash.

In Durban there was no such thing. Otherwise I wouldn't have bothered with sleeping accommodation. I would have done what I used to do back in Johannesburg: made love to one of the working girls and lived with her, even if living in the back yards of white men's houses is not without its ups and downs.

I'm reminded of one night when I went to my girl's room at the back of a white man's house. It was late when I got there and my girl must have long been through with her duties. What I really remember about that night, is that it was so cold that my nose wouldn't stop running. When I got to the room I knocked. But there was no reply. I tried again, still with no results. I made for the spot where she always kept the key for me to find when she was on her day off, but I drew blank.

Again I repeated the knock and still nothing happened. I was afraid to knock loud for fear of waking up the house. That time of night they have a dangerous tendency of shooting first and asking questions after. After repeated knocks, I gave up. I decided to think.

One thing stood out like the point of a Zulu warrior's spear, and that was that if I tried reaching Sophiatown at that time of night, I would end up in jail for not having a night special.

I looked around for a place to spend the night, but could see none. Then I realised that I was leaning against one of those giant trees that are so frequently found in white gardens. Without a moment's hesitation, I climbed the tree, meaning to spend the remainder of the night there. Better a human bird than a jail bird.

I must have dozed off because something startled me. I would have fallen head first to the ground if I hadn't taken the precaution of tying my belt to a branch and then around my arm. I peered into the night hoping to see what it was. Then I heard a noise coming from my girl's room. Someone unfamiliar with the mechanism of the lock was fumbling with it from the inside.

Hurriedly I undid my belt from the branch. My fingers were numb with cold and my descent was not without hazards. Finally, I made the ground with little more damage than bruised hands and a tear in my pants. I was in time to see a stark naked figure emerging from the door and making his way to the toilet which was situated on the other side of the garden. Like lightning I went into the dark room and locked the door behind me. I groped towards the bed where the bitch was deep in sleep. Undressing quickly, I crawled into bed. As my icy body came into contact with hers, she moaned and said, "Why so cold, dear?"

"Shut up, you bitch." I felt her shiver, and knew it was not from cold.

I waited. Then it came. First softly, then loud, then louder, then frantic. It was the naked bum outside. Unlike him, I raised my voice triumphantly and said, "Climb the tree, pal, climb the tree." As usual, I'm not the brainiest of men. There are people with far more. This son of a bitch pushed the mouth of the garden-hose through the small window, and before I knew what was happening, the water tap was turned on full force, soaking me, bitch, blankets and all.

I checked to look at the time on my wrist, then remembered that my watch was in the pawn shop. It was dark outside, time for me to get going. I groped for my walking-stick, then decided to stick around a little longer. Think before you move. Having reviewed the wealth of accommodation alternatives, I turned my attention to thoughts of transport. Four hundred miles, more or less. Do I walk it? Thanks. Stow away on a train, ride in the toilet? My jaw itched, thinking of the sturdy fist of the law. Which left me with one alternative. The one I hit Durban in when I came down starry-eyed to book halls and accommodation for my players. I call it my Jonah trip. You know the Bible story of Jonah and the whale? That's the story, except Jonah began in a ship. I began in the whale.

At eleven o'clock every Saturday night there is a special closed news van that leaves Johannesburg to deliver the Sunday newspapers to Durban. This van arrives here in Durban about two hours after midday.

That night at Marshall Street I was drunk. I watched them feeding the red monster with endless bundles of newspapers. There was a Zulu man who worked inside the mechanical whale. Every time a bundle was heaved into the van, he would drag it further in and pack it. When the van was finally loaded, I walked unsteadily nearer so as not to be left behind. The driver was about to close the doors when he chanced to look over his shoulder. "Get in. get in," he said. I nearly asked, "In where?" because I could see no place to perch myself. But that would have been looking a gift whale in the mouth.

I found myself lying flat on my back, both arms pressed tightly to my sides. The tip of my nose was two inches from the roof of the van. The driver slammed and locked the doors, shutting out the only light that came from the street, leaving the insides of the van in complete darkness.

Man, sardines were a hundred per cent better off. The damn things were at least dead. The four-wheel monster started to move. At the same time my misery which was hitherto only misery, became painful misery with every turn. The knob of my walking-stick, which was pressed close to my side, seemed about to cave my ribs in. If my presence wasn't illegal, I would have taken the matter up with the news manager. Then I made a hair-raising mistake. I dozed off. When I came to, I nearly screamed. You see, I had forgotten where I was. As I tried lifting myself, my head banged against the ceiling, leaving a lump as big as a dove's egg on my forehead. I tried lifting my knee but only succeeded in banging it. As for the top half of my body, it wouldn't move at all. This brought me to the logical conclusion that I was in a nailed coffin.

I was about to fill my lungs with whatever air there was and scream like hell, when I heard a baritone voice praying in the Zulu language. I was damn sure it was my ancestors, though I didn't think I wanted to meet them. Not if they were going to inquire about my past. Imagine my relief, when my drink-befuddled brain slowly recalled the incidents of the past few hours. As for the voice that seemed to come from the long departed, it really belonged to that African worker who had been packing the bundles into the back of the van. To ease my fear, I began a shouting conversation with him.

He told me that in spite of the fact that he was on this run for three months now, he was damned if he could get used to these trips. Just the idea of being locked up in a closed van with only one door that couldn't be reached in an emergency because of the bundles of newspapers, and even if you could reach the door wouldn't open because the lock was on the outside, was enough to make any man cling to God's apron. I didn't blame him for drowning his fear in prayer. I know I would have done worse.

That was how I came to Durban, and that was how I was going to have to go back. But this time, I wouldn't have to worry, because, when the van goes back, it goes back empty. No newspapers, no inconvenience. . . .

SIXTEEN

A knock sounded through the whole house. Police, I thought; never underestimate an Indian landlord. The door was flung open and someone was shouting my name. It was Tim. I'd know that voice anywhere.

"What's up?" I called.

He was out of breath as he said: "You remember you told us to go to Hakkeltjie for our tickets?"

"Yes," I said.

"Well, Hakkeltjie took the money, all right, only he bought his own ticket to Cape Town. He's gone, I tell you, gone! Gone! Gone!"

I groaned. I had forgotten Hakkeltjie's soul-dream. In fact it was no different from ours. He was forever dreaming of the day when he would return to his happy hunting grounds armed with a bottle of red wine in his back pocket.

"You tell me how the Coloureds make out by living off the next man, yet you still send us to them. If I didn't see him jump on the Cape Town train with my own eyes, I would have said that you're in with him. What I want to know from you here and now is how the hell are you going to get us out of here? What are we going to do?"

"Wait, Tim. Let me think."

"Don't!" he almost screamed "I don't trust your thoughts—just get us out of here!"

"I know how to get myself out of this mess, but definitely not all of you."

"Why not all of us?"

"Because that Dutch driver will never agree to a mass removal—it might get him into trouble."

"What driver? What the hell are you talking about?"

"Hang on," I repeated, "let me think."

"But I don't trust your thoughts. . . ." Tim began again.

I was tired of hearing these words, so to shut him up I said, "There's only one thing we could do, Tim." His eyes brightened up. I could actually see the whites of his eyeballs in the gloomy room.

"What, Duggie, huh?"

I let him stew a bit before saying, "We could sell your trumpet,"

"Sell my trumpet? Are you mad?" He was shaking visibly. Sometimes I had wondered who came first, himself or his trumpet. Now I knew.

"Where the hell will I get another outlet for my misery? Tell me, man, tell me that!"

"You can always buy another," I said slowly, hedging away.

"This trumpet to me, Duggie, is like that artificial leg is to you. Inseparatable, inseparatable, see? So see that you keep your dirty mind out of it."

"All right, Tim, I was only pulling your leg."

"Pull something else, you bastard. And," he added meaningly, "if anything should happen to my trumpet, I'll know who's responsible!"

I cursed myself. Now I was stuck with the job of seeing that nothing did happen to his bloody trumpet. This task would have been easy if Brother Joe wasn't living amongst us.

"All right, all right, damn you, forget it! Where's the rest of the gang?"

"Zani went wild, she dashed off shouting for the police at the top of her voice."

"Hey, she could get us all into trouble!"

"No, we caught her. She led us one hell of a chase, but we managed to bag her just off Smith Street."

"Where are they now?"

"At the Esplanade. Fana is trying to talk some sense into her. She'll be O.K."

Poor Zani, I thought. That running must have opened the sores on her feet.

I could understand Tim's horror at having to part with his instrument. In Johannesburg, whether you're working or not, it's hard to have ten whole pounds all at one time. As for twenty-five, the approximate price of Tim's trumpet, well, that's completely out of the question. If you buy it on the Play-While-You-Pay scheme you are sure to be the loser in the end.

In fact, many things can happen to you before you come to the last instalment. You'll find most of them listed in your pass book which more or less tells you not to get sick, see that your rent is paid on time, plus your tax, be out of any white area by ten p.m., do not choose work, just take work, because as I told you before, you are only allowed three work-seeking permits and when you go for the fourth, they hang a vagrant sign on you, then send you to the nearest potato farm. When you come back, they endorse you out of town. How the hell can you finish instalments with odds like that stacked against you?

Tim certainly wasn't exaggerating when he spoke of his trumpet as the only outlet to his misery. He was not going to be long for this world. He put too much emotion in his playing, tugging and tugging at God's apron strings like a jealous disciple that wants to be noticed. I sat in the yard with Zani and the old washerwoman. His sound came through the back door. A mournful, bleeding sound.

Jesus! The old washerwoman—it was as if she was in a trance of some sort. She was rocking from side to side in time to the wailing of Tim's trumpet. The balls of her eyes were protruding. She was not of this world. Even poor tired Zani with her raw painful feet was fascinated.

Suddenly, the music broke off. There was a slight commotion. I got up to go and find out why Tim had so suddenly shut off his sweet, haunting music. As I side-stepped the old lady at the door step, she said, "You know why I don't mind so much when you boys crook me out of my money?" Before I could frame an indignant reply, she said, "It's because of the beautiful music that that boy makes."

Inside, I found Joe. He was with three American merchant seamen. They were in search of drinks and girls. This was good. It meant we were going to eat. After that, anything might follow. Negro seamen are noted for their generosity. We could expect anything.

Something did follow. We got money for food, plus a promise of some second-hand clothing. When their ship sailed for some distant port, blues settled on us again.

Without a moment's hesitation we agreed that Joe should take and sell the second-hand clothing at the rickshaw sheds where they buy and sell anything, including fat from a white woman's rump. They claim this fat, if rubbed on the right spot, could secure you the post of boss boy in any firm. Or if you want the dirt from a monkey's toenail, to stop a leaking ear, that's the place to get it.

They even sell gent's socks. You can get new ones, second-hand ones, dirty socks—you've got to wash these yourself. Then there are the darned socks. The ones with holes in them are the cheapest.

While Joe was gone, I tried to think of a way to get the gang out of town. I was becoming desperate. I thought of selling my guitar, but it wouldn't amount to much. Also, I wouldn't get a fair price for it.

We had a hundred-and-twenty bass piano-accordion that we didn't often use. We agreed to sell it for food money, and I was elected salesman. There was a teenage Indian boy who was very interested in the accordion. I took it to him. When I got there he suggested I leave the accordion with him and come back later when his father would be present. Apparently he couldn't do anything during the absence of his old man.

Later, when I got there, I walked right into a family row. The father was giving the son hell for doing things without his knowledge. I was completely ignored while it went on.

"You know I can't stand noisy things!" said the father. "In fact, I hate musical instruments of any kind. Now here you are, the only son that I have confidence in, actually trying to buy this thing behind my back. What's going to happen to your studies once you get busy keeping the family awake with the noise of this thing?"

Turning to me, he said, "I'm sorry, friend, but this boy of mine is getting out of hand. He's trying to do things without my consent. And I shall never allow it. This is a respectable family, not a noisy family. Music should be left to snake-charmers. Now, my friend, take your instrument and go. I'm sorry he has wasted your time." While all this was going on, the boy didn't say a word. He just stood there with his head bowed. I felt sorry for him.

I was struggling to go through the door, bent double under the weight of the accordion, when he called me back.

"Look, my friend," he said. "The boy tells me that you people are stranded and need some money. Well, I'm not a bad man at heart. I'll tell you what I can try and do for you. I'll give you five pounds for the instrument to help you out. That's all I can afford. I'm losing because I'm not a music man. I just don't want to see another man suffer."

So saying, he produced five single notes. He didn't even glance at them. It was if they were just lying in readiness for this very purpose. Come to think of it, maybe they were. Fearful that he might have a change of heart, I took the money and hurriedly made him out a receipt.

That night my surprise turned to disgust as I stood in the same shop buying food with part of the money he had given me. In a backroom of the shop, I saw the same music-hating old man surrounded by an admiring family of fifteen. He was singing an Indian song in a high-pitched wailing voice to the accompaniment of a wrongly-harnessed accordion.

Ever since that night, I toyed with the idea of meeting that teenage boy in some dark doorway, because something told me that he was in league with his father.

Joe's voice interrupted my dirty intentions. "Duggie!" he shouted. He was carrying a ten-pound bag of cornmeal and a paperbag full of pork bones. As he unloaded the stuff he said, "Duggie, we'll never starve again, I found a hole where we can get pork bones bone-cheap."

"Better tell the boys," I said, "in case we need some when you're not around."

While Brother Joe was explaining the whereabouts of the pork bone hole, I went to the washerwoman for the loan of a pot to cook thick porridge. This kind of porridge not only gives you stamina, it also keeps you fed for quite some time. If my mind wasn't always working overtime, I would have thought of thick porridge, instead of bread, bread. After all, porridge is our staple food. It's cheaper than bread and more filling.

I stirred the porridge, thinking that the Government guards our movements so jealously that I sometimes wonder why we should feel so lost. Christ! I'm glad I'm already mad, otherwise I'd worry about myself. Take these boys, for instance. Not one of them has ever seen the insides of a prison, but just because one rubber stamp is missing from their books, they face a two-year prison sentence at Leeukop where their thighs are going to be used as piss-pots by some long-term convicts.

There was one sure method of getting them to Johannesburg, but it was such a round-about way that it would take a hell of a long time before it could be made to work. The only snag was Zani. If she wasn't so feverish about going home, I could have talked her into remaining with me until a suitable way presented itself. But her itch for home itched worse than the sores on her feet. What made this way unsuitable for Zani was that it was a man's way.

In each large town in South Africa there's an office with a sign board that boasts a picture of a well-built African standing spread-legged and smiling in a miner's uniform. Printed around this impressive picture in bold colourful letters, are the words: "Native Recruiting Corporation." The illiterate Africans refer to these offices as the Join because they are the depots where they join, or sign contracts for work in the goldmines in and around Johannesburg. This is one place where they never bother about asking for your pass. Why should they, when you're about to sell yourself for thirty shillings a month? All they do is put a dog label with an engraved number around your neck like they do in the army, then escort you to the mines. After your three-year contract has expired, they escort you back. You're not permitted to wander around.

Now, if I could get Tim and the rest of the boys to agree, I could get them to sign on and then when they get to Johannesburg Station, they could easily give their escorts the slip. Maybe. . . .

"Duggie!"

"Huh?" It was Zani.

"Can't you smell something? The porridge is burning."

"Sorry, Zani, I was far away."

"Then come back, man. You're starving us. The boys are impatient, they want to eat and go!"

"Take over, Zani, and leave my share in the pot."

SEVENTEEN

I was happily swinging my artificial leg down the main street of Durban as if there was nothing better in the whole world to have than one leg and two-legged people didn't know what they were missing. It was only when I looked over my shoulder at the taut, naked breasts of those beautiful Zulu maidens who were selling beads to passersby that I swung the leg too fast. The sharp contact of the heel with the cement pavement would send a sharp pain up my thigh and acid words from my lips. I had every reason to be happy, I had at last hit upon a plan of how to get my crowd out of Durban. I stopped at the corner of Field and Smith Streets. This was where the phone-book told me I'd find the social worker's offices.

It didn't take long to tell them the whole story of how we landed in Durban and what had happened ever since. I made a clean breast of everything. After I was through, the nice white lady said, "Wait a minute, aren't you the boy who lost an artificial leg in Umbilo Park?" I nodded gravely. I didn't want to be reminded of it.

"Sorry," laughed the social worker as she looked at my gloomy face. "I can't help laughing whenever I think of that incident." More seriously she said, "You do get into strange kind of troubles, don't you?" I swallowed and nodded my head. "Go to the address where you are staying, I'll see what can be done." I left, knowing in my heart that something would be done.

The next day the social worker came to the cottage. She told us that she would give us a loan of fifteen pounds and that she'd keep one instrument as security. She assured us that we could take our time in paying the money back. Meantime we needn't worry about the instrument. It would be quite safe.

That night I sighed with relief as the Johannesburg train pulled out of Durban Station. The strains of "Blues in the Night" from Tim's trumpet kept me rooted to the platform until the train was long out of sight.

For me, it was the news van. I wanted to save my ticket money which I was sure I was going to need once I got to Johannesburg. It was Thursday. I had two full days before Sunday. There was nothing for me to do except go back to the cottage.

When I got to the cottage, I found the old washerwoman at home. She was busy cooking on the old stove. I sneaked into the gloomy room, not wishing to meet her. I went straight to my favourite corner and sat down on the floor-boards. I was about to take my artificial leg off and rest my stump, when I heard a soft knock on the door. It was the old lady. Without a word, she bent awkwardly and placed a plateful of thick porridge and meat in front of me.

Straightening up, she said, "They gone?" I nodded. "I feel sorry for the girl." As an afterthought she added, "And you, too." She left closing the door softly behind her.

I didn't feel like eating anything. There was nothing that my stomach could take. It was too bloated with defeat. All I wanted was to sit in this gloomy corner and not even think. Tim was right when he said, "Don't think. Your brains are not to be trusted."

Everything I touch becomes black sticky liquid, like tar. I had thought the loss of a leg would encourage or somehow force me to lead a serene life. Instead it was the other way around. Pass laws are tough, but pass laws combined with one leg add up to sheer hell.

The bladder in my stomach was still swelling with defeat when Joe came in. He was sweating and out of breath. In his grip was a large suitcase. He dumped it unceremoniously on the floor, and sat heavily next to it. I winced as his buttocks thudded on the floorboards. His fingers started fiddling with his shoe-laces. I got up and opened the window. Brother Joe's feet are noisy enough when reposing in the shoes, but once out of there, they shriek. He kicked them away one after the other. His socks were hopelessly torn. They reminded me of ankle-guards, because that was as far as they reached. The ankle. Like soldier's puttees. Between the toes were wet, bluish stains of dirt. Regardless of that, Joe started massaging his toes one by one, as if rubbing the wet stains into the skin.

After studying his socks critically, he said, "You know, Duggie, there are only three things worrying me in this whole world. Socks, underpants and a pass. If I could get those three things, I think I could grow fat. I just wouldn't have a care in the world."

I sat thinking, "Joe has very little worries."

"Mind you, Duggie, it's not the money. I get that now and again just like I got this suitcase."

Disinterestedly I asked, "What is it, Joe?"

"It's, it's . . . hell, I don't know," he said impatiently. "But everytime I have some money I forget I need these things. They are just not in my mind. I never find myself walking into a shop and telling the shopkeeper to give me a pair of socks and underpants. Just one, Duggie; not many, mind you, just one. Like I do when I go into a shop for cigarettes, or a shebeen for liquor."

Still without interest, I asked, "Why, Joe, why can't you go into a shop and buy your own underpants, if they worry you so?"

Musingly he said aloud, "If someone could snatch my money from me and run into a drapery shop and buy me underpants, maybe that could help." Still looking at a spot between his toes, he added, "But I mustn't catch him."

I spat.

"I just can't understand myself, Duggie."

"Why?"

Irritably he said, "You keep on asking why. Isn't that what I want to know? For instance," he went on, "when I'm penniless, and my intestines have tied themselves into reef-knots because of hunger, in every shop window I pass, I see all kinds of juicy cold meats and fried fish that have me drooling. But when there's money in my pocket, I don't see these things. They are just not there. You know that upstairs shebeen house in Grey Street before you get to Leopold Street on your right-hand side from the direction of Victoria Street where cane spirits are being sold left and right? At five shillings a quarter?" I shook my head, he was too fast for me.

Ignoring my headshake, he went on, "There's a drapery shop at the entrance where they sell underclothing dirt cheap. You can get a pair of underpants for as little as two and sixpence. Upstairs is the shebeen. Duggie, you won't believe this, but I never see those underclothes when I go up. I only see them when I come down. Every time I come downstairs from the shebeen above, I see these underpants. Then I swear on the head of my late mother that the next time I go there, I'll start with the underclothing. But these vacant promises have been going on for six months. Now I've stopped patronising that shebeen because it shows me my true self by dangling what I'm made of right in front of me. No man wants to be shown exactly what he is and that's what that place has done. I can afford a quarter of cane spirits, but I can't afford a pair of underpants. Hell," he finished off lamely, "I had to stay away from that place. After all, I've also got a conscience."

"What's in that suitcase?"

"How the hell should I know? I haven't opened it yet. Had to run like blazes."

"You don't have to jump down my throat, I was only asking."

"Sorry, Duggie, for a moment I was feeling bitter with myself. Is the gang gone?"

"Yes, Joe; they pulled out."

"Good riddance. They were more of a burden to you than a help. Now you and me will be able to think better."

"There's nothing to think about, Joe, except, maybe, how to get back."

"Whose plate of food is that, Duggie?"

"Have it, Joe, I just don't feel like anything."

Joe was wiping the plate with the last bit of porridge, when he screwed up one eye and said, "It's funny."

"What's funny?"

"That rickshaw."

"What rickshaw?"

"The owner of that suitcase."

"Oh, what about him?"

"He caught me red-handed lifting the suitcase from his cart. I ran like hell down Smith Street with him not far behind, in his hand he had a chumenchu. Why I didn't abandon the suitcase I'll never know, because the damn thing kept on banging on my knee. Anyway, even if there was no suitcase I would never have won the race. Running is the man's daily bread—he earns his living from it.

"But here is the funny part. At the corner of Grey and Smith Streets I decided to stop trying to outrun a Zulu stallion, and start fighting for my life. I dropped the suitcase and turned. He in turn jumped high up in the air and landed on his haunches reciting the 'Thanks of Chaka'. They all do that when they are about to put up a good fight.

"Just then, a white policeman came. I was panting heavily.

" 'What's going on here?' asks the policeman. The rickshaw dazed me by saying, 'It's nothing, baas, was just running.' Then he backed away, turned and left me gaping at his muscular bare back. The policeman said, 'It didn't seem like nothing to me.' Before he could think further, I picked up the suitcase and walked away. This is it. Now can you tell me why the hell the man didn't lay a theft charge on me? After all, it is his suitcase and I did steal the damn thing!"

"I think we better let the suitcase explain," I said.

"What the hell do you mean let the suitcase explain?" asked Joe densely. "Suitcases can't talk!"

Calmly I said, "Open it."

He did. When he stood back from the open suitcase, he said only one word, and there was disgust in his voice, "Ganjha!"

Ganjha is the Indian term for the South African drug known as dagga. Marijuana. A few puffs from it could even make your pass book look like a Bible.

"There's your answer."

"Christ!" said Brother Joe, badly shaken. Beads of perspiration had gathered on his forehead.

"That was a fast-thinking rickshaw, Joe."

He was staring at the suitcase as if it was full of wriggling snakes.

"Duggie, do you realise that this load is worth five years' hard labour? Plus the four I'm wanted for—hell, my previous convictions plus all this can get me a twenty-year jail term!" The thought made Joe groan. I looked at the stuff and automatically got up to close both the door and window.

"Joe," I said, "you see five years' hard labour, I see two hundred and fifty pounds. From where I stand I can tell you that that stuff in that suitcase is first-grade stuff. It will go like butterfly wings in a strong wind."

"While I go to jail in heavy chains! No, Duggie, take the stuff if you want it, but leave me out of it. Just give me my share after you've got rid of it."

"O.K., Joe, just do me this one last favour. Take this half-crown and go to the shop at the corner and buy me a small padlock. On your way back, get me a rickshaw."

"A rickshaw?"

"Yes, Joe, any rickshaw, and I don't want the owner of the case!"

When Joe and the rickshaw came, I loaded the suitcase, and told him to drive me to the hall where our band had enjoyed so many flops. When we got there, I took the suitcase into the hall. I was in luck. The hall was empty. Behind the stage, leading from one of the dressing-rooms, was a trap door. This door lead into a cellar that was built directly beneath the stage. To see this trap door, you had to take real notice. All I had to do to secure it from intruders was to padlock it. To make double sure, I got Joe to unscrew a red sign from some electrical power house which read: "Danger. Keep Out."

Then I started work. I worked until the small hours of the following morning. In spite of my non-stop labour, when morning came, the suitcase was still half full. After counting the small brown paper packets of dagga that I had been folding, I saw that they amounted to four hundred. At a shilling a packet, I had a ready round figure of twenty pounds. That is, if I was not arrested first. Everything seemed like a godsend right up to Hakkeltjie's customers. I knew them all.

Upstairs in the dance hall there were rooms to let at seven and sixpence a week. Now I had a room upstairs with business downstairs. There were many risks, but they were tolerable. Like crossing a street in heavy traffic. When Brother Joe saw my success, he became an active partner. We ordered the drug from as far away as Goleli, the border that divides Swaziland and Natal. We had call-girls who tipped us off whenever foreign seamen wanted the stuff.

The dial of my watch, which was always too slow or too fast, told me it was eight o'clock. Not that I cared, time meant nothing to me. I was just living, and enjoying every minute of it. It was Sunday morning. The dance hall hadn't been swept yet. Evidence of the Zulu choir competition of the night before was strewn all over the dance floor. Cigarette stubs, cold-drink bottles and a womanless stocking, were lying around, the only evidence of a packed gala night.

I was playing "Danny Boy" strictly by ear on the old battered piano and thinking strictly nothing, when a curious face peeped around the curtain. It must have been peeping for quite some time, because when I looked at it, it smiled mischievously.

I saw the dimples before I saw the smile. When the

figure beneath the dimples started toward me, it was as if I was seeing a woman for the first time. Her story was brief and simple. She was a probation nurse from Baragwanath Hospital. She was on her first seaside holiday. Originally, she was from Swaziland, and would I please show her around the town. Hell, three weeks later I found myself before a magistrate monotonously saying, "I do, I do, I do," even if it wasn't called for. I was married! Me, Duggie Boetie! What's more, I loved what I married.

With the money I had, we entrained for Johannesburg. After taking her to the hospital where she practised, I went straight to the offices of the British Empire Service League, an organisation that looked after ex-servicemen. Without any difficulty, I was allocated a house at Dube Township under the ex-servicemen's scheme. Then, before returning to Durban to wind up my business, I went to Dube for a last look at my future dwelling. It was really my last look.

Back in Durban, I arrived just in time to hear Brother Joe telling me that the Indian who owned the corner shop wanted two bags urgently. My mind immediately went to furniture money. This being an emergency, me and Joe decided to hire a car for a quick run down to Zululand. We filled a trunk full of the stuff, and packed it in the back seat. Then we filled a sugar bag and loaded it in the boot of the car. It was the first time that we had ever taken the risk of travelling by road. We usually did the runs by train with the help of a fifteen-year-old school girl.

To draw suspicion away from us, we used to dress the girl in school uniform and pack her luggage with the stuff. That way, we were nearly always sure of reaching Durban without any trouble. But this being an emergency, we discarded all formalities. We were zooming past a town called Verulam when the car developed engine trouble. It gave one cough and finally went dead. That was nothing, no trouble at all, just a bit of engine trouble like any other car. Only this damn car had chosen the queerest of places to conk out.

I don't know who noticed it first: Joe, the Indian driver,

or myself. That was not important. The important thing was that directly opposite our car, dutifully flying in the wind, was the Union Jack flag. We were stuck right in front of the Verulam police station.

I don't know who left the car first: Joe, or the Indian driver. But that was not the point. The point was that there they were walking rapidly away. The Indian was trying to catch up on Joe's rapid strides, but Joe wouldn't let him. Soon they broke into a run. Again I was left holding the baby.

Slowly I got out of the car. To my relief the pavement was empty. There wasn't a soul that mattered. Except for an Indian woman carrying the broadest basket I had ever seen on the crook of her arm. The street was as deserted as the broad step that led up to the police station.

I was about to follow the two cowards, when the corner of my eye caught sight of the trunk in the back seat. Greed took over. I stood rooted to the spot. This is how Jeegar must have felt when he tried to drive that Chinese car away to safety against terrible odds. Then two of my life-long corns appeared at the top of the stone steps in the form of uniformed police.

I left the car door wide open on purpose hoping that the air would clear the dagga smell inside. Then I crippled boldly up the stairs towards my legal guardians. When I was three steps away from them, I looked up and said in faultless Afrikaans, "Baas, my car doesn't want to start." One of them looked up at the other and grinned. He took a match box out of his trouser pocket and made as if to give it to me. The one said, "What's wrong, my boy?"

I shrugged my shoulders, still in Afrikaans I said, "I don't know, baas."

"Come," he said to his friend, "let's see if we can't help this boy." His friend looked at the palms of his spotless pink hands, and shook his head.

The policeman didn't bother to close the car door as he tried the starter of the car. It whined like a hoarse child, but wouldn't catch. He tried it again with the same results. In the meantime, the dagga in the car was smelling like a witch doctor's burning headgear, or so it seemed to me. I stopped inhaling in case I panicked and gave the game away. The blocked air in my lungs nearly caused me to black out.

Hurriedly, I took a cigarette out of my pocket and started puffing furiously on it, hoping to kill the dagga smell with smoke from my cigarette. Maybe his nostrils were blocked like most of the white race. I didn't know, but I hoped so. He got out of the car, and opened the bonnet. Then I really started pulling on the cigarette. After bending for a few minutes over the gaping bonnet, he straightened up and whistled amazed. "Kosie," he called. "Come here and take a look." I got out of the smoke filled car and had a look with Kosie. The constable pointed at the carburettor. It was chockful of sand.

"No wonder your car wouldn't move. Take that out and clean it. I'm not going to dirty my hands. Then pump some petrol into it and we'll see if she won't start. When you're finished, call me."

When I was through, I signalled to him again. He got into the car. This time he closed the door. While I started saying my prayers the car started with a roar. He released the clutch and it shot forward at a reckless speed. He let her go for five hundred yards, then he stepped on the brakes hard. After that he reversed with the same speed. Getting out of the car he said, "Careful next time."

"Dankie, baas," I stammered. I still couldn't believe that the man didn't smell anything.

I got into the car and used my left hand to place my artificial leg on the clutch. I pushed the artificial knee down with the palm of my hand until the clutch was flat against the floor boards, then I pulled the gear out of neutral and into first. After that I eased the pressure from the palm of my left hand slowly. I felt the clutch lift and I lowered the gas pedal slowly with my right foot. The car moved.

While all this was going on, the policeman up the stairs was wondering why was I taking so long to get going. He was just about to come down the stairs when the car moved.

Once the car was on the go, I was all right because I didn't need the services of my left leg. My right leg did all the necessary press work. I reached Durban without mishap.

I've never seen two men so surprised as Joe and the Indian when they saw me the following morning. I told them that the police had taken the drugs for themselves and had allowed me to go. The hell with it, didn't they run out on me? The Indian was too relieved at getting his car back to bother about the charges. As for Brother Joe, he resigned on the spot. Next I heard from him, he was selling corn beer at the Victoria Street beer hall. A much safer business, as he put it. All he did was buy a pound's worth of corn beer and sit around in the beer hall till the beer tanks closed. Then the latecomers bought it from him at twice the price.

I was in my room, sitting spread-legged on the floor. In front of me was an old newspaper. It was strewn with dagga. My last bag. After this, I intended washing my hands of the business. At my elbow, within easy reach, was a bottle of brandy. It was three-quarters full. This brandy was not for drinking purposes. It was there to make third-grade dagga into first-grade. You spread the dagga out before you like it was now, then you sprinkled a little brandy on it. The spirits shrunk the stuff. When it was dry, there'd be hard little knots. At the same time, the colour changed from green to a reddish-green. In other words, from third-grade to first-grade.

I wasn't around. Only my nimble fingers were. They were fast rolling the stuff into little parcels while my mind was at Baragwanath Hospital. First time I ever believed in witchcraft. That nurse had me. I was like somebody possessed. To me she was my mother, my father, my only friend, all wrapped in one.

That was why when someone tapped me on the shoulder, I payed him no mind. Not until an authoritative voice nearly broke my eardrums by barking, "Get up!" I looked over my shoulder, and my breath became hot. My stomach muscles contracted and my mouth behaved like a fish that had just been landed.

When things like these start happening, confusion sets in fast. Otherwise there would be a lot more dead policemen in the world. You become too bewildered to think straight. It was one of those times when you fight till your arms fall off, or you become a complete idiot. I became the latter.

I was so engrossed with thoughts of my wife, that one of the most important things escaped my mind. Namely, to bolt the door from the inside, and have a lock hanging from the outside. "Mister! This is a police raid!"

I was hauled to prison, where I was kept three months awaiting trial while they checked my previous convictions.

This all goes to show the part the police play in my life. It has been going on ever since I was born, and it will go on till I die. They are out to ruin me, always have. This time they succeeded.

Like all the magistrates that I have come across, he found me guilty. After preaching me a sermon about the behaviour of cripples, he sentenced me to three years and three months. Three years for dagga, and three months for the brandy. When I asked him to waive the three months, he pointed at my pile of records and told me that was the reason why I awaited trail so long.

EIGHTEEN

What was three and a quarter years even in a place like Intaba Zo Sizi (Mountain of Sorrow), my new jail, when my mind was forever on the woman I loved.

I was in group A, with the staff job at reception. I was not going to start any trouble, because I was no longer irresponsible. I had a wife to think of.

The prison was divided into three sections. A, B and D. They start you off in A section. B stands for bad, from there it's D prison for you. D means dangerous, or "Hyenas' Cage". The inmates of D section are real inmates. They were never allowed out. As a result, any kind of smuggling was out of the question. Their favourite pastime was to kill one another off. Me, I was going to do my utmost not to grace that section with my presence.

It was the longest prison term I ever pulled in my life. My five years at the Fort was nothing compared to Intaba Zo Sizi. Here, minutes were like hours, hours like days. I suppose the tortoise pace was caused by my being in love.

Maybe I should have written to her, I don't know. But I didn't want her to know that she was married to a reformed criminal. Since meeting her, I knew deep down that I had reformed. These thoughts sped through my mind as I stood, a free man, outside the big prison gates waiting for the prison truck to haul me to Durban Station.

My three years were served to the full; I didn't do the three months, thanks to remission and good behaviour. I took a last look at the formidable iron doors and unconsciously read the three chalk words that were written boldly on them: "Kilroy was Here". Kill-joy would have been more appropriate, I thought, as I spat and walked away without waiting for the prison truck.

As the train carrying me back to Johannesburg and home rumbled through the Italian prisoner of war tunnels near Pietermaritzburg, I couldn't resist looking at my reflection in the compartment mirror. The hair on my head was scraped clean by the convict barber, giving me the look of a hairless pink monkey.

At Johannesburg Station I got off the train and made my way to the station's butcher just in case there was no food at home. After all, nobody was expecting me. There was a lot of confusion on the platform. People were running up and down, especially old ladies with washing bundles and babies tied on their backs. They were jumping into the wrong trains then jumping out of them again, only to find they had jumped from the right train. They kept asking people who didn't know either but were too proud to admit the fact. A mess of human frustration, pushing, pulling, and tramping on one another as they fought to get into the narrow single doors. The loudspeaker that was announcing the destination of the train succeeded only in giving a fair imitation of a horse being slaughtered. A hell of a bedlam.

As a train was being mobbed, I asked a struggler where it was going to. He said Nancefield. A girl's voice behind me said, "You're mad; this is a Dube train." The man shrugged his shoulders and pushed. A woman next to him screamed, at the same time the guard's warning whistle shrilled. The train started to move while people were still dangling outside. A teenager who was trying to get in through the window had succeeded only with the top half of his body. Inside, the train was so crowded that it was as if someone had added more sardines to an already packed tin, and was trying to reclose the tin. I pushed through. The vacant seat I found was worth the two missing buttons on my jacket.

On nearing Braamfontein Station, a surprising thing happened. Occupants of seats started getting up. I thought they had reached their destination. Instead, they climbed on to their seats and stood on them. To me this was unusual. I always thought it was better to sit than to stand. I was not going to follow any mob psychology. The result was near disaster. At Braamfontein Station, the train was again mobbed. This time, in real earnest. Maybe it was because Braamfontein is an industrial area.

Funny, when you're in distress, your mind wanders over irrelevant things. There I was thinking of industrial areas when I was slowly suffocating to death.

Suddenly there was an eclipse. I looked up, then blinked. My head was under a woman's skirt. I saw big buttocks covered by white bloomers. Hastily I looked down, not wanting to smell anything in case there was something to smell. This nightmare journey took three quarters of an hour. When at last we reached Dube Station, I staggered, minus my walking-stick, dazedly out of the train, vowing never to board a train again, even if it was going to fairyland.

I looked at my watch with distrust, and saw that it was five-thirty. I shrugged my shoulders and started to walk home. I transferred the flat parcel of meat from my right hand to my left to sort of balance the weight, since my walking-stick was gone. My progress was painfully slow, but I couldn't have cared less, since I'd soon be resting.

A big lock on my gate kept me from entering the yard. I hadn't bargained for this. It was all adding confusion to an already confused mind. I looked around, then decided to enquire at the next house. I was just about to walk away, when I saw someone familiar walking toward me. I waited, at the same time wondering where had I seen him before. I was leaning against the gate. It was a good thing I did, otherwise I would have fallen. Because I had never laid eyes on the man before: what was familiar was the suit he had on. It was mine. My wedding suit! It was cut by a West Street tailor just before my marriage. My best and only suit. The last time I had seen it, it was neatly folded and resting at the bottom of my wife's trunk.

Now here was someone dressed to kill in it. I wasn't mad, or even angry, or any of those things. Just a little foolish. As usual, when I was being deeply hurt, my bowels wanted to work. The slight headache that I had had since getting off the train, suddenly became a splitting headache.

"Hello!" he said.

"Hello!" I said, conscious of a slight tremor in my voice. He whipped out a key ring from the side pocket of his (my) jacket, and started unlocking the lock.

"Can I help you?"

"No. Yes. Where can I get a drink?" That was all I could think of saying.

He laughed, "Not here!"

The gate opened. I limped aside.

"You look tired," he said.

I nodded, paralysed.

He looked closely at me. "Come in, have a rest. We don't sell drink, but I can get it for you." He had a nice pleasant face with strong white teeth—no prison teeth like mine. He helped me inside. I just stood. My lips couldn't speak. "Sit down," he said. "I won't be a minute."

From where I sat, I could see into the bedroom. He took off my jacket, I mean ours, then he hung it in a wardrobe. He stopped at the door and looked closely at me again. I was scared he might have seen a photograph. But I was very thin now, and without my hair.

"Can I give you some water?" he asked. I shook my shiny head. "Well, what can I do for you then?"

It was a trembling hand that passed over the money to him.

"A nip of brandy, please."

"I won't be long. I have to get my children from the woman who looks after them during the day. My wife is a staff-nurse. She should be here any minute. But don't worry, just make yourself at home. I'll be back before her." With that, he was gone.

Make yourself at home, the man had said. But this was my home. I got up to go and have another look at the number. Maybe it was the wrong number. Sure enough, it was my number. Thirteen-o-two. As I reoccupied my seat, all kinds of thoughts sped through my mind. I thought maybe this was my wife's cousin, or maybe it was her brother, or . . . oh, hell.

I looked around more carefully. A wedding photograph. My wife. My suit. There the relationship ended. Stuck in at the base of the wedding picture was a picture of two kids. One about eighteen months old, the other about six months. The older one looked like a boy. The exact replica of my wife. My bowels wanted to work. This time it was even worse. I started to cry. And that doesn't come easily to me. I thought I heard someone coming and rubbed at my face, but it was just a woman passing. I got to the door and climbed out cautiously. No him, no kids, no staff-nurse. I just walked and walked not caring the hell where I was going, cursing myself, cursing him, cursing her, cursing the whole damn world. Despite myself I couldn't help seeing it her way. She marries a man. He's an angel for three weeks. He goes back to Durban to wind up some business and then he doesn't show up again. So she waits and she hunts and she waits. Still no husband. So she meets up with this smiling saint and it's sweet dreams, Duggie. Most probably adverts in the *Bantu Earth* and *Natal Moon,* which is the beginning of divorce proceedings. And while I'm still cuddling my scruples in jail my suit gets married again.

The sharp hoot of a car jerked me from my misery, and with a jeering finger showed me my surrounding hell. I found myself at the bottom step of the bridge that led to Dube Station's platform. Sighing with self-pity, I started mounting them painfully, without my walking-stick. My entire body was screaming for a rest and the Dube beer hall would do me good.

I roamed around the beer hall in the hope of seeing someone I knew. But luck was against me. I bought myself a shilling's worth of beer and perched myself on a bench. Now there was my rotten pass book to worry about. Nothing short of a lighted match could fix it.

I sat on the corner bench slowly sipping my drink, when I heard the drummer. He was standing directly in front of me, as dirty and nauseating as ever. More and more bad luck. It was the mad teacher. There was pus as thick as condensed milk at both corners of his eyes. I avoided the face and looked away. Maybe in six months time I'd be just like him. If only he'd go away.

Abruptly the drum stopped beating and I heard him say, "I crave for your wisdom and hate your scorn ... I pray for guidance with hope forlorn. . . ."

He started beating on his drum holding it close to his ear and whispering and blowing on it. Not one of the drinkers were taking notice of his ravings. For that matter, I don't think he did either.

I was about to take my mug of beer and move away when someone near me shouted, "Hey, you! *Futsek* away from here, we want to drink." He walked away singing "Nkosi Sikelele e Africa".

I was about to put the mug down between my legs after having taken a deep drink, when I saw Zala, a string bass player. We had once shared the back of a police van together after being arrested for being without night specials.

I went over to him and glanced at the newspaper over his shoulder. There was a state of emergency declared in

South Africa. My eyes travelled away from there to the crime column. I noticed Zala's eyes were also there.

"Zala," I said.

He spun round, "Christ! Duggie, where the hell've you been? The last I heard of you was when you and Tim toured Durban! How did it go? Tell me, man, how did it go?"

"First tell me whether you can put me up for the night."

"Sure, Duggie, but I'm not at Orlando anymore. I'm now at a place called Naledi."

"Where the hell is that?"

"About an hour's ride from town and twenty minutes from here."

As we got off the train at Naledi, Zala became unusually quiet.

"What's eating you, boy?"

"Huh?"

"Why so quiet?"

"I'm thinking, Duggie, thinking of that stone."

"What stone?"

"It's getting on my nerves."

"What are you talking about?"

"Never mind, you'll see."

It was late when we got to Zala's house. His young wife met us at a fenceless gate. I noticed the area was newly built. The whole place, as far as you can see, was rocky. Inside, there were four doorless unplastered rooms. As usual, the lavatory was built a distance from the house. There was no bathroom.

When I entered the fourth room, I stopped and gaped. In the middle of the room was a huge boulder. A channel was built around it. Next to the boulder stood a fire-galley. It made the tiny room unbearably hot. On the fire-galley, about to boil, was a four-gallon tin of water.

Zala said, "This is the rock that gives me sleepless nights. The rock of Gibraltar. Duggie, I sweat morning and night trying to get rid of it. You see that channel I built around it? Someone advised me to continually throw boiling water around it to get it to crack."

"But how did it get here?" I asked, amazed.

"It didn't get here, it was here. The house got here. I mean, they built the house around it."

"Why don't you report this matter to the superintendent?" I asked.

"I did. The bastard told me to carve a table out of it."

I wanted to laugh, but it wasn't funny.

"They build these houses so fast, you'd think they use a magic wand. You leave a vacant plot to go to work, when you come back, you find a house." There was disgust in Zala's voice.

"I've been fighting this boulder for a week with a sure feeling that I'm losing. All the wood and coal I'm buying and carrying is making me physically weak and financially broke."

"What made you leave Orlando Township?"

"I didn't leave, I was elbowed out. I lived in Orlando Township all my life. That house was what you call an inheritance; I took it over when my parents died. It had a bathroom, with hot and cold water, and a kitchen sink and house gutters and cement right round the yard. Then one morning I was summoned to the superintendent's office. He told me I must make way for people who get less wages and go to a new township—Moroka—where the rent was higher. When I pointed out the money I had spent to make the place look decent, he told me that the house didn't belong to me, that it was Government property. And as for the improvements on the house, they were done at my own risk.

"Hell, Duggie, we were hardly three months at Moroka Township when I was kicked out of my job. A good job. I was locked up twice at Kliptown police station for being hopelessly behind with my rent. I was transferred to Jabavu. There the houses are worse, Duggie. They are built Siamese-fashion. If your bed-springs squeak, the family next door hears. If you quarrel with your wife, you have to quarrel in whispers. What nearly drove my wife mad was the wood and coal smoke from the next house.

"You see, the walls that divide the two families don't go right up to the ceiling. They go half-way. So when the family in the next house makes a fire, we get at least half their smoke. Hell, Duggie, maybe we are not civilised yet, but we are more civilised than these houses!

"Then my luck changed. I got a better paying job. The first thing I wanted to do was to go to the superintendent's office and ask him for permission to extend those walls up to the ceiling to keep the smoke out. But my wife said nix. No more money was going to be spent on a house that didn't belong to us. Not when we might be told to get out any time. She was right. When the superintendent found out that I was earning four pounds a week, he transferred me to where I am now. If I lose this job . . ." his voice trailed off. "I tell you, Duggie, what a black man needs is a caravan. If the man says go, you go, man. But I'm boring you with my house difficulties. Tell me about Durban. What happened there?"

"Tomorrow," I sighed, "or the next day. For now, just show me a little piece of floor."

"Seriously, what are you going to do now, Duggie?"

"Try and get this hopeless pass fixed, I think."

"Let me see." I gave it to him. He thumbed through it, then gave it back to me.

"What do you think of it?"

"Nothing."

"What do you mean, nothing?"

"I mean it stinks."

"O.K. Now, where's that piece of floor?"

NINETEEN

Next morning I was at Influx. I was careful not to show the police guards at the gate my pass. Upstairs at the social workers' offices I was told that things were different now. They told me to try and get a doctor's certificate. But I wasn't sick, I told them, I was in prison, and there were my prison discharge papers. "Yes, we see them," said the man, "but where were you before you went to prison?" I'd often heard about questions that can't be answered. This was one of them.

I took my battered pass and prison papers and went downstairs. There I took a chance and went directly to the work-seeking permit officer, thinking that he might take pity on my being legless. He took one look at my pass and personally shouted "Escort!" before I could even blubber. The beginning of the end, I thought.

While he was holding on to my pass, I reversed, meaning to lose myself in the black throngs of misery. I would have succeeded if I hadn't tramped on somebody's corn while reversing. He took it upon himself to push me forward into the hands of the escort. It was hopeless to try and run. Hell, what am I talking about? Running had long been out of the question for me.

"I wonder what caused him to do it? I saw him only a few minutes before he did it, and he seemed happy and cheerful." What they don't know is that the reason why you've been so happy the last few minutes is because you have at last pounced on the only way out. You wonder why you didn't think of it before. You are going to smite your miserable life to death, and enjoy every minute of it. It's your secret and yours alone. You giggle when you think of it. You're as smug as a hanged man at the end of a rope. People believe that there's a mysterious happiness in the last hours of a dead man's life. But it's not for them to know, because the secret belongs to the dead. They regard death as an unfair evil. What they don't seem to understand is that only death can play a noble part when endurance is exhausted.

All this was passing through my mind as I was escorted upstairs to the prosecutor's interrogating room. The policeman knocked and opened the door. He clicked his heels smartly and motioned me to enter. He gave my pass to a tall white man, then came and stood next to me.

"Now, what's this?" he began, as he scrutinised my

pass. He looked up at me and said to the policeman, "Why bring him here, why not lock him up? This book is hopeless, man."

The policeman said, "Is cripple, sir."

Irritably he said, "That doesn't mean anything."

Turning to me he said, "Where are you cripple?"

"One leg, sir."

He stood up to have a better look.

Then, "I see two."

"Artificial, sir," I said, knocking on the leg.

"What happened?"

"War!"

He coughed and directed his attention back to my pass. Musingly he said, "I see here you've only worked once—why?"

"It's difficult for a man like me to find a job."

"Why?"

" 'Cause I got no leg."

"Nonsense, you're just lazy, that's all."

"Not lazy. It's painful and discouraging to walk every day to the pass office only to be told there's no work."

"Don't talk nonsense; I say you're lazy." Banging his fist on the desk, he said angrily, "I don't accept that excuse! I happen to know men in worse positions than you are, going through life without a complaint!"

Good for them, I thought.

"Have you ever heard of Lieutenant Bader?" I nodded. We used to hear in camp about the legless British ace's exploits. How he was a prisoner of war and how they flew his two artificial legs to him from England and dropped them by parachute over the German prison camp.

"Well," said the prosecutor, whom I was slowly beginning to dislike, "I was in the Air Force myself, and I happened to know Bader personally. Legless as the lieutenant is, he never made capital of his disability. The man used to walk around and dance with his artificial legs. Yet you with the advantage of one, have the nerve to tell me that you find walking with an artificial leg difficult!"

I heard myself reply, "Sir, in the first place, Lieutenant Bader has expensive legs. Not legs that weigh fifteen to twenty pounds and produce blisters every second week. Secondly, he is well-off, and last of all, he doesn't have to walk up and down the streets trying to fix a pass. I'll change places with him any time!"

"Have you ever been to prison?"

"Huh?"

"Have you ever been to prison?"

"What's that got to do with this?"

"Look, I'm asking the questions. Have you ever been to prison?" I looked down and nodded. When I looked up, he was grinning.

"Look," he said, wiping the grin off his face, "I'm going to deal with the man in you, not with your crippleness. That has nothing to do with me. My business is you! If you can prove to my satisfaction where you've been since leaving your last place of employment, I'll see what I can do for you, and not before."

"But that was years ago."

"I don't care whether it was one week ago. I'll give a two-week special, and if you are ever brought before me again, without documents, *ek sal jou gal werk!* Now get out of here!"

Slowly I made my way to the station to catch the Dube train. I was going to the beer hall to think, and there was no suicide in my thoughts. I'd been in tighter spots than this. As I climbed the steps that led from the station's platform to the bridge and the beer hall, I saw them. Pass raiders. The fresh two-week stamp special in my pass book allowed me to ignore them.

Two hours later, I was still wondering whether this was really the kind of life I was cut out for. Homeless, passless, and legless. And suddenly I knew what I was going to do. I stood up sweating, my beer half-finished.

I took a train to Pretoria, capital of the Transvaal. There, I was directed to the bus rank. I boarded one to the Union Buildings. I walked up three flights of stairs. When I came to the third floor, an arrow sign drawn on a board directed me to the Coloured Identification Department. Win, lose, there was no draw possible. I was taking the bull by the horns. This time there was no going back, for man or mouse.

At the office entrance, there was a long bench. It was empty. Worriedly I perched on it. From inside the office came hilarious laughter. That made me a little nervous. My courage threatened to desert me. I gripped the bench tightly so as not to bolt and run. The laughter inside continued uproariously. At least they are happy, I thought, that's something.

I wasn't there long before a burly white man came out of the happy office and stood at the door. He was red in the face from laughter, and wiping his eyes with a khaki handkerchief. He looked up and down the long corridor. Then he saw me. Controlling himself with difficulty, he said in Afrikaans, "You—come here." I followed him meekly into his office.

He pointed to a figure that sat squirming in a chair. Before he could say anything, he burst into laughter. He was joined by two others. I looked at the figure on the chair, and saw a pitch-black man. His shoes were worn out. After controlling himself, the white man said, "Boy—" it sounded like "Booy". "Now you tell me, boy, does this man look like a Coloured to you?" Again there was laughter. I looked at the poor man and felt sorry for him.

"Come on," urged the Afrikaner. "Does he now, does he?"

I was about to say, "I don't know, baas." Then I remembered my own position, and through my mind flashed the story of the monkey. I looked at the man and I grinned. My grin was not beautiful. It must have been ugly, because it brought forth more laughter.

A pet monkey once followed the aroma of frying peanuts into its master's kitchen. There, strewn on the hot stove, were the frying nuts. He looked around, to make sure that there was no one around. Then he reached out with his paw. As the tips of his fingers made contact with the hot plate, he screamed, somersaulted and sucked his scorched fingers. He tried again, with the same results. He was still sucking his poor fingers and trying to scratch out an idea from the crown of his head with the fingernails of his left hand, when the cat came in. At the sight of the cat, the monkey grinned. In one swift move he snatched the cat up, and with it swiped the strewn nuts from the hot stove. The cat screamed and bolted through the door. Grinning, the monkey started picking up the nuts leisurely from the floor. I was sorry, but I was going to do to this man what the monkey did to the cat.

Spacing each word, and in faultless Afrikaans, I said, "If you, my friend, as black as you are, claim to be a Coloured, then what the hell should I claim to be?" From the top pocket of my jacket I pulled out a pencil.

"Here, take this pencil, and push it through your hair. If the pencil goes through without a hitch, then the baas will issue you with Coloured clearance papers, but if the pencil sticks in your hair, then you're nothing but a kaffir."

The office vibrated with laughter.

"Yeh, yeh!" they screamed. "Go on, take the pencil. Yes, yes," continued the voices.

The poor man made no move. That uncombed bush of crinkly hair could have gripped a broom stick. As for a pencil, it could have lived there for years.

"Yes, yes, stick the pencil through your hair. If it falls off, we'll issue you with a Coloured pass." If eyes could kill, I would have died where I stood. Still laughing, the baas said, "Here is a man who could claim to be Coloured. Just look at his complexion, I'm sure if there was a hair on his head, the hair would have been straight."

My smooth-shaven head was once more coming to my rescue. In Cape Town, I wanted to have my drinks in a pub that catered for Coloureds only. Africans were prohibited from drinking in pubs. I knew that if I tried entering one, I'd only be thrown out because of my crinkly hair.

For a solution I went to a barber and told him to remove my hair. "All?" he asked surprised.

"All," I assured him. After the hair-cut I went to the pub. I pushed open one bat-wing door and held it until I was sure that the bartender's eyes were centred on me. Instead of going in, I turned my head towards the street and swore volubly at an imaginary molester using juicy rude words like a real Cape Malay. Then I pushed both doors open and danced a jig towards the counter. "A glass of sherry." I ordered. And was served. From then on, I was a regular customer. But from the way the barman eyed me every time I entered the pub, I knew that he was waiting for my hair to grow, so as to see whether it was crinkly or straight. He was going to wait a long time, because I was equally anxious to see that it didn't grow.

The baas behind me said, "Now stop wasting our time and get out of here before we have you locked up." Shakily the man got off the chair and walked toward the door. I didn't meet his eyes, I knew how Judas felt.

"You!" The voice was directed at me. I braced myself. "I suppose you also want a Coloured identification card?"

"Yes, baas."

"Where were you all the time, that you want one now? Why didn't you come before?"

"Before, baas, it wasn't so important, but now it is very important that I should have some kind of paper to say who I am."

"So you want to know who you are?"

"Yes, baas."

He grinned. "Who the hell are you anyway?"

"Duggie Boetie, baas."

"Why is it so important now, when you've been going without it all your life?"

"It's because I want to marry, baas," I stammered and looked down.

"Marry!" he exclaimed. "Who wants to marry a cripple?"

"I think it's because she's twenty years older than me, baas," I said shamelessly.

The office exploded with laughter. "So that's the case, heh?" he said, wiping his eyes. When the din had subsided, he turned to the young one and said, "Take down his particulars and give him a temporary form to go with until we can issue him with a real identification card."

Turning to me he said, "Next time you come here, bring two passport photos with you. . . ."

Two passport photos. And I was a Coloured. Just like that. I limped out in a daze. My head was spinning, my heart was double-timing and my ears were going ping. I wanted to sing or dance or something. I wanted to fly. I needed my guitar. No more pass! No more pass! No more Influx Control! No more sit here, not there, no more shut up, take your hands out of your pockets, no more where the hell do you think you're going, no more you are a liar, do you know who you're talking to, no more move, wait, line up, fall in, no more can't you see I'm busy—No more! No more! It was now somebody else's shit—everybody else's—not mine! I wanted to start shaking hands, banging everybody on the back, buying booze for the whole of bloody Joburg! I looked around wildly.

Standing forlornly at the building's entrance was the unfortunate black man.

My hand fished into my pocket and came out with a shilling. I went to him and placed the shilling in his hand, then quickly walked away. I was a few hundred yards from him, when something flew with terrific force past my head. It went *zinnnng,* narrowly missing the tip of my ear. It clinked once and fell into the gutter. It was the shilling piece. I bent down, picked it up and walked on without looking back.

EPILOGUE

This book was written by Dugmore Boetie and finally edited by me. It was meant to be the first volume of his autobiography. Now I don't know what it is. A book, certainly. A book covering years (early 'thirties to early 'fifties) that he knew, and set mostly in places that he knew.

Duggie was essentially a con man; so that attempts I have made to establish the facts of his life have led only to chaos and contradiction. Perhaps, in time to come, a kind of "Quest for Duggie" will be another book. One is tempted. Just yesterday I spoke to somebody who claims to have been a student of a sort of Duggie Boetie school for junior thieves. Then, in contrast, there was the lovely young African nurse in Zululand, where I took Duggie to die, who gasped and wept when she saw him: "I know this man—from Johannesburg! I grew up under him! He used to play the guitar for us when we were children—he used to tell us stories!"

I met Duggie roughly two years before he died. Which is about how long it took for the first draft of this book to be written. It was some time in 1964, towards the end of the year. I was running (it was a little easier then) an improvisation group of African and white actors and writers. We attempted to investigate, through improvisations and monologues, the everyday encounters between us. Not the dramatic ones; the seemingly simple ones, where the convolutions were as complex, the poisons as insidious.

"The Last Leg," an edited version of what is now Chapter 14, had appeared in *The Classic,* a South African literary magazine, as a short story. It excited many people. The then editor of *The Classic,* the late Nat Nakasa, was a very lively member of our improvisation group, and I asked him to bring Duggie along. He did.

Duggie was small, dapper, vivacious, sharp. He carried a walking stick which helped compensate for an artificial leg. At improvisation, he was inventive, unobvious, bold. He filled the place with his presence, his anecdotes. Nat, sophisticated, urbane, was irritated by him; the rest of us were fascinated, relishing all the rogue that showed. He claimed to have served seventeen criminal convictions in his time; to have lost his leg in the Sahara, serving against Rommel.

One day when I reiterated my admiration for his story, he put forward what must have been a pretty carefully prepared proposition. Or no, considering the way it developed, it could quite well have been improvised. If we *really* admired his work, he had to ask, what were we going to do about it? Working at a radio factory, travelling to and from Germiston every day with an artificial leg exhausted him, made writing virtually out of the question. If we could provide him "just with a roof over his head, food and paper for three months", he would write the "true, hot book" that was "bursting to come out".

When I took reasonably to his request, he adjusted it swiftly. A roof, food, paper and, say, £15 a month. Finally I committed myself to matching his present wage, £30 a month, for three months by collecting from friends as well as myself. He was to write what he liked.

After about six weeks, he came to see me with some pages of manuscript, about an African gang of criminals which had somehow ended up in the army. After the war, each returned to South Africa with a single purpose—to beat the others to hidden loot. In trying to reach it, they all get killed, one by one, through the most extraordinary fates. One died by shark, another by his mother. . . . Beside the humour, irony and vitality of "The Last Leg," this was very disappointing. The influences were obvious: comics, movies, Agatha Christie, Peter Cheyney, and a little—just a very little—life. What was marvellously, uniquely Duggie hadn't even been touched on. We discussed it extensively, passionately. I explained that this kind of writing was valid in itself, and that if it was what he wanted to do he might quite easily get good support. But that it was not writing that interested me, that I truthfully did not know enough about it to help in any way.

I quoted Dickens—*David Copperfield.*

"Do you want it *all?*" Duggie asked. "As it was? All the dirt?" I assured him that I did. "We'll get into trouble," he said. I asked him to tell what he knew, what mattered to him, as best, as simply, as truthfully as he could. So he began again. Not with "I was born ..." but a kind of equivalent.

At about this time, Nat Nakasa, who was not a politically involved man, was given a Nieman Scholarship for a year's study at Harvard University. He was not permitted a passport, so he left on an exit permit. This meant that he could never return to South Africa under the present regime. I took over the editorship of *The Classic* (named, incidentally, after a shebeen). Some months later, Nat committed suicide in New York.

I earned my living as an advertising copy-writer. Very few people in the agency knew about my theatrical or literary activities; I preferred it that way. Duggie couldn't meet me in the evenings, and during the day there were not that many places where we could easily get together. He used to come to the office. Not *into* the office, but to the downstairs foyer of the building. The watchman, a gentle, cross-eyed man, used to come up and call me. I used to go down, receive the new manuscript and give back the old one. With questions. Opening questions, I hope; I tried not to intrude, only to provoke.

We had many meetings in that pale, marble-faced foyer or, when it was cold, out in the winter sun on the pavement. The three months extended themselves and the book was barely begun. Laurens van der Post had been granted a literary award, and he asked that some part of it be spent on the development of African writers. I managed to get £100 of it for Dugmore. £20 a month. At the end of the five months, the book was just halfway there. When the money came regularly, he didn't write regularly. I became aware that in many ways I was just another con to him. This was fine, as long as a book was happening. He sometimes stayed away for a whole month. When the £100 was finished, I kept him going, which meant that the visits and the writing became more regular. God knows what Dugmore's life was; I can't judge completely by what he told me. There was a woman he lived with who he said was mad and beat him. There was the difficulty of having a place to write in peace. He had no family, just a dead sister's children who were being looked after by an old woman he had to give money to. Often he smelt of brandy. Once a job interview was arranged for him and he arrived drunk. And there was that leg, that I watched from afar sometimes, heavy, stiff and cruel, that seemed to propel the rest of him like a punting pole.

I decided to get him to complete the book, imperfectly, and then work back. With a sense of pattern, of a whole, it might be easier to sustain his interest. It wasn't the end of what he wanted to say, but it could be the first volume. He completed it, ending off with: O.K. BARNEY—HERE'S MY WRATH! We had been working so close to things that I had lost perspective. Seeing the book as a whole was a revelation. It was, quite simply, the book of a shit. Magnificently vital, funny, strong and ironic at its best. Hopelessly sentimental and inaccurate when he attempted to care. There was a lot to question, a lot of work to do.

And then suddenly, frighteningly, Duggie, without money, disappeared. I waited for about three weeks and then began to search for him. After a month, he phoned me. He had been sick. His right arm, the one above his stump, was going into violent spasms. He was coughing badly. He thought that he had pneumonia and was going to hospital. Duggie had two passes: one issued to Africans; the other a Coloured identity card. The first because he preferred to live among Africans, the second to get the privileges that came with it. He chose the superior attention of the Coronationville Hospital for Coloureds.

Then began a new ritual; visiting Duggie in hospital. He had no family. His friends seemed to have forgotten him. I went twice a week after work. His arm, except for occasional spasms, was now virtually immobile. He lay and dreamt about sour milk and pigs' knuckles, and so I brought them to him. At first he was relatively cheerful. We discussed things. Shoes. He was going to get a £20 pair of American Freeman shoes when he left the hospital. Food. I remember once listening to him boast about how splendid a cook he was. He could cook a seven-course dinner. "A seven-course dinner?" I asked. Duggie and crêpe suzettes. I leaned back indulgently while he listed the seven. "Meat. Potatoes. Beans. Pumpkin. Rice. Carrots. Cabbage. Even more."

As soon as he was better he would finish off the book. It needed some juggling, some rewriting, a fortnight or so's work. I brought him books, but he never read; paper, but he never wrote. It was summer. The ward was hot. Radios were loud. Pop music. Commercials. Two beds away from him was a tiny, toothless, legless old man making rugs. He had a thin, piercing voice, a wild cackle, and yelled at people far across the ward. Duggie hated him, said that he was cruel, that he mocked and frightened the very sick.

Duggie's condition seemed to worsen. I went to speak to the doctor in charge of his ward. Duggie had cancer of the lung; it had spread, affecting his arm. He wasn't sure how long Duggie would live. Perhaps months. A year. They took him once a week to the General Hospital for radium treatment. It seemed to me quite simple that Duggie should know, but the doctor advised against it: one can never predict exactly how a patient might react. His condition, however, would reach a kind of plateau of comfort when he would quite likely be able to work again.

So my ritual became more significant. I was the only man visiting a man dying of cancer, the only friend who knew. When I came a day late, he'd say, "Hello, stranger." Nadine Gordimer, tiny, transparent, exquisite in the vast brown ward, came with me once and then began to visit him occasionally during the day. Sometimes Lionel Abrahams, another friend, went with her. I continued to come in the evenings, after work.

Duggie went what he called "stir-crazy." He couldn't bear to be in the hospital. He desperately needed to get out. He began to fight with the staff. He refused the bed-pan and demanded to be taken to the toilets. He weakened, lost weight. His hair fell out as a result of the radium treatment. Without his dentures he looked like Gandhi. He seemed neglected, dirty. He nagged violently about the book. I said we could wait. He nagged Nadine and Lionel. They nagged me. I spoke to the doctor again. There was not much that he could say. The radium treatment would be effective only up to a certain point; thereafter, nothing more could be done. When that point was reached, Duggie would have to leave the hospital. Not enough beds. Where would he go? That became a case for the social workers—a familiar phrase in Duggie's life. I contacted a friend who ran a mission hospital in Zululand. When nothing more could be done for Duggie, would he take him in? He would be happy to help. I told Duggie that when he was well enough to travel, I would take him down to Zululand to recuperate. He wasn't particularly comforted. I began to despair of him ever finishing the book.

Visiting him became more difficult for me. Nadine and Lionel were always confronted by a warm, brave, humorous invalid. I would come there and sit paralysed through monologues like this: "You see that fucken little bastard over there," indicating the legless old man two beds down. "Tonight I'm going to get his neck in here," indicating the crook of his knee, "then I'm going to hold on," he held his only foot with his only moving hand, "and then I'll fucken well strangle him to death. . . ."

At that time, I was between jobs and in need of a radical change. I decided to take a three-week excursion overseas. I had the book typed out virtually as it stood. Dugmore was threatening to leave the hospital. Where would he go? To friends in the township. What friends?

Friends. Where were they now? No answer. I begged him to wait until my return. He wept.

I left the book with an agent in London. I asked him to explain to the publishers that they should judge it by its best parts, that the rest would be improved upon. I even argued unfairly. I stressed how important to Dugmore a letter of interest would be. The book was accepted for this publication a year after Dugmore's death.

On my return, Duggie insisted on leaving the hospital immediately. Nadine had been in communication with the woman specialist who had administered his radium therapy at the General Hospital. He was at the end of his treatment. I consulted her and the doctor at Coronationville and was advised to wait a week or so before taking him down to Zululand. I saw Dugmore at Coronationville on a Wednesday, and promised to revisit him on the Friday. With a pig's knuckle. He said that he wouldn't be there. He wasn't. After his therapy at the General Hospital, he had had himself carried to a taxi and driven into the township. There was nothing to do but wait.

Then a week later, at my new office, a phone call. The woman specialist. Dugmore and his mother were at the General Hospital. (His mother! I had read about her death, questioned it, heard about it in detail.) She could no longer look after him, and had brought him back. The hospital would keep him until the end of the week. Then would I drive down to Zululand? I dashed up to the hospital and was taken to his ward. Dugmore was lying propped up in bed under a grey blanket. On his shiny bald head a knitted cap had slid askew. Beside him stood a little old woman, unquestionably his mother. He lay there like a snake with his one leg and lame arm. It was as if all his cancer was in his eyes. They were staring at me, phosphorescent.

His mother spoke. "Mr Barney, I'm sorry, I've wanted to meet you often, but Duggie wouldn't let me. I wanted to meet you at Coronationville Hospital but he wouldn't let me. Me and my daughters used to visit him all the time there. I'm sorry, I couldn't look after him. I have to do the washing, Mr Barney, I have to look after the children.

He was too heavy for me to lift, Mr Barney, I couldn't turn him over. And he was cursing all the time. I couldn't, Mr Barney; I'm too old, I'm too tired ... I know he got money from you, Mr Barney, but he never gave me a penny...."

As she spoke, Duggie spoke in counterpoint, ignoring her words, acknowledging her as the old woman, never as his mother. "All she has to do is make some black coffee ... I came here just for some treatment ... I won't stay ... I'm going back ..." All the time he spoke he stared at me. Terrified. Mad. An open declaration. Now I knew the score. The lies. The cons. Those hospital trips to the "loner". Even the money for the old woman hadn't reached her. But he was there. On my back. For the rest of his life at least. I hated him. He hated me. I just wanted to walk out, to be left alone. I took the old woman out into the passage.

She spoke on. Duggie had always been a difficult child. He lost his leg at the age of eight. One day he came home screaming from a pain in his leg. The leg turned black; it had had to be amputated. He'd been to gaol only twice to her knowledge. He'd never been up north in the army.

The following Saturday, after promising his mother that I would cover the cost of bringing his body back to Johannesburg, I drove Duggie down to Zululand. Lionel sat beside me. Duggie reclined among cushions and blankets in the back. It was a beautiful, gentle journey through the flat yellow landscapes each of us had a special feeling for. We all relaxed into an acceptance of the situation. At one point, passing a group of washerwomen, Duggie leaned back and said, "You know, I'm really enjoying this drive."

When we arrived at the mission hospital, he was skilfully settled between clean sheets and soft blue blankets in a ward of his own. It was there that the young nurse exclaimed, "I know this man, I grew up under him ... he used to play the guitar ..." We left him radiant, a pile of manuscript paper beside his bed to encourage him to begin working again.

Parts of the book began to be published in newspapers.

The first chapter was published by *London Magazine*. There were letters, clumsily typed.

Dear Barney
First let me thank you for having brought me here. Otherwise Iwould have been dead by thistime.
The treatment is ex celent everybod is so nice.
Barrney, Iha tobe certain I haven't written a thing due to continuous headaches and a irritating pain inmy chest. The stuff is just orbiting in my brain wantigg to beplaced on paper. The Dr says I should take things easy for a while.
PLEASE except this as a fact.
NO JOKE.' BARNEY,
XXXXIE. Whenare you coming?
Barney can you organise a second hand battery shaver?
BY,
DUGGIE.
And BARNEY, PLEASE GET MESOME "FIT" RE-LEAVING PILLS FROM Dr Broadie or Mr Tana.

Then, six weeks after taking Duggie to Zululand, a cable:
"FEELING WORSE. COME FETCH IMMEDIATE-LY. DUGMORE."
I phoned hospitals in Johannesburg, tried doctors I knew. None would take him. I spoke to his mother. She couldn't possibly cope. It was pointless writing or phoning. I drove down with Lionel again.
Duggie was delighted to see us. "Good!" he said. "When d'we leave?"
"I'm sorry," I said, "I've driven here to tell you that you can't come back. Not yet." I was still not to tell him that he had cancer.
"You're taking me," he said.
"You are very sick. No hospital will take you in now. Your mother can't. You're being fed here, looked after, kept clean. Please, you must stay. When you're better, you can come back."
"You can't keep me here against my will. . . ."
We argued on and on, Lionel sitting silently by.

"I'll get the police on to you," Duggie threatened.

"Duggie, I can't take you."

"I want to go back to Joburg."

"Where? Where to in Joburg?"

"I don't care! Leave me in a gutter—I want to go back to Joburg."

I knew what he meant. It was hard to argue.

"If I take you to your mother it will be hell in a week."

"Take me to Joburg." He started to weep. Then finally he said to Lionel, looking at me, "I know why Barney doesn't want to take me back." We both sat silent. "He thinks I'm going to die." We said nothing. We got up to go. Dugmore began to curse me.

"I'll come again," I said. He went on cursing me. We left. It seemed like the end of everything.

Before we left the mission, I said goodbye to the doctor in charge. He was very quiet and sympathetic. It seemed to me that he knew exactly what had happened, how final, how terrible this last interview had been. Lionel and I drove back to Johannesburg saying very little. I remember seeing some washerwomen, this time across a pale spring field, and, I think, watching them, that I learned something, changed a little. I remember wondering about Duggie, what remark he might have made or even yelled, seeing these women. He could have been passing, but he wasn't. The book might not have happened, but it did. Those papers beside his bed, his work, my work, might be burnt or blown away. These women would still be there in exactly the same way. But the world *would* be different without what we had attempted. There was both a serenity and a finality to what I was feeling. It was prophetic. I never saw Duggie again.

Occasionally I received letters from people at the mission. They mentioned always that "Dugmore would like to hear from his friends." On each occasion, I phoned those of his friends I could and asked them to write. It was some weeks later, when I phoned the mission, that I discovered that the "friends" included me. I was told that he spoke constantly of me. I promised to come down and see him over the weekend.

On the Friday they phoned me to say that Duggie was dead.

I contacted Duggie's family. I was working alone in the office that Saturday. His mother and his two sisters came swollen-eyed and weeping to see me there. We spoke about him for a while, exchanging anecdotes and even managing to laugh. Then they handed me the bill for the funeral. £107.10.0. A coffin for £75. I was stunned. Somehow it *did* all seem my responsibility, but all my savings had gone on the trip. I phoned Nadine who had offered to help. We agreed that £75 was a lot for a coffin. That kind of money would be better spent on living writers.

A sister asked if I couldn't use some of the money from the story. Which story? The one that was sold overseas. I tried to explain that *London Magazine* had only paid £15. They were obviously not convinced. How much did they think it was? Duggie had said that he was going to get £150. Oh no. I felt sick, drowning, then a bit angry. I phoned the undertaker to ask the price of a good, polished coffin. £25. That was how much we would contribute towards a coffin. If they wanted a more elaborate one— well, then it became their problem.

Duggie's youngest sister went with the undertaker's van to Zululand. I asked her to collect the manuscript for me. It was important to the revisions that I would now have to make. A few days later, she came to see me. She had a scab on her forehead. The van bringing Duggie back to Joburg had overturned and his face was bruised. She had collected the papers, but had left them in the township.

I went to Duggie's funeral with Lionel and an African friend who showed us the way. We didn't go to his mother's house, but straight to the cemetery. There was a heavy traffic of hearses, battered American cars and big rattling lorries coming and going. We found the grave, empty still. The cortège had not yet arrived. We sat in my car. The sun was white-hot. A long line of cars moved in and stopped nearby us. In a long, gleaming black hearse driven by a handsome young Indian was Duggie's coffin.

Carved, trimmed in silver and covered with flowers. The £75 one.

Lionel and I were the only whites. A large crowd gathered around the grave. Duggie had a brother, too. The brother spoke. The preacher spoke. About Duggie's reverence. His goodness. There were several children there, weeping bitterly. I thought of the nurse in Zululand and the Duggie in her childhood and found myself close to weeping too. Then suddenly I was called upon to make a speech. There was a terrible pause, and then I managed to grope through a few words. I said something about Duggie being a man of talent and great vitality and that the world was a lesser place without him. The faces around me looked bewildered.

We all went forward to drop earth on Duggie. As I bent, I looked down the four raw clay walls at his beautiful coffin. I thought of his dream of Freeman shoes when only one foot really knew the difference. The coffin was the same. I felt ashamed for having argued.

Afterwards, I went to shake hands with Duggie's mother. There was a tension. I tried to mention the manuscript papers to his sister. She looked blank. As we began to get into my car, a young man came up to me. He was asking, he said, for the family, about the money from Duggie's writing that was sold. I repeated my story. I showed him a letter from London. Car doors were slamming all around. There was dust. It was too hot. I just stopped talking. Perhaps this was Duggie's final con. I knew that it would be a long time before I got the papers back. It was.

Barney Simon
Johannesburg 1968